Conquest

Conquest

Elizabeth Walker

GUILD PUBLISHING
LONDON · NEW YORK · SYDNEY · TORONTO

This edition published
1990 by Guild Publishing
by arrangement with
Piatkus Books Ltd, London W1

CN 8336

Phototypeset in Compugraphic Times 11/12 pt by
Action Typesetting Limited, Gloucester
Printed and bound in Great Britain by
Butler & Tanner Ltd, Frome and London

Part One

Chapter One

The cow looked up from its nonchalant munching of a straw basket, waved its tail at an irate shopkeeper and sauntered off. Flora picked her way down the street after it, delicately avoiding a rotting cabbage and other assorted filth. It had rained last night and it would be hours before the sun, filtering through the thin pale air, steamed the mud into dust.

Embroidered bags, hung at head height, threatened to entangle her. She veered round them, almost colliding with a cyclist who yelled with typical good humour. The Nepalese were a charming people, they often smiled when it wasn't strictly necessary. Flora mumbled an apology in halting Nepali, though the man was already pedalling vigorously away.

She felt slightly sick. One of her fellow aid workers had taken her out the night before, determined to show her 'the real Kathmandu' as he called it. They had eaten *dal bhat takari* at a grubby, noisy cafe off Freak Street with a smiling proprietor and a dog scratching fleas at the door. No wonder she felt ill.

But even her upset stomach couldn't spoil the day. It was so good to be here, at last. She had waited all her life for excitement, wrapped in a cocoon of care and consideration. She wondered what her father would be doing now. Sending a telex probably, demanding that she be returned. Flora giggled to herself. It had never occurred to him that once she arrived at the aid agency's office in Paris she would manage to persuade them to send her out here. He would be furious.

Suddenly she visualised him, stamping up and down his vast office, yelling into 'phones and at secretaries, insisting that someone send his daughter home. Tears flooded her eyes. She stopped and blinked, cursing herself for being so silly as to be homesick. It was only because she felt ill. All the same, at that moment she

3

would have given anything to be back in Scotland, watching her father rustle the morning paper, with a bowl of porridge on the table before her and the silver gleaming against a starched white cloth.

Abruptly, she turned aside into a cafe. It was moderately clean, and by last night's standards impeccable. An old man sat in a corner, turning a prayer wheel and avoiding her eye, but his son came out smiling from the back. He summed up Flora at a glance. 'Tea?' he enquired. 'Good English tea?'

She nodded dumbly. Let it be anything but Nepalese tea, with globules of rancid butter floating on the surface. Thankfully when it came, it had no milk, no sugar and certainly no butter. She drank the bitter liquid, feeling it coursing through her, letting it scald its way down her throat.

Her spirits began to revive. The old man in the corner twirled his prayer wheel and muttered; outside in the street a little boy from a hill village trailed dreamily after his father. The child was submerged in clothes: a bulky coat made of layers of what looked like flannel; an embroidered hat with earflaps framing his flat-cheeked face. The day would be warm later on, but even then the child might not be unwrapped. These people seemed to have a horror of fresh air. Flora smiled at the little boy and after a moment he smiled back.

She would have liked more tea, but it was time she was getting on. She paid, handling the unfamiliar money awkwardly. Tom, who had taken her out last night, handled cash with wild confidence, as if he had lived here for years instead of just three months. Still, he'd short-changed the waiter and caused an argument, so there was something to be said for caution. Tom seemed to be trying very hard to impress her, she thought. Sadly, she wasn't impressed.

Out in the street again she hurried towards the aid office, taking two wrong turnings although she had been there several times. She began to feel panicky. Tom said they never started the meetings on time, but she didn't want to be late anyway. Not in her first week. When at last she recognised the shrine or whatever it was at the end of the street, and the battered frontage of the aid office, she felt a surge of relief. She rushed through the door with what must have appeared to be anxious haste, because someone said 'Where's the fire?' and laughed. Flora felt herself blushing.

'I was told to come for the planning meeting,' she blurted.

'First floor. Want a coffee?'

'No thanks, I had tea just now.'

4

'Take some up for the others, will you?'

She was handed a tray and staggered up the rickety stairs with coffee sloshing from the mugs. Plaster was peeling from the walls and the wooden steps were steep and narrow. The door at the top was shut. She kicked at it with her sandalled foot and sidled into the room.

'Ah, Flora Kincaid!' said a voice. 'What a charming sight.'

'Can you take the tray?' she managed. 'I'm sorry but I'll spill it otherwise.'

'My dear girl, it wouldn't matter if you did.' James Kennedy, the district officer, took the tray and set it down. 'Flora thinks we're going to eat her if she makes a mistake,' he announced genially to the rest of the room. There was a chorus of indulgent chuckles. Thoroughly patronised, Flora sidled to an insignificant chair and sat down.

From the very moment of her arrival she had felt too young for all this. There was such a world-weary air about the other workers, against which she felt pink and over-exuberant. Except for Tom, everyone else was very much the seasoned professional; they had weathered earthquake and famine, mudslide and war, bringing succour to the needy all over the world. They had skills which she could never hope to match, and an effortless grasp of geography. They chatted knowledgeably about Bhaktpur and Pokara, Sunauli and Namche Bazar, but even when Flora stared for hours at a map, within minutes she had forgotten where they were. She never had been able to tell left from right.

She shifted on the hard chair, gripped by a sense of unreality. The gentle sound of temple windbells was drifting in through the open window.

'Where the devil is Tom?' demanded James Kennedy. 'Can't he ever get here on time?'

'Probably throwing up,' said Winifred, grey-haired and stringy, as if years of struggle had burned away the flesh to leave bone and sinew. 'Silly boy thinks it's clever to eat in slums and get Delhi belly.'

Flora kept quiet. James said, 'Well, if he isn't coming we'd better get started. I'll run through the situation here for Flora's benefit. As I'm sure you know, Nepal is one of the poorest countries in the world. It's a monarchy, with some democratic representation, based on the panchayats, and in general it seems to work pretty well. But it's got very few natural resources. Generally speaking, there are too many people. Outside the towns there's been massive deforestation for fuel, with resultant landslip and erosion.'

5

'The two main industries are tourism and climbing, I'm sure none of you can fail to be aware that there's another bloody Everest expedition arriving today. God knows why they want to have yet another go at the thing, but there's no accounting for taste. You'd think they could instal a bloody lift – elevator to you, Franklyn.' He grinned at one of their American members. The charity was bewilderingly cosmopolitan.

Kennedy went on, 'Anyway, leaving that aside, we are here to do a land survey, instruct on primary health care and undertake tree planting. We've tried to encourage new industry here, on the smallest possible scale, to improve standards in the villages. They are so dependent on farming, you see, Flora. And the land is divided and divided again, you find whole families trying to live on the produce of a fraction of an acre. We get a lot of malnutrition.'

There was a general rumble of assent. 'If I could have your reports please?' said Kennedy, smiling round at everyone. 'Winifred, you first. How are things around Lete?'

Winifred stretched her neck, as if it ached. 'Not good, I'm afraid. We had an exceptionally bad monsoon and a lot of landslides. Some of the fields have been reduced to little more than stones. The rice crop was poor, and the maize looks not a lot better. But Finn is making progress with his health education programme, we have some local people trained. And I'm hoping Flora will be able to give us a hand with paper making. It's a traditional product,' she explained, 'but we're trying to improve quality and set up a central market. We want people to have the money to buy the food they need.'

Flora nodded enthusiastically. 'Oh,' added Winifred, 'the Italians are having a go at Annapurna. We've had an amazing trade in the bazaars lately: spaghetti, tinned tomatoes, and some incredibly fashionable ski suits.'

Everybody laughed. 'These climbers are such goddammed exhibitionists,' said Franklyn. 'Yesterday I saw a guy who was a cross between Che Guevara and a Buddhist monk. And I know they bring work, and I know that's good, but they exploit the local people. They use men who need money so bad they're prepared to die for it.'

'Not for us to complain, old chap,' said Kennedy.

'But you have to admit, James, some of these people are so crass,' said Winifred. 'Just because a man will shoulder an eighty pound load, that doesn't mean you should let him. We see the porters going out, half-starved, killing themselves carrying crates of champagne or foie gras, and the climbers stroll along weighed down by a little light reading. That has to be exploitation.'

'The government is clamping down,' interposed James. 'Sherpas have to be insured nowadays.'

'And about time too,' said Winifred. Suddenly she laughed. 'Do you know, the French expedition actually took along a coffee grinder and a sack of Arabica beans?'

'Got to keep our standards up,' said a small, grizzled man. 'And it was wonderful coffee, I had some.' Everyone chuckled.

At that moment Tom burst into the room. He looked pale and dishevelled, with dark rings round his eyes. 'Sorry I'm late,' he muttered. 'Bit of a tummy upset.'

'Dear, dear,' said Winifred coldly.

'Sit down now you're here,' said James. 'You've brought the planting figures I asked for?'

Tom became still paler. There was an audible chorus of irritated sighs. 'I think we'd better have a talk later, Tom,' said James. 'Now, Flora, as I say, I want you to work with Winifred, out in the villages. You'll be leaving on Friday, and between now and then I want you to familiarise yourself with the language and customs. We can't do anything if you offend people out here, so in these few days I want you to use your time well. Ask us anything, any time. We're all here to help.' He smiled at her, exuding fatherly reassurance.

When the meeting ended Flora waited for Tom downstairs, watching one of the clerks update records in an enormous and very dusty filing cabinet. In Edinburgh, where she had enrolled, the charity had seemed wonderfully organised, with computers and photographs of smiling children being fed. Out here it all seemed rather small beer. Winifred had shown her how she was to teach paper making, spreading the pulp of a wild shrub on mesh screens, letting it dry in the thin mountain air. It was an upgrading of a rough and ready local product, and success meant covering a stony hillside in drying frames. It seemed unimportant, frivolous almost. A drop in an ocean of need. Even here in Kathmandu there were children going blind from eye infections.

Tom came heavy-footed down the stairs. When he saw Flora he deliberately turned away towards the street.

'Was he cross?' Flora hurried to keep pace with him.

'He's sending me back.'

'What? Just for being late? He can't!'

'Well, he's got you now, hasn't he? Flora this and Flora that. Don't flatter yourself it's your work he's interested in.' He sidestepped a dog gnawing something in the gutter.

Flora said, 'Shall I ask him not to send you home? I do feel guilty, you got ill taking me out.'

He turned on her furiously. 'Just — just mind your own business! We all know why you're here. You're not going to be any use. But Daddy promised a million and in return we show his daughter some excitement. Let her gawp at some unaccustomed poverty!'

He stalked off, leaving Flora standing. It was true, of course. But Dad had only meant her to go to Paris, it was her own idea to come out to Nepal. She was sure they wouldn't have sent her if they hadn't thought she'd work.

She took hold of a strand of hair and twisted it into a tight band, and when she let it go it frizzed into red curls. The dust got into your hair out here, turning everyone grey. Did they know how she came to be there? All the kindness she had been shown came back to her, and this time the smiles seemed false. The day stretched ahead, empty now that Tom had stormed off. She wondered what she ought to do.

She was staying in a house the charity rented for its Kathmandu workers, but she couldn't go there. Tom would be back and besides, conversations stopped when she entered a room. Perhaps they were all talking about her. There was nothing to do but follow James's instructions and get to know the place, she decided, starting with the bazaar. Tom had whisked her through a couple of times, but he never let her stop and look. She had left her map back at the house, but she turned in what she hoped was the right direction. Her thoughts went round and round on themselves, she took little notice of where she was going. Within five minutes she was hopelessly lost.

The streets became narrower, the bustle less intense. A man was leading a train of yaks across a road, almost jostling a yellow-robed monk, striding purposefully by. Women shook cloths from upstairs windows, and children played with puppies in the dust. Now and then a car would try and pass, disrupting everything. Even this temple city wasn't safe from them, thought Flora. It seemed that if a people wanted food, prosperity and education, then they must also have the motor car. Some of the main streets were clogged with traffic.

She blundered on, stopping from time to time to look hopelessly at street signs. She had no idea where she was. Every so often she would turn and try to head back to the centre of town, but the roads weren't straight and the shrines and temples merged one into the other. When she asked for directions, saying 'Durbar? Hotel Annapurna?' or anything else she thought might strike a

8

chord, people smiled and gave a fusillade of directions, none of which she understood.

Eventually she sank down in a heap at the side of the road, letting the skirt of her pretty cotton dress trail limply in the dust. She felt exhausted, thirsty and sweating. If she ever found the bazaar she would buy a compass, she decided. Or tie a piece of cotton to the bedpost first thing in the morning and twine her way around and around the city until she returned to that same bedpost at night. She closed her eyes for a second, and when she opened them saw a pair of long brown legs crossing her line of sight, with hiking boots at one end and khaki shorts at the other. Western legs. 'Hey! If you don't mind?' She scrambled to her feet.

'Yes?' An immensely tall, angular man towered over her. He had curly brown hair, held in place by a red sweatband, a scrubby beard and the palest grey eyes.

'I — I'm lost. If I could get back to the centre I know I'd be all right, but I seem to be going round in circles.'

'It's all in that direction.' He waved his arm vaguely and started to move away.

'Please wait! I'm sorry, but — I know I'll get lost again. Can you tell me properly? Is there something I could aim for?'

'Like I say, you'll be fine if you keep going that way. Look, I've got to get on.'

Flora rubbed her hands down her skirt. 'Yes, I'm sure you have. Sorry.'

As she turned away, drooping, the man said, 'Would you like me to walk back with you? I've got a couple of things to do here, then I'll be going back.'

'Will you?' Flora beamed. 'That would be wonderful. Thanks.'

They walked together down the street. 'Don Harrington,' he said abruptly.

'Flora Kincaid,' she returned. 'I'm with a charity out here.'

'I'm with the Everest expedition.'

'Oh.' Flora assessed him beneath her lashes. He looked forbiddingly fit, a collection of long, lean surfaces covered in muscle and skin. His hands were huge, great square palms with long, calloused fingers. 'You look like a climber,' she remarked diffidently.

'Well, you don't look like a charity worker. Far too young and far too pretty.'

Flora giggled, and pushed her red hair back with a dusty hand. 'I really am working for a charity,' she said breathlessly. 'I'm being sent out to the villages to teach paper-making. And I've only just learned it.'

9

'I'm sure you'll be able to teach the poor natives a thing or two. Don't worry, they're far too polite to tell you to get lost, they'll put up with you.'

'I didn't want to be tolerated. I wanted to help.'

He grinned. 'Good for you. You might. Just don't assume that everything Western is good and everything Nepalese a waste of time. Life's hard out here. They can't change quickly, they can't risk it. For instance, on my last trip I got permission to bring a new maize variety, lots of yield, fast growth. Gave it to a farmer friend and nearly bankrupted him. No disease resistance. And the ground's almost played out, and he can't afford bags of fertiliser. See what I mean? He was right, and I was wrong.'

'Winifred says climbers exploit the country.'

'Winifred might be right.'

Suddenly he stopped and knocked on a door in the wall. Flora looked up at him, waiting for him to explain, but he said nothing. Vague anxiety nagged at her. What was this place? Why had he brought her here? Just because she was in Nepal she had taken up with someone in a way she would never have done at home. She felt like Red Riding Hood and hoped she had not encountered the wolf.

The door opened. A man stood there, his face creased with wrinkles that might have been age, or simply hard living. He smiled at them, his eyes disappearing into folds of creased flesh. 'Ang Stupa!' Don Harrington put out his hands.

'Donald Harrington!' The man returned the embrace. Flora felt embarrassed, intruding on the meeting of such old friends, and when Ang Stupa stretched out his hand to greet her too, she stuck out a stiff, unresponsive fist.

'You are welcome to my home,' declared Ang Stupa. 'Come, come, into my house.'

Flora hesitated and shot an anxious look at Harrington. 'I can always wait,' she whispered.

'He'll think he's offended you. Come on, it won't take long.'

Flora followed the men into a bare, low-ceilinged room. A fire burned, the smoke funnelling erratically up the chimney. The air was pale grey, perfumed with the aroma of sweet wood, a soft cloud of smoke hanging just under the ceiling. A table and chairs stood in a corner, and there was a sofa covered in a colourful Tibetan blanket. Ang Stupa waved them towards it and they both sat down.

There was an awkward silence. Flora glanced from one man to the other, wondering if she was the cause of it.

10

'I shall bring you *chang*,' said Ang Stupa. 'I remember your taste for *chang*, Don Harrington!'

Don laughed obediently, cutting the sound off the moment their host left the room.

'Why don't you tell him who I am?' hissed Flora. 'He thinks we know each other.'

'We do. Flora, wasn't it? Just stay quiet. Don't make a fuss.'

Before she could say another word, Ang Stupa came back with a jar. Looking from one to the other he gave an almost lecherous grin, and poured out three glasses of milky liquid. Flora took hers and sipped. To her surprise it tasted quite bland and she sipped again. The climber knocked his back in one gulp.

Again there was silence, but this time Ang Stupa looked enquiringly at Harrington. He sat turning the empty glass in his large hand. The silence stretched on, until Flora too found herself watching Harrington with an almost desperate attention. At last, when she felt that at any moment she would burst into hysterical giggles, he said, 'Ang Stupa, I need porters. And Sherpas for the climb.'

Ang Stupa let out his breath. At last they had come to the point. He shifted in his seat, and sniffed. 'You have porters,' he said mildly. 'I hear you have many porters.'

'The man who hired our porters was not a good man. These porters want too much money and they won't walk far. And his Sherpas won't go on the high mountains.'

The other man stared at a point somewhere to the left of Harrington's head. 'If you wanted my help you could have asked me,' he said in an aggrieved voice. 'I have waited for you. I did not go on the Japanese climb because I knew Don Harrington was coming. I did not go with the Germans because Don Harrington would need me. And then I find that another man is to serve you.'

'I did try, Ang Stupa. I'm not running this expedition, if I were I'd have come to you straight away. As I come now. Ang Stupa, I need your help.'

The Sherpa sniffed again, a little less stiffly. He too turned his empty glass in his stubby fingers.

'You knew I wouldn't go without you,' coaxed Harrington. 'Remember that night above the snowline?'

Ang Stupa shook his head, as if refusing to remember. He took his head between his own two hands and shook it, saying 'Aaaaaahhhh' in a long, throaty chuckle. Then his wrinkled face split into smiles, and he and Don Harrington stood up and embraced each other.

When, finally, they left, Flora staggered a little. 'Steady on.' Don caught her arm and held it.

'*Chang* is stronger than it tastes,' she remarked. 'And surely you're not going to take that old man up Everest, are you?'

'As far as he can go, yes. He's not that old. Besides, Ang Stupa's been on every major expedition in the last ten years. He knows all there is to know.'

'He seems very excited.'

Don laughed. 'He thought we'd decided he was past it. But we're having a hell of a lot of trouble getting things together, the Japanese have put the prices up and everyone wants too much money. And they all tell lies about their experience. Too many expeditions, that's the trouble. You used to be able to get to the mountains for peanuts.'

'Sounds like exploitation to me,' said Flora.

'Do you think so? We all enjoyed it more. Nowadays you have to pay for bloody great helicopters to fly doctors in and out. And a million porters, and half a ton of camera equipment. There won't be room for more than a couple of blokes who actually mean to get to the top?'

'Will you? Get to the top?'

He looked down at her and grinned, his teeth very white against his tan. 'That's what I came here for.'

The day was appreciably colder and a nasty wind was swirling the dust. She shivered. 'I ought to be getting back.'

'What? Oh, we'll go back in a minute. There's someone I've got to see, a Thakali. He's going to sell me shoes for the porters.'

'Don't they have shoes?'

'Boots. The expedition always provides them, it's part of the deal.'

He turned up an alleyway, firing a few words in Nepali at a man walking by. The man gave directions and Don strode off, Flora trailing behind. She was very hungry. Gooseflesh stood up on her bare arms.

At last Harrington knocked at a door. A man in a belted tunic answered, his face distinctively Mongolian. Don shook his hand, friendly but not effusive. The man watched him out of brown, almost lidless eyes. 'I am pleased to help your expedition,' he said carefully, and it was clear he said the same to everyone. He ushered them in, accepting Flora's presence without comment. He gave them whisky to drink.

The business took over an hour, and when it was done Flora knew she was drunk. Harrington walked quickly down the street and she scurried after him, her head spinning. Suddenly the world slid sideways, she lurched, and saved herself by clinging to a carving protruding from a wall. 'Wait,' she squawked. 'I'm dying.'

12

Harrington turned. 'Thought you were a good Scot with a head for whisky.'

'I haven't eaten anything all day. And I threw up everything I ate yesterday.' Flora straightened up and took careful steps towards him. Her pale dress billowed in the breeze.

'I'll hold on to you.' He reached out and put his arm around her waist, drawing her close. The side of her breast rested against his chest, she could feel his warmth through his shirt. 'Your hair's a pretty colour,' he said.

'It's all full of dust.'

Flora knew she should pull away, but she was warm there. She felt relaxed, almost sleepy. Suddenly a gust of cold wind swirled her skirt and she and Don clutched at it together.

'Don't,' she said, gathering her wits. 'I can manage.'

'You shouldn't wear see-through skirts.'

'It isn't see-through! It's broderie anglaise.'

'I don't much care what it is, actually.' He reached out to take hold of her again.

Flora squirmed out of his grasp. 'Are you going to take me back or not?' she demanded, pushing her hair out of her eyes. 'I think I'm better off lost than looking to you for help.'

He looked down at her, his expression unreadable. 'I'll take you back. But first I think we should stop off and have some food. I know a good place round here. You can get superb *masala dhosa*.'

She nodded. Only one thing was clear: that Harrington knew his way round Kathmandu rather better than most. Going about in the company of Tom had been simply embarrassing, watching him pretend friendship with people he hardly knew, demand price reductions on perfectly fair deals. Harrington had shown her more Kathmandu in one afternoon than Tom had seen in three months. What's more, she wasn't in any real danger from this man. She felt almost sure she could handle him.

They came out on to a wide dirt road, with trees growing on either side. It was quite crowded, and it seemed natural to link hands.

Flora said, 'I'm getting very cold.'

'When we get to the restaurant I'll ask the owner to lend you a coat.' He looked down at her and grinned. She smiled back.

The restaurant was small, dark and warm. It smelled delicious, of curry and hot bread, and when Flora asked for tea they brought her an earthenware bowl with fresh green leaves floating on the surface.

Harrington said, 'You like that better than whisky, I can see.'

She rested an elbow on the table. 'I like them both. Whisky makes me silly.'

13

'I'll remember that.'

When the food came they ate with concentration. The curry was thick and creamy, it soothed even as it satisfied. Flora's stomach hadn't felt so content since she left home. As the edge went from their hunger they talked a little. 'Where are you staying?' asked Harrington. 'Do you have a room to yourself?'

'It's a cupboard,' said Flora. 'There's only just room for the bed.'

'Sounds fine.'

She looked at him. 'I told you whisky makes me silly. I didn't mean anything. I'm sorry if you thought I did.'

After a second he dropped his eyes. 'You're too nice a girl for that sort of thing.'

She laughed. 'And you won't persuade me, either. It's my own fault, I should wear jeans like everyone else. But then they're too tight. I've got too round a bottom.'

'Have you? You'll have to show me. Or let me see for myself.'

His voice was slightly husky. Flora felt her nerves quiver, as if someone had run their fingers the length of her naked spine. Oh God, she thought. Oh God, is this what they mean by lust? If he stood up now and drew her to him not a fibre of her body would resist. She swallowed down a piece of the flat, Indian bread, keeping her eyes on his hand. He reached out and touched her fingers.

'Did I tell you I was going to teach paper-making?' she said jerkily.

'And you've only just learned how.'

'Yes.'

She looked up and met his eyes. 'Why do you want to climb Everest? It isn't as if it hasn't been done before.'

He sighed impatiently. He'd been asked this a hundred times. 'It isn't what everyone else does that matters. It's me. For me. My own achievement. I vowed I'd do it before I was thirty.'

'How old are you?'

'Twenty-eight.'

'Oh. I'm nineteen.'

Flora drank the last of her tea. The wind was rising again, sending a draught whistling under the door. It was dark; through the uncurtained window could be seen many pinpricks of yellow light. Don called the restaurant owner and borrowed a coat, a thick padded jacket that smelled of woodsmoke and alien sweat. Outside, Flora felt normality return. She was bone tired, and wanted nothing so much as her own bed.

They walked together, Don holding her hand and seemingly

14

unaware of the cold. The air seemed to fall down from the mountains at night, tumbling into this central zone straight off the snowcaps. Raucous Indian music came from a bar, and voices raised in argument. She felt suddenly grateful to Don for his large, reassuring presence.

At last Flora recognised her street, and turned thankfully for home. At the door of the house she stopped. 'Thanks, Don. Look, I must pay for my meal.' She fumbled in her bag for some money.

'Let's talk about it inside.'

'But everyone's there. All the others.'

'Not in your room they're not.'

'I can't take you up to my room! They'd have a fit! Here, have the money. And the coat.'

'There's no need to rush.' As she opened the coat he slid his hands under it and round her body. Flora gasped and stood rigid, letting him hold her. His hands almost circled her waist.

The door of the house opened behind her.

'Flora! Flora, is that you? Where in heaven's name have you been?' Winifred stood in the light, her short grey hair standing up in spikes.

'I've been exploring,' said Flora, turning with guilty haste. 'Mr — er — Don lent me a coat.'

'How cosy,' said Winifred in icy tones. 'And who might you be, Don?'

'Donald Harrington,' he said calmly. 'Flora, keep the coat. I'll come for it tomorrow. About ten.'

'Yes. Yes, all right.' Flora stepped away from him, into the circle of light from the door, into the safety of Winifred's world. When she looked at him he seemed dark, a threatening stranger. Then he grinned at her, a wide, white smile. 'It was a good day,' he said.

Flora smiled back.

Chapter Two

When Flora came down to breakfast she found Winifred sitting alone at the long wooden table, drinking coffee and making notes. 'Ah, Flora,' she began ominously.

'Good morning, Winifred.' Flora fetched herself some coffee and sat down. Yesterday's dress was gone, she was wearing jeans and a green bush shirt, her red hair tied up in a green bow. The bow was an act of defiance. 'I'm sorry I came in late,' she said cheerily.

Winifred put down her pen. 'This isn't school, Flora. All we ask is that you behave in an adult and responsible way.'

'I thought I had.'

Winifred folded her hands, in preparation for the lecture she felt duty bound to give. 'I think I should make one or two things clear. We're in a position of trust in Nepal, at the invitation of the king. If we abuse that trust − '

'I don't think having a meal with a friend is an abuse of trust,' said Flora hotly. 'I haven't done anything!'

Winifred snapped, 'You've been playing at this since the day you arrived. You dress as if you were on the French Riviera! I am trying to impress upon you as best I can that this is no holiday. And yet yesterday, the first day we let you out alone, you pick up some hippy.'

'He's with the Everest expedition. James told me to explore and I did.'

'That is not a justification!'

Flora's pale skin flushed dark red and two high spots of colour had appeared in Winifred's cheeks. 'At least you won't be able to get up to much in the hills,' said the older woman forcibly.

'Except wasting my time making rice paper.'

Flora pulled the bow from her hair, letting the red curls fall in a tangle on her shoulders. Winifred had disapproved of her from the

16

first, had insisted that Flora should work on the rice paper project, had made things difficult in every way, in fact.

'Tell me, Winifred,' said Flora in a voice tight with anger, 'why are you being so unkind to me? There must be lots of really important things I could be doing. I want to work, I want to work hard! I don't want to be given some pointless job just to keep me out of mischief.'

Winifred sighed in irritation. 'Don't you realise, you silly girl, that you have an awful lot to learn? All right, making rice paper isn't going to change the world, but at present you know nothing about the country or the people. And it is important — to the little communities eking out an existence on their barren fields. It could be vital. What's more, if the rice paper's successful we can go on to more complicated things. We can't just waltz into a community and teach them nuclear physics!'

'I thought perhaps — basic hygiene? Obviously they don't understand about germs and things — '

Winifred started to laugh. 'Oh Flora! If it were only that simple. You'll learn, child, you'll learn. There's a whole way of life here you don't understand, a vast and complicated culture, and until you grasp that you can't begin — oh dear! I'm sorry to say this, but you'll know better when you grow up.'

Flora was silent. At length she said, 'Are you cross with me because I got Tom into trouble?'

'I'm not cross with you, you silly girl! If anything I'm cross with the people who sent you. You're young, you're pretty, you're idealistic. There's nothing wrong with any of those things, provided they don't come together in an aid worker. Now, there's no need to get depressed about this. Perhaps you won't achieve much in Nepal, but you might be in India next, or one of the African states. Sooner or later all your experience will come together and you'll make a real contribution.'

'I don't know why I'm here at all,' said Flora bemusedly.

'To learn, dearie. To learn.'

Winifred began to tidy her papers. As she stood up to leave, she said, 'Let's have no more cosy little dinners with our handsome friend, shall we? We've got a lot of hard work to do, and I don't want you agonising over whether you're pregnant or not. Conduct your romances in your own time, not ours.'

Left alone, Flora could have wept. It was part rage, part frustration. Nobody in this entire country took her seriously; they all thought she was silly and frivolous and irresponsible. She almost ground her teeth in fury.

17

The front door clicked as Winifred went out, leaving the house absolutely silent. Everyone else was about their proper business, only Flora had nothing specific to do. She thought about writing to her father, but in her present mood she could not possibly generate the bubbly letter she knew he would expect. To make Winifred happy she should spend the morning studying the language, reciting verbs and tenses, but she was too unsettled. Outside it was dull and windy, the sun and the far mountains hidden by thick grey cloud. She went up to her room and fetched the coat she had been lent. She would go out in it, and feel part of the local scene.

Her spirits lifted the moment she left the house. Winifred didn't know everything, her word wasn't law. A procession was passing the end of the street, and Flora stopped to let it by. It was Hindu, with the masks of gods held aloft and young girls with gold nose-rings, dancing. They wore red head-dresses and twirled their bare feet in the dust, holding their hands up in an elegant pose.

When it was past, Flora headed for the bazaar. She was determined that today she would not get lost, and instead would stay close to home. She took exaggerated care to note which buildings she passed, like a blind man counting lamp-posts with his stick. When at last she reached the bazaar she paused for a few moments, trying to get her route straight in her mind. But the sight of a man carrying a young goat distracted her, and a woman selling belts called out. She wandered through the stalls, looking at this and that, and shaking her head whenever anyone tried to tempt her with food.

Although she had only been in Kathmandu for such a short time, she could sense something new in the atmosphere. There was an excitement, a sense of bustle, that had been missing before. There seemed to be more Westerners than usual, and more of the hill people were pushing their way purposefully through the crowds. It was the expedition, of course. There was money to be made by those quick enough to seize their opportunity. Suddenly, coming through the crowd towards her, Flora saw Don Harrington. He was wearing nylon climbing trousers and a bright red padded jacket, and he towered above three or four Nepalese trotting along beside him.

'Hello,' she called out.

He barely acknowledged her. 'Hi. Look, I'm busy right now, I've got to find a dozen men before dark. I'll come round about six and take you out.'

'I can't.'

'Course you can.'

He walked on, but Flora struggled out of her coat and ran after him. She caught at his arm. 'Here.'

'Flora, I said I'd see you later.'

'But I can't come! So take the jacket and give it back to the man who lent it to you.' She pushed the bulky coat into his arms.

'What's so important that you can't eat dinner?'

She shrugged, feeling the colour rise in her face. 'I'm in trouble. Winifred's forbidden me to go out with men.'

'You're not going to do as she says, are you?'

'Well — yes.' As he began to laugh she went on, 'I have to! If I don't they'll send me home. And she's right, I'm not here to have fun after all. And neither are you.'

'As long as I climb I can do what I damn well like, and as long as you work so can you. Don't be such a baby, Flora!'

'I'm just doing what I'm told — '

'Sitting with your hands in your lap — '

' — and it isn't any of your business — '

' — like the little convent schoolgirl you are!'

Flora's blush went to the roots of her hair. 'Oh — just go away, will you?' She turned on her heel and stalked off.

'You're going the wrong way,' yelled Harrington, and she stopped, turned round and hurried past him. 'See you at six,' he said.

'Don't bother!' snapped Flora.

The men with Harrington were laughing, and Flora hated them all. As it happened, she had been very happy at school. It wasn't a convent, though it might as well have been for all the freedom they had. It was only now that she wondered if it had been far too protected an education, with men as some distant and tantalising goody. And she had to admit that she liked Don Harrington. She liked his size, the way he moved with such long-limbed, easy grace, his assurance in this strange country. It made everything terribly difficult.

She got lost on the way back to the house, and when she reached it Winifred was there. 'Just in time for lunch,' she said.

'Yes. Good,' said Flora. She felt an almost shameful relief that the row was over. Squabbling wasn't in her nature, and all her friends discovered sooner or later that with Flora the first flash of temper was followed minutes later by a flood of urgent conciliation.

'I gave the coat back,' she said quickly, like a little girl.

'I am glad.' Winifred smiled, and Flora knew she was quite forgiven.

But Harrington turned up at six o'clock. Flora was reading Winifred's notes on Nepali, after a virtuous afternoon making frames for rice paper production, at which she was neat, quick and efficient. The moment the knock came she knew who it was.

19

She sat rigid as James Kennedy turned from the door and said, 'It's for you.'

She rose under the weight of their combined accusing stares. From the kitchen came the unappetising smell of boiling vegetables, heralding a dull meal to come. And Harrington had brought his different world to the door, a place of excitement and unknown opportunity. He filled the entire doorframe, still in his red jacket. And he had brought her some flowers.

'Here,' he said cheerfully, 'are you ready? I've arranged for you to meet some of the blokes.'

Flora swallowed, well aware that everything she said was being overheard. 'I told you, I can't come.'

'I'll get you back nice and early. Thought you'd like to meet some of our Sherpas, practise your Nepali.'

He grinned wolfishly, knowing he had put her in an impossible position. She was lost for words. 'I − I −'

Winifred swept past her. 'Now see here, young man. Flora is not here to enjoy herself. She's a working girl and she hasn't any time for your shenanigans. Talking to your Sherpas, indeed!'

'Not going to learn much about the country sitting in and reading her Bible, now is she?' snapped Harrington.

'I think the sort of education you have in mind can well be curtailed,' retorted Winifred.

'That isn't fair,' broke in Flora, but neither took any notice. 'I do think − I mean − '

James Kennedy appeared round the door. 'This house wasn't too warm to begin with,' he said mildly. 'Leaving the door open is freezing us half to death. Did you want to go out this evening, Flora?'

She looked in anguish from Don to Winifred. 'Well − I − I did want to meet the Sherpas − '

'Then I'm sure if this young man brings you back before ten there can be no reasonable objection.'

'We are in loco parentis,' declared Winifred.

'Flora is over eighteen, Winifred. And I'm sure she'll be sensible.'

As they walked down the street together Don said, 'Was that the boss? Seems a nice old boy.'

'He is.' Flora pulled her Gore-Tex anorak round her. Her father had made her buy it for hill walking at home, at tremendous cost. It was wonderfully warm, but not the most seductive of garments. She tried to tell herself that she did not wish to look in the least seductive.

20

'Come here.' Don took her arm and pushed her into the shadows. A temple towered above them, the dome an exotic black shape against a paler sky. Don's head came down, smelling of tea and soap, blotting out everything. Hadn't he noticed the anorak? she wondered. She felt his lips, cold and strange, his tongue meeting hers in the soft, dark moistness of her mouth. Shards of feeling pierced her, like molten glass.

'Don't! You mustn't!' She pushed him away, but he held her in the circle of his arms.

'Don't let them get at you Flora,' he murmured. 'We could both be dead tomorrow.'

'You don't die making rice paper.' He was nuzzling her forehead, where her skin met her hair.

'You've got beautiful hair,' he whispered. 'And skin like white marble. Let me kiss your eyes, your lovely dark blue eyes – '

'Please don't,' she whispered. 'I'm supposed to see your Sherpas.'

'I could be dead in a month. An avalanche, an ice-fall and I'd be gone. Undo your anorak.'

'No!'

She pulled free and stood out in the light, her head thrown back, watching him. 'I won't,' she said sulkily.

'No. I can see that you won't.' He sighed, and sunk his hands into his pockets. After a moment he said, 'I suppose we could go for a drink.'

'I thought we were going to eat,' said Flora. 'I'll pay if you like.'

'I don't think one meal is going to bankrupt me. Look, we can eat with the Sherpas. Give you a real tale to tell.'

'Weren't we going to see them at all, then?'

He grinned. 'Possibly. Afterwards.'

They walked along in silence for a while. Flora said, 'It isn't that I don't like you. But obviously, working for a charity, I've got responsibilities.'

'You don't say!' He glanced down at her. 'You don't have to apologise for not fancying me. I'll get over the blow, I suppose.'

'But I do! I mean – well, obviously, if things were different, and I wasn't here doing a job – but even so I don't want it to be like that. Just sort of, not important. Not for the first time.'

Harrington took a long breath. 'I was beginning to wonder if you knew what you were doing,' he remarked. 'You ought to be more careful. What do you think you're up to, wandering round Kathmandu on your own? Anything could happen.'

21

'I can take care of myself,' said Flora in an aggrieved tone. 'Everyone always assumes I'm quite helpless.'

'And so you are. Don't wear that dress again, it gives people the wrong idea.'

She chuckled. 'So I've gathered.'

The expedition had taken over two guest-houses, and by the time Flora and Don arrived everyone had eaten. But there was bread and stew left over, and one of the Sherpas went to get some. The bulk of expedition support would be recruited at Namche Bazar, a Sherpa village near the Everest range, but the old hands and the senior men came down to Kathmandu. Flora looked round in bewilderment. There were at least thirty people in the room, a dozen or so Western, and all around were heaps of gear; ropes, rucksacks, boots, ice-axes, oxygen sets minus the cylinders, and a case of Johnny Walker whisky.

'You don't take that up the mountain, do you?' she asked Don, pointing to the scotch.

'Certainly do. We need something to cheer us up.'

'Winifred said you were a lot of self-indulgent layabouts.'

'Bloody Winifred!'

One by one the climbers shambled over to be introduced. There was John, the expedition's doctor, newly qualified and nervous. He was treated with kindly contempt by Eddie and Mike, two joiners who only worked to finance their climbing. They were clearly experienced and had been to Nepal the previous year in an abortive attempt to climb K2.

'What do you see in our Don then, sweetheart?' asked Mike.

Flora took a steaming bowl of stew from a Sherpa. 'He feeds me,' she said. 'What more could a girl ask?'

'Lucky bastard,' leered Eddie.

A big man, shorter than Don but very wide, nodded from across the room. Don waved a hand.

'Who's that?' asked Flora.

'Van. He's Dutch, doesn't talk much. We climb together.'

Flora looked across at Van again. He was older than Don, perhaps ten years older, with a face that was smooth and unlined except for a fan of creases at the corner of each eye. When he spread his hand Flora saw that the tip of one of his fingers was missing.

'How can he climb with his hand like that?'

'Better than most,' said Don shortly.

Mike leaned across and said ghoulishly, 'It was frostbite, my girl. Frozen off above the snowline on Annapurna. Lost two toes as well.

22

Our Don was out that night too but he only lost his little willy. You'll know all about that, Flora. If you look close enough you can see where they had to graft it back on with — '

'Shut up, Mike,' said Don. 'Flora doesn't want to hear that sort of talk.'

'Christ all bloody mighty!' said Mike. 'The man's in love.'

The room was warm, the food filling. People drifted in and out, discussing this, complaining of that. The expedition leader was having dinner with a government official and in his absence Eddie and Mike seized their chance to complain about the officious way he was running the expedition, his ignorance of the mountain and his high-handed refusal to let Eddie and Mike make the summit bid. Flora listened in horror. According to them there was too little food, too little gear and the radio sets were useless. According to them they were all doomed. She looked anxiously at Don. Perhaps he would die, with no kindness from her, and she would have it on her conscience forever!

Towards ten the Sherpas gathered in a corner to talk and smoke. One of them began to sing, and other voices joined in. When that song ended another began, and Flora almost felt an intruder, enveloped in warmth and comradeship that did not belong to her. She nudged Don. 'I've got to go.'

He nodded and stood up. As they left Eddie and Mike shouted obscenities and Van lifted his huge hand in farewell.

The night air smelled of woodsmoke. A dog was barking in the next street, and windbells were chiming in the evening breeze. 'You oughtn't to go,' said Flora suddenly. 'Not with such terrible organisation, it could be very dangerous.'

'It's the name of the game,' remarked Don carelessly.

'But the radio sets! If they won't work you could be trapped somewhere. And obviously there isn't enough food, and Eddie was saying there isn't even enough rope!'

'That's a load of balls, and they know it.'

Flora stopped and stared at him. 'You mean it isn't true?'

'Course it isn't. They moan about every expedition. What they're really pissed off about is me and Van making the summit bid. But then, we wouldn't have come otherwise and they damn well know it.'

'Oh. Oh, I see.' But she didn't. Why must Don and Van be enticed to climb when Eddie and Mike would come without such inducements?

'I'll be going to Pokhara tomorrow,' he said suddenly. 'There's some stuff there I've got to pick up.'

'Oh. I'm going off on Friday.'

'Yes. We'd better say goodbye.'

The charity house was a scant hundred yards away. Harrington put his arms around her and suddenly Flora wanted to hold on to him, to go on talking and discovering with no need for goodbye. Her mouth opened under his, and she heard him moan. 'Oh, Flora, I wish you were coming with me.'

'So do I. I wish you weren't going!'

His mouth slid from hers down to her neck. His hands struggled to find her breasts under the bulky anorak. 'I've got to go,' whispered Flora, and when he still kept on she said again, 'I've got to go.'

'All right. Yes.' He straightened, looking down at her in the gloom. 'Going to wish me luck?'

'If you want. But I wish you weren't going. Really I do.'

He touched her face. 'I like you being worried. It turns your eyes almost black. See you when I get back, OK?'

Flora's spirits, momentarily squashed flat, revived at once. 'Will I? Truly? Oh yes please, Don!'

As she came in the house Winifred looked at her sardonically. 'What an educational evening you seem to have had, Flora. I'm off to bed. Good night.'

When she had gone, Flora turned to Franklyn. 'What's the matter? What have I done?'

Franklyn chuckled. 'I may be wrong, but I think it has something to do with the lovebite on your neck.'

Flora blushed a dark, fiery red.

24

Chapter Three

The charity's paper project was based on a cluster of villages near Lete, a mountain village looking on to the great peaks of Dhaulagiri and Annapurna. The people were Magars mostly, and their lives followed a grim pattern, struggling to wrest food from barren soil. They kept yaks, and yak-cattle crosses, and foul-tempered water buffalo for their milk. At some seasons there were no men in the villages at all; they were all away, serving the expeditions. And when they came back, they brought transistor radios and Western clothes and the knowledge that elsewhere in the world life was not as hard as this.

Flora and Winifred took a plane to a short take-off strip some miles from their base, and then walked for two days. The country was spiked with mountains, the peaks almost bare of soil, the lower slopes cut into an endless pattern of terraces. The valleys were green and gave an illusion of fertility. From the trail Flora could look down and see the buffalo pens, and the women endlessly carting fodder. The houses, of mud and thatch, were a dark, rich red.

They were already very high, and breath came quickly, in short and painful gasps. She rested, taking in the scent of lentil bushes, pungent in the sun. Coming from a land of mountains herself, she was nonetheless astounded by Nepal. Peaks so jagged they seemed to prick the clouds, cliffs so sheer that nothing could cling to them. They seemed unreal, as if they might be hanging from the sky rather than rising from the earth. Yet rise they had, so little time ago that primitive man had walked this land when it was flat. What had they done to cause all this? It was like some extreme and beautiful punishment.

The porters, carrying their gear in wicker baskets on their backs, were waiting at the top of the next rise. 'Come on, Flora!'

called Winifred, waving her sturdy walking stick. 'Stop admiring the view.'

Flora took a breath of the thin mountain air and set out on the trail once more. Far below a river crashed and bubbled through the narrow valley, brown with silt washed from the fields. The silt caused flooding, the erosion ate away at people's livelihoods. Even on this calm and sunny day Flora felt a sudden surge of urgency. They ought to be doing something! They ought to be doing more!

They had started to walk very early and stopped to eat at ten, high above the thatched roofs of a farmstead. It was up to Flora and Winifred to fit in with the porters, who ate twice a day when trekking, once in mid-morning and again at night. It was again *dal bhat takari*, the soup, rice and vegetables that had made Tom ill, but so far from the fleshpots of Kathmandu it was good and very filling. The sun was warm. Crimson hibiscus seemed to flow out of cracks in the hillside, like a torrent of blood-red.

Winifred said, 'Don't you love this country? Couldn't you die just looking at it?'

It was an odd comment for Winifred, usually so stern and unemotional. Flora said, 'It's very beautiful. And I feel I understand it. The problems here aren't so different from Scotland.'

'Good heavens! What an odd comparison.' Winifred leaned back against a rock, her sturdy boots stretched out in front of her.

'Not so odd perhaps. The mountains are always hard places, you can't live easily there.'

The food made Flora sleepy and when they set off again she trailed behind, listening to the hum of insects in the flowers. When she rounded a corner she was surprised to find the whole party gathered. They had stopped at a narrow wooden bridge, stretching across a gorge some fifty feet deep. Although the bridge was no more than two feet wide, a yak train was coming the other way, led by a toothless old man and followed by his wife. The porters yelled at him to hurry, the old man waved his stick, and one of the yaks stopped in the middle of the bridge and bellowed a protest. Flora's stomach heaved.

'These bridges are much sturdier than they look,' said Winifred bracingly. 'Anyway, think what that friend of yours will be doing. Dangling hundreds of feet up held by no more than a piece of rope.'

'Not yet, surely?'

'Oh, of course not yet. When they get there. One of the porters was saying he's much admired, I gather he's a star climber. I never will understand what motivates these young men.'

'He didn't talk about it much.'

'Really? Well, I suppose even a fanatic has to take time off for other things occasionally.' She smiled, and Flora grinned back. Winifred wasn't such a bad old stick, and underneath her brusque manner she was very kind. The porters knew her well and teased her a little, saying she walked so fast that young men like them couldn't keep up. Winifred brought Mars bars to give them after meals.

'They do so love them,' she said apologetically to Flora. 'But I do worry about their teeth. With all due respect, Flora, I could wish that your appointments board had sent us a dentist.'

At last the yak train was across, wending its way down the path with gentle purpose. Until the roads, built only recently, and the still more recent airstrips, the trek was the only means of travel. There was a timelessness about it, and an air of long tradition. People met and parted on the trail, news was passed from traveller to traveller, as if the paths themselves were the country's blood vessels, carrying vital fluid up and down. Were the foreigners enriching? Or were they like cholesterol, clogging up the system and ruining the spare, simple efficiency of the whole?

The porters, followed by Winifred, began to amble across the bridge. Far below, in the shaded gorge, the river bubbled and boiled, white as soapsuds. The bridge was almost as wide as a garden path, decided Flora, and set a tentative foot on it. Then she stood back. The bridge trembled, not violently but enough.

'Come along, Flora!' called Winifred impatiently.

They wouldn't wait for her. If she was scared now, if she lacked the courage to conquer that fear, then she was no use to anyone.

Resisting the urge to bend down and scrabble across on all fours, Flora walked out on to the bridge.

That night they stayed in a village, spreading their sleeping bags on the floor of a hut. Buffalo stamped outside the door and the porters lit cigarettes and chatted with the farmer. Winifred said softly, 'There are probably fleas, so put some powder in your sleeping bag. Otherwise you'll have a miserable night.'

Dubiously Flora sprinkled the powder. She had an altitude bag, recommended by one of the people in Paris, and when she had tried it out one night there she had almost suffocated from the heat. It seemed cosy and welcoming on the flea-ridden mud floor of a hut. She wondered if Don Harrington had a bag like it, trying hard to imagine him bedding down in a tent somewhere. He might not even have set out. He was weeks away from any danger.

She was very tired, so tired that sleep eluded her. Winifred said softly, 'Is it like you expected, Flora? It's not very glamorous, I know.'

'I didn't want glamour.' She turned over in the dark, looking up at the roof of the hut. 'But are we doing any good, Winifred? I mean the aid agency as a whole. I don't feel as if I'm going to be any use at all. You can't change the land, you can't make it flat.'

Winifred grunted. 'We all think like that sometimes. I worked for six months once in Bangladesh, setting up a workshop, and then soon after I left the rains came and it was all washed away. Gone. As if I'd never been. But the skills were there still, the people I'd taught were still alive. And when I went back, nearly two years later, a woman had begun making simple metal goods in her house. I'd taught her, and she had remembered. It was a nice little industry, making money enough to send the children to school. We do what we can, Flora. What happens after that is up to God.'

Flora lay awake long after everyone slept. Her sleeping bag was a haven, and her mind wove patterns in the dark. She wanted more than Winifred, much more, she didn't want her work to be measured in grains of sand, lost in a desert of need. When her father had banged on the table and insisted 'Flora, it's just the way it is!' she had never believed him. Change had to be possible. The people of this village had to eat better, live longer, have their children grow up educated and strong.

The buffalo grumbled outside the door, stamping softly. Would she see Don Harrington when she went back to Kathmandu? She might go back and find him long gone, without even a note. She let out her breath in a sigh. And slept.

They reached their village, Khola, late the next day. Winifred tutted angrily, because only half a hillside was covered in wooden frames.

'They won't make it if they can't sell it at once,' she said testily. 'We want to build up a stock of course, and then sell that, but they don't believe we can do it. And I dare say all the men have gone off after that damned expedition.'

'All the way to Kathmandu?'

'Good heavens, no. They pick it up on the trek. Somebody's always dropping out, and on really bad trips the porters stage walkouts and our people get the work. And they'd rather live in hope of some climbing excitement than in the certainty of hard work leading to a fair return.'

They climbed the slope to the house allotted to them by the villagers. Flora went in warily, taking time to assess what was to be her home, perhaps for months. An upstairs loft for sleeping,

28

and a mud-floored lower room for everything else. A paraffin stove stood in a corner, and a table surrounded by rickety stools. Against the wall stood a pile of files and papers.

'Is there a bathroom of any sort?' asked Flora dubiously.

'Two tin buckets behind a curtain in the bedroom,' said Winifred. 'There's the river if you want a bath. The toilet bucket empties into a latrine trench out the back. Do make sure you cover everything with earth every time, otherwise the dogs make a nuisance of themselves.'

Flora wrinkled her nose. She wondered if she would ever overcome her very Western liking for a clean, flush lavatory. Fleas she did not mind, bad food did not revolt her, but a tin bucket was very hard to learn to love. She had a sudden vision of her father's face, if he could be transported here and see where she was living. It made her laugh.

'That's better,' said Winifred. 'You've been looking very dismal since that climber went. Don't worry, if he's worth anything you'll see him again.'

'He said I would,' said Flora ingenuously.

'Well then. Just make sure you don't waste your time here worrying about what might not happen there. Go and get some water, Flora, you'll see the pump on the hill. We pipe direct from a fresh spring, to keep the villagers from drinking diluted yak droppings. That's a tip for you — whenever you start somewhere new, clean up the water supply.'

Flora took hold of a large copper water urn and went up the hill. Two village women were getting water too and they smiled at her, one with a baby slung on her hip. Flora took the child while the woman used the pump, and to stop him crying she held him up above her head, jiggling him to make him laugh. A soft evening breeze came hurrying along the valley, touched with the ice of the high snows. The baby chuckled and kicked his legs, and the women, all three of them, laughed.

Base camp was more than usually chaotic. As the Sirdar, Ang Stupa did his best, but whenever he set out on the climb the late-coming porters straggled in and dumped gear anywhere. What's more John, the expedition doctor, was proving all too popular and was continually setting off to answer this or that call for medical aid. He always seemed to be gone.

It was up to the leader, Simon, to put a stop to it but for one reason or another he refrained. Don was beginning to have misgivings about this climb. Eddie was having trouble with his feet after the trek,

29

Mike was taking the altitude badly, and the doctor was nowhere to be seen. Don knew they were wasting time, and they didn't have time to waste.

He tried to curb his sense of impatience. He was always bad tempered before a big climb, tense with the weeks of preparation. As usual, the Sherpas were taking great care that the expedition should be blessed, chanting prayers and waving flags to ward off ill fortune. As always with an Everest attempt, everyone had visited the monastery at Tangboche, where for a not so small fee Lama monks gave sacred protection. Somehow it irritated Don. It seemed to reduce his effort to nothing more than a few coins in a begging bowl.

He found himself spending more and more time with the Sherpas. They seemed casual, almost exuberant, but like many apparently light-hearted people that was not the whole story. They were superstitious, and here, in the high mountains, who could blame them? Life and death often seemed to be in the hands of some whimsical god. Every morning, as they set off with their loads, each man threw a handful of rice on the fire. Don did the same. The Sherpas looked for omens in the high mountains, and if the signs weren't good sometimes they would leave and go home.

Omens. Don told himself he saw none, but they were all around him. The lack of organisation, the time-wasting, the bickering about tiny details. Not that quarrelling in itself told against a climb; there had been many occasions when the only peace for weeks had been out in front on a big face, with behind him the squabbles and personality clashes of a dozen self-centred men. Climbers got on with each other very well some of the time, and very badly most of the time. The odd man with humility and grace had the imprints of climbing boots left all over him by those with fewer principles.

Everyone was busy carrying gear up to Camp I. The logistics of a big climb were always the same, the trail blazed by one or two men, and behind them the vast power and resources of a strong team, carrying food and equipment from one camp to another, going up and up again. Carrying was sheer drudgery, following the ropes laid down by others, perhaps risking your life in the cause of a load of oxygen cylinders and a tent. Only the day before one of the Sherpas going to Camp I through the Khumbe icefall slipped into a newly opened crevasse. He got out using his ice axe, but he had been badly shaken. If he regained confidence he might be a candidate for third man for the summit, because it was always good policy to let a Sherpa get to the top, but he had become very quiet and withdrawn. He, as well as Don, knew that this year the weather was bad.

Hard frost was best for Everest, with the ice sound and not too much new snow falling. Yesterday the snow had fallen wet and soft, and in the midday sun today there was an odd tinkling, as pinnacles of ice collapsed and fell. Higher up, where it was always cold, the danger was not so acute, but down here in the comparative warmth of what to the uninitiated looked like endless snowfields, a man could die in an instant.

They were of course tackling a difficult route; neither Don nor Van would have come otherwise. Don stood for hours at Base Camp, studying the mountain through binoculars. He and Van planned to take a line over an overhang in the rock band; technically difficult and at that height terminally exhausting. It was a direct route, and might take two days off a summit bid, if the men that climbed it were in any state to go on. He and Van were as fit as they could be for it, big men both who reacted well to altitude. Others had tried and failed, which made it more interesting of course.

Eddie was moaning about his feet again. 'Is that bastard never coming back? What the fuck's the point of having a fucking doctor if he's never fucking here?'

Simon, as always, was conciliatory. He had his points, did Simon, the main one being that he charmed his way into the embassies and palaces of the world, obtaining concessions and permission to climb. But, when it came to the crunch, he was too inclined to think he was better on the mountain than he was, and he was congenitally incapable of laying down the law.

Don picked up his load and headed out. If he had to stay here and listen to the squabbling for a minute more he'd kill someone. Even as he left Eddie's voice went on and on, nagging like a bad filling. Don concentrated on stepping out into the snow, fresh last night. Every footprint virginal, every breath cold, clear and pure. Here he was, almost at the roof of the world, alone in a hard, white circle of light.

Nothing to hear but the sound of your feet crunching in the snow, your own harsh breathing in the thin mountain air; nothing to think of except the next step, the next resting place. As always when he stopped he lifted his snow goggles and studied the route up the mountain yet again. A good route, possibly a great route. He and Van were the only two who could do it, the only two strong enough, perhaps even stupid enough, to try. When they climbed together they barely spoke, there was no need. Each knew that what he was thinking the other was thinking also.

Don turned round, and sure enough, there was Van, coming up behind him. Yet they never saw each other between climbs, and they

31

arranged the next one with just a terse 'phone call, one to the other. It was sometimes possible to wonder if they were even friends. Don waited until Van came steadily up beside him, digging the handle of his ice axe into the snow with each step. Without speaking he took off his goggles and scanned the route up the face. He nodded. 'Yes,' said Don. They shouldered their packs and went on.

By the time Camp IV was set up, Don and Van decided they needed a rest. They holed up there for two days, leaving the others to ferry the supplies. It had been hard pushing up to this height. Powder snow avalanches seemed to pour endlessly down the mountain. There was no understanding the Everest weather, one minute sunshine, the next the bleakest storms, minus forty degrees some nights and then a sunlit morning. If the cold didn't get you or the avalanches finish you off, then the sun turned the snowfields soft and the ice friable. On one pitch a nut pulled out and Van came off, falling twenty feet. The rope held, sawing dangerously over rock. 'Well,' he said, as Don hauled him up. 'The gods are playing with me today.'

It was a good time to rest. The sun was hot on the slopes and every now and then another slab avalanche thundered down the mountain. Far below they could see the Western Cwm, filled with boiling white. The whole mountain seemed to be slipping, the snow cascading in beautiful drifts down every gully. They had set up the camp in the lee of a giant boulder, that — hopefully — wasn't going to fall. They sat out in the sun, perched high above the toiling men on the ropes below, drinking tea and reading.

Towards noon on the second day, with storm clouds gathering and the sudden wind so typical of the mountain whipping plumes of snow high into the air, they cooked lunch. They were a little concerned that no one had come up to them that day, but on this expedition anything was possible. They needed supplies, though, and Simon knew that. With the big push to come they were becoming anxious. Hours passed with no sign of activity. As it began to get dark they were both relieved and surprised to see someone coming off the end of the fixed rope and heading towards them. It was Mike.

'You idle bastards,' he snarled, staggering into the camp under the weight of a piled up pack. 'Glad to see you're so cosy.'

'Did you bring the rope?' asked Don.

'Course I brought the sodding rope! Waiting on you hand and foot we are. I'm telling Simon this can't go on. Either you do some work or me and Eddie make the summit bid.' He fell to his knees, almost sobbing, and as one man Don and Van went to take the pack. He looked ghastly, almost hysterical with fatigue.

32

Putting his hand on Mike's chest Don could feel his heart, galloping like a scared rabbit. His breathing was becoming stertorous, exhausted muscles calling for oxygen that Mike could not obtain. Don ran through the pack, but of course Simon hadn't thought to send up any oxygen yet. Stupid bastard. 'Have a cup of tea,' he said matter of factly, and Van held out a mug. Gradually, sipping the tea, Mike seemed to calm. Don and Van exchanged glances.

They had both been surprised when Mike was chosen for the expedition. He was basically a good climber, but he lacked stamina when it counted, and once it had been Don's task to half drag him off a face. It wasn't Mike's fault he wasn't suited to high altitude, though he ought to have the sense to recognise it. And if not, Simon should have pointed it out to him. Still, later in the evening, as Van melted snow on the stove, that endless, laborious task, he came back again to the unfairness of things.

'You two ought to do more,' he insisted. 'We all should have a chance of getting to the top. We're not here just to service our two star climbers, ripping our guts out hauling up and down those damned ropes. Eddie and me can do the rock band. We've got it all planned out.'

'We're working hard enough,' said Don calmly. He handed Mike a mug of Bovril. 'It's getting colder. Me and Van are going to push on tomorrow. We'll bivvy for the night and then look for somewhere to set up camp. The usual site's been swamped by avalanches today.'

'It's time someone else had the lead. I'm going to have a go at Simon about it.'

Mike sank down and cradled his mug. Even the dark stubble on his chin couldn't hide his weariness. He was taking fast, shallow breaths, and his hands were shaking.

'You should go down to Base Camp,' rumbled Van. 'You would feel better.'

'I don't feel ill.' But Mike lay exhausted while the others warmed some stew. When the meal was ready he had fallen into restless sleep.

'He ought to go down,' said Van again. 'And he should not go down alone.'

'If we take him, we'll lose days. Someone's got to come up.'

Every evening Simon held a radio call, talking to each camp on the mountain. Don and Van rarely said anything, but tonight Don cut across all the chatter. 'Simon, we've a problem up here. Mike's dead beat. We want someone to come and take him down.'

'What do you mean, dead beat?'

'Just that. It's the altitude, he needs to go down. And now it's getting colder Van and I are pushing on. We want someone to come up here and get him.'

Eddie's voice came on, thoroughly scornful. 'Oh, come on. Don! If he's that bad you and Van can waste a day bringing him down. And if he isn't he can have a day off up there, living the high life.'

'We haven't a day to waste,' said Don. 'I mean it, Simon. The weather's against us. If we use the next two days to set up the new camp then we could be at the rock band by the end of the week. We're in an avalanche track now, it's difficult, we've got to get on. Someone's got to come up and get Mike.'

The argument raged, with Simon trying to conciliate and Eddie leading the opposition. In all the days Don and Van had been out in front on the climb resentment had been building against them. Everyone wanted to be where they were, and no amount of reason would make them think that it should not be so. No one was prepared to climb to Camp IV just to take Mike down.

The night was very cold, and twice Mike woke and tried to blunder out of the tent. He seemed confused, unable to grasp what was said to him. But in the morning he ate some of the porridge they cooked up for him, holding the bowl close to the growing beard on his face.

'Don't feel so good this morning,' he muttered. 'I'll get on down.'

'Make it by yourself, will you?' asked Don.

'Yeah. Sure. Of course.'

He seemed all right when they saw him down the first fixed rope. His movements were slow and deliberate, and at one point he brushed against the rock and sent a flurry of snow into space. The camp below was visible from here, and on a fine day seemed unnaturally close. Further down it moved out of sight, obscured by the mountain's shoulder.

'He'll get down,' said Don, and bent to lace his boots for the day's climb. They had wasted an hour seeing Mike on his way, they should have been up earlier, well before dawn. The wind was blowing in cold, unfriendly gusts.

'What was that?' Don looked up, suddenly.

'I heard nothing.'

'A cry.'

Both men moved to the edge and looked down. Below, far beyond the end of the first fixed rope and way to the left of the second, lay a spreadeagled figure. Mike's blue duvet jacket was all too recognisable.

'Oh Christ!' Don ran to the tent, grabbing his gloves, rope, his ice axe and snow goggles. As he came out Van stopped him.

34

'No. We will lose a day.'

'He may be a pain, Van, but we can't leave him there.'

'Someone could come up and get him.'

'It could take hours. We can be there in ten minutes.'

'And what can we do? He's dead. Certainly dead. Mike's a climber, he knew the risks when he came.'

They went to the edge and stared down at the prone figure below. It made no discernible movement. 'Leave him,' whispered Van. 'If we go today we can climb this damned mountain. Look at it, Don. Look at it!' The big Dutchman turned and gazed up at the towering mountain face, rock and ice gleaming through the endless white of the snow. It looked majestic.

Don looked back at his partner. Van's face was smooth, expressionless. If they did this thing no one would ever know that they had seen Mike fall. Neither Don nor Van would ever say. And after all, Mike had come on this climb of his own free will; he had accepted the danger, as they all had, with eyes wide open. Simon had forgotten what they were here for, he should have sent someone up to fetch him. Don felt a longing, an almost painful longing, to be up on the face, climbing, just climbing. But there was only one thing to be done. He forced his mouth into a rictus that was supposed to be a smile. Mountains had been paid for by death many, many times, but when it came to deliberate sacrifice, the price had to be too high. 'It's only a bloody hill,' he said. 'Let's go and get him.'

Mike was unconscious, although whether he had passed out before or after the fall was hard to tell. He had skidded down a snow field and slithered to a stop against a rock. One leg was twisted horribly, broken in at least two places. Pulling it roughly straight, they lashed both legs together and began the long task of carrying the casualty down to Camp III. Halfway down they met Eddie, Simon and a Sherpa, carrying loads. When Simon saw Mike's condition he went pale.

'This is all we need. John's away again, what are we going to do?'

'Get a chopper and have him taken out,' said Don shortly. 'He's got one broken leg, possibly two. Look, why don't you two leave your gear and take him down? The wind's getting up. If Van and I don't climb today we might not get out tomorrow.'

'I don't think a day's going to make that much difference,' said Simon. 'I think we should all go down and discuss strategy. There've been one or two niggles surfacing, it would do us good to have them out in the open.'

Frustration almost brought tears to his eyes, Don couldn't speak.

35

He turned on his heels and started back up the slope. Van lifted a coil of rope from the pack Eddie had been carrying and followed him.

'Here!' yelled Eddie. 'That's my bleeding rope. And I'm fucked if I'll let you two stay out in front. Give us a fucking break, Don! Van!'

But the big men took no notice. They began to jumar up the fixed rope, heading back to their barren ledge. If and when they were no longer the best men for this job, then they would give way. Not before. Never before. All they wanted was to get on with the climb.

Many excuses were given for the failure of the expedition, from poor weather to altitude sickness to the basic impossibility of climbing the rock band by the direct route. But Don and Van both knew that without that one lost day they could have made it. The next day was impossible, with high winds and snow blowing horizontally across the mountain. In a bivouac all night, the two men waited only for dawn before crawling back down to Camp IV, and the dubious comfort of dried food. If they could have climbed further the bivvy would have been in the lee of another giant rock, where they could have rested for twenty-four hours. Instead of which, when the weather improved they were faced with a day's climb to that spot, and then a two-day wait before the weather cleared again. They were running short of food and rope, and there were too few men on the mountain to ferry supplies up. Simon had got his logistics wrong.

Don and Van came back in despair to Camp III. They both knew they were tiring, that each day at high altitude was sapping valuable strength that they would need for the rock band.

'We should go down,' said Van.

'If we do, we won't get back up,' said Don. 'Listen to that wind.'

The gale howled and tore at the little box tent. Don felt lethargic and depressed, every action an impossible effort. If things were going well, if he was full of hope, he knew the altitude wouldn't get to him so badly. But he had a crashing headache, and an unquenchable thirst. What's more, Van couldn't raise Simon on the radio.

Snow was piling against the walls of the tent, pressing them in. Don forced himself to get up, go outside and clear it away. His brain wouldn't work, he felt mindless, almost a zombie. The climb was going bad, he was going bad, his feet hurt, his head hurt, how he wished he could escape it all and be gone from here. Where would he go if he could? Somewhere soft, warm and scented. Somewhere quiet, where the wind didn't howl and shriek like a

36

long-dead ghost. And instead of Van, with his billy-goat stink that was as much Don's as his, there would be Flora. Clear, virginal skin, spread like transparent paper over veins that throbbed with blood; her hair, smelling of roses, and as red as a winter fire. Crouched there, scraping at snow with stiff, gloved hands, his beard frozen on his face and the very tears in his eyes turning to ice, Don longed for her.

The next day, to their unending surprise, Ang Stupa brought food up to their camp. He staggered in exhausted, coming out of the snow like a personification of the yeti. But, if the food was welcome, his news was not.

'A Sherpa died yesterday,' he said. 'Avalanche. There is almost no one on the mountain now, the avalanches come down two and three times a day. Camp I was all covered up.'

'Was anyone hurt?' Don munched slowly on a biscuit. He was starving hungry, but his actions seemed as slow as his thoughts, ponderous and heavy.

'A Sherpa full of snow. The doctor is treating him.'

'At least the doc's come back. How's Mike?'

'Took him out by chopper. Not too good.'

They sat in silence, letting the wind's roar fill their heads. Don noticed that the end of Van's finger was splitting, at the point where his fingertip had been amputated. That night came back to him: no food and no fuel, just ice and cold and the wind. Wriggling your toes in frozen boots, taking the boots off and putting your feet in each other's armpits; feeling nothing and wondering if you would ever walk again. When he was away from the hills he remembered that night as a dream, with no reality. You had to be here again to taste the fear.

'Is Simon calling us off?' he asked. 'We can't get him on the radio.'

'He's hoping the weather will clear.'

'If it cleared tomorrow we'd be in no state to tackle the rock.'

Neither he nor Van looked at each other. They had known it for two days past, and neither had said a word. But if a man couldn't lace his boots without two pauses for breath, if he couldn't string a dozen words together in a coherent sentence, then his chances of tackling a big, dangerous climb were precisely nil. A week ago, yes, they could have done it. The moment had come, and been lost.

'We'll go down in the morning,' said Don.

Ang Stupa let the breath out through his nose. 'The signs were bad,' he remarked. 'In Kathmandu I knew it. This is as high as I will ever climb again.'

37

Suddenly, Don felt like crying. A man had died, the climb had gone bad, and high adventure had turned sour. But his sadness was for Ang Stupa. For Don it was over for this year, but for Ang Stupa, it was over forever. It was given to few men to join the elite, to scale the great mountains and triumph over them. If death took one of their number it was almost right, almost a worthy end. But for age to drag a man down, to condemn him to the fireside, to take him back into the mass of creatures too weak and too afraid to look at the high snows and try, that was a tragedy.

Don looked down at his own big hands, clasping a mug. Strong, brown hands, each muscle working in perfect co-ordination with the rest. Fingernails thick with grime that would almost be a joy to wash off. He looked at Van's hands, every bit as huge, the deformity a living testament to the illusion of strength. But Ang Stupa's hands were worn, crabbed, the skin ridged over vein and sinew; aged hands.

Don closed his eyes. There was no time, he thought, nowhere near enough time! All the hours and the days added up to nothing, you were here and then you were gone, the sum of your achievements a pitiful tally on a crumbling wall. Soon, in the blink of an eye, it would be too late. He would be old, as Ang Stupa was old, the great climbs would be over, the memories would grow dim. And he still had so much to do! He would come back. Before God, there in that little tent, he swore he would come back.

That night the wind died to a whisper. The three men woke to bright sunshine, reflecting fiercely from the snowfields, brilliant in the thin, mountain air. The world was clear and beautiful, the peaks around like a gathering of veiled women, cloaked in snow. In the distance they could hear the rumble of yet another avalanche. They filled their packs, dismantled the tent, and went down.

Chapter Four

Flora was becoming expert at paper-making. Naturally dextrous, she could turn out the neatest, smoothest batch of rice paper that anyone could want. In fact, left to herself she could produce enough to keep Winifred happy forever; more than the rest of the village could make in a month.

'Flora dear, you're supposed to be teaching, not doing it yourself,' said Winifred, quite exasperated.

Flora put down her latest stack. 'Everyone's busy. And if I've got nothing to do I might as well make paper. Anyway, they all know how to do it, but half of them aren't interested and the other half are useless. They're so clumsy!'

'All they need is practice,' snapped Winifred. 'Which they don't get when you're doing it for them! Think about what we're trying to do. The western world could send enough food to Nepal to keep everyone going for two years, no one here need ever work again. They'd do it if they thought it would keep out the Chinese. Would that be good for the country? Would it make anyone happy? Of course it wouldn't! We're teaching self-sufficiency. Self-respect. Pride.'

Flora went and sat out on the hillside. She wasn't enjoying this as much as she had expected. The people seemed to tolerate her, no more. Their thickly accented speech was hard to understand, they made jokes which she was sure were about her. And they were so poor! They seemed to live on a diet of *tsampa* and stewed greens, even their hens were so thin and scrawny they were barely worth killing. It was no wonder there was so much disease. The people used a clump of bushes as a latrine, a place swarming with flies and filth; they left wounds unwashed, they drank water out of ditches, they withheld liquids from a child with diarrhoea and then mourned it when it died. But she could not help them. They didn't listen to a word she said.

39

That evening another worker arrived in the village, a man called Finn McDonald. Flora was fascinated. Everyone in Kathmandu had spoken about him, Finn this and Finn that. He was a doctor, one of that rare breed prepared to spend his life amidst the heart-breaking disease of the very poor. He spent his time touring the region, and news of his progress ran like electricity along the paths, carried from porter to porter. They had been expecting him for days, weeks, but there was always some reason for him to be elsewhere. Flora had begun to doubt that he would ever come. And at last he was here.

When he came to the hut Winifred got up, smiling. 'Finn! I expected you days ago. Meet Flora, our newest recruit.'

'Ah! I've heard about you. The little rich girl who wouldn't stay safely in Paris. Glad you could come, Flora. It's good to see you.'

She took his outstretched hand. He was black-haired and bearded, an unmistakable Celt. His face was thin and alert, and in Flora's mind she recalled old Bible pictures, of John the Baptist perhaps. To enhance the image he was wearing a khaki shirt washed almost colourless, shabby trousers and open leather sandals.

Winifred patted the rug. 'Sit down, Finn, and tell us your adventures.'

'No adventures. Just eye infections and worms. Oh, and a good breech birth. A fine little boy, the mother was delighted.'

'No casualties from the Italian climb?'

'A couple of porters who dropped out with retinal damage, that's all. I imagine the expedition doctor will deal with most of the stuff.'

He leaned back against the wall. In an attempt to minimise the divide between helpers and helped, they tried as much as possible to live as the people did, and in the evenings they sat on rugs, with a foam mat surreptitiously placed underneath.

Flora looked at Finn's thin, drawn face.

'You must be very tired,' she said reverently.

He smiled at her, the years dropping away. He would be no more than thirty, perhaps less. 'And so I am. How are you finding Nepal? It's a great mixture, isn't it?'

'Oh, yes. That's what I like about it. But I don't feel I'm earning my keep just now.'

'Flora thinks she's wasting her time on the paper,' said Winifred. 'I keep telling her to take things steadily.'

'Don't you like paper-making?'

Flora shrugged. 'Nobody but me has any time to do it. The women are so busy − in the fields, cutting grass for the stock, fetching water − they don't think it's worth the return. If they could see proof of money earned they'd make time I think.'

40

'Perhaps you should send a load away, Winifred. As Flora says, it might give people an incentive.'

Winifred sighed. 'I was hoping we could have ten loads at least. But all right, Finn, if you and Flora are ganging up on me I suppose I'd better give in.'

Flora beamed at her, and shot Finn a look of gratitude. He at least was taking her seriously.

'You'll have to come out with me for a while,' he said. 'You can see what I do.'

'I'd love that,' said Flora. 'Really, I'd love that more than anything. Winifred, can I?'

'If you wish, dear. Finn, you look exhausted. May I suggest you take yourself off to bed?'

When he had gone to his hut, Winifred said, 'I don't know what we'd do without Finn. He's quite dedicated.'

'Yes.' Flora wondered if Winifred was angry with her for giving up the paper-making so joyously. 'I hope I don't get in his way. When he came in he looked like something out of the Bible.'

'I know what you mean! Tall and thin and fiery. I think he's a Roman Catholic, actually.'

Winifred went back to her book. Flora tried to read too, squinting in the fumes from the paraffin lamp. The wind was beginning to gust under the door, making the lamp flicker. At this height the storms could be sudden and vicious, falling as rain here, although afterwards Dhaulagiri would be wearing a new shawl of snow. The thatch leaked in places, one of the village men had promised to lash some more straw on to it in time for the monsoon. A sense of peace came over her, almost of relaxation. Steadily, gradually, she was finding her feet.

Several days later Flora rose early, and dressed in her trekking gear of jeans, anorak and lightweight rucksack. Finn was taking her to a neighbouring village on one of his regular visits. 'There's nothing very exciting,' he said. 'We might get the odd broken limb, but if it's serious they usually bring the casualty to me. If they know I'm due to visit they wait though. That's why it's so important not to let them down.'

'I won't be late,' promised Flora, and was standing outside Finn's door before it was barely light. After twenty minutes or so two porters turned up, yawning and stretching, with big wicker baskets on their backs to carry the doctor's gear. Finn loaded up quickly and efficiently, with everything boxed and labelled.

'I don't know how you manage out here,' said Flora. 'Everything's so disorganised.'

He grinned. 'I was driven mad at first. But in the end you learn a double standard, to do everything right yourself and just accept what others do. They have a different culture, a rich and varied one. It's not for us to judge.'

Flora nodded humbly. She had the disloyal feeling that it was her humility that made Winifred and Finn approve of her. She longed to know enough to give it up.

The track was steep and arduous. The porters and Finn went effortlessly along, and Flora puffed and panted in their wake.

'If it's any comfort you're acclimatising quite well,' said Finn, reaching in a shirt pocket for a packet of glucose tablets to share. 'It's time, Flora, your body needs time to adjust to lower levels of oxygen. In a week or two you'll be fitter.'

'How long have you been out here?'

He sucked on a tablet. 'About two years. I come from Glasgow. We know all about your father there, I can tell you.'

Flora flushed. 'It's nice of you not to hold it against me. Most people do, you know.'

'And you think they do even when they don't, I suppose.' He laughed at the expression on her face. 'Come on, girl, we'd better get on. I've better things to do than stand here chatting.'

The village seemed very poor. It was set on a steep hillside, and the terraces were small and stony. Three goats were grazing, herded by a child with rickets. When he saw their arrival he hurriedly chased his goats back to his house, following behind on twisted legs. As if by magic twenty or thirty people appeared out of the houses, and gathered expectantly.

Finn unpacked his wares. 'I hope your Nepali's good,' he said to Flora. 'I'm going to send the women to you for a talk about good food and food hygiene.'

'Oh.' She was taken aback. Then she felt an enormous wave of pride. She determined not to let Finn down.

He worked quickly and decisively. As he said, there were many bad eyes and open sores, and several of the children had infected cuts on their bare feet. 'They will wade in the filthy mud of the rice fields,' explained Finn, injecting a local anaesthetic into a cut that needed stitching. 'They understand nothing of infection.'

Flora watched, holding swabs and sutures, preventing light-fingered children acquiring pills and potions while no one was looking. The queue began to grow shorter, as patients became onlookers. Finn called for quiet.

'This young lady is a very good cook,' he said in Nepali. 'She is going to tell the women about food that will make your children strong and your husbands potent!'

Flora grasped what he meant from the shrieks of laughter. She moved to one side, and the women followed her with curiosity, squatting down on broad, bare feet to listen. It was as if the doctor had kindly provided them with an amusing entertainment.

'I want to tell you about how we get ill,' said Flora in halting Nepali. 'About the bad things that come from flies on to our food.' The women chuckled. One or two of them nudged each other, as if this was a joke they had heard before. 'The flies feed on the dung from cattle and pigs and people,' went on Flora. 'And when they settle on your food they leave invisible pieces of dirt − '

One woman, unable to contain herself, fell over in a paroxysm of mirth.

'You'll tell us about the magic creatures next!' yelled a woman. 'The ones we can't see!' A wave of hilarity rocked the audience, and when it subsided they sat, bright-eyed, and waited for more.

'They're not magic,' said Flora shrilly. 'You can't see them because they're so small. And − and in the hot weather − they − they − ' she couldn't think of the word for breed, so she dashed on recklessly ' − they marry and have many, many children − '

Tears began to pour down one woman's face. An old woman with her forehead marked by years of contact with a load strap trumpeted laughter down her nose. It was hopeless.

'I managed to tell them about protein,' she said to Finn, as they began the trek back. 'But they didn't believe me.'

'You did well. And it was cruel of me to throw that at you. I knew what they'd do. But I thought it the best way of teaching you what we're up against. They think hygiene is just another form of superstition, one peculiar to our race.'

'Invisible spirits coming with the flies to make you ill,' sighed Flora. Then she giggled. 'You can see their point, really. It is a bit far-fetched. I'll have to tackle something that will work, like giving babies clean fluids. They might listen a bit more if I gain a reputation for getting things right.'

'Ha! I'm a genius,' said Finn. 'You've learned a great lesson.'

The walk back was peaceful. Finn went in front and Flora seized the opportunity to study him. He might only be twenty-five, she thought. Twenty-seven at the most, he had come here straight after qualifying. But although he was friendly, and took a flattering interest in her, he gave away nothing of himself. In fact, he was so reticent as almost to be guarded. Winifred said he had only been

43

as far as Kathmandu once in his two years in Nepal. She said he was a difficult man to know.

Gradually the weeks passed. The trips with Finn became commonplace, pleasant interludes between bouts of paper-making. Winifred was supervising a tree-planting project, utilising a primitive system of irrigation for this, the dry season. But soon it would be the monsoon, and nothing could be done until it was over. Then they would plant in earnest, and so would the villagers, turning the stony terraces into rice paddy.

'We can't do much here during the rains,' said Winifred. 'We'll head back to Kathmandu.'

Flora blinked. 'I'm not sure if I'm glad or sorry. I'm just starting to get to know everyone.'

'No doubt we'll be back. You've done well, Flora. I'm very pleased. I thought you were going to be difficult and I was pleasantly surprised.'

The compliment made Flora blush with pleasure.

Finn was staying. 'Give everyone my regards,' he said.

'Shall we send you some new books?' asked Flora. 'You must have read everything for miles.'

'If my copies of the *Lancet* have arrived you could send those. And anything that isn't about Western consumerism – it doesn't seem to make sense out here.'

'Franklyn's got a stack of *National Geographic*,' said Winifred. 'I'll send some of those.'

They listened to the radio daily, following the progress of the monsoon. Day by day it advanced through India, and clouds began to gather over the hills. One evening Winifred turned off the radio and said, 'Time to go, Flora. We'll be off in the morning.'

'But I'm not ready! I haven't said goodbye!'

'There'll be time in the morning,' said Winifred. 'Oh, Finn, the places we've left in our time. Places you leave running, what with the tapeworms and the bedbugs and the terrible food. You lie awake at night praying to be rescued!'

'Tomulo,' said Finn, and they both laughed. The place was a byword amongst aid workers.

It took an hour to organise the porters in the morning. They left Finn the radio, and the cooking pots stayed in the hut, ready for their return. Every now and then a villager would come up and press a present into their hands, some *roti* bread wrapped in leaves or a parcel of rice. As she set out on the road one of the children clung to

44

Flora's hand. 'Send him back, dear,' said Winifred matter of factly. 'And keep looking forward. You're leaving a job well done.'

But Flora did look back. She stopped on the next rise and stared down at the little cluster of huts. If there was a ladder of knowledge for her to climb then she had at least ascended the first rung. She felt a great warmth, almost a love, for the strange, smiling, complex people of Nepal.

The air was heavy with heat. Walking was torment, like struggling through a hot blanket of air. The fields and hillsides had taken on a grey colour, as if the sun had bleached them. Over the mountains the monsoon clouds gathered in purple towers, and the hot wind scorched their faces. Flies fed on their sweat, and it was an agonising choice between the heat of enveloping clothes or the pain of scanty ones. Even the porters grumbled.

They stopped for the night in the same village as on the outward trip. This time Flora chatted with the people, and took the toddler on her lap and played a Nepali counting game. The man of the house teased Winifred and said she should be proud to have such a lovely daughter. She would be worth a great deal as a bride.

'She's not going to get married,' said Winifred. 'At least, not for ten years or so. She's got work to do.'

They reached the airstrip around noon the following day. There was a tea stall at one end, and buffalo were tearing at the yellowing grass on the runway. Flora hated buffalo, they were always wildly unpredictable. Finn treated a great many injuries caused by the beasts. She skirted cautiously round them and went to the stall for tea. In the heat it was like nectar.

'The monsoon should break by the end of the week,' said Winifred. 'After the heat it's quite delicious. And everything stops for a few weeks, and the roofs leak and your clothes go mouldy, and rats come and camp out in the houses.'

'Yuk!' said Flora.

'You get used to it,' said Winifred. She shaded her eyes and looked towards one of the paths. A line of porters was approaching, led by the taller figures of Westerners. 'We're going to have company,' she remarked. 'I do believe it's a climbing expedition.'

'Really?' Flora jumped up to look. The colour rushed up into her face. 'I think you're right. Winifred, it's him!'

'I don't see how it can be. Good heavens, so it is.'

Flora dragged her fingers through her hair. It was odd, watching Don Harrington when he did not know he was being observed. He was wearing a singlet and his face and arms were burned mahogany brown. He had a sweatband round his forehead, holding back long hair in need of a cut. The giant rucksack on his back overflowed with ropes, hooks and slings, and a set of crampons dangled from the back straps. Van walked next to him, the porters followed behind and bringing up the rear came the other climbers. One of them was Eddie.

'Hello, Don.' Flora stepped out of the shade of the tea stall. Don's face took on a comical look of amazement. 'Flora! My God, I thought you were a ghost. Flora.'

One of the buffalo extended its neck and bellowed, rolling the whites of its eyes. Flora squeaked and retreated behind the tea stall again. Laughing, Don shook a fist at the beast and it bellowed again, pawing the ground alarmingly.

'Don't, Don! I never know what those things are going to do.'

'Most irascible creatures in history, they are. Come here and say hello.'

He held out his arms, but under Winifred's gaze Flora gave him no more than a chaste peck. He hugged her just the same and Flora whispered, 'She's watching! She'll be furious!'

'I don't give a damn. Oh, Flora, you're a dream come true. You even smell good.'

'You smell like the buffalo.'

'I know, we're filthy. We had to race back or the monsoon would have got us. And our permits are running out. No time for niceties like washing.'

In truth, he didn't smell bad. There was sweat and woodsmoke, oil and leather, an aroma that was headily, deliciously male. Standing so close she felt as if her bones were turned to soft, pliable metal, like the purest, softest gold. She put her hand on his arm where the sweat gathered, and her fingertips tingled.

'Oh, Flora, it's good to see you.'

Winifred's voice broke across them. 'What are you doing here, Mr Harrington? I take it the Everest venture failed?'

'Afraid so. Weather turned bad. We lost a Sherpa.'

'That doesn't usually put expeditions off. They shed the odd crocodile tear and get on with the climbing.'

'Depends on what the Sherpas themselves decide. They accept the risks and if it gets too bad they quit. We don't try and persuade them.'

He turned away. Simon, the leader of the party, was coming into camp. 'I think we'll sort the loads now,' he called. 'Everybody unload their packs and we'll sort out what's going where.'

The porters, squatted on their haunches drinking tea, moved not a muscle. Don said, 'We'll see to that when we've had tea, Simon.'

'There may not be time. Heaven knows when the plane comes in.'

'Not before four,' supplied Winifred. 'May I offer you some tea? You look quite exhausted.'

'Yes. Thanks.' Simon wiped his brow with a handkerchief and took his cup of tea.

'Is he always so worried?' murmured Flora to Don.

'Right now he is. After Everest Van and I wanted to slope off and do some more climbing. Simon's permit wasn't in order but we persuaded him that it would be OK. Quite a few of the blokes wanted to come with us and Simon thought he should come along too, and since we all thought he was something of a plonker on Everest he hasn't been too happy. The porters won't do a damn thing for him.'

Eddie sidled over to them. He dropped his bulging pack on the floor beside Don's. 'You'll be back, will you, Don?'

'Should think so. When I can next get on an expedition. But I've got to put in a bit of time at the climbing school, it won't run itself forever.'

'Look – if you need a bloke, count me in. I'm not kidding. Me and Mike'll have to split up anyway, he's bust his legs and he never was any good at altitude. I know we haven't got on that well but I'd put in some slog if I had to. We could make it to the top next time.'

A porter offered more tea and Don took it, nodding his thanks.

'Everest's booked up for years.'

'Get a sponsor and buy your way in. Someone's bound to want to sell permission. Get out and run the show, Don! We need a climber in charge, not some damned poofter.'

It was said loudly enough for Simon to hear. He pretended he had not. Eddie looked at him challengingly for a minute or so, and then said to Don, 'I'd take it kindly if you counted me in. I wouldn't let you down.'

He picked up his pack and moved away. Flora said, 'I didn't think he liked you.'

'He doesn't. But we've done some good climbing these last few weeks. Reckons I'm his best chance of getting back here. I'll bring him if I get a permit. He might be bloody difficult, but he's got what it takes. Never bottles out, does Eddie.'

Flora became aware that Winifred was signalling to her. She left Don and went over. 'Don't let him dazzle you, Flora,' said Winifred sharply. 'He might look glamorous here but imagine introducing him to your father.'

47

'Honestly, Winifred! I hardly know him.'

'I'd rather you didn't get to know him. That sort of man has scores of women and I particularly don't want you adding to his quota. Have some fun, dear, by all means, but please don't sleep with him.'

Flora went scarlet. 'I wouldn't! You know I wouldn't!'

But, oh, how much she wished she could. She had a breathless, gasping sensation in her chest. Her groin felt hot and tight, her breasts heavy with wanting. He was the most physically powerful man she had ever seen in her life, and she wanted him. She wanted him.

She forced herself to look away. There was no use staring at him like a lovesick cow. The Sherpani women were notoriously easy, he'd probably had half a dozen on this trip. He'd use her and leave her, just as Winifred said. But if only he would kiss her, and his big hands touch her waist, and his long, hard thighs press her down into the hard, dry earth − she felt herself shudder. She mustn't think of it. But if only she could.

The plane was late. They watched it circling the airfield, and at the last moment one of the buffalo sauntered out on to the grass. The plane banked steeply away and the men rushed out to chase the creature. It bellowed and swung its horns fiercely from side to side, making the porters yell and leap to safety. Eventually they sent it trotting down the field and after a cautious interval the plane came again. This time it landed, bouncing over the rough grass.

The porters were being paid off and surplus food distributed. One of them held up half a bottle of Johnny Walker and most of them had hats and gloves that the expedition no longer needed. An air of jollity came over the place, an echo of Christmas on a hot, dusty, flyblown afternoon.

'Come along, dear.' Winifred shouldered her pack and headed for the plane, with Flora close behind. Don fell in at her heels.

'Don't run away from me,' he murmured. 'You know I want to be close.'

'I've got to sit with Winifred.'

'She can sit with Simon. I can't believe your skin. All these months and your skin's like golden silk.' He touched her cheek, and then, as they ducked to go into the plane, slid his hand quickly under her T-shirt. His palm was against the bare skin of her back, sticky with sweat. Every fibre in her shuddered.

The plane was loaded remarkably quickly. The porters left even before they had taken off, anxious to get their money and presents back to their villages before the monsoon. The buffalo was ambling back towards the airstrip. Yelling at everyone to fasten their belts and hold tight, the pilot revved his engines, swung the plane round and executed a short and wrenching take-off. Like a fly buzzing in a bowl, it swept along the ground and then began its steep climb, above and beyond the encircling mountains.

'One step nearer a decent beer,' yelled Eddie.

'And a decent bit of roast beef,' yelled someone else.

'Are you glad to be going back?' asked Flora.

Don glanced down at her. 'Not really. I run a climbing school in the Lakes. It never goes right when I'm away, and now it's back to work and worry and bank loans. I ought to stay home I suppose. But I'm damned if I'll give this up.'

'Who looks after it when you're not there?'

'That's the trouble. People don't stay. Climbers want to climb, they don't want to waste time teaching other people how to do it. I've got a woman comes in to teach beginners, I do the blokes trying to grade up. They don't know what they can do until they try.'

'There must be women who are very good.'

He looked at her assessingly. 'Not many, no. There's the odd one that's brilliant, of course, but it's a very odd one. Climbing's all about bottle, having the right sort of nerve. Girls don't have the same physical courage as men. Or perhaps they give in too easily. I get sick of some woman yelling "Get me down" when she's five feet off the floor.'

'Perhaps we're braver in other things,' said Flora.

He slumped down in his seat and took her hand. He played with her fingers, bending them down one by one. 'Perhaps you are.'

The steep slopes of a mountain pass stretched up on either side, the little plane darting like a gnat between massive peaks. Was it something like this Don had climbed? It wasn't even as high as Dhaulagiri, so he had climbed something immense, unimaginable. Someone began to sing, and soon everyone was singing, 'Ten Green Bottles'. Don's massively corded arm pressed heavily against her. They were a different breed, these men.

Chapter Five

The airport at Kathmandu was as always quite chaotic, and to add to the confusion a storm broke soon after they landed. It was one of the pre-monsoon hailstorms, a vicious assault of ice. Flora and Don ran back to the plane and sheltered under the wing. The noise of the hail was like gunfire. When it stopped, as suddenly as it had started, the lumps of ice deliquesced instantly into shining pools, already steaming in the sun. Some of the clammy heat of the day was gone.

'You'll have dinner with me tonight,' said Don. It wasn't a request.

'I might have to go to a meeting or something.'

'I don't suppose they'll miss you. If I read the situation right, Winifred is very happy to keep you as her eager pupil, hanging on her every experienced word. She won't mind you being flighty.'

Flora laughed. He had summed up Winifred in a nutshell. 'I really like Winifred,' she said. 'I know she seems a bit gruff but she isn't. A baby she helped nurse died and she went up the hill and cried for half an hour. She thought I didn't know.'

'Did you cry?'

Flora shook her head. 'I couldn't, really. I didn't know it. I only saw it once and it looked like a little monkey, and Finn said I wasn't to get involved because it was sure to die. He said it had a serious heart defect.'

'And who is Finn?'

Flora grinned. 'He's a doctor. Very nice. Handsome and dedicated and really quite young. We did so much work together – '

Don reached out and grabbed her hair in a mock attack. 'You were supposed to be pining for me, woman!'

'Ouch! Let go! I'm sure I would have pined. If I'd had the time.'

As Harrington let her go she shot him a look of conscious coquettry.

'Flora! Flora, do come on!' Winifred was waiting.

'I'll come round tonight,' said Harrington, and as Flora walked away she lifted her hand, waggling the fingers in acknowledgement. He watched her go, the mane of dusty red hair swinging. Her bottom bounced deliciously as she walked.

'Bloody scrumptious,' muttered Eddie, at his elbow. 'A bloody Sunday dinner of a girl.'

The thought of an evening with Flora cheered him up. Letters were waiting for him, one from the man he had left in charge of the climbing school, handing in a month's notice as from three weeks ago, and someone had taken the trouble to forward a circular for double glazing. An envelope that had once been crisp and white informed him that one of his regular schools was giving up climbing, as a result of government cutbacks. It would make a serious hole in the climbing school's cashflow. He thrust the letters into his pocket, deliberately refusing to think about them. Coming back was always the same: problems, problems, and never enough money.

He had a bath in lukewarm water, and got a shock when he looked at himself in the mirror. The sun had bleached his eyebrows white, and there were deep hollows where his cheeks should be. He looked years older than when he had left, although good food would soon perk him up. But it depressed him. The time was coming, and coming all too soon, when he would be years older, when the life still left was less than the life so far. He was sick of the climbing school. He taught for the money, no more than that, he wasn't cut out for it. The same rocks, the same mistakes, yet another nervous beginner who thought he'd let them fall — whatever patience he once had was gone.

He went early to collect Flora. He waited on the doorstep while she rushed around collecting her coat and her bag. People called out to her: 'It's your turn to shop in the morning. I'll leave the list on your bed.'

'I bet you're glad to have your dogsbody back.'

And Winifred's voice: 'Just you go with Flora and help her carry. Honestly, you men!'

She came out in a rush. 'Sorry. We were chatting and I didn't notice the time.'

'I was early. But you seem very at home in there.'

Flora nodded, bright-eyed. 'Everyone expected me to take fright and go home. It's so much better now. I feel I could stay here forever.' She spread wide her arms, taking in the cluttered, smelly

51

street with its paving of broken tarmac, the scramble of buildings, the blue-black, velvet night.

'I've got to go home,' said Harrington. 'My permit's run out.'

'Oh. Yes, I suppose you must. I didn't realise.' For a second she looked crushed. And then she smiled at him. 'At least we've got tonight.'

They went to a restaurant that was almost glamorous by Nepal's standards. Although the room was smoky there were fingerbowls and hot towels and fruits suspended in glistening syrup. Don ordered everything, and more of everything, and he and Flora ate with silent dedication. After a while they paused.

'I'm so glad I came,' said Flora. 'It's heaven.'

Don said, 'I can't decide if the food's really superb or we're just desperate.'

Flora wiped a scrap of bread round her plate. 'It's wonderful. Just wonderful.'

'I do like a girl that retains her standards whatever the situation.'

Flora threw back her head and laughed. Don grinned too, taking pleasure in watching her. Her red hair was a mass of newly-washed curls, gleaming in the lamplight. She had found a white blouse from somewhere, and he could follow a trail of freckles from her cheeks to her throat and down into the tantalising shadows.

At that moment the door opened and James and Winifred came in from the street. They all said hello, but as soon as the older couple had settled Winifred made a face.

'Did you see that? He's like a wolf preparing to dine on young spring lamb.'

'You shouldn't be so strait-laced. They're only young.'

'Too young, in Flora's case. I didn't think they produced nineteen year olds quite so innocent these days. She's dazzled by all that clomping around draped in thongs and hooks and ropes. And this Harrington creature is altogether too much. He's a strong, passionate, wild young man, and he isn't good for her.'

James tapped her wrist. 'You were the one who really didn't want her out here in the first place.'

Scooping her short hair behind her ears, Winifred said, 'You'll have to forgive an old cynic for being so mistrustful. Her background put me off. But she's a very sweet girl who ought to be married off to some clean-living aid worker. Do we know any?'

'None. It's like the foreign legion − they're either homosexuals or they all have murky pasts.'

The food came and they began to eat, trying to ignore the

murmuring and muffled laughter from across the room. 'Have you heard from your wife?' asked Winifred lightly.

'Yes. A letter was waiting. She's keeping busy, involved in the church bazaar. We're getting the funds.'

Winifred wrinkled her nose. 'Knitting tea cosies to feed the starving. How very demanding.'

James kept his eyes on his plate. After a moment Winifred said, 'That was uncharitable of me.'

James looked up at her. Just for a second his face registered deep and painful unhappiness. 'I'm sorry, Winifred,' he said. 'Believe me, I'm sorry.'

She took a deep breath and hiccupped on a sob, seizing her glass and taking a gulp of strong Indian beer. 'Twenty-five years of us both being sorry are rather hard to take, James,' she remarked. 'Sometimes I wonder what we're doing it for.'

Flora leaned across to Don and said softly, 'Do you know, I think there's something between them. Winifred and James.'

'Having an affair, you mean?'

'No! In love. There's something about the way they look at each other.'

Don grunted and gave them a cursory inspection. 'Probably talking about tree-planting. Did you hear about Mike?'

'Was he the one who swore all the time?'

'He and Eddie took turns at it. The dark bloke. Broke his legs on the climb. They've stuck him in some hospital here and he can't get out. They've got him flat on his back with his legs up in traction and he spends his days yelling for a decent pint of beer. Simon's going to have to get him shipped out by ambulance plane or something.'

'Poor Mike.'

'If it was me, would you come and visit?'

She closed her teeth on a piece of bread. 'I might. If I could fit it in.'

He chuckled and she laughed back. He murmured, 'You know, Flora, your eyes reflect the light. It's like the afternoon sun on a fathomless mountain lake.'

'Oh! And to think I said you weren't romantic.'

'But it's true. Are you sure we can't go back to your room?'

'Quite sure.'

'Let's go find a room someplace.'

She looked fearfully across the table at him. His face was oddly intent, the eyes pale as water. He took her hand, squeezing it with some force. 'Come on, Flora. Join the grown-ups.'

She took a deep breath. There was something delicious about this moment, when she knew that he wanted her quite desperately. She felt suddenly capricious. 'And will you love me for ever and ever?' she whispered breathlessly.

'Until the world stops turning. I just want to hold your naked body, to love your naked body – '

Flora leaned back, away from him. The actual physical image of what they might do repelled her. She wanted it wrapped in mystery, like a miraculous happening. 'Don't,' she said sharply. 'I don't want to do it. Let's go.'

His eyes seemed to blaze at her. But then he said, 'Yes, let's go.'

He threw some money on the table, they nodded to Winifred and James and went out.

When the temperamental electricity supply allowed, some of the temples of the city were illuminated. Don stopped outside one, staring up at the long sequence of carvings that decorated the roof. Giant phalluses stuck out at obscene angles, figures twined and contorted in leering union. Don pointed at a symbol, repeated and repeated again.

'Lingam and Yoni,' he told her. 'Penis and vagina. You can see it everywhere. This whole country's founded on sex.'

Flora said, 'I know. Everything seems to be doing it. No one does in Scotland. Not near me, anyway.'

Don glanced down at her. He had expected to shock her, and had failed. He felt a sudden and surprising rush of tenderness. She was so young, so lovely, she had such deep and untrammelled innocence. He drew her into the thickest shadows and started to kiss her, letting his tongue caress hers, but when he reached up under her shirt she pulled sharply away. He cursed himself. She was a virgin, and needed coaxing down this path. His fierce need only frightened her. 'I'm sorry,' he said. 'I know I'm being rough, I can't help it. I find you very desirable.'

'I don't mean to be difficult,' she said shyly.

'You're not. Look, I was going to leave tomorrow, but I can squeeze another week. Let's get to know each other.'

'Yes! Oh yes, please.'

He took hold of her again, and as they kissed he cradled her bottom, rocking her against his imprisoned erection. He was so hard he could have broken through concrete, and suddenly she gave a soft, wanting moan. He couldn't bear it. All at once he was trying to get into her jeans, and she was beating at him with small, work-roughened hands. He couldn't wait, he had to have her. Suddenly she pulled away from him and began to run.

'Flora! Flora, wait!'

She was running the wrong way. He raced after her, and when she glanced over her shoulder and saw him she turned into a side alley, as dark as Hades. He heard the thump as she fell. Her blouse, no more than a glimmer in the darkness, lay ominously still.

'Are you all right? My God, you're not hurt, are you?'

'Go away,' she said thickly. 'You're a rapist.'

'I am not! Come on, get up. Your beautiful blouse is a mess.'

She was covered in mud and the unspeakable slime of Kathmandu. He took her to a wayside fountain and washed her hands and face. Her cheek was grazed. She was crying. He said, 'You're being a terrible baby.'

'I don't think I want you to stay after all,' she said thickly. 'If I did sleep with you, I'd never see you again.'

'Of course you would.'

'Would I?' She looked up at him with such hope that he was ashamed. If she was here and he in England there was no future for them. But the present, the here and now, beckoned with such tantalising insistence. 'You never know what might happen.'

He had lost her. In that moment she went back inside herself. He felt enraged, because if he had lied she would have come to him, and truth ought to have some of its own reward. He took her arm and began to hustle her along.

When they reached the aid house one of the workers said, 'Why don't you bring your friend in, Flora?'

'No thanks,' she said shortly. 'I fell in an alley, I'll go up and get washed.'

'I'll say goodbye then,' said Don. 'I'll be on tomorrow's plane.'

'Yes,' said Flora. 'I think you should.'

He made no move to kiss her. She turned her back on him and went quickly upstairs, and he said nothing, did nothing. She knelt in the dark at one of the windows and watched him walk away.

It was dark when they woke her. At first she was bewildered, assailed by nameless fears coming to her out of the darkness. 'Where am I? What is it?'

'It's all right, Flora.' Winifred, calm and pale, in her clean blue pyjamas. 'There's been a telephone call. Are you properly awake?'

Flora sat up, pushing her hair out of her face. 'I think so. What's happened?'

'It's your father. He's had an accident in a car. You're needed at home right away.'

The words didn't make sense. Instinctively she put her hand out towards the letters she had opened only that day, all of them written in his strong, curling hand. 'He isn't ill,' she said incredulously.

'I'm afraid he is, dear. An accident, he was hurt. If you get up now I can help you pack. James has rung the airport and got you a seat on the early plane.'

It all seemed impossible. She staggered about her room, doing what Winifred said, cramming a great stack of unwashed clothes into a bag. Sleep clogged the mechanisms of her brain, and still there was no belief. She said 'Who telephoned? I don't see how – '

'Someone contacted the consul. You forget how important you are.'

'Dad is. I'm not at all.'

'I'm sure you are to him.'

Later, she sat in the kitchen drinking tea. Her eyes felt hot and dry. Franklyn, wearing a sweater in what was already solid heat, said, 'It may not be all that serious. We don't know what happened.'

'Oh, Franklyn! What shall I do if he dies?'

Her mug shook, and the tears brimmed up, dammed by her dark gold lashes.

'Don't think of the worst,' said Franklyn. 'Perhaps he's making an awful fuss to have you back home again.'

Flora swallowed down her tears. 'I bet that's it! He never wanted me to come. It'd be just like him, you know.'

They drove her to the airport in the agency's battered truck. The sun was coming up, filling the horizon with glorious pink. In the distance the mountains seemed like a child's fantasy, a dream of a foreign land. A woman in a red skirt walked by, carrying a load of fodder.

'Remember us, won't you?' said Winifred.

'I'll be back. Whatever happens, I'm sure I'll be back.'

'I hope so, dear. I really do.'

A line of businessmen in crumpled tropical suits was waiting at customs. They had been on the incoming Indian flight on which Flora was to leave, chasing the sun into the morning. A motley crowd of people was getting ready to board the plane, and amongst them was Harrington. Winifred went up to him. Circumstances conspired to make him seem a welcome constant in Flora's life.

'I'm so glad you're on this flight. Flora's had some bad news, her father's had a car crash. She has to go home. I wonder if you'd be kind enough to take care of her?'

He looked across the room. Flora was watching him. She was very pale, the shadows under her eyes as dark as the eyes themselves. She was as tired and wary as a young hunted deer.

'I'll take the greatest care of her,' he said.

Chapter Six

In the beginning they were distant with each other. Flora sat by the window, watching the mountains come and go, until all at once they were engulfed in a storm. The little plane lurched and stuttered about the sky, lightning sparking off the wingtips. Some of the passengers reached discreetly for paperbags, and a businessman said loudly, 'At least I'm well insured. If this goes down my wife will be able to buy herself a Scottish estate.'

'I don't think I'd mind if we crashed,' said Flora.

'Rubbish!' said Don. 'Death's a lot more frightening than you think. And it's permanent. Believe me, I know.'

As the turbulence increased a rumour spread that they would turn back. But the little plane battled on, thrown around the sky like paper in the wind. Don held out his hand and Flora took it, because warm flesh held wonderful comfort. At last they broke out of the clouds, and the airport lay welcoming before them, gleaming under a sheet of water. They landed in a haze of spray. Everyone clapped.

'I've got to sort out my onward ticket,' said Flora.

'So have I. I'll do us both.'

She followed him into the terminal. People, bags and boxes thronged the place: a lady of the greatest elegance in a gold sari was trying to refrain from rubbing shoulders with the masses. Umbrellas were everywhere, like some strange form of flowering shrub. The noise was indescribable.

'Miss Kincaid? Miss Flora Kincaid?' An urbane Indian in white tunic and trousers was approaching them.

'I'm Miss Kincaid.'

'We are so delighted to have you with us. Let me take you out of all this upheaval. We shall find you a quiet place to sit and take tea, your flight is not for one more hour. We were so sorry to hear of your father's accident.'

Flora smiled shakily. 'You're very kind. Do you mind if Mr Harrington comes too? He's been asked to look after me.'

'Then Mr Harrington may of course accompany you. Will you require an onward ticket also, sir?'

'Er – yes, please. If you can arrange that.'

'Of course.'

Porters were summoned for the luggage and their benefactor led them away, cutting a swathe through a forest of humanity. They were deposited, with their luggage, in a small, very English air-conditioned room furnished with sofas and a tray of tea.

'If you would be so kind as to make yourselves comfortable. I shall let you know directly your plane is ready.'

Harrington flung himself down on a sofa and stretched out his long, khaki-clad legs. 'Who the hell do they think you are?' he asked incredulously.

'Me, I suppose. Flora Kincaid.'

'And you habitually get the red carpet treatment?'

'I do if Dad asks for it. It's quite heartening really. He can't be too bad if he's gone to all this trouble.'

'Flora – who is your father?'

'Malcolm Kincaid. You might not have heard of him. He owns KORSEA.'

Harrington said nothing. Flora reached across to the tray and poured them both a cup of lemon tea. A bowl of spiced nuts tempted her and she nibbled a few.

'He's a multi-millionaire,' said Don at last.

'I know he is. It's a bit difficult to get away from, actually. He always does things like this, throwing great chunks of money around to try and make things easy for me. He doesn't realise how often he makes things difficult. But he's an old darling. I do love him, you know.'

Harrington thought for a moment. 'You're not nearly nasty enough to be the daughter of someone that rich.'

Flora sipped her tea. 'I think people are only nasty when they don't have what they want. I've always had everything I wanted. And I went to a girls' boarding school and learned very quickly not to rush about telling everyone how rich I was, especially since I was the absolute richest. I couldn't bear Dad turning up in the helicopter.'

'Oh, Christ,' said Harrington, laughing.

Flora had to grin. 'Everybody's so worried about the poor little girl on an assisted place whose parents come on the bus, they never stop to think about me at the other end, being smarmed over by the headmistress because she wants an extension to the science block. So

I learned to be normal. And I don't shop. I can't bear shopping.'

Harrington looked at her. 'Where did you get last night's blouse from?'

She had the grace to blush. 'Actually, it was Chanel. It's easy there, you just – and it's bound to last.'

'It should. It could probably keep a Nepali family for a year.'

Flora sat on the sofa and hunched her knees up. 'Don't get at me. Everyone always does when they know. It's only when you've got money that you realise how much more important other things are. Like effort and reward for effort. I'm sure we could land you on Everest by helicopter, but I don't suppose you'd appreciate it. You want to climb there.'

'While you sit by in your designer jeans.'

'It would be a bit stupid of me to dress like a pauper! Honestly. I knew you oughtn't to know.'

He came and sat on her sofa, encircling her ankle in his fist. 'I'm not teasing. I'm just a bit taken aback, that's all. Here's me, going to impress you with an invitation to visit my climbing school, all of three wooden buildings and some cliffs, and you live – where do you live?'

'Castle Melchior,' said Flora offhandedly. 'Were you really going to invite me?'

'Yes.' He took both her ankles in his hands, and pulled her legs an inch or two apart. Flora lay back, her eyes half-closed, watching him.

'Will you come?' he asked.

'I don't know. It depends how ill my father is, I suppose. But you can come to the Castle. I'd like you to.'

He said nothing. Instead he drew her legs further apart, until her denim-covered crotch was fully exposed. It was a position of stark abandonment. 'We should be lovers,' he said softly. 'If we were lovers now it wouldn't matter what else we were. The money's going to get in the way.'

Flora closed her knees, twisting away from him. He let her go.

Starting high in the mountains, for the first third of its length the river Delyn falls as a fast-flowing stream. As the gradient lessens and the water increases it harbours salmon, the rich man's lawful prey and the poor man's secret theft. Malcolm Kincaid began by renting the fishing and ended by buying ten miles of the water, in the midst of which, on a knoll in a bend of the stream, stood Castle Melchior.

There had been a defensive dwelling there since time immemorial.

Surrounded on three sides by the river and raised up on its granite plinth, many a warlord found he could lie easy there. The final castle, the one whose remains Malcolm Kincaid decided to own, was over four hundred years old, a turreted, battlemented ruin of a place, with arrow slit windows and shrubs growing out of cracks in the walls. Never conquered, never overcome, the castle was crumbling under the weight of time, and some said had been beaten to death by Kincaid.

Not that he had forgotten the building's history. On the contrary, he relished all that was ancient and great. He put battlements where they had existed before, and turrets where turrets should be. When the extra wing was constructed he insisted that it should be in keeping, and since by this time he was coming to like turrets and battlements, he encrusted the place with as many as it could hold. Winding stone stairs delighted him, although of course they were impractical. So wide, grand staircases in the Hollywood style rested cheek by jowl with medieval stonework, and many a vast and flaming log fire turned out to be run on gas.

Idiosyncratic, in some ways absurd, the castle sat on its hill like a child's dream of such a place, like Malcolm Kincaid's dream. Loathed by historians, the local people loved it, because it was extravagant, and unembarrassed. Like the robber barons before him, Kincaid did as he wished, and stood by it.

The estate stretched for miles all around, encompassing the whole village of Delyn Cross, a grouse moor and a deer park. Much of it was wasted, because Kincaid hated shooting. The thought that a creature might get away and die horribly tormented him, although he had no such sentiment about fish. Or men for that matter. But the Kincaid estate was swarming with foxes, stoats and pine martens, ospreys and eagles and kites. They fed on grouse living wild on the moor, disturbed only occasionally, as this evening, by the Kincaid jet landing on the tarmac strip nearby.

The sun was going down, and the castle cast long shadows across the river. A white peacock hung from one of the turrets, and another paced slowly across the lawn. Kincaid's own flag, that flew on all his ships, on his offices, on his buildings, on his factories, on his farms, fluttered bravely from the flagpole, because Kincaid was in his castle and all was supposed to be well.

Flora climbed from the plane and stood for a moment, her hair blowing across her face. She swept it back and held on to it, gazing down hungrily. 'It looks just the same,' she said to the pilot. 'I can't believe he's not the same.'

The car was waiting, a chauffeur in a tam o'shanter holding open the door.

'Good to see you, John,' said Flora, shaking hands. 'Do you know how he is?'

'Angry I think, Miss Flora. Because he's upset. Mr Darnley was driving, at your father's request, they had some private business to talk over. And Mr Stephens was in the back. Swerved to miss a deer, the police said.'

'How are Mr Darnley and Mr Stephens?' Her father's two closest associates were well known to her.

The chauffeur looked down. 'They are dead, Miss Flora,' he said gently. 'Mr Kincaid was on the other side of the car, you see. They were on the side that hit the tree.'

She felt very cold suddenly. She got into the car, saying nothing. Her heart beat in an uncomfortable rhythm, as if she was in Nepal again and climbing a steep track. He must be bad to call her home like this. Why had no one said that people had been killed? Suddenly she wished that Don was there, to bind together these two separate parts of her life, of her; the Flora Kincaid that lived at Castle Melchior was not the girl that was coming home.

The journey was over in minutes. They drew up before a great oak door, studded with iron. At once it was flung open. A grey-haired woman stood beaming, neat in dark blue, with a starched lace collar.

'Marie!' Flora scrambled out of the car. 'Marie. How good to see you, how are you? And how is Dad?'

'Not as well as he'd like to be, Miss Flora. He's in the white turret, with more space for things, and that's upset him, he wants his own room. But the doctor couldn't manage with all that armour around. Your father swore at the doctor and spat at the nurse so you see the state we're in!'

She threw up her hands in exasperation and Flora giggled in nervous relief. 'He can't be so bad, then. I've been so worried. I'll pop up and see him right away.' She ran through the hall and up the stairs in a whirl of red hair.

The housekeeper wiped her eyes. 'He'll be a piece better now she's back,' she said confidentially to the chauffeur. 'This place is a barrack without her.'

Flora herself was at her father's door. She knocked softly. Not softly enough it seemed. A cracked voice called, 'Flora? Is that you, Flora? Come in, girl, come in! Let me see you.'

She went in, brushing her way past a nurse and her assistant rising hurriedly to intercept her. Stretched out on a high bed, surrounded by drips and instruments, lay her father, Malcolm Kincaid.

He had always been a striking looking man. Now, in old age, he had the wrecked grandeur of an ancient monument. His hair had once been as red as Flora's, but now it was silver grey, with just a badger stripe of the old, bright colour flashing back from his forehead, like a flame in the mist. There was a gash in the midst of it, criss-crossed with bloody stitches. Flora met his eyes, so like her own, that strange dark blue, but in Kincaid they were misted to purple. He had never been tall, only a chunky five feet eight, but he had held himself like a ramrod. That was the greatest change. He lay in the bed with his great head rolled against the pillow, hiding the side of his face. His skin, once ruddy, was deathly grey. A graze, scabbing over, marked his cheek and the bedclothes were held up on a cage.

'Flora! What kept you, I've been waiting.'

'Hello, Dad. I'm sorry, I came as soon as I could. You don't look nearly as bad as I expected.'

'Then God knows what you expected. They want me finished off, out of it. Lie down, go to sleep, take the pills. Recipe for death. These women are in the pay of my enemies, Flora!'

She bent over and kissed him on the forehead. One side was quite stiff, she realised. His eye and his mouth seemed to be dragged down, as if by an unseen hand. A linen cloth, the greatest humiliation, was pressed against his cheek to catch the dribble.

'How are you hurt?' she asked thickly.

He swallowed, grunting. 'Broken my pelvis and cracked some bones in my back. Trussed like a chicken I am, enough steel in me to build half a ship. Bloody fools wanted me to stay in the hospital, I told them what to do with their pap and their fussing.'

'But — your face looks different.'

There was a silence. The nurse stepped forward. 'I think you've noticed a slight degree of brain damage, Miss Kincaid. Your father suffered a severe blow on the head. Doctor scanned of course, but it was decided — they felt it best to see what time can achieve.'

'Frightened of turning me into a vegetable,' muttered Kincaid. 'Don't care how many pills they give me but they won't operate, oh no. Don't have the nerve for it.'

'Three specialists agreed that it was best left alone,' said the nurse soothingly. 'It's important that you rest.'

Kincaid flared at her: 'How can I rest? I've a business to run, things to do! The world doesn't stop just because some harpy in a white apron says it should. What have you done in your life, hey,

63

Nurse Collins? Seen off a few dozen old duffers who would still be here today if they'd had a chance − got out of bed instead of lying here − waiting to die −' His head rolled feebly on the pillow.

'Has Mother been?' asked Flora, sitting down beside him.

'She came. I sent her off with a flea in her ear. She never wants to see me when I'm fit, can't bear the sight of me. And the minute I'm ill and she thinks she can get the upper hand, round she comes telling me to lie down and take the bloody pills. You know what she's like, Flora!' He looked at her with a hint of pleading.

'I know what you're like. Oh, Dad, it would be nice to have her here.'

'Not with me like this. I won't have her see me like this. Flora, if you could have seen Darnley − Stephens − and she would talk about them. As if I can bear it!' He closed his eyes for a brief, tortured second.

She took his hand. He had never been a man for weakness. When she was a very young child, when Kincaid was fighting for his commercial life, he hadn't come home when he was losing. He came home in triumph or not at all; he cast his wealth before his wife and asked her to take that as proof of love. For him it was the ultimate proof. For her it counted for nothing, and he had never understood that, not even now.

'She likes to think she can help you,' said Flora softly. 'You shouldn't drive her away.'

'I did not drive her! She went because − oh, you know your mother. Lilian never did understand me. I'd rather she was away from here. I don't want her sympathy, I don't want to die with her hanging over me, watching my eyes fall out.'

Nurse Collins was preparing an injection. 'If you'll calm down you won't die at all,' she remarked. 'And I've never yet seen anyone's eyes fall out. Mine nearly did when I saw this place, of course, but that's rather different.'

Kincaid chuckled. 'Made of stronger stuff than your mother, isn't she, Flora? She won't run out on me.'

'I will if you spit medicine at me again. Hold still.'

She injected into his hand. Kincaid's fingers twitched, the most feeble of movements. He tried to laugh 'Feels as if it doesn't belong to me. Lump of wood, almost. Strange.'

Flora took a dragging breath, forcing herself to optimism. 'It's bound to get better. Like a bruise, or something. Oh, Dad, I was so worried! At first I thought you'd died.'

'I swear I told them not to worry you. Wanted you home, of course. Wanted you worried enough to up stakes and come and see your poor old dad. Not much for a man to hope for in life when his little girl's off round the world not thinking of him, not caring about all he's set up for her.'

'Dad! After I've come all this way to see you.'

A sudden grin lightened his grey face. 'So you have. Just as pretty and fresh as the day you were twelve. What are those earrings you're wearing?' He squinted at the brass hoops she had bought in a bazaar. 'They suit you. I'll get them made up in gold. Now if only this damned nurse would see sense we could have a proper family dinner, tell Marie to do some salmon, with venison pie. We'll have Château Margaux and a decent port −'

'You'll have a lightly boiled egg and like it,' snapped the nurse. 'I'm sorry but Miss Kincaid is going to have to leave. You've got to get some sleep.'

Kincaid subsided, grumbling. The nurse went with Flora to the door. 'He's been so worried that you wouldn't come. In quite a state. I think he'll rest now.'

Flora looked back to the bed. Already her father's eyes were closed. 'How bad is the brain injury?'

The nurse sighed. 'It isn't easy to say. He was never unconscious, not for a moment, but he was very confused. There's an area of pressure, some bleeding has occurred. It may clear. In the meantime − your father has a severe loss of function on his left side.'

Flora swallowed hard. He was alive, she told herself. He would get better. She gathered her wits. 'Was he horrible to my mother?'

'Unforgivably. But I gather it's his way.'

Flora nodded and went out.

Her room was ready for her, a clean cotton nightdress laid out on the vast drawn-thread quilt on her bed and a small tray of sandwiches standing nearby. She nibbled at the corner of one, then went to run a bath. She felt bone weary, and her nerves shuddered under the strain of everything. There was no use crying, no use at all. Her father's state appalled her, as it so clearly appalled him. Malcolm Kincaid had spent his life bending men and circumstance to the force of his will, and now that circumstance had turned and broken him.

Flora stripped off, throwing her clothes in a bundle into the linen basket. At school she did everything for herself, and at home she did nothing. Early on she had learned double standards, that it was as wrong to be competent at home as it was to be helpless outside it. She had learned two personalities too, one for her father and one for everyone else. Only occasionally did the two converge, and then always to her father's fury. He adored his daughter, and he would never stop, but that did not

65

prevent him from bullying her unmercifully if she was not as he wished.

She stepped into the huge bath, letting her hair hang back in the water. The tears that she had tried to suppress seeped out beneath closed eyelids, and nothing she could do would stop them. Everything had changed. She had gone out into the world secure in the knowledge that she could always come back, and stand safe and surefooted on the rock that was home. But there was no rock. Her father was mortal, as mortal as the men who had died, and never in her life before had she known that.

Flora slept well into the next morning. Five minutes after she awoke a breakfast tray appeared, and she knew from experience that a similar tray had been brought every fifteen minutes for at least the past hour. After Nepal the waste seemed horrific. Flora ate porridge and munched hot buttered toast with thick Dundee marmalade wondering how she could ask Marie to be more frugal without causing a disturbance. 'Your father will not like it, Miss Flora,' was always Marie's irrefutable defence. Perhaps the servants benefitted, and shared four or five breakfasts between them.

It was a bright day, but cool after tropical heat. She dressed in pale grey trousers and a white cashmere sweater with huge sleeves gathered into a cuff. As she was finishing, the telephone by her bed rang. Flora recognised the brisk, bright tones of the nurse. 'This is Nurse Collins, Miss Flora. Your father's a little woozy after the night and he doesn't feel too happy about visitors. He'd like you to come and see him after lunch.'

'Is he worse? Is that what you're saying?'

'No, the same as usual. He wants to be at his best for you, my dear. He made a big effort yesterday. He's quite exhausted.'

'I see. I'll come after lunch then.'

She went slowly downstairs. What was she to do, if her father would not see her? She had come home to see him. Disconsolate, she wandered into the library. She must write to Mr Darnley's wife, although Mr Stephens was divorced long ago, his marriage succumbing to the pressures of his job. Perhaps he had a sister, a brother. But after that, what? She could ride perhaps, or take the keeper's dog for a walk. A visit to her mother would take the whole day, and must be postponed, but she could perhaps go into Aberdeen and look round the shops. As she had told Don, she hated shopping, unless it was for something she particularly needed. She had the money to be profligate, and profligacy offended her soul.

Someone cleared their throat. She turned and saw Forbes, the

66

butler, so silent and so discreet that he would have qualified as a cat burglar. 'I'm sorry to intrude, Miss Flora, but Mr Mactee is here. He wants to see your father.'

'But he can't. Dad's not nearly well enough.'

'He's very insistent, I'm afraid.'

'Show him in, Forbes. I'd better talk to him.'

While she waited she wandered over to the window, gazing out across the river. Swans were gliding elegantly along, and a gang of ornamental ducks were squatting on the bank, quite ignoring the specially designed jetty constructed entirely for their convenience. In the distance, on the hill, she could see faint brown smudges that meant deer, the hinds fanning out from their stag. She turned when the door opened, and greeted James Mactee with outstretched hand and a welcoming smile.

'Mr Mactee! I'm so glad to see you. It's been ages.'

'It certainly has, Miss Flora. You've quite grown up.'

He was a man nearing sixty, with pepper and salt hair and heavy rimmed glasses. After Darnley and Stephens, Mr Mactee was the most senior man in the firm, responding to orders from above. He had been Kincaid's chief clerk for over fifteen years, a cautious, reliable employee at the limit of his potential. Flora sat herself in one of the huge leather chairs and invited Mactee to sit down also. Her father always said Mactee had no mind of his own, so it was no wonder he was lost.

Mactee leaned forward on the edge of his chair. 'I must see your father, Flora. We've been negotiating the purchase of a small diving concern, and I cannot possibly agree a price without his approval. He wouldn't expect me to.'

'How much is it?'

'About two hundred thousand pounds.'

'But you can agree that, surely? It isn't very much. Dad doesn't need to be bothered, and he really is far too ill. You go ahead, Mr Mactee. I'll take the responsibility.'

'But it might not be what he wants to do, you see. Sometimes he pulls out of these things. He has a nose. Of course if Mr Darnley was here — or even Mr Stephens — it's a tragedy, Flora. You should have seen poor Mrs Darnley at the funeral, it was a pity. And a greater pity that you weren't there to represent the family, if I may make so bold.'

'I was in Nepal,' murmured Flora, knowing that to Mr Mactee that was no excuse. In his view, as in her father's, she should never have gone.

Mactee drummed his fingers on the little marquetry side table.

'There's no one knows what to do, and that's a fact,' he declared.

Flora clasped her hands together. 'I think we've got to learn to manage, Mr Mactee. What's wrong with this diving business?'

The man looked affronted. 'How am I to say? It's Mr Kincaid decides these things. The business looks a fair bargain, I'll give you that, but he might be thinking that the market is closing down, or their equipment is past its best, and there's no way I could commit money just on your word. If it was Mr Darnley or Mr Stephens, but as things are — he'd be angry, and rightly so. I think I'd better do nothing.'

'If my father wants to buy this firm then you should. You really are going to have to learn to manage without him, Mr Mactee. For a while at least. Perhaps forever.'

There was a silence. Mactee looked dourly up through his heavy glasses. 'I cannot believe he's so bad.'

'I'm afraid he is. There are a lot of broken bones, and there's a brain injury, you see. A slight brain injury.'

'I did not know it was his brain!' said Mactee, suddenly round-eyed.

'It isn't! I mean — he had a blow on the head. It's like a sort of stroke. A minor stroke. It's bound to get better.'

The man sniffed. 'We'll not want people to know it's his brain,' he murmured. 'If I could just have a wee word with him, Flora, I could put minds at rest.'

'I'm sorry.' She stood up, indicating that the meeting was over. 'The smallest thing exhausts him, even seeing me. Please, Mr Mactee, try and imagine what my father would want. You have to manage without him. Please.'

When he was gone she felt unsettled. What was to happen to KORSEA, to all Kincaid's numerous projects? He had come so far in so short a time, beginning with two trawlers left to him by his father, a skipper. He had built up the fleet to more than twenty, and then, when the oil boom came, overnight he turned the firm into an oil rig supply venture. It was still the backbone of his empire, with tugs and supply vessels, helicopters and support crews. He already had two specialist diving teams, engaged in oil contracts all over the world. Whatever his strategy in seeking to purchase another, he had not told Mactee. Kincaid and his two henchmen had always played their cards very close to their chests.

The 'phone rang. It was a small engineering factory, engaged in constructing specialist equipment for the oil industry. Where was Mr Kincaid, what were they to do? They had completed a big order for another company, but rumour had it they were going out of business and wouldn't pay. Should they deliver? Normally they'd consult Mr Stephens, but in the circumstances Mr Kincaid would know. What would Miss Flora advise?'

'I haven't any idea,' she said desperately. 'Make some enquiries. Really, my father's too ill to be bothered and I can't help. I'm sorry.'

But the calls kept coming. This problem, that problem. The range and scope of her father's activities amazed her. And the risks he took – she went cold thinking of the millions involved in deals, all hanging precariously in the balance. She simply didn't know what to do.

She visited her father straight after lunch.

'How are you Dad?'

'Fine. Just fine. Up and about tomorrow.' But he looked so ill. His eyes were filmed with weariness.

'I want him to take some sleeping pills, but he refuses,' murmured Nurse Collins. 'He's too anxious about his business.'

'I need to be worried,' said Kincaid in a breathy, urgent voice. 'You can't just leave things and hope they'll survive. What's happening, Flora, can you at least tell me what's happening?'

She sat down and put her chin in her hands. There was no use fobbing him off, he was worried to death about things. 'Everyone's running around in a panic,' she admitted. 'Nobody knows what to do. Mr Mactee was here this morning and I've had a dozen telephone calls from different people about different things. You didn't tell anyone what you were doing, you see. They don't know how to go on.'

'You don't advertise your hunches,' mumbled Kincaid. 'Don't want everyone jumping on the bandwagon. Darnley – Stephens – either one of them could have taken over. Stephens most likely, Darnley had that ghastly woman in tow. The wolves will be gathering, no doubt of that, waiting their turn to rip at KORSEA's carcase. We must look as if we're managing, Flora!' He glared at her in impotent entreaty.

'We'll try.' Even to her own ears it sounded weak.

He let out his breath angrily. 'Don't let Mactee buy that diving company, I never meant to go through with it. He must – he must watch the markets. There's a recession coming. My God, he's bound to be caught napping!'

His eyes seemed to glaze. 'Lilian?' he mumbled. 'Lilian, is that you? Get that damned dog off the bed.'

'It's me, Dad,' said Flora in a high voice. 'There isn't a dog.'

'What? Course there isn't. Why isn't there somebody – any-body – to help? Oh God, Lilian, why did we never have a son?'

Nurse Collins moved Flora firmly away from the bed, administering an injection whether Kincaid wanted it or not. Flora waited until her father's eyes began to close. She folded her arms across her breast. If she had been a boy so much would have been different. There would have been pressure, pressure to succeed, to follow Kincaid in footsteps scorched hot with brilliant achievement. Instead there had been gentleness, indulgence and love. Kincaid had never wanted her to take an interest in the firm, and besides, the sly opportunism of business had never attracted her. She and her father had always known she wasn't cut out for the firm. But he had always wanted a son.

She went downstairs, back into the library. The Kincaid family tree hung on the wall, a fabrication made up of thin fact and wishful thinking. Kincaid's father had been a man from nowhere, making good with iron determination. In Kincaid himself that iron had turned to steel, but in her − she knew herself all too well. She had her father's looks and her mother's brand of gentleness.

The telephone rang again. She wondered helplessly if she should ask Forbes to stop putting the calls through. But she picked up the receiver just the same. 'Hello. Flora Kincaid.'

'Hi. It's me.'

'Don! Oh, Don, if you knew how good it is to hear you.'

'I was worried. You sound a bit frantic. Is your father OK?'

'No, he's really ill. And nobody seems to be able to manage without him. It was a terrible crash, you've no idea. My father's two most senior executives were killed, there's no one running the firm at all. I thought you were another company wanting to know what to do, and I can't tell them. I didn't even know we owned half these things. He's even got a turkey farm. A turkey farm!'

'You'll never be short of a Christmas dinner.'

'Perhaps we will. They're supposed to be expanding. But I don't believe the man in charge, I think he's taking advantage while Dad's ill. He sounded like a crook.'

'What do crooks sound like?'

'Not like you. Oh, Don, it's so good to talk to you. I feel it's been years since I got home and it isn't even a whole day.'

'I know. Flora, there was something I wanted to say. I should have said it before and I wish I had, because everything was simple then. I love you.'

For a long second words deserted her. 'Oh, Don,' she said at last.

'You don't have to sound so disappointed!'

'I'm not! But it makes me want to cry.' Her voice strangled and she was silent.

'Don't cry, Flora. I hate to think of you alone there. Look, I'll telephone tomorrow.'

'Oh yes, please!'

She put down the 'phone and sat for long minutes, her arms wrapped around her knees. For his part, Harrington swung his receiver in a long-fingered hand, looking at nothing. The climbing centre dog sat staring at him, and at last he noticed. 'What are you looking at?' he demanded. 'A man's entitled to fall in love once in a while. She's beautiful. A lovely, very special girl. You old cynic.'

The collie sniffed, contemptuously, and lay down on the worn office rug.

Chapter Seven

The Harrington School of Climbing had been in existence for only six years or so. Before that it was quaintly called the Lakeland Outdoor Centre, consisting of a sharp rocky outcrop, some collapsing huts, a dozen canoes and a long walk to a river in which to put them. As a failed business it cost very little, and Don bought it with the aid of a loan from his parents, who were only too pleased to have him doing something positive with his strange desire to climb.

He had paid them back within a year. Another twelve months and he had the huts refurbished, a practice wall built in an old barn and two part-time teachers helping out with a seemingly endless stream of schools, detention centres, women's groups and rambling clubs who all wanted to scramble about his rocks, finding themselves. The true climbers, the ones who needed his help to stretch and grow, were thin on the ground. Or perhaps they weren't on the ground at all but were up in the hills, discovering for themselves the things he wanted to teach them. It wasn't what he had intended – not at all what he had planned. Leaving aside his relative affluence, the job gave him more in common with the history master at the comprehensive than the men in the hills.

Gradually, almost without conscious thought, he found himself spending more and more time away. The school provided the money to climb, and its momentum kept it going for a surprisingly long time. But gradually the rot set in. Teachers who had been filled with enthusiasm lost it to a steady drip of dissatisfaction; decisions went unmade, repairs undone, sometimes even wages were hard to come by. Don was never there, nobody could ever get hold of him for long enough to complain. So they left, and sent him their notice, in the post. And the clients fell off, one by one, sometimes literally when worn equipment broke. There were a couple of insurance claims for broken ankles. As Don moved up in the climbing world so the school

72

moved down, in exact counter-balance. Now, when he was truly in the front rank of the world's best, the school teetered on the edge of collapse.

He glanced through the bookings; a couple of local schools sent their more difficult boys for the odd afternoon, in the hope that they would kill themselves no doubt, but he could get someone else to take care of them. Apart from that there was only one good engagement, a party of three students. Don knew them slightly, they were from a club in Calderdale. They were looking for some thrills, a dose of terror that would take them through the hard graft of finals. Don grinned to himself. He had got his own degree, in engineering, largely through sitting in climbing huts in the rain, reading a book by the light of a torch. If the weather had been fine that year he might never have graduated at all.

Until then he had ten blank days. He glanced round the office, furnished with an unpleasant desk that someone had thrown out, a row of iron filing cabinets and a series of highly detailed maps, each with worn spots where endless fingers had stabbed. He should go and see the bank manager, talk about a loan, promise commitment and dedication and hard work. But he would far rather go and see Flora.

He wasn't much of a romantic. And yet, how could a climber not be all romance, what else was it that spurred you on, to that mystical, joyous loneliness at the top? He had never courted a girl in his life before, there had been no need. Women tended to fall off the tree in front of him, like ripe plums. Flora was ripe enough, more than sweet enough, and if she wouldn't fall he saw no reason why, for once, he shouldn't shake the tree.

He allowed himself a moment of erotic fantasy; Flora, naked to the waist, struggling to get out of a pair of tight jeans. He arrived at the moment when her damp forest of pubic hair came into view, and she looked at him, full of shocked virginal horror to see him there, but smiling ... He groaned. The dog scowled at him and pointedly got up and went to the door.

'I just wish she wasn't so damned rich,' said Don as he let it out. 'If she offered me a loan I'd have to crucify myself not to take it.'

The dog wasn't listening. Instead he sauntered off down the track to the neighbouring farm, where he stayed when Don was away. He could tell when the boss was off again, on some new enthusiasm. He might be a dog but he wasn't stupid.

Flora was seated at the desk in the library. She had devised a filing system for problems, listing each one under whichever heading seemed most appropriate. The biggest section was KORSEA, then Farming, Estate, and the last was Absolutely Stupid Little Queries that Even I Could Answer.

She was wearing a plain grey jersey dress, and not even its simple lines could disguise its pedigree. She found it essential to be smart, since the removal of all the firm's top brass resulted in managers and executives arriving daily with their distress in person. It needed all her authority to deter them from insistence on seeing her father.

In the distance the doorbell rang yet again. Flora glanced round the room, checking that everything was intimidatingly formal. She wondered if she ought to find herself a pair of glasses to add to the executive image. Forbes knocked on the door. 'A Mr Harrington to see you, Miss Kincaid.'

Flora let out a gurgle of surprise and joy. Don held out his arms and she ran into them, and then they parted to stare at each other.

'My, my,' he said in admiration. 'This, for a girl who doesn't shop.'

'You look very − sportsmanlike,' replied Flora. Don was wearing flannels and blazer, and his university tie. But he was so tall, and she felt dwarfed by him, and the room seemed somehow diminished.

Forbes, still at the door, cleared his throat. 'Shall I bring tea, Miss Flora? And some of Marie's scones perhaps?'

'Oh. Yes please, Forbes. Are you staying, Don? Do say you are. It's just terrible here on my own, you can't know.'

'That's why I came. You sounded so fraught I couldn't sleep.'

She giggled. 'You look very well rested to me.'

Don clapped a hand to his heart. 'I am exhausted, ma'am! Worn out with the strain of our parting.'

They both laughed, and somehow they were holding hands again. Don lifted her wrist to his lips and pressed feather kisses along the path of a thin blue vein. Shivers of delight coursed through her.

'Excuse me, Miss Flora.' Marie, with the teatray.

Flora said, 'That was quick, Marie. Forbes can hardly have had time to tell you we wanted some.'

'I thought you'd be thirsty. You and your visitor. He'll not be staying, with your father so sick.'

'He is staying, actually. I shall enjoy his company. Be an angel and organise his room, Marie, please?' Flora gave her most winning smile, but Marie glowered in return.

'It isn't fitting, Miss Flora,' she hissed. 'With you alone!'

'There are almost two dozen people in this house, Marie.'

'Only the servants, Miss! It isn't proper! What will your mother say?'

'I think she might say I was old enough to invite who I like to stay. Put Mr Harrington in the blue room. That should keep everyone happy.'

When she had gone, Don said, 'What's the matter with the blue room?'

Flora grinned. 'Nothing. But it's so far from mine it's almost in England. Honestly, sometimes I wonder who's in charge here. It certainly isn't me.'

The telephone rang and Flora spent ten frustrating minutes saying that no, her father had not recovered, and no, he was not receiving visitors. When she hung up she looked glum and Don said, 'Is it really falling apart?'

She shrugged. 'Hard to tell. Possibly. He kept everything so close, you see. It was all between him and Mr Darnley and Mr Stephens. They even stopped talking when I came into the room, let alone anyone else. It was Dad's way, it was easy for him, and he never took holidays. Half the time he'd set people chasing hares he never intended to catch, and there are companies half bought, and schemes half-finished, and no one knows what to do. Least of all me.'

'And he's really not going to get better?'

Flora shook her head. 'Not for ages. He's so ill, Don. Even I'm only allowed to see him once a day. Ten minutes exhausts him. His mind starts to wander.'

'Don't look so anxious, love! Don't.' He put his arms round her and she nestled her head into his shoulder. They were so close, thigh upon thigh. A mutual heat began to build. Flora lifted her head and he kissed her open-mouthed, crushing her to him.

'If I might show Mr Harrington to his room?' Forbes. Flora went red with mingled rage and embarrassment.

Don followed Forbes at some distance, taking time to look around. The house was unreal, unbelievable. He passed walls swathed in tartan, each one different, and swords with silver-gilt handles set one above the other. Yet there was nothing museum-like about the place; it was all too extravagant, too touchable for that. Thick Persian rugs lay scattered on the floor and the heavy, damask curtains were held back with silver chains. Everywhere was the evidence of Flora; a book left on a chair, a scarf and a pair of gloves set down on a table, some sewing abandoned in a passageway. Forbes was waiting for him at a door.

'Does Flora always leave things around?' asked Don.

'Always, sir. At the end of each day we send a boy round to collect them for her.'

He ushered the guest into the blue room. There was a four poster

75

bed, draped in blue and red, against walls lined with pale blue silk. The carpet was creamy white, and white roses stood in a vase on a table. The flowers impressed Don more than anything, hinting at endless gardens from which flowers of all colours could be summoned in an instant.

His bag was already in the room, and his clothes hung in the cupboards. When Forbes had gone he sat on the edge of the bed for a moment. A door led off to a pale marble bathroom; from his window he could see a peacock steadily pacing in the park. 'What the hell are you doing here?' he whispered to himself. 'What the hell makes you think you can look at Flora Kincaid!'

He pulled off his tie defiantly. She was the same girl now as in Nepal, and all this was only money.

Flora ordered a special dinner that night. She was feeling optimistic, because Nurse Collins' policy of sedation seemed at last to be helping her father. He was resting peacefully, and his colour had improved. When she discussed the menu with Marie, Flora put an arm round the housekeeper's broad waist and said, 'You don't have to look so po-faced. Don's only a friend. Dad's a little better and my friend's come to stay, so tonight I'm going to enjoy being home.'

She dressed in jade silk, tight in the bodice and waist, flaring to a wide skirt. She caught her hair up in emerald clips, and put plain gold earrings in her ears. Joy was her perfume, from a huge bottle that must have cost hundreds of pounds. But tonight she felt joyous.

Don was waiting in the small sitting room. He executed a mock bow. 'My lady. I am yours to command.'

'And I command – that you should kiss me.'

Even as she said it Forbes came in with a tray of drinks. 'I swear they listen at the door,' said Flora incredulously. 'I can't do anything.'

'It's no time to be upsetting your father,' said Forbes meaningfully.

'But you're upsetting me,' said Harrington. 'We want some privacy, Forbes. You can come and tell us when it's time to eat, and until then I don't want to see a damned soul. Except Flora.'

Forbes turned dark red, and left. Don poured them both a drink, whisky for him and sherry for Flora. 'Damned autocrat,' he muttered.

'You sound just like Dad,' said Flora. Suddenly she sighed. She wasn't fooling anyone. There was nothing to celebrate. She took a gulp of sherry to still the ache in her throat. 'Oh Don, I know he's better but he's still desperately ill. What's going to happen? What do I do about the business?'

76

Her eyes swam with tears. He couldn't look at her. 'You need a manager. Someone to run things for a bit.'

'Mr Mactee's past it, and even if he wasn't he hasn't got the guts. Don – I keep thinking I should try.'

'Can you?' He sounded incredulous, and he was. She was soft through and through; soft breasts, soft belly, soft, soft heart.

'I don't know. But things couldn't be worse than they already are. Would you help me – just for a few days? Just until I know something about what I'm doing?'

He reached out and brushed the tip of her nose with his finger. 'You know I'll do anything you want,' he said gruffly.

They drank champagne and laughed at nothing. The food was exquisite, with home made petits fours and the vegetables served in little pastry cases. Don held up a gilded serving fork and studied the crest. 'I have never lived like this,' he said bemusedly. 'I never knew people could live like this.'

'I'm glad you're here,' said Flora. 'You make it so much fun.'

The candles flickered in their sconces, and Forbes drifted silently from his post by the door and neatly trimmed the wicks. A telephone began to ring in the next room, an irritating break in a warm and golden mood. Forbes went quickly to silence it.

'They shouldn't put calls through to the library at this time of night,' said Flora. 'They know I'm entertaining.'

'Perhaps it's urgent,' said Don.

Forbes came to the door and said, 'Miss Flora, if I could ask you to spare five minutes?' and she got up at once, casting down her napkin and widening her eyes at Don.

He waited in the doorway while she spoke. Her voice was tight with tension. 'Yes – yes – of course – do you think I need to come? I will if you want. Yes – if you think I should. Thank you for 'phoning.'

As soon as she hung up Don said, 'Crisis?'

She nodded, twisting the 'phone cord round her fingers. 'One of our helicopters has crashed. Some men may have died. Mr Mactee's at a golfing dinner somewhere and no one can reach him, and they want a company representative to go to the quayside. Dad would go normally, he always got involved in these things. Now I've got to go.'

Don took her shoulders. 'We'll both go. I'll get my car.'

'Don't be silly, we'll go in the Bentley.'

It was a strange night for an accident. The weather was warm and still, the air shot through with pearly summer moonlight. So far north it never became completely dark, and they drove through a

77

perpetual twilight, still and beautiful. They hardly spoke. It was late by the time they reached the quayside, but everywhere was abustle. The chauffeur, John, approached the dock gates with confident speed, and sure enough they parted majestically in front of him. Everyone knew the Kincaid crest. Blinding lights almost hurt the eye. The lifeboat had come in.

Don got out and Flora followed him. In the yellow light everyone looked like aged ghosts, from the reporters to the bedraggled survivors. Beyond, dawn seemed to hover on the horizon, as the sun skirted the edge of the earth.

'Let Miss Kincaid through,' called Don. Men stood aside to let her pass. She felt helpless and irrelevant. A man in uniform who might have been the harbourmaster said, 'This is the helicopter pilot, ma'am. You'll be wanting to talk to him.'

'Yes – ' said Flora, and looked nervously at a man wrapped in a blanket. He was shaking with nerves and shock, and someone had given him a cigarette. He threw it down on the quayside.

'I don't smoke,' he said waveringly to Flora. 'I think it kills you.'

His hands went up to cover his face. Before she could think what to say Don stepped past her and said, 'You're in shock, mate. I know, I've been there. Don't mind us, we can talk tomorrow. But people need to know what went wrong.'

'That's easy enough.' The man swallowed convulsively. 'Bloody engine packed in, didn't it? I thought the fuel line was blocked, the way it died – did anyone die? We were in the water for bloody ages.'

'A good half hour,' said a broad, oilskinned lifeboatman. 'We're checking the manifest but it looks as if everyone got out. We've a man near gone from the cold, though. The only one not in a survival suit.'

The pilot huddled deeper into his blanket. Flora said, 'There's an ambulance here, you'd better get off to hospital. I want to thank you for all you did.'

'I couldn't tell if everyone was out,' he whispered, and choked on a rush of tears. Someone led him away to the ambulance.

A television camera team lumbered up, the sound recordist almost shambling under the weight of the powerpacks and a girl reporter circling frantically, asking questions.

'Who's here from KORSEA? Is anyone here from KORSEA?'

'We are,' said Don.

'Great. We'll do a short spot, can you get under these lamps. Howard, we've missed the survivors, we'll pick them up at the hospital. Which one of you is the spokesman?'

78

'Me,' said Flora in a small voice. 'I'm Flora Kincaid.'

'Great, let's get it in the can. Howard, are you ready? Helicopter crash, Take 1. Miss Kincaid, was this an old helicopter? It seems strange that it should crash on such a fine night.'

Flora swallowed. 'Yes – I thought it was strange too.'

'There have been a number of cases of metal fatigue in planes lately, do you think this helicopter has fallen victim to the same disease?'

'I suppose – it could be – '

'KORSEA'S profits have been exceptional in the last two years. Has it been the result of cutting down on investment in new machines?'

Flora blinked. 'I haven't the faintest idea. Don, I don't know anything about any of this.'

The reporter grimaced at the camera. 'Scrap that one, Howard. Do you want to try again, Miss Kincaid? We were hoping to get this out on breakfast television.'

'I can't answer any of those questions,' said Flora. 'I don't know any of the answers.'

'Right, we'll say we approached the company and a statement wasn't forthcoming. Howard, let's get off to the hospital.'

'I'll do the statement,' said Don.

The girl looked him up and down. 'You from KORSEA? OK, we'll give it a try. Howard, Take 2, helicopter crash. Was this an old helicopter? It must be unusual to have a crash on such a fine night.'

'We should be grateful it was such a fine night. The rescue services got into action immediately and first reports indicate that everyone was picked up. Our pilot acted with commendable presence of mind.'

'Was metal fatigue behind the crash?'

'Obviously firm statements can't be made at this stage. But the pilot reports sudden loss of power, perhaps due to a blocked fuel line. All KORSEA helicopters are grounded as from now until checks on the fuel systems have been given the all clear.'

'Were all the passengers wearing survival suits?'

'All except one, and he's seriously ill with hypothermia. I've got no idea why anyone was aboard without basic survival protection and we won't rest until we know how this came about. We take the most stringent safety precautions at KORSEA, and the fact that so many people were saved shows that we're doing the right thing. But that one man worries me. There's no room for slackness where North Sea safety is concerned.'

He directed a single, piercing look right at the camera. The girl clicked off her microphone. 'Great. What's your name? We may want to come back to you in the morning.'

'Harrington. Don Harrington. I'm staying at Castle Melchior.'

'Where? Oh, Castle Kincaid. Right, got it. We'll be in touch.'

The girl bustled off, followed by the cameraman toting his load on his shoulder, and the soundman struggling behind, still linked by a cable, like an umbilical cord.

'I don't know how you could say any of those things,' said Flora.

'If I hadn't they'd have minced you. All the press want is an easy story, they won't chase too hard for the truth. Still, we'd better do what I said we'd do. We'll have to kick someone awake to get working. Why wasn't that man wearing a survival suit? We've got to find out in time for the morning TV. And we've got to ground the other choppers — do you have other choppers?'

'Lots, I think. I don't know what we've got.'

'Are the offices round here? You'll have to get hold of someone.'

Flora telephoned Mr Mactee from the car 'phone, only to find he had returned from his golfing dinner somewhat the worse for wear. 'If you could just give me some telephone numbers for the staff,' she coaxed. 'No, really it can't wait till morning, Mr Mactee. I'm sure your secretary will know, but what's her number?' He mumbled, swore audibly to his wife, and at last found the entry in his address book.

Dorothy, the secretary, the real brains behind Mactee's office, was more rewarding; within half an hour she was at the KORSEA headquarters with the office keys and a list of relevant names. Don gave instructions and she began telephoning. The telex machines chattered aggressively.

'You mustn't mind Mr Mactee. He's not used to managing on his own, Miss Kincaid.' Dorothy, middle-aged and ruthlessly efficient, pulled out crew lists and rosters even as she spoke.

'We need whoever's in charge of maintenance of these damned machines,' said Don. 'Is there a safety manual somewhere? I want to be able to flourish it on TV.'

'Suppose Dad doesn't like it?' worried Flora.

'Dad is going to have to lump it. There'll be a Board of Trade enquiry, you don't want the firm coming out of it with a bloody nose.'

'Will you be coming into the firm, Mr Harrington?' enquired Dorothy sweetly. 'We could certainly use someone like you now dear Mr Kincaid's so unwell.'

'They've got you, what more do they need?' said Don.

Dorothy chuckled. 'He's certainly a charmer, Miss Flora. You'll have your hands full with him.'

'We're just friends, Dorothy,' said Flora tightly. 'He's keeping me company while my father's ill.'

'Oh, I see. Sorry, I'm sure.'

Don shot a look full of laughter at Flora, and she went pink. He thought how lovely she looked, in the green silk dress, her hair a tangled cloud of red. But there was no time to talk, people were coming into the office in ones and twos, unshaven, just in tracksuits; one man had simply flung his coat over his pyjamas. 'We'll have to ground the choppers,' he yelled. 'Tell the old man I'm getting on to it.'

'They're grounded,' said Don. 'I'm waiting for someone to run a check on the fuel systems.'

'Blockage, was it? Thought it must be that. I'll see to it right away.'

'Thanks.'

Dorothy held out the 'phone. 'TV people want you over there, Mr Harrington. Here's the safety manual. And that particular machine was only two years old.'

'They've had the same problem in the Far East,' yelled the man in pyjamas. 'It was the heat there. And the weather's unusually good for this time of year.'

'Not exactly tropical,' prevaricated Don. 'It'll be something else. Thanks a lot, folks, I'll blind them with science.'

Flora hurried after him out of the building. 'I feel dreadful, having you do this,' she said. 'I know it isn't fair.'

He took her wrist and pushed her through a door in front of him. 'You realise if someone finds out who I am then we're sunk? I suppose they might think I earn the odd crust working for KORSEA, though. Amazing the way everyone talks about your father. He's God to these people.'

'A very noisy, bossy God. But they all love him. So do I.'

They came back to the castle at two in the afternoon. Flora was exhausted, and Don's chin was thick with dark blond stubble. Marie met them at the door. 'I've laid out some luncheon in the small dining room,' she said respectfully. 'Some salmon and a few venison patties. There's a wee bowl of raspberries too. I thought Mr Harrington might be hungry after so much talking on the television. We all watched.'

'Is my father all right?' asked Flora, yawning.

'Nurse Collins says he's a mite restless. He'd like to see you, Miss Flora.'

'Do you mind, Don? I'll go right up.'

But she went to her room first to clean her teeth and put her wrists under the tap. She was surprised to see herself still in the same green dress. She must change or her father would know something had happened. She unzipped herself, revealing harsh lines where the whalebone had bitten into breast and torso. It was a relief to pull on a skirt and jumper. She paused a moment to compose her face into carefree lines.

Her father was sitting up in bed. 'Hello, Dad,' said Flora brightly. 'How are you? It's a lovely day.'

'Not when one of our helicopters has gone down.'

Flora hesitated in the very act of sitting down. She shot a glance at Nurse Collins. 'How does he know?'

'You all think I'm bloody senile,' said Kincaid. 'Even I can watch television.' He gestured to the remote control set on his bedside table.

'I didn't know he shouldn't,' said the Nurse.

'What else are you hiding? Who else are you hiding? Who was that creature, sitting there talking as if he runs my firm? Can't I trust even my daughter to tell me the truth?'

'I don't lie, Dad,' said Flora. 'But I don't worry you. Lots of things have happened, of course. The crash was an emergency. I've got a friend staying – Don, Don Harrington. He seemed to know what to do.'

'Someone staying? Here?'

'In the blue room. I met him in Nepal.'

She tried to meet her father's eyes with total frankness. A blush crept towards her hairline. 'Get him,' said Kincaid suddenly. 'Get him here, now. Now, I said!' He fell back against the pillows, suddenly breathless.

'You can see people later,' said Nurse Collins. 'You must not disturb yourself like this, Mr Kincaid. The doctor particularly said – '

'Will you shut up, woman?' hissed Kincaid. 'I've got business to see to. I haven't spent my life building an empire to see it fall apart because of the strictures of some frigid schoolmistress! If I die it will be when my work is done. Not now.'

'I'll get him,' said Flora. 'I'll go right away.'

'And I'll see him alone,' said Kincaid.

Harrington came slowly up the stairs. The nurse was waiting for him at the door. At once she murmured, 'I've called the doctor. He could kill himself like this. Please remember he's a very sick old man. I'll be outside the room if you need me.'

Don nodded. He was possessed of an enormous curiosity about Kincaid, and he was dreading disappointment. Kincaid's castle, his empire, were so entirely magnificent that if the man himself was only ordinary it would be as if he climbed Everest and found a tea shop open on the top. He forced himself to turn the heavy brass door handle. His feet drowned in thick carpet, making no sound.

'At last. I feared the women wouldn't let you come. I'm Malcolm Kincaid.'

'Don Harrington.'

'Won't you sit down?'

Don pulled out a chair. Kincaid was staring at him openly and he returned the compliment. It was odd to see so much of Flora — those eyes, that streak of hair — and yet to see it in ruins. Still there remained traces of some quality of presence.

'You're a handsome bastard,' said Kincaid suddenly. 'You get girls by the handful no doubt.'

'When I was younger.'

'You're not in your dotage yet. And now you've got Flora Kincaid.'

Don laughed. 'A poor guess. What I would like to have and what I've got are not the same thing.'

'And what is keeping you? There was never a girl yet could resist a man of charm and good looks if he decided to have her. My daughter's my own, but she's a woman for all that. A very young woman.'

'Perhaps you don't know her as well as you should. She's got a mind of her own, has Flora. And so have I. We'll make our own history and we don't need help.' He met Kincaid's eyes with calm defiance.

Kincaid snorted. 'Mind my own damn business, in fact. And why don't you mind yours? What were you doing today, blethering about my company, my affairs? How in God's name do you know we've got ten choppers, this or that safety record? How dare you get on that damned box and behave as if you own my company, my own company?'

'I'm sorry you didn't like it. No one else seemed to have a clue what to do.'

'Doesn't surprise me. Mactee's an old woman, I should have got shot of him years ago. I was waiting for him to retire. And there's always something you never plan for. I never thought, never

83

guessed – Darnley and Stephens, both together – good men, both.'
He paused, dragging himself back under control. He went on tightly,
'You never think you're going to go. Never think it can happen. Year
after year you keep going, and after a while you start to think you'll
keep going forever. I was a fool. I made provision for everything
except this.'

Harrington said nothing. Kincaid leaned back against his pillows,
gesturing for a glass of water. Don held it to his lips and he sipped.
'You think I was a fool, don't you?'

'No. You ran a tight ship. You couldn't know there'd be an
accident. You can get new people to take over, but in the meantime
there's bound to be a bit of panic.'

'If I'd run things differently it would have been better. But it was
good to have just three of us, no one looking over our shoulders,
asking questions. I like to do things my way.'

Don grinned. 'Yes. So do I.'

He found the old man looking at him. Those dark, pain-filled
eyes had none of the sharpness, the hardness that he had expected.
Kincaid was a subtle man, he realised. He pretended bluntness only
for effect. 'You did well,' said Kincaid, and he was almost humble.
'I owe you my thanks.'

Don cleared his throat. 'I wish I could say I did it for Flora, but
it wouldn't be true. I couldn't resist getting hold of things. It was –
like the best sort of game.'

'Like sex,' said Kincaid. 'The buzz is the same.'

'But it doesn't put you to sleep,' said Harrington. They met each
other's eyes and laughed.

Kincaid studied the man before him almost genially. 'Where did
Flora find you?' he asked. 'Did she say Nepal? I sent her to Paris,
you know, and the hussy got herself taken on as a field worker.
The only time in her life when she hasn't done as she was told.'

'You're lucky. She's very sweet. The sweetest girl.'

'Are you in love with her?'

Harrington glanced at him. 'That's private. Nothing to do with
you.'

Kincaid gestured with his good hand. 'You don't understand, my
boy. You think I'm prying into my daughter's love affairs, for no
good or worthwhile reason. But, you see, Flora isn't just any girl,
not even any rich girl. She's Kincaid's daughter, his only child. And
I am one of the richest and most powerful men in the country.'

'I realise that.'

'Do you? Sometimes I can hardly comprehend it myself. The
beginning was so hard, so desperately, painfully hard. I lived for

84

the work, it was real to me. Now, it isn't so real. It's all kept at a distance. And yet I know, I can't sleep for knowing, that if someone isn't there, caring, living it, as I cared and as I lived, then soon there will be nothing! There's no old money. No blocks of shares in national institutions that I can leave to my girl, to my wife even. It's just living, breathing enterprise, the ships, the gear, the men. What can I do? Who can I ask to step into my own shoes? There's only Flora.'

In a dead, hard voice Don said, 'She'd hate every minute of it.'

Kincaid nodded, wearily. 'She never saw the point of it. I never showed it to her. I never wanted one of those tough girls, tougher than the men. I wanted to keep Flora soft.'

For a second his eyes closed. When they drifted open again there was a moment of confusion. He said, 'Who — ?' and Don said, 'We were talking about Flora.'

'I'm sorry — my mind goes. They think I don't want to sleep, but I'd give anything to let go. How can I? You know my girl. I would never want her any different, God knows she's been a joy to me, but I cannot see her lying and fighting and sacking good men, just to keep ahead. All she has ever wanted is to make the world better, and all the money, all the tat, it means nothing! She tells me she loved Nepal. She lived in some shack, eaten alive by fleas, and she loved it.'

Don took a long breath through his nose. 'She did. But I know she appreciates what you've done.'

'Don't flatter me!' All at once Kincaid found he was crying. His face contorted. 'She loves me and she tries to be kind. But it wouldn't matter to her if she had to go out scrubbing to get enough to eat. I've built an empire for her and for her children, and when I'm gone it's going to fall apart.'

Harrington tried to think of something to say. There was nothing. Kincaid was only saying what was true. 'I fancy a brandy,' murmured Harrington. 'Shall I get one for you?'

'What a bloody good idea. They've put pins in me everywhere, they give me hell. There's a bottle in the cupboard, if the damned nurse hasn't thrown it out.'

There was only one glass, and some paper medicine cups. They each had a paper cup. 'We can hide the evidence,' said Kincaid. 'They make me live like a criminal. Right, Don, tell me about yourself. Where do you come from?'

Don recited his own history. A modest home, a minor public school, university. But he talked most about his climbing. He had begun at school, on a small granite outcrop, taught by a cautious master who was both horrified and bewildered to see a thirteen year old disappear up a chimney the master himself had never managed to climb. To Don it was neither difficult nor frightening and it took other, fiercer rocks to show him that a climb could be both. And it was then that he truly began to enjoy it.

'But it's a hell of a waste of time,' said Kincaid teasingly. 'A hobby. No more.'

'And your business is a hobby. You don't need what you make.'

'Oh, I do. My ego needs it. A very hungry beast is that.'

Don grunted. In climbing his ego didn't come into it. His spirit perhaps − but he hated emotional indulgence. If he was the sort of man that wanted psychological analysis he wouldn't be a climber. Or perhaps the climb did whatever needed to be done. Sometimes it felt as if one's whole mind was being taken apart and reassembled, in either better or worse order.

'So.' Kincaid roused himself to effort. 'You've done OK for yourself and no more than that. But then, you haven't been trying. Do you think you can try?'

Harrington's pride was stung. 'When I want to do something, I'm the best,' he said shortly.

Kincaid chuckled. 'Oh, are you now? Oh, are you?'

The two men looked at each other. Kincaid was very tired, there was a tremor at the corner of his mouth. Harrington felt a tightness in his chest.

'Well,' said Kincaid, 'are you going to marry her then?'

'I don't know if she'd even have me.'

'But if she would? If by chance she'd developed some level of tolerance towards this big, glamorous, clever young man? In the unlikely event of such a thing?'

'Then of course. Of course I would.'

Waving his hand, Kincaid said, 'You must know what I'm asking. Why I ask it. It isn't just Flora. I want someone − need someone. You would step into my shoes, custodian of the great rambling empire I have built. I didn't build it for you, I wouldn't give it you if there was any other way. But for Flora, for her children − your children.'

Don got up and wandered over to the window. There had been little rain recently. The Delyn crawled along between dust dry banks. If he lived here he would know that river in all its seasons, from spate to ice-bound winter. He would step from his castle each morning into a world that cared about his lightest whim. Silver and gold, the bellow of stags and the rustle of silk − and he would have Flora.

The old man was watching him. Did he imagine it or was there pleading in those strange, purple eyes? Whatever Don was given it was less than he could give to Kincaid, an old man waiting for the freedom to die. Above his bed hung the crossed swords and the bonnets of long dead highland warriors, and Kincaid had their spirit, if not their blood.

'We must talk to Flora,' he said.

By the time she came into the room Kincaid was almost at the end of his tether. 'More brandy,' he told Harrington. 'For God's sake, more brandy.'

Don poured him a small measure. 'We don't have to talk now, Dad,' said Flora. 'Later. When you've had some rest.'

'I can't rest − until this is settled. You don't know − how it preys on my mind.'

Flora looked in bewilderment from one man to the other. There was something in the air. 'What have you been deciding?' she demanded.

'Nothing,' said Don. 'We can't decide unless you do. Flora, I want you to marry me.'

She went white, and then the colour surged up into her skin. 'What on earth − Dad, what have you been saying?'

'The truth. I'm near the end, girl. And there's no one − no one to take care of things. He can do it. And it goes without saying he loves you, there's nothing he would want in a woman he wouldn't have in you. All I need to know is that he is what you want. If he isn't − I don't know what will happen. But if he is, Flora, if this is the man you want for your husband, then marry him, don't take time I haven't got, marry him!'

'I'm not even twenty yet.'

'And I am damn nigh dead, girl! I'd give you time if I had it. I'd give you forever. Why do you think I let you escape half across the world? To give you what you wanted. To let you go. And now there's chaos everywhere, and all I've worked for all these years is going to pieces. Think of your children, Flora. Think of your mother. Think of me.'

She stood quite still. Don said 'You know we were coming to this anyway. We both knew that.'

'But − it's all got so serious. I was still playing a game.'

'There are no games in real life,' said Kincaid harshly. 'It's time to grow up, Flora. I have asked nothing from you in all your life except that you should be happy and that's all I ask now. Be happy. Marry him.'

Why did she hesitate? She loved Don. She loved her father. They needed her now as never before, the cog without which the machine could not run. And she wanted all that marriage offered, the security, the companionship, the constant warmth of love. Only not yet. Not quite yet.

The dribble was oozing unheeded from the slack corner of her father's mouth. His life was ebbing away before her eyes, every moment's hesitation taxed him a little more. He was holding to consciousness by willpower alone. She looked at Don, and his face was strained and wary. She couldn't hurt him, she could never hurt anyone. All at once she flung out her hand to him, and he reached out to catch it, the hardness dissolving into a crack of laughter.

'Will you do it then? Will you honestly do it, Flora?'

'Yes. I honestly will.'

Chapter Eight

It was as if a weight had been lifted from Kincaid. He slept without sedation, slept for three days and nights. When he woke, clear-eyed and peaceful, he called Marie to him.

'Miss Flora's getting married, Marie. And I want you to see to things. She's to have the best, the very best. You know what she's like, ready to slide off to some nasty place if we don't stop her. I want her married in the chapel. Invite everyone, right back from the early days, from before my wife left. And make sure she has a nice dress. Something – you know – special.'

Marie chuckled. 'Oh, Mr Kincaid! Everyone's going to be thrilled, we thought it might be a nothing sort of wedding.'

'Because I'm like this, you mean? Hell's teeth, woman, if anything's going to perk me up it's seeing Flora walk down the aisle. I only hope her mother comes.'

Marie sighed. 'Aye. There's no saying what Mrs Kincaid will want to do.'

There was nothing Flora could do to change things. She pleaded fruitlessly with Marie, and then tried Don. 'I don't want a great big production! It should be small. Romantic. Personal.'

'It's only one day, Flora. It's going to make him happy.'

'But it isn't what I wanted.' She looked helplessly at Don. He reached out and pulled her close to him, nuzzling her hair. 'You should want people there. It's important. We're declaring in front of everyone that we're in love and that we promise to stay together.'

'And we're going to make love.'

'You're not frightened, are you?'

She pulled back and looked at him. 'Yes. A bit.'

'There's no need Flora, honestly. Look, let's do it. We'll go up to your room and lock the door and take the 'phone off the hook, and we'll do it.'

89

'And everyone would know what we were up to. There's no privacy here! And I don't want to go to a hotel or anything. We'll do it then, when we're married, and it'll be just one more embarrassment in a terribly embarrassing day.'

'Embarrassing is one thing it won't be.' He pushed her hair aside and nuzzled her neck, hearing her suck in her breath. 'It's going to be wonderful. And all you've got is a bad attack of stage fright.'

The days flew by. Don went with Mactee into Aberdeen on a couple of days, but then he excused himself and went back to the Lakes. He had his climbing engagement to see to, he said, and things to clear up.

'I'll have to put the school on the market,' he told Flora.

'Won't you be sorry? Won't you miss it?'

He thought of bolshie teenagers refusing to listen, and impressionable girls mooning after him. No, he wouldn't miss it. He ran a finger down the freckles on Flora's nose. 'I'll be back as soon as I can. The firm won't fold in a couple of weeks, love. Mactee can cope. And if he can't he can ring me. And I'll ring you. All the time.'

She laughed and hugged him. He was wonderful, strong and kind and good. But when he was gone she was at Marie's mercy, pushed hither and yon, choosing menus and flower arrangements, hymns and seating plans, not to mention the all important dress. She felt beleaguered, pressganged into a production for which she hadn't even wanted to audition.

One morning she rebelled. Instead of seeing the photographer she went out to the garage and accosted the chauffeur.

'I want the Land Rover, John. I'm going to see my mother.'

'I see.' Like all the servants, John kept a close eye on Flora's life. 'I was of the understanding that Marie had some appointments for you this morning,' he said sternly.

'Nonetheless, I'm going to see my mother.'

'Then I'll fetch the Bentley.'

'John, I am driving myself! I shall take the Land Rover. I am sick to death of this dreadful wedding, so will you please let me have the Land Rover and get away for a bit?'

'Have a cup of tea and feel better,' he advised kindly.

'John!'

Afterwards, reporting to Marie, he said, 'It's the only time I've ever seen anything of the old man in her. " – John! – " she says, and her eyes flashed like his used to do when he was going home the worse for wear and I wouldn't stop to buy him a bottle.'

'He was never a drinker,' said Marie loyally. 'Except when Mrs Kincaid left him.'

'Aye. He was then, right enough.'

They nodded together, secure in many years of service to Kincaid. John had a second cup of tea and they shared a plate of homemade biscuits.

Flora took the country road away from the castle. It wound up and over hills, climbing high into the mountains, passing through moorland thick with heather. The chill of autumn was in the air, and the few trees were losing golden leaves. There was ice in shadowed dells, and the Land Rover squealed on a corner. Flora stopped and put it into four wheel drive.

After about an hour she came to a padlocked gate. She got out and unlocked it with her own key, and then carefully locked it again when she had passed through. When her mother first left the castle no one knew where she had gone, and when Kincaid finally discovered her he had driven a car straight through this gate, and had sent a team of workmen to tear the fence out stake by stake. He dragged his wife out too, put her in his ruined car and drove her back to the castle. But she left again. And the gate went down twice more before he gave up and left it there, locked against him.

Nowadays there was a more prosaic reason for its existence. Lilian Kincaid kept goats, skipping about her three poor fields with exuberant abandon. As Flora drove to the croft they followed the car, shaking their heads and bleating, expecting titbits.

'Flora! Goodness me, I didn't expect you.'

'Hello, Mother.'

Next to her mother, Flora always felt garish. Lilian was pale, with silver-blonde hair, and dark, toffee-brown eyes. She dressed in pale mauves and pinks, echoing, almost blending with, the landscape all around. Her face was marked with lines, set by the weather into fine, delicate Celtic skin. But she was still very beautiful.

She stepped aside to let Flora enter the croft. Lilian lived with oil lamps, a peat stove and water from a spring, because there was no electricity, or anything else for that matter. Even the turf was cut by herself, although Kincaid annually sent men to do the work for her. Each year she declined to have them on her property and laboured herself, using a donkey to cart the turves and a long-handled spade to cut them. Her hard-won independence was all that mattered.

Flora looked round the dark little room. Nothing had changed. There was still the old sofa, and an armchair for guests, and an old elm rocker in which the cats slept. The fire let out wisps of peaty smoke and some strings of onions were hanging up in front of it.

'The weather's too damp to dry them outside,' explained Lilian. 'Last year they went mouldy, so I'm trying this.'

Flora sat in the armchair. 'Didn't you get my invitation?'

'Why, yes, I did.'

Her mother said no more and Flora waited. At last she said, 'Don't you want to know about him?'

'About the man? I don't know. Perhaps I shall be unhappy if I know. Will it do any good if I tell you you're too young?'

'He's twenty-eight.'

'And you're not yet twenty. Younger than me when I married your father.'

Flora met her mother's eyes. 'I do love him, Mother.'

'Who? Your father or this man?'

'Both, of course. But Don. I love him. The firm's in chaos without Dad and he's been marvellous. Everyone trusted him right away. The only trouble is that Marie's organising an enormous wedding and I'd really much rather have something small and private. I only want the people I care about.'

Lilian removed the wooden lid from a water butt at the side of the hearth, and ladled water into the kettle. Then she hung it over the fire, gave the flames a blast or two with the bellows and turned to Flora. 'Most of this seems to have been foisted on you,' she said. 'Were you planning to marry this man even if he wasn't needed in the business?'

Flora hesitated. 'I – I was going to sleep with him. But I was taking my time. I didn't want to be just one of the crowd for him.'

'Very sensible. And somehow your erotic passion has been translated into wedding bells.'

'That isn't fair! I'm sure we would have married anyway. We're right for each other. He's witty and fun, and now that Dad doesn't have to worry any more he's so much better – '

'Oh, Flora, when will you stop doing what other people want? Put the wedding off. Wait six months, a year. Go back to work for your aid agency. This man can run KORSEA if that's what your father wants. Don't let them shackle you!'

'But I'm not! Really, I'm not.'

She felt tearful suddenly. Her mother so often upset her, and it was difficult to know why. But it was always over Kincaid. It was hard for Lilian to accept that those things which had crushed her in her marriage were not now crushing her daughter. Flora didn't mind doing things to please her father, even when she was small and it had been no more than making sure she was on the steps when he came home, because he so loved to see her there.

'Have some tea,' said Lilian. 'You must tell me about Nepal. And then you must come and see this year's kids, I've had a wonderful crop. All but two were nannies and I'm keeping the billy boys to breed. I shouldn't, of course, but they're so beautiful.'

'Nepal was fascinating,' said Flora dully. 'It seems a lifetime away.'

'How much more of a lifetime when you're married and no longer free.'

Flora said nothing.

Don telephoned that night. He'd come in from climbing and drunk a few beers, and he was relaxed and sleepy. 'Do you love me?' he murmured, and Flora, anxious and a little unhappy, said, 'Of course I do. You sound half asleep.'

'Do I? We had a good day, did a great route. Mactee was on earlier. My God, how that man worries. Tell me what you've been doing.'

She wanted to tell him about today and her mother, but the words would not form in her head. He didn't know her mother, and the tale would only prejudice him. She folded the day up, like a parcel in her mind, and swallowed it down hard.

In the morning Marie woke her with a guest list on her breakfast tray and photographs of flowers by her bath. 'Just have a wee think about this and that,' coaxed the housekeeper. 'My, but it's going to be grand! Where shall we put the Sheriff, that's the question?'

'I don't know the Sheriff! I don't want the Sheriff! You can put him – where the monkey put his nuts!'

'Miss Flora!' Marie went red as a beetroot and stormed out.

Childishly Flora stuck her tongue out at the closed door. She would have to apologise later. But, oh, this damned wedding!

She was sitting in a window seat, trying to read, when a small red sports car zipped across the park and squealed to a halt in front of the castle. The door opened and two very long, very slim legs emerged, sheathed in skintight red leggings. They were followed by a long, slender torso, and at last the head, aquiline-nosed, almost regal, with a mane of curled black hair. The girl stood looking up at the castle.

Flora fought the window catch and won. 'Shalimar!' she yelled. 'Oh, Shalimar! Wait, I'm coming down!'

She raced through the corridors and down the stairs. But Forbes was before her at the door. 'I'm sure Miss Flora will be delighted,' he was saying. 'Do come in, Miss Lucas.'

93

'Oh, Shalimar!' cried Flora, and flung her arms around the visitor.

They repaired to the library. 'The place hasn't changed,' said Shalimar, pacing like a giraffe. She was immensely tall, well over six feet, and she wore towering red high heels. Next to her gaunt height Flora seemed rounded and almost bouncy.

'You know Dad's ill?' said Flora. 'You got my letter.'

'I was in Antigua, I only got back last week. How bad is he?'

'Better now, I think. I'd take you to see him, but he gets tired — I'll get the nurse to tell him you're here.'

'The things you do, Flora! I'm away for five minutes and not only does Malcolm have an accident, but you're getting married. Suddenly, just like that, a wedding invitation! What are you up to, Flo?'

Flora giggled. 'Nobody ever calls me Flo any more.'

'And everybody calls me Shalimar. Except Forbes, of course. Oh, I love coming back to this place. Exquisite, unchanging isolation.' She threw herself down on a sofa and stretched out her legs, dangling the excess length over the arm at the end. Heavy eyelids dipped in languor, bushy lashes momentarily dusting creamy skin. She was an incredibly beautiful girl.

'Did you get anywhere with the film director?' asked Flora.

'No. In the end he didn't want to marry a girl six inches taller than he was, and a half-caste into the bargain. He just wanted to screw me. And he did.'

'Shalimar!'

'Don't look so shocked, Flora. You are out of the Ark, you know that? He was just — like people are. Lots of people. We had good times, and I can't have liked him that much because I'm not broken up now that he's gone.'

'Aren't you?' Flora looked dubious.

'No. Anyway, one of his friends has got me a part in a film. A good part. So I don't have to spend my days being a dumb model any more, what do you think of that?'

'It can't be that boring, being world-famous,' remarked Flora. 'I even saw you in Nepal. A man in Kathmandu had an old cover of *Vogue* pinned up on a wall.'

'But I'm tired of wearing swimsuits! I've spent a lifetime on the beach. Last week I stood for eight hours with my legs apart in the surf and a man I hardly know crouched underneath me staring up at my crotch. He got so excited it was nearly pornography, they should have found someone gay. And the suit was cut so high I had to shave off all my pubic hair, and now the itch is driving me mad.'

94

'I thought you were supposed to wax,' said Flora, feeling a total innocent.

'I am not into masochism. And it was OK in the end. We had dinner afterwards, and when it was dark me and this guy went for a swim. Naked. It was so delicious! Like warm silk on your skin. And when we came out he started kissing me, right where he'd been staring all day. Flora, you've no idea! All day thinking about it, and at last having it happen. It was heaven. Absolute send you into orbit stuff. Then, when he finally had me, the waves were bubbling all over us, and he was thumping away like a machine, and I was — worried about getting sand in my hair. I've got a marvellous new shampoo, it saved my life, I must give you some. And then I come back home and find you're about to rush into marriage with some bloke I've never even heard of. Are we best friends or what?'

Flora grinned. She was wearing a green shirt and matching cord trousers, with a cream Aran sweater over the top. Next to Shalimar she felt dull and sexless. 'I met him in Nepal,' she said shyly. 'He's a climber. Dad's letting him take over the business.'

'What? Malcolm Kincaid is handing over to some climbing bum? He must be desperate, Flora. You must be desperate. Where is this Donald character, I've got to see him.'

'He's teaching some climbing for a few days,' said Flora. 'Honestly, you will like him. He's very tall and very brown, and he's got very pale grey eyes, like looking through water.'

'So, he's sexy,' said Shalimar, sitting up. 'But is he nice? Is he a nice kind man who won't run off the minute you get wrinkles and go grey?'

'He's clever,' said Flora doggedly. 'And everybody at KORSEA loves him. Dad's delighted. The worry about the business was almost killing him. Don's got this climbing school he's selling, and —'

'You don't know him very well, do you?' said Shalimar suddenly.

There was a silence. Flora said, 'I don't think you can know someone terribly well after just a few weeks. But we're sure. If it wasn't for Dad we'd wait, but he's so ill — we need Don. We both do.'

With the air of a barrister cross-examining the witness, Shalimar said, 'Tell me, Flora, what's he like in bed.'

'I don't know. We haven't. Yet.'

'And you are going to marry this man? He could be a psychopath!'

'Of course he isn't! Anyway, we can't sleep together here. There'd be Marie at the keyhole and Forbes would tell Dad.'

'Not to mention John on a ladder at the window,' agreed Shalimar. 'But you could go somewhere.'

'Doesn't seem worth it,' said Flora. 'We're getting married in three weeks. And I don't want it to be rushed, and furtive and embarrassing.'

Shalimar got up and wandered around the room, looking at the books on the shelves. She came across a copy of *Anne of Green Gables* and chuckled. 'Look at this! Remember when we were new at school and we read it together? You were Anne and I was Diana. Do you remember playing at being them?'

'Oh, yes. And I was going to marry someone just like Anne did and have six children. And that's when you stopped wanting to be Diana. She married and settled down with a drip.'

'I might be Diana again one day,' said Shalimar. 'When I'm tired of being Shalimar.'

The girls had been friends from their first days at boarding school. It was an alliance of misfits, because neither of them blended well into the fabric of school life. Flora was governess taught, and had never before been away from home; red-headed, shy, and known to be fabulously rich, she couldn't help but stand apart. As for Shalimar, even at eleven she towered over her classmates. What's more, her mother brought her on the first day, and as one girl hissed to another: 'That new girl's mother wears a sari! Shirley Lucas is black!'

Yet there was no one sweeter than Shalimar's mother. Flora came to know her well. The cultured daughter of an Indian diplomat, she had met Henry Lucas at an ambassador's party when she was seventeen. Hugely tall, charming, and still at almost fifty a single man, he lost his heart in an instant to the lovely Indian girl and married her. They travelled the east together, posted to first this and then that embassy, and when their daughter was born, a long thin mixture of the two of them, they were ecstatic.

But, when that daughter was ten, Henry Lucas died. Since it had always been their intention to send Shirley to school in England, Mrs Lucas entered her in a select Ladies' College and bought a house nearby. She found herself friendless, alone in a cold and alien country. Shirley, deeply aware of her mother's unhappiness, suffered at school. And it was Flora Kincaid who went up to her one day and said 'I saw your mother. She looks so nice. I thought she was terribly pretty,' and won herself a friend for life.

They invented the name Shalimar together. Shirley was a disaster name for such a tall girl, inspired by a Shirley Temple film the Lucases had seen on a balmy night in some tropical posting when everything seemed touched with romance. They had never imagined they would have such an un-Shirley like daughter. It was so obviously unsatisfactory that the two girls decided it had to go, and spent three days trying to think of something better. 'You should be something exotic, like Zanzibar,' declared Flora finally. 'Shanzibar. Shalibar.'

'Shalimar!' declared her friend. And Shalimar she was.

She would answer to nothing else, and besides, the name suited her. She had that indefinable touch of the exotic, in the blackness of her hair, the thickness of her lashes, the dark lustre of her eyes. What's more she was a natural sensualist, taking after her father if she did but know. His bachelor career had been littered with wild liaisons, until he had finally fallen in love. As she grew up, his daughter stood up straight, threw her hair back from her face and took on the world.

Her mother died when Shalimar was seventeen, of tuberculosis. The bacillus had entered her system years before, perhaps even when she was a child, breathing the air of the hot Indian plains. Coughing, breathlessness, high fever, all these had been part of Shalimar's experience of her mother, and she had thought nothing of them until one of her mother's hardwon friends came to school and said, 'Is there somewhere you could go in the holidays, dear? Your mother's got to spend a week or two in hospital, nothing serious.'

And the weeks spread to months, to a year, while Shalimar spent her summers and Easters and Christmases with Flora at Castle Kincaid.

That evening the girls lay on a rug in front of the fire and giggled hysterically at photographs of Shalimar. Each one was accompanied by some story or other.

'You see the girl there is looking so cross? She'd been promised a job, and then they saw me and I was offered it. Naturally I accepted, but then she was so sour I realised what they'd done and told them I couldn't poach someone else's work. And if you look at this picture —' she held out a shot of four beaming girls ' — you can see we're all the best of friends. Except the next day I went out for a drink with a guy and discovered he was her boyfriend! Now, look at the venom in that shot, you could poison a regiment. So I gave up. Let her hate me.'

'No one could hate you,' said Flora loyally.

Shalimar sighed. 'You are just such an idealist. People hate me because I look like I do, earn so much, because I'm half black. And

97

as for you, there are hundreds of people poorer, uglier, nastier than you who all hate you for being what you are.'

'Not people I know,' said Flora.

'Yes. Even people you know.'

The girls stared at each other. Flora had the feeling that Shalimar had leaped ahead of her, into knowledge and worldliness.

'We'll see The Dress tomorrow,' said Shalimar suddenly. 'I've got the feeling that Marie wants to put you in something so frilly you'll disappear. I saw a wonderful wedding dress in Antigua, it's a body stocking covered in white lace. I modelled it. Looks like I'm naked, and it's so tight my ribs and my nipples show. Just the business. That's what I'm wearing when I get married.'

'Not quite Marie's thing,' giggled Flora. 'I wish − oh, I wish I was you! I could just do what I wanted and not worry about what anyone thought.'

'And if you could − would you marry at all?' asked Shalimar softly.

Flora's eyes were large and very dark. 'I don't know.'

A shower of cold rain slashed across the rock. Don leaned back in the slings, screwing up his eyes against the flakes of mud displaced by the wind. He liked this overhang, liked the belly of it, the great fat solidity of the thing. You only realised how much you had progressed on rock when you went back to something that had once been tough.

'Are you OK?' The cry of his second, half hoping that Don wouldn't get up and he wouldn't have to follow.

'Can't see a bloody thing. I'll be up in a minute.'

He reached back and up, feeling out under the overhang. A camera shutter clattered, someone was recording this for posterity. It was the other lads, less confident, going up the adjacent chimney. Those two could do a couple of traverses this afternoon, no one came out to learn from Don and got away lightly.

The muscles in his arms twanged like wires, a sensation so painful as to verge on the delicious. That hold was further over than he remembered − he looked around for the wrinkle that would take his right foot, wondering with a sudden chill if the boy down there was concentrating. It could be stupid entrusting the rope, your life, to someone you barely knew. He cleansed the thought from his mind and made the next move, but then he thought, that diving business. What had Mactee said? The words slid across his consciousness. Christ!

He clung limpetlike to a Godgiven spur.

98

'Don?' The boy below, too inexperienced to know he had seen his leader nearly kill himself.

'It's OK,' he called. 'I lost concentration for a moment.'

Time enough to think about KORSEA when he was back in Scotland. Kincaid might have devoted every last waking hour to the thing but Don would not. It wasn't necessary.

The fright had been good for him. He made his mind cold, clear, diamond-bright. The rain started again in earnest. He felt a delicious sense of immediacy, of his own unbounded strength. The top came too quickly, these pitches were always too damned short. He sat in the rain, waiting for the boy to come up to him, leaning down now and then to give advice. His nerve gave out, he needed a tight rope on the crux of the overhang. It was the mind that conquered rock, Don decided. Like an oriental mystic, you expunged everything from your consciousness but the here, the now, opening your thoughts to every last nerve in toes and finger-ends.

There was nothing like this, he knew. To be here was to be happy. A sudden charge of euphoria ran through him. Wasn't he the man who had everything? This, Flora, and riches too! The ultimate good fortune.

When the boy came up to join him Don got up without speaking and walked across the grass to meet the others. They walked on, in the rain, to the next climb, and to the next. In the evening the students went to the pub without him, and said to each other, 'He's amazing. A natural. He lives for climbing.'

'Don — this is Shalimar.'

They stared at each other, Shalimar in tight black leather, Don in battered jeans. He was browner than she, his face burned to the colour of light oak by wind and mountain air.

'How do you do?' He put out his hand, unused to a woman on a level with himself.

She flashed her immense white smile. 'Flora didn't do you justice,' she remarked.

'And your photographs lie about you. I'm overwhelmed. Flora, you shouldn't subject me to shocks like this.'

'You look pretty unshocked to me,' said Flora.

Don reached out and took her plait of hair in his hand. He used the end of it to tickle her neck. 'How are you?' he asked.

'Fine.'

There was an awkwardness between them. He wanted to talk to her, but the presence of this statuesque beauty prevented it. Shalimar had a magnetic quality, he noticed, it was hard not to sit and watch

99

her. Every movement, every change of expression, seemed to possess some mysterious quality of importance. 'You'd be great in films,' he said.

'I'm going to act, actually. But I'm so tall, they'll have to start getting bigger leading men or something. My first part's as a witch.'

'You never told me that,' said Flora.

'Didn't I?' Shalimar let her smile expand towards Don. 'Perhaps it's Don making me relax.'

'I'm known for my hypnotic gaze,' he said, and they laughed.

Later, Shalimar talked to Flora on her own. 'I'll go,' she said. 'I don't want to get under everyone's feet before the wedding.'

'But you're not! Honestly, Shalimar, I won't know what to do if you go. There's the dress to finish, and the goddammed flowers, and guest lists and everything. I'm relying on you to help.'

'But Don can help!'

'Don's busy. He's going to be in Aberdeen at KORSEA most days. Please don't go. I feel I need moral support.'

So Shalimar stayed, knowing full well that she should not. Donald Harrington — when Flora first told her his name she had inwardly sneered a little, and decided he was dull and safe. How could she have been so wrong?

The wedding crept daily nearer. Each night Shalimar forced herself to go to bed early and leave them, and then found herself engineering some other casual encounter. If she met Don in the hall she rested a light, detaining hand on his sleeve. And when he touched Flora, letting his hand linger on her brilliant hair, she was conscious of the most cruel emotion of her life: green, poisonous jealousy.

Chapter Nine

Shalimar stood tall behind her friend, holding Flora's veil in out-stretched hands. She let it fall, the embroidered gauze settling into perfect folds. It was a very long veil, almost to the ground, divided at either side to allow the bride's hands to emerge. Beneath it Flora looked ethereal.

'Wonderful. I could cry just looking at you.'

Flora giggled waveringly. 'Please don't, you'll start me off.'

'Not nervous, are you?'

'Yes. Petrified. I keep wondering if Mother's going to come.'

Shalimar made a face. She had always been slightly wary of Lilian Kincaid, and her obscure hold over her husband. By rights he should have divorced her years ago, but he never had. They hung together, joined like the twin towers of a suspension bridge, each on opposite banks.

'She must realise it makes things difficult.'

'I don't think she minds. She thinks I'm being pushed into marriage.'

Shalimar snorted. 'As if anyone would need pushing into marrying Don!'

An uncomfortable silence fell. Shalimar could have bitten out her own tongue, she couldn't bear to Flora to know – but perhaps she knew already. It was always wrong to assume that Flora's calm, pleasant manner was all there was to the girl. She could be worryingly perceptive.

'I've told them to leave a space even if she doesn't come,' said Flora. 'That way there doesn't need to be any horrible shunting up.'

'I feel really cross with her. She ought to realise how difficult it makes things, for you, not your father.'

'I suppose she does realise. That might be what she wants.'

101

The dress designer strode in, and knelt down to make the final adjustments to the flounces on Flora's skirt. The whole thing was a confection of extravagance, with a pearled Elizabethan stomacher, hooped skirt and a neckline that plunged over Flora's young breasts. A single large diamond hung in the shadow of her cleavage, suspended from a chain of white gold.

'Perhaps the iron − there's a slight crease here −' the designer was fussing, unable to leave his creation alone. Under Shalimar's high fashion urging he had excelled himself.

'I think it's perfect,' said Flora, placing a gently insistent hand on his shoulder. 'Perhaps you'd like some champagne? I believe there's some downstairs.'

'That's very kind of you, Miss Kincaid.' The man withdrew, impressed by his tactful dismissal. He frequented many houses of the great, and was not often treated with such charm. She was a lovely girl, he thought. A perfect bride.

From the window Flora could see the guests trooping into the chapel. At least half the men wore the tartan, as her father himself would have done if he had been well. She saw Don crossing the lawn, resplendent in morning suit and grey top hat, Van at his side. They had spent the night at the inn in Delyn village. 'Don's early,' said Flora. 'I suppose John insisted on leaving hours to spare.'

'Only five minutes,' said Shalimar, also watching. She took a grip on the velvet curtain. How would he think she looked? she wondered. She had dressed so carefully, in a tight suit of cream satin, its skirt high above her knees. She wore a lace hat with a short, flirty veil.

Flora glanced at her. Suddenly she wished that Shalimar wasn't there, that instead she had her mother. Her heart was pounding, her palms were wet, she had no wish to appear before all these people, most of whom were strangers, and make the most binding, the most private of promises. With my hand, I thee wed − with my body − his body − 'I think I'm going to faint,' she whispered.

'Don't! You can't! I'll ring for some sherry.'

'No, I'll breathe fumes all over the minister. I'll be all right if only we can get on with it!'

A soft knock came on the door. It was Marie. 'Mr Kincaid says to come down, Miss Flora. He wants to start on time.'

'I thought we still had five minutes,' said Shalimar.

'He's a wee bit on edge, Miss. Making a terrible fuss all morning.'

Flora looked round for her bouquet, a fall of exquisite white roses, interlaced with greenery and white heather. The flowers were

Shalimar's choice, ensuring that the only colour was in the red of Flora's hair.

'Oh, Miss Flora, you look so lovely!' Marie pressed a handkerchief to her mouth.

'Go on down, Marie. I'm coming, I promise.'

The chapel stood across the lawn from the castle itself, a gothic building with an oddly modern interior. The walls were of cream plaster, stretching up to a glorious painted ceiling in blue and cream and gold. Kincaid had ordered the place to be crammed with flowers, candles, people. It hummed with noise and the air was redolent of the scent of many hothouse blooms. The only vacant seat was Lilian Kincaid's, an elegant velvet cushioned chair set apart at the front. Kincaid himself sat at the back, hunched in a wheelchair, a tartan rug over his knees. He glared out at everyone, daring them to pity him.

Don sat immobile. He had never imagined that he would feel quite this nervous. For some strange reason he was wondering if she was going to go through with it. He had felt closer to Flora on the very first day they met than he did now. His mind tossed thoughts around. The climbing school, KORSEA, Flora. This felt like the first moment of true reflection since — almost since Nepal. He looked around at the magnificence that only wealth could provide. It was like the court of a great Scottish king. What was he doing here? What was he taking on?

He eased his collar. Suddenly he wondered what everybody thought of him, who they thought he was. He was almost an impostor — well-dressed, apparently well-intentioned. And underneath it all he was just a climbing bum, his business collapsing, his friends shuffling in their seats, wearing shabby suits. Who was he to take on all this? At his side Van tapped his fingers on his knees, feeling his pocket for the ring at regular thirty second intervals.

The organ music began to swell, the great pipes filling with air to burst out into the triumphal march Malcolm had chosen for Flora's entrance. It was grand, imposing music, crashing and rolling around the church. In the midst of it, with all heads turning to see, Flora came in.

She seemed too young, too fragile for such music. Her dress billowed about her, the red hair only slightly dimmed by the veil. As she walked, the diamond, her father's huge and outlandish present, gleamed in the valley of her breasts. She seemed ghostly, grave as a statue, pacing at a speed that kept her in line with her father's wheelchair, pushed by one of his men. There was something

103

medieval about the scene, the laird's daughter being offered up like a sacrifice, white, pure, her dowry so great that a single precious stone must be its symbol.

'Hey, man,' whispered Van to Don. 'Lucky bastard.'

Don felt his breath catch in his throat. He didn't believe in such luck, he couldn't believe in it. He had chatted up a girl in Kathmandu and with the wave of a magic wand she had turned into a princess. He looked at Kincaid, and saw the grey sheen of exhaustion lying heavy across his face. He was making one last bid for what he wanted. Ever the gambler, Kincaid was staking everything on one last throw, and by some magic, by some miracle, Don was the winner. Last night, in his lodgings in the village, he had thrown a handful of rice on the fire.

He and Van stepped out before the altar. Flora was walking very slowly now, and her face beneath the veil was stiff with nerves. Instinctively Don turned and held out his hands to her, drawing her firmly to his side. And she stood, almost bewildered, until Shalimar stepped forward and drew back her veil. Don looked down into Flora's white face. Again he felt that misplaced sense of pity.

The service began. It took the old form and the old words, reinforcing the strange sense of timelessness. Flora's hands, relieved now of her bouquet, trembled visibly. The minister began to hurry a little, because Kincaid was sagging in his chair and the bride looked pale enough to die. He raised his voice a little. 'If there is any person here present who knows of any reason why these two may not be joined together in Holy Matrimony, may they speak now — or forever hold their peace.'

He took the briefest pause, a mere half breath of space. A woman's heels sounded on the old stone floor. 'Donald Alexander Harrington — ' began the minister, and Lilian Kincaid's clear voice said, 'Please wait. I'm not sure that this marriage should take place. I have to talk to my daughter.'

Flora put her hand on Don's arm. Kincaid, suddenly turning a dark, livid purple, spluttered: 'Damn you, Lilian! What are you doing here? We can't stop now!'

'Please, Malcolm.' She came quickly down the aisle, wearing a dark pink dress and a paler coat, a long grease trail marking the hem. 'I wanted to see Flora earlier, but the car broke down. I can't let her marry until I know that she's sure.'

'She is sure,' said Don thickly, and he took firm hold of Flora's hand. 'She wouldn't be here if she wasn't.'

'I think it quite possible she might be. Flora's father has always been able to bully her.'

104

The minister said, 'Perhaps we should adjourn for a few moments — if you'd like to come into the vestry — '

And Kincaid said, 'Like hell we will! The harpy wants to ruin Flora's day, that's all. Like she ruined my life!'

'If you don't mind — the vestry — ' The minister was ushering Lilian to one side.

'No,' said Don. 'It's too late. She's had weeks to talk to Flora.'

'All she wants to do is get at me,' muttered Kincaid venomously. 'We'll take no damned notice. Get on with it minister, at once!'

'I do have to ask Mrs Kincaid why she feels — ' began the minister, and Kincaid yelled: 'What she feels has no bearing on a damn thing! She's always wanted to ruin me, could never stand to see me succeed! Flora's my daughter, mine! She wants to marry. She at least wants to give her husband sons!'

'Oh, Malcolm, will you please let that rest!' begged Lilian. And Flora fainted.

Don carried her into the vestry, her veil trailing on the floor like a shroud. Lilian brought out a bottle of eau de cologne and dabbed Flora's face, and Don said murderously: 'How could you do such a thing to her? She never deserved that sort of humiliation.'

'I meant to come earlier,' said Lilian. 'I wasn't going to say anything, and then yesterday I decided I was letting Flora down. You don't know each other. Flora deserves to be given more time.'

The girl stirred and came round, leaning groggily against a line of choirboy cassocks hanging from pegs.

'There is no time,' said Kincaid. 'The time was lost years ago, when you wouldn't let me touch you. If I had a son I wouldn't need Flora now, and God knows, I pleaded with you — begged you — '

'We tried for years to conceive again,' said Lilian, fighting bitter tears. 'And why do you talk about this now? All I want to do is spare Flora our level of misery!'

Flora's quiet voice cut across them. 'Will you please stop? I'm getting married today. Why don't you both go back in.'

'You could wait for a year,' said Lilian. 'You can pay people to take over companies, you don't have to drag them into the family!'

'We're getting married,' said Don. 'We're both single, we don't need anyone's consent, and we know each other as well as we need to. So there's nothing further to discuss.'

Kincaid gestured angrily, and was pushed back into the chapel. Lilian said, 'I have a feeling about this, Flora. I never distrust my feelings.'

'But they're your feelings, not mine.' Flora turned her face stiffly aside.

They were briefly alone with the minister. 'We could delay,' he said. 'You might feel better in an hour.'

'No,' said Don. 'She'll be better getting it over with. Won't you?'

Flora nodded. He held her against him for a second, and the diamond dug into the soft flesh of her breasts. She gasped, and Don felt a sudden rush of desire. Married or not, tonight nothing would stop him. He took her wrist and led her firmly into the church.

An odd mood of euphoria broke over the castle, once the wedding was done. The guests were wild with excitement, and became wilder with the flowing champagne. Kincaid sat through no more than half the meal, and was taken up to bed, but Lilian stayed, watching the proceedings with a blank, white face. Just before the speeches Flora leaned across and said, 'It's all right, Mother. It's over now.'

'I should have come earlier,' said Lilian.

Don had got up to exchange a brief word with Forbes, automatically assuming Kincaid's role now that Kincaid wasn't here. Flora said, 'Don't you like him?'

Her mother made a face. 'No. I think he's aggressive.'

'I think he had every right to be.'

'But can't you see, Flora? He may be right for KORSEA, but that doesn't mean he's right for you! You'll never stand up to him.'

'I'm not that much of a doormat, Mother.'

'Then you'd better become one. Men like your father, men like Don Harrington, need women that let themselves be crushed flat. Then they despise them. And if you won't be crushed they hate you – and make you miserable.'

Don came back and sat between them. He said to Lilian, 'I'm sorry we didn't have a chance to get to know one another earlier.'

'Yes,' said Lilian. 'I always welcome visitors.'

'But I dislike visiting without an invitation.'

She looked at him calmly. The lines at the corners of her eyes were a soft web, exactly matching. 'I'm sorry if I've upset you,' she said. 'But I would do anything to spare Flora my sort of marriage. I know rather better than either of you the strains imposed by a business like KORSEA. I didn't want Flora to marry you, but she has, so all I ask is – be kind to her. Let her have some space in which to live and grow.'

106

Don said nothing. He felt an enormous irritation with the woman.

The meal was finished, the tables cleared, and the party began. People swept through the castle's great rooms, laughing, drinking, dancing, and two pipers took turns to play. The sun faded, and the bats came out round the battlements. Flora danced reels, her veil streaming out behind her as Don whirled her and twirled her, pushing her this way and that with steadily increasing violence. Shalimar danced, first with Van and then with one of Kincaid's stockbrokers, a man of thirty-five who had arrived in a Porsche. Lilian sat quite still, watching them.

Kincaid had ordered magnums of champagne, and the giant bottles popped and gushed, one after the other. Flora knew she was drunk, her head spinning, sweat running between her breasts. The great hall was very hot, men with red faces spilled champagne on girls' dresses and laughed.

It had been intended that at some point in the evening Flora and Don would slip quietly away upstairs. They were spending the wedding night at the castle, in the bridal chamber. Tradition had it that all the castle brides spent their first night there, and Kincaid had prepared accordingly. There was a vast, muslin-draped bed, a log fire, and erotic plaster mouldings on the ceiling.

And somehow, by some strange telepathy, the whole gathering had come to realise that Flora was to be taken upstairs, her maidenhead to be ritually sacrificed at the appointed time, in the appointed place, to the appointed man. Lascivious eyes watched them dance and Van, very drunk, shouted out: 'Go on, man! Stop tormenting yourself and take her to bed!'

A great roar went up and Don lifted a fist to acknowledge it. Lilian rose from her seat and went to catch Flora's arm. 'Sneak away, darling. Get changed and go and take a room at the pub. This is primitive.'

'So it is,' said Harrington. His eyes glittered strangely.

Lilian let go of Flora's arm. 'He's very drunk, darling, why don't you sleep apart tonight? Start off tomorrow, when all this is over.'

'What?' Don let out a crack of laughter. 'Not have her? Are you hoping for a quick annulment in the morning and everything undone? Sorry, Lilian. Flora and I are going to bed.'

He grabbed her round the waist and ran through the hall, and everyone cheered and whistled and ran with them. Shalimar threw off her shoes and ran barefoot, and the stockbroker hung on to her

107

wrist and let out a hunting yell. Up the stairs, along the passages, higher and higher, a yelling throng chasing them. A button burst from Shalimar's jacket and the man grabbed at her, bursting the rest. She ran with her breasts naked, longing for Don to look back and see. A man pushed his girlfriend into an alcove, urgently opening her clothes. Another girl fell sprawling, and lay on her back laughing hysterically. As the crowd raced past, leaving her, a man she didn't know stopped, undid his trousers and came down on her. The laughter abruptly halted.

At the very top of the stairs the door to the bridal chamber stood open. Don thrust Flora through, her veil streaming behind, momentarily blinding him. He fought free, turned and slammed the door. The mob hammered on it, howling, shouting. The stockbroker grabbed at Shalimar's hard breasts. She turned from the door, pushed him away, and dragged her jacket shut.

Inside the room, Flora sank in a heap on the floor. 'They've gone mad,' she said shakily. 'Did you see them?'

'I saw. Get on the bed, Flora.' He ripped off his tie and dragged at the buttons of his shirt. His new gold cufflinks, a present from Kincaid, would not undo quickly enough and he snapped them in two, casting them and the shirt on the floor. In one movement he stripped off his trousers. Naked, and hugely erect, he stood astride the girl on the floor. Flora put her face in her hands.

'Get on the bed.' He reached down and dragged her to her feet. She brushed against his penis and he gasped. 'Get out of this dress and get on the bed!' he said urgently. 'Do it, Flora!'

'You'll have to help me.' She turned her back to him and he threw the veil over her shoulder while he wrestled with hooks and eyes. The dress peeled off, inch by inch, freeing her breasts to fall naked; freeing her belly, white and soft; falling away to reveal her dark red forest of pubic hair. When she was quite undressed he turned her. The veil still fell in a mist behind her head, and she still wore the diamond, like a drop of frozen water, placed exactly between nipples suffused with blood, the colour of her lips. Harrington bent his head and sucked each one in turn, and her head fell back, as if she was drugged.

He picked her up and took her to the bed, laying her on heavy white linen sheets. The covers were turned back but he dragged them off altogether, spreading Flora's white body on a stark white sheet, her veil crushed cruelly behind her head. She was breathing hard, her eyes, those navy-blue eyes, fixed on him in fascination. It had to be now, now!

He pulled her knees apart, reached up and found the place. A mat of wet hair guarded it. She had soft, fleshy outer lips, the inner folds protruding like pink frills. The smell of her came strongly to him, the smell of an aroused woman. He pushed his hand up and in, and Flora moaned, writhing at the touch of his fingers. He said nothing, there was nothing to say, his erection was anguish to him. He came down on her, guiding himself in, and she clutched at his shoulders. In the last millisecond before she had him all, he thought of Malcolm Kincaid. He drove himself home.

She let out a long, surprised cry. They were together, at last. If this was what her mother wished to save her from, then she did not wish to be saved. He began to move in her and she held on to him, writhing under him, closed tight round him like the finger of a glove. Heat centred there, around this alien hardness, her tissues holding him in wet, blood-gorged thrall. In torment, stranded, Flora arched her back upwards, driving him deep into her flesh. Harrington, in a moment of tremendous power, felt himself explode within her, felt his whole being gather up and discharge into her womb. Flora cried out. Tense as a bow, she arched rigidly upwards, and her head thrashed briefly from side to side. All at once her body seemed to collapse. He felt himself held by long, shuddering convulsions.

They discovered afterwards that she had bled, a trail of bright drops across the sheet. 'Might as well finish the job,' said Harrington. 'Complete this tribal ritual.' He rolled Flora to one side, ripping the sheet half off, then rolling her back to take it off completely.

'You can't,' she said sleepily.

'I bloody well can. They ought to know. Your father should know. I'm the first, and I can prove it.'

He walked naked to the door, unlocked it and flung the sheet out at those of the guests who were left, lying around in the passage fortifying themselves from champagne bottles. They looked bemused, not understanding.

'My virgin bride,' said Harrington, and he laughed at them. Standing there quite naked, he threw back his head and laughed.

They woke from a deep sleep at almost lunchtime the next day. Someone was knocking on the door.

'What do you want?' called out Don thickly.

'I've brought Miss Flora some food. Mr Kincaid wants her to have something.'

It was Marie. Don got up and went to the door, pulling a pair of underpants on. Flora curled up on the bed, dragging one of the covers over her hips. Outside, on the floor, the sheet still lay in a revealing heap. Don grimaced at it. He certainly must have been far gone last night. Marie said smugly, 'I'll not be washing it now. A thing to be proud of, that is, in this day and age.'

She pushed in an entire trolley of food, loaded down with a silver coffee pot, bacon, eggs and oatcakes, fruit, fresh bread, and a vase of pale pink roses. Flora lay with her eyes closed, her naked breasts bruised and fingermarked. 'Shall I run your bath, Miss Flora?' asked Marie, her tone almost reverent.

Flora opened her eyes a crack and shook her head. 'Leave us alone, Marie,' she murmured.

'I can always fetch the doctor to you,' whispered the woman.

'Go away! I don't need the doctor.'

Flora sat up, pushing her hair out of her eyes. She winced. She was sitting on the diamond. The chain had broken at some time during the night and they had let it go, intent on something far more important than a mere hundred thousand pound jewel. Now Flora fished it out and tossed it to Marie. 'Get that mended, would you, please? They can shorten the chain. I don't want always to have to be half naked when I wear it.'

'I like you being half-naked,' said Don. 'I like you being whole naked.' He knelt on the bed and kissed her shoulders, and Flora put her head back against his. Marie almost purred with delight.

They ate the breakfast lying in the chaos of the bed. Flora felt that she had never tasted anything so good. The bacon was sharp with salt, the oatcakes crisp and floury. It was as if her senses had come alive, awakened to a world that had existed before only in dull, muted colours. Today the world was brilliant, the sky more blue, the day more lovely than ever before. 'Are we going to get up?' she asked.

'No,' said Don. 'In a while we'll have some more champagne. And I'll love you again and again and again.'

'Good,' said Flora. 'I'll have a bath in a moment. I feel I must smell.'

'You do, but it's delicious. I'll get in with you.'

It was while they were lying in the suds, half sleepy, half aroused, that Don said, 'I wonder if I've made you pregnant.'

'It doesn't happen at once,' said Flora. 'Not on the first night.'

Don burst into delighted laughter. 'Who told you that old wives' tale? It isn't true, Flora. We didn't do anything to stop it, which means that you could very well be pregnant. You must have several million sperm swimming around in there.'

Flora sat up. 'But I don't want to be pregnant.'

'You should have thought of that before.' Don put his arm round her and drew her back down, silencing her with his kiss. But, when he

110

finished, Flora got out of the bath. 'I've got this diaphragm thing,' she confided. 'I'll put it in now. It might do some good.'

'Don't bother. Flora, I want you pregnant.'

She stood holding the box, looking mystified. 'But not yet, Don! I want us to have some fun together.'

'Sweetheart — there's not going to be much time for that.' He saw her bemused expression and he climbed out of the bath, dripping suds. He tried to explain. 'Your father wants the firm sorted out, and I don't know a thing about oil, I'll have to start from scratch. And obviously there's the climbing. Quite honestly I can't see that I'm going to be around all that much.'

'You never said this before!'

'Flora, it's obvious! But if you have a baby then at least you'll have something to do. You'll be a brilliant mother, you know you will.'

She felt bewildered. Her life had taken a whole new turn, and instead of love and companionship she was to be given motherhood. 'I'm too young to have a baby,' she said feebly.

'The younger the better. And think how it would please your father.'

Flora's expression stiffened. 'He can wait until I want a baby, I won't have one for him. He's only my father, Don.'

'And he's given me everything. This is the best thing for all of us. If you have a baby we'll all be happy. Please, Flora.'

She held the rubber semicircle in her hand. Don came across, took it, picked up a pair of nail scissors from the shelf and neatly sliced it in two.

She suddenly remembered her mother's face, beautiful, drawn with anxiety. All at once she was afraid, as her mother had been afraid, of something she couldn't see. Did she want what he wanted? Suppose she did not? The future seemed formless, like a white cloud, with nothing clear or solid. She had given her life into the hands of someone she didn't know.

Chapter Ten

After a few, sensual days at the castle, Don and Flora went away. Kincaid wanted them to go abroad, to the Greek Islands perhaps, or the Caribbean, but Harrington preferred a series of luxury hotels throughout Scotland, driving Flora from one to the other in the Bentley. He took obvious pleasure in sweeping up to the front of some ancient house, Flora at his side, the boot full of matching luggage and everything within his grasp. He enjoyed the food too, the superb fresh salmon, venison, quails' eggs. Flora, used to luxury from childhood, loved it because he was there and they were together.

She felt sleepy most of the time. But then, they hardly ever slept. They would go to bed early and rise late, and in between they revelled in one another. One morning, the sun streaming through a mullioned window on to a priceless Persian rug, coffee in a silver pot at his elbow and Flora at his side, Don murmured, 'This is so wonderful. Flora, Flora, you're my good angel, my wonderful girl.'

'So I am.' She yawned and curled up against him to catch five minutes more sleep.

He lay on his back, wondering what they could do that could possibly enhance their paradise. Never in his life had he been so idle for so long, with every one of his senses satisfied. Flora's hair tickled his bare arm, and the slight discomfort irritated him. He moved out of the way. Beyond the double glazed window lay a crisp late autumn day, the sky as pale as washed linen. Energy fizzed in him suddenly, taking him by surprise. What was he doing here, wallowing in pleasure? What was the use of muscle and flesh if not to strain one and bruise the other? It was time to do something.

'Wake up, Flossie.' He patted her bottom. 'Let's go out and get some exercise.'

'I'm asleep.' She reached up to pull the lace-trimmed pillow over her head, but Don twitched it out of reach.

'It's a beautiful day. Let's go climbing. I'll teach you to climb.'

'I can't. Let's stay in bed.'

'I forbid it. If we stay here much longer we'll turn into suet pudding, so up with you, woman! Up! Up!'

'I'm not a blasted circus lion.' She sat up, glowering in mock rage. Her hair was a mass of tangled curls and he couldn't resist kissing her. She sighed against his tongue, a soft, erotic, half-sleepy sigh.

'None of that.' He got off the bed. 'If we do it much more the equipment's going to break. Today's exercise day, wear your jeans. I'll go and see if I can scrounge some gear from the hotel, they're bound to know where I can borrow something.'

'What sort of thing?'

'Rope. I'm not going to let you break your beautiful neck, sweetheart.'

When he had gone the bed tempted her again. But instead she yawned, got up and turned on the shower, delighting in yet another delicious sensation as warm water cascaded on to sleepy flesh. They might as well go out. Perhaps they'd make love in the car; they had before, giving in to a desire that would not wait until the next corner, let alone the next hotel. She felt drunk with love.

She dressed in jeans and trainers, with her cream Aran sweater and a matching hat. Scanning herself in the mirror she wondered if she ought to want to look like Shalimar, sexy, exotic and beautiful enough to turn heads in any room. But Shalimar was in her very person a statement about herself; she demanded a response from people, from men. Flora was pretty, sometimes very pretty, but her looks didn't ask for her to be considered on a different scale from the rest of womankind, as Shalimar's seemed to do. She wasn't only her looks.

'As long as Don likes me, I do too,' she murmured, and settled her hat firmly on her head.

Don was waiting for her in the hall. 'I've got us some sandwiches,' he said. 'You've taken forever, we'll be climbing in the dark.'

'I can't climb,' said Flora. 'And you'll find out I can't. I felt sick even on those bridges in Nepal, and little children run across them.'

'Everybody gets scared sometimes. And you're going to love it, I promise. But let's get moving!'

He hustled her out and into the car. After the hotel's central heating the fresh air felt like spring water. 'Oh, what a lovely day,' burst out Flora. 'What a beautiful day to be alive.'

'Told you. Let's go and do something to justify being alive!'

He sent the Bentley purring up the road, turning off to the left and then left again, following a scribbled map he had obtained from somewhere. The houses fell away behind them. Sheep spotted the heather like lost handkerchiefs, and the cold wind had the trees in a perpetual shiver. They saw no other vehicles, and only the occasional abandoned croft. Soon the rolling heather moors began to give way to rocks and barren peaks, with eagles circling high in the clear mountain air. At last Don stopped the car at the foot of a rocky crag.

Flora looked up in amazement. 'This is ridiculous.'

'It's a scramble. Don't worry, I'll put a rope on you, you're not going to die. You'll like it.'

She was distinctly dubious. She looked at her trainers, clean and smooth-soled, but Don was wearing a similar, if dirtier pair. 'It's so cold. I didn't bring a coat.'

'You'll be fine on the rock. The sun's on it. Look, I'll show you how to rope up.'

He talked to her about knots and rope technique, but she wasn't paying attention. She felt a strong sense of unreality; there was no way she could climb this crag, and Don's assumption of possibility seemed laughable. But he didn't appear to think so.

'I'll lead,' he told her. 'Don't worry about the rope, just let it hang, don't jerk it or anything. Wait until I'm about up to that bush and then come after me. I'll call.'

'But I can't. Really I can't!' She smiled at him reasonably. Whilst part of the crag was theoretically navigable, the bush was growing on a wide ledge some forty feet above a rock face inclined only a degree or two from the vertical.

'I'll pull you up if necessary,' he told her, in what was intended to be comfort.

She began to wonder if he meant it and decided to be firm. 'No thanks! Honestly, Don, I'd rather not. I'll wait here.'

'Oh, for Christ's sake, Flora, don't be a wet!' He spoke with real irritation. For an instant she saw herself as he did; pathetic and cowardly. Perhaps it was easy, perhaps it was only amateurs that saw difficulties in such a thing. She stood silent and watched Don prepare to climb.

He moved to the rock face, rubbed his hands down his trousers and – ascended. All he seemed to do was extend his long arms and even longer legs, suspend himself from this or that crevice and move quickly up the wall. There hardly seemed to be effort in it, and there was certainly no indecision. Sometimes he would try a move, stop and try another, but generally he barely paused in his quick, light progress up the rock. When he reached the bush, he seated himself on the ledge and yelled, 'Come on up, then! You can't fall, I've got a good belay.'

Flora stood away from the face to see him better. 'You know I can't do it!'

'Course you can. It isn't hard, you'll love it once you try. Start. Find a route. You'll manage.'

She felt angry with him suddenly. She was frightened and he didn't care, he was high above her and expected her to achieve the impossible. It would serve him right if she fell and broke her neck. Her father would be furious.

She went to the rock and scrambled up the first, easy boulders. The rope round her waist tightened, but much good it would do her with a ten foot stretch of barren crag before the next possible step. 'To your left,' called Don. 'Hand on the spur.'

She took hold as he said, and quite fortuitously it seemed there was a niche for one of her toes. 'Reach up on the right,' called Don again. 'A crack. Jam your hand in.'

She had to. The rope was tight, so tight she couldn't go back. She put her hand in the crack. 'It hurts!' she grunted. 'Hurts like anything.'

'Put your left hand on the ledge. Reach for it, you can't fall.'

And she did reach, feeling the skin peel from her right hand, her toes cramping with the strain of hanging on. 'I want to get down!' she wailed. 'I'm going to fall!'

'You can't, I've got you. Left foot, up to your waist. You can do it, you're fit enough. Good girl. I'm getting horny just watching you. Come up here and let me get into those jeans. I love the way your backside bounces up and down.'

Flora clenched her teeth, hanging on for dear life. But she opened her mouth enough to shout, 'Let me down! I want to get down!'

He paid no attention and continued hauling her up. He had taught a couple of lads this way, breaking through the initial fear and tension with one dramatic climb. But Flora was making heavy weather of it. She was exhausted after twenty feet, but whenever her foot or handhold slipped the rope held her. Another ten feet, she was almost there. He called to her, advice and encouragement, and she struggled on in barely controlled panic. Glancing down to place her foot more securely, she saw the drop below. Her blood froze.

'Don! Don, let me down, I want to get down! I'm going to fall, I know I'm going to fall. Please, please, let me get out of here!'

'Shut up and keep climbing.' His voice was like a whip. If she panicked she could get hurt, she had to listen to him.

'I hate it! Please, I'm going to fall!' She was whimpering with fear, her face pressed against the rock.

'Come up here, Flora. Now.' She must not freeze. She simply must not. He couldn't imagine what he would do if she did. The pull on the rope became insistent once again. When she still stayed frozen against the face he jerked, hard, and she squealed in fright. 'Don't! Please, Don!'

'Climb, Flora. Right hand up. Go on.'

With a sense of wild desperation Flora flung herself upward. She felt her nails go, her chin scrape the rock, and all the time the rope at her waist was cutting her in two. Her legs were trembling violently, beyond her control. Her hand reached the ledge. Don reached down, took hold of the waistband of her jeans and hauled her to safety.

'Good girl. Wasn't so bad, was it?'

Flora lay face down. Tears were turning the dust into mud. 'It was horrible,' she whispered.

'You ought to feel proud of yourself. Not many novices could have got up Jacob's Crag, I tell you. I climbed it once before, when I was at school. Odd how your body remembers when your mind can't. You see, it was all possible, you didn't have to be scared. Turn over. Come on, turn over and let me clean you up.'

She rolled on her back and when he saw her tears he laughed. 'Silly girl. You should have known I wouldn't let you fall.'

'But I didn't want to do it, Don. It was horrible. I was terrified.'

'Next time won't be so bad.'

'There won't be a next time. Never ever.'

After a moment he said, 'Going to stay here forever, are you?'

Flora sat up and looked around. Above, below, and to both sides stretched barren rock. As he said, unless she climbed she would have to stay there forever.

'I hate you,' she said incredulously. 'You said we were going for a walk.'

'Don't be a rabbit, Flora! You can enjoy this. Make an effort.'

She glared at him. If she had dared she would have hit him, but the ledge, which from the rock had seemed so safe, now felt narrow and precarious. 'You're only doing it to torment me,' she burst out. 'You've dragged me up here to amuse yourself. You don't care if I'm scared out of my wits!'

'There's nothing to scare anyone, you're not going to die. Look, you're spoiling the day. You'll feel great when it's over. Hang on here until I get to the top then I'll bring you up after me. It's a walk down from there.'

He went away again, moving easily up the rock. Flora felt her breath coming in shallow pants, her guts felt as if someone was stirring them with a paddle. She wondered what she would do if he fell and was hurt, because she couldn't get down by herself. But of course the rope would drag her off and they would both be dead. She felt a hopeless sense of doom, and then of abandonment as Don moved out of sight. A moment late he yelled to her to climb.

The second pitch was slightly less hard, but it seemed more difficult because Flora was tiring. She felt acutely conscious of space beneath her feet, of how easy it would be to look down and become immobilised by horror. Don became annoyed at each missed hold. 'Reach for it! Flora, you're not trying. Make an effort, woman!'

On and on it went, a purposeless exercise in torture. At last, at long last, Don reached down and hauled her on to the sweet mountain grass. It was over.

That night, at dinner, she was frosty. Her nails were broken, her knuckles skinned and there was a graze on the point of her chin. Don was pleased with himself, and wanted her to be pleased too, but it was impossible for her to pretend that everything was fine. She felt bruised, mentally and physically. He had forced her up that cliff, paying not the slightest attention to her distress.

Eventually, after trying for an hour to talk, Don put down his knife and fork. 'Are you going to sulk all night?' he asked quietly.

'I'm not sulking.' She lifted her wine glass and avoided his eye.

'I don't know what else to call it. Little girl sulks.'

'As opposed to big boy bullying!' Now she glared at him. 'I think the least you can do is apologise! It was cruel and pointless.'

'Of course it had a point. I wanted you to share it with me. I wanted you to understand. Flora, if you don't know why I climb then you don't know me. I thought you should.'

She ducked her head down. 'That wasn't a beginner's climb. It was too high and too hard, and you know it.'

'It wasn't high! It wasn't even hard. No one learns anything on easy pitches, they're for schoolgirls and wets. You were slow because you were scared, but that's what climbing's all about. Being scared, and overcoming it.'

Flora felt a chasm in their understanding. There was nothing to gain from fear, nothing at all. She had been scared enough almost to lose control, and afterwards she had hated herself for being afraid,

117

and him for causing it. Perhaps, just perhaps if there had been a
child to rescue from a fire, or an urgent message to be carried, she
might then have scaled the cliff and felt good about it, but as it
was all she felt was shock. Only days ago Don had promised that
he would take care of her forever. And now this.

When they went up to their room she was distant still. Don said,
'This is starting to annoy me, Flora.'

'Poor you.' She sat at her dressing table and began to file her
broken nails.

'I've apologised, there's no more I can do.'

'You have not apologised!' She swung round on the seat and
faced him. 'You haven't once said sorry. I wouldn't mind if you
said that. But you didn't care how scared I was, or how much I
hurt. You don't care now. All you're worried about is not having
me to play with tonight.'

'I'll have you regardless, Flora.' He stripped off his tie and flung
it over a chair.

'You will not.'

Their eyes met. Realising he had gone a shade too far, Don said,
'You're being stupid. Making a fuss about nothing.'

'I don't think it's nothing. It's important to me.'

'Is this the way you mean to go on? Blackmailing me with sex
when you can't get your own way?'

'I'm not doing that! But I don't want to make love when we're
fighting. I am allowed to say no sometimes.'

'If you were ill, I suppose. Not for this. I'm not letting you decide
when you will or will not allow me the odd favour. You can lift
your pretty finger as often as you like, Miss Kincaid, but you're
Mrs Harrington now. You'll do as you are told.'

'No!'

He said nothing. She was a spoiled brat who had never had to
face difficulty in all her pampered life. One easy climb, when he
was trying to teach her, give her pleasure – she couldn't possibly
have found it frightening. He began to take off his clothes, throwing
them in a heap on the floor. She said shrilly, 'Don, don't. Please
don't be horrible.'

He ripped off his trousers and flung them at a chair. 'I won't be
told what to do, Flora. Not by your father and certainly not by
you. For the last time, come to bed.'

'What if I don't?' she almost whispered, cold with apprehension.

'Nothing. And I mean nothing. Ever.'

This morning they had been happy, blissfully happy. In the blink

118

of an eye almost it had all gone wrong. He wouldn't love her any more. He wouldn't want her any more. She dropped her head like a suffering child and began to cry.

Harrington sighed furiously. 'Flora, there's no need for this. No one's hurting you.'

'You do hurt me. I think you must hate me.'

'I think you're making this up out of nothing. There was no reason to quarrel in the first place.'

She put her hands over her face and Don ran a violent hand through his hair. He hated to see Flora cry, he realised, he could almost want to hit her to make her stop. He went over to her, took her by the shoulders and shook her. 'Will you shut up? Will you just shut up?'

For a second she couldn't breathe. She felt as if her teeth were loose in her head. When he let her go she fell against the wall.

'I'll tell my father!' she yelled shrilly. 'He'll make you sorry.'

'You dare, Flora! I'm warning you, you're going too far!'

'I haven't done anything! I didn't want to go on the beastly climb and you haven't − you won't even − why won't you say you're sorry?'

He went over to the tray and poured himself a stiff drink. He didn't trust himself to look at her, she aroused more rage in him than he knew he possessed. The sound of her sobs sent red hot pulses through him.

'Will you just stop crying?' he said tightly. 'I don't trust myself if you keep on crying.'

'What can I do then? If you won't even let me cry?'

He spun on his heel and yelled, 'You can get into bed and behave yourself!'

In complete silence, Flora got up and began to undress. He watched every movement, from the shrug of her shoulder to the lift of her knee. Against the red of her hair her skin was like milk, marked by a two inch gall round her waist. 'I had the rope too tight,' he said gruffly. 'That must have hurt.' It was as near as he could get to apology.

'Yes.' She was naked, and made no move to cover herself. She went to the bed and got in.

'What now then, Flora?'

She didn't meet his eyes. 'I don't want to fight. We can make love if you want.' He put down his glass. 'I don't want to argue about this again. Do you understand that?'

'No. Yes. It isn't my fault if I don't like climbing!'

'And it isn't my fault if I go off and do it and leave you behind. I tried, Flora. Just remember I tried.'

He stepped out of his underpants and came towards the bed. She watched him, eyes wide with anxiety. He pulled back the covers and threw himself down, she could almost smell his anger. She closed her eyes and tried to let her mind drift, tried to enter that world where neither heat nor cold nor anything existed except feeling, but the door was closed to her. He held her on her side, pushing her leg up so he could enter her. A second later he swung on to his back, pulling her with him. She pushed herself up, her hands braced against his chest, and her round, hanging breasts aroused him utterly. He held her buttocks, thrusting up, and then the feeling came. She gasped, hanging her head, and involuntarily moved on him. It was beguiling, deceiving, dishonest. At that moment she loved him not at all, and yet the act, the expression of love, was still the same. She climaxed first, shuddering almost painfully, and lay on him while he finished.

'Beautiful girl,' he whispered. 'You see? There was nothing to fight about.'

She let out her breath in a long, soft sigh.

The row blew over, as rows do. It was a symptom perhaps of the end of the honeymoon, a sign that they were ready to go back. Besides, Flora's period began and she was embarrassed and upset.

'I thought you didn't want to get pregnant?' Don watched her from the bedroom, halfway to being cross.

'I didn't think I did. But I'd like to know I could. This makes me feel a bit of a failure.'

He felt a rush of warmth towards her and went to take her in his arms. 'It's all right. Another time, you can't rush these things. The moon's got to be full or something.'

'You can't say we didn't try,' said Flora, aggrievedly.

'It's God telling us to keep on trying!' He clutched her bottom lewdly and she squealed. He pursued her round the bathroom, leering like a maniac. She ran, and he cornered her by the basin, declaring, 'Now I've got you, my pretty!' She put up her face to be kissed.

Chapter Eleven

They returned on a bright, cold morning, the castle seeming sugar-coated, windows shining under a crisp dusting of snow. There was a new coat of arms over the door, with the letters K and H entwined. Flora got out of the car and stared at it.

'He didn't waste much time,' said Don.

'I don't know why he has to do these things,' she muttered. 'He always has to go over the top where I'm concerned.'

'It's flattery. Because he loves you.'

'But he never thinks what I want! Only what he wants, what he thinks is right!' She stamped into the castle, unreasonably cross.

Kincaid was sitting up in bed waiting for them. Flora felt her anger evaporate in the face of his weakness. Her unconscious mind always expected him to be as he used to be, strong and well.

'Hello, Dad.' She went and kissed him. 'You look as if you've been overdoing things.'

Kincaid shook his head. 'Someone's got to keep things ticking over. They won't let me out of bed any more, not since your wedding. I – I get so tired. You don't recover the same, at my age. Blasted nuisance. Don, there are some matters I must discuss with you. You should not have bought that diving concern. I never meant to.'

'I know that. But I decided to go ahead.' Don leaned on the tall press, easy and comfortable. The room was very warm, almost like summer.

'There's over-capacity. We need more work, not another team.'

'We've got more work. Last I heard they were heading out to California.'

'I don't like getting involved in that market! We're nowhere near close enough, we'll get our fingers burned.'

'My fingers. Not yours. Don't worry about it.'

Only a little time ago it was Kincaid making the choices, taking the risks, urging others to quell their anxieties.

'We saw the coat of arms,' said Flora.

'Did you? They only showed me the sketches. Means what it says, though. Kincaid and Harrington — together. You and me, Don. Don't forget, I came up from nothing, or almost nothing. You can't forget me.'

'I don't think that's very likely,' said Don.

'I don't know — a few years on and there'll be all Harrington and no Kincaid. You'll be glad to get rid. Glad to see the back of me.' He glared at them, daring them to agree.

'Why don't you sleep?' suggested Flora.

'I'm always asleep. Your mother came. All she talks about is goats.' His head drooped with weariness, and the nurse rose from her unobtrusive corner. She went to the bed, easing its occupant down against the pillows. He sighed throatily, and his eyes closed. Flora and Don left.

It was time to start their married life, and Flora wasn't sure what on earth she was supposed to do. Don had KORSEA, and would presumably go into the office every day, but for her, active, healthy and not pregnant, there was nothing. On the first day she went into town with Don, and did some shopping.

She bought two shirts for herself and a pair of soft Italian leather shoes for Don. Only forty-five minutes had passed. She decided to buy presents for everyone, and found a pink angora cardigan for Marie, a watercolour of Highland cattle for her father, and a length of good tweed for Lilian. A gauze shawl spangled with sequins caught her eye, and she bought it for Shalimar's Christmas gift. A feeling of doom came over her. There was nothing she could not buy, and yet there was nothing she really wanted. Suddenly she longed for the spartan life of Nepal, where the definition of need was of something without which you could not survive. Perhaps her need was to be needed, they said everybody's was. And just at the moment she was not.

When she went back to the office in the afternoon Don was nowhere near ready, so she waited another hour. She was rigid with boredom. Finally he prepared to leave, still talking to Mike, one of the project managers. 'So KORSEA have these two ships being built and no work for them? Do we have to take delivery? The old man must have included an exit clause somewhere.'

'He didn't expect a downturn in the market. No one did.'

'He wouldn't have ignored the possibility,' interposed Flora. 'If you think he did then you don't know Dad.'

Neither of the men said anything. She knew they were being polite, that they thought Kincaid had lost his grip even before the accident. His habits of secrecy had infected the whole firm, there were no records, anywhere.

'You ought to ask him about those ships,' she said to Don, in the car. He grunted. 'I will. When he's up to it. Know anything about oil rigs, do you?'

She shook her head. 'But I've been on a few. Dad used to make me dress up and go and present things on them.'

'I'm a bit more interested in the cranes that supply them. Damned complicated this business.' While John drove he immersed himself in technical papers.

She didn't go into town again. There wasn't any point. At home she could at least paint and draw, walk in the park and ride the frosty hills, watching the deer reaching up to strip bark from the trees. When she was served an elaborate and excessive lunch she picked at it, causing Marie to exclaim, 'Really, Miss Flora! Don't you know a bride needs a good appetite? It encourages things.'

So it seemed that everyone was waiting. She began to think too much about being pregnant. She put a little chart in her handkerchief drawer and consulted it each day. There was little else to think of. Don, aware that she was bored, said, 'Why don't you take up charity work or something? Isn't that what women do?'

'It's what I did in Nepal,' said Flora morosely. 'I thought you'd taken me away from all that.'

He laughed and put his feet up on the sofa. 'Did you ask Dad about those ships?' asked Flora.

He glanced up briefly from the technical paper he was studying. 'I tried. He can't remember. And I don't like bullying the old boy.'

'No.'

That night, when they made love, she was stiff and unresponsive. When he finished, rolling aside, he said, 'What's the matter?'

She lay looking up at the ceiling. 'Nothing. Everything. I'm bored.'

'Like I said, get involved in something. Homeless families, orphans, something like that.'

'There isn't anything like that around here! Believe me, I know. If I get involved in the village, they think I'm being superior.'

'And I think you're being defeatist. You could do anything, start a shop, whatever you wanted.'

'Don't you think that would be a bit silly? I don't need more money, I can't spend what I've got.'

'Then buy something that makes you happy. You can do anything you want, Flora. There must be something you can do around here. Look, I'm exhausted, I've got to get some sleep. We'll talk in the morning.'

When he was sleeping she lay beside him and stared up into the dark. She loved Don, and because of it the days stretched ahead of her, blank and unrewarding. There was no one to blame but herself. Her mother had foreseen this, but Flora hadn't listened. Making people happy had seemed more important, Don, her father. She had the sensation of a great weight on her, a stifling, suffocating commitment.

To everyone's surprise, at the end of the week Van turned up. He walked in, carrying a rucksack, from the country bus which dropped him in Delyn village. 'Hello, Flora,' he said, rubbing frost from his beard. Lumps of snow were melting from his boots on to the shining parquet floor. He seemed utterly out of place.

'Perhaps you'll take tea,' she ventured, and when he looked at her askance, added, 'and stay the night? Don won't be home till gone six.'

'I would have telephoned but I did not know when I should arrive. I did not wish to cause inconvenience.'

'And you haven't. Come and have tea.'

It was fun to have someone to entertain. Only when the world outside made itself felt did she realise how quiet and insular the castle had become. She lived in a nursing home, in polished splendour, smothered by love and care. She curled up on the sofa and saw that one of Van's socks had a hole in it.

'Have you been climbing recently?'

He nodded, his mouth full of good Dundee cake. 'I climb always. But without Don it is not the same. We are good together. I climb once with Eddie, chatter chatter, all the day, and with some Germans. They plan too much. If the weather goes bad they do not put up a tent, they look up the plan. Madness! When did a plan ever stop you freezing to death, hey?'

She laughed, and he grinned at her. 'I don't grudge you him,' said Van. 'But I should like to borrow him for a week or two. Men should be married, but not all the time, yes?' He often finished his sentences with a question, and it made disagreement seem almost rude.

Nonetheless she said, 'Actually Don's terribly busy at the moment. The business needs him.'

Van took a crumpet. 'Of course. If he cannot come then that must be. But I am going and I think to myself, "Van, what would it be if Don could have come with you and you had not asked him?" So I must ask, yes?'

124

Flora said nothing. Forbes came unobtrusively into the room and put another log on the fire. Van let out his breath in a long sigh. 'I have never known a house so comfortable. At your wedding I thought it magnificent, but now, in the winter – paradise.'

'Thank you.' Flora poured them both another cup of tea. 'Do you see many people that were on the Everest expedition?'

Van shrugged. 'Some. Mike, that is a bad business. Him I wish not to have seen.'

'I thought he was going to be all right. What's the matter with him?'

Van shook his great head. 'The leg. A thrombosis developed, they took it off, above the knee. Now – he has nothing. No one. The climbing gone, his job gone, his wife run off. I gave him money, but it was no good. A bad business.'

Flora schooled her face into concern. She wished she had liked Mike more. 'You don't want to go back to Nepal, do you?' she asked fearfully.

'For a married man with business commitments? Naturally not. This is almost home. Almost on the doorstep. The Eiger Direct.'

'The Eiger? You mean – *the* Eiger?'

'But yes. Don and I did the original route years ago. The Direct is more difficult, of course. We shall climb in the classical style, none of these camps and fixed ropes. There is an American, and a boy called Neil Kindler who I think climbs in your Lake District, and myself. Another man is needed.'

'People get killed on the Eiger.'

He nodded. 'Some, yes.'

Flora was silent. When Don came home he would be sure to tell Van that he could not go, and there would be a tense and unhappy evening. She hated people being at odds with one another. When Van went to his room to wash and change she called Marie and asked for a special dinner that night. It was up to her to do everything possible to save the occasion from disharmony.

But the lobster bisque, steak au poivre and floating island pudding were enjoyable but unnecessary. The two men greeted each other quietly enough – but their eyes gleamed. Over the soup Don said, 'What have you been doing? I heard you'd been in Chamonix,' and Van said, 'Ah, you keep your ear to the ground still!'

Flora had no idea he still kept in touch with climbing. They conversed in a shorthand she barely understood: the Dru, North Face Fiescherhorn, Gervasutti Pillar. Van's Alpine winter had been crammed with incident it seemed. 'I saw Reinhard go,' he said at one point. 'One moment laughing, then a rock fall, and he was

125

gone. Berthold was on the same rope, he was badly shocked. But it's always a shock, yes?'

'Always.' Don lifted his wine glass and drank. 'Did you see Mike? I hear he's in a hell of a mess.'

Van nodded, exhaling a huge sigh. 'We should have left him, Don. I said at the time. Sometimes a man is better off dead.'

A shiver went down Flora's spine. This horrible, horrible climbing. She hated it. The telephone was ringing in the next room. They heard Forbes answer. 'Mr Harrington's at dinner, Mr Mactee. I'll tell him you called.'

'Flora says you are indispensable,' said Van, tucking into a second helping of steak.

'Depends who wants me and what for. I'd do a lot to get rid of Mactee nagging at me for a week or two.'

'You didn't tell me he was nagging,' said Flora.

'It isn't your problem, love. He doesn't like me taking over. It's understandable. His first response is to give up all decision making and dump everything on my desk. He's hoping to expose my ignorance, which is all too bloody obvious already I should have thought. I don't know a damn thing about the oil business.'

Van chuckled. 'When has ignorance ever stopped you? Come and have a break, Don. Two weeks, no more. Classic Alpine ascent, Eiger Direct. Nowadays it's a stroll.'

'The dear old Eiger. A Sunday afternoon outing.' They met each other's eyes in silent accord.

'You've only just got into the firm,' said Flora reasonably. 'You can't swan off just like that. And the Eiger's dangerous. Mike, this Reinhard person – people are always getting hurt.'

'We've done it before,' said Don.

'Then why do it again?'

He didn't reply, instead asking Van who else was on the expedition. He wrinkled his nose at the name of Neil Kindler. 'Bit of a bloody whizz kid, isn't he? Likely to try and make his name and get himself killed.'

'Afraid of the competition, Don? He's good. Going to be the best.'

Don contemplated. A little desperately Flora said, 'But you can't go Don! It simply isn't possible!'

'Anything's possible,' he murmured. 'But it depends on what you want.'

Flora went to bed early, but couldn't sleep. When at last Don came up, she said, 'Well? Are you going then?'

He looked at her. 'You're very pretty tonight.'

126

'Don't change the subject. Are you going?'

He cleared his throat, guiltily. 'Yes, I am.'

'Oh, Don!'

He began to get undressed, and the silence was as thick as treacle. Suddenly he stopped. 'Look, it's only a fortnight. Things won't fall apart in two weeks, for Christ's sake. If the weather's bad, if things don't go right, I'll come home, I'm not sitting it out for three months waiting for a fine day. I never meant to give up climbing, Flora. We got married in a hurry because your father was sick, and that's fine, that's what had to be. But I don't have to give up climbing. I never intended to.'

'I had to give things up.'

'So did I. I never used to have to justify going climbing.' He grinned at her, but she turned her shoulder to him.

When he was in bed she said, 'It's the North Face that's dangerous, isn't it? If you were climbing that it would be different.'

'Would it?' He sounded rather strained.

'Well, of course it would! Loads of people get killed there, even I know that.'

He said nothing. Then, after a long moment in which it seemed he was wrestling with himself, he burst out, 'It *is* the North Face. It's the Direct route from bottom to top, no veering, no shirking, just straight up. It's usually climbed as an expedition, with fixed ropes and camps. We're doing an Alpine push. Straight up, fast.'

She lost her breath. 'And – and what am I supposed to do if you get killed?'

'Whatever you would have done before. Without me.'

She flung out of bed and stormed to the door. 'I'm not staying here! You don't ask, you don't consider, you just decide. I'm married, but you're certainly not, so you can be as single as you like and sleep by your horrible self!'

He caught her halfway down the corridor. 'Stop it! We don't want everyone knowing we're having a row.'

'Row? Who's rowing? You're going off to climb, leaving me stuck at home with a sick old man, worried out of my mind in case you die and leave us both in the lurch. You promised, Don! Less than three months ago, you promised!'

'I'm not going back on it. I will never go back on it. And all I want is two short weeks to go climbing. For Christ's sake, Flora, can't you see that I need it? KORSEA is one hell of a place to watch yourself growing old.'

He was holding tight to her wrist. 'You're hurting me,' she said dully.

'Come back to the room. The staff know every damn thing about us as it is, we ought to try and maintain some areas of privacy.'

She allowed herself to be led. But when he released her she sat on the dressing table stool, as far as possible from the bed and demanded, 'Why is it so bad? You haven't said anything.'

'There's nothing to say. But it isn't easy.'

She laughed, unkindly. 'I can't imagine what made you think it was! That business has been my father's whole life. It ruined his marriage, ruined his health, and took every ounce of his brain and strength for over forty years. But, of course, it was bound to be easy.'

'All right, Flora. Have your little dig. But part of the trouble is the mess he left. No one knows what's going on. You can have some bloke ringing up talking about a contract signed by Darnley or Stephens or even him, that no one's ever heard of. Sometimes he remembers, sometimes not. Sometimes he thinks he's fifty again. Last week he gave me the name of someone to talk to, and it turned out he'd been dead ten years. Mactee doesn't help, of course. I'd retire him, except he's one person with a clue to what's going on. I need a break, Flora.'

'Oh, Don, I do understand, really I do, but I'm pretty sure the business can't stand it.'

'It's going to have to. I thought — don't know what I thought. I never meant to give up climbing altogether. This has been the longest time in my life when I haven't climbed. I'm going. I'm sorry, but that's that.'

She got up from her stool and flung over to the bed, sitting stiffly on the edge. He got in too, and put a firm hand on her back. 'I never thought you'd be the sort of woman who'd make this sort of fuss,' he said grimly. 'A moaner who wants her husband locked up safe in a plastic box. It never works. The men go just the same.'

'What about the women?' asked Flora. 'Don't they ever go?'

He chuckled. 'No, they do not. And most of them have very much more to complain of than you.'

'How lucky I am,' she said thinly.

He turned off the light. 'Yes.'

Chapter Twelve

She sat on a sofa, watching him pack his climbing gear; ropes, slings, crampons and ice axes; nuts for jamming in crevices, jumars for ascending ropes; the bright red duvet jacket she remembered from Kathmandu, when he had worn a beard and seemed wild and dangerous. Which, of course, he was.

'I wish you'd say when you're coming back.'

'Can't. If we get good weather we could be done in two weeks, a few bad days and a month's gone. I won't stay more than a month.'

'KORSEA can't last out a month.'

'If there's anything urgent they can get in touch. Mactee can manage.'

She said nothing. Her heart seemed to be stuttering in her chest, choking on a mass of unexpressed emotion. An odd thought came to her − at that moment her most conscious feeling was envy. He was packing, he was setting out on adventure, and she − she was staying at home.

'I could come,' she muttered. 'Dad has his nurse.'

He zipped up a waterproof bivouac sack and tossed it down next to his double boots. 'I hope they don't mean to use bolts,' he said thoughtfully. 'I'm damned if I'll go if they do.'

'Then I hope they use a thousand,' snapped Flora. 'I want to come. Please, Don!'

His pale eyes almost seemed to look through her. 'What's the point, Flora?' he said eventually. 'Your dad needs you, I don't. Not out there. You'd be in the way.'

She felt herself start to shake. He had their lives so compartmentalised, his things, her things, and he had everything and she − she looked round at her beautiful home. It never had been enough and it wasn't now.

129

Don went to see Kincaid before he left. He was up, sitting at the window in his dressing gown, legs stretched out in front of him, his good hand flicking the remote control for the television. He was studying the share prices on the information channel.

'Recession's coming up,' he said, casting a glance from beneath his drooping eyelid. 'You want to be careful.'

'Yeah. Sure.' Don eyed the old man, trying to assess him. He looked better today, and less vague than for a while. 'The new ships are about ready for launch,' he said.

'What? What new ships?'

'The supply ships. You remember, don't you?'

'I wouldn't order new ships now! What are you thinking of, man?'

Don sighed. 'It doesn't matter. Look, I'll be away for a couple of weeks or so. Flora's going to be here, of course. I'll come and see you as soon as I get back.'

Kincaid's head jerked up. 'And where the hell do you think you're going?'

He sounded like a headmaster interviewing one of his naughtier boys. Don felt irrationally guilty. 'I'm going climbing,' he admitted. 'Just in the Alps, nothing much.'

'And you'll bloody well not go. The City's watching us like a hawk, they know what a mess we're in. I expect you to stay here and do your work, not go swanning off to some party! I forbid it. Absolutely.'

They glared at one another. Kincaid said, 'No need to bite your tongue. Say what you think, I won't die in a second. What do you want to go for, anyway?'

'I don't need to justify myself.'

'Oh, but you do! We have a bargain. God, don't think I don't know what it's like. Hellish responsibility. Something you can't get away from. But you can't go off as you please, when you like, where you like –'

'Why not?' said Don. 'The firm can cope. It's not for long. I'm running things my way, not yours. Before I met Flora, you, my whole life was climbing. You can't expect me to give it up.'

Kincaid swallowed. 'I do expect it. We agreed.'

'Then I don't think we agreed to the same thing.'

As he turned to go, Kincaid called, 'Wait!' Don hesitated, big hands looped in his belt. 'I just want you to know,' said Kincaid, 'that whatever happens – whatever! – I hold you personally responsible.'

'That's fine by me,' said Don.

Little changed with Don gone. The afternoons lost their focus, that was all. There was no need for Flora to go and change, to make sure that dinner was on time, that her father was happily settled and wouldn't wake in the evening and demand to get up, thinking morning had come. She couldn't sleep herself. Once in the night she got up and wandered the corridors, looking out at the frosty gardens. A thin sheet of ice coated the river, gleaming like diamonds in the moonlight. She couldn't imagine how Don was living.

Suddenly she couldn't bear it. She looked at the clock, trying to guess what time it would be on the west coast of America, and decided she didn't care. She went back to her bedroom, leafed through her address book and extracted a scrawled postcard. 'Here for the next six weeks,' it read, the writing so large it left little room for the address and number. Flora dialled and waited, trying to imagine the unimaginable; some impulse travelling instantly and invisibly across half the world, just so she could speak to her friend.

'Hello?' said a voice.

'Shalimar? Shalimar, is that you?'

'Yes! Flo, what is it? It's not your father?'

'No, it's nothing important. At least – I didn't mean to frighten you. Are you busy, I mean really busy? Can you come back?'

There was a pause. Flora could hear her saying something to someone in the room. Shalimar laughed voluptuously. 'I can spare a few moments,' she murmured. 'It's all right, he's going into the next room. Is there a crisis or what?'

'No crisis.' Flora sighed. 'I know you can't come. Don's gone climbing and I'm all by myself. He's on the North Face of the Eiger.'

'Flora!'

There was a long pause. Then Shalimar said, 'I'll come and hold your hand. You must be terrified for him. He'll be killed.'

'Funnily enough, I don't think so. Oh, Shalimar, it's not the climbing I'm worried about. It's – it's everything. I wish I wasn't here. I wish I hadn't got married. I haven't got a life, I haven't got a future, I haven't got anything. I sit here in this damned great house and watch my father get no better, and half the time he doesn't know I'm there. It's so strange, Shalimar. Some days I feel as if he's forgotten who I am. I don't know what to do. Oh, Shalimar, I'm so miserable!'

'I'm coming over,' cut in Shalimar. 'I'll be there in twenty-four hours. Go and take a pill, or better still don't take one. Don't take anything, not even a glass of sherry. Go to bed and read something comforting. *Winnie the Pooh*. That's an order.'

'I've made such a mess. I wish I knew what to do.' Flora found she was weeping suddenly.

'And I'll tell you what to do. Go to bed and read that book. The only alternative is *Wind in the Willows*. I'll be there. I'm coming.'

'Oh, Shalimar, I do wish you would.'

The receiver clicked into silence. Flora wiped her tears with the flat of her hand, amazed at herself. She had never done that before. And still she cried, a silent, unstoppable river of scalding tears. Wrapping her dressing gown around herself she padded along the passage to her old room. The books were still there, rows and rows of them in a high glass cabinet. She found *The Wind in the Willows*, illustrated with glossy drawings of Mole and Rat, and took it quickly back to bed. Shalimar was right. There was much comfort to be had from remembering a time of innocence. That time had long gone. She had been given the world, and found it wanting.

Twenty-four hours later the jet collected Shalimar from Heathrow and delivered her to the castle. Flora stood on the airstrip, wrapped in a sheepskin jacket, gripping her hair in one fist as the wind whipped around her head. Shalimar was wearing a long black skirt, high-heeled black boots, and a short leather bomber jacket over a red sweater. Huge silver hoops hung from her ears.

'Flora! Make way, make way, I'm heading straight for bed. I'm a zombie.'

'You look great. Do you really have to go to sleep? Can't you drink coffee and talk to me?'

'Half an hour, no more. This isn't jet lag, it's brain damage.'

Shalimar collapsed into the car, groaning when she had to unfold herself minutes later at the castle. Cold rain was starting to fall, and she shuddered. 'Why did I leave California for this? It was raining there too, but at least it didn't give you frostbite. Talking of which, how's the mountaineer?'

'He sent me a postcard when he arrived, but he can't write. They don't collect mail from tents on mountains.'

'Oh.' Shalimar followed Flora into the library, and warmed her hands at the fire. 'It must be terrible, worrying,' she said jerkily.

'Honestly, I don't. Don's so − so competent. He can't fall off, it's impossible.'

'What about avalanches?'

Flora's eyes widened. 'Do they have those? I thought perhaps it was just sort of rock.'

'It is. And lumps of it fall off on people's heads, and the snow hangs on in great slabs and then slides off, tons at a time.'

Flora had paled visibly. 'I see. I didn't know. Oh, Shalimar.'

The girl slumped into a leather chair. 'I'm supposed to be cheering you up, not frightening you to death. Flora, the men in California are — different. A million queers of course, but the rest are just so sensual. They regard making love as sort of practical work on their therapy, they're all going through therapy. When this bloke lay on top of me, panting, "I want you to know I respect you as a person," I realised it was time to take the initiative. I didn't need respect, I needed fucking!'

'Shhh! Marie will hear.' Flora leaned forward avidly. 'What did you do?'

'Tied him up. A gag and his wrists tied to the bedposts. He didn't mind, it was all a new experience, and there aren't a lot of those in California. I had a — wonderful — time.' She stretched her arms and extended her fingers like a cat's claws. 'But I didn't mind leaving,' she added. 'The fruitcake wanted to marry me.'

Flora sighed expressively. Shalimar lay back with her eyes closed, and Flora gazed into the fire, letting her thoughts wander. She visualised Don, spreadeagled against the rock, on a larger, blacker version of Jacob's Crag. She tried to imagine him drowning in snow, and could not. He was too alive, too autocratic. He would never let himself be tied to any bedpost, not even by Shalimar.

She glanced at her friend. Head cushioned on a forest of black hair, she was fast asleep. Quietly, Flora got up and fetched a rug, spreading it tenderly over her.

Morning dawned cold and blustery, with the remains of yesterday's rain gusting across the park. Shalimar, fully restored by a night's sleep, said, 'Let's go riding. We can get soaking wet and frozen stiff. Then we'll really enjoy lounging around playing Scrabble.'

The ride, which would have been dull and uncomfortable by herself, delighted Flora. They raced across the park and pushed the horses through the ford in the Delyn, with the water up to the animals' bellies and their nostrils wide with fright. Snow buntings hopped from rock to rock in the stream, and one of the villagers waved from the bridge, shouting, 'Good day to ye, Miss Flora!'

By the time they reached home again their fingers were stiff on the reins. It was a joy to lead tired horses into stables thick with straw, and the groom bustling up with buckets of warm bran mash. 'A raw day for a ride, miss,' he said contentedly. 'I'll see to the horses, that I will.'

Back in the house the girls peeled off sodden gloves and dripping

133

oilskins. 'I've made a toddy, Miss Flora,' called Marie. 'Ye'll have it before the fire just now.'

'Everyone here always loves doing things for you,' said Shalimar.

'They get bored, I think,' replied Flora.

'I don't mean that. They like to help you, you personally, Flora Kincaid. I should be jealous. You seem to have the ability to make everyone want to be your friend.'

Flora padded through to the library in her stockinged feet. Glasses in silver holders stood before the fire, and a jug steamed invitingly. She poured them both a drink. 'People think I can't cope,' she confided. 'That's all it is.'

'Rubbish! In Nepal I bet everybody liked you. And they knew who you were, they knew your dad had bought your way in. You're nice, and people respond to it.'

Flora looked at her over the glass. 'I'm not nice at all. If I was I wouldn't have telephoned like that. It isn't Dad's fault he's ill, it isn't even Don's. But I feel so angry at them both. I feel – I feel as if I'm wasting my life.'

'But you knew what you were doing. You wanted to get married and stay home!'

'Did I? I wanted to get married, I think. And Dad wanted it. But after that I didn't think much at all.'

Kincaid was well enough that day to join them for lunch. The girls chatted about their morning, and rain rattled on the windows to give point to the tale. The old man chuckled and sipped wine, dabbing at the drops that fell from the corner of his slack mouth. 'Good to see you both here again,' he said. 'This house needs people, it needs Flora's children. She won't keep me waiting.'

Flora shot Shalimar a look of weary amusement. 'They're not likely to appear with Don halfway up the Eiger,' she remarked.

Her father snorted. 'I know what I think of that! What was he thinking of? I don't understand the man, I don't at all.'

The rock face gleamed as if polished. It was ice, covering the black stones like a varnish. Yesterday's snow, hanging in the gulleys in great slabs, was hard and dangerous, likely to avalanche in a heavy, sustained fall. Don took a rest under the insubstantial protection of a lump of loose stones, frozen together. From here the view was magical, a miracle of white. Some tourists were watching from the Eigerwand station, that incongruous piece of railway engineering cut out of Eiger rock, which somehow placed absolute danger and absolute safety in mind-blowing proximity. He glanced down but all he could see of Van was a slice of orange helmet, as he craned his neck round the overhang. Neil and the American, Greg, were only just getting their act together. Last night's camp, tied insecurely on a miserable ledge, had taken its toll. In an hour or so he would let Neil lead and take a rest, but now – he looked around for a suitable place for a protection bolt.

'Have you frozen to that damned rock?'

Van, finally admitting that he was tired of hanging around on the end of this rope. Deciding against the bolt, Don gave the yell that over the years had come to mean 'climbing' and swung out on the rock. The loose stones just above him creaked. With these moments of thin sun it was getting marginally warmer and the ice was losing its grip on the face.

As if to contradict his thoughts, Van yelled, 'The clouds look bad. Perhaps it will snow.'

Perhaps it would. Don didn't think about it. His right hand found a hold, but he reached again and found another, at the extent of his arm. Right foot up, braced against the rock, left foot, left arm extended to a comfortable half inch ledge further up. It was confidence climbing, forcing the mind to exclude all thoughts of avalanche, rock fall, the possibility of his fingers pulling through the friable surface.

Time for another protection bolt. He fished around in the sack dangling from his waist, noting that the clouds were indeed massing behind him. A dark yellow light was descending on the face. In a moment he would call Van up with the sacks, they might have to find a perch and stay put for an hour or so; a day or so. More than a few days and the food would run out, and that would be that. Climbing the Eiger was always a matter of luck and the weather.

The bolt went in, a good one. The day was not far off when even a protection bolt would be looked down on by climbing aesthetes, leaving the real hard men to die for their mistakes. That would separate the men from the boys. As it was, after a period when people virtually drilled their way up cliffs, cruelly defacing the rock with every device known to man, now they were back to basics; you climbed the rock as it was, with the minimum of artifice. Getting up was only half the game, doing it unaided was the other half. The odd nut or piton, the occasional bolt that might stop you dying if you fell off, these were things Don could reconcile with his conscience. Anything more seemed to him to be cheating.

A few flakes of snow drifted past his face. God, but he was cold. He made the next few moves quickly, consciously increasing his speed. When he reached the ledge he gave the twitch on the rope that was the signal for Van to follow him. Neil and Greg were waving. Were they coming on? He couldn't tell. If they chose to sit out the storm there he couldn't blame them, even though they had the chocolate and the books. He fancied a brew. Eyeing the neighbouring slab of snow he wondered about a snowhole. The sky was darkening by the minute, and a snowhole would mean relative comfort at least.

In those minutes, waiting for Van to come up with the shovel, he let his thoughts drift. Flora would be having lunch now, dining off beautiful porcelain. And that fool Mactee would be ordering his usual plate of egg sandwiches. Suddenly he felt wildly thankful that he was here, in this wild loneliness, his legs hanging in space. Flora, Mactee, the whole circus, it would all wait. When the time came he would go back willingly, but now – he huddled himself further into his duvet jacket, feeling his lips crack and tasting salty blood. Now he had to climb this mountain.

The short day was coming to a close. Shalimar was drawing, the high fashion styles that might one day launch her into the world of the designer, when she had tired of modelling and films. Flora tried to write letters; to Winifred, still in Nepal, to Don, to her mother.

Forbes knocked on the door and came in. Flora blinked at him, her thoughts lost somewhere. 'Mr Mactee has called to see you, Miss Flora,' he said.

She sat up, pushing her hair aside. 'Mr Mactee? Here? Er – show him in.'

She hurriedly put on her shoes and pushed papers and magazines aside. Shalimar looked at her quizzically. 'Shall I go? Do we have to make an impression?'

'Do stay, please. He thinks I'm frivolous, so I try and look sober. Quick, get a book out, something worthy. Not that, idiot! Even he's not going to believe I'm sitting here reading a dictionary!'

Forbes cleared his throat. 'Mr Mactee,' he announced. Both girls stood unnaturally still, and then, as the man entered, Flora smiled and extended her hand.

'How nice to see you, Mr Mactee. Do sit down.'

'Thank you. I prefer to stand.'

'Oh.' Flora and Shalimar sat down themselves. Mactee stood over them, his hands behind his back, rocking backwards and forwards on the balls of his feet. He waited until Forbes had left the room.

'It's about the new ships, Mrs Harrington. And I should prefer to talk to you alone.'

'I'm sure we can trust Shalimar,' said Flora mildly.

'Then let's be sure that Mr Harrington knows it wasn't my idea to make our troubles public.'

136

'Troubles? What troubles?'

'Those ships are about due for delivery, Flora. And there's no work for them. No money to pay for them. Your father would have stopped work building them nigh on six months ago, and try as I would to speak to your husband he seemed incapable of listening to me. Seems to think he can spirit work, capital, out of nowhere. I talked to the bank today, and they are not willing for us to make the final payment. It's due on Tuesday.'

Flora said, 'I'm quite sure Don must have made some sort of contingency plan.'

Mactee sucked his teeth. 'Apparently not. No doubt he was optimistic that I would think of something.'

Flora stood up and walked over to the window. She pressed the bridge of her nose with her fingers. 'Let me get this straight,' she said slowly. 'Three years ago my father ordered two supply ships to be built. We've made stage payments up to now but there's a final tranche due. We can't pay, and even if we could perhaps we shouldn't. There's no work for those ships.'

'Precisely.' Mactee rocked still more firmly on his feet.

'But I'm sure my father must have thought of something! He wouldn't go blithely on without covering every possible contingency.'

'I think we have to assume he was failing long before his accident,' said Mactee smugly. 'I thought so myself, often. He was a little more short-tempered, forgetful, incautious. We can none of us escape the failings of age, Flora.'

She bit back the hasty words. If her father ever recovered his old form Mactee should be the first to know it. 'No. I'm sure you're right, Mr Mactee. Will you take some refreshment? No? Then I think the best thing is if I come into the office tomorrow and see if anything's occurred to me. I'll talk to my father tonight, he's sometimes at his best in the evening.'

'I'll look forward to seeing you, Flora. No doubt between us we can do something to remedy the mess Mr Harrington saw fit to leave.'

'Pompous fool,' said Shalimar, the moment he was gone.

'He's old. It isn't his fault.' Flora leaned her chin on her hand.

'For God's sake, Flora! He's got a bad word for everyone except himself. Why didn't he do something about these ships, he's had long enough.'

'It's Dad's fault. He wanted someone with no ideas of their own.'

'I suppose even Malcolm can make a mistake.' Shalimar shook her head wonderingly.

'I bet he didn't. I'll bet anything.'

'Dad. Dad? Are you awake?'

Flora hung over the bed, watching the slit of dark blue just visible under her father's lids widen to a crescent. He gazed at her without comprehension for a moment, before wakefulness dawned.

'Flora? What time is it?'

'About nine. Nurse Collins is going to settle you for the night soon. And I wanted to talk.'

'I don't need to be woken to be told I've got to go to sleep,' he grumbled. 'Bloody ridiculous.'

'I suppose it is. Look, Dad, do you remember those ships? Two that were being built on Tyneside. They're about ready.'

He turned his head restlessly. 'Never had a ship ready on time in twenty-five years. Forgotten how, if you ask me.'

'This time they're on the button. And we've got to pay. Dad, did you mean us to use those ships? I'm sure you didn't.'

For a moment he stared full into her face. 'I could do with a cup of tea,' he said.

'Yes, Dad, but about the ships. What were you planning? To use them, to sell them, what?'

'No market for supply ships,' he mumbled. 'Too many already.'

'I know that, Dad. That's why we don't want two more. We can't afford two more. Dad – what on earth did you mean to do?'

His expression blurred 'Not supply ships. Wouldn't build those. Much better – tugs – '

He was sliding back into sleep. Flora got up. The nurse said, 'I'm sorry, dear. He never has his good days when we want them, does he? But that's how he's always been, by all accounts. Contrary to the last.'

138

Chapter Thirteen

KORSEA had its offices in a shiny new block, its mirrored walls reflecting the ancient granite of Aberdeen. The city had changed in recent years, its fortunes fluctuating with those of the oil industry it served, boom and bust following one upon the other in an eternal circle. But Kincaid never went down. Somehow he kept on making money.

Flora and Shalimar presented an odd contrast, the neat redhead in her beautiful black velvet cape next to something that was all arms and legs and a mass of dark hair, swathed in a red dress that appeared to be no more than a bag of material with holes punched for movement. Shalimar wore a diamanté necklace round her forehead, the central paste star positioned over her nose. Flora sported four rows of pearls.

'Something for everyone there, pal,' muttered one of the junior messengers.

'You couldna afford the time of day,' said one of the managers. He advanced towards the girls, cracking his face into a beguiling smile. 'Would you be looking for Mr Mactee, Mrs Harrington?'

'Possibly,' said Flora. 'Unless you can help me?'

'Certainly, anything. I'll get you some tea. Coffee. A sandwich, perhaps?'

'Nothing, thank you. Can we go into your office? Shalimar, I've got to hide you, everyone's staring.'

'I think it's at you,' said Shalimar, looking about her.

'Me? I doubt it. Mr Andrews, isn't it? I need to ask a favour.'

Mr Andrews was aware of the entire staff grinning. He glanced at Shalimar and quickly looked away again. The girl was absolutely — magnetic! The sweat started on his brow. He preferred to look at Flora Kincaid, a delightful girl. 'If you'd come in, Mrs Harrington. Anything I can do —'

'I need to see anything and everything about the two Tyneside ships. And I need you to explain things to me. In absolute confidence. I don't want anyone inside or outside KORSEA to know about our discussion.'

'But Mr Mactee — '

'I'm quite glad Mr Mactee's not here at present. Not even Mr Mactee.'

Andrews felt his collar start to prickle. Whose back was she going behind then? Mactee's, her husband's, or both? This was the moment to complain of stomach pains and have to be taken home, but — he felt Shalimar's dark eyes on him. She smiled. He looked back at Flora's ingenuous face. 'Anything I can do,' he said huskily.

They flew down to Tyneside before lunch, Flora, Shalimar and Andrews, in the private jet. Over a glass of champagne Andrews asked, 'Have you heard how the expedition's going, Mrs Harrington?'

She gave him a brief smile. 'No, I haven't. I'd rather not know. It seems very — complicated.'

'It certainly is. Everyone at the office has the greatest admiration for Mr Harrington. Did you see the article on him in *Alpine Climber*? He's rated one of the top men of his generation.'

'I'm sure he is.' Flora looked away, down at the expanse of fields, dotted here and there with houses. The distance was too short for much height to be gained. The world appeared as a miniaturised village.

'I never realised he was that good,' said Shalimar wonderingly.

'If you saw him climb you would,' remarked Flora. 'But it's such an odd thing to be good at.'

'It's the challenge,' said Andrews. 'A challenge in a world that's grown too safe.' The plane hit an air pocket and lurched. He clutched nervously at the armrest of his seat.

Flora was greeted with respectful consternation by the shipyard. Cold flurries of snow were blowing between the buildings, and from the office, amidst the mahogany and grandeur of a past age, could be seen an icy river. The cranes reared up into the sky, like giraffes on some alien plain, a species steadily dying.

'We were delighted to hear that our ships were going to launch on time,' said Flora confidingly.

'Indeed. We were pleased ourselves. And we've been hoping for some guidance.' The director looked earnest.

'Yes,' said Flora blankly.

'We've gone as far as we can on the original specification. If Mr Kincaid's plans have been finalised we need to know. The engines are coming from Germany, I believe.'

'And what do you need to know?' Shalimar leaned across, smiling.

'Obviously, whether he's going to introduce the tugs as part of the KORSEA fleet. He may want to sell at this point, I know the Norwegians are interested. Mr Kincaid was well ahead of the game here. These small tugs are in great demand and short supply.'

Flora went slightly pink, the only indication of her delight. From outside came the faint sound of hammering, and welding sent brilliant blue flashes of colour into the dark afternoon. She asked to see the ships, and they went out on to the dock, picking their way across cables and sheets of metal. When they stopped at the KORSEA boats she almost laughed. Why had no one else come to see? These were obviously tugs – small, broad and stocky – even Andrews had seen that from the specification. They weren't half big enough for supply. But, canny as ever, her father had played his cards close to his chest. Let others think what they might, he had quietly set about plugging a gap in the market.

The hooter went for the end of the day. Men streamed out of the yard, pouring through the gates into narrow streets of houses only feet from the noise and turmoil of the dock.

'We could do with a dozen orders like this,' said the director, stamping his feet against the cold.

'Yes.' Flora held out her hand. 'Thank you. We'll do what we can. And someone will be in touch first thing tomorrow about these.'

Frost rimed even his nostrils. He rubbed a hand over his face, watching Van trying to jam his feet into frozen boots. It was very early, not yet four, but this was the last day, whatever happened. The wind had dropped. Neil and Greg were ten feet further down, and he could hear them cursing and muttering as they too prepared for the day. Don decided to lead the first pitch, and leave Neil the second. The boy was hungry for achievement, and he was good, very good. For a second he felt anxiety. Suppose he was losing it? Suppose his right, his automatic right, to the hard place, the hardest lead, was ending? One day it had to come, but surely not yet. This kid was younger even than Flora, by a month or so.

'Bloody stove.' Van was struggling with a cold gas canister. They'd have a brew and get off at first light, be up good and fast before the sun melted the ice and loosened all the rocks and scree just waiting to slide them off the face. For a brief moment Don thought about home; good food, warm bed, and Flora – Flora. He stopped himself. Death was so close, up here. Only the other day they had seen the rescue teams go out, not bothering to use a helicopter. Nowadays if they brought the body down themselves it was a death. It might be someone he knew, and in all probability it was. Tomorrow he might think of it, but not today.

His arms and legs felt stiff and weary, although when he started to climb the tiredness fell away. The sun was coming up over the mountains, a spreading stain of crimson and gold. He felt happy suddenly, with that wild surge of feeling you remembered long after the reason for it. If there was a reason.

He finished the pitch and let Neil through. The boy was good, but he took hellish chances. They were the chances Don himself took, but he knew what he was doing; he doubted the boy did. He watched him try a spur of rock and almost commit himself. At the last moment he stopped and the piece fell away, thundering down into the abyss. Neil was learning about Eiger limestone, good if it was grey, lousy if red, with yellow the unknown quantity. The sun was too damn hot — there would be avalanches soon.

They all met up on a ledge towards mid-morning. 'We're going to make it,' said Neil. 'Two hours, no more.'

'Bit hot,' said Don. 'But we should be OK on the pillar.'

They could hear the rumble of falling snow, and a cloud of spindrift rose from a far gully. Van passed round Mars bars and they all sat chewing. Neil threw his wrapper over the edge.

'What the hell did you do that for?' snapped Don. 'Have some respect for the place, can't you.'

'It's only paper.'

'And you're a damn fool. Throw any more down and I'll kick you after it. Greg, do you want to lead or shall I?'

'I'm going,' said Neil truculently. 'I'm strong enough.'

'We've got to get down as well as up,' said Don. 'Let Greg, he's fit.'

The American swallowed. He wasn't enjoying climbing with Neil, who was impatient as a second and pushed his partner into climbing faster than his natural speed. 'Neil can go if he wants,' he said.

Don scowled. Neil was tiring, but this was no place for a row. He and Van sat it out, waiting for the boy to reach a stance. It was warm for once, with no hint of the Eiger storms that so often lashed this face. He heard a distant, unalarming rumble, and suddenly a body flashed past him, falling fast. It hit the rock, swung on the rope, and struck again.

'Christ!'

They looked for Greg. He was clinging, shocked, to a ledge. Even at this distance they could see the blood on his hands, used to brake the rope as it snaked out with Neil's flying dive.

'He should have put another bolt in!' cursed Don. 'He's fallen nearly forty feet. Was it an avalanche?'

'Rockfall,' rumbled Van. 'What in God's name are we going to do?'

'I'll go down to him. They'll have seen him fall from the valley. We'll have half the SRFW up here to rescue us in a minute.'

They dropped a rope and Don went over the edge on it. Already he could see Neil stirring, causing the rope to pendulum. 'What's the damage?' he called.

Neil looked at him wildly. 'Can't move my legs. I think I've broken my bloody back.'

A vision of him hitting the face came back. Yes, it would be his back. The worst, the ultimate hurt. 'Might just be bruising,' said Don. 'Don't worry, I'll get you down. Keep still, let me do the struggling.'

God, but it was hairy. They hung like the bait on two fishing lines, suspended in space. Van sent down a rucksack frame and Don lashed Neil into it, keeping his back as rigid as possible. The boy was crying quietly, and Don said, 'Don't know why you're so bloody miserable. You're one hell of a lot better at this than I was at your age.'

'Am I? I only came off because I wanted to impress.'

'And impress you did, son. I was feeling old.'

He could hear the helicopter taking off from the valley. He wrapped his legs round the boy and held him as the draught hit, sending snow and shale blasting past them. Thoughts of breaking ropes filled his head, he could almost see the fibres parting. The winchman started to come down. 'Bloody party down here,' yelled Don.

'I hope he's brought a bottle,' said Neil.

There was a swift confab about Neil's condition. The rescuer, bearded and burly, wanted to bring Don off the face as well.

'No!' yelled Neil. 'You fucking make it, mate. Knock the bastard off.'

Don clung to the rock, his face turned away, as the chopper howled off down the valley. It took a moment to reorientate himself to climb. He felt dreamlike, as if he could step out into space and fly, and land a second later back home.

Van yelled, 'I'm bloody freezing up here!' and Don realised he too was very cold. He had to climb. Van had him on the rope, he had nothing to do but climb.

When he reached the stance he found Greg there, nursing his hands. 'Can you make it?' asked Don.

Greg nodded. Van sucked his teeth, making an odd whistling sound. They messed around for a few minutes, wasting time, feeling the wind get up and the storm clouds gather. Without a word to either man, Don suddenly started to climb.

They were down in the valley late that night. The press were there, and a few cameramen, because a dramatic accident on the Eiger was always news. But the three men went straight to the hotel, and sat in the bar drinking brandy.

'We ought to go to the hospital,' said Greg.

'Tomorrow,' said Van.

'Where the hell is it?' asked Don. 'If it's near enough we could go.'

'I will drive you,' said the hotelier. 'My pleasure.'

'Not the words I would use,' said Greg.

He was white underneath the grime and the tan. They were shocked, all of them, to a greater or lesser extent, held up by the adrenaline of the climb. At least at the hospital Greg's hands could be attended to. Rope fibres and pieces of his gloves were embedded in the palms.

No one wanted to let them in, of course. Eventually Greg's hands persuaded them, and Van and Don made so much noise that eventually they were permitted to see their friend. They clumped along the corridors, trying to tiptoe in their double boots, leaving a trail of snow and mud. In this pristine environment they were as welcome as a barrowload of muck. Neil was awake still, but drugged. He looked blearily at them. 'Did you make it?'

Don nodded. 'Yup. We were nearly there when you took that dive. Bloody spectacular.'

'Always a show-off, that's me.'

It was uncomfortably near the truth. Van said, 'Have they said anything yet?'

'Not a lot, no. Doubt if I'll climb again, though.'

There was an intake of breath. What was life without climbing? What was the point of it?

They stared down at the boy in the bed, suddenly aware of their own strong backs, their legs supporting them in unconscious ease.

'Think you'll walk again?' asked Don.

'Dunno. I can move my toes a bit. If I couldn't walk, if it was that bad − I'd be wishing I'd never got down at all. You should have cut the bloody rope, Don, that you should!'

There was an uncomfortable silence. Don thanked all the gods that ever were to be straight and whole and unscathed, to have his life still his to use. He could not have borne to be Neil now, he knew that absolutely.

Going back in the car, Don said, 'It was my fault. I let him push himself too hard, I let him go over the edge.'

Van rumbled, 'Since when can you stop eager boys hurting themselves? He may get away with it. In a year he could be back, who knows, hey?'

Greg said, 'He shouldn't have come with you. You're his idol, he had to be better.'

'And I was bloody scared that he would be. Oh God! If that's me any time, you let me fall. Just let me go, got it?'

The others said nothing. Don glared at them and Van gave a slight shrug. Who could tell what would happen, who could say what would be done? Don sighed. 'Well, at least I can pay for the chopper. I'll settle your bill too, Greg.'

'Thanks. You know, I don't think I've ever had such a weird and wonderful day in all my life.'

They knew what he meant. Disaster and triumph, side by side; civilisation and eternity, cheek by jowl; it was the same sensation Don had felt when he saw the faces watching from the railway station, a sense that the strands of life were too close together, without a decent distance in between. The brandy was starting to hit him, he felt weary suddenly. His neck ached and he realised he had eaten nothing in hours. What was the point of climbing if it did this to men? And what was the point of life if a man couldn't climb? Scenes crowded in on themselves, cluttering his memory: Mike on an Everest snowfield, Neil's face just now, and the first man he had ever seen fall, taken unconscious from a scree slope in Wales. The price paid, again and again. The lucky ones died. He was tired enough to die. Tomorrow, early, he would go home.

Flora crossed her legs demurely. Shalimar crossed hers seductively. The Norwegians, large men in lounge suits, asked if it wouldn't be more pleasant to continue the discussions over dinner.

'Why don't we conclude this first, and then talk about it?' said Flora.

'Yes, money talk is dreadfully dull,' agreed Shalimar. She got up and began to look through the even duller bookshelves in this, KORSEA's boardroom, full of tracts on North Sea development and the breaking strains of wires. Her narrow, muscled bottom rose and fell within her dress, attracting all eyes.

'So we're agreed on the price then?' murmured Flora.

'Er − no, we can't agree. Too much.'

145

'Oh. Oh dear. I thought we'd decided.' Flora found her mind wandering. All this haggling and jostling had gone on for hours. She was so new to all this, and most of her information had been acquired in a hurried briefing session half an hour before. She felt like a nursery school child given a sword and told to go to war. Grimly she dragged herself back into the fray. 'Right. Let's go back to basics. We'll undertake free delivery to your yard, and it's our responsibility to get Board of Trade approval. Taking all that into consideration – I think it's a fair price. Isn't it?'

The Norwegian tore his eyes away from Shalimar's undulating body. 'Let's go out to dinner and talk about it tomorrow.'

'But we must settle this today!'

The moment she said it she knew it was a mistake. Desperation was all too evident. In an instant they guessed at the angry bank, the shipyard penalties for late payment, Mactee's old womanish refusal to think any further than the constant repetition of 'It's not my fault'. Like an angler playing a salmon, the fish had gone from the edge of the keepnet to open water in the flash of its tail.

The Norwegian leaned back and smiled. 'Tomorrow,' he said expansively, reaching for a cigar. 'There is no need to rush this pleasant discussion, Mrs Harrington. Let us go out and see what your town has to offer.'

The girls exchanged alarmed glances. Everything had been going so wonderfully well. Flora struggled to regain the initiative. 'Sadly, I can't be with you this evening. My father's ill, and he likes me to sit with him. We'll talk again tomorrow, shall we?'

'I think tomorrow we'll have a day sightseeing,' purred her guest. 'Shall we say – next Monday perhaps? A little later?'

'I don't know –' Flora flailed around for an escape route. None presented itself. She cast her eyes down to the notepad on the table in front of her, willing the figures to give her some clue. She should not have let her concentration lapse. God, how she hated all this!

The door opened. Flora looked up, thankful for any interruption, even if it was the cleaner. A tall, bearded man stood there, in a bright red duvet jacket. It took her a moment to realise it was Don.

'So there you are, Flora.'

'Don! Oh, Don, I am so glad to see you.' She got up and ran over to him, putting her arms round his neck in an enormous hug. He hugged back, burying his face against her neck for a long second. Then he put her aside. 'What's going on? Shalimar. Everyone.'

'These gentlemen are buying some tugs of ours,' said Flora, trying to regain some poise.

'What tugs?' He looked from Flora to the Norwegians and back again.

Flora said hurriedly, 'I'll explain. Gentlemen, shall we meet again tomorrow?'

'No,' said Don. 'We'll ring you. I haven't got a clue what's going on.'

Shalimar saw the visitors out. Left alone, Don said, 'Tugs? What tugs? I didn't even know we had any.'

'Nobody knew. It was those supply ships, they weren't that at all. Mactee was having a fit because we couldn't raise the final payment before launch, and — '

'We had raised it. A lien through a merchant bank.'

'But — why didn't anyone know anything about it then?'

He shrugged. 'I knew I'd be back in time.'

'And suppose you weren't? Suppose you'd been killed?'

'I can see how that would have upset you. You'd have had a nasty moment worrying about the ships.'

'Oh — don't be so unkind.'

She found she was starting to cry. She wiped her fingers across her eyes and said, 'We were trying to sell the tugs to those Norwegians. Apparently there's a shortage of tugs, Dad spotted it and commissioned these two secretly so no one else would follow his line of thinking and jump on the bandwagon. I knew he'd be ahead of the game.'

'You've got more faith in him than in me, I notice.'

She met his eye. 'That's hardly surprising. Dad didn't swan off and leave me in the lurch.'

He said nothing for a moment. She was conscious of him watching her, his eyes very clear and grey. He seemed bigger than she remembered, an absolutely huge person that she didn't know. 'Aren't you going to ask how we got on?' he said quietly.

Flora shrugged. 'Does it matter? It wasn't important.'

'The lad, Neil Kindler, broke his back.'

'No! Don, that's terrible. Such an appalling waste.'

'But we got up. That's what was important. Even he thinks so.'

'I don't suppose his family would agree.'

She went to the cupboard and got her coat, making ready to go home.

Don said, 'Did you finalise this deal, then?'

She didn't look at him. 'No. I made a mess of it. They were about to sign and I let them know we had to sell. Except now I find we don't. So it was all a waste of effort.'

'I think you could have guessed I'm not that irresponsible.'

She stared at him, her face white, her eyes dark with rage. 'How dare you say that! How dare you! Leaving me on my own, leaving my father worried to death about the business, leaving the business in the lurch! All to risk your neck and other people's on some pointless piece of rock. You knew it was dangerous, you knew it was terribly dangerous, and you didn't care what would happen to me if you died. It that isn't irresponsible, I don't know what is.'

'You don't own me, Flora. Your father didn't buy me lock, stock and manhood. If I want to risk my life that's my affair, you were never going to starve.'

'Oh God! Why do people who never had money always think it matters? It doesn't. Not a bit.'

Don laughed, cruelly. 'And there speaks the daughter of a multi-millionaire.'

The door opened. Shalimar said diffidently, 'I told them we'd call the hotel sometime tomorrow.'

'You won't do a damn thing. I will,' said Don.

'Oh, thank you,' retorted Flora. 'Swinging back on the end of your rope, like Tarzan to the rescue.'

He took hold of her shoulder and propelled her willy nilly through the door. 'Sad to say, it appears you needed rescuing. You were never cut out to be a businesswoman, Flora my love, and it's about time you realised it.'

She was speechless with rage. If Shalimar hadn't been there she would have screamed at him. But there were people in the office, and John driving the car, no privacy anywhere in fact. The silence in the Bentley became oppressive. Flora sat in the middle, between the others, and Shalimar began a frenzied chatter. 'It must be such a relief to get home, Don. You look exhausted. And I know Flora's been missing you, haven't you, Flora?'

'Desperately,' said Flora in a dead voice.

'Well, of course you have. Everyone at KORSEA is fascinated by your climbing, you're almost a hero to them. They wouldn't be surprised if you shinned up the outside of the building and climbed in the window instead of using the lift!'

Don yawned and said nothing. Shalimar looked pleadingly at Flora, but her friend was stony-faced. Leaning forward to make sure the glass partition was shut, Shalimar said, 'I wish I knew what you two are really fighting about.'

For a moment Flora considered. 'Selfishness,' she said at last.

'Freedom,' said Don.

Flora glanced at him. Couldn't he see that his freedom meant her servitude? Suddenly she was ashamed of herself. Here she sat, in a luxury car, surrounded by more comfort than most people ever dreamed of enjoying, and she was sorry for herself. It didn't hurt to give more than you thought was due, to exert yourself beyond what was fair. She reached out and took Don's hand. 'I am glad to have you back,' she murmured. 'Very glad.'

Constrained, because Shalimar was there, he squeezed her fingers.

They smoothed a veneer of good humour over the evening. Don bathed and changed before sitting down to a huge meal and a lot of wine. He told them little about the climb, replying to their questions with laconic and factual answers that did nothing to help their understanding. It was a state of mind not unfamiliar to Don, the dip in energy and spirits that always followed a time of great exertion. It was as if his nerves were made of strong elastic; they had been stretched beyond the norm, and instead of returning to their usual tension they hung in loops, waiting for quiet days to restore them. To Flora he seemed wilfully uncommunicative. When she told him about the tugs, about discovering what they were, he interrupted halfway through and said he was going to bed.

'He must be exhausted,' said Shalimar in his defence.

'He's had too much to drink.' Flora picked up the wine bottle and poured herself a large glass. They could both play at that game, she decided. Her head was starting to spin, but all the same she emptied her glass. 'We'll have some brandy, too,' she declared, and reached an unsteady hand for the decanter.

Shalimar looked broodily down into her glass. 'I'll go in the morning. Time I was back in California, actually. They want me to be filmed lying naked on a bed while my Roman slave eats grapes from a bunch tastefully positioned over my crotch.'

'All right as long as no one you know sees it.' Flora leaned her elbows on the table, holding the glass to her lips with both hands.

'They might. It's not a porno movie, it's art! Real grapes.'

'You'll be famous then,' said Flora.

Shalimar sighed. 'Sure thing.'

She thought then how much she wished she was Flora. So what if Don wanted to go climbing now and then? As long as he came back in one piece she wouldn't mind. Flora didn't know when she was lucky; she didn't know that she had somehow landed one of the world's most desirable men.

'I think I'd better go to bed,' said Flora, and got up, staggering a little.

Shalimar watched her wavering path to the door. She found herself imagining Flora and Don making love. He'd grow tired of her, Flora was always the lady. A man like that needed a tigress in bed – Shalimar closed her eyes on her own disloyalty. Tomorrow, first thing, she would go. And she would not come back. Not while Don was here.

Chapter Fourteen

Flora was too drunk for love. The brandy was seeping into her system, making her drunker by the minute. When she reached her bedroom she staggered to the bed and fell on it, feeling her head spin sickeningly.

'Come here.' Don, naked, reached for her.

'Get off. No. I feel ill.'

He took no notice, pushing her on to her back. Her limbs felt like jelly. 'Feel sick,' she mumbled, but he didn't seem to hear. She might have been a doll, something not alive at all. He pushed her skirt up, stripping off her tights and pants. She tried to hold her knees together to stop him, but the jelly feeling made her feeble.

All she wanted was to be allowed to go to sleep. He dragged open her blouse, cupping her breasts in his big hands, pulling them free of her bra. He began to tease her nipples with his teeth, and when she pulled back, held on.

'No! Don't! I don't want it.'

He hung over her, huge and menacing. 'Don't try and stop me. You're not in charge here. I am.'

He pushed himself into her, so hard that he hardly seemed like flesh. His mouth came down on hers, she felt like a doll, but a ragdoll, her arms and legs spread out uselessly while the owner did what he wanted. She felt his body tensing, felt him come, filling her up. His hands cradled her head, he feathered her face with kisses. 'I love you,' he whispered. 'You've got to understand that I do.'

He rolled aside. Suddenly the booze rose in Flora's gorge. Jerking up, she half fell from the bed, staggering drunkenly into the bathroom to be sick. Hanging over the basin she stared at herself in the mirror. Her clothes were torn, her thighs blue with a man's fingermarks. One breast was marked, and her lips were swollen and bruised. She had been crying.

151

In past centuries men came home from wars to wives left guarding the castle. Did they too take back the power quite so blatantly? He was on top, she underneath, and no passing variation, no momentary lapse, could alter that fundamental. He went when he liked, came back when he liked, and made sure that he marked his claim.

In the morning Flora lay like the dead. Don brought her a tray of coffee and dry toast. She squinted at him between swollen eyelids. 'Shalimar's gone,' he said. 'She left a note. I imagine she feels a bit of a gooseberry.'

'She only came to keep me company. She had a film to make. Oh God, I feel ill. That brandy!'

'Have some toast. Look, I'm sorry about yesterday. It's always a bit odd after a climb. Everything used up, nothing left.'

She sat up and her ill-treated breast fell painfully clear of the covers. 'You found something last night,' muttered Flora.

'Here, let me put something on that.' He went to the dressing table for a pot of cold cream, and dabbed carefully at Flora's nipple.

She closed her eyes and lay back against the pillow. She had a headache. Suddenly she moaned, surprising herself. Her body didn't care about last night, it craved some satisfaction. The cold cream touched her other breast, and when he reached a sticky hand under the covers she opened her legs. Oh, but it was cold. His hand slicked against her in oily rhythm. She put her arm over her face and climaxed. It was odd, feeling so divorced from her own flesh. He pushed the tray aside and got back into the bed.

Afterwards he said, 'I've been thinking. I'm putting a manager into KORSEA.'

Flora, half-asleep and still hungover, sat up. 'You can't. Dad could have put a manager in. He chose you.'

'And I'll still oversee things. But we rushed into everything. I've got to be honest, love, I can't see myself sticking it out at KORSEA month after month. You saw what it was like yourself, you can't take your eye off the ball for half a second. If I'm going to stay sane then the climbing's got to fit in somewhere. The only sensible arrangement is to appoint someone competent who can take control when I'm not there.'

'We had an agreement!'

'What we've got is a marriage and a business. How we keep both those going is entirely up to us, no rules and no agreements are going to make us happy.'

She got out of bed and went to turn on the shower. He leaned in the doorway, watching her. 'Flora! At least say what you think.'

'I can't hear you.'

152

'Yes you can. It isn't my fault you're not pregnant.'

'Are you saying it's mine?'

'No! You've got to find something to do, Flora.'

'A job, you mean?'

'I don't know. Look, you didn't make a mess of that deal, you almost had it. All you need's some experience. Do you want to work in the firm?'

She shook her head. 'No. I never did. I can't take it seriously.'

'You've got to take something seriously. I love you, Flora. Your father needs you and so do I. But you've got to do something. You need a hobby.'

He thought stamp collecting would make her happy. She turned her back on him and ducked under the spray. Her head hung back, letting the water fall over her face and hair in a deadening stream. Dimly, through the rushing water, she heard the 'phone ringing. Don stuck his head round the door. 'I've got to go. KORSEA. Your Norwegian posse is on the doorstep demanding two tugs and the shipyard's squealing for money. Back for dinner, OK?'

'Yes — yes, OK.'

Another empty day. She banged her forehead against the tiled wall, only just holding back from force.

Somehow the KORSEA offices seemed less real than the Eiger, and at times that had been dreamlike enough. Don's business suit constrained him. He ran a finger round the inside of his collar, and tried to concentrate. On the Eiger, on any mountain, there were only two considerations, survival and getting to the top. Here, in this other life, it was this against that, take the good with the bad, digging your way towards a whisky at the end of the day. He'd get used to it again. It was the transition that came hard.

Dorothy, his secretary, buzzed the intercom. 'Shall I ask the gentlemen to come in, Mr Harrington?'

A none too subtle hint that they had been waiting too long. 'All right. Send them in.'

He rose from behind the desk to welcome them. 'Since yesterday we heard about your achievement,' said one eagerly. 'It is an honour to do business with you, Mr Harrington.'

'I'm not sure we can do business,' said Don. 'The tugs were finished sooner than we'd planned, it took my wife by surprise. I'm considering keeping them.'

'Really? Are you sure this is the time for KORSEA to enter so specialised a market?'

153

Don grinned. 'Certainly could be. There's a lot of activity just now.'

'Some. Yes, some.'

The Norwegians cast gloomy looks at each other. Why had they not clinched yesterday, before the husband got back? They needed the tugs, and greed had deprived them. 'We could of course take delivery from the yard,' said one.

The other followed the lead. 'And as for the Board of Trade Certificate — you need hardly concern yourselves with it. Let's do business at your wife's price.'

'Let's not,' said Don, and leaned back. He wondered what Van was doing. Probably still in bed. 'I'm going to look around. See who else is buying.'

'Indeed.' The Norwegians sighed. There was nothing for it but to start the bargaining all over again.

Kincaid came down for dinner that night. It was the first time in weeks, and Marie cooked chicken in cream and herbs. Prudently, Nurse Collins brought an oxygen cylinder down and stood it discreetly behind the curtain.

'She thinks I'll pop off and you'll sue,' said Kincaid. 'But no one's going to be sorry to see me go. Not even my wife.'

'Rubbish,' said Don. 'Sold your tugs today. The ones you called supply ships. Made a packet.'

Kincaid looked up from under his heavy brows. 'Sorted that one, did you? Good man.'

'You didn't tell anyone what you were doing,' said Flora. 'It made things awfully difficult.'

'Good for the lot of you. Never win in business if you don't play poker, and no one ever said it was wise to show your hand at cards.'

As the plates were being cleared, Don said, 'I hear you took the plane out, Flora. Where to?'

'Edinburgh.' She drank some water. Last night's wine had been more than enough for a week or so.

'If it's shops you want, why not take the plane to Paris?' demanded Kincaid. 'Your mother used to.'

'I wasn't shopping. I went to see the aid people. I thought I might address envelopes or lick stamps or something, but they don't need me. They've got hundreds of old ladies to do that sort of thing.'

Don said, 'Bit of an odd idea anyway, wasn't it? Commuting to Edinburgh to lick stamps. You could have paid for a dozen stamp lickers with just the cost of the fuel.'

154

And suddenly Flora blazed at him. 'I don't want to know what you think! You've got your life all sewn up, everything shipshape. You don't care what happens to me. Neither of you gives a damn!' She leaped up and ran from the room.

The two men looked at each other. 'Not like Flora to be bad-tempered,' said Kincaid. 'Should ask yourself some questions.'

Don sighed. 'She's mad at me, that's all. And I was – heavy-handed. It's nothing serious.'

'Hmm.' The old man watched him speculatively. 'There are two things I want from you,' he murmured. 'To take care of my business and my girl. I shouldn't like to think you were neglecting either.'

When Kincaid had gone back to bed Don went looking for Flora. She was in the library, writing to Shalimar.

'Your father thinks I'm having an affair,' he remarked.

'Does he? Poor Dad.'

'More like poor us. Why aren't we getting on, Floss?'

She shrugged. 'Perhaps you are having an affair. With your life, your life before. You go through the motions here, nothing else.'

'I've only been away once.'

She looked at him, her dark eyes misty. 'So far.'

He felt himself losing his temper. 'I don't understand you. I honestly don't,' he said tightly.

'It's quite easy.' She threw down her letter and stood up. 'Imagine yourself in my place, leading my life. You wouldn't like it. And funnily enough, neither do I.'

That night, feeling her lying rigid on the edge of the bed, Don put his hand in the small of her back. 'It's all right,' he said. 'It's going to be all right, I promise.'

She rolled suddenly towards him, the speed of her capitulation taking him by surprise. 'I know it's not your fault,' she sobbed. 'It's mine. I got married and I didn't think. I wanted to marry you, I want to be married to you. But it's so hard – you don't know, I was going to do so much.'

He held her close, feeling her body shake down its whole length. 'You will, you will,' he murmured. 'We're together in this, you and me. I'm sorry about last night, I wasn't myself.'

'You shouldn't have gone away!'

He breathed against her ear, 'I know, I know. I won't leave you, I won't leave you again.'

'Yes. Stay home.' Her sobs began to lessen. 'I was frightened and lonely, you can't know.'

155

'Go to sleep now,' he whispered. 'We can be happy. Remember, I'm home.'

During the next weeks Don found himself a manager. He had spent time working for one of the American oil companies, and had the disconcerting habits of frequent firm handshakes and constant use of first names. The KORSEA staff, Scottish to a man, took against him on sight.

From Don's point of view George Williams was knowledgeable, enthusiastic and hard-working. He seemed to find interest in even the most tedious of KORSEA's many tasks, not to mention the turkey farm.

'Keep us in turkeys for Thanksgiving,' he declared, forgetting for the moment where he was.

'Since when did we celebrate the loss of a colony?' demanded Andrews, dumping a pile of files on his desk.

'I'm actually Canadian,' said Williams, with careful friendliness. 'With Scottish ancestors.'

'You don't say? A Mountie in a kilt. A sight for sore eyes, no less.'

Don reported the skirmishes hilariously to Flora each night. 'They're going to have to accept him. But they've got all the suspicion and deviousness of a very old nation, and he's full of new world openness and enthusiasm.'

'You're being very understanding,' said Flora, toying with some fish.

'It's my new technique. There's nothing you can say to me that I won't understand. Provided it isn't in Gaelic.' She giggled and he said, 'Can you come in on Friday? We're having Mactee's retirement party.'

Flora nodded. 'I'll buy him something. I always buy the presents.'

'That's OK, we had a whip round and I put in enough to get him a set of golf clubs.'

'Oh. Yes. Great.'

But it was still her duty to turn up in her glad rags and grace the occasion. On the morning of the presentation she scanned the clothes in her dressing room, racks and racks of beautifully tended silks and wools and linens. Her shoes were arranged in a cupboard by themselves, all on shoe trees, the legs of her boots stuffed with tissue paper. Two dresses hung separately, awaiting the attentions of the seamstress who came in once a month to sew on buttons and catch up hems. In Nepal Flora had gone around for weeks with a blouse held together by pins. Yet still so much care was lavished upon her.

She put on a cream wool suit over a pale green silk camisole. She had darker green shoes, and a pillbox hat to match. Checking herself in the mirror she stopped in surprise. Reflected back in the pier glass was someone she wasn't sure she knew; paperwhite face, huge dark eyes. Some of the rounded contours had fined down, she seemed older, sadder perhaps. But something else was different – it was as if her lips, her eyes, even her skin, had all been touched with light, imbued with a subtle inner glow.

John brought the Bentley round early, as always. Flora delayed, because if she arrived before four no one would be ready and there would be nothing to do. Her father was sitting up by the library fire, writing.

'What on earth are you up to?' asked Flora.

He scribbled on, busily, the notepad wedged against the arm of the chair. 'My memoirs. They're right, you know. When you get to my age the past comes back as clear as day.'

She glanced over his shoulder. 'No one's ever going to be able to read it!'

'What? Won't they?' He glared at the pages of his scrawl. 'Perhaps I should dictate. Have the tapes locked up till I'm gone.'

'Surely it's not that bad.'

'Bad enough. Yes, it was bad enough. All that wheeling and dealing. All those fights!'

He was tired. Flora took the pad and pencil away and sat talking for twenty minutes, about an early fawn born into frost and snow, about Mactee and his retirement present.

'Perhaps I should have given up. Played golf,' said Kincaid.

'You always hated golf.'

'Bloody waste of time.' He glanced down at her, curled up on a footstool by the hearth. 'You look pretty today. In fine style.'

'And all for Mr Mactee's golf clubs. I'll be off now, Dad. See you later.'

Left alone, his mind drifted. For an hour, perhaps two, he could imagine himself as well as ever, except for a little weakness here and there. But the weariness, the utter, desperate weariness, always overtook him. Thinking, remembering, making connections between hand and brain, all these forsook him. No wonder he remembered his childhood. He was a baby again, dependent and without skills. All the brilliance and ability he had developed in his life were falling away, to leave him much as before. The words of the funeral service came to him: 'We brought nothing into this world and it is certain that we carry nothing out'. Perhaps he was one of the privileged, to witness his own deprivation. A quick heart attack and he'd have missed the lot.

He remembered, suddenly, how his wife had looked when she was pregnant with Flora. Always a beauty, Lilian, and then so very beautiful. Like Flora tonight.

George Williams had his points, the KORSEA folk decided. When it came to a party he knew how to be extravagant. There was champagne, and a cake inscribed 'James Mactee – Thanks, Friend', and plates of vol au vents and sandwiches. Mactee himself appeared somewhat overwhelmed by the lavish display, and stood in a corner swallowing hard. Flora made it her business to talk to him, gradually thawing his fierce reserve. At last he said, 'I shall be glad to relax a wee bit now, Flora. We've had anxious times since your father's accident.'

'You must go on a trip,' she said. 'Visit the Far East, or America.'

'I'll do no such thing. I shall stay home in Scotland and play golf.'

'You'd think I'd suggested a girlie bar in Bangkok,' murmured Flora to Don, later.

'What do you know about girlie bars?'

'I hope about as much as you!'

They exchanged a look full of laughter and understanding, and then parted again, to continue the social round.

Flora's legs began to ache. She drank a glass of water to clear her head, and nibbled on a sandwich. The party was going splendidly, and now included the wives, husbands and friends of almost everyone. She wondered if she could sit down for a moment in Don's office, but when she got there found it full of caterers and the golf clubs were on Don's chair. Her hands felt clammy with sweat and her heart was beating rapidly, as if she was running for a bus. Back in the corridor she leaned against the wall for a moment, resting her forehead.

'Flora?' It was Don, looking for her.

'I'm all right. All this standing, I felt strange for a minute.'

'Come in here.' He pushed her into a room that held a photocopier, a telex machine and two chairs. She sank into one thankfully, and tried to laugh. 'It isn't anything to worry about. Perhaps I should have worn flat shoes.'

'You might be getting 'flu. Look, forget the presentation, I'll call for the car and have you taken home.'

158

'There isn't any need.' She glanced up at him, and his face was full of worry and concern. 'I didn't mean to tell you till I was sure. But I think I'm pregnant.'

'Good God. Really?'

She nodded. 'I'm a week overdue. And I feel so – well, peculiar. Aren't you pleased?'

'Yes. Are you?'

'Yes. Terribly.'

She felt a strange sort of triumph. It was as if her womanhood had been confirmed, as if she had shaken off the last lingering bonds of the young girl. It had happened the night he came home, she was sure of it, a good thing coming out of turmoil and pain.

He bent down to kiss her and she put her arms around his neck, and at that moment the telex rattled into action. They pressed their noses together and giggled. 'This is hellish unromantic,' murmured Don.

'I don't care. Had we better go out and give old Mactee his golf clubs?'

'In a minute. You are such a clever girl.'

'Yes, aren't I?'

They went home early, leaving the party in full swing. At the Castle, before they went in, they stood looking up at the night. The moon was almost full, pinned improbably on to a velvet blanket of stardusted sky. Everything was going to be all right. Don held Flora's hand in his, warming it with his own body heat, until finally they went inside to bed.

Chapter Fifteen

When Flora was three months pregnant Van came to stay. It was the signal for Don to down tools at KORSEA, leave George Williams in charge and go climbing. They went out each day in the estate Range Rover, loaded down with climbing gear, and returned tired and hungry, ready to eat and go to bed.

'How good of you, Don, to live in such wonderful climbing country,' said Van one night. He had his mouth full of Marie's steak and kidney pie, but he had a casual approach to table manners.

'How good of me to have married such a wonderfully tolerant wife,' said Don, and raised his glass of beer to Flora. She smiled wanly. He well knew that she was bored to tears sitting at home, her waist expanding far beyond the bounds of decency.

'Why don't you come with us tomorrow?'

'What?' Her thoughts had been miles away, her chin in her hands, her hard round belly resting on her thighs.

'Now you're feeling so much fitter you can come out for the day. There's a good walk to the cliffs and we'll take a picnic. Bring a book, sit in the sun and fill your lungs with good fresh air.'

'Won't I be in the way?'

'You are never in the way, Flora,' rumbled Van. 'The one woman I know who is always good-tempered. We will take a rug, you can have a sleep when you feel tired.'

It sounded delicious. The cold northern spring was well under way, and the crocuses were blooming in the shelter of the castle walls. Up on the crags there would be aconites and purple marsh flowers, and some new lambs perhaps. She borrowed a pair of her father's old trousers, because none of hers would do up round her embarrassingly large waist. Marie provided a picnic in a large wicker basket. 'How much does she think you eat, Flora?' demanded Don. 'If we take all this we'll need a mule.'

'We could take a pony,' said Flora.

'Not unless it's prepared to take a back seat in the car.'

But at last they were off. They saw few other cars on the roads, only the odd shepherd and two other men loaded up with climbing paraphernalia. Birds nested late this far north, but even so they saw hawks circling above the high crags, and a silhouette that might have been an eagle.

'When do you go and see the baby doctor, Flora?' asked Van, leaning back to talk to her.

'Next week. Why?'

'You have such a large belly,' he said bluntly.

Flora's face flamed. Don said, 'Shut up, Van. What do you know about pregnancy, anyway?'

'But I have two of my own children! And Flora is big for so early.'

'I never knew you were even married,' said Flora.

'Not now, sadly. Climbers are not good husbands. My wife is now married again, to an accountant.'

Don slid the car on to a patch of mud at the side of the road. A thin sheep track marked the path, heading across heather to a distant line of cliffs. 'Flora's fit as a fiddle,' said Don, helping her out of the car.

'Fitter,' she said. 'As fit as a double bass.'

They began the walk, Don with the hamper and Van loaded down with books and a rug. Unburdened by so much as a handkerchief, Flora skipped along, waiting every now and then for the men to catch up. It was quiet up in the hills, with only the wind whispering across the land, shaking the grass and heather into shivering compliance. She felt calm, almost tranquil; it was a mood of pregnancy, a gradual and insidious relaxation of all that was not concerned with that condition.

They came to a cleft in the rock, a place of cold shadows. 'Bit bloody gloomy,' said Don. 'I don't fancy it.'

He walked back into the sunshine and scanned the eastern face. The rock was grey on the surface, and yellow where the covering shale had scraped off, with a growth of vegetation on most ledges. A buttress protruded halfway up, extending suddenly out of a sheer cliff, and jutting with brief indentations all the way to the top, like the underside of a teapot spout. 'Fancy that better,' said Don, rocking back on his heels to look at it. 'Has it been done?'

'No bloody idea,' said Van. 'We do it and see. But if you fall off Flora will be upset.'

Don hesitated. It was very exposed. When swinging out over the

161

buttress he would be a hundred feet off the ground, suspended from friable rock. But the route tempted him. It had the purity of line that he loved, the sweet direct curve that allowed for no compromise. He could almost feel the rhythm of the climb before he had even begun. 'Have a doze, Flora,' he advised, starting to unlace his boots. He would climb this in the flexible shoes he had had for at least three years, wearing through at the toes and the laces knotted into tangles. The sun was warm even if the wind was cool. He stripped down to a singlet and tied a sweatband round his head.

Wide-eyed, Flora said, 'Are you sure it's safe?'

'As houses,' said Don. He stepped into his harness and felt for his pouch of French chalk, already starting to breathe in the deep, rhythmic swoops that controlled his nervous excitement. Van began to whistle through his teeth.

They began quite quickly, up through the first twenty feet without a pause. Don called Van up to join him, and they hung from the rock discussing the line with all the ease of commuters comparing bus routes. 'To the right there is no way,' said Van. 'You could put a bolt in, perhaps.'

But Don was climbing free, belayed to a couple of slings hanging from spring-loaded cams jammed into cracks, part of the high-tech climbing armoury that made these routes just possible. He looked out to the left, but the holds, such as they were, lurked invisibly under moss.

'At least you can see what you're doing to the right,' he said. 'I'll try it.'

'Then I will settle myself and wait for you to come off.'

Van belayed himself to the rock, running the rope through a sling. Don would fall no more than ten feet if he did come off, and that was only to be expected; this was the crux of a severe climb.

From below they heard Flora call: 'What are you doing? Why don't you come down?'

'Go and start the picnic,' yelled Don, and then under his breath: 'Bloody hell! I wouldn't have brought her if I thought she'd watch.'

'I told you she wouldn't like it,' said Van.

'Get stuffed.' Don dipped his fingers into the chalk and began a short traverse followed by a reach up over the buttress. His feet began to slip against the stone, the damned moss had left a slime on his shoes. He let his mind dwell on the drop, it was amazing how motivating thoughts could be. The hold he was searching for did not oblige. His foot slipped, his hand found nothing and he was off.

162

Flora shrieked and ran forward, putting up her arms to catch him. But he hung in space, the cams creaking, as he turned the air blue with curses. 'Next time bloody listen,' yelled Van.

'Sod off,' retorted Don. He took time to wipe the soles of his shoes, dangling with apparent unconcern, supported by only a thread of rope. Flora's heart was catapulting from front to back in her chest, she couldn't breathe. Somehow he got back on the rock.

'Take the other way,' called Van.

But Don tried again, this time traversing further before reaching up. Again, a moment's pause, a grunt, and he was swinging.

'Fuck the bastard!' he bellowed.

'Ladies present,' purred Van.

'I'll get it this time. Just you watch.'

This time he spread his legs wide in a straddle. From the ground Flora could see muscle straining against the fabric of his jeans, and in the peace of the day his breathing sounded short and harsh. The sun glistened on sweat-slicked shoulders and arms. She watched him arch his back and slide his feet inch by inch up the rock. He was braced against the face, spreadeagled on the underside of the buttress. He grunted, lunged, and was up.

'You bastard,' yelled Van.

'Just match that, sunbeam!' Don was gathering his breath on a tiny ledge. With that out of the way the rest was comparatively easy. He belayed himself and sang out for Van to follow, but two inches less in height made the move impossible. Van struggled for an hour, going this way and that, exhausting himself. For the first time Flora glimpsed something of the competition between them. They were a team, but only because they each had strengths; if one of them proved weaker then he might not lose his partner's respect, but he would lose his own.

Finally, when Flora had long since despaired of Van ever getting up, he amazed her. 'Watch that bloody rope!' he screamed.'This time I make it!' He brought his feet together, jumped them up the rock until he seemed to be kneeling on the face, and then threw himself out and up. For a moment there was nothing holding him, he was in space. But his fingers found the hold. He let out a howl of triumph.

It was around three in the afternoon when they came down. They were euphoric, delighted with themselves. Flora opened the picnic hamper and doled out crusty rolls filled with cheese, home-cured ham and salad, and unwrapped pasties kept warm folded in cloth inside a hay box. 'I thought it was a damned heavy picnic,' said Don. 'What have you had, Flora?'

'I wasn't hungry.'

'Well, eat now. Come on, you must.'

She shook her head. Her stomach was churning still, and if she held her hands out in front of her they shook.

'You would do it, Don,' said Van, munching a pasty.

'Oh, for God's sake, no one got killed. You saw how safe it was, Flora.'

'I gave up watching after the first two falls. And that was worse. I kept expecting one or other of you to land with a loud crump right next to me, with your brains coming out.'

'People don't often get killed,' soothed Don.

'Liar.'

'Even on the Eiger, Neil didn't die. He might even walk again, one day.'

'Big deal!' declared Flora, with massive sarcasm. 'I hope you'll be very happy together, in matching wheelchairs.'

She got up and headed back towards the car. After a hundred yards or so Don caught her up. 'You're going the wrong way.'

'No, I'm not. I'm following the track.'

'There are two tracks. If I let you go this way you'll end up a great deal more dead than me, lost in some bog or other. You don't have to climb to die.'

Flora stopped and stared at him. 'I wish you cared,' she said softly. 'I wish you would think about how much you're needed. I need you, my father needs you, KORSEA, everything, not to mention this baby! It was your idea to have it. And if you go on like this it's going to be born without a father.'

He sighed. 'If I'd known you'd go on like this, I would never have let you come.'

'That way you could go on risking your neck, with no embarrassing questions asked about responsibility, I suppose?'

'It's my life. I've got the right to do what I damn well like with it.'

'But if I said the same I could be a drug addict and make the baby a drug addict even before it's born, and presumably that wouldn't matter to you or Dad or even the baby, because it's my life and I can do what I damn well like.'

There was a ghastly sort of logic in her words. He took her arm and steered her none too gently back through the heather to the picnic site. He threw things haphazardly into the hamper, ramming the lid down with the sound of breaking china.

'That was the mustard,' said Van, aggrieved. 'It will run out all over everything.'

164

'Hot and vicious, just like Flora,' snarled Don.

'Don! Flora is never cross without reason.'

She felt a sob rising in her throat. How she hated rows, hated anything that meant people screaming at each other, saying the harsh thing, the cruellest word. If she could she would take back everything, try and put back the day as before. But she was right. She knew she was right.

They walked back to the car in silence. Flora was tired now, and lack of food made her weak. She stumbled over roots and into holes, until Don put his free arm round her waist and guided her. The anger gradually abated, she began almost to feel foolish. He hadn't killed himself, he was here, helping her, taking care. She was getting agitated about his climbing only because she knew nothing at all about it.

When they reached the car he put the rug over her knees, still without speaking. 'Thanks,' she said. He met her eyes. Without a doubt it was for her to give in, to make the unconditional apology. 'I suppose I was being silly,' she murmured.

'No,' interrupted Van. 'You are right and should not pretend otherwise.' They both stared at him. He hadn't even heard their conversation.

'Belt up,' said Don. 'This is nothing to do with you.'

'It has to do with me. It has to do with everyone who climbs. With my wife I argued many, many times. I chose to go on climbing, and it cost me dear, because now it's all I have. But you are very lucky. You have Flora, a baby, responsibilities. There is a bill for everything we do, and it is not always up to us to pay it.'

Don sat behind the wheel, gazing out across miles of countryside. The hills marked the horizon, a range topped by another and still another. Clouds, as darkly blue as Flora's eyes, were gathering above them. In a low voice he said, 'There's no point in thinking I'm going to stop. If you're right then I don't want to know. One day perhaps I won't want to do it any more, it might be tomorrow and it might be never. Until that day comes – I go on.'

There was nothing more to say. Flora pulled the blanket up and wrapped herself more warmly in its folds. Don watched her in the mirror, but she would not meet his eyes. He started the car and drove home.

Van stayed on, two weeks stretching into three, then four. George Williams took to telephoning the castle at night, the only time he could be sure to catch Don at home. He took the calls in the study, a room furnished with giant leather chairs and a mahogany desk.

165

One evening Flora stood outside the door and listened, feeling treacherous.

'There's nothing that can't wait,' Don was saying. 'I'll be in next week. I know it's a big decision, but we'll take it together next week.'

She opened the door and stood there, watching him. He glanced up. 'All right, George,' he said. 'Next week. Promise.'

As he replaced the receiver, Flora said, 'You should go in now. If he's worried, it must be something important.'

'You want to know what the problem is? Is that it?'

She nodded. 'He keeps ringing and you keep putting him off.'

'This great, earth-shattering difficulty is one ship with a dicky engine that keeps giving trouble. I've told him to get it overhauled and lose a couple of days' work, and he's being anxious and wants the ship put in for a refit. I don't think it's necessary. Anyway the responsibility's mine, so he can sleep easy in his bed. Still he keeps on about it. He's an old woman.'

'I thought he was very experienced?'

'Flora, if you know so much about it, *you* go off and discuss it with him.'

She picked up the onyx-handled letter knife and played with it. 'I'm going for another scan tomorrow,' she said. 'Will you come?'

'But you had one before.'

'I know, but Mr Mitchell wants another. He's taking a very close interest in me actually. Please come.'

He looked down at the desk for a moment. 'I should have kicked Van out weeks ago. Shouldn't I?'

'I do like him, Don. I like him a lot.'

'But we go climbing all the time! OK, OK, we'll send him off on the train tomorrow and go on for your scan. What's the doctor looking for, do you know?'

She shook her head. 'He doesn't seem gloomy or anything. But when I come in whole squadrons of students are summoned from wherever students go when they're not prodding people, and he says things like, "I'm sure you can all observe the expansion of the perineum" or something like that. And everybody murmurs agreement.'

'What's the perineum?'

Flora shrugged.

So it was with mild apprehension that they sat in the flower-bedecked waiting room of the private wing of the hospital. Don, who had never been subjected to anything except National Health treatment, was fascinated by the free coffee and biscuits, the current

166

copies of *Vogue* and *Country Life,* as well as the chintz-covered arm-chairs. No vulgar summons by loudspeaker, nor yet by brass-voiced nurse, but a tender murmur from a receptionist who escorted them all the way. Mr Mitchell himself welcomed them, resplendent in a pinstripe suit with a rose in his buttonhole.

'Mrs Harrington, Flora! Mr Harrington. Do sit down. Delightful day, isn't it?'

'Wonderful.'

Mr Mitchell had the charismatic charm of the ultimate obstetrician. He inspired such confidence that Flora always came out of his consulting rooms feeling that her entire life would be perfect if only it could be examined by Mr Mitchell from time to time. Yet his nurse, in an unguarded moment, had revealed that he was on his third marriage, so perhaps he wasn't quite so infallible as she supposed. Perhaps he couldn't resist making good use of his charm elsewhere.

'Now, it is good to see you both together. You've been having us rather puzzled, Flora. At first we wondered if your dates were wrong — but now we don't think that.'

'No?' She looked at him wide-eyed.

'No. And today's pictures should help us make up our minds about something. Go along with nurse now, and get changed. We'll take a little look.'

She could tell from Don's expression that he was far less impressed with Mr Mitchell than was she. Perhaps he was a bit patronising, rather in the manner of the intelligent white man speaking to the primitive African tribe.

'They get so worried about these things,' she heard Mitchell saying. 'The pregnant woman needs to be handled more sensitively than a wild beast.' The two men chuckled together, and it was no longer a surprise to reflect on Mitchell's chequered relationships. But he was a good baby doctor, all the same.

She lay on a low bed while a technician oiled her belly, moving a heavy probe over her skin. Whatever picture was revealed was shown on a television screen, turned away from her and towards the others.

'Good Lord, Flora,' said Don. 'This poor kid is swimming around in a fog.'

'Hmmm.' Mitchell twiddled a knob on the screen, and the technician concentrated his attentions on the left side of her abdomen. 'Nurse! Nurse!' yelled Mitchell. 'Do call the students. They oughtn't to miss this.'

'The greatest show on earth,' muttered Flora, and Mitchell said,

'Exactly, dear girl! You should be very proud of yourself – there are two nice babies growing away in there.'

'Two?' Don peered uncomprehendingly at the screen.

'Yes, look. One head – and a heart here – the other head – the other heart. And the shape of the limbs, at this stage of course no definition. We suspected something from the first visit, and it's wonderful to be proved right. How do you feel about two for the price of one, Flora?'

'I – I don't know.'

The students came in and there was a general air of excitement. Don came and took her hand. 'Bit of a shock, this.'

'You can say that again.' Barely had she come round to the idea of one child than she was faced with the prospect of two. 'I don't know anything about babies,' she whispered. 'I thought I could muddle through with one, but two –'

'You never do anything by halves, you.'

At last she was allowed to get up and get dressed. Mr Mitchell was as excited as if the twins were his own creation.

'Now, Flora,' he said, 'I shall want to see you every two weeks from now on. And you'll be coming into hospital a few days before the birth, just so we can be there the moment anything starts to happen. You never know with twins, they can get themselves into terrible tangles, so we want to be prepared. Are you happy, my dear?' He smiled down at her warmly.

'Yes. Thank you, Mr Mitchell.' He stood on the steps as she and Don were ushered out of the building.

'Something of a ladies' man,' said Don. 'I suppose you have to be in his game.'

'I think he's wonderful,' said Flora. 'I'll be wife number four if he asks me.'

'He's already behaving as if he's the father of our twins.'

'Dad will have a fit if they're both girls.'

'He'll celebrate for a month if they're boys.'

'Yes.'

She felt tired suddenly. 'Don't tell him,' she said. 'Or Mother. Let it be our secret.'

He said nothing. 'Odd seeing that picture of your insides,' he remarked. 'Brings it home to you. I'm not even sure I like kids.'

'A fine time to discover that!'

He considered. 'I liked them in Nepal. But Nepalese children are gorgeous, all smiles. They don't whinge and throw up in supermarkets.'

'Is that what you're expecting?'

168

'Yes. Aren't you?'

'No! They'll be pink and cuddly and adorable. And you are going back to KORSEA tomorrow, aren't you?'

'Flora, George is in charge! Will you please stop worrying about that damned firm.'

Chapter Sixteen

Flora woke feeling sticky. She put her hand down the bed and felt a damp patch, and when she brought her fingers out she was frozen in horror. Blood! The skin on her face felt stretched suddenly, tight over her cheeks and teeth. With her other hand, the clean one, she reached out and shook Don's shoulder.

Mr Mitchell drove out personally. The castle held an air of doom; no one spoke above a whisper, no doors slammed, no delivery boy dared to whistle. The consultant took a stand for optimism, clapping his hands together and demanding loudly: 'What on earth's all this, Flora? Too much dancing, I dare say.'

The tears she had held back began to fall. It was her fault, without a doubt her fault, but she couldn't tell him why. Last night they had made love, to her own satisfaction. He held her hand and patted it, saying soothingly, 'These things happen, my dear. Nine times out of ten it means nothing, but we'll have a look at you, shall we?'

She lay rigid during the examination. She felt that if she could only hold tight, hardly breathing, hardly moving, then nothing could be lost. He was very gentle, but even so it seemed a dangerous exercise. When he finished she curled herself up in a protective ball.

'Bed rest, for at least a week,' he commanded. 'After that, no lifting, no strenuous activity, no long car journeys. And no sex.'

Flora felt herself blushing. He knew. She hadn't told him but he knew.

'We've got no idea if any of those things cause miscarriages,' explained Mitchell, settling himself convivially in a chair. 'But if there's a threat, and this is a clear threat, we like to be on the safe side. This pregnancy means a very great deal to very many people, so we must do our best, mustn't we?'

Flora nodded. She wondered if everyone knew that she was expected to produce the long awaited male heir. All she wanted was a healthy baby, she would be more than satisfied with one. To want two seemed then to be impossible greed. Dubious from the start about her abundance of blessings, she saw it now for what it was, a gift so lavish as to be unacceptable.

Don came in and he and Mr Mitchell shared a pre-lunch drink. The consultant was staying to lunch, he and Don would sit down together in the small dining room, while Flora had her meal on a tray. As they prepared to leave her, Mitchell said, 'My dear, you look far too worried. Nothing terrible's going to happen. I'd stake my reputation on getting you through to week forty, because you're sensible, because you have excellent care, and your husband's a fine fellow who understands. Relax, have a well-earned rest. When these two are bouncing around the place, you're going to need it.'

Flora smiled wanly, and kept the expression pinned to her face until she heard their voices fading away in the distance. She looked round for something to read, a magazine, a book. Nothing caught her interest. She felt very lonely suddenly, and very afraid. Without climbing, without sex, what would Don do?

Don went into KORSEA in the afternoon. Anything was better than hanging around the castle. Somehow Kincaid had got wind of the pregnancy crisis and was being impossible, demanding Flora's instant hospitalisation.

'She should stay in bed,' he declared. 'Flora should know better than to gad about, doing this and that. Bed rest, that's what she should have had from the start.'

But Don thought it was bed that was the trouble. He felt unreasonably guilty. A moment's pleasure, forgotten almost as soon as it was past, reaping this sort of harvest. He imagined it felt about as bad as one drunken screw giving you Aids. It was so trivial a cause of so dramatic a retribution.

George Williams was glad to see him. He brought sheaves of papers into Don's office, and began flicking through one thing after another that he felt needed the chairman's attention. Share deals, contracts, an argument with an oil company over apparent shortfalls in supply delivery. 'It's the men on the rig pilfering,' said Williams. 'But our crews are at fault. They've got to get cargo properly checked and signed for, otherwise we can be accused of anything.'

Lazily, Don said, 'I thought part of the problem was half empty boxes? The bottom half stuffed with newspaper and so on. That's most likely a problem with the people who supply us.'

'I reckon they're repacking the boxes on the rig,' said Williams. 'We just can't prove it.'

171

'Get a special seal for the boxes,' advised Don. 'We'll check and then seal. That way we know we're in the clear.'

Williams nodded. He sifted through his papers once again. 'There is just one more thing, Mr Harrington. The ship *Rosamund*. We're going to have to refit.'

'Really?'

This problem had rumbled on and on. Williams was determined to refit *Rosamund,* the ship with a doubtful engine, and Don was equally determined to prevent him. Somehow the issue had come to mean more than a simple logistic decision: it was about one man being right and the other wrong. It was about power and responsibility.

'There's a lot of vibration on the main shaft,' explained Williams. 'We're going to have to take the whole bearing assembly to pieces, and while we're at it we might as well improve the crew accommodation.'

It would be expensive. They would need to charter another ship to take over the contracts *Rosamund* would be unable to fulfil, not to mention the cost of the overhaul itself. Don wondered what Kincaid would have done in this position. A man like that would never spend money on something that wasn't yet bust, that was for sure.

'Let's wait until something goes really wrong,' he said.

Williams gaped at him. 'But − but − ' He couldn't find the words. A seaman through and through, he had no doubt that if an engine was going to go, it would make sure it was in a Force 9 and on a lee shore. Did this man Harrington know anything? he wondered.

Don was moving on to the next thing, a project that interested him more. They were researching a new design for the small deck cranes without which oil rig supply would be virtually impossible. There was real progress to be made here, with lightweight materials replacing cumbersome struts, and high tensile cables adding the necessary bracing. The practical engineering problem had always attracted him. If the mountains hadn't beckoned, which were themselves a practical application, he might well have been a construction engineer.

He wrote some suggestions and amendments on the report and gave it back to George Williams. It wasn't the manager's thing. He went on the defensive, unsure if he was deliberately being made to feel uneducated and crass. All his experience had been gained in the open and effusive atmosphere of an American company. This English/Scottish mix of reserve and suspicion confused him. He went back to his main complaint.

'Mr Harrington, the realtime loss on the *Rosamund* − '

'Realtime? Realtime? What sort of expression is that?'

172

'Sorry, Mr Harrington. The downside of our policy – '

'Oh, for Christ's sake, George! Don't worry about it. All this downside, upside nonsense is just so much hot air. Relax. We'll worry about engine failure if and when it happens. Not before.'

Outside, in the office, Williams fumed. Harrington didn't seem to know what he wanted. Either his manager ran the company, or he did not. But Kincaid's legacy had been a structure that demanded secretive men at the top who engaged in day to day personal involvement, and Don was following that line. He had given Williams power, but only to a certain degree; it wasn't enough.

Andrews wandered up to him. 'Having trouble, George?'

'What? No. Don and I have one or two things we need to discuss, that's all.'

'Don and I, is it? Don and I?'

Andrews had put his finger on the sensitive spot. Harrington had not requested that Williams use his Christian name, and made it plain that he preferred that he did not. Instead of a trusted colleague, in the chairman's full confidence, George was made to feel like a lackey.

He went home that night bitter and tired. The usual crammed briefcase was left at work. He didn't see why he should slave his guts out for someone that ungrateful. Did Harrington want a manager, or didn't he? The job move that had seemed so promising suddenly looked very ill advised.

Don was asking himself the same question. Why had he appointed a manager? He was paying someone to do work that Kincaid had expected him to do himself. When he was away he needed someone, but when he was back there was no clear division of labour. He was aware that he hadn't given Williams a free hand, but if he did, what would Harrington's own role be when he returned from here or there and looked for work? He'd be an unnecessary spare part. It was the eternal dilemma of a mother with a nanny – wanting help, needing help, but jealous of any signs of true competence.

Perhaps he was jealous of KORSEA. For the very first time he felt some sense of personal pride in the company, the urge to do things himself, keep them to himself. Always before he had thought of the company as Kincaid's, and if he had any role to play it was simply as a cameo in someone else's production. All of a sudden he had the urge to play the lead; in rehearsals, perhaps, not necessarily in performance. But at least he wanted to know that if he wished he could play that part – he wasn't Kincaid's stand-in any more.

He was surprised to get home and find that Van had been

173

telephoning all day. 'Didn't you tell him to reach me at the office?' he asked Forbes, handing the butler his coat.

'The gentleman preferred to speak to you privately at home,' replied Forbes.

Before going up to see Flora, Don went into the study and called Van back. It was a London number. He didn't recognise it.

'Van? It's me. What's all the fuss?'

'My God, man, I've been choking all day on excitement. You won't believe it. I don't myself.'

'What? Get on with it.'

'Everest. There's a team leaving in six weeks, Dougie West's team. The permit has been theirs for four years, I think, and all that time he's been planning. Yesterday Dougie fell in Wales. Concussion and a fractured pelvis. They want us to go. They want you to lead.'

For a long moment Don felt suspended outside reality. He was hearing what he wished to hear, and Van was saying something quite different. 'Repeat that, would you?' he said flatly.

Van did, once, then twice more. 'They want you to lead! For once we can do it our way. Can you believe it, Don?'

'No. Frankly, I can't. Look, who's running things? I'll call them and have a talk.'

'I have several numbers here. I'll give you everything. I didn't say yes, only maybe. There's no need to sound too eager.'

'Yeah. Let them think themselves lucky to get us. OK, Van, I'll ring back. Stay by the 'phone.'

He telephoned, talked, telephoned again. Forbes came in twice but each time Don waved him away. The third time the butler brought the whisky decanter on a silver tray, and Don poured himself a shot and sat sipping as he talked. The man on the other end was an army colonel, because half the projected team was made up of army personnel. 'We know you've a company to run,' he was saying. 'But we do very much hope you'll be able to come and head us up. We need your depth of experience.'

It sounded like cattle ranching. Don suppressed the urge to chuckle; he had long since learned that the army tolerated the undisciplined, uncouth civilian climbing fraternity only with difficulty. They could not hide their deep conviction that every one of the shower, however talented, would benefit from a good dose of National Service. It would be Don's job to meld the groups together, and he could begin now. 'I'd like the team members to meet up,' he said. 'How about here, at the castle? We can do some climbing, find out about one another.'

'Great, first class, righto.'

There was no light in the room except the fire. Don sat in the gloom, watching the flames flicker, reflected in polished wood, glass, the brass studs on the furniture. All at once he remembered Flora. God, Flora! He shot out of his chair, out of the room and up the stairs.

She was reading by the light of a small bedside lamp. Her hair was plaited in a thick braid hanging over one shoulder, she looked desperately young. When she lifted her eyes to his he could hardly bear to meet her navy blue gaze.

'I – er – I had to telephone someone.'

She closed her book. 'It's all right. Forbes told me what it was about.'

'How does he know?'

'He listened, of course. You don't imagine anything in this house happens that they don't know about, do you? You've been asked to go on an Everest expedition and they're all terribly excited.'

'I haven't just been asked to go. They want me to lead it.'

'Do they?'

That dark, steady gaze. He looked away, and the silence stretched into a taut rope of accusation. 'It would be months,' said Flora. 'Four, five months perhaps.'

It would be all of that. He said, 'Not so long. I'd be back for the birth. I mean, you should know I'd not want to be away for that.'

'And KORSEA. Mr Williams hasn't been there five minutes, he doesn't know what's going on.'

Don rubbed his hand over his face. 'He's a good man, experienced. It's probably time he had complete responsibility.'

Flora made no reply. He could feel her watching him, knew that she was steeling herself against all the bitter, justified accusations. He was deserting her. When she needed him, when she needed not to be alone, he was leaving. He met her eyes. 'I'm sorry,' he said. 'I can't pass it up, not for anything. I never said I was going to give it up.'

'Sometimes would be all right. Not all the time.'

'This could be the last time, it could cure me forever.'

'Death tends to be permanent,' said Flora thinly.

'Believe me, I don't intend to die.'

She wondered why he didn't say that he loved her. Not that she would believe him. You didn't love someone and then leave them like this, you didn't care more for your own life than you did for theirs. She kept her body very still, as she had all day, and she dared not scream at him as she wished. They had her trapped, docile and obedient.

175

Don was watching her. He looked different, as if the man of this morning had undergone subtle surgery to become the man of tonight. Everything was sharper, brighter, more alert. He always looked like this when he was leaving, she realised. Only when he was going did he truly come alive.

It was a small expedition, only sixteen climbers. The army contingent ensured that they were moderately well equipped, although the others looked askance at heavy tents and army issue oxygen bottles. They arrived at the castle in dribs and drabs, and were each in turn dumbstruck by the sheer magnificence. 'You fell on your feet, boy,' said Idris, a Welshman known to Don through odd encounters in the climbing huts of the world. 'Last time I see you it was up to our necks in snow we were.'

'And you pinched the last of the rum,' said Don. 'I remember, you bastard.'

'We've been offered several cases of single malt whisky,' confided Howard, the army man in charge of provisions. 'They want us to be seen drinking it on film.'

'What film?' Don looked curiously about.

'Er – we've got a television crew coming with us. Good men, not much climbing experience though.'

'Oh, shit.'

They all chuckled at his discomfiture. He relaxed, because there was no point in pretending that he knew what was going on. He could take his time and admit ignorance, because amongst these men he was known and understood. They lounged around, the army types instantly distinguishable in expedition blazers, short hair and controlled gestures. The others were a languid collection of shaggy, bearded individualists. Idris wore small wire spectacles, a great nuisance to him at altitude but one which he always overcame. Tom Daventry, an American with much rock experience at Joshua Tree National Park, was making his first trip to the high peaks. The grittiest member of the group, the one Don put above himself to get to the top, was Geoff Barclay. He had begun work as a miner, and the fitness he had gained down the pit still paid dividends. He had tremendous strength, and more than once had proved that it did not desert him when the air became thin. But he was uncompromising, and often returned from a trip at daggers drawn with everyone else on it.

Don said, 'First of all, I should tell you that I'm changing this expedition somewhat. I don't want a big, army-style push, a ponderous trudge up to the top. Takes forever, costs a bomb, no

176

decent climbing. My choice is for the direct route and a modified Alpine-style ascent. I'm also debating whether some of us could climb without oxygen.'

The army men looked from one to the other. As a group they had the least experience. Peter, Howard's close chum, cleared his throat. 'A lot of us have wives and families, Don. We want to get back from this expedition.'

'I'm married,' said Don. 'And my wife's pregnant. I think we've all got to accept that we could be killed. The risks are no greater this way.'

'Get your brains scrambled with no oxygen,' said Idris, and put his feet up on the sofa, still in his shoes.

'I'm game,' said Geoff, and swiped the shoes back to the floor. 'Let's do it the clean way. Hard, fast and brilliant.'

For Howard, the change of tack was too swift. 'Er − I think we should consider the logistics,' he began. 'There's a lot to consider.'

'Come on, Howard!' Don leaned forward, grinned and coaxed him. 'More fun this way. We don't need two hundred porters, a vast camp kitchen, latrines, shower cubicles. All that's been done before. We'll get in fast, hit it, and get out.'

'What about bad weather?'

Van spoke for the first time. 'On Everest, the weather can always win. Sometimes it chooses not to, that's all.'

'We're not making big camps on the mountain,' said Don. 'If it's too bad we all come down. We can sit out quite a few weeks at the bottom, and have another crack at it when we get a break. Saves a hell of a lot of struggling up and down with loads, servicing the camps.'

They talked amongst themselves. Gradually the idea began to take hold in their minds. They moved from caution to enthusiasm through to excitement. Don signalled to Forbes to top up all the glasses. Then he sang out for silence.

'Just one more thing. I'm leading this, but I also want to get to the top. To be honest, me and Van are one of the best hopes for getting there. We're a strong team and we know what we're doing. The chances are we'll come through from behind, take the lead and finish the job, without oxygen. But we could be hurt, it might not work like that. If there's a problem, if I can't function, then Idris is my deputy.'

'Bloody hell, Don! I've never organised a vicar's tea party.'

'And you probably won't have to. But that's the way it is. You're it.'

They all laughed at the man's appalled expression. The army men looked askance, and Don knew why. For the sake of unity he should have put one of them in the position of deputy. But he had not. He didn't know the soldiers, and their army manners made them seem difficult to know. One of his hardest tasks in the weeks ahead would be to turn this disparate group of men into something resembling a united force.

Lilian called the next day. She stood transfixed in the hall, gazing round at a scene of utter confusion. Rucksacks, boots, axes and gloves, all lay heaped about on the polished floor like the residue of some panicked evacuation. Only the army had achieved anything like order, with neat piles of kit gathered together by the door.

'What's happening, Forbes?' asked Lilian faintly. 'Does Malcolm know anything about this?'

'It's the pre-planning meeting of the Everest expedition,' said Forbes smugly. He was becoming very free with the jargon. 'Mr Kincaid — he's a little upset, I believe.'

Lilian hurried up to see Flora, bursting into the bedroom trailing a length of brown wool scarf, her hair everywhere.'Darling, what can Don be thinking of? Is he really going on this expedition? Now?'

Flora put aside some embroidery, saying glumly, 'Yes, he's going. Is it chaos downstairs? It sounds terrible.'

'It's worse than chaos. Some troglodyte types, all hair and those puffed up jackets, and then some neat, clean-cut boys who look so reliable and good that you feel they must all be convicted rapists. Don tends rather more towards the first group, I feel.'

'He was like that when I met him,' said Flora wistfully. 'He's a bit more civilised now.'

Lilian said nothing. She took her daughter's hand, trying to convey some sort of sympathy. There was no point in stating the obvious; that Flora should not be left here, alone, in her condition.

'I thought you might be up by now,' said Lilian.

'Mr Mitchell says another week. I think he meant to keep me in bed for ages right from the start, but he's letting the news out bit by bit. It's so boring. And I don't believe he will let me get up on Friday, whatever he says. His credibility's gone.'

Her mother sighed. Reaching down into her bag she pulled out some books, an old jigsaw and a battered piece of knitting. 'I thought you might like to finish this off for me,' she ventured. 'It's supposed to be a sweater. I know you don't need anything, but I do. You'd be such a help.'

Flora was touched. Lilian was not perhaps the most supportive of parents when things were going well, but in a crisis she was invaluable.

She gave encouragement, quiet help and a level-headed feeling that all would be well provided one was sensible. Up here, stuck in a bed which Don visited increasingly rarely, Flora felt herself falling back on the old affections, the tried and tested bonds.

'Have you been to see Dad?' she asked.

Lilian shook her head. 'I'll go now, shall I? Then I can tell you how he is. It's most peculiar, having everyone in bed at once. I don't remember you ever being ill as a child.'

'I wasn't much.' It wasn't true. Flora had endured mumps, measles and chicken pox after her mother left. But it was Marie who had nursed her then. Lilian's memory was accurate, but incomplete.

Kincaid was sitting up, by the window of his room. When Lilian entered he said to her, exactly as if she had been there all the time, 'Can you see, Lilian? Now they're trampling the rose bushes. I'm damned if I'll have these people taking over my home!'

His wife stood beside him and watched them load two transit vans and the Range Rover. 'I think they're going climbing. I don't know where Don is.'

'Keeping out of the way! And well he might. It's the damnedest thing, Lilian. The damnedest. You know he's going and leaving Flora?'

She nodded. 'I didn't think he was the stay at home type. All the same –'

'Why now?' said Kincaid, filling in her thoughts. 'If he cares for the girl, why now?'

'I had such a feeling – right from the start I wondered about him. You wanted someone settled, reliable. I could see from the first he wasn't that.'

'Damn it, of course he is! He's just young. Adventurous. Just the sort of man we need in KORSEA.'

'To be honest, Malcolm, I think he's been finding KORSEA a little dull.'

He seemed to fold in on himself, dropping his head into his chest like an offended bird of prey. She had insulted his pet, his baby, the hobby that had fascinated him through all his adult life. Lilian had once told a steam train buff that she found old-fashioned trains dirty, slow and boring. The man had never spoken to her again.

'Nothing ever goes right,' mumbled Kincaid. 'Can't get it – can't make it – don't trust this man Flora's seeing. Doctor. Doesn't understand the importance –'

'He seems very sound,' said Lilian. 'Really Malcolm, pull yourself together. You're making poor Flora feel persecuted. If she never had

179

a baby, never ever, it wouldn't be the end of the world. It would be one of those things. That's all.'

He lifted his head to stare at her with evident outrage. 'Sentimental claptrap,' he muttered. 'The firm needs someone, and Don's no bloody good. A Kincaid! A good, strong Kincaid, that's what I want!'

Lilian prepared to go. But at the door, her fingers on the handle, she turned. 'You can't be reincarnated, Malcolm,' she said softly. 'However many children Flora has, you can't have your chance again.' He watched her, balefully, until she was gone.

Don sat on the edge of a crag, watching the men toil up the rock towards him. It was interesting. On the plod out the soldiers had been dogged and determined, maintaining an even pace to arrive in good time at the rock. The climbers, on the other hand, carried less, started late and messed around more. There were lots of minor crises, of the 'Where the hell's Idris?' variety, and inevitably someone had forgotten some vital item of gear.

But when they came to the rock, ages later than the soldiers, they shinned up it with amazing competence. For them there were no collective decisions but as many answers as there were men to ask the questions. It was team players versus committed individualists, and it gave Don a headache just thinking how he was going to blend the two.

The soldiers were a bit ponderous on the rock. They needed to speed up, to gain confidence. Trained in good sense, it took a huge effort of will for them to tread the finely balanced tightrope between calculated risk and foolhardy exhibitionism. However well belayed, for them it was a failure to come off; for the others, on rock like this, coming off was part of the game. But on Everest they didn't need great climbing skills: much of the climb was a fight against exhaustion and cold. So in the end the soldiers might win. Climbers were too often big babies, deeply involved with their own bad cough or sore toe. The soldiers had been drilled out of such childishness. But then, thought Don, the big peaks were no place for mature men. Anyone of real maturity wouldn't be there.

He chuckled to himself. Oh God, what was he doing? At KORSEA George Williams was in a sulk, at home Flora was silent and unwelcoming. He had no doubt that he was being supremely selfish, but damn it, he'd done the best he could. KORSEA had a manager, Flora was pregnant, and if none of them could see that this was a chance he could not pass up, then they didn't know him.

Idris slipped and hung in space, yelling Welsh obscenities.

Hidden by an overhang ten feet below Don's feet two soldiers exchanged muttered words. 'They're a load of bloody wildmen! Do you think Harrington's got any idea of what he's doing?'

'Buggered if I know. Thank God Howard's doing the food. We'd end up at Base Camp having to eat each other. And that lot look most unsavoury!'

Don smothered a chuckle. Those two had come the wrong way, so he lay down on his face and spoke to them. 'You've missed the route. Get back to the spur and go right, the short traverse.'

He watched them exchange glances, wondering if he had heard. Let them worry. They were fit these boys, but not climbing fit. They lacked the pumping muscle strength to force their way up faces. Although they had enough rock climbing stars for this climb, perhaps too many. He leaned down again, saw that they were stuck and gently guided them out of the problem. Once he had thought that teaching would be enough, once he had thought that KORSEA would be enough. Perhaps there would never be enough. One after another his men scrambled up the crag, and came obediently over the grass towards him.

The days, the weeks, passed like rushing clouds. Always Don was fighting his way through seemingly unimportant distractions. The ship *Rosamund* was laid up in Rotterdam with engine trouble, but they wouldn't refit there, it would cost an arm and a leg. George Williams dithered over what to do, until at last Don yelled at him: 'Don't bother me, man! Get her patched up and bring the bugger back. Get our own men to look at her.'

'She'll need to be in ballast,' said Williams nervously.

'Oh, for Christ's sake. Put a cargo in her and make some cash. And if she needs this bloody refit get it done here, where we can keep an eye on the bill! Do I need to think of everything around here myself?'

The KORSEA people overheard and smirked. They were against Williams, with his alien way of doing things. If Don had backed him, that would have been different, but he had created a whipping boy who took all the blame.

'It's going to be better when Harrington's gone,' consoled George's wife one evening. 'At least then you'll have a free hand.'

He stared glumly down at his dinner. 'I think it's too late. They've got so used to ignoring what I say and waiting two days until he comes in and decides something different. He doesn't know what the hell he's doing and he doesn't care. But they all worship the ground he walks on.'

181

'They call it charisma,' said his wife.

'I'll give him bloody charisma!'

But if George could be left at the office, Flora seemed ever present. Out of bed but confined to the house, she wandered from room to room looking at lists, listening to telephone calls, opening cases of equipment. In a rare moment when he gave her his full attention, Don wondered if she was being deliberately irritating. One evening, at dinner, when he was telling her about the walk-in from Kathmandu, thinking aloud, she got up suddenly and said, 'I'm going to see Dad. Then I'll have an early night.'

He looked at her. 'OK,' he said finally, with heavy sarcasm. 'So you're not interested. We'll talk about something else. Marie's latest witticism perhaps.'

She stood at the door, swathed in black jersey. 'Mr Mitchell came today, but that doesn't concern you, I suppose. You wanted me pregnant, you made me pregnant, and now that I am you couldn't care less. I get in your way, don't I? You don't want to have to think about me when you've got really important things on your mind, like whether or not you can get your own precious self up to the top of a mountain that's been climbed so often before no one's even going to notice when you've done it!'

'Shut up, Flora, everyone's going to hear you.'

Her eyes flashed fire. She yelled, 'I don't care if the whole world hears me! The one sure thing is that you certainly never do!'

He got up and went to her, and she tried to slam the door in his face. They wrestled, he could have won easily but dared not. 'I thought you were supposed to be taking things easy!' he hissed.

'It's none of your business! Nothing I do is any of your business any more!'

He managed to get his hand round her wrist and gripped tight. She gasped and let go of the door. It hit him on the side of the face.

'Bitch,' he said.

'Let go of me! How dare you, leave me alone!'

He glimpsed Forbes peeping round the corner of the hall and he dragged Flora back into the comparative privacy of the dining room. She was shaking with rage. He tried to put an arm round her shoulders but she hit him away. He let her go and stood back, and suddenly she collapsed into a chair.

'You're being stupid,' he said dully. 'You must see this is an opportunity I can't pass up.'

'All I see is an overgrown schoolboy. I need you, the firm needs you, and all you can think to do is go off playing games.'

'But if it's a game I want to play then I shall play it.'

182

She stared at him then. 'And what about any games I might have in mind? You seem to be as free as a bird, but you've got me firmly locked up in the proverbial gilded cage.'

He put his hands in his pockets and sighed. 'I'm sorry. I know things are difficult for you at the moment but I can't see why you're making such a fuss. It's not my fault you're a woman, it's not my fault women have the babies. You came back from Nepal because your father was ill, not because I made you. And you had every chance not to marry me. But you're married, you're pregnant, your father's ill. Can't you just learn to accept that?'

'About as well as you learned to buckle down to real hard work.' Her voice was edged with contempt.

'Thank you for your encouragement,' said Don softly. 'I really appreciate the way you support me in everything I do.'

'Don't mention it,' snapped Flora. 'I learned my sensitivity from you.'

'My God, I never thought you had such a vicious tongue!'

'Didn't you?' Sobs threatened to swamp her. 'But then, I never thought I'd have so much time to practise.'

He left a fortnight later. Flora came out to the airstrip to see him off, and stood in the wind, her hair blowing about her head.

'Take care,' he said. 'I promise I'll be back for the birth.'

She nodded. 'I'm sure you'll try.'

'Look, I said I promise. That means I will. I'm not going to die, I'm not going to forget you, I'm going to get to the top of that mountain and come straight back here to see that you're all right. I love you.'

'Good luck. Don't get hurt. Please.'

They kissed, and his lips tasted of salt. Somehow their hands entangled, and she found herself gripping his thumb as tight as she could hold. She forced herself to let him go. As he got in the plane he found himself wondering, suddenly, why he was there, why he was going. In the brief seconds before take-off he hung in limbo, watching a red-headed girl standing in the wind. She turned away.

Chapter Seventeen

In Kathmandu Idris decided he needed a new pair of boots. He wandered the side streets, calling at the dozens of shops trading in used expedition kit. Finally he picked up a stylish Italian pair. 'Well, boys, now I do look the part,' he said happily. 'A fairy amongst men.'

Howard looked at him sourly. He had taken a survey of biscuit preferences before they left Britain and Idris had held out grimly for custard creams, although no one else liked them. A request to the manufacturer had brought hundreds of packets of custard creams, with no one but Idris to eat them. No other free biscuits had been forthcoming.

'Sell 'em in the bazaar,' advised Don. 'No point in taking them for the sake of it.'

So Howard had been forced to stand haggling over boxes of biscuits for a day, swapping two cartons of custard creams for one of chocolate digestives, and trading these in turn for a dozen highly prized Mars bars. It had been fun until the film crew arrived. Howard now had the dubious pleasure of knowing that wife, mother-in-law and commander-in-chief would all witness him being chatted up by two flirtatious Nepali girls who clearly didn't want anything to do with custard creams. But, as Idris said, 'Travel broadens the mind, they do say. Give us a biscuit, boy.'

They set out from town in a straggling line. Geoff Barclay got up late and wouldn't hurry, so Don left him. He trudged in at the end of the first day, as grumpy as ever. 'Too bloody keen, you lot,' he snarled. 'Too much bull and blanco.'

Geoff never joined any team, on principle. If it was decided to stop and eat at twelve, he continued until one, but if one was decided upon then he took his snack at twelve. It annoyed everyone, soldiers and climbers alike, but Don did nothing. Grumbling at Geoff gave them all something in common.

Day by day they drew further and further from Kathmandu. Several men went down with stomach problems, and the doctor, Dave, was kept busy. On one day they rested and a post runner caught them up, with letters for everyone. Don tossed all his aside except Flora's. It was short, crisp, uneffusive. She wasn't forgiving him easily, that was certain. For his part he wrote masterpieces, saying how much he loved and missed her. He was sure she would soften. Flora was not a woman to bear grudges.

The rest of his mail was to do with the expedition, and a letter from George Williams requesting an authorisation for a chemical cargo. Don skimmed through and then wrote back, a stiff note saying George could do what he thought best. He added: 'Try to understand that I can't be concerned with any day to day business while on this expedition. I expect you to see to everything.' What was the man thinking of? It took at least two weeks to get mail out, even to Kathmandu.

They reached Namche Bazar. A friend of Ang Stupa was waiting for them, with a reference and a crumpled photograph of himself on a nameless mountaintop. 'Have you been to Everest?' asked Don. The man, Poteng, nodded. 'My brother lost in the icefall,' he confided. 'Many times I travel through the icefall. With the Japanese.'

Don hired him. The Japanese climbed with elaborate hardware, taking forever to hammer and nail their way up a route. If Poteng had endured the Japanese way then he had stamina indeed. His wife and children came to see him off. The children were small, perhaps two and four, and his wife was a short, attractive girl with black button eyes. Poteng kissed them, lifting the children up for an extra hug. His wife began to cry.

Somehow it upset everyone. Even Geoff Barclay, who as far as was known had never been pleasant enough to anyone to persuade them to sit next to him, let alone marry, blew his nose fiercely. Don thought, suddenly, that he might never see his child – his children. He might never see Flora again. They marched out, no one speaking, and at mid-morning Don passed round a flask of *rakshi,* the local spirit. Even so, they were still low at the end of the day. Subdued, they went to bed and thought of home.

Dear Mrs Harrington,

It is with regret that I find I must tender my resignation. My time at KORSEA has been made difficult by Mr Harrington's absences, and I have been fortunate enough to be offered a position of seniority in my previous company. In view of the fact that my contract of employment with KORSEA was never finalised I should be grateful if you would consider my resignation effective as from the end of the month.

Yours sincerely,

George G. Williams

Flora blinked at the page in front of her. It was rather badly typed, as if his wife had knocked it out at home. Glancing at the calendar she saw that the end of the month was no more than two days away. She picked up the 'phone.

'Hello? Mr Williams, please. It's Mrs Harrington.'

She waited a long time. She imagined him debating whether to refuse to take the call. But at last she heard a cautious, 'Mrs Harrington? Hi.'

'Hello, Mr Williams. I − I got your letter. I'm really sorry you're leaving.'

'I'm sorry too, Mrs Harrington.'

'I wondered − would it be too much to ask you to stay on? My husband won't be back for months yet, and I'm pregnant and not very well, so I thought − '

'I've another job to go to and I'm expected. I'm sorry, but that's the position. As I said, I never even had a contract.'

'I don't know how that can have been overlooked! Surely you could delay for just a little, couldn't you? This is leaving us so much in the lurch.'

She heard him take in his breath, to say in a tight, unhappy voice, 'I have to leave. Believe me, I'm sorry.'

He hung up on her. She sat looking at the receiver for a while, and then put it down carefully. What was she to do? Mr Mitchell was adamant that she should do nothing more strenuous than lift a teacup to her lips. She thought of Mactee refining his golf handicap, Andrews at the office with his narrow view. She thought of her father.

When she went upstairs her father was sitting up in bed, the paper open at the financial pages and the share prices flashing on the TV. He squinted at the screen, grimaced, and made a note on a pad at his side. Soon he would make one of his infrequent calls to his stockbroker and ask him to switch in or out of something. It was a sign that he was feeling well.

She wondered why no one had ever thought he might completely recover, or at least get well enough to resume something of normal life. But as the months went by he was getting better, it was undeniable. His pelvis had mended, and although he had a weakness in his lower back he could walk, after a fashion. The hair had grown back over the scar on his head, a thick mane of white streaked with red. The only residue of the accident was the weakness down one side, most evident in his slack mouth and dragged down eyelid. But all in all he was remarkably well.

'It's amazing what you can do with electronics,' remarked Flora.

'Don't spout platitudes, Flora.' He clicked the remote control switch and changed the screen.

'With the right equipment you could almost run a business from this room.'

'Indeed you could – get me that directory down, will you? The nurse puts it away, she thinks it excites me. And if I'm not much mistaken there's a takeover in the wind.'

'You don't say.'

She sat watching him while he pored over the entries. 'The manager at KORSEA just quit,' she said.

'Which manager?'

'George Williams. The man Don put in to look after things.'

Her father's good hand groped wildly for his glasses. He dragged them off his face. 'Now? The man's gone now? I don't believe it.'

'Apparently he didn't have a contract, so he can do what he likes. I wondered – Dad, why don't you take over for a while?'

Kincaid let out his breath in a long, angry sigh. 'There's never anything like doing it yourself. You give people work to do and they make such a complete and utter mess of it that you can't stand by and watch. I'm old, Flora. I'm sick. My mind plays tricks, I don't remember things.'

'There isn't anyone else,' she said. 'Even at your worst you have to be better than no one. And at your best – Dad, you know you're unbeatable.'

He chuckled and dropped his eyes. From above, his eyebrows looked like the wings of some captured bird. 'I could still have my nap,' he murmured. 'I need that. Forbes must make sure I don't get too many visitors, they tire me so. Get the telephone men in. I need a fax in the dressing room, a telex and a couple more phones. God knows what the nurse is going to say.'

The nurse said quite a lot. She telephoned the consultant and he said even more. But Kincaid was unstoppable, an old war horse with the scent of battle in his nostrils. He made Flora ring a secretarial

187

agency and engage a lady to work in the mornings, perched at a desk in the corridor outside his room. She was middle-aged and efficient. At lunchtime each day she covered her typewriter, plugged in an answering machine and went into the kitchen to enjoy a pleasant meal with the staff.

'I always knew the old man wasn't finished,' said Forbes with satisfaction. 'Old soldiers never die.'

'He couldn't have been more wrong in Miss Flora's young man,' added Marie. 'After the money, he was.'

'Mark my words, we've seen the last of him,' said Forbes. 'Best if he gets himself killed, if you ask me.'

They arrived at Everest Base Camp on a dull, windy, piercingly chill day. A cold was going the rounds and everyone looked miserable. Don got the Sherpas making tea almost at once, and gradually the tents went up, the stores were stacked, and each man's personal kit given its home. It was amazing how cheering it was to have a place that was entirely yours. Don and Van shared a tent as usual, and Don had an upturned case as a desk in the main mess tent. The film crew, grumbling and feeling ghastly, pursued him round the camp taking footage of everything he did.

Tom Daventry, himself something of a film expert, was scornful. 'They'll never get to Camp 1,' he said loudly, in their hearing.

'Don't think I bloody want to,' muttered the cameraman. He had a splitting altitude headache. 'What am I doing here? Why can't I be back down the local in Potters Bar?' He struggled about, his plight studiously ignored, even by the doctor.

Don was pushing on. The weather was relentlessly cold, but he wanted to get through the ice fall. At night the seracs creaked alarmingly, and the Sherpas muttered to one another that conditions seemed exceptionally bad. The place was littered with ladders and bridges from previous expeditions, and Peter went around gathering them up. He was the ice fall specialist, commissioned to lay a secure trail over ice and snow crevasse. The camera crew crouched against a snow tower and filmed him doing it, lowering ladders on ropes across bottomless splits in the surface. It was a nightmare place, ripe for haunting. No one knew how many men lay under it, and at night, listening to the ice creak, it sounded like the wailing of lost souls.

On the third day it snowed heavily. The climbers slummocked around, creating mess and muddle everywhere. Peter lost his temper with Geoff, who shared a tent with him and Howard. Rummaging without permission through Peter's climbing gear, he had spilled a tin of insecticide all over the tent. It smelled like badly disinfected drains.

'You stupid pillock!' snarled Peter. 'Haven't you any understanding of the word privacy? Get your fucking self over here and sort this mess out.' Geoff sniffed, but did nothing to help clean up. Howard went to Don and demanded that Geoff be moved out, but Don said, 'I'm sending you and Geoff out tomorrow, if the weather clears. He can lead. You'll have fun.'

That evening the soldiers took to muttering in the mess tent. Clearly Don favoured his own kind, and wasn't going to give the soldiers a break. There was a suggestion that Howard should refuse to climb with Geoff, and remembering the custard creams Howard was tempted. But they were disciplined men; in the morning he and Geoff set off to break trail.

It was a bright, blue day. For once the wind had dropped and fresh snow covered the sour detritus of man. Everything was brilliant white and silver, the colours so vivid that even an hour's neglect of goggles could bring on snow blindness. Geoff worked his way solidly up, moving quickly and lightly across the ground. Howard found it tough keeping up. His breath came in shallow pants, he had to force himself to breathe deeply. When Geoff rested and he caught him up, Geoff said, 'You move well. Don said you did. Dump that fart Peter and stick with me, we'll get to the top.'

Howard didn't know whether to be flattered or appalled. He looked behind and saw Sherpas coming on, carrying the tents for Camp 1. Things were moving suddenly, with disconcerting speed.

'What are you here for if you don't want to get there?' Geoff sneered at him, and Howard, goaded, pushed past and took the lead. Twice, three times, he went up to his waist in snow and floundered, exhausting himself. Geoff passed him and took up the lead again, saying nothing. Howard wondered how he was going to explain to Peter.

At night the wind seemed to be alive, a deep-sea grampus taking grunting breaths only an inch beyond the tent wall. As always at altitude, it was hard to sleep; Don had pills if he wanted them, but mostly he preferred to lie awake, moving a little to keep his feet warm, thinking about the problems of the day.

The film crew were being pathetic; if Don had been involved earlier in the planning he would have chosen people who were climbers first and film men second, whereas these were the other way round. They were unused to the squalor, no washing, camp food and a lavatory that was only a hole in the snow. They would never get any distance up the mountain, and one of the objects of the expedition,

189

certainly from the army point of view, was to get a decent film out of it. Who else could manage the cameras? Tom Daventry. Don fumbled for his notebook and wrote the name down.

But if he was sent through, another climber preferred, the soldiers would rightly be annoyed. He would have to team with Peter, like it or not, although there was no way of telling if Peter had any film experience. He was going to gain some, that was for sure. But was Tom up to the carrying involved? He had had a bad fall in Yosemite a couple of years ago, and one of his shoulders was weak. But if Peter was asked to carry more kit he would think he was only a beast of burden – which brought the question of the Sherpas. They worked at their best if they knew one of their number was destined for the top. So far, it didn't look as if it was going to happen, because they were climbing fast, with as few men on the mountain as possible. Don wondered if the Sherpas realised the probable outcome. He would have to discuss things with them soon.

He tossed and turned in his bag, thinking, always thinking. Beside him Van lay in apparent unconcerned slumber and for a surprising second Don hated him. Where was the sharing now? Where was the companionship? Van slept and Don worried, about the men, the supplies, the weather, a hundred variables that changed a hundred times a day.

KORSEA was like this. The thought took him by surprise. Decisions, choices, rolling on and on. He had been mad to take on KORSEA and he was mad to take on this. How much more peaceful it was to be Van, asleep and unaware, waking in an hour or so to think only about himself, his fitness, his climb. Don felt a headache starting and had a sudden mad wish to get seriously altitude sick and be taken out of it. When you grew up everything was spoiled: the tree house became a real house and had to conform to building regulations; scrambling rocks turned into mountaineering and cost money. Even romance turned into marriage and responsibility. Like Gulliver, tied down by a thousand tiny strings, he was steadily succumbing to imprisonment.

The turkey farm was losing money, the divers in California were fighting for work, and someone had sabotaged the compressor; and what was the good ship *Rosamund* doing stooging about from one port to another? Kincaid flipped pieces of paper around, his glasses slipping further and further down his nose. He felt tired suddenly. In the months since his accident he had forgotten how unremitting it all was, and he had got out of the habit of concentration. He

190

leaned on the buzzer for his secretary and began to dictate a note about turkeys. But in the middle he found his mind drifting off to think about California. He had never wanted to get involved in that market. He looked thoughtfully at his secretary.

'Tell them to sell.'

'Beg pardon, Mr Kincaid?'

'California. The divers. Send them a message. I want the business sold.'

Dutifully his secretary wrote the message down. Kincaid was silent for long minutes and at last she cleared her throat. 'The turkeys –' she reminded. He tried to remember. What the hell was it about the turkeys? Stupid birds. Manipulated out of flight and into freezers. He could think of nothing he could usefully advise. Was it time for his nap? He felt so weary, he would give anything to slide down the bed and sleep. He was like a flat battery, giving a spurt of energy after each period of rest, and then dimming, dimming. He waved his hand at the crisp woman opposite. 'Tomorrow.'

When she was gone he closed his eyes. The papers slipped off the bed. Tomorrow would be soon enough, he decided, tomorrow, Monday – he fell into delicious, welcoming sleep.

Flora fielded call after call. 'He's having rather a bad day, I'm afraid. If you could leave a message – I'll find out. Yes, I promise.'

In the end she instructed Forbes to say she was not at home. There was no point in talking to these people, she didn't know what to do. Balance sheets meant nothing to her, quoted prices were so much double dutch. She glanced down at the last message on her pad. It said *'Rosamund* – why not docked? Work waiting.'

It seemed a straightforward query, and she was angry that no one at KORSEA seemed capable of answering it. But enquiries went round and round. This was the third such message she had passed through to her father.

The 'phone rang again. She picked it up angrily, saying, 'Forbes, I thought I said –' but a delighted laugh greeted her.

'You do sound cross,' giggled Shalimar. 'I don't think I'll come and see you after all.'

Flora almost choked. 'Where are you? London? Then you must come. You don't know how desperate I am.'

She arrived in time for dinner. When she saw Flora, swathed in a blue print tent, she exclaimed, 'My God! You've swallowed a balloon!'

191

'Two balloons,' said Flora. 'Don't tell anyone, but it's twins.'

Shalimar was dumbstruck. She sank on to the sofa, her long legs folded up like a giraffe's. She was wearing her usual high heels, a tight top and a pair of silk Turkish trousers gathered at the ankle. Her face, always thin, seemed gaunt. 'What does Don think?'

Flora shrugged. 'How should I know? He's seen fit to go off to scout camp, leaving an inadequate manager, who has now left. Dad's having to try and run KORSEA and it's making him ill. And I don't know anything. But every few days I get a letter from Don saying how much he's missing me. Him, missing me! What the hell does he think is happening here, may I ask?'

Shalimar said nothing. Flora looked at her a little more carefully. There was a slight nervous tremor at the corner of one eye. 'Did the film go all right?' she asked.

The girl nodded. 'Fine. Fine. I could be famous.'

'You already are. But you look a little − tense.'

'Do I? I hoped it didn't show.' She took a deep breath and forced a laugh. 'I've got myself down, rather. Too many parties, too much coke. I − I made the classic mistake and went to bed with the producer. He was getting divorced, and I thought − and it helped. I got my part rewritten, it's huge. But he took to coming round at lunch and soon everyone knew. What the hell, I'm not ashamed of it. But there was an Englishman there, one of the crew. He had it in for me, he wouldn't help, cut me out if he could, wouldn't light me, anything. It got so bad I went to talk to him and he said: "You're just a half-caste slag. You want to be made to look like the Virgin Mary and you're nothing but a cunt."'

Her voice dropped to a whisper. Flora saw that her eyes were filled with tears. 'Was he gay?' asked Flora shrewdly. 'Sounds like a woman hater to me.'

'He might have been.' Shalimar blew her nose on a tissue.

'I just wonder why you let it upset you.'

The girl looked up, making a pathetic attempt at a smile. 'Because he's right,' she said. 'My mother would be shocked at the way I behave. *I'm* shocked. Some of the men I sleep with I don't even like, but if I get good sex then I'm happy. But − oh God, Flora, it shouldn't be like that. I want to love someone. I want someone to love me. I want to wake up in the morning in a bedroom full of sunshine and make breakfast for two and dinner for the same two, and in between go out shopping and choose curtains for the nursery.'

Flora grimaced. 'You want to get married.'

'Yes! Yes, I do. And there isn't anyone.'

192

All at once, Flora felt very depressed. Shalimar was free and still she wasn't happy; Flora, the captive, knew only too well what her own life felt like. 'We ought to change places,' she said, sighing. 'You can be the milch cow and I'll be the sex object. No one's ever made love to me except Don. I'd love to know what it feels like.'

'Lonely.' Shalimar lay back on the sofa. 'You don't know them, so it's OK to make them give you what you want. "Touch me here, touch me there, this way, that way." He does the same. "I want to put it in here, God but you're beautiful, why don't you open your mouth?" It's like grabbing apples off a tree, each snatching handfuls, wanting the most. There's no sharing. And afterwards you've got to be polite. If he's at your place what you really want to do is kick him out and take a shower, but if you're at his and he wants you to go that's an insult. Mostly I don't ever want to see them again. And a month later you meet him in a parking lot and he says, "What did I do? I thought we had a good time together." I just wish you could have sex with robots.'

Flora looked down at herself. 'I don't have sex with anybody. I don't have anything with anybody.'

Shalimar said nothing.

Unusually, Don was troubled by an early morning erection. It was a rare event at altitude, in fact when the Chinese invaded Tibet they found themselves rendered almost impotent. Presumably the locals adjusted. Judging by the Sherpas, for whom sex was the national sport, they had no problems in getting it up.

It was a sign of acclimatisation. Don rolled out of bed into the grey dawn. No one else was awake and he blundered around the camp rousing cooks and climbers. Peter only grunted when kicked. He must have taken a pill. Yesterday he and Tom Daventry had been caught in the trailing edge of an avalanche, and for an horrific few seconds had not known if they were alive or dead. The camera had been filled with snow, and Tom had taken enough in to alarm everyone. Peter had got him down. But if Tom was having a rest day, Peter was needed. Exhaustion or no, he had to get out and get up the mountain. Howard and Geoff were climbing again today, and someone had to film them.

Idris had fallen asleep with his diary in his hand. Don glanced at it. 'For once Don hasn't bottled out,' he read. 'At the start I was sure he'd head up the mountain and let everyone else sort out the mess below, but he's doing his job. My worry is that he still thinks he and Van can get up without oxygen, and if they try the whole expedition could crack up. In the end, after all, Don's a bloody selfish climber.'

Don flicked the book shut and shook Idris. 'Get up, damn you,' he murmured. 'Get up and get cracking.'

Idris groaned and opened his eyes. 'I thought it was you. I was dreaming of bacon and eggs in Pontypool. And the telly. A terrible film on a wet afternoon. Bliss.'

'It's porridge and snow. As for the telly, we'll get one of the army lads to flick through his training manual very fast, showing us the pictures.'

'All those blokes think about is murder and eating nettles. God, what a life.'

Gradually the day began. Don was stiff with tension. Howard and Geoff, at a high camp, had been half buried in snow during the night, but had radioed in to say they were pushing on up. Don did a carry through the icefall, for the sake of doing something. It was better to be at base, taking the calls, sending people up or down. The intervals of idleness troubled him, the times when there was nothing to do but wait. He was conscious that Van was angry about something. Finally, after a tasteless lunch of corned beef sandwiches made with some disgusting tinned bread, Van cornered him.

'What are we doing here, Don? Wasting our time.'

'We're doing fine. A good fast climb, and no one hurt.'

'But you and me. We came to climb. I came to climb. I do not want to hang around down here.'

'No. It's not what I came for, either.'

They were silent. At last Van said, 'What do you want, Don? For them all to be so pleased with you?'

'Get stuffed.'

'I don't believe you are scared. If you were scared you would do it just the same. Why won't you climb?'

'It's not 'won't'. I can't. I'm here to lead, that's what I have to do. And I can't lead if I'm up in some camp with an avalanche belting down and my feet freezing. I'll go high when I need to, not before.'

'That could be never.'

'Yes. So it could.'

Van began swearing in Dutch, a long, complicated tirade. Don said, 'Look, I didn't know it was going to be like this. I should have known better, I admit, but as it was – you can't be a star climber and lead the troops. Simple as that.'

'Let Idris take over down here. He can do it.'

'It's not his job. He came to climb, not lead.'

194

'And I came to climb! I came to achieve something, to get up without oxygen, the two of us, together. There is no stronger team, Don. We're the best.'

Don looked at him. Suddenly he felt old, a hundred years older than his friend. 'Are we the best? Were we? Think of all the trips we've been on, where the thing broke up, where men died. We got what we wanted all right. I just wonder if we got it at the expense of everyone else.'

'That's climbing! That's what it is! These soldier boys have infected you with this team spirit, when there isn't anything in the mountains but you!'

'When we climb by ourselves, perhaps. But I owe these boys something. I've got to do the job.'

Van stood for a moment, his brown eyes uncomprehending. Then he turned and stormed to the mess tent. Loads were waiting there, stacked ready to be carried up through the ice fall, through the camps. It was late, no one was setting out now. But Van shouldered a pack and Don didn't try to stop him.

'I'm going up,' said the Dutchman. 'I stay at the camps. Tomorrow I ask Idris if he wishes to climb with me and make the summit bid.' He waited, as if he expected Don to speak. But he said nothing.

Gradually Van's plodding figure became no more than a black dot against the snow. Some yaks were wandering, taking a rest after bringing in supplies. Don felt lonely suddenly. His hands were cold, and he put them in his pockets. The yaks had brought letters, but none for him. From a nearby tent he could hear Tom Daventry coughing and the radio crackled. Geoff Barclay's voice saying, 'Don't suppose anyone down there wants to know what it's like up at the sharp end then?'

Don knew what it was like at the sharp end. Now, for the first time, he was learning what it was like down here.

195

Chapter Eighteen

Shalimar leafed through the pile of letters, facsimile documents, telex messages and files. She began by putting them in two piles, 'Important' and 'Less Important', but soon gave that up in favour of 'Understood' and 'Haven't Got a Clue'. Tracing the history of projects was hard enough. There had been so many changes of style and management, so many interruptions. Everyone had a different idea of what should happen, and the company had lurched from side to side like a ship tacking in rough seas. One thing was certain; they were not making progress.

'What is all this about the ship *Rosamund*?' she demanded. Flora, resting with her feet up and a file propped open on her belly, said, 'I don't know. I think George Williams wanted a refit and Don wanted a patch up job. Why it's now trundling around the Channel ports I do not know.'

'I'll get in touch with the captain.' Shalimar hooked the telephone towards her. She rang KORSEA and put through her request. It would take a while, they would have to patch through on the radio, they'd ring her back. 'I don't know why it's full of chemicals,' she said thoughtfully, leafing through papers while she waited. 'I mean, why fill a dicky ship full of chemicals?'

'It's supposed to be on oil rig supply,' said Flora. 'The whole thing's falling apart.'

She looked dismally at a note in Kincaid's scrawled hand: 'Ship *Rosamund*. Get the hell out of English Channel. African port.' What on earth was he thinking of? What on earth was she thinking of, putting a sick old man in charge?

The babies kicked in her stomach, a churning maelstrom of movement. She couldn't imagine what they were doing. She couldn't imagine them, boys, girls, arms, legs, jumbled up in her thoughts. A great fear nagged at her, that they would love each other more than her. She wanted to be loved, wanted to enter into an exclusive relationship. It would be too terrible to give her all and find that they gave only half.

The telephone rang. Shalimar picked it up, and smiled triumphantly at Flora. 'Got it,' she mouthed. Then, loudly, 'Captain? Captain – er – Longley? I'm speaking on behalf of Mr Kincaid. Can you tell me just what you are supposed to be doing at present?' She switched the receiver to transmit, sending the reply over the telephone loudspeaker. A voice, roaring against a background of engine noise, came tinnily into the room. 'We are – trying to dock,' yelled the captain. ' – repeated engine failure – hazardous cargo – request instructions.'

'What is your hazardous cargo?' Shalimar shot a look of amazement at Flora.

'Security – cannot divulge – check manifest.'

'Where on earth's the manifest?' muttered Flora, fumbling through papers. There was nothing there that told her about the cargo.

She heaved herself to her feet and padded in stockinged feet through to the other room. Shalimar continued her bellowed conversation with the captain, asking about the engines and about ports. Flora buzzed the intercom to her father's secretary. 'Do you have the manifest for the *Rosamund*?' she asked.

'Mr Kincaid has it, Mrs Harrington. It's confidential.'

'Oh. Oh, I see.'

They couldn't do anything until they knew what the ship carried.

Still wearing no shoes she went quietly upstairs, stopping to catch her breath on the half landing. The secretary, on sentry duty outside her father's room, glared. Flora replied with a smile, tapped on the door and went in. The nurse was bending over the bed. She looked up and said, 'No visitors today, please. He isn't well.'

'I won't be a moment. There's something I need.'

Kincaid, lifting his head painfully from the pillow, said, 'Flora?' in an old, weak voice.

'It's all right, Dad,' she said. 'I was looking for something. The manifest for the *Rosamund*.'

'Drawer. In the drawer. Get a tug to it!'

'A tug?' But he had closed his eyes and turned his head away.

'I've given him something to help him rest,' explained the nurse.

Flora felt like shaking her. He wouldn't rest if he knew the mess KORSEA was in. Why couldn't he be better? She had so much wanted him to be. She opened the bedside drawer and looked inside. A

197

handkerchief, penknife, some cough sweets. And a sheet of paper. The manifest.

She glanced at it while going down the stairs. Her legs went weak. She reached out for the banister rail, hung on, and then sat down with a bump on the stair. Shalimar was still talking to the captain, she could hear the raised voice. Grimly Flora got to her feet once again and made her way downstairs. Shalimar fluttered her fingers in a wave. As Flora unfolded the paper on the table in front of her, Shalimar's voice lost strength and faded.

'Er – I'll call you back, Captain,' she said. 'I'm checking the manifest.'

'You do that!' yelled the captain. 'It's about time somebody did!'

The two girls stared at each other. 'Who authorised it?' whispered Shalimar.

'Don. George Williams, perhaps. Nobody. It's been such chaos at KORSEA, no one knows what's supposed to happen. No wonder they can't get to port.'

'No one will have them. What are we going to do?'

Flora scrabbled frantically for her father's note. 'Get the hell out of English Channel. African port.' A sense of shock ran through her like electricity. Had he really thought they could do that? The ship might never have got as far as Africa, and if it had – the thought was horrible.

'We must inform the authorities,' she said in a tight, unhappy voice.

'We can't. We could be sued. Think of the consequences.'

'Think of the consequences if we don't!'

Shalimar looked wildly from Flora to the manifest and back again.

'We've got to tell Don,' she burst out.

'Don? Why? It's probably all his fault.'

'Flora, it can't be! If he knew about this he wouldn't have gone. And he'll come back and sort everything out. All we have to do is tell him!'

'It takes weeks to get messages through. And the chances are he'd look at it, throw it on one side and say he had more important things to think about. He isn't interested, Shalimar! He's gone off on an ego trip, leaving me pregnant, Dad sick and KORSEA in chaos.'

Shalimar stared at her for a long moment. Then she sighed. 'OK. So we have to do something. What?'

'Confess.' Flora's eyes were dark and troubled. 'The ship

Rosamund, powered by one inadequate engine, is staggering about the Channel loaded to the brim with hazardous nuclear waste.'

Shalimar squeaked and clutched her head. 'It sounds so terrible!'

'It *is* terrible. KORSEA has never done anything like this before. We've never touched anything shady – anything!'

Shalimar swallowed. 'It could be only mildly hazardous, of course.'

'It isn't. If it was there'd be no need for it to go for reprocessing. Don't they turn it into glass blocks and lock them up for a million years or something?'

'God knows. Oh, Flora, suppose there's a storm.'

Grimly Flora reached for the telephone. 'I've already thought of that.'

It was strange to watch the story permeate the news media; a small item at first, a disabled ship and the threat of bad weather. Then, like the storm clouds themselves, the story grew and expanded, through speculation about the cargo towards a nagging suspicion. For some hours it seemed that the ship was carrying chemicals, and nobody denied it. Somebody somewhere had decreed that the public were not to know everything at once.

Shalimar talked to the captain again. He was tense and cryptic. 'Surrounded by Navy boats,' he snapped. 'It's upsetting the crew.'

'Do they know?' asked Shalimar, aware that the whole world could be listening.

'No,' said the captain flatly. 'The weather's blowing up. We need a tow.'

Flora hung on the other line, talking endlessly to KORSEA. Could they get a tug, where could a tug come from? Gradually, as suspicion grew, the salvage companies drew back. They didn't want to be involved, not at any price. 'Double the offer. Treble it,' snapped Flora. But still the salvage men stood back.

Rain rattled on the castle windows, driven by a cold east wind. Flora prayed that in the south it would be fine, prayed for a calm, clear night. She turned on the television and watched the forecast, and a jovial man put computer clouds in the Channel, and made rain fall magically down the screen. Gales were on their way. The telex clattered from KORSEA, Lloyds was involved, disclaiming liability. No one wanted to be blamed.

199

At midnight they got a tug. It was a Frenchman, terse and mercenary. This one job would make his fortune, it was worth the risk. An hour later, in the dead time of night, the story finally broke.

Van and Idris were in the highest camp, if a two man tent and a rucksack of food could be dignified by such a name. They had no oxygen, although Geoff and Howard in the camp below were using it even at night. The weather was closing in. Peter and Tom Daventry were clawing their way up icy ropes, trying to get high enough to film a summit bid. The jumars slipped constantly. Through binoculars Don saw Peter slide back twenty feet, saved from death by a fortuitously tied-off rope.

The official film crew were getting excited, following people around waiting for a row or a breakdown. They wanted a death, Don realised, they were ghoulishly rubbing their hands and hoping for a corpse to be brought off the face. They even invaded the privacy of the radio calls when Idris was panting, 'Fuck this, Don. I can feel me bloody brain cells popping.'

'If you want oxygen I'll send it straight up,' said Don calmly. 'Four hours and you can have it. There's a stack with Geoff and Howard. Are you cold?'

'Freezing. Bloody freezing.'

'Make a brew. Take a pill.' They all had pills to ward off frostbite. The effect dilated all blood vessels and wasn't at all safe, but anything was better than taking off a pair of socks and with them several toes. 'You've got tomorrow and no more,' said Don. 'Have you got that, Idris? Van? If you don't make it tomorrow you come down regardless. That's an order.'

A low growl came over the radio. 'We do what we like up here,' snarled Van. He began to cough, the thick, painful spasm caused by altitude. Don felt desperately helpless. Did they know how slow they were? There came a point when lack of oxygen induced not only lethargy but a euphoric acceptance of it. He clicked on the radio again. 'For God's sake, drink,' he said. 'Best of luck. We're thinking of you.'

Afterwards he went outside and stood looking up at the dark bulk of the mountain. It was so huge that it couldn't be contemplated in its entirety. The human mind could only break it up into sections of possible achievement, this rope length, that camp, this day's struggle. A few stray wisps of cloud trailed across the moon; from the Sherpas' tent came the sound of raucous laughter. He'd go in there in a moment and talk, keep on binding the expedition together. If only he could be up on the mountain now. His breath came quickly, as

200

if he too was starving for oxygen, he felt an almost physical longing for that pain. He might never come here again. To climb at the edge was for certain kinds of people, prepared to lay down everything on the altar of achievement. The time had come when he wanted to hold some of that back. Whatever it was the mountains gave to him they never surrendered the right to take it away.

He turned back to the tents, and the unblinking eye of the camera. At least Van and Idris could suffer in privacy. The anguish Don suffered was definitely going to be public.

Nuclear protestors were refusing to allow *Rosamund* to dock anywhere on the south coast. The safest solution seemed to be for the cargo to be landed and transferred to rail, for onward transmission to the reprocessing plant, but no one wanted the huge lead cases in their harbour. It should go all the way by ship, it was decided, but the tug captain was reluctant to haul his luckless charge through the heaving Irish Sea.

'We'll return it to the port of origin,' decided Flora. 'We should never have taken it in the first place.'

But they wouldn't have it back. No one would even admit to knowing where the waste came from, and in the muddle of paper at KORSEA there seemed little chance of laying the blame at the right door.

By the middle of the next morning the news bulletins carried pictures of waves crashing over harbour walls and drenching passing cars. Someone chartered a helicopter and got film of the *Rosamund* wallowing, her escort gathered round her like royal attendants. A government minister was wheeled out to pontificate about 'gross irresponsibility', and a regional news team showed the KORSEA offices, looking glossy and uncaring. Flora dismissed the secretary and had the television set taken out of her father's room. The telephone never stopped ringing. She had a permanent crashing headache.

Some nameless government official insisted on speaking to her. 'This is to inform you that the *Rosamund* is to dock at Dover. The weather makes it imperative. And we must insist on a KORSEA representative on hand for immediate consultation.'

'Oh.' Flora felt helpless.

'Will somebody be available, Mrs Harrington?' That unctuous, and at the same time supercilious, voice. She hated it.

'I don't know.'

'Mrs Harrington, if I might emphasise the urgency of the situation. The *Rosamund* —'

201

'Yes, yes, I know! I was the one who blew the whistle on this as it happens. I'll be there. Dover you said.'

'If you'd like us to arrange a flight – '

'KORSEA can still manage an aeroplane, I believe. Goodbye.'

Shalimar was pouring herself a large gin. Flora wished desperately that she could have one too. 'You can't go anywhere. I will,' said Shalimar.

'Rubbish. You can't afford to be associated with this. I can't even ask anyone at KORSEA, they've all got friends and futures too. It's up to me.'

'You know perfectly well Mr Mitchell won't allow it.'

'Mr Mitchell can – jump in a nuclear reprocessing plant. If Don was here now, I'd kill him.'

She went upstairs and dressed in her black maternity frock. She looked gargantuan, but at almost eight months pregnant that was to be expected. Don should be home in two weeks. She felt a great desire to have him here and to hit him, hit him and hit him again. She slipped the fat *Rosamund* file into a briefcase, wrapped a purple wool cloak around herself and rang down for the car.

It was months since she had done more than walk gently round the garden. An odd excitement ran through her as she was helped heavily into the plane. She sniffed the warm scent of coffee and leather, mixed with the tang of aviation fuel before they shut the door. The pilot welcomed her personally, there was a bustle of attention. It soothed her slightly. Locked away in the castle, watching her plague ship struggle, she had begun to feel cursed herself.

The country sped by beneath her. Flora took out the file and leafed through, taking the time to read the papers carefully. They told a sorry tale. Poor *Rosamund*, ailing, sick, pushed from one port to another, her engines patched up with less and less hope. She had spent three days powerless at sea while the engineer righted first this and then that fault, finally limping into harbour and begging for a refit. But Don wouldn't have it. He had decreed that she was to be brought back with a cargo, but *Rosamund's* plight was known by now and no one wanted her. George Williams had sent an order down the line, to find her a cargo, any cargo. And someone had. Some containers, their contents ambiguously described, had appeared from nowhere.

There was no telling where they had come from, or why. Perhaps big money had been paid for disposal, and someone had taken the waste and looked for a cut price solution instead. Everything had passed through agents, several on each side, the ship and the cargo only counters on a board. Time had passed, weeks in which

Rosamund sat in harbour, forgotten. Eventually she was loaded and put to sea. Only then did George Williams see the manifest. He had quit.

Flora felt weak. It was the effect of so much exertion after so long, so great a challenge to be faced. She put the file away. They were circling ready to land at a small, private airport. The moment had come.

As she stepped from the plane a gusty wind was blowing. A car was waiting, and she wished suddenly that she was going home, back to the castle and safety. Instead they headed into Dover, and swept importantly up to the dockyard gates. Cameras crowded at the windows. She kept her face still and calm. Her stomach churned sickeningly. She wanted to cry.

At last they were through. There were placards everywhere: KORSEA KILLER, CAPITALIST PLAGUE SHIP, NO DEATH HERE. It was terrible to think that KORSEA could be involved in all this; something so sordid, so terrifying. All because Don had decided, on no more than a whim, that the ship would not be brought home in ballast.

A small delegation of dark-suited men was on the quayside to greet her. They were frighteningly calm and polite. 'We wanted you to be on hand to agree any decision we might make,' explained an official. 'Obviously if there should be an accident, then we want it absolutely certain that all procedures were agreed.'

'I don't have any technical knowledge,' said Flora in a low voice. 'I'm here simply because I couldn't ask anyone else. This isn't something you can pass down the line very easily.'

'I'm sure we understand.'

They were trying not to sympathise. She represented a company that, on the face of it, had tried to capitalise on a filthy trade. They were not even sure that her arrival wasn't some publicity gimmick, an attempt to gain hearts instead of minds. Pregnant, pretty, with a touching gravity of manner, she was quite out of place.

They marched her quickly along corridors, at a pace which made her breathless, and into the radar room. Someone tapped the screen. The central moving dot was *Rosamund*, led by her tug, and all around clustered naval vessels forming a giant escort. The scale of the operation came home to Flora for the first time. For such an exercise, the danger must be immense.

'Would it be very terrible if *Rosamund* sank?' she asked.

'Only if her cargo broke open. But, of course, it might. And that would be a disaster. The sea might be polluted for generations. It would affect wildlife, fish, and people of course. A great many people.'

'The cargo isn't leaking now, is it?'

The man shrugged. 'Difficult to tell. No one on *Rosamund* appears to have any equipment that might detect it. Yet another oversight, apparently.'

The weight of KORSEA's guilt fell heavily on Flora's shoulders. All her life she had felt pride in the KORSEA name, knowing that good men and good ships sailed under it. A lifetime of pride and achievement was lost and irrecoverable.

'I think we should go out in the pilot cutter,' said an official.

Flora nodded, not thinking. The men clustered round her, much as *Rosamund* was escorted by her ships, almost an arresting force.

It was a grey afternoon, dark clouds whipping across the horizon. The ships were visible with the naked eye, coming steadily towards harbour as other traffic stood off, waiting for the convoy to pass. This one small freighter had disrupted the entire Channel. Ferry queues stretched out into the town; dockside fire boats were testing their hoses, sending gouts of water into the air. A dozen men in white radiation suits lumbered across Flora's line of sight. Suddenly she felt very cold.

They sat her in the wheelhouse of the cutter, looking out through spattered panes of glass. 'There's *Rosamund*,' someone said. A small, rusty little ship. Huge grey containers were stacked on deck, tied down with chains. 'Is that it?' asked Flora. 'The cargo? It looks so harmless.'

'Don't you see the way she rolls? She's top heavy. Those lead containers overbalance her.'

'There ought to be another tug. No one wanted the job, of course.'

'She's nearly there now. With a bit of luck – oh, my God!'

A black snake of steel whipped across the water between *Rosamund* and her tug. The line had gone. Suddenly the radio was alive with chatter, and the voice of the Frenchman bellowing, '*Rosamund! Rosamund!* Is anyone hurt? Over.'

A pause, and then Captain Longley came on. 'One of my boys went in. We've got him back but he's hurt. Send us another line, quick. Over.'

'At once. Stand by. Over and Out.'

Rosamund was leaning broadside to the wind. The tug dug its little snub nose into the waves and tunnelled towards her, giant engines screaming. A line went across and was made fast. Flora found she had dug deep crescents into her palms with her nails.

'This is the *Rosamund, Rosamund*. Our cargo has shifted. Request permission to heave to and secure.'

'Christ!' Everyone except Flora crowded to look. She hid her face in her hands, sure that this waking nightmare would never end. There was no point in hoping for the best, the worst was bearing down like an express train. The load would be lost, the containers broken, the sea turned foul. It was all KORSEA's fault.

'*Rosamund, Rosamund,* you must continue to harbour. Can we adjust the tow to compensate?'

'Look, my men have had enough, we've someone injured here. We'll enter harbour in the morning.'

'We must insist that you continue, Captain. Your ship must not heave to, you are a hazard. You must come into your berth.'

'I suppose it's too much to ask for a chopper to take our man off? We're just the hirelings, pushed hither and yon with never so much as a by your leave − '

Flora pushed her way forward. 'Captain Longley' she said into the microphone. 'This is Flora Kincaid. Flora Harrington. How badly injured is the seaman?'

She could sense the man gathering his wits. 'He's − he's all right. Broken leg, perhaps. It might only be bruising. But I won't take the blame for all this, I'm damned if I will. We were told what to do and we did it, as we've always done for KORSEA, and here we are in the middle of what looks like the biggest naval exercise this side of Pearl Harbour − '

'I know it's not your fault,' said Flora quietly. 'Believe me, I'm sorry. KORSEA won't hold you responsible.'

'There'll be other people that will,' said the captain. 'Mark my words, someone's going to have my guts for garters.'

It was all too true. No one was going to come out of this unscathed. The grey sea heaved and rolled. Men struggled on the decks of the *Rosamund,* tying down cargo that could crush them in a second. The tug dragged her onward, the tow making an oblique angle with the bow of the ship. A navy cruiser charged past, catching the pilot cutter in its wake. Flora's stomach heaved, she had never been the best of sailors. A helicopter hovered over the *Rosamund,* the downdraught sending hats and clothes spiralling into the water. It had been chartered by newsmen, more anxious about a story than the fate of the ship, coming like scavengers to peck at the carcase of a condemned beast.

Flora moved out on deck, opening her mouth to let the cold wind scour her very soul. She felt so sad suddenly. Nobody had meant this to happen. It was because Don wasn't interested, because Williams didn't care, because she didn't understand − and KORSEA, her father's triumph, was finished. If the claims didn't finish them the publicity would. It was the end, she was sure of it. The end.

When the *Rosamund* berthed she was boarded by a specialist team. The KORSEA crew came off, including Captain Longley. Flora was waiting for him in a shabby seaman's lounge.

'Mrs Harrington.' A stout, greying man. She remembered seeing him now and then. He had been with them a long time.

'Captain Longley. Did they ask you to come off?'

'Wouldn't let me stay on. I queried the cargo, you know. Was told to accept it. Can't be that dangerous, wrapped up like that, on the deck for all to see.'

'I think it's deadly,' said Flora. 'I only hope no one's come to any harm. There's been a fiddle somewhere, someone promising to dispose of waste safely and then looking for a cheap dump. They'll take it off tomorrow, when the weather clears.'

'Yes. Yes.' The captain looked tired and worried. 'Better telephone the wife,' he muttered. 'She'll be worried. Been worried awhile, about poor old *Rosamund*. Should have had a refit months ago, poor old girl. They'll scrap her now, I daresay. Poor old girl.'

He wandered off, a good seaman puzzled and distressed. The sadness came again, like a wave of regret. Flora turned and saw a suited official bustling towards her. 'Do you want me to stay until tomorrow?' she asked wearily. 'I would very much like to go home.'

'We do need someone on hand. I'm sure we can arrange a hotel room – something suitable –' He looked disdainfully about him, and Flora sighed. She would have to get used to being despised.

It was a long, cold night. She was restless and when she rang down for a hot water bottle or some extra bedclothes there was no one there. She put her cloak on the bed and lay in the shabby, dockside hotel doing penance for KORSEA's sins. In the morning, when she came wearily down to breakfast, she found the driver of her limousine making earnest enquiries at the desk.

'Mrs Harrington! I've been to all the hotels.'

She smiled grimly. 'This is the one they thought suitable for me. I'm sorry, I should have contacted you. I hope to be leaving this afternoon.'

'I've a message for you, ma'am. Mr Kincaid's flying down.'

'Mr Kincaid?'

'Yes.'

'You mean, my father?'

'I imagine it must be.'

'He can't! He mustn't!'

She ran to the desk and seized the telephone, without so much as a by your leave. The receptionist said 'Do you mind?' huffily, but Flora took no notice, dialling with determined speed. 'Forbes? Forbes, it's me. What's happening?'

She listened for a long minute. 'I see. Yes, I know. Don't worry, I'm sure you all did your best.'

Turning, she met the curious eye of the driver. She shrugged. 'Would you believe it? My father hasn't been out of the house in months. And he's flying down here.'

'Might do him good. The outing.'

'I don't think this affair is doing any of us good.'

She was at the airport to meet him. They lifted him off in a wheelchair, and after him came Shalimar, her lovely face distraught. She ran across the grass. 'Flora! I couldn't stop him. His pills wore off and he demanded that the nurse tell him about the ship. The silly woman did.'

'It's all right. He had the manifest, he knew.'

She walked to meet the wheelchair. Kincaid was bundled up in a tartan rug, with only his head exposed to the wind. Strands of reddish hair blew frivolously over his forehead. 'You should be at home, Flora,' he rapped.

'And so should you. There's nothing you can do, Dad.'

'I can speak to the press. And I will.'

They lifted him bodily from the chair into the car, and then struggled to fit the chair into the boot. As Flora settled beside him, he said, 'One hell of a mess. One hell of a shocking mess.'

'The ship's berthed at any rate. But the claims – the expense –'

'You're bound to be insured,' said Shalimar.

Kincaid almost growled. 'There's no insurance in the world would pay up over this. He's wrecked my company, Flora. That man of yours has wrecked it.'

Shalimar said, 'Don wasn't all to blame.'

'Then I don't know who was.' Flora reached out and took her father's hand.

The news conference was held at the dockyard. Officials tried to prevent it, and left alone Flora would have given in. Kincaid was made of sterner stuff. He snarled, 'Since we're paying, you can let us have our say. Or do you want to be accused of suppression of the truth?'

'There'll be time for news conferences later, Mr Kincaid.'

'Later doesn't concern me. Let them in. Now! Quick!'

He was used to getting his own way. He sat muffled in his rugs while cameramen and reporters jostled to get close. Flora perched on a chair at his side, feeling a strong sense of unreality. Shalimar, like a glamorous stork, lounged spikily by the window.

'You'll want to know how this happened,' said Kincaid. 'You're not the only ones. I built up KORSEA over forty years, and never in all that time have we done anything underhand or dishonest.'

That wasn't true, thought Flora. They had never been discovered doing anything underhand or dishonest. But they were no less guilty than any big company. Their hands were clean enough.

'When I had my accident,' went on Kincaid, 'I gave the control of the company into the hands of my daughter's husband, Donald Harrington. It was a mistake. A great mistake. He wasn't interested. He dabbled at first but in the end he went back to his climbing. He is on Everest at this moment, quite unaware of all this drama. I wish that I could be just as unaware.' A sympathetic chuckle ran through the audience. Kincaid had great charm. 'A manager was appointed, with limited responsibility. It wasn't satisfactory. The KORSEA staff struggled to cope, because that's the people they are, loyal, dedicated. But despite all their efforts everything became disordered. No one knew who was in charge. And because of this – this weakness – KORSEA was taken advantage of. Some unscrupulous foreigner dumped this unlabelled cargo on us with no regard for the potential hazard, and if that is in general great it is considerably greater for the KORSEA crew. They will be compensated for their ordeal.'

He looked round grimly. 'I know many people wish to blame KORSEA. They are right to do so. We must bear our part in this sorry saga. But let us look for the true culprits. Those who seek to profit from this – dirty trade.' He stopped, breathless, and Flora used her handkerchief to wipe his mouth.

One of the newsmen waved a hand. 'What was your first reaction when the true nature of the cargo was discovered? Weren't you tempted to dump it?'

Flora thought of the note her father had written. God forbid that anyone should see it. Had this man seen it? They might have been betrayed. Kincaid glared at his questioner. 'There was never any question of anything except complete honesty.'

'Has this ruined your company?'

'I hope not. I shall do everything in my power to save it.'

'You're a sick man. Will you ask your son-in-law to come home?'

'There seems to be very little benefit to the company when he is here,' said Kincaid thinly. 'But I suppose he should come home. My daughter seemed quite fond of him at one time.'

208

The conference broke up. A few photographers hung back for shots of Shalimar, but for once she put up her hands and wouldn't co-operate.

'You shouldn't have come,' said Flora in a low voice.

'I had to. He was amazing, wasn't he?'

'Tremendous.'

They watched Kincaid being pushed to a window overlooking *Rosamund's* berth. Cranes were being wheeled up, ready to unload. Those same men who yesterday had been so stiff with Flora were today being deferential to Kincaid.

'I'm not cut out for this,' she said grimly. 'I don't have what it takes to kick my way to the top.'

'Don has,' said Shalimar. 'I don't care what your father says, he has.'

They waited all day, watching the containers come slowly off the ship. A Greenpeace demonstration was being held outside the dock-yard gates, and the chants and singing rolled on like some impromptu church service. Kincaid demanded to see railway officials, and grilled them about safety. Instead of a mere observer, guilty and therefore reviled, he had somehow assumed the role of a trusted statesman. When all was done, the last container trundled off the dock, he made a television statement. 'I have been held responsible, and rightly so,' he said. 'But I will not rest until reparation has been made. KORSEA has never shirked its responsibilities.'

Exhausted, in the car on the way back to the plane, he murmured, 'Flora, for God's sake get hold of someone at the office and make sure KORSEA doesn't pay out a single penny. We'll get the lawyers on to it.'

Chapter Nineteen

At home, in the castle, Flora fell into bed. Sleep seemed a luxury, a delicious benison. Marie brought a bowl of soup and some fresh bread, but she ate nothing; it was enough to lie in the warm peace and close her eyes.

When she woke it was still dark. The curtains were open and the moon was shining on the river, a silvery, ghostly light. Deer walked in the shadows, picking delicately at shrubs and other titbits, pushing the gardeners' defences aside with a firm hoof. Flora felt wet. When she touched herself she closed her eyes and wouldn't look, because if it was blood again, blood — she had an urgent desire to go to the bathroom.

Her hand was wet, but not with blood. Fluid leaked from her in spurts and trickles, she didn't know what to do. There was no pain, no discomfort, just this strange leaking, a full five weeks too early. Holding herself tightly in, she crossed to the 'phone.

The day had been so long, a hundred years could take no longer. Howard and Geoff Barclay were clearly visible through binoculars, making their steady way to the summit. They would make it, there seemed no doubt. But Van and Idris — high on the face Peter had his camera trained on something that only he could see. It must be them.

At base the wind had been blowing hard all day, although in a typical Everest quirk it seemed calm on the face. They had been there forever. The filth of other expeditions lay everywhere; the piles of oxygen bottles, the oil drums, the heap of tins that someone had ineffectually tried to bury in iron-hard ground. It was the antithesis of Don's philosophy, which was to leave each mountain exactly as before, without a nail, a nut or a piton despoiling it. This shambles was all that he hated in climbing. It was as if men came and robbed the mountains, taking away mystery, and beauty, and peace. No wonder the mountains fought back.

He looked up again to the cold, white face. Geoff was moving well, appreciably faster than Howard, and if it came to it he would go on alone. That was the difference between them, because Howard would turn back rather than abandon his partner. There was no real team in climbing, only the illusion of one. In the end you must care for nothing except yourself.

He thought of Flora suddenly. Whatever happened he was leaving Everest in two days' time. He'd walk to Namche Bazar and get a plane. One of the quirks of this mountain and its thin air was that you couldn't fly in but you could fly out. A body took time to adjust from high oxygen to low, but the reverse could be done in an instant. He never knew if post altitude euphoria was the result of more gas, or a return to baths and decent food. He hadn't heard from Flora in weeks. Anxiety settled in him like a stone.

The day crawled on, edging into night. Geoff and Howard were no longer visible; if they made it then they would have to bivouac. Don grinned wryly at the thought of a night spent rubbing Geoff's sour feet. The others would have to get down, there was no surviving another night without air and warmth. If they died, as they might, he would be blamed for letting them take the risk. Perhaps he should have stopped them. Perhaps, in fact, he should have done the stupid thing and gone himself.

It was almost dark. The radio crackled and Don's heart leaped, but it was only Peter. 'Tom's snowblind,' he said. 'Took off his goggles to film. He's in hellish pain. We're coming down first thing.' In the background they could hear an odd, harsh sobbing. Snowblindness was hell, there was no pain like it, and even tears caused anguish.

'Try putting snow on them,' said Don. 'It sometimes helps. Any news?'

'You saw Geoff and Howard. The others — I don't know. They were close, very close, but they were going so slowly —'

'Yes. OK, come down early, we'll have the doctor standing by.'

He sat by the radio, turning a cup of something nameless in his hands. Minutes ticked by. If they didn't come down they were dead. What was the use of getting there if you never got back? Another statistic, another pointless end. This mountain could be built again with the bones of the men who had died here.

'Don? Don. It's us.' Van's voice. A roar went round the tent, there were people everywhere, people that Don hadn't even noticed. For

211

hours past he had thought himself alone. He took up the microphone. 'So, you old bastard. You made it.'

'So we did. Idris has frost nip on his toes.'

'Get down first thing and we'll see to it. What's the view like from up there?'

'I do not remember.' Van's chuckle came clearly into the tent. 'It seemed much like any other mountain. And I was quite bothered about myself, there seemed to be two of me. And four at least of Idris.'

'The place was bloody crowded,' agreed Idris from the background. 'Odd, really, boyo.'

Mr Mitchell had sent an ambulance. They had rumbled through the park in the dawn light, sending birds clattering up from night time roosts in the trees. But the hospital was in full morning bustle, with nurses changing shifts and trolleys moving importantly around. Flora felt disorientated; nothing was happening, she had no pain or discomfort. Even the dripping had stopped.

They put her in bed in a private room. She felt very lonely. Then Mr Mitchell came in, and she got high on his confidence and charm, it seemed foolish to waste her time worrying. The nurse brought them coffee and they drank it together, having a convivial chat. 'We'll have you in theatre this afternoon, then,' he remarked.

'What for?'

'Your section. By tonight we should see two bouncing babies.'

For a moment Flora was speechless. 'You never said anything about an operation!' she accused.

'It's often best with twins, Flora.'

'But — why can't I have them normally? I'd much prefer it.'

'My dear, they don't want to come. And your waters have broken, which concerns me. I'd like those babies out.'

'Couldn't I try and have them — please?'

The door opened and Shalimar came in. Visitors were always a problem in private rooms, they wandered in and out endlessly. Mr Mitchell drew in his breath in unaccustomed irritation, and Shalimar said, 'Oh, I am sorry. Shall I come back, Flora?'

'No,' said Flora. 'Mr Mitchell won't let me have my babies properly. He wants to operate.'

'They do that in the States all the time,' remarked Shalimar. 'That way the doctor feels he's covered.'

'I was advising on purely medical criteria,' said Mitchell, his exasperation poorly veiled. Flora wondered if he had been up too late the night before. Baby doctors with young wives couldn't get

212

much sleep. 'A trial of labour can be exhausting for the mother, and with twins – '

'Those operations make horrible scars,' said Shalimar. 'They leave your stomach a funny shape too. You have to do sit-ups every day of your life.'

Flora grimaced. 'That sounds more tiring than labour!'

'You think so?' Mitchell got up. 'We'll put you on a drip and see what happens. If it doesn't go perfectly you're in theatre. And no complaints.'

'I don't complain.'

'No. So you don't.' He stopped at the door. 'Just remember, my dear – we want two healthy babies. Let's keep our eye on the ball.'

When he went out Shalimar flopped down into a chair. 'He's worried you're going to want to give birth upside down in a bath of asses' milk.'

'I might. But I read so much I got confused. What with bonding and singing and music and what you shouldn't eat – I don't think I'm going to be much of a mother.'

'I'll be a wonderful auntie,' said Shalimar. 'Tolerant, intelligent, experienced – I'll send beautiful presents. But you can't send presents to rich kids. They've got everything.'

Flora made a face. 'Who's rich? I shouldn't be at all surprised if Marie has to start turning the sheets sides to middle before too long.'

'Pessimist. Your Dad's back in charge.'

'If you can call it that.'

Flora lay back on the pillows, looking up at the bare hospital ceiling. She had known all along that Don wouldn't be here. He was up on his mountain, doing what he wished, with the outside world locked out and unimportant.

Two nurses came in and started setting up a drip. Flora felt detached, and watched them with objective interest. One was West Indian, cheerful and quick, the other a quiet-spoken Scot.

'We felt sure you gonna be a Caesar,' said the West Indian. 'We'll get these babies out the right door. No point in knocking down walls when the door just needs opening, is there?'

'Ring the bell if you're worried,' said the other nurse. 'We're just down the hall. Got something to read, have you?'

They left, and the girls looked at one another. 'We could watch television,' said Shalimar. 'But it's all about the *Rosamund*.'

'Perhaps we'd better see.'

They watched the news glumly. 'Some news just in,' announced

213

the newscaster. 'The climbing and services Everest expedition led by Donald Harrington has today radioed news of their success. Two climbers ascended with oxygen and two without. It's the first time the mountain has been climbed by this route without oxygen, and the team have established a new speed record. It's believed Mr Harrington, who is linked to the KORSEA nuclear waste scandal, is flying home.'

'Turn it off,' snapped Flora. 'Just turn it off!' She dashed away tears.

'Don't you think you should be pleased?' said Shalimar.

Flora shook her head. 'When he wants something he gets it,' she muttered. 'And if he doesn't want it he won't lift a finger. If all that effort, all that energy, had gone into KORSEA, we wouldn't now have a name as black as ditchwater.'

Shalimar said nothing. There was nothing to say.

The weather was bad on the walk out. Rain brought down bridges and sent rivers into spate. They were delayed and Don wrote up his log. 'There's a certain smell about a climbing tent. It's a stink of feet and bodies and Bovril, and I'm going to miss it like crazy if I give up. Perhaps it's a very male thing, a sort of primitive desire to be in a band like this, but when it's going well there's nothing better. This has been a good trip. Even festering like this the blokes are in control.'

Everyone wanted to get home. Geoff Barclay was telling Howard of climbs they could tackle together.

'You can't go with the pillock!' said Peter incredulously. 'He'd eat his own grandmother if he thought it would help him get to the top.'

Howard grunted. He'd been a backroom boy all his life, doing the food, doing the carrying, making the weight. With Geoff he would go places. If grandmothers were on the menu he might consider eating a piece himself.

They moved on, into the cold and sterile valleys of the high Himalayas. Idris was having trouble with his feet and they rested for a night in a village, the wind whipping across bare, winter fields and flaying exposed flesh. It seemed colder here than on Everest. The climbers sat in a smelly hut, muffled in their clothes, watched by silent, large-eyed children. Fleas hopped visibly on a blanket by the fire, and the tea tasted of woodsmoke and gall. Don thought of home, always of home. He couldn't wait to be home.

Lilian arrived in a rush. 'The call took me quite by surprise. Oh, Flora, you do look white, shall I ask them for a cup of tea?' She shook her head.

Shalimar uncomfortably gave up her seat. In her mother's presence Flora seemed to retreat into herself a little, showing less spark, less drive. They were the things Lilian most disliked in her, of course, the things that reminded her of Kincaid. It could be the reason Flora had so determinedly rejected the business. To be involved in that would seem to Lilian to be a terrible betrayal.

The pains were beginning. Gradually Flora's conversation faltered and died. Lilian settled down by the bed and opened a catalogue of baby products, lingering over the pictures of charming infants. It was meant to encourage, but Flora was beyond believing in babies at all.

Shalimar said, 'I'll ring for the nurse, Flora.'

'There's no need,' said Lilian. 'Have you heard from Don, Flora? I really do think he should keep more closely in touch. You shouldn't have to be on your own at a time like this.'

'We're both here,' said Shalimar. 'I will ring, Flora.'

Flora nodded, mutely. She felt frayed and weary. The past days were taking their toll.

The nurse came and gave her something and things seemed easier. Shalimar and Lilian kept sparring, and when Mr Mitchell came he was gloomy. 'If you don't make some progress soon we're going to operate.'

'I really think you should,' said Lilian. 'Better sooner rather than later.'

'She doesn't want an operation,' said Shalimar. 'Do you, Flora?'

She shook her head. 'I'd be ill for days.'

'You're not going to be dancing the hornpipe however it goes,' said Lilian, a trifle desperately. 'I think I'll go for a little walk. You'll be all right, won't you, darling?'

When she had gone Flora grimaced at Mr Mitchell. 'Perhaps I should have the operation.'

'You'll get it if I think fit, my girl. Another hour and we'll see. Look at your glamorous friend and think how thin you're going to be when all this is done.'

Left alone, with only Shalimar, Flora closed her eyes. The only sound was the blip of the foetal monitor, the only sensation that of a gradually gathering wave. This wave came on and on, building into the next and the next again, higher and higher. Shalimar put her finger on the bell and kept it there.

Mr Mitchell appeared within seconds, summoning cohorts to whisk Flora to the delivery suite.

'Get the anaesthetist here,' he said, striding determinedly in front

215

of the trolley. 'It's going to be forceps. Mrs Kincaid, Shalimar, if you'd like to go to the waiting room, nurse will bring you some tea.' The drip was gone, and Flora felt less panicked. But there were strangers everywhere. Even Mr Mitchell was hidden behind a green surgical mask. She didn't know it was him until he spoke.

'I know it seems terrible,' he said gently. 'It gets better, I promise. Not long now.'

She would have given anything to escape. They laid her flat on a hard table, which made the pains worse, and the anaesthetist was taking his time fiddling with a mask. She thought suddenly of Don, striding comfortably down a trail, wondering when he would eat supper. How could he do this to her? How could he leave her like this? She hadn't even wanted a baby in the first place!

The mask was coming down on her. 'I wish my husband was here,' she said shrilly.

'He'll have a surprise when he gets home,' said Mr Mitchell.

She took a long breath of plastic-tasting air. Thank God, she could go to sleep.

When she woke it was night. She was in a long room, with a light on the table at the end. Everything was very peaceful, and now and then a soft rain rattled at the window. The past hours, dreamlike, haunted her consciousness. What had happened? Had it happened? Where was she?

She tried to move, and it hurt. There was a tube between her legs, desperately uncomfortable. Everything felt sore and ripped, even her hand hurt where the drip had been. There was no sound of babies. She felt a terrible foreboding.

'Nurse! Nurse!'

At once someone got up and came to her. 'Hello, Mrs Harrington. How do you feel?'

'My babies?'

'They're in the nursery. One little boy and one little girl. The little girl's had rather a rough ride, she came out feet first, so Mr Mitchell's sent them both up to the special care nursery.'

'Are they going to be all right?'

'They certainly are. You can see them tomorrow.'

Flora lay back, exhausted. A while later the nurse brought her some tea but she couldn't drink. It was almost like being in shock after some terrible accident. Bits of the scene floated constantly across her mind, snatches of things people had said. She tried to feel her stomach, to see if it had gone flat, but the effort of moving her arm seemed impossible. She couldn't feel worse if she'd been run

216

over by a steamroller, she thought. Why hadn't anyone told her it would be like this?

Sleep dragged her inexorably back, claiming her like a victim. Her last thought was of Don, finding the energy, the strength, to climb Everest. He didn't know what hard work meant.

Excitement filled the room. The nurse lifted a bundle and gave it to Flora to hold. There was a shock of bright red hair above a face as old as the hills. Flora touched his hand and felt soft skin, which amazed her. This doll was real.

Before she had gathered her thoughts she was handed the other child. 'This is the girl,' said Mr Mitchell. 'She's much the lighter. The other chap's a bruiser if ever I saw one.'

The girl had dark hair, laid delicately against her skin. Her eyes were Don's, already a piercing blue-grey. A forceps bruise marked the skin of her forehead.

Flora looked from one to the other. 'They don't look at all like brother and sister.'

'Odd that, isn't it? But twins need be no more alike than other brothers and sisters. One more night on the ward upstairs and you can have them with you.'

The nurse began to bustle around the room. 'I think Mother had better try feeding now,' she said pointedly. 'We'd like some privacy please, Mr Mitchell.'

Flora laughed. 'They don't allow you anywhere near once they've been born.'

'Not when they're healthy, no. We had quite a struggle in the end. Are you pleased?'

She nodded. Her heart was hot and heavy within her. It was a strange feeling, almost like sadness, overwhelming in its intensity. If this was love, she thought, then she had never felt it before.

'Hey, Don! Look at this! You're a dad.'

Don stared at the hastily scrawled message, brought out from Kathmandu.

'Have to inform you that Flora has given birth to boy and girl twins. To be called Alexander and Anabel. Kincaid.'

He looked up in bewilderment. 'She can't have had them yet.'

'Time, tide and birth pangs wait for no man, mate. Well done. Congratulations.'

He felt cheated. They had packed up in double-quick time, marched in rainstorms and snow flurries — for this. She had managed without him. He had left life frozen in limbo for his

217

return and unaccountably it had revived and gone on. He couldn't imagine it. Flora was as he had left her, pregnant and alone. They should have encountered these new people together; she should have waited, not rushed ahead on her own.

The hut was draughty and unpleasant. Suddenly he hated it, hated Nepal, everything and everybody. That morning he had heard one of the soldiers say, 'Hell of a bloke, Harrington; twice the man I thought he was.' He dared not think what Flora thought of him.

Chapter Twenty

It was thought best for Flora to remain in hospital for a week. She didn't mind. The outside world, brought to her through her television screen, seemed dangerous and full of threat. The hospital sheltered her, and her babies, when she felt there was nothing else to stand between her and chaos.

Kincaid ran KORSEA with an erratic hand. The sharks were after KORSEA blood, tearing at each and every unprotected limb. The firm reeled under the onslaught of insurance claims, suits for damages and the multiplicity of lesser mistakes in spheres that had nothing to do with the *Rosamund*. It was the inevitable result of the thrashings of a headless monster.

One afternoon Lilian came in, pale and obviously shaken. She cooed distractedly at the babies, nibbled at Flora's grapes and gazed blankly at Shalimar when she too came to visit.

'What's the matter?' asked Flora, filled with a sense of nameless foreboding. Anything could occur and she wouldn't be surprised. 'Has something happened?'

Lilian sighed. 'I don't know. I always thought I hated KORSEA. I do hate it. But, Flora, if it went down — I had a writ served on me today. Apparently your father's never removed my name from the list of directors. And as I came out two more men chased the car, with more writs I suppose. It's killing your father. I called to see him and he looks — ghastly. He's on oxygen, it's all they can do.'

'It's only some days,' said Shalimar quickly. 'Honestly, he's not at death's door. But obviously it's a strain. There's going to be a government enquiry.'

'I could kill Don,' said Lilian hysterically. 'How could he leave everything in this mess? How can he justify it?'

'He doesn't bother,' said Flora.

She got out of bed and went to pick up Alex, who was starting to

219

bleat and wave his fists. Annie, also awake, lay staring at her mother, her wide eyes struggling to focus. Flora gathered her up too, and took her burden back to bed. She wrapped her arms around them both, keeping them safe near her heart.

'Malcolm's arranged a giant coming home party for you,' said Shalimar.

'I thought he was on oxygen?'

'He is. But he still finds the breath to celebrate the production of a male Kincaid. At last.'

'Yes.'

Flora stared down at the tiny, red-haired boy. He seemed all Kincaid, barely Harrington at all — whereas long-limbed Annie was her father's daughter in everything but the colour of her hair. Where that thatch of black had come from was anyone's guess. Already she seemed aware of subtle differences in the attention she received, the perfunctory admiration that was so soon turned on Alex, the big, red boy. Everyone was guilty, Lilian, Shalimar, even Mr Mitchell — 'My, but this chap's his grandfather's spitting image and no mistake. What a bruiser!' Alex bicycled his tough red legs and glared out at them impatiently.

She went home on a cold, windy morning, feeling strange in outdoor clothes once again, the babies muffled in shawls and blankets. When the castle came into view her throat closed on tears; all her emotions were dangerously near the surface, she could swing from joy to sorrow in the blink of a baby's eye. The whole staff was lined up before the door, waiting for her, and on a banner held high over the coat of arms, she read 'Welcome to the New Young Laird.'

'Did my father have that put there?' She nodded at the banner.

'He did indeed, Miss Flora. And it's a great day for us all, to have you and the young boy home.' Marie beamed and reached to hold a baby, but Flora moved aside.

'I've had two babies, not just one. I think it a little odd that you shouldn't find it in you to welcome them both home.'

She stormed into the house, alight with anger. That she should be forced to defend one child against the other, when they were barely a week old — her stomach was heavy, full of churning misgivings. Everything was as bad, worse, than she had feared.

Forbes was holding a silver tray, with a letter in Don's handwriting. 'Not now, Forbes,' she said distantly. 'I'll go and see my father.'

'Let me take one of the infants,' said Shalimar. 'I can't get enough of them. I could eat them both up, every last morsel.'

Flora handed her Alex. Together the girls went upstairs, their footsteps quiet on the carpets. It seemed immensely strange to think that when last she was there she had known nothing of these two children, and now she knew nothing but them. Flora felt oddly disorientated.

Kincaid was sitting up, his hair brushed, the oxygen mask hanging loosely round his neck.

'Hello, Dad. Look.' Flora walked to the bed, holding out Annie. 'This is Anabel.'

'Let me look at the boy. Shalimar, do you have him? My God, he's a fine one. I'll wager he'll grow up strong as an ox.'

'Don't you think Annie's lovely too?' Flora offered her girl, her second-best child. Kincaid took no notice. He put out his finger for Alex to grasp, and chuckled to himself when the boy clutched at it.

'Annie's got thick black hair,' said Shalimar, watching Flora's appalled expression.

As if she hadn't spoken Kincaid said, 'I've set up a trust for him, of course. God knows what's going to happen, he needs his money assured, there was no time to waste. Bad time to take it out, but his father could have lost the lot by the time he's eighteen, and I'll not have him struggling, not as I struggled. I only wish I could be around to guide him. That's what he'll need, you see. The guiding hand. What would I have done if only I'd had that?'

He looked up, bright-eyed, at the girls. Flora's face was flushed dark red. 'Go and rest, Flora, do,' he said. 'I'll be down for dinner, and what if it does kill me? I'll celebrate this chap's arrival, and I'll do it in style. Even the ghillies can drink a dram tonight. And when that damned husband of yours comes back he can say what he likes, we'll have welcomed a Kincaid!'

But Flora was gone. She cradled Annie to her and ran up the stairs, along the corridors, to her room. Two cradles were there, each decked out in a welter of white frills, but on one there was a tiny pink bow and on the other a giant blue rosette. Flora put Annie carefully in her crib and then ripped both symbols off, tearing them up with vicious fingers.

Shalimar came in behind her, and gently laid Alex down. 'You can't change anything, Flora. It's just the way he is.'

'And this is the way I am! Angry. Bloody angry.'

'Who with?'

'Dad. Don. Everyone. If Alex turned out as selfish and stupid as them I should be ashamed. Really ashamed. All they think of is what they want, what they need, there's never a thought for anyone except themselves. They ruin everything, and then look for more people like themselves, who can go on ruining things. I won't have it. I won't have any part of it!'

Shalimar sat on the bed, curling her long legs up underneath her. She was wearing a black catsuit, clinging to every contour of her lean body. Next to her Flora felt fat and ugly. Her breasts ached with milk. Suddenly she wished that Shalimar would go, that everyone would go, and leave her alone. Then she would love her babies, love them equally, without the need to compensate for the unequal loving of others. It would be wonderful to be quite alone.

Kincaid was at dinner that night, presiding in the hall over a feast to which servants, tenants, friends and neighbours were all invited. Long tables stretched the length of the room, covered in white cloths and an ancient pewter service that Kincaid kept for just such occasions. The stags' heads on the walls were draped in spruce and the great candle sconces were ablaze with light. To Flora it seemed macabre, fiddling while Rome burned. Her babies were born into more trouble than she had ever known, and yet she was supposed to laugh and celebrate, and look not at all into the abyss of her future.

'If only Don was here,' said Shalimar.

Flora turned her head. 'He could be. If he wanted. He doesn't think we're important enough, you see.'

Shalimar couldn't contradict her. Perhaps he could have come home. She felt uncomfortable. It was hard to talk to Flora these days, she was walling herself up behind silence.

One of the tenants, a stocky young farmer, came and asked Shalimar to dance. She accepted, stepping out on spiky heels, towering over his swinging kilt. 'I'm sorry I'm such a giant,' she apologised.

'You're a wee bit taller than me,' he agreed. 'But I'm not a man to quibble about trifles. Keep light on your feet, I'm no such a good dancer.'

They cavorted together, the farmer doing his own brand of waltz and Shalimar hopping bravely in front of him.

Flora watched and some part of her was amused. But her mind could not cope with everything, there seemed no area of her life that was settled and secure. Conflict, quarrelling, they seeped into every corner, the very things she most hated.

'Take heed, Flora,' said Kincaid, slumped in his chair. Flora jumped. She had thought him asleep. 'This may be the last time you see a sight like this.'

She pulled herself together. 'Are we going to go under?' she asked.

'Damned if I know. I've done all I can to protect the boy. When he's older, when he can understand, you must tell him. I didn't let him down.'

The dancing changed to a wild reel, and Shalimar shrieked and teetered on her high heels, flung to the end of her brawny farmer's arm. Trays of whisky arrived at each table, but as a concession to modern celebration there was also champagne. Corks popped like a fusillade of gunfire and Marie, that pillar of respectability, sank back against the chauffeur in a fit of drunken giggles. Forbes reached for her thigh-high skirt and pulled it back over her suspenders. 'You'll pull yourself together, Marie!' he said sternly, and she collapsed with laughter again. Flora took herself off to bed.

That night, feeding the babies in the early hours of the morning, she felt a fugitive peace. No one knew that she was awake. For this brief time she could do as she wished, and no one would know. She reached out for the letter Forbes had placed coaxingly next to the bed and opened it awkwardly, anchored as she was by the sucking mouths of children. Sitting cross-legged, the babies balanced on her thighs, she hunched over them and read what Don had to say:

My Darling Flora,

I was stunned to hear that the twins had arrived. Naturally I'm coming home as soon as I can. I should arrive on the 23rd, it's the soonest we can get everything sorted. I'm longing to see you and the twins. I haven't heard from you so I imagine you're upset, but believe me, we can sort out everything when I get home. I love you.

Yours ever,

Don

Her hand closed on the letter, crushing it to a hard ball of paper. What could be sorted out? KORSEA was in extremis, no magic wand could set that right in a moment; her father was intent on slighting one child and worshipping the other, what wonderful solution did Don have to that dilemma? And for Flora herself – she felt a charge of anger that was like lightning. She wanted to hit back at him, at them all, for making decisions and assumptions about her and her life with no real thought for anything she might truly wish for herself. She did not shout, she did not rage, and the result was that no one listened. The least she could do for her own daughter was spare her that same long training in humility.

She packed as the babies slept, two suitcases crammed with

223

essentials. Shalimar, in the next room, stirred in her sleep. She was due to leave for America in a day or so. Flora scrawled a note:

Dearest S,

I've got to go. Please try and explain to my father. I need to be by myself with the twins, and I don't want to be here when Don gets back. I know I'm letting everyone down but I simply can't go on like this. I'm sorry not to say goodbye, but it's impossible to talk. When I'm settled, I'll write and tell you everything.

All love,

F

She opened the door and heaved the suitcases downstairs, one at a time. They bumped on every step, but the household was lost in alcohol induced slumber and no one woke. Flora slipped out of the side door and crept round to the garage, noticing a couple of empty bottles gracing the flowerbed. Everyone had certainly made the most of last night, as if it was the last celebration ever to be at Castle Kincaid. An era was ending.

She took the Land Rover, capacious, solid and reliable. Its diesel engine chugged noisily in the early morning air, but no one appeared from the chauffeur's flat, nor yet from the house. Flora loaded her suitcases and then the twins, each in a carrycot, and since still no one was awake she added a coat and boots, because the cases were mostly crammed with baby things. Neither child was awake. She looked down at the crescent eyelashes, one pair red as her own hair, the other black as night. They would remember nothing of this. She started the car and drove quickly away from the castle.

Her mother stood shading her eyes as the Land Rover bumped down the track towards her. She had a goat in her other hand, a tall white nanny with a pendulous udder. Both the goat and Lilian stood in silent accusation as Flora got out.

'Hello, Mother.'

'I don't think I want to know why you're here.'

Flora put her hands behind her back. 'I couldn't stay. Dad was impossible, doting on Alex and taking no notice of Annie at all. And he threw a huge party, and I hated it. And Don's coming home.'

'There is no good reason in any of that for running away. Your father needs you, he's in terrible trouble. And you're married. You haven't tried to make it work.'

'You can't try on your own! It takes two to be married, and only

224

one of us ever was. And I can't be responsible for Dad any more. I've got my own children to worry about, and I won't have their lives ruined by people wanting things and needing things that you shouldn't want from children! I want them to be free of all that. I don't want them to be like me.'

There was a long silence. Finally Lilian said, 'What an indictment. You're right, of course. I left you to do what I couldn't any longer.'

'I didn't mean it,' said Flora tearfully. 'I was a happy child, very happy. But I want something different for these.'

Lilian went to put the goat in the paddock. It didn't run off but stood at the gate watching them with shocked yellow eyes. Lilian rubbed her hands down her skirt. 'Do you want to live here, then?'

Flora shook her head. 'I want the key for Eryn Cottage.'

'Good God! There is no way you could manage there!'

'You manage here. It's no worse than this.'

'It is the bleakest, wildest place on God's earth.'

They went into the house and Lilian made tea. When Flora took the mug she saw that her hands were shaking. She hoped her mother hadn't seen. Lilian said, 'You'd better stay here. Or better still go back. When Don comes home he's going to be furious.'

'I think he'll be relieved,' said Flora. 'He's found me a terrible shackle. And he doesn't really want children. He thought he ought to oblige Dad, I think. The reality is something else again, he admitted as much.'

'There! I knew you should never have married him!' Lilian sat down, shaken and upset. It was only at times like these that you realised how old she was, that age was sapping her resilience. 'I will go to the cottage,' said Flora. 'After all, I can always come back.'

Eryn Cottage was all the dowry Lilian had ever had. Set on a promontory on a wild and rocky coast, she had spent endless family holidays there as a child, too often huddled round a smoking fire as storms blasted the windows. Flora had been there twice, with her mother after the separation, but the house depressed Lilian, speaking as it did of long ago hopes and long dead friends. Kincaid had never seen it. As far as he was concerned Lilian had nothing that he had not given her, and what she might have had was of no account. He wanted her to be entirely his creation.

There were no other houses on the narrow coastal track. The nearest dwelling was a mile away in the next cove, best reached by small boat. Eryn Cottage had its own jetty, stout oak beams set out into the water, green with age and seaweed. The cottage itself, small and hunched, wore its roof like a hat pulled well down against the weather. There were three rooms, two upstairs and one down, and a long low byre at the side, stacked high with ancient peat.

The door unlocked with difficulty. Housemartins had nested against it that summer and their mud nests jammed the hinges. Flora shoved hard and was showered with brown crumbs and the smell of old feathers. Shaking the bits from her hair she took in the rusting range, the dusty table, dresser and chairs. Everything was cobwebbed. There were plates on the dresser but the pattern was obscured by dust. Vague memories came back, of a pack of cards in a drawer, a patchwork quilt on the bed upstairs. She wandered about, touching things.

The babies were crying. She went out to the Land Rover and fetched them, and sat on the floor in the open doorway to feed. The ocean confronted her, a fugitive sun gleaming on rolling breakers, churning into washing machine suds on the rocks. Shags flew calling, and gulls, and small waders picked their prim way along the shoreline. There was a smell of salt and rotten seaweed, and suddenly a sheep rounded the end of the byre and stood staring at her, as if Flora had blundered into the wrong house and not the other way round. Flora laughed.

How good it was to be here. She felt safe. No one but her mother knew she was here, and Lilian wouldn't tell. Neither Don, nor her father, nor yet Shalimar could find her. When she chose she would go back, if she so chose. There was no certainty except that she could please herself.

Alex let go her nipple and belched, sending a trail of milk down her skirt. She soothed him, watching his face smooth into calm, but anxiety caught at her mind. She was so alone here, and without her the twins would die. They might die anyway, without a doctor on hand, if she in her ignorance failed them. But she looked down at their soft heads, and then out to sea. A rare and unexpected peace was growing in her. It wasn't unknown, she had felt it once before, in Nepal. At last, she was following her instincts, doing what to her seemed right. And her reward, earned through suffering, was tranquillity.

No executive jet met him at Heathrow; Don made his way home on the scheduled flight, and still there was no chauffeur to meet him. He got a taxi and spent the journey leafing through newspapers. The KORSEA debacle, though no longer front page, ran through the columns like lettering in a stick of rock. Everybody had an interest, everyone felt involved, and no one doubted that he was to blame.

He asked to be dropped at the end of the drive and walked up to the castle, rucksack slung over one shoulder. Kincaid's flag still fluttered in the clear afternoon air; the coat of arms still hung above the door, K and H entwined. Don felt tense, like a man about to start a fight, or to finish one, bloodily.

Marie answered the door. She stared at him, her face blank and hostile. 'You'd best come in,' she said frostily.

'I will. I live here.' He stepped past her. 'Where's Flora?' Marie said nothing. Don repeated, menacingly, 'Where is Flora?'

'The old man wants to see you,' snapped Marie. 'We knew you were coming. So did she. And if she doesna want to know you, who can blame her?'

She turned on her heel and flounced back to her kitchen. Don dropped his rucksack on the floor, a loud clatter in the deathly quiet. Everyone seemed to be hiding away, not daring to come out and look at him. He couldn't stand it a moment longer. He ran to the stairs and went up three at a time, to see Kincaid. His fist hammered on the door, but he went in before anyone replied. Kincaid sat in the bed and glared at him, an old, sad man, the streak of red no badger stripe now but a thin line against the silver.

'Where's Flora?'

Kincaid said nothing. Harrington crossed the room and towered over him, saying again, 'Where's Flora? I warn you, I will know.'

'And — I don't.'

'Is she at her mother's? Was she ill, was it the twins?'

'If you had been here you would know. Instead, you went off gallivanting. And in the process destroyed — everything.' Kincaid's voice was low, controlled, with a seething undertow of anger. Suddenly it bubbled up. 'God damn it, I gave you everything! And look what you've done! Look what you've bloody well done!'

Eyes of old, hot purple met those of clearest glass. Don didn't flinch. Kincaid felt weak suddenly, overwhelmed by this strong, brown, good-looking man. He fell back against his pillows.

Don said, 'It's a mess, I admit it. My own fault. I'll do what I can, but that's not important. I have to see Flora.'

'Flora! Flora! Now, she has importance, when before she had so little. It's entirely your fault. I lay all the blame at your door.'

'For what?'

'If you had been here you would know.'

Don put his face very close to the old man's, an inch from his glaring defiance. 'Where is she? Where has she gone?'

'If I knew that I'd have her home. Not for you but for me! For

227

my heir! The girl's left you and taken the boy, and for that I shall never forgive.'

Don retreated back from him, and Kincaid reached his good hand for the bell that would call the nurse. Harrington sank into a chair, dropping his head into his hands. He had known all along she'd gone, but he hadn't believed it. When the letters stopped coming, weeks ago, he had known. But he'd still expected her. There was nothing that couldn't be put right, no vast rift in understanding. He had upset her by going, surely he could please her on his return?

The nurse was clucking anxiously over Kincaid. Harrington lifted his head. 'Why don't you get out of here?' said the nurse venomously. 'You'll not even stop at bullying a poor, sick old man.'

Don ignored her. 'You must know where she's gone,' he said helplessly.

'If I did I wouldn't tell you,' snarled Kincaid, secure in the protection of the nurse. 'You never knew what you had, I don't believe you'll mourn it now it's gone. You took my firm, and you took my daughter. And you've destroyed me.'

Don got up and blundered downstairs. It was raining, the showers spatted on the windows like a thousand dying flies. As he turned the corner into the hall he glimpsed Forbes, his pale face set, disappearing into the servants' hall. Don ran and caught the door.

'I've got to see her, Forbes. You've been here forever, you know where she is.'

'The butler glanced quickly through the door. No one was there. He let it shut and went quickly and silently into the dining room. Like conspirators the two men stood in the corner, away from the windows.

'It wasna your fault she left,' said Forbes. 'Not entirely. The old man was favouring the boy, didn't want the girl at all. It upset Miss Flora something terrible. Marie wouldn't see it. We had words. And the next thing is, John chauffeur has his hand in her drawers! And her giggling and squealing like any young slut from the docks. We've been walking out these twenty years, she and I, and – '

'Flora,' reminded Don. 'You said she was upset.'

'Aye, and so she was. Wouldna read your letter. I left it by her bed and we found it there, afterwards, all scrabbled up. But it was the old man mostly. Favouring the boy.'

Don swallowed. He had sent a dozen letters to which she hadn't replied. Had they all been scrabbled up? 'When did she go?'

'Last Wednesday,' said Forbes. 'Very, very early in the morning. After the shenanigans of the night before Marie was bedfast, and I'd

228

had a dram too many. To console myself. He had his hand right up her skirt, and I'll swear she let him handle her bosom! Her blouse was fastened all wrong.'

'But you know where Flora went.'

'Oh, aye, I've guessed that. Not another soul knows, but that's no surprising. Brains of mashed neeps, Marie has. What can you expect from a woman with instincts of that nature, no better than a beast of the field? When Miss Flora went I thought Eryn Cottage, first off, she'd get the key from her mother and be away. Miss Shalimar was here you see, or she might have gone to her. She wouldn't stay with her mother. The old man sent a car there the moment he knew, she'd have had no peace. But it's her mother's cottage, you understand. By the sea. Away from anywhere.'

Chapter Twenty-one

There had been a storm the previous day, and it still raged, out at sea. The waves told the tale, crashing in on the shore with unnecessary force, quite at variance with the sunshine and gentle winds of today. Salt spray was white on the windows of the cottage. Flora put the babies to sleep in their cots by the front door and fetched a chair to wash the windows with clear, spring water. The cottage existed because of the water, a bubbling source of exquisite purity that her mother had always assured her, as she herself had been assured, came from thousands of feet below ground. She would tell the twins the same, thought Flora, but her imagination failed. She could think no further than the next hour, the next feed or bath or change; the children her babies would become were unknown to her.

She had decided that if anyone came then she would hear them long before they arrived. It would give her time to decide what to do. But she had reckoned without the storm-tossed waves, filling the air with crashing, and neither had she expected that Don would park the car half a mile away and walk. So she was washing the windows, scruffy in jeans that wouldn't fasten and an old maternity smock, when he walked up.

He stood and watched her working, oblivious to him. Her arms, rounded and lightly freckled, moved with neat efficiency. She was humming to herself, some Scottish air, and he was conscious of a surge of rage; how could she be happy, here, in leaving him?

'Flora.'

She turned, her mouth gaping in astonishment, and clutched at the window to stop herself falling off her chair. They stared at each other, he in his old red jacket, his face as brown as mahogany, and she turning whiter by the second.

'Go away,' she said throatily. 'You're not supposed to come here.'

'I've come to take you home.'

She got off her chair and stood behind it, as if protecting herself from him. 'I'm sorry, Don. I suppose I should have written you a letter, but I couldn't. I'm staying here, with the twins. I don't want to be married any more.'

He swallowed. 'I suppose the birth pulled you down.'

'I'm not unbalanced, if that's what you mean. Be honest, Don. You don't want me, you don't want KORSEA, you want your climbing. There's no use pretending that isn't so.'

'You don't know what I want. I love you, Flora. My God, you've had my babies! And you didn't even hang around to let me have a look!'

She put her hands behind her back. 'Isn't that best? What you never have you never miss and all that.'

'Don't be so bloody flippant!'

He crossed the rough heather between them and went to peer into the cradles. Flora came out from behind her chair, hovering anxiously. Don put his hand down, to draw the cover away from Annie's face.

'Don't touch.' A new and fierce aggression.

'I'll touch if I like,' said Don. 'They're mine.'

He stared down at Annie's starlike hand, her little mouth pursed up in dream suckings. He looked at Alex, active even in sleep, his tough little limbs fighting invisible battles. His heart dissolved in love for them. 'Oh, Flora, how could you take them away from me?'

'You didn't have them to lose. You were the one that left, and you can't drop and pick up just as you please. Go away, Don. I've decided I want a divorce.'

Her eyes were huge and purple. He stared her down. She pushed her way into the house and put the kettle on the range, swinging it over the peat fire. The room was so low-ceilinged he could barely stand up, and she had hung bunches of flowers and heather from the beams to tangle in his hair. Everything was homely and organised, there was none of Lilian's sluttish clutter. Babyclothes hung drying in a corner, some books were propped on a shelf, and a small transistor radio stood on the dresser. She had all she wanted, and at the castle she could have everything she might ever want. He knew that would never tempt her.

'If I knew you'd leave me, I'd never have gone.'

She shrugged. 'Would it have made any difference? You'd have gone somewhere else. You'll go somewhere else. Whatever you say you won't settle down and be married.'

'Is that what you want? Someone around all the time, out of the

231

proper mould, reliable and well-intentioned, clockwork man? I can't be that. And you don't want it, you only think you do.'

'I want what I've got,' said Flora. 'To be here, with the twins. I'm happy, really happy, and I haven't been happy since — since I got back from Nepal. Everything since then has been other people telling me what to do, none of it's been me. And I want to be me. Here.'

'Oh God, the women's libber! She needs a man to fuck her, she needs him to pay the bills, but will she admit it? Not her. She's independent. She's being herself. She's stealing my children!'

He lunged at her. Flora turned and ran for the door. Don tried to follow, hit his head a crack on the beam and reeled back. By the time he made it outside Flora was running towards the rocks. He followed, gaining with every stride, and caught her easily. As he held her she fought him, her body soft with the aftermath of pregnancy, unwittingly stimulating him to desire. He held her in an iron hand, grinding his crotch against her, letting her feel his arousal. Men pretended to be civilised, they played the pansy game, but in the end it came down to this; she was his, he was a man, and he would hold on to her.

'You don't love me!' wailed Flora, her voice breaking. 'You only want to hurt me!'

'I want you to come home. Now. Back where you belong.'

'What, to the castle? If it's my home, it isn't yours. You didn't earn it, you didn't work for it. All you've done is shake it to the foundations.'

He let her go. She stood, breathing shakily, putting her hair back with a trembling hand. 'I'll get you a home,' he said. 'If you don't want to live at the castle I'll find somewhere you do want. Our home, to live in, you and me, and there won't be anyone can say I did it on the back of your father's money!'

'Oh, if it was all so easy.' She made a face at him, knowing that if she went too far he might hit her. 'I don't want your home, I don't want anything but what I have. I'll stay here until there's no more money in my account, and that will be quite a long time I should think. After that I shall decide what to do. I can't go back to Dad, he doesn't understand about children. About my children. And I won't go back to you.'

'For Christ's sake, Flora!'

He stood glaring at her in impotent rage. She felt a deep sense of satisfaction; at last she was reaching him, at last he understood. It took this to make him see what he had done. 'You thought I was a doormat,' she said. 'I certainly behaved like one. But this doormat got up and walked away, and I'll be damned if I go back again. Ever.'

She pushed past him, back to the cottage. Annie was crying, that shrill, insistent squall that was her hallmark. Alex had a robust bellow, twice as loud but nowhere near so urgent. Flora picked up the crying baby quickly, aware that she would have to feed her in front of Don. It was embarrassing. She couldn't relax and the milk did not come easily. Annie glared at her with an outraged eye, but Flora could think of nothing but the intimacy of this situation; his face was set as if in stone.

Alex woke halfway through the feed, and Don said, 'Should I pick him up?'

'No,' said Flora shortly. Don went anyway, and tried, his big hands for once clumsy, he didn't dare grip. Alex, alarmed by such ineptitude, arched his back and screamed. 'I told you, leave him,' said Flora irritably. 'You've only upset him, you're upsetting all of us. Why don't you go away?'

Above the yelling baby Don said, 'We've got to have a proper talk.'

'There's nothing to say. I don't know why you came here if you just wanted to make the babies miserable.'

Annie had finished. Flora got up and put her in her cradle, then lifted Alex and cuddled him close. He kept on yelling, letting her know how offended he had been by amateur handling. Flora's cheek was against his hair, she murmured soothing words.

'This isn't the end of it, Flora,' said Don, conscious that he had quite lost the initiative. 'I shall be back.'

She said nothing. Alex was calming, and the two of them, mother and child, locked in such exclusive unity, made Don feel desperate suddenly. When Flora had needed him he had gone away, and now that he was back she had no need of him any more. 'I won't let you do this,' he said. But he could do nothing to stop her. When she sat down and began to feed the boy he turned on his heel and left.

The day was golden and warm, but to Don it was bleak as snow. He felt drawn with cold, as if he had been out all night in thin clothes. It was all so unjust. The full sense of triumph he had experienced when Everest was climbed had been as great, if not greater, than if he had personally stood on the top. Not only had he beaten the mountain, he had conquered his own selfish soul. He knew the full measure of his fault and he was back to make good. Surely he deserved some measure of reward.

He was guilty, yes, of neglecting KORSEA and Flora both. That did not mean he would go on being guilty. The full extent of the KORSEA

233

crisis wasn't clear, he didn't understand quite what had happened, but he would put it right. Everything could be put right. What Flora didn't understand, what no one understood, was the briefness of life; the flame was lit, and in the blink of an eye it was snuffed out. Living was for now, the present, chances were for taking, and if the fall-out from that was chaos then so what? The world had come out of chaos and would go back to it. Each person made their own journey through.

Suddenly he stopped, although the car was only yards away. Tears scalded his eyes, and he hadn't cried since he was ten. The sensation was ghastly, like the breaking down of a giant dam, but he had been so sure that Flora would relent. She loved and she gave, and he had trusted that loving and giving. He had never thought that one day she would refuse him, because he had taken everything and given nothing back. He had travelled his own road, thinking that he could turn back at any time and find Flora, that his life would be a long series of partings and renewals. He had taken no notice of her unhappiness. Had he hurt her so very much?

'Bloody Kincaid,' he whispered to himself, screwing his eyes up against scalding tears. 'It wasn't just me. You did it too, you bastard. Bloody Malcolm Kincaid.' It was easier to blame someone else as well. He couldn't bear the whole weight of it alone. If he hadn't known how she felt then he might have had an excuse, but he had known and chosen to ignore it, as her father had done. There had been no easy answer, that was the trouble. He should have found a hard one, perhaps. At least he might have looked for one.

He didn't know where to go. He drove aimlessly for a while, until it was almost dark and the wings of owls were brushing the tops of the trees. He couldn't go back to the castle, that was certain, and all he wanted was a bed and some peace. He turned the car towards Aberdeen, thinking that he would find a room in one of the oil hotels. They were used to single men wandering in and out. But when he came to the city and the lights he was uncomfortably aware of his tear-streaked face. God, what was happening to him? He was falling apart, that's what.

He needed somewhere private, somewhere quiet. The KORSEA offices perhaps. It was Friday, he had the whole weekend to pull himself together. He still had the keys, he was still in charge. Without further thought he put the car into a U-turn, narrowly missing a taxi and a group of teenage boys crossing the road. 'Who d'you think you are, Jackie Stewart?' yelled one. The taxi driver sounded his horn angrily.

The KORSEA office building was in darkness. Don wondered if

the police would notice lights and investigate, so he was careful to switch everything off as he went along, finally drawing the blinds in his office. He sank into his chair, letting his head loll back. Now he could cry if he wished, there was no one to see, no one to hear. But the tears had subsided, leaving his eyes dry and painful. In a minute he would stretch out on the sofa and try to sleep, but the thoughts kept racing through his head, like a video of a race, endlessly repeated. The image of Flora's breast seemed burned on his brain, a firm white globe, blue-veined, her nipple oozing milk. He hadn't had sex in months.

When he settled on the sofa he couldn't sleep. After ten minutes or so he got up and switched on the lights again. He needed something to read, anything to blot out the thoughts that kept crowding in. A stack of newspapers stood at the side of his desk, and his in-tray was piled with memos. He started to read.

Two hours later he stopped. He didn't want to know any more. In the time he had been away KORSEA had gone from relative order to total madness, worse by far than he had suspected. The *Rosamund* scandal might be off the front pages but it reverberated endlessly in the corridors of power. Without anyone to save it, KORSEA was being sacrificed as a scapegoat. And everything else suffered. Even the turkey farm, tarred with the KORSEA brush, was teetering on bankruptcy, the public seeming to think that the birds were being reared on nuclear waste.

It was disaster, no more and no less. George Williams had seen it and had cut and run. Now, with Kincaid sick and failing to cope, with no hope for the future except ruin, other managers were doing the same thing. Wandering through the dark offices Don saw on several desks the telltale specialist magazines, thumbed at the job advertisements, and cryptic notes that, decoded, meant interviews. The oiled machine that had so impressed him at the start had proved to be no more than a lurching, rusting heap of junk. It was the same machine, but the oil had been good management, and it had dried up.

The guilt was inescapable. Kincaid, Flora, they had trusted him, and he had let them down. Don put his fist to his forehead, groaning because there was no way he could escape. What a foul night this was. He had spent terrible nights before, trapped on a mountain in fear of his life, but this was like being eaten up by rats, from the inside.

He went back to his desk, pushing aside the papers and instead bringing a pad of plain white sheets before him. He spent ten minutes sharpening a pencil, and when it was drawn to an exquisite point he wrote in big letters at the top of the page 'KORSEA - Survival Plan'. It was no time for half measures, there was no room for anything except clear, cold thought. The government was even contemplating taking action against the directors of KORSEA personally. But Kincaid had been quick, he had extracted what he could and put it in trust for Alex, well aware that it left KORSEA more bloodless than before. And Don would be damned if he let the firm die. He took out a ruler and divided the page into four quarters; KORSEA would be divided like that. Oil rig supply in one section, *Rosamund* litigation in another, engineering and diving in a third, and for the fourth – peripheral activities, probably to be sold off. The first thing to go would be the turkey farm, a nuisance that had never fitted into KORSEA's structure. There was a fish farm somewhere too, and a chain of launderettes. Kincaid needed diversions to sustain interest, but KORSEA couldn't afford them. They would go.

Putting the page aside he started another, writing a list of names of people he wanted to meet. The Secretary of State for Scotland came first, followed by the local MP, the Euro MP and the Minister for the Environment. He moved on to the head of the local council, oil company men and the coastguard. Lastly he added the names of KORSEA people, the people who had to know, to believe, that he would save them. There was no alternative. He must.

Dawn broke, and he was still working. The blinds shut out the daylight, it was only when he went into the outer office that he realised it was morning. He hunted through his desk and found his secretary's home telephone number. 'Dorothy? It's me, Don Harrington. Can you come in? Right away, if you would. Thanks.' He called another dozen people, and some were reluctant. It was Saturday, and they had suffered enough for KORSEA. But they all came in the end, to find Harrington pinning up huge cards on the walls. 'CRISIS DAY ONE' he was writing, in red pen on the first. He followed it with a list of tasks, 'Organise', 'Rationalise', 'Inform'. Then he turned and spoke to them.

'Is everyone here? Good. I want to thank you all for coming. As you know, KORSEA's in a mess, and it's my fault. I went off doing my own thing when I should have been minding the shop. I've called it a crisis and it is. If we're going to survive we have to pull the thing together, now, this minute, today. First, we re-organise. Then we stop doing anything that isn't vitally important. We forget cleaning, the office party, complaint letters, pension schemes, everything. It all stays on ice until I take down these cards and the crisis is over. And we tell everyone, staff, media, government, exactly what's happening and why. I'm going to try and get the government on my side, stop them trying to finish us. Now, my office is there, the door's open and it's staying open. If you need me just yell 'Don' and I'll come running. It's the least I can do.'

Nobody knew what to say. They were tired, worn down by weeks of problems. But something stirred in them. It was the chance to begin again, to do a wonderful spring clean and wipe away all the disorder and muddle they so hated. Andrews, who had been offered a job in London, was the first to move to his desk. He had a couple of weeks before he need make up his mind about the new job. And he didn't like London. The housing would bankrupt him and he wouldn't be able to fish. Most of all, he hated to see the old firm in such trouble.

'It's impossible, the thing's too far gone,' said one of the technical men, sotto voce.

Andrews grunted. 'He's good at the impossible — Everest without oxygen and all that.'

Dorothy was telephoning, getting the duty officers in various ministries. 'I have the Secretary of State's private number,' she called. 'Shall I get him for you, Don?'

'Thanks. Yes.'

The others exchanged glances. He meant business then, did Harrington. They got up, some brisk, some slow, rubbing their hands together or putting them deep in trouser pockets. It was hard to know where to begin — or even why they should. But Dorothy's voice said, 'Yes, sir — I have Mr Harrington, head of KORSEA, for you.' She mouthed at Don, 'It's him!' and Don, tall, loose-jointed, wearing jeans and a twenty-four hour beard, went to take the call.

Weeks passed. For Don one day ran into another. He had a bed put up in an empty room and went from work to sleep and back again, never stopping. Food was sent in from outside, or he lunched with this or that important person. The government was persisting in its attack. They seemed determined to bring down KORSEA; ministers were gaining votes by their uncompromising stand over the company's role in the *Rosamund* debacle. No one had anything to lose from KORSEA's end, except the people who worked for the firm, and they hardly counted when set against the good opinion of the nation.

Don put on his best suit, blue silk tie and matching handkerchief, and went to do battle in London. He took a scheduled flight down; no more glamorous extravagance for KORSEA. He felt a pang for the grandeur of the company jet, and at the same time wondered if Kincaid's flamboyance had contributed to this downfall. He had

237

been too rich for too long, and in Britain it never paid to be that ostentatious.

They kept him waiting in a small outer office. It was a calculated snub, he wasn't even permitted to sit with a secretary and listen to the murmurs from within. After twenty minutes he went in search of someone, and prowled corridors, opening doors. He heard voices. He turned a brass handle in a heavy rosewood door and discovered the minister, having a convivial drink with some parliamentary friends.

'Hello,' said Don. 'I believe I have an appointment.'

There was a visible freezing of the atmosphere. 'And you would be − ?'

'Harrington. Don Harrington, head of KORSEA. You know us, the nation's favourite, leaky nuclear waste containers a speciality. You're trying to drive us into the floor.'

The minister put down his glass and silently led the way into an office. An aide followed, notepad and pencil poised. 'Can you give me any good reasons why we shouldn't put you out of business?' enquired the minister. 'You were guilty of the biggest pollution scare this century.'

'And it was only a scare. Nothing happened.'

'No thanks to you, I might add.'

'No thanks to me. I was in Nepal at the time, as I'm sure you know. Look, I won't beat about the bush. I don't think you realise just how many people are employed by us, in farms, factories, on the ships, in the office − we even have diving teams. And obviously I'll be contacting the newspapers explaining why all those people are going to be unemployed. But then, you've hardly got votes to lose in Scotland.'

'We have very little support at all,' agreed the minister. He put his fingers together in an arch. 'So you can't exactly use votes as a threat, can you?'

'I could as a promise,' said Don.

'What on earth do you mean?'

Don leaned forward in his chair. 'Suppose we worked together? Suppose you actively supported us? The *Rosamund* thing was a one-off, and no one's got to the bottom of it yet. We'll help do that. All our resources, all our information at your disposal. No more lying, no more obstruction − I know you haven't been able to get a thing out of us. Kincaid always did play his cards far too close to his chest, and he decided to keep you out.

'Things are going to change. KORSEA will undergo a transformation − we're going to go green. Led by the government we'll be

238

the most environmentally friendly company ever, a big employer, high profile, persuaded to see the light by you. The government. Marvellous PR. You might even get a Scottish MP next time round.'

'You can't really expect us to let you off the hook, can you? The disposal of the waste involved vast expense, and we believe the polluter should pay. It's a fundamental tenet of policy.'

'Of course we'll pay. Over time. What you're doing at the moment is taking your pound of flesh in one solid lump out of the company's heart. You're killing us.'

The minister glanced at his aide. He raised his brows. Then, to Don, he said, 'I wonder if you would care to wait outside? We need to discuss one or two things. I'll call for the detailed reports, and we'll look through them. Colin, get Mr Harrington a drink, would you?'

'Thanks.'

He was promoted to a more comfortable waiting room, and given a large scotch and water. He felt disorientated. Outside there was sunshine. Perhaps Flora was hanging out washing or walking along the beach. Barely an hour of the day passed without him wondering what she might be doing. Soon he would visit, soon he would go to her and say, 'Look, I've put it right, I've made it better. Now you can forgive.' If he couldn't put it right she would never forgive him. Like a knight serving his lady, he was wearing her colours into battle.

He finished his drink and no one came with another. It was almost lunchtime, but he wasn't hungry. So much rested on today. He stood at the window, hands in his silk-lined trouser pockets, and wondered bleakly what he would do if he failed.

The door opened. It was the minister himself. 'Ah, Mr Harrington. Sorry to have kept you so long. Look, why don't we have a spot of lunch? We can chat while we eat. There are one or two points I'd like clarified.'

'Certainly. Only too pleased.' Don smiled, casually. His heart was thundering, a veritable paean of joy. The blood rushed in his ears so loudly he could hardly hear what the minister was saying, but still he nodded and smiled and answered with just sufficient eagerness. 'I'm saved,' he kept thinking, and the words resounded again and again, 'I'm saved.'

Chapter Twenty-two

'I can't go on,' said Shalimar. 'I don't care what you say – I simply cannot go on!' Her voice rose into trembling hysteria. Her face, drawn tight with emotion, was beaded with sweat. She looked like a woman about to kill herself.

'She'll win an Oscar,' murmured one of the make-up artists. 'I'd put money on it.'

'Ten dollars,' agreed his friend. 'I'll go for Meryl Streep. This one's too fucking gorgeous. She'd get it if she was a dog.'

The set was crowded. Everyone who had the slightest reason for being there had turned up for Shalimar's scene. She was playing a politician's wife, a society beauty who was hiding her drug addiction. They had made her learn to inject herself with sterile water, and she had snorted more chalk than it took to write the Bible on a blackboard. But that wasn't the attraction. Everyone was hoping they would get to see her do the sex scene, the horrific culmination of her steady slide into prostitution.

'Clear the set,' called the director. Everyone groaned. They should have known. But they, like the rest of the world, would have to wait until the film was made before they could sneak a look at what was reputed to be the most beautiful body ever.

Shalimar wrapped her diaphanous robe around her and went to sit in her dressing room. Her maid put a plate of sandwiches down and Shalimar chewed one, morosely. 'I hate this film,' she grumbled.

'It sure don't hate you, honey.'

'Can't think why I ever said I'd do it. It's just an excuse for everyone to leer at me.'

'I guess they do that anyway. Good thing men's minds are secret, that's what I say. Thoughts like that don't deserve to be around in public.'

Shalimar laughed. When she began in this business everyone had seemed hostile, but nowadays she found friends in strange places. The man playing her husband, Jack Monaghan – most evenings they had dinner together, sucking crayfish claws in weary companionship. His wife was running around with someone, but he didn't seem to mind. She had the feeling that he saw her as a replacement. That was the trouble with films, they created a hothouse which forced relationships into premature bloom, and as soon as the film was over the flower died in the cold fresh air. She'd stick to eating crayfish with Jack, she decided.

'I don't want to do this scene.'

'You're going to get beat up, you're not supposed to want to do it! I'll keep your wrap handy. And watch him when he hits you. I've known times they've got carried away, and really let fly.'

'Oh, thanks. So I lie on the bed and wait for him to really bash my head in.'

'Punch you in the mouth, most like.'

It was time to do the scene. Shalimar went out with a feeling of doom. She could barely look at the man she was playing with. He was big, heavy, a brilliant character actor. Too brilliant. She was scared of him already. They had done the pick-up scene weeks ago, and ever since then she had been dreading this moment. It was like a nightmare come true.

'You won't really hit me?' she heard herself say.

'As long as you don't kick me in the balls.'

She grinned. This maniac was in fact a family man who played bad tennis. The words she had to say revolved in her head, and suddenly she had forgotten that none of this was real. She was the woman, going down, perhaps forever. Her husband thought she was off the stuff, he kept her so short of money she had to beg to buy a stamp – even the children's pocket money had gone. They treated her like a child herself, they deserved nothing, those prim-faced, neat people with their gossip and their hypocrisy – but she was scared. Here, in this dingy place, there were no deceptions any more. Everything was raw, elemental. Dangerous.

When it was over she was shaking and in tears. 'You were brilliant, honey. Just so good,' said Jack, and she tried to smile, as if she felt normal. The director, an Italian American, waved to her to come over, but she ignored him and went to her dressing room. The maid poured her a glass of mineral water. 'You don't need nothing but that, honey. You go and dance the night away. You been so good they'll let you come in late tomorrow.'

The director knocked and came in, waving the maid away. Shalimar didn't look at him. She blamed him, somehow, for the

241

way she felt. Silence, like thick custard, slowed her movements to stiff caricatures. Her face was strained by the effort to appear calm.

'You've got a problem,' said the director.

'I thought you liked it.'

'That's not your problem. You know how good you were. The best.' He took out some gum and began chewing it. He was a reformed smoker who couldn't live without some prop. 'This part's getting to you. All your parts do. You get weird.'

'I'm not weird now, am I?'

'Just about cracking up, I'd say.'

It was true. Her hands were shaking, she felt sick and ill, and all she'd been on was white wine and crayfish.

'I just wonder if you're going to hold out.'

'It's only another couple of weeks.'

'Some rough scenes in those weeks. Look, go somewhere, get away. You can have ten days. It'll put us over budget, but I don't give a shit. This film's going to be big box office.'

'I've nowhere to go.'

'Everyone's got somewhere. I'd say to take Jack, but I'm going to need him. We'll buy you a ticket, anywhere in the world. How about India?'

Shalimar smiled. 'I've been there. I've friends in Scotland, though. There's someone I've been meaning to see.'

'Don't get too tanned, that's all I ask.'

'In Scotland?' She looked at him blankly and he shrugged. He always took his holidays in Jamaica.

The next day, instead of the dawn run to the studio Shalimar found herself on a plane. She would turn up at the castle and see what was happening. Lilian had written once, to say that Flora was living by herself with the twins, but since then there had been no news. What was Don doing? How was Kincaid? She had the feeling that she had left them all in crisis and that she should have done more, although heaven alone knew what.

A man sitting next to her tried to chat her up. At first she was cool, until suddenly she caught herself thinking that no one knew where she was, and if they had a stop-over in some hotel he might give her good money, and she could use some. It had been days since she'd got really high . . .

'No!'

'I'm sorry?' He looked blank, a little startled.

'Nothing – I meant – sometimes I forget who I am.'

'But you're the actress, aren't you?'

'Yes. I suppose I am.'

242

He took out a magazine then, and began to read. The plane seemed airless, claustrophobic almost. She had a fierce longing for the cool, wide moors around the castle, where she could breathe at last, where people knew her for what she was. The stewardess brought her a drink, vodka or something, and she gulped it down. But the feeling persisted, nudging at the edge of her mind; she was playing the part of Shalimar, and reality, horrible reality, was lurking inside her head.

She reached the castle late in the afternoon. The sun was casting long shadows, and Kincaid's flag flapped in a lazy wind. A capercaillie squawked from somewhere, and a small flock of grouse shivered upwards. Shalimar pulled at the giant bellrope, which in typical Kincaid fashion was attached not only to a clanging bell but to an electronic signal in the servants' quarters. The door took a while to open, as if few people came and no one was expected. The butler gawped at her.

'Hello, Forbes. I think I've come to stay.'

'Well – Miss Shalimar! Of course! You'll know about Miss Flora, no doubt. She's away from here just now. And that man of hers given his marching orders, I understand. So it's only Mr Kincaid to see you, and he'll be delighted. Marie! Marie, see here, Miss Shalimar's with us again.'

The old pair clucked and fussed, unable to conceal their delight. If anywhere was home this was, thought Shalimar. A great joy rose up in her, that she was here and welcome. She ran up the stairs to see Kincaid, to tell him that she was home.

Two large oxygen cylinders stood outside the bedroom, next to a stainless steel trolley. Shalimar knocked and waited to be called to enter, but she heard nothing. Knocking again, she opened the door cautiously, calling, 'Malcolm? It's me, Shalimar. Are you awake?'

A nurse was sitting beside the bed. She got up quickly, putting a finger to her lips. 'Not now, please! He's sinking.'

'What? You mean he's going to die?'

She pushed the nurse aside and ran to the bed. Kincaid lay quite still, his face already as pale as death. The only sign of life was the gentle rise and fall of the sheet over his chest. Shalimar let out a shriek. 'Malcolm! Malcolm, wake up!'

The nurse grabbed her. 'Get out of here, Miss! Keep your hysterics for the stage, if you please!'

'But you're letting him die. Malcolm? If he's dying Flora should be here, and his wife! You haven't the right to keep him like this.'

The patient's heavy lids lifted a fraction. 'Shalimar. What in God's name are you doing here?'

The nurse gave a squeak of surprise. Shalimar swallowed. 'Panicking about you, as it happens. I thought you were dying.'

'Rubbish. Had a slight stroke, so the doctor says. Minor thing. Follow on from the accident, they've been expecting it apparently. Makes you damned tired. Flora's taken the boy, you know. Taken him off somewhere. But she's kicked out that bastard Harrington.'

'I thought she'd be back by now,' said Shalimar, taking his hand. He tried to grip, but his fingers were like limp asparagus.

'That's what I thought. Sent me a birthday card last month though, and a painting she'd done. Paints well, does Flora.'

The sketch was propped up on his bedside table, water colours of rocks and tumbling seagulls. Flora had captured the spirit of the place, wildness and acres of sky. Shalimar grimaced. She recognised the scene so well her friend might as well have written the address on the bottom: Eryn Cottage.

'What's happened to Don then?' she asked.

Kincaid snorted. 'He's gone back to KORSEA. First he ruins my business then he tries to stick it all back together. You can't mend broken china, you can't go back. It's carnage. Selling this, finishing that. I was so wrong about him, girl! Thought he was all fire and brimstone. But he's a bloody damp squib. Doesn't give a damn about Flora, doesn't give a damn about anything except himself.'

He swallowed dryly. Shalimar said, 'Would you like something to eat?'

'He's not on solids,' intervened the nurse.

'I bet you could use some of Marie's cake,' coaxed Shalimar.

'Hmmm. Bit of shortbread, perhaps. And some cake. They give me stuff to drink like thick milk, you know.'

She put her arm round his shoulders and struggled to lift him into a sitting position. He smelled familiar, of eau de cologne mixed with a dry tang of skin. She said, 'They don't know you like I do. They think you're going to die.'

Under the flattery of Shalimar's attention, Kincaid revived. Some of the old spirit came back. He called in a secretary and dictated long letters of instruction about the upbringing of Alex, his male heir.

'Flora's just like her mother,' he told Shalimar. 'Followed her example, if you ask me. Took off into nowhere. The man had nothing about him, of course, or he'd have hauled her back.'

'Like you did?'

For a moment Kincaid said nothing. 'It was different with us,' he said in a gently reflective tone. 'Lilian couldn't give me a son.

I held it against her. I didn't think that I did, but now I realise it must have been so.'

'Daughters are more faithful,' said Shalimar.

'Like bitches,' interposed Kincaid, and they held hands and laughed.

On the third day Shalimar drove to the cottage. It was summer still, and the apples were not yet ripe, but a cold wind was blowing rain in gusts along the shoreline. Shalimar had only been there once before, a wet halfterm which Lilian had endured while the two girls passed the time hunting for crabs in the rock pools and making up stories about treasure and romance. As the car drove up Flora's head appeared out of the door, wearing an expression of controlled panic. When she saw Shalimar she came running, in stockinged feet, wearing old cord trousers and a huge collapsing sweater. She looked slim and fit, her hair shining with health. 'Oh! Shalimar, how glad I am to see you!'

'I thought you wanted to see the last of me. You didn't write.'

'I know I didn't. I've been asleep here. Come in, do.'

Shalimar reached back into the car. 'Wait a minute, I've a hamper. Forbes sends three bottles of good wine, and Marie's packed a ton and a half of food. Everyone sends their love, Malcolm included.'

Flora said nothing. She led the way into the house, and it was bright with oil lamps and the fire. Alex was asleep, but Annie lay on the floor, rolling from side to side, her bare gums chewing on a creamy white shell. 'It makes a wonderful teething ring,' explained Flora. 'She does everything first. It's as if she knows she's in a race to beat Alex.'

'Is she?'

Flora was hunting for a corkscrew, and finally came across one in the table drawer. She uncorked a bottle with brisk efficiency. Everything about her seemed brisk and determined. 'Dad wasn't even going to acknowledge she existed. That's partly why I went. I could see he was going to put Alex first in everything. Don would be just the same, he'd have Alex halfway up a mountain before he was two.'

'Are you sure?'

The wine sloshed into two thick glasses. 'Pretty sure. He came once and made us all miserable and he hasn't been again. Tried to pick up Alex, never gave a thought to Annie, so I could see how it was. And he was violent.'

'Did he hit you?'

'No. But it was there — bubbling.'

Shalimar sipped her wine. Flora was making her feel angry, and

245

she didn't want to feel that, not with her best friend. But what were friends for, if not honesty? 'A lot of men would have hit you. Taking off with his babies like that.'

'He took off. Not me.'

'But he came back! He tried to make it better!'

'Since he only came the once, I don't think he tried very hard.'

'Flora, you can be so unfair.'

'And you always take Don's side.'

They said nothing for a long moment. But theirs was a friendship of years, a never-ending link, past to future. Whatever happened in the present, the friendship would go on.

'Have you finished your film?' asked Flora.

'No. I'm on sick leave. I was going off my head.'

'That doesn't sound very true.'

'Believe me, it is. I've got a mental hang-up. When I was a fashion model I thought of myself as a clothes horse. I *was* a clothes horse. I believed that's what I was. Now I'm an actress, I seem to think I'm whatever people try to make me. A witch last year, a screwball this. At the moment I'm trying for an Oscar as a drug-crazed socialite housewife. Look at my clothes, I even dress like her! A little tacky at the edges.'

Flora scanned the clothes; they were certainly not quite Shalimar. A suit of good blue wool, silk blouse, high heels. Over the top she wore a mink jacket, and Shalimar never wore fur. Her hair, heavily lacquered, was slightly wild, as if she had suffered some rough experience since leaving home that morning. 'Didn't you think you should put on something a little less formal? Coming here?'

'Not me. My husband has a position to keep up.'

'Even drug-crazed socialites have weekends off, don't they? You need a couple of dozen pairs of Calvin Klein slacks.'

'So I do! You're right, my husband won't like me looking out of place at election time. I'll get some.'

'Shalimar!' Flora leaned across and poured them both some more wine. 'You are in a mess.'

'But the film's going to finish. I think I'll keep on until I do someone really happy and successful, and I'll stay like that forever.'

'I shall hate you,' said Flora. 'You'll be unreal.'

'But I'll be happy. After all, you don't care what people think. You're doing just what you like. No father for the kids, no future for your dad, but it suits you. Great.'

'You can't accuse me of being selfish! I was so damned unselfish I nearly expired!'

'It isn't my fault you always go to extremes.'

'Who's extreme? I'm being a good mother, not some mentally unbalanced misfit.'

It was the wine, loosening tongues. A little subdued, they opened the hamper and ate patties and pastries, bread and biscuits. Marie had included a jar of fruits preserved in brandy and elderberry wine, and when they ate that their heads began to spin again.

'They won't be able to finish the film, I'll be too fat,' complained Shalimar.

'They can rewrite you to being pregnant. Except you'd get pregnant, just for authenticity.'

'I wish I could.' Shalimar yawned and let her head fall back.'You should go home, Flora. You're being a coward out here.'

Her friend said nothing. She got up and went to the window, watching the rain slip under the eaves and splash whispering against the glass. The longer she stayed here the more settled she felt. This was her home, the place in which she would rear her children.

'You know your father nearly died?' said Shalimar. 'Oh, I thought you might not. He had a slight stroke. When I arrived they were getting ready to put the pennies on his eyes. You've kicked the heart out of him, you and Don between you.'

Flora took a shuddering breath. 'I couldn't let him eat Alex up. I couldn't let him turn Annie into a pale copy of me. I'm not responsible for my father's life, I can't be!'

'We're all responsible. We all have to take care of each other. If not, what's the point of everything?'

On the way back to the castle Shalimar felt depressed. It was a good feeling, because it was her own, caused by the real world and real problems. Her socialite didn't get depressed, she got suicidal or she got high. Everyday blue moods touched her not at all.

But Shalimar's blue mood persisted. She got lost in the maze of small roads that led hither and yon across hill and heather, until eventually she followed the signs to Aberdeen, from which she could find her way home. The KORSEA building was very visible, a tall, glossy structure, and she was surprised to see that even at this hour of the evening it was ablaze with light. She stopped in the car park and walked to the door. A girl sat behind a desk, cutting clippings out of a newspaper. 'Can I help you?'

'Er – is Mr Harrington in? I'm a friend.'

'He's upstairs. Take the lift to the third floor.'

'Don't you have to announce me or anything?'

The girl grinned. 'All that's changed. If he gets a crank he throws them out himself, he's big enough.'

247

Shalimar went up in the lift. It stopped at both the first and second floors, and people got in, giving her glimpses of busy offices humming with noise. 'Is this some sort of night shift?' she enquired of her fellow travellers.

'Most people work till nine,' said a shirt-sleeved young man. 'It's the opposite of martial law, and by God it's effective. We're on an employee profit share, so we're all pretty keen to make a profit.'

Another man rapped on the pine panelling of the lift. 'Don't you adore our renewable wood? The rain forests love us, the ozone is so friendly people are starting to talk, and the government is going to put us in their election video. I hope that coat isn't real fur, we don't approve.'

'Neither do I,' said Shalimar feebly. She was bewildered.

On the third floor she saw Don wandering about the office holding a piece of paper. He was wearing jeans and a sweatshirt bearing the words 'Clean the Sea With KORSEA'. 'Doesn't anyone know a fucking thing about this?' he was demanding, brandishing his paper. 'Who took the message? Which minister is coming to see me tomorrow?'

'Since when did you get visits from ministers?' demanded Shalimar.

Don spun round on his heel. 'Well, good God, where on earth did you spring from?'

She spread out her hands, and he took them, putting a comradely kiss on her cheek. She leaned into him, pressing herself affectionately to him for a second, saying, 'It's good to see you! You don't get any smaller.'

'You don't get shorter but you do get thinner. How are you? Have you seen Flora? The old man?'

She nodded. He looked different too, she decided. It was in his eyes, determination mixed with reserve. Before he had sometimes seemed hardly to be paying attention to what was going on, as if he was passing the time with life until he could move on to something that interested him. But now she interested him, or at least what she had to say. 'Come into the office,' he said softly.

She followed him, conscious that they in turn were followed by many pairs of curious eyes. She minced slightly, the socialite again, always ready for a quick screw if it would get her someplace. 'What the hell are you playing at?' said Don, surprising her.

She blushed. 'I'm sorry. I've been acting, it's some kind of hangover. Every now and again I flip.'

'I know all about flipping. Has Flora come down to earth yet?'

'I don't think she was ever up in the air.'

248

He closed his office door, a rare event if she did but know. 'I — I daren't go and see her,' he confessed. 'I made a mess of it last time. Next time I'm going to be calm, reasonable and persuasive. I've got my eye on a house we could buy, and I'm going to show it to her, see if she likes it. The share price is coming back up, it should take off when the results come through. We've not included the *Rosamund* debt, of course, that's going to tie us down for years, but apart from that we're looking good. I wanted — can you tell her that?'

'Perhaps you should write to her.'

'Yes.'

He turned his back for a moment, as if pulling himself together. Glancing round the office she saw a television, books, a couple of cartons of orange juice and four pairs of trainers. 'Are you living here?'

'What? Yes, I am. I clear all this out if someone big's coming in. Which reminds me, who the hell is coming in tomorrow?' He stared again in puzzlement at the note in his hand.

'Malcolm's had a slight stroke,' said Shalimar.

'What? Oh God, I'm sorry. Poor bastard.'

'He's over the worst now. But he thinks you've ruined KORSEA. If he knew what you'd done here he wouldn't feel so bad. But losing Flora, and the business — it's taken the heart out of him.'

'I don't think it's done any of us any good, actually.'

He looked strained and suddenly unhappy. 'All my life I've been using women,' he said. 'Pick 'em up, drop 'em, find another. Flora was different, I knew that, but she wasn't that different. I came and I went, doing what I wanted. Now, when she's given up on me, I can't — it's hard. I'm not going to let her finish like this. She's the mother of my children, damn it! I love her.'

'What? Because she's the mother of your children?'

He ran a hand through his hair. 'Oh Christ, not you as well. Nowadays if you can't justify your emotions they don't count. Flora and I have two children, and they need two parents, whatever she thinks. Like it or not she should come back and try.'

'You incorrigible romantic, you!'

He looked away, unsmiling. Shalimar said, 'Sorry.'

'I won't wear my heart on my sleeve,' he said tightly.

'Just as long as you've got a heart! I've never known Flora be so determined before. I mean, she's persuadable. You only have to look unhappy and she gives in, she's never had an ounce of bitterness in her. I wish I knew what you'd done.'

He turned on her, suddenly fierce. 'You wish you knew! All

249

right, I wasn't a model husband, I should have stayed home and worked, but I'm doing that now! We had good sex, we had good times, we lived with her father because that was the way I thought she wanted things to be. So, what was so wrong? What makes her want a divorce?'

Shalimar looked at his strong, bewildered face. His eyes were shadowed under jutting brows, as if he wasn't sleeping well, but he seemed so utterly desirable that her knees felt weak. This wasn't the socialite responding, nor yet the clothes horse, but Shalimar, from the essence of her soul. 'I don't know why anyone would want to divorce you,' she said bleakly. He glanced at her, something in her tone alerting him. Hastily she added, 'For those sorts of reasons, I mean.'

'Yes. Well, I don't understand it. I'll come back with you. It's about time I saw Malcolm.'

He picked up his jacket and strode out. 'Turn the lights out when you go,' he yelled. 'And someone find out who on earth it is who's coming to see me tomorrow.'

There was a general murmur of acknowledgment and farewell. Shalimar followed him, taking an obscure pleasure in appearing to be enticing Don out for the night. How wonderful if they thought she and Don were sleeping together. How wonderful if they were.

They went in her car, but Don drove. Sitting beside him, watching his strong, lean hands on the wheel, her stomach melted with desire. This man had a devastating effect on her. If he touched her, however briefly, even for a handshake, she trembled. But he was Flora's husband, and that alone made him the one man in the world she could not try to have. If they were divorced, though – Shalimar pushed away the unworthy thought. She would not put herself before her friend. Flora was married, and must stay married, and while that was so there was nothing for Shalimar but sad, hopeless longing.

Chapter Twenty-three

The castle was not as Harrington remembered it; dark, silent, almost brooding, it had none of its old lightness and energy. Once it had seemed the centre of a world, and now it was a dark planet, allied to a dying sun. Strength and power were not timeless, though they might appear to be so; they came, too quickly, to this.

He followed Shalimar quietly up the stairs. In Kincaid's room, someone coughed, and the nurse murmured soothingly.

'I'll go in first,' said Shalimar, but Harrington caught her arm, feeling her shudder.

'No. We'll go in together.'

He knocked on the door and entered. There was a screen between the bed and the door, and he said 'Malcolm?' before he rounded the screen and saw him. Lying back against his pillows, the old man went suddenly pink. He stared at his visitor with outrage.

'And what do you want here?'

'Shalimar said you weren't too good. I wanted to see you. Tell you what's been going on.'

'He should be asleep,' said the nurse crossly. 'Please, he can't see visitors.'

'Rubbish, woman,' snapped Kincaid. 'I sleep all day, I can't sleep all night as well. Have you seen Flora?'

'I didn't come to talk about Flora.'

Shalimar came up to the bed and took the old man's hand. 'He's turned the firm round, Malcolm. It's doing brilliantly.'

'Correction.' Kincaid glared beneath bushy brows. 'Though saddled with debt, the firm is managing to remain solvent. In twenty years' time it may struggle back to the position it held before Donald Harrington saw fit to ruin it.'

'Make that five years and I'll agree,' said Don.

Both men were silent. After a moment, Kincaid turned to Shalimar.

'My dear, Don and I have a number of things to discuss. I wonder –'

'Oh. Yes. Of course.' She withdrew, feeling foolish and angry. It was cruel of them to exclude her. Didn't they trust her? She went downstairs and hung around in the cold hall, waiting to see Don before he left. Nobody lit the fire here nowadays, with no one to relish it.

Her mind drifted over the day, over past days. She began to walk about, her arms folded round her, feeling aggrieved that her husband the politician was leaving her by herself with nothing to do but wait. In this cold hall, too – she sighed angrily. He deserved everything he got. No wonder Flora had left him.

She sat down on the stairs, putting her head against the banister. Oh God, she was definitely cracking up. She didn't know who she was, where she was, anything. Footsteps sounded on the stairs above, and she looked up, terrified. Of course it was Don.

'What's the matter? You look scared to death.'

'I am. It's – the house, everything. How was he?'

He shrugged. 'I don't know. The last thing he said was "If you're buckling down at KORSEA at last you'd better move back here. I prefer to have you where I can keep a very close eye." By which I think he means he's forgiven me. I might be wrong.'

'I shouldn't think so. He's lonely. This house is a morgue. Oh, Don, I don't want to sleep alone tonight!'

Her dark eyes, huge and luminous, met his. He said, 'You wouldn't say that if you thought she'd come back to me. Would you?'

'I don't know. Forget I said anything, I didn't mean it. Flora's my friend, she means more to me than you and – and I won't spoil that. Like I said, I've been confused lately. I need a teddy bear, that's all.'

'But she must have said something. Did she say she wanted to see me? I need to know.'

Shalimar turned on him. 'And I don't! I have just offered myself to you and all you can do is wonder what this means about Flora! You don't see people, Don, you don't see them and you never listen to what they have to say. No wonder she doesn't want you back. Living with you must have been like talking to a dead man, with as much hope of response.'

'What response do you want? A quick fuck on the carpet and no questions asked?'

Shalimar gasped. She drew herself up, rubbing her hands together. 'You might at least have the grace to be polite.'

'Strange as it might seem, just at this moment I don't feel very

252

polite.' After a moment he added, 'Look, don't listen to me. I'm not rational. I'll get away. If I don't talk to anyone I can't insult them. Be seeing you.'

He strode to the door, and then realised that he couldn't get back. He had come in Shalimar's car. 'Can I borrow your car?' he asked abruptly.

'No! Or at least – yes, if you like. Come and pick me up tomorrow. We can go and see Flora.'

She watched his face change and stiffen. 'All right,' he said slowly. 'After I've seen whoever this minister is.'

She nodded and he was gone.

But the next day he didn't come until six in the evening. Shalimar had waited all day, finally putting on a velvet caftan and relaxing in front of a small fire. She felt angry and misused, so that when he did come she looked up at him with challenge in her face. 'What took you?'

'It was the Prime Minister. A bit of a shock to the system, that. Everyone swears they didn't know.'

'And what was she like? Abrasive?'

'Like sandpaper. The Tories think we're a load of undisciplined lefties. After today I feel bloody left of centre. She told me off about mess in the ladies' loo. I thought she was going to ask to see my fingernails as well.'

Shalimar got off the sofa, aware that the gown was unbuttoned halfway down her body. The material stood away from her and if Don cared to look he could see that she was naked. 'Have you got dirty fingernails?'

'Not so far.' He moved across and looked thoughtfully down her dress. 'Do you show this off in the film?' he asked.

She nodded. 'A man has me and then beats me up. It's very realistic, so I'm told.'

'Did you do it with him, then?'

She shook her head. 'Actually, nowadays I'm fairly particular.'

Under his gaze her nipples hardened to dark grapes. She put out a hand and touched his crotch, feeling him iron hard in his trousers. But he moved away, and she let her hand fall. 'We're going to see Flora,' he said. Shalimar went to change.

In the car he apologised. 'I'm being foul to you. I'm sorry. I'm mixed up at the moment, about Flora and the kids.'

'That's all right. I'm more than happy to be used as a turn-on.'

'She says, in an icy tone!'

Shalimar chuckled. 'What a good thing we're both so moral.

253

Otherwise we'd be driving along with our lusts slaked and one hell of a load of guilt instead.'

Don changed down for a hill. 'Actually, I've got a lot of time for marital fidelity. But it gets a bit hard when I'm denied my conjugal rights.'

'Poor old you.'

He accelerated up the hill, sending a couple of sheep racing away across the heather. Why was he going with Shalimar? He was using her as an insurance policy, in the hope that Flora would be reasonable and listen to one of them at least. And they would have to be civilised with Shalimar there.

It was getting dark by the time they finally drew up at the cottage. The waves were playful, slapping down on the rocks and beach, sending plumes of spray into the evening air. Gulls hung in the spindrift and sat on the roof of the cottage, like vulgar lodgers, yelling abuse into the street. There was no movement in the cottage. Shalimar went to the door, calling, 'Flora! Flora, it's me.' She knocked, lifted the latch and went in. Don felt his heart hammering in his chest, where was Flora? He followed Shalimar into the cottage.

She was sitting by the fire, wearing a dressing gown that was as homely and unattractive as Shalimar's kaftan had been alluring. Her hair lay like a tangled flame against dull brown wool. 'It's only a cold,' she was apologising. 'Both the twins have got the sniffles, too. I don't know where we caught it, we only go out to the shop in the village.'

'You should take them out more,' said Don. 'You don't give them a chance to build up any proper resistance.'

Taken by surprise, Flora spun round. 'Why on earth did you bring him, Shalimar?' she demanded. 'You didn't need to stir his conscience, we were quite happy being forgotten.'

'I hadn't forgotten you,' said Don. 'I was busy.'

'I'm sure we came to mind occasionally. Like a film you only saw up to the interval. Don't worry, we're finishing the reel without you.'

Don said nothing. A little desperately Shalimar said, 'He's been saving KORSEA, Flora. He's reorganised, got government backing, everything.'

'Oh. Good.'

She pulled out her handkerchief and blew her nose. Don's heart twisted. She looked so young and so vulnerable, her nose red and sore, her eyes pink as a rabbit's. 'How are the twins?' he asked gruffly.

254

'They're fine. Really. Upstairs asleep.'

While he clambered up the stairs to see, he heard Flora say, 'He wouldn't have come without you to back him up. And you shouldn't have bothered. Next week I'm going into town to see a solicitor, I've decided.'

'But he isn't climbing any more! He's given it up.'

'Oh no he hasn't! Nothing good's been offered, that's all. And look, he's put KORSEA where climbing used to be. He doesn't want a wife and children, not real ones. He wants a plastic family, that you get out to play with when you've got time.'

Don bent over the cradles, putting a big hand against each soft cheek. Plastic? These? He had never felt such emotion, like a river running underground, a hidden torrent of feeling. He had so much to give these two, and Flora, only Flora, stood in his way! Anger surprised him. It would take very little for him to go downstairs and hit her, he was so right to have brought Shalimar. One of the children stirred and a small hand touched his. He could have cried.

When he went downstairs Flora was sitting hunched up, poking the fire desultorily. 'They look – well,' he said, his voice husky.

'They haven't got much of a cold. Only sniffles.'

'Your father – Malcolm's asked me to move back.'

'Oh.'

'So you see, even Malcolm's forgiven him,' said Shalimar breezily. 'He had the Prime Minister visit today. That's why we're late. And it's going to be wonderful for Malcolm to have him back, it is really.'

'I – I might not go,' said Don.

'You can't stay at the office forever,' said Shalimar.

'Actually I've got my eye on a house. I thought you might like to look at it, Flora. It's ideal for a family.'

Somehow it sounded pathetic. He was begging, for the first time in his life. He almost hated Flora for bringing him to this, so unnecessarily. 'So you can stop fucking about here and be sensible,' he snapped. 'You've had long enough to play games, Flora. I've done everything you wanted and this has got to stop. You've got to come home.'

'I haven't got to do anything.'

'My God, and I used to think you were so sweet! Do anything for anyone, I thought. And it was all an act, which you dropped the moment it stopped paying dividends.'

'When you walked all over me, you mean. When have you ever done anything I wanted? You do what you want, all the time, even now!'

255

'You wanted a house, didn't you?'

'No! You decided I wanted it. I want to stay here, I like it here. Except when you come round screaming and yelling!'

Shalimar stepped between them. 'I don't think this is helping.'

'Well, you heard her! You heard how stupid she's being! She's waiting for me to crawl. She knows I'll do anything to get the kids and she's determined to see me crawl!'

'You, the concerned father!' screamed Flora. 'You couldn't care less about them when they were born!'

'Stop it, stop it, STOP IT!' Shalimar put her hands up between them. 'You never fought like this before. What are you making such a fuss about, Flora? You could try, couldn't you? Don's prepared to try. He's giving you what you said you wanted. For the twins, you should try and make up.'

'No.' Flora looked at neither of them. Tears brimmed in her dark blue eyes, like diamonds on her lashes. Next to Shalimar she seemed almost gaudy in colour, prettiness set beside beauty, but Flora had charm. Don remembered how he had felt when first he set eyes on her, a girl he knew he would like on sight.

'I know I seem very hard,' she said in a low voice. 'I have to be. If I went back with you, Don, everything would be just the same. Life would be your way, not mine. I've lived like that all my life and I don't mean to do it any more. I can't do it.

'And I remember what it was like when my parents split up. It seems to me far better to end our marriage now, so the children won't ever remember a time when things were different. When they're older you'll see them, of course. You'll marry someone else. In a week or two I shall start taking them in to see Dad as well. I'm being quite sensible, really.'

Don took a shuddering breath. 'You don't expect me to take that lying down, do you?'

Flora shrugged. 'We spent far too much of our marriage lying down. We got married for sex, and not much else. We didn't know each other.'

'We do now. And I will not let you divorce me!'

'Strange as it seems, I don't need your permission.'

He leaped at her, sending a cup spiralling to shatter on the floor.

'No!' shrieked Shalimar, and pushed herself between them. Don clutched at her, thrusting her out of the way. She clung to a handle on the range and it came off in her hands. Flora backed away, up the stairs, and Don got rid of Shalimar and came after her. Halfway up, she stopped. 'Not near the children,' she said. 'I'll come down and you can hit me there.'

256

The matter of factness of it unmanned him. Tears choked his throat. He turned and thundered down the stairs, out of the door and into the night. Shalimar, nursing her wrist, started to laugh hysterically.

Don drove home fast, too fast. Beside him Shalimar sat silent until a corner loomed up out of the dark and they took it on two wheels. 'Don! Surely you can slow down. It was you losing your temper that ruined everything.'

'There was nothing to ruin. She wasn't going to come back whatever I said.'

'If you'd cajoled her a bit she might have done. All that ordering and yelling wasn't very bright.'

He stamped on the brake and brought the car to a shuddering stop. His hands banged impotently on the wheel. 'I can't act for her,' he said desperately. 'I can't pretend I'm not angry. She sits there, all defiant and determined, and she makes me so mad I want to take her across my knee and show her what happens to little girls who think they can do as they like!'

'And big men who think the same end up living all alone,' said Shalimar in a sing-song voice.

Don sat in silence. His emotions were wound tighter than a spring. He felt that at any moment he would explode, fall apart, disintegrate into a thousand pieces. Shalimar was watching him, her eyes dark and unreadable. She was wearing loose black trousers and a red jumper, with no underclothes at all. Her hard breasts were clearly outlined. He put out his hand and touched her crotch, suddenly aware that he was desperate.

'You don't want to do this,' she said shakily.

'Of course I want to! I need to. If I don't have you, I think I'm going to go insane.'

'It's Flora you want.' His fingers had found their mark and she writhed, involuntarily arching her back.

'We don't want anything but this.'

He pushed across, kneeling astride her on the seat. He dragged the jersey over her head, and dug his fingers into her naked brown breasts. She had abnormally large nipples, and he held them between finger and thumb, pushing her to the verge of pain. Her breath came quickly and he put his hand down and rubbed her, watching her face contort as she came. She opened her eyes and stared at him. The skin of his face was stretched tight across his nose, and he met her gaze without blinking. Suddenly she wanted him inside her. It was more than desire, it was need. Flora didn't want him, Flora had sent him away, and Shalimar needed what he had to give.

257

She pulled at his trousers, trying to free him. His penis was hot and thick, already oozing semen from the tip. She licked the end quickly, and he gasped. As she wriggled out of her trousers she felt her excitement surge unbearably. She put her arms round his neck and lifted her naked body up to him. She cried out as he went into her, and writhed under him, sure that he was going to come quickly. But he settled to a steady, rhythmic pumping, barely pausing even when she came again, and he had to hold himself into her. His fingers bit into her buttocks. She put her legs up outside his arms, spreading herself wide for him. Their eyes met, his glassy and hers dark and moist. He pumped on, reaching out to hold her breasts, and she gripped his shoulders where the muscles ran thick as saplings.

'Hurt me,' he said thickly. 'Go on, hurt me!'

She reached behind him and raked her fingernails down his back, scoring red stripes in his skin. His hips drove hard into her. She felt his whole body begin to pulsate. She jerked up and sank her teeth into his shoulder, feeling salt blood rush into her mouth. He cried out and fell on her, lost in his climax, and she lay quite still, completely filled up.

When he rolled away he said, 'I've never had an orgasm like it. You saved my life.'

Shalimar said nothing. After a moment he reached out and touched her arm. 'You're not going to get pregnant, are you? I was too far gone to think. I'm sorry.'

'It's all right. I'm on the pill.' She wished desperately that she wasn't.

'I suppose you do this quite a bit, do you? Quick bang in a car with a bloke.'

'I don't, actually. But you needed it. We both did. Don, that was important to me. If you want just to sleep with me then all right, you can, but if you want more − I'm ready. More than ready.'

He glanced across at her. Her hair cascaded down like a curtain of black. She was long, strong and desirable. She reached out and touched him, and at once he felt his own response. If he'd been himself tonight this would never have happened. It should never have started. He pushed her hand away.

'I don't think we should take this any further. What's done's done, but I don't want more. You've been a good friend, Shalimar, to me and Flora.'

'And you think we should stay good friends.' Her voice cracked on the last word.

He pulled his clothes roughly together and started the car. Shalimar hunted for tissues, and wiped herself. She only dressed when they saw the lights of the castle. 'You should stay,' she said then. 'Not in my room, they'd talk. But you shouldn't drive back. Have a drink and go to bed, you're exhausted.'

It was tempting. Upstairs in his old room the bed lay waiting, and at the office he only had a sleeping bag laid out on a sofa a foot too short. He felt bewildered by conflicting emotion, and wrung out by sex. Shalimar watched him, her face soft. He turned away from her and made his way up to bed.

She went the next day, and in the days that followed he found himself struggling to find a reason to continue. From his office window he could see the street, and the slow, plodding mothers pushing their children along the pavements. None of them looked like Flora, and yet every one of them reminded him of her. Why did she hold him responsible for things which were not his fault? What did she want from marriage? Or had she never wanted marriage at all?

In the evenings he went back to the castle, and it was a relief to be alone there. He could pay the obligatory visit to Malcolm and then sit and brood, his glass of whisky growing warm in his hand. Damn Flora, damn her pig-headed contrariness! She knew only what she didn't want, with no hint of what she did.

One night Van telephoned. It was a call out of the blue. They hadn't spoken in months. 'Hi.' Don felt awkward, remembering how they had parted.

'Hi.' Van said no more, sending heavy breaths down the 'phone.

'Where've you been then?' asked Don.

'Yosemite. Good climbing.'

'Good.' He felt no envy, but a strong sense of remembrance. Hard, yellow rock, the dust like sandpaper in your throat; birds, giant birds, turning lazily in the beaten metal bowl of sky; shouting to one another and the words echoing from cliff to cliff, like an Inca chant.

'Good,' he said again.

Van sighed, as if he was about to impart terrible news. 'Dhaulagiri's on offer,' he said lugubriously.

'When?'

'Spring. They want you to lead. Small, tight group, you know?'

'Yes. Who's going?'

Van rumbled away, giving names and potted climbing histories. Involuntarily Don's brain clicked into gear, assessing strengths and weaknesses, who he would be pleased to have and who would be dead weight. When Van stopped he was silent.

'You know something?' said Van.

'What?'

'You made it. The time you don't climb is the time you make it. Everyone says "Don, he's the man. The best." And I think, "Clever bastard".'

It was as near to an apology as Van would ever come. 'I knew the lack of oxygen would get to your brain,' said Don. Van chuckled, relaxing.

'So, you going to come?'

'I — I don't know. You know the problems here. Christ, the world must know the problems. Give me a few weeks, will you? To see what I can do.'

'You got till spring, man. They'll wait for you. So get off your arse and do some climbing, hey?'

'I'll let you know. Thanks, Van. Good to hear from you.'

He went back to his chair. The ice in his whisky was well and truly melted by now. Every evening Forbes poured the drink and every evening Don sipped at it, like medicine, until at last it was gone. Now he sipped and the taste came to him, a long-forgotten pleasure. Outside it was blowing hard. Leaves rattled in muffled panic against the double glazing. He went to look out across the darkening parkland as the moonlight was snuffed out by rushing clouds. Dhaulagiri, he thought. White of face and with a shawl of ice. Dhaulagiri.

One of the trees in the park thrashed its arms in terror, bending this way and that in a swirl of wind. As if in slow motion, one of the branches detached itself from the trunk and turned, lazy and suddenly controlled, to bounce on the grass. 'Christ,' muttered Don, and went out into the hall. 'Forbes? Forbes, there's a hell of a wind blowing. Are the cars put away?' John had a habit sometimes of leaving some out.

'I doubt it,' said Forbes, who was determined to despise John for a lifetime if need be. 'I'll ring through to the garage.'

'Someone had better go round and shut the windows. I must 'phone the office, we've got half a dozen ships out.'

When he rang through there was no reply. He glanced at the clock, and saw that it was almost ten. They had to go home sometime, he supposed. So he telephoned the Met Department and a bland voice said, 'It's surprised us a wee bit as well, Mr Harrington. A depression somewhat deeper than we'd been led to expect. A rough night out at sea, I fear, for some.'

He wondered if there was any point in driving into the office. Probably not. The chances were that the road would be blocked by a tree, or even that a tree might block the road by falling on him. Damn, he hoped those ships were all right. The North Sea was no place to be on a nasty night, with oil rigs littering the ocean like man-made wrecking harbours. The wind grew in strength, and began to howl around the battlements, a thousand angry ghosts. When at last he went upstairs he saw Kincaid's light on.

The old man was awake. 'O hear us when we cry to Thee,' he murmured. 'This is definitely a night for prayer. How many ships are out?'

'Six, I think. One may have made harbour this afternoon. This was supposed to be a Force 6, and it's storm going towards hurricane. God help the poor bastards.'

Kincaid nodded. 'I'm a lousy sailor, you know,' he said. 'If I hadn't been I'd have ended up a trawler captain, most like. My dad was. Had a few boats, but he was a captain, through and through. And I threw up and disappointed him.'

'Like hell you did!'

Kincaid grinned. 'He couldn't understand it. Knew I was tough, and couldn't see why I turned green in harbour. Still affects me, you know. But they say Nelson was always sick.'

Don nodded. Kincaid, still in the same tone, said, 'You ought to get hold of Flora. Show her who's boss. She's not like her mother. It only ever needed a bit of a threat to bring Flora into line.'

In a tight voice Don said, 'She thinks − she thinks it's better for the children if we get divorced. Do it now, instead of later. As if we're bound to get divorced.'

'Bloody hell, that's her mother's fault! I can't abide all this feminist nonsense, I thought I'd made sure Flora wasn't tainted with it. The girl doesn't know what she wants, and it's time you made her behave. If I had my strength again I'd do it. No woman ever objected to a strong man, that's my view.'

On the way up to bed, listening to the frantic twirling of the weathercock on the roof, Don felt the first stirrings of anxiety about Flora. What was it like on her beach tonight? If it was like this here − he thought of the waves, crashing like mountains against the rocks, against the little stone house. But it had stood for generations without crumbling. Far better to think of the men at sea, rolling and tossing to the point where walls became floors and the world itself a seething cauldron of water. He went to bed and tried to sleep, but it eluded him. At dawn, with the wind still roaring like a wild beast, he got up and went to work.

Chapter Twenty-four

Trees were down everywhere, from light sycamores to giant oaks. People ran around in the still-eager breeze, looking anxious and upset. Don passed a house where the chimney had landed in the garden, and a fireman was eyeing the remains, belligerently.

At the office the telex was clattering out messages: rigs needed this and that, ships and harbour installations required immediate repair. And there was one more message: 'KORSEA ship *Helvellyn,* listing and taking water. Request assistance.'

His first thought was that they were sinking, but that was rubbish; they were not in distress, merely difficulty. He went down to the radio room where the skinny lad with the pebble glasses was just taking off his coat. '*Helvellyn's* taking water. Get on to them and find out what's up, will you?'

The lad nodded and settled at the set. He was a computer buff who had been weaned away from the keyboard to the knobs and dials of a radio, with barely a withdrawal symptom. 'KORSEA calling *Helvellyn.* KORSEA calling *Helvellyn.* Come in, please.'

'*Helvellyn* here. You're bright and early.'

The line crackled, due to wind and storm. If necessary they could go over to morse, but it was last resort. They preferred to speak direct. '*Helvellyn,* this is Don Harrington. What's up?'

'Not a lot, sir. We're taking water but the pumps are coping. Should make harbour later today. But we've a wee problem. We didna make it to the rig, and we've some machinery they need in a hurry. It's no going to suit anyone to have us take it all the way back home, now is it, sir? And the company reputation isn't so sweet we can afford to let people down, not when it can be avoided.'

Don grinned at the man's patient tone, evident even through the static. 'I take your point. What do you want us to do?'

'Well, it's no so heavy stuff. Could go off by helicopter. And

262

we've Geordie with his broken arm could go too, and not get thrown about here for thirty-six hours, if you take my meaning.'

'Rough, is it?'

'You could say that. The cat won't come out of the lifeboat, and she's seen a thing or two. Been with us fifteen years.'

Don was laughing as he turned away. Some of these men, some of these captains, how he admired them! In the worst of conditions they remained calm, measured, even somewhat humorous. They put up with storms, delays, oil company tantrums and KORSEA mismanagement, each running his own little empire with the benevolent hand of a father. Not that they were always benevolent – there was the odd Captain Bligh in the KORSEA fleet, who nonetheless had a loyal crew. They might hate him, but they trusted him above all others to get them home.

Don wandered into the office. He felt restless and confined, trapped in a man-made box when his natural home, his element, was air and space. If he could he would go today and climb, claw his way up greasy rocks and foaming chimneys until there was nothing in him but exhaustion. His eye fell on the clothing locker, a room housing all the hard-weather gear of a seagoing firm. It was emergency gear, seldom used. 'Get me a place on the chopper going to the *Helvellyn,*' he said absently.

'Yes, Don.' Dorothy was almost too quick in her reply. He glanced at her and she made a face. 'We don't mind if you sometimes go out to play,' she said. 'We just prefer it if most days you come to school.' He felt foolish. They knew him too well.

The chopper was big, spartan, with a floor of non-slip rubber and first aid kits in bulky boxes on each wall. Don, in his survival suit, wedged himself against a metal spar, nodding to the doctor and the two winchmen. From time to time the helicopter pad was swept by gusts of heavy rain, and the men outside had hair plastered wetly to their foreheads. It was a filthy day.

The ride out was bumpy, buffeted as they were by wind and rain. The rigs stood like insects above the waves, long-legged with antennae spiking up into the sky. Lights twinkled on them, like eyes. This was the first bad storm of the season, and winter was hard out here, bitter cold. But this wind was a product of the autumn, the changing moon and tide. The doctor passed round a bar of chocolate and they all had some. It left a thick paste on Don's tongue.

He was the first man down on to the *Helvellyn*. He'd never done it before, but his past career seemed to make advice unnecessary. The consequence was that he was unprepared for the deck list and the rotor blast, and cannoned into the deck housing. 'Want to watch yourself,' said the captain. 'Break your collar bone that way.'

The ship was OK. They were crawling uncomfortably back home, and the cat was indeed in the lifeboat, curled up under the cover so tight that she barely lifted her head to glare balefully when Don looked in at her. He poked his finger into her warm centre and she blinked at him.

'Come and have some cream, Tibby,' coaxed one of the deckies. 'There's a good cat.'

But Tibby stayed where she was, court and plead as they might. She knew all about storms.

Don chatted and listened, while others did the work. They were thrilled, he realised, to have him aboard. After all he had done to damage their livelihood, they were still pleased when he took time off and came to talk to them. When it was time to go he nodded to the captain. 'Sorry you've got such a rough ride back. When you're in, come round to KORSEA and have a drink. The lot of you. You deserve it.'

Back in the chopper, the man with the broken arm was tongue-tied. The doctor found some more chocolate and they all had some, squinting out of the window at another helicopter buzzing off a rig. A forty foot flare of burning gas lit the sky to the left, and Don found himself thinking that in an ugly business, these rigs had a strange sort of beauty. They were like sculptures on an iron grey backdrop, forgiven by nature to the extent that she would frame them wonderfully.

As they crossed the coast the doctor said, 'Look at that.' It was a row of cottages, the roofs quite gone. A police car stood by and four men were trying to spread a tarpaulin over broken timbers, fighting the flapping folds. In the gardens the remains of the tide had left sand and seaweed in ungainly heaps, no doubt mimicking more heaps inside the houses.

'Bad night last night,' said the winchman. 'The worst.'

The moment the chopper touched Don peeled off his suit and headed for his car. Dorothy said, 'Don, I've a hundred calls –' But he said, 'Later. Something's come up.' She was left looking disconsolately after him.

He drove fast. Why hadn't he gone to Flora? Why did he find it so hard to think of her living a life of which he had no part? He pushed his family to the back of his mind, because it hurt less there. But as the weeks passed he found he was concealing a steadily increasing pain. He had never expected that she would last out this long, he had never expected that in the end this might be something he would have to accept.

He stamped on the accelerator. Damn her, he would never, never accept it!

As he drew nearer, windblown sand covered the road. The car's wheels ground shrilly, losing traction. But the cottage itself looked unharmed, except for a slate gone from the roof and the garden fence down. Two or three sheep huddled in the shelter of the barn, their fleeces sodden, and moved not at all as he went up to the door.

'Flora? Flora, are you there?'

The fire was out. The room was cold and full of damp air, as if the crashing waves had saturated the atmosphere with moisture. Without the fire the room seemed small and dark, a dingy place without charm of any kind. But where was Flora? Feet sounded on the narrow stair, and she came cautiously into the room.

'My God, you look terrible.' She was white, with dark shadows under her eyes.

'I've been ill.' A voice grating like old cheese. 'My cold went to my chest.'

'But the kids are all right, aren't they?'

'Yes. Yes, of course they are. I've put them to bed.'

She sank into a chair with such evident, dragging weariness that he was silenced. He went to the table and picked up a spoon, stirring the remains of some mashed vegetable or other, a baby meal. 'Why have you let the fire go out?'

'I didn't. The rain put it out. Down the chimney.'

'I bet that smoked.'

She tried to laugh, but coughed instead. When she recovered she said, 'We were nearly suffocated. I had to take the twins into the barn and the rain came in. No windows, you see. But they're fine. They didn't seem to mind much.'

Her head drooped and her eyes closed. She wasn't asleep, he knew, but conserving what strength she had for whatever must be done. 'You need a doctor,' he said.

She opened half an eye. 'I'll go. Next week.'

'I meant now. You can't stay here like this, it isn't safe.'

The cough came again and she suppressed it, as if to avoid pain. Don could hardly bear to watch. Instead he went up the stairs to the twins.

'They've grown huge,' he called down. 'Absolutely massive.'

Annie woke up with a jerk and her face crumpled. Quickly he gathered her up, warm and sweet-smelling against him. If he dropped her ... He climbed carefully downstairs.

'What are you doing?' She was gripping the chair arms, staring at him fearfully.

265

'Taking you home. All of you. Just for now, just till you're well. I can't leave you here, Flora, you know that.'

'I'm fine. Really. A good night's sleep – ' Her voice tailed off and he realised she was crying. 'It was the fire,' she sobbed. 'We'd have been all right but for the fire. And I thought you'd come this morning, I didn't think you'd wait all day. You worry so – with babies.'

He wanted to cuddle her and couldn't, his arms were full of baby. That he should have left her here like this! He went out to the car and tried to wedge Annie on the back seat, although he couldn't see how it could be done. Didn't they have things for babies? He remembered the carrycots and came back into the house to fetch them. Flora was coughing quietly.

The night was full upon them by the time they were ready to go. Flora staggered the short distance to the car, hunched over like an old woman. The sheep still stood against the barn, sodden, the cottage behind them like a dark, cold rock. He didn't lock the door.

By the early hours of the morning Flora was in hospital. She had pneumonia, untreated perhaps for weeks. 'That's not serious, is it?' Don asked the doctor. 'I mean, with drugs nowadays – people don't die?'

The man glanced at him. 'You'd be surprised. But she's a good strong girl. She's sorely neglected herself lately, that's the problem, and she's fretting about her children. But you can look after them, I suppose?'

'Well ...' He had hardly considered up to now. 'Yes, I suppose I can.'

Although when he returned it was to the sound of wailing children. Marie and Forbes were fussing like anxious hens, but both babies were beyond being calmed. Their howls made a wonderful counterpoint, Alex taking the bass with low, rhythmic bawls and Annie providing the shrill, jazz-inspired melody. Don picked up Annie and jiggled her, to no avail. Suddenly the door opened. It was Kincaid's nurse in her dressing gown, a look of purposeful scorn on her face.

'I have never heard such a noise,' she declared. 'Not even when I was in the Maternity Unit at St Hilda's and we had upwards of forty babies in the nursery.'

'I've been feeding them,' said Marie guiltily.

The nurse cast a withering eye over the array of cups, spoons, pans and unsuitable forage. 'One imagines you have given them both indigestion. Put the child down, Mr Harrington!'

He almost did as he was told. Then he recovered himself. 'She needs to settle. Now if you take Alex – '

'I shall do as I see fit.' She knotted her dressing gown cord more firmly. 'Some gripe water, a nappy change, and some peace and quiet are all that's required. May I suggest that you all retire to bed?'

Reluctantly Marie and Forbes gave way. Don hung on, fighting the cowardly impulse to hand everything over to Nurse Collins and go too. He was so tired. He could think of nothing but Flora's face, all shadows and hollows, no colour anywhere. The nurse removed Annie from his inexpert grasp and laid her on the table. At once the screeching abated, becoming an unhappy grumbling. 'If you must stay, then change the boy,' ordered the nurse. 'These poor children. These poor, poor children.'

Both babies seemed robustly healthy. Alex kicked like a rough-house fighter, and stared up at Don in fascination. Suddenly he grinned, gurgled and belched, letting out a long trail of saliva. 'Tough guy,' said Don, and tickled his hot, fat middle. The baby opened his mouth and yawned capaciously, and so did Don, in sympathy.

When at last they both slept, Nurse Collins was quietly smug. 'Routine, Mr Harrington,' she said, tapping his arm. 'Calmness and routine. Inevitably they'll miss their mother, but ultimately she can only relax if she knows they're well. I suggest a nanny, someone competent.'

'Er – no.' Don put his hands in his pockets. 'I haven't had enough to do with them as it is. Would you mind helping out, Nurse Collins? I can work from home for a week or so, just until we get settled.'

The nurse considered. Caring for Kincaid was all right in itself, but the job lacked challenge; she hungered for the old days of under-staffed wards and crises. A little variety wouldn't go amiss.

'Very well,' she agreed, with no little condescension. 'We shall see what we can do.'

Three days later Van telephoned. 'Have you thought about it, Don? We have to move, get the gear together.'

Don, with Annie balanced on his knee and her tea congealing on a spoon, was distracted. 'You'll have to give me a bit more time. Flora's ill, I'm looking after the twins.'

'You mean she's come back?'

'No. She's in hospital. Look, I want to visit tonight. I'll be in touch, OK?'

'If the answer's no then say so and stop keeping us all guessing. Is it no? Is it?'

267

Don caught his breath. At the table Alex was expertly dodging Nurse Collins' proffered spoon; Annie, as always, was watching him, she spent little of her mealtimes eating. The room was bright, warm, homely – and all at once he shivered. He could feel the wind on Dhaulagiri, the cutting blast of snow, he could even smell the foetid stench of the tent with its packed and unwashed bodies. A nightmare world surely.

'I'll go. For a month, no more than that. OK?'

'Yeah. More than OK. Bloody good, Don, hey?'

Annie's curious face looked up at him, with his own pale eyes, growing paler by the day.

'If you would feed that child, Mr Harrington?' said Nurse Collins pointedly.

Don grunted, watching Annie suck disinterestedly on the spoon. She didn't care about food, she was far too fascinated by the world to waste time being fed. She grew long and thin while Alex, the red child, was simply robust.

That night he went to see Flora. He went every night, but always before had done no more than look at her for a few minutes, lying wired up to instruments, unconscious and untouchable. Her hands were rough and scarred, the nails broken down to the quick. Sometimes, looking at her, he couldn't imagine that he and this woman, this stranger, knew one another; that they had ever made love.

This time she was conscious, propped against pillows, her red hair caught up in a pony tail. She looked incredibly young.

'Hi. You look fine.' He bent to kiss her cheek.

'How are the twins?'

'Fine. Well, all right, anyway. They were miserable to start with, wouldn't settle. But your father's nurse took charge, the place runs like a military encampment. Annie doesn't seem to eat very much, though.'

'You have to bore her into it. Face the wall and maintain total silence. Otherwise she finds something else to amuse her.'

'Yes. I'll remember that. Alex shovels it down like a hoover, of course. And hits you on the ear if you're a bit slow with the spoon.'

She gave the ghost of a smile. 'Does he do that to you? I thought it was just me he liked beating up.'

'No. He knocks his old dad about a bit too.'

The conversation petered out to nothing. Don got out the obligatory bunch of grapes, but in this hi-tech ward there was nowhere to put them. So he laid them on the bed in the hope Flora would like some, and they sat, untouched, like a votive offering.

'So that's settled,' said Don huskily.

'What?'

'When you come out. I mean, it seems obvious – we won't stay at the castle if you don't want. We can buy a house. But the doctor says you'll need weeks of convalescence.'

'He hasn't said that to me. He says I'm doing well.'

'I don't suppose he wants to discourage you.'

She closed her eyes suddenly. 'I don't want to go back,' she whispered.

Rage swelled up in him so violently and so suddenly that he almost failed to contain it. He pushed his chair back from the bed, pushing so hard that the grapes rolled like miniature cannonballs on to the floor. He mashed some as he left, leaving a trail that resembled dark blood. If he had looked he would have seen Flora watching him, with huge eyes.

In the car afterwards he drove fast. Damn it, she would have to come back! Her whims, her problems, were as nothing compared with that truth. The children needed what he could offer, and Flora must not be allowed to deny them that. Whatever selfishness he had shown was being matched now by hers.

But she was ill. He wished suddenly that he had stayed longer, although at the time he thought the place would choke him. When she was better she would see that he was right.

To his surprise, when he got home Kincaid was sitting up in the library. Nowadays it took a major effort to bring him downstairs and it was rare that he thought the effort worthwhile. Tonight he sat with a velvet smoking jacket over his pyjamas. 'Ah, Don! How is she? Back to her old self?'

'You could say that.'

He flung himself down in a chair and glowered.

The old man said, 'Still stubborn, is she? Don't know what you're worried about, man. You've got the children.'

'What do you mean?'

'What I say. She can do as she likes but she won't get them back. If she wants to see them, she lives here.'

'But – I couldn't do that to her. And it wouldn't stand up for a minute in a court of law.'

Kincaid chuckled. 'I never thought you such an innocent, Harrington! Does it matter? She'll give in the moment you tell her that's what's going to happen. Might think you a brute, of course, but you can soothe her down.'

'Can I?' Don swallowed. Flora had changed. When he first met

269

her, so pretty, so young – and even then he hadn't been able to persuade her into bed. He'd expected to. When she set her mind to something it was hellish hard to sway her.

They drank some brandy and talked of other things. Kincaid was happy that night, charming, ebullient, with an astuteness which belied his years. Don chatted about the company, the reorganisation.

'I should have done it right away,' he confided. 'We needed a more open style of management. I've got a team now, some good blokes.'

'The dictatorship becomes a democracy,' murmured Kincaid. He viewed the world through his balloon glass. 'I do not doubt that Alexander will change it all back. I have to admit, you and Flora surprised me there. I didn't think you could produce that boy. I've adjusted my will, of course.'

'What do you mean?'

'Well, obviously he gets the firm, I've set up a trust. It was left to Flora, but that isn't a tax efficient arrangement. This is. You have control until he's twenty-five, and I've given you a slice of the equity. Incidentally, Flora gets nothing unless she's living with you.'

'Christ! That's a bit strong, isn't it? And what about Annie?'

Kincaid flapped a hand. 'Jewellery, that sort of thing. She's going to be pretty, she can marry a fortune if she wants one. Or you can put something away. I don't mean to slight the child, but I will not split the firm. In years to come companies are going to need big muscle to stay afloat, and breaking bits off to leave here, there and everywhere is absolutely not on.'

Don leaned back in his chair. He felt slightly shocked. 'Does Flora know what you mean to do?'

'I imagine she has guessed. Don't you?'

It was the cause of all the trouble, or at least half its cause. He felt a sense of relief; she wasn't rejecting him alone, but him and Kincaid together. 'I think you're going to have to reconsider that will,' he said.

'Oh, come on, Don! You know I won't. But you can tell Flora I have. If you want. I won't give you away.'

'And when you die and she finds out the truth?'

Kincaid grinned devilishly. 'You were all deceived, weren't you? What a shocker the old man was. Don't let the women bugger you about, Don. There's no need.'

Flora came out of hospital two days later. Don took the Bentley to fetch her, and they sat in the back together, awkward and silent.

270

She was very pale still, and her voice sounded weak and shaky. Two young doctors came to the door to see her off.

'Best of luck, Mrs Harrington.'

'Do come back and see us. We'll miss you.'

In the car Don said, 'They seemed pretty friendly.'

She grimaced. 'Young and bored, that's all. They work such long hours, they don't get time to socialise.'

'Speaks the old lady! You're younger than they are.'

'Am I? I don't feel it just at the moment.'

She leaned her head back against the leather squabs. Don opened the cocktail cabinet and got out a silver flask, pouring them both a measure. 'Here. It's cherry brandy.'

'Isn't that what Prince Charles got caned for?' She sipped the thick goo, letting the medicinal taste slide soothingly down her throat. 'It's lovely. Thanks.'

Don checked that the glass panel was tight shut. 'I'm back in our old room,' he said. 'And I want you there too.'

Flora said nothing for a moment. Then she looked out of the window. 'Honestly, I'm not up to it, Don. I cough half the night. No.'

'I wasn't talking sex, damn it! Marriage. I don't care if you keep me awake, but I do care about being married. It's important.'

'But — just while I'm ill. I'd prefer to be on my own.'

'And I won't have it. If you don't want sex then so be it, but at least I want us together. Give us a chance, Flora! A chance to be a family.'

Weakness made her easy prey for tears. She struggled against them. Sitting so close to her, Don seemed huge, an invincible man. His long thighs dwarfed hers; his hands were brown and knotted with muscle. She was too ill for sensuality, his strength only served to make her still more feeble. Dimly, she remembered how much she had been hurt; he had left her, neglected her, ignored and forgotten her. He had arranged life to suit himself and expected her to be suited too. And she was tired, so tired that when the car stopped she could barely put one foot in front of the other to walk to the castle door.

Nurse Collins was there, with the children. Suddenly Flora's feet had wings. 'Alex! Annie! My darlings!' she cried, and put her arms round babies and nurse together. Alex shrieked with delight and Annie began crowing, a throaty warble she had made all her own. Now Flora cried in earnest. 'I thought they might forget me,' she sobbed, sinking to the stairs and letting Nurse Collins put the children in her lap.

271

'As if they'd forget their mammy!'

Don felt a lump in his throat too. Her face was joyous, bright with happiness and love. She had once looked like that for him. He turned briskly to Forbes. 'Have my wife's bags taken up to our room, please. We'll have tea in our room today. Flora's ready for bed.'

'Am I?' She looked up at him in surprise.

'Yes. The twins are exhausting you. Give them to Nurse Collins and come on up.'

But she wouldn't give up the children. Instead they came to the bedroom with her, and wriggled about the bed as Flora sat in it, cuddling first one and then the other in an orgy of reunion. When Don picked them up they screamed and kicked to get back to Flora. He felt an unreasonable hurt.

That night he joined her in bed late, with too large a brandy under his belt. He, who risked his life as a matter of course, needed dutch courage to go to bed with his wife; it was humiliating. What's more, Flora was still awake, propped up against the pillows reading.

'Do you want the light off?' she asked. 'I find it hard to sleep at the moment. I wake up thinking I'm suffocating.'

'Keep it on if you like.'

He wouldn't retreat to the bathroom and undress there. Flora watched with huge eyes as he took off his clothes, almost as if she was frightened of him. This was all her fault, he found himself thinking. If she had been patient and sensible, none of this would have happened.

Suddenly she said, 'What on earth's happened to your back?'

He froze. 'What do you mean?'

Flora half knelt on the bed. 'It looks as if someone's scratched it.' He turned round quickly, and saw the blood drain from his wife's face. 'I don't think it's any use hiding it,' she said shrilly. 'There's a bite mark clear as anything on your shoulder.'

He glanced down. Clearly outlined against his skin were the blue puncture marks of teeth, still only half healed. Why hadn't he seen them? Because he didn't look. He shaved and dressed each morning like a robot, barely glancing in the mirror.

'Who was it?' she asked.

'It − it wasn't anybody.' His mind raced, trying to think of something that would placate her. He would have to admit sex perhaps, but who with? A prostitute? Someone at the office? Marie?

'You can't have forgotten. Those marks are recent.'

'Not that recent. A month, perhaps.'

272

'Don, who?'

He turned away from her and went to the window, lifting the curtain aside to look out. Blackness met him, there wasn't a light anywhere. 'I don't think you've got the right to ask,' he said. 'I was desperate. Because of you, I needed someone. You wouldn't come home and I couldn't see any way out, and she was just there! We did it once, in the car, and that was that. One wild, painful screw.'

He turned to face her, and her eyes were so dark they might have been black. Her breasts swelled against her nightgown, arousing him to untimely desire. 'Was it Shalimar?' she asked.

He said nothing. He could think of nothing to say. The colour surged in Flora's cheeks, bright red draining instantly to ghastly white. 'I always knew she liked you,' she said shrilly. 'But I never thought she'd do anything about it. You I could understand, but Shalimar. Shalimar!'

'It wasn't her. It was a girl at the office, one of the typists.'

'Don't lie, Don! It only makes it worse.'

He could see no way in which things could be worse. Flora was betrayed, by her husband and her friend. 'You drove us to it,' he said desperately. 'It was that night. You wouldn't come back and I was going mad. I'm a man, I need sex, you can't have expected me to become a monk! And that night wasn't sex – it was a way out of torment. Flora, you were sending me mad.'

She got out of bed then, and went unsteadily across to the door. She held it open. 'I think you'd better go.'

'You're not being sensible.'

'Yes, I am. You don't have to explain, I'm not angry. There isn't any point. But you do see, don't you, that we can't go on? We didn't have much of a chance before, but now we haven't any. It's over.'

'No it isn't.' He took her by the arm, her fragile arm, he thought it might break if he gripped hard. 'Shalimar sleeps with anyone, it meant nothing to her and nothing to me. We're married, we can be happy. Flora, please!'

'I can't. I don't want to. I could have got over it with anyone else. But not with her.'

He took her in his arms, he hugged her tight, crushing her against him. Flora was crying, her sobs muffled against his skin. She thought of Shalimar, Shalimar, raking her nails down Don's back in an ecstasy of passion, biting deep into his flesh. Revulsion swept through her, she couldn't bear his embrace. She put her head back and screamed.

He let her go and she fell on the bed, sobbing horribly. He put out a hand towards her, longing to comfort and not daring to touch. 'Don't,' he whispered, 'Please don't.'

'Go away. Please − go away.'

There was no help for it. He must go. His eyes fixed on his wife, he backed slowly from the room.

Flora's recovery was agonisingly slow. It was as if she had no wish to get better, and she spent her days in her room, resisting all Don's attempts to talk to her. He decided to concentrate instead on the twins. When she saw that he loved them, when she saw that he was prepared to do all that he could, surely then she would see that everything else was unimportant?

But, day by day, they became set in opposing camps. There was no anger any more, just a steadily spreading ice. When Flora began to get up and come downstairs, she was civil and restrained. Yet somehow she had erected a wall against him, a structure as solid and impregnable as concrete, for all its invisibility.

Don turned this way and that, searching for a way through to her. He brought her chocolates, flowers, holiday plans, for which she thanked him, civilly, and declined. Never in his life had he worked so hard for so little reward. It left him speechless with frustration.

Finally, a month after Flora's return home, he v.ent to see Lilian. He took the Land Rover, taking pleasure in bouncing uncomfortably over the ruts and potholes in the road. Physical suffering was so straightforward, he thought. For real torture you had to experience the mental variety.

Lilian was mucking out goats, spreading straw and piling hay in place of barrowloads of muck.'Do you want me to help you with that?' asked Don gruffly.

'No, thank you. I prefer to do things myself.'

'But I should like to help.'

So she let him, and he did the job with easy efficiency. Lilian stood watching him, her eyes very steady in her pale face. She herself was steady, thought Don. She had quietly remained herself against all Kincaid's attempts at transformation.

When the pens were finished, Lilian said, 'I don't imagine you came here to muck out goats. How is Flora?'

All at once he couldn't speak. He put his hand up to his face to hide the sudden tears. What a time to show such weakness − here, in front of this woman who had never wanted him to marry Flora at all!

'Oh dear,' said Lilian dully. 'Oh dear.'

'It's as if she's made up her mind and nothing's going to change it,' he burst out. 'I can't explain to her – she won't listen – but we have to try again.'

'Why?'

He drew in his breath. 'Because – I can't bear not to. I'd lose them all. Everything.'

'And isn't it a little late to realise you don't want to, Don?'

They went into the house together, and washed in the same bowl. Lilian made tea. When they were settled by the fire she said, 'Are you giving up the climbing then?'

He shook his head, denying her assumption. 'It wasn't the climbing that was at fault. Not completely.'

'What then?'

He sighed. 'Me. Us. I had everything I wanted and she had nothing. And now she's taken the things I really need.'

'You haven't lost anything yet!' She sounded scornful and he said dully, 'She's going to leave me. I know she is. She's going to take the twins and leave.'

Lilian sat looking at him. Her emotions surprised her. She had felt such rage against this man, such impotent rage, and now that he sat there, hurt, brought down, she felt nothing but understanding. Wanting everything from life, trying to cram it in, had left him with hands full of dust. Powerful and used to success, he couldn't believe that he had broken something that couldn't be mended.

'Perhaps you'll have to let her go,' she said gently.

He shook his head, slowly, like a creature at bay.

'You will only hurt the children if you resist.'

He looked at her then. 'It's going to hurt them if I give them up. They need me. She doesn't see it but they do. They need what I can give. You know Malcolm, you know what he's like, plotting and planning to give Alex everything and shut Annie out. Flora thinks I'm going to stand by and watch, when surely she must know that I won't. If I left now he'd do his worst. I can't leave them to that! And if she goes – I won't have them living in some poky cottage again. They could have died.'

'So, what do you suggest?'

He took a shuddering breath. 'We don't sleep together any more. If you would just talk to her – make her see – we could make it different.'

'Some things just insist on staying the same.'

He was home early, a full two hours before his usual time. As he drove up he saw a cluster of people on the doorstep: Flora, Nurse

275

Collins, Forbes, Marie – and Kincaid. The old man was between his nurse and his butler, and he was furious.

'Flora, you will do as I say! I'll have the constable to you, that I will! I'll have you certified! I'll not let you take that boy away, and not one penny of mine will you have if you do!'

Both carrycots were in the back of the Bentley. The screams of frightened children were audible for yards. Don pulled the Land Rover across the bonnet of the car and got out. Flora's face was white with strain, and as he got close she flinched, as if he might hit her.

'Thank God you're here,' said Kincaid. 'She's insane. We'll get the doctor to her.'

'If we get him for anyone it'll be you,' said Don quietly. 'Get inside, man. You do nothing but harm.'

'If she goes, she goes,' bellowed Kincaid. 'We keep the boy!'

Don stepped away from Flora. He turned very slowly towards Kincaid. 'Listen,' he said softly, 'these children have two parents. I will not take my children from Flora, any more than I wish them to be taken from me. And if you persist in this ridiculous – this criminal – attitude towards Annie, I will not be responsible for the consequences. The children will go, all right. We all will. And you will live in your damned castle all by yourself.'

'Sentimental claptrap,' said Kincaid. 'I need that boy.'

'Balls!'

He turned back to Flora. She shook her head at him, miserably. 'He won't change.'

'He must. Where were you going? Not the cottage again?'

She gestured vaguely. 'Somewhere. A hotel to start with. I couldn't – we can't go on.'

'Oh, she can't go on!' mimicked Kincaid. 'No guts, that's her. Like all women, no grit when it comes down to it.'

'Right,' said Don. 'What else do you need, Flora? I'll help you pack.'

They stood, all of them, in a moment of frozen silence. Kincaid almost hiccupped with surprise. 'After all I've done for you,' he said wonderingly.

'I'm nobody's lapdog. For once in your life, old man, you have to realise you have gone too far! Get inside, Malcolm, and let me see what I can do to put right this mess.'

As he was led back inside Kincaid snorted, defiantly. Flora sank down on to the steps. Don sat beside her, and then called: 'Marie! Take the children in, will you? They shouldn't be left to cry.'

'All this is so bad for them,' muttered Flora, putting her hands over her eyes and rubbing with her palms.

'It's bad for all of us.' He reached out to touch her arm but she moved away. 'Your mother thinks we've had it,' he remarked.

'She's right.'

'At least − at least we could try. The house is big enough. We needn't see each other if we don't want. There's nowhere better to bring up children, provided Malcolm keeps his nose out. And he will.'

'I don't want you to touch me,' said Flora dully. 'I keep thinking you'll try.'

'For Christ's sake!' He dragged his temper back under control. 'All right,' he said tightly. 'You'll be spared my obnoxious presence in the bedroom. You ought to feel safe, I haven't been near you in weeks. And actually I'm going to Dhaulagiri soon − '

Flora snorted, in exact imitation of her father. 'Oh, surprise me! I wondered how long the model husband and father act would take to crack! You can't hang around long enough to let your boots dry, can you?'

'Would it help if I did?'

She dropped her eyes. 'No.'

John came out of the house and discreetly climbed into the Land Rover to return it to the garage. Then he returned for the Bentley. Still they sat on, side by side, saying nothing. It couldn't go on forever, Don told himself. Climbing or no climbing, living as they must, side by side, she would come to see that there was nothing to be gained by coldness. He was putting right all that he could, and anything he couldn't undo must be buried. Damn Shalimar, he thought. And damn himself!

Flora turned to look at him. 'We must never argue in front of the children,' she said. 'In fact, we mustn't argue at all.'

'That's impossible.'

'We've got to try.' She pushed her hair aside with a small hand, and the flesh of her neck flashed blue-white. He wondered if he wanted her so much because he knew he couldn't touch her. How long would this continue? There might be a cool three months perhaps. He could take that.

'We shall be terribly civilised,' he said soothingly. 'We'll pass the marmalade at breakfast.'

Flora got up, dusting her skirt. 'I would rather you took breakfast alone.'

After a while he followed her into the house. He stood in the hall, and servants passed him carrying clothes and books, records

277

and stacks of papers. Flora was removing all trace of him from their room, every sock and cufflink. The familiar, dangerous rage rose up in him and he bit down hard on it, mastering himself. Patience, that was his weapon. Sooner or later she must come round.

Chapter Twenty-five

Dear Winifred,

Congratulations! I was delighted to read of your appointment, I'm sure it's very well deserved. Nonetheless I imagine you'll find it strange working in Edinburgh again after so long abroad.

I must confess that I've got a favour to ask. Previously when I've asked the agency if there was any work for me they've always said no, but since you're now such a bigwig I wondered if you could find something for me? The twins are almost two now and I could leave them for two or three days a week and come and stay in Edinburgh. In fact, that might be good for them. Things do tend to get a bit tense around here sometimes and I know Don likes to have the children to himself now and then.

Please believe me when I say I'm not asking for any special favours, but since you do know my work I thought you might be able to find something I could do. I would be most grateful.

Yours ever,

Flora

She sat for some minutes after the letter was done. The children were playing on the lawn outside, watched over by an indulgent Marie. One thing was certain, she could not continue as she was. She had to find some joy in life.

She had never imagined that so much time could go by, living like this. Nowadays when Don went climbing she watched him go with relief. When he was home they did their best, both of them, not to argue, and somehow that made the inevitable fights all the more bitter. They were sudden, vicious and unrewarding. The children had taken to hiding in corners with their hands over their ears.

It was as if tension built up over weeks, and finally had to explode.

Lately Don had badgered her, pleaded with her. Last night, drunk, he screamed: 'What shall I do then? Give Shalimar a call and see if I can't get her into bed? That's bound to give you something to complain about and you've got absolutely no bloody right! What do you want, Flora? Will you be happy with my head on a platter?'

Nowadays, nothing made her happy. She was trapped in loneliness and pain, not knowing what she wanted, only that it wasn't in Don's power to give. If it all could be put right by letting him into her bed then she would, she would. Living like this was torment. His hands fascinated her, in all their calloused strength. She found herself watching the way his shoulders moved beneath the soft silk of his shirt. If she let herself remember how he felt, how he tasted, she couldn't sleep, and when she did she dreamed. But there was no way she could take that and nothing else.

If she surrendered her body, she would have nothing left. She wanted her own life, she couldn't live as an adjunct to his, as the woman in his bed, the mother of his children, the dinner partner. To live as part of a couple, it seemed to Flora, you had to be whole yourself, not a pale moon to a brilliant sun. If Don bought her now, giving satisfaction to her crying sexual need, it would be the end, she knew. Flora Kincaid would make nothing of herself. Flora Kincaid, like burned heather, would wither before she flowered.

She was prepared to wait a week before despairing, but Winifred's reply came within three days. It was all that Flora had hoped.

Dear Flora,

How delightful to hear that you want to come back to us! Of course we can find you something, and to begin with I should like you to be my assistant, sorting out the dreadful paper. Something of a muddle has developed here in the past year or so and it needs a clear mind to deal with it. You will do admirably, my dear. I shall expect you next Wednesday, at nine.

Best wishes,

Winifred

The ease of it amazed her. A step had been taken, small and surely harmless, to make something of herself. Enough of this trapped, false existence. She was making a new beginning.

It had been a hard week. Flora kicked off her shoes at the door, flung down her capacious leather bag and padded across to her desk. Forbes always piled the letters there for her to read, topping them

280

with a chased silver dirk that it was said Bonny Prince Charlie had used to cut meat. Flora used it to slice open each letter, glancing quickly through. She opened one blue envelope quite slowly.

My dear Flora,

I know you don't want to hear from me but I feel I must write. Don telephoned me last weekend in quite a state, I gather you'd had yet another row. I know you'll think I've an axe to grind, but honestly, don't you think it's time you moved out? Don seemed to think I might be able to convince you that it's time you forgave and forgot, but it seems to me that if you haven't by now then you're not about to. So what are you doing? Whatever it is, you're driving him nuts.

Couldn't you at least write back and tell me what's going on? I've stood on the sidelines all this time, waiting for you two to sort things out, and if it's not going to happen then I'd like to pick up where we left off. I've said sorry till I'm blue in the face, so can't you at least talk to me? You're my dearest friend, and I can't believe that we won't ever speak to each other again.

Yours ever,

Shalimar

Did the woman never give up? Flora moved to add the letter to the unanswered pile in her drawer. Then she hesitated. Lately she had found it hard to summon up anger against Shalimar. One evening in Edinburgh she had gone to see her in a film, playing a hard-edged, sassy girl who gave as good as she got, and so much of it had reminded her of their youth. She and Shalimar drew from a shared past, and when she doled out her wisecracks and erotic sighs Flora thought again and again of their carefree, united girlhood. The time had come to make amends. Flora picked up her pen, determined to write now before the impulse faded.

Dear Shalimar,

Thank you for your letter. I'm sorry if Don's upset but there's not a lot I can do about that just now. As you probably know I've been working for the agency for over a year now, staying away a few nights a week. I may have to be away for rather longer in the future, I haven't decided.

As for Don and me, that is most definitely over. If you could help him accept it you would be doing us both a great favour. We're parents, of course, and always will be, but nothing more.

281

Anyway, I don't believe he is utterly heartbroken, merely peeved that he can't have his own way. He's still climbing half the time, he simply manages to run the business more efficiently these days so things don't fall apart while he's gone. Then he comes back and plays Superdad and annoys me by being so good at it. You may feel sorry for him but believe me, if you lived here you would see he doesn't need anyone's sympathy. Life may lie down and do Don's bidding but I won't.

I enclose some pictures of the twins that you might like. They're beautiful and full of themselves, almost three and a half now, an adorable pair. They come to no harm at all while I'm away, if you discount the spoiling. If I'm not there in the evenings Don is, and after him there are dozens of adoring helpers.

Actually I might telephone you myself in the next few days. There are one or two things it might help to talk to you about. I don't know − I thought I never wanted to speak to you again, but good friends are hard to come by, however treacherous they may be on occasions.

I think I should scratch that out, but I won't. It was treacherous. But it's over, and in the end I don't think it made any difference. So that's the hatchet buried, on my side at least.

Love,

Flora

She clasped her hands on the paper, and then unclasped them again. There was no help for it, she must look. She took up a flimsy, official missive, stamped with the agency's logo, and unfolded it. She had told no one, so if the news was bad there would be no humiliating confessions, but somehow Don suspected what was in the wind. He had the knack of awareness, forcing her to erect barriers against his knowledge of her. She smoothed the letter with a shaking hand.

Dear Mrs Harrington,
It is with great pleasure that we write to offer you the position of Assistant Supplies Co-ordinator (India). As explained at the interview, this full-time situation is based in Delhi and is a minimum two-year posting. Our salary scales and UK holiday allowances are detailed on the attached sheet, and we should be grateful if you would let us have your acceptance, or otherwise, within twenty-four hours.

Should you accept the post we feel sure that you will be a worthy addition to our staff in the Indian sub-continent, and

282

that you will make the most of the opportunity we have been able to provide.

Yours sincerely,

J.A. Holdsworth

Flora wrinkled her nose. Mr Holdsworth was making the point that without Winifred's strong support they would have given the job to the would-be clergyman who was on the short list with her. Why had she ever listened to Winifred? She should never have let her send in the application, because if she refused this offer they might never consider her again.

She put both the letters under her blotter, although she knew Don might look there and read them. He watched her every move nowadays, as she detached thread after thread from her wings and spread her feathers tentatively to fly. First it was the part-time job, which soon became full-time, although she managed to work for two days at home. Responsibility came next, as she learned to make decisions and to stand by them. The logical onward step was an overseas posting, and logic had made her apply for this position, as trainee dogsbody in Delhi.

She pulled the letter out again and looked at the holiday schedule. Every four months they would let her have three weeks at home. Big deal. What would three and a half year old twins think of that? On second thoughts she pushed the letter into her pocket.

She went upstairs to the nursery, an airy room with windows on three sides, where they tried vainly to contain the mess and muddle that the twins seemed to create from nothing. On a raw afternoon it was a good place to be, with its deep sofas and piles of picture books, as well as the army of kilted toy warriors Kincaid had given to Alex. There was an equally numerous collection of Scottish farm animals Don had obliged him to hand to Annie, although the old man hadn't needed more than token persuasion. It was strange, thought Flora, with a wry smile. For all that he pretended the girl didn't matter, no one could help but warm to her. She had such determined, clear-eyed charm and defeated her brother's strength with intelligent guile. Alex would always be his grandfather's favourite, but Annie was not unfavoured, after all.

To her surprise, Don was there, although she had thought him still at work. He sat silent on the sofa, Annie on his lap, sucking her thumb. He barely acknowledged Flora's arrival and she hovered on the threshold, not sure what to do, but Alex stomped towards her waving sticky hands and said, 'Make my castle work, Mummy.' So she found herself up to her elbows in flour and water paste, trying to model with collapsing dough. Finally she got up, went over to Annie and put a clean inch of wrist against the girl's forehead. 'She's so quiet. I thought she might have a temperature.'

'She's too darned sensitive, that's all.'

Don looked up at her bleakly. Flora rubbed her hands together, collecting the dough in balls between her fingers. This was hurting the children so much. She said, 'I didn't know you'd spoken to Shalimar. She wrote.'

'I had to speak to someone. Who else is there?'

She shrugged. Suddenly Annie crawled off Don's lap and hid under a cushion, her narrow little bottom in its red tights poking incongruously into the air.

'We're not cross, Annie,' said Flora despairingly. 'Really we're not.'

But Annie didn't move. Alex tipped the bowl of water abruptly on to the floor, adding his wordless protest to Annie's. Where was the point in trying to pretend? For the good of them all she must go, and she knew it was going to break her heart. Flora pulled her letter from her pocket and thrust its crumpled pages at her husband. Then she turned on her heel and left.

They talked, finally, late that night. He was in the library, drinking hard, which so often had the perverse effect of leaving him almost sober. In a green dress, long and flowing, Flora sank to a stool on the other side of the fire, and gazed into the flames without speaking. Don reached up above the fire and took down an ornamental silver cup. He poured Flora whisky, cutting it with the minimum of water. 'Here.'

She took the cup and sipped. 'I haven't accepted,' she murmured.

'But you will.'

'Will I?' She stared at him, her eyes like black pools. 'I decide and then I change my mind. Do you want me to go?'

He sighed, heavily. 'I want – something. I want our children not to flinch when we're both in a room together. I want lightness and happiness in my home. I want an end to being celibate.'

'Have you found someone else?' asked Flora breathily.

He shook his head. 'But I might. You're not the only woman in the world. I don't have to spend my life like a dog at your locked door. It seems to me we've reached a crossroads. Either you stay and we try again – or you go. And that's an end of it.'

'I'm not giving up my children!' burst out Flora. 'You haven't won, you know. I shall be back. Officially it's every four months, but if I save up off-duty I could grab a week in the middle. Most people can't afford to come home, but I could. It's got to be better. Hasn't it?'

He said nothing. At that moment everything seemed pointless and without hope. He had been so sure that everything would work out as he wished. But gradually, month by month, Flora had slipped further and further from his grasp. Looking back she seemed to have been moving steadily towards this day, when she could safely leave them all. He felt an explosion of unexpected anger, which at once felt like sorrow, hot and sore. 'Why doesn't it hurt you?' he asked desperately, coming out of his chair towards her. He knelt on the rug, feeling the heat of the fire burn his face. Her hair was like fire itself. He took it in his hands and crushed it. 'How can you bear to turn away?' He bent his head and kissed her.

For a second she leaned against his shoulder. Her lips opened, he felt the warm welcome of her tongue, and the pleasure startled him into helplessness. He heard her sob. When she left him and he reached for her, he even failed to catch the hem of her dress.

He sank down before the fire, stretched out on the rug. Stags' heads gazed down at him and he put his hands over his face to shut them out. The air smelled of her, he could taste her still, and at last, finally, he knew that she was gone.

Part Two

Chapter One

A hot wind blew the dust around the village. Peasant women covered their mouths and pulled shawls over the babies on their backs. Flora blinked gritty eyes and scratched absently at a mosquito bite on her arm; these hot Indian afternoons before the monsoon were unbearable. Families squabbled, aid workers snarled and even the yellow dogs turned on one another, to be chased from the streets in fighting tangles. Flora tried again to make sense of the list; tractor parts, high energy biscuits and grain. The grain had been pilfered, the parts sold off, but she was expected to sign for it just the same. She wouldn't, of course, and if necessary she'd call on the magistrate. But it really was time they sent someone as shotgun with these consignments: she wasted days over things like this. Whoever was doing her old job as Supplies Co-ordinator was certainly not doing it well.

'This is just complete rubbish,' she said in Urdu, and the man in front of her looked hunted. 'If the rest of the stuff doesn't turn up by tonight I shall see the authorities. May I have the keys please?'

He didn't want to give her the keys to the padlocks, but eventually he did. Thieving was a way of life in India, difficult for the Western mind to understand, but you couldn't hold it against them. You just took every precaution.

She went wearily back to her bungalow, her skirt stuck to her body with sweat. Her servant, an ex-leper, hovered with a jug of lemon squash. Flora took a glass, drained it and set it down. 'I'll have some more when I've showered, Abdul. Thanks.'

He bobbed up and down, gripping the tray with almost fingerless hands. Even after months with Flora he still seemed to half expect to be shunned.

'The letters have arrived,' he said shyly. 'I have placed them in your room.'

'Oh! Oh, wonderful!'

The shower could wait. After months out here, in charge of a dozen eager young hopefuls, contact with civilisation was blessed. She ran to her room, grabbed the pile of post and sorted quickly through. Letters from the children, a treat! And one from Don. One from Shalimar too, postmarked Singapore of all places, and a pile of official mail. She opened that first, in case of bad news; they might be sending her another student. They seemed to regard her station as a worthwhile training ground for young idealists, and after six months with her they either gave up and became stockbrokers or grew up and became useful. The last one had fallen in love with her and had taken to leaving impassioned poems on her pillow. She'd sent him even further up-country.

The news was relatively good; she was losing her able Indian woman doctor to a senior post in Bombay, to be replaced by a man. The promotion was deserved, but a man? Half the work here was childbirth, and a male practitioner could drive so many women back into the hands of the dirty and unskilled. She would write back tonight suggesting that they think again. And there was a note about fertiliser, a WHO communique on malaria, a request for a report on diseases of cattle – she pushed it all to one side. Not another moment could be wasted. She would read her letters from home.

Dear Mummy,

They've made me prop forward in the under fourteens. It's quite an honour, but it does hurt my ears. I'm tight end, of course, I'd much rather be loose. Dad says it hurts less if you really shove, but Smith major's lending me his scrum cap. He got trodden on last week and lost a tooth, he can't play for a bit. We all wrote our names in his blood.

How are the starving Indians? Dad says to ask if you're coming home for Christmas. Grandad's got a new nurse, she's a dragon. Can you ask Dad if we can have a dog? He says not because we're all away at school but Forbes would take care of it, he likes dogs. I want a lurcher, for the rabbits. Don't tell Grandad, he doesn't approve of bloodsports.

I got C in my Latin, and a detention. I want to drop it, please tell Dad. Can you send photographs of the starving? We're doing a project. Do come for Christmas.

Lots of love,

Alex

Dear Mum,

I absolutely hate this school!!! The girls in my form are foul, Patricia Wilkes is REVOLTING, she picks her spots in French. Everyone's sure the Head is a lesbian, she's so butch it isn't true. They're having a pogrom on skirts again, anyone with less than ankle length is going to be crucified. I am THIRTEEN YEARS OLD and some old biddy presumes to tell me how short I can wear my skirts. Anyone would think we were a load of tarts.

I asked Dad if I could leave, but he's being pigheaded as usual. He seems to imagine it's healthy to be in a community entirely obsessed with hockey and spots. I LOATHE hockey. All that shrieking, and it turns your thighs blue. Dirty old men from the village come and peer at us, we ought to have ankle-length skirts for hockey if anything, instead of those ghastly grey nappies, they must be out of the Ark!

Alex and Dad are both sport mad, we've got absolutely nothing in common. Are you coming home for Christmas? I do hope so, you could take me back to school and refute all the rumours. They're saying you're locked up in a lunatic asylum, like Mrs Rochester. Every time Dad brings me back all the girls peer at him and swoon, it's sickening. If they had him for a father they wouldn't think he was so great. He's just the most old-fashioned disciplinarian there has ever been. He sends me to bed at NINE O'CLOCK! In the HOLIDAYS! Do come for Christmas.

Lots of love,

    Annie

Dear Flora,

Thank you for your letter. It's good to hear things are going so well. I'm afraid we've got one or two problems on the home front. Your father's not too well and we thought he'd have to go into hospital. But he seems to have come round a bit, thanks to an Intensive Care nurse. She's not exactly charming, but at least with her around he can stay at home.

Alex is fine, feet taller than the rest of the boys in his year, and in the school rugger team. He sends his love. As for Annie, I was delighted to see the back of her at half term. She is just the limit. Skirts up to her knickers, wants her ears pierced, weighs her eyelashes down with soot, plays rock music loud enough to crack the walls and spends all morning in the bath. In the evenings she comes down and rabbits on about boys, spots and the lesbian Headmistress, who isn't — rumour has it she's shacked up with

291

a socialist. Daren't tell Annie that, the whole school would know. She hates her pony, says he's "putrid", but had hysterics when I suggested we flog it.

Are you coming home for Christmas? Annie clearly needs you, and if the starving Indians can starve alone for five minutes I think your own deprived children could do with a bit of attention. Besides, I want to go climbing. Let me know.

Yours,

Don

Flora brought her knees up and rested her chin on them. A wave of longing to be home rose up in her; she would give anything then to be back. It was over eight months since her last visit. It was so hard to get away and there wasn't so much point in the trips with both children away at school. If she went home now she would take Alex out to tea and talk rugby, not that she knew anything about it, and as for Annie, they'd go shopping for clothes and be scurrilous. How Flora loved her! All that excess, all that wild thrusting at life. No wonder Don couldn't cope.

She got off the bed and went into the shower, leaving her clothes in a sweaty heap on the floor. The water cascaded over her face and hair, she stood and let it wash the day's exhaustion out of her. In a moment she would put on her robe, go out on the verandah, drink more lemonade and read the letters again.

But people kept arriving and disturbing her. She tried to suppress her irritation, because she always sat on the verandah at this hour. It was a convenient time to tell her things, seek her advice or confess some mistake, and normally she didn't mind. But today she had her letters. They all thought she had no real home life, of course, they saw her as wholly dedicated, like Winifred. In the end she'd be exactly like Winifred, she decided, an old dried-up cynic with no life but this. She was retired now, and instead of a rose-covered cottage in England lived in a hut in Bhutan, dispensing health care.

Would she go home for Christmas? She didn't always. To begin with, when she had the dreadful supply job, she went home every eight weeks or so, laden down with guilt and presents. Gradually the intervals had lengthened, largely because she seemed to disrupt things by going home. An air of calm had settled over the castle, a welcome condition of peace. When she returned Don at once became tense, the children anxious and her father vindictive. He was sure that if he yelled at her enough she would see sense. 'What sort of a mother are you? Don't you think your own children need some care? I warn

292

you my girl, much more of this and you're out of my Will. Out, out I say!'

She had finally come to see that he wasn't going to forgive her. Perhaps his rage was good for him, as year by year, month by month, he lost his grip on things. It was three years since he last walked, two since he used his left arm, a full twelve months since he remembered the month or the day. Only when raging at Flora did he seem undiminished. But Don was going to be away this Christmas. Perhaps she should go home.

Flora suppressed a yawn, trying to generate some interest in the tale of woe the young man before her was telling. 'So I asked him if he'd understood the question, and he said yes, but when I asked him again what he'd do if the crop failed, he kept on saying "Pray"! I mean, we were talking about spraying for disease. It isn't so hard. I'm sure I made it clear.'

'Did you give him the spray?' asked Flora.

'Yes! Weeks ago.'

'Then he's probably sold it. Don't dole stuff out indiscriminately, Matthew, it's pointless. You're lucky his children didn't drink it. Give him some more, stand over him while he uses it, and then go back to inspect progress. If it works, he'll remember. If it doesn't, so will you.'

'I − I haven't got any more. I gave it all out.'

'Oh, Matthew, you bloody idiot!'

'Hello, Flora.'

She turned at the unfamiliar voice. A thin man with dark hair and beard, going grey at the temples. And bright green eyes. 'Is it − yes! Finn. Finn McDonald!'

'The very same.'

She swung her legs off the long verandah chair, and he put his hands out to help her up. They stood looking at each other. 'You've hardly changed at all,' said Flora. 'Just as thin, just as brown.'

'And you are more delicious than ever. I'd convinced myself I'd imagined your navy blue eyes, but here they are, like a midnight sky. Oh, you always were the prettiest little girl. And now you're glamorous too.'

She pushed her hair back, blushing. 'I wish I was. I'm not even dressed, we're not used to visitors. What are you doing here, Finn?'

'Ah! When do they ever send a wire? I'm your new doctor. Your excellent lady, Bana Subhai, is being promoted.'

'They did send, I got it today. But − you? Finn, you're far too senior for this! I thought you were running a hospital.'

He said nothing, and to fill the silence she called Abdul and asked for drinks. The others were gathering round, eager to see who had come, because a new face in their small circle inevitably caused shifts and changes. Finn was charm itself, and once the introductions were done Flora slipped away to change. Wearing nothing but a towelling dressing gown left her at a distinct disadvantage.

She decided to put up her hair, she knew it made her look older. As she put in the last pins she remembered that she hadn't quite finished her mail. There was still Shalimar's letter.

Dear Flo,

Just a note to tell you that I went to see Don last weekend. I know he won't say anything, so I thought it was up to me. Your father's quite ill, and if you want to see him again I suggest you make some travel plans soon. Of course you may not want to, and that's up to you.

I was also a bit worried about Annie. I know Don thinks she's just being teenagerey, but when we went to see her at school she did seem somehow wild, a bit more than the usual bolshieness. We were bad enough, but underneath we were settled I think. Annie doesn't seem to be.

Incidentally, I think I'm going to give up going to see Don. The children are beginning to suspect what we're up to, and really, it wouldn't matter if we were going anywhere, but we're not. I can't go on wasting my life waiting for Don to find somewhere to fit me in his, and I think it's finally dawned on me that he's not going to. When I found myself fantasising about getting myself pregnant I knew it was time to get out.

So, don't you think it's time for a visit? I may fly out and see you if the schedule permits — I'm playing a murderous Rani at the moment, you should see my nails!

All love,

Shalimar

Flora folded the letter very small and put it in her handbag. Sometimes it amazed her that she and Shalimar had stayed friends, but, unaccountably, they had, even after Shalimar and Don had revived their affair. They had done it with an air of defiance, watching to see what Flora would do. There was nothing to do. She was well aware that she had no right to complain.

Besides, it was better if it was Shalimar than some total stranger. At least Shalimar told her what was going on. Don told only what

294

suited him; Shalimar told the truth. And if she also warmed Don's bed, wasn't it better that he slept with someone nice, and not some floozy who would disgust the children and alienate the staff? Flora was brisk about sex these days. It was a weakness she had determinedly overcome.

She went into dinner in a mood of brittle charm. If Finn was witty, she was wittier. When she drank a glass of water she felt the eyes of the men on her throat. She dipped her fingers in the glass and reached into her dress to dab them on the skin between her breasts, because for once she didn't care what anyone thought of her. Except perhaps Finn.

They didn't get a chance to talk until well after dinner. As always before bed, she went for a stroll down the village street, carrying nothing but a torch. Everyone said it was dangerous and they were probably right, but she loved the warm night air, the sounds of the bazaar closing down and the soft munching of stalled cattle. Besides, everyone knew who she was; attack wasn't likely.

'Do you mind if I join you?' Finn stood beside her on the verandah steps.

'Not at all. I should like that.' He strolled beside her, and she felt constrained.

'Politeness aside, Flora, I think you'd rather be alone' he murmured.

'Not at all! Or rather — I'm sorry, Finn. I'm used to my own company, I deserve to have my routine disrupted. If I'm not careful I shall get terribly spinsterish.'

'But aren't you married? I heard you had babies.'

'Yes, twins. They're at home, in Scotland. Thirteen now. Don and I — we're sort of separated. But since neither of us wants to get married again, we haven't bothered getting divorced. When I go home we live in separate parts of the house, or he's away climbing or something. The children don't seem to mind, but then they've never known anything different. I had letters from them today, it made me quite homesick.'

'I haven't been home in years.'

They walked on a little. The butcher's shop was still open, with sides of scrawny lamb hanging in the lamplight. Flora exchanged greetings, noticeably cool. 'That man's an absolute rogue,' she murmured to Finn. 'I'll swear he had two of our sheep last week, and he knows I know. I'm going to talk to his wife tomorrow, and make him sweat. He can give us a present of something, out of fright.'

Finn chuckled. 'You have grown tough.'

295

'Not as tough as his meat. He sells the rankest goat in history.'
She glanced up at him. It was very dark, she could barely see his
face. 'Why are you here, Finn? Why really?'

He took a deep breath. 'I'm testing my vocation,' he said. 'I
feel that I'm being called to be a priest, a Catholic priest. The
hospital confused me. My whole day was taken up with work, and
half the night as well. I needed more space. I needed naturalness.
And the director seemed to think that you would be good for me,
Flora. His exact words, if I can remember, were, "That woman's
efficient, hard-headed and practical. She's also sexy enough to test
any ideas you have on celibacy, so prepare yourself." I'll be taking
cold showers.'

'We don't have them, the water's always warm. That awful
man! He makes me sound a tart.' Her daughter's word came
back to her.

'Oh no! He didn't mean that, I'm sure.'

'Didn't he?' Flora felt ruffled. Well, she knew the rumours that
circulated about her, living alone out her, surrounded by young men.
Perhaps even the director thought she extended their education in
more ways than one. It was grossly unfair.

'I'm sorry. I shouldn't have told you.'

She sighed. 'I'm glad you did. It's why I'm not getting promoted,
I think. Everyone's wife would think I'd got the job the easy way.
If it is that easy, perhaps I should try it. I'm getting bored, Finn.
I want to do more.'

'Yes. You do seem to have outgrown this pond.'

She turned, as she always did, at the baobab tree, and started
back to the bungalow. The moon was coming up, hanging like a
ripe fruit just above the horizon. She switched off her torch and
walked by pale moonlight. 'Why do you want to be a priest?'

'I don't.' She looked at him and he said, 'Really, I don't. But
I feel as if I'm being coerced in some way, and if it's God or the
devil or my own bad conscience then I need to know. I've been
fighting it for months, perhaps years. And at last I've decided to
give up the fight. I'm opening myself, laying down my weapons,
letting whatever is going to happen take place. The responsibility
isn't mine any longer. I'm giving it to God.'

Flora felt embarrassed, as if he might at any moment try and
convert her. 'I do hope you realise it's going to be difficult having
a male doctor around. A good deal of the work is childbirth.'

'I'm used to that. Perhaps you'd come with me the first few times.
Until they gain confidence.'

'Me?'

'Yes. Bana Subhai is leaving tomorrow. There has to be someone they trust, someone who speaks the language. Is there anyone else?'

Flora shook her head.

So it was that she found herself in an airless hut, crouched with her torch over the pelvis of a mountainously pregnant woman while Finn wrestled with a breech birth. One of the young girls was administering gas and air, and every now and then the woman moaned a little.

'It's all right,' Flora kept telling her. 'It won't be long. It's a boy.'

The woman smiled at that. This struggle would be too much if it was only for a girl, she already had three daughters. A contraction came and Finn was working again, compressing the tiny chest and at the same time easing the head through the woman's pelvis. Out it came, a slimy monkey of a child, ominously silent. Finn was decisive, at once starting to suck the airway clear. The woman sobbed, and Flora gripped her hand. Long seconds passed — and the baby coughed, sneezed, and came to life.

Afterwards, walking back, Finn said, 'She shouldn't have any more, of course. God knows how she's still alive as it is, she's got a tiny pelvis. Who delivered the others?'

'Bana. I told you she was good. I'll get someone to talk to her about birth control tomorrow, now she has a son she might listen. But her husband probably wants two. And he can always get a new wife.'

He glanced at her. 'Are you getting disillusioned, Flora?'

She grunted. 'No, not yet. Just realistic. This job is all about the art of the possible, you can't change the world overnight. That's why I'd like to be in charge, so I can direct things, do what can be done. So much of our effort is wasted.'

The young girl who had accompanied them said, 'Is it all right if I go to bed now, Mrs Harrington? I've got to get up at five.'

'Yes, of course, Sandra. I'll take the gear.' She shouldered the strap of one case and Finn took the other. When she had gone Finn said, 'Is she any good?'

Flora sighed. 'Not really, no. I'm trying to convince myself it's only youth, but she isn't a hard worker. I'm going to send her back.'

'You are a martinet, aren't you?'

Giggling, she said, 'I'm not at all. I have to fight against being soft, actually. Perhaps that makes me harder than necessary. I always want to give in and let them have their dream, even if it does mean hardship for the people out here. I've had to learn to be tough.'

297

They went first to the medical centre, two rooms in a whitewashed building. Finn put the instruments in the steriliser and switched it on, while Flora put the swabs and used dressings in a refuse sack for incineration. Suddenly she became aware that Finn was close. She turned. 'Oh dear. You are taking the director's words seriously.' It was a situation she was familiar with. The light touch always worked best.

'I didn't need him to tell me how lovely you are. When we were in Nepal you gave me sleepless nights.'

'You never even noticed me!'

He laughed and touched her hair. 'Of course I did! You were the talk of the place. Young, lovely and exuberant. And I was too old. But you've grown up – and I'm not that old.'

'You frightened me,' she said. 'All that burning vocation.'

'I keep wondering if it's burned itself out.'

He took her in his arms and kissed her. Flora stood without responding, and then her lips parted under his. Don, Shalimar, even that girl Sandra – everyone was doing it except her. And they all thought she was. She felt herself melting, their bodies moving together until they touched, breast to breast, thigh to thigh. There was such physical joy in this, she thought. It was food to assuage starvation.

Gradually she pulled herself free. 'No thanks,' she said. 'I make it a rule not to sleep around.'

'You haven't been celibate since you came out, have you?'

To her chagrin, she blushed. 'Almost. When I first came I was battered from my marriage, I felt I had to sleep with someone I wasn't married to, just to prove that I could. I went with this absolute lecher from the Italian Embassy, and I hated it. I felt everybody must know. They probably did. So there was no one after that. After all, you don't meet many possibles out here, and if you do have an affair it get's terribly complicated. I'm always having to send people off, pregnant, lovesick or something. What about you?'

'I haven't slept with anyone for over ten years.'

She gurgled with laughter. 'So me saying no won't be too great a strain! Honestly, Finn, do you simply think you'd better have one last milkshake before you give them up?'

'Not exactly, no.'

He reached out and took her face between his hands. 'You seem so tired and strained. I can't look at you without wanting to pick you up and carry you. I feel I was meant to come here, that we were meant to meet. I want to stop turning aside from the things

298

that beckon me. I was more than half in love with you on the day we met.'

'And how in love are you now?'

'I don't know. That's something I want to find out.'

He pushed her back on the little office desk, half lying across her body. He began to mouth her neck and she moaned, involuntarily parting her legs. He was pulling her down to the floor, and she said, 'We'll get filthy. Put a blanket down or something.' He got up to look for one and as an afterthought locked the door. Flora began to undress. She turned her back, unfastening her blouse very slowly.

'Are you sure you want to?' Finn asked suddenly.

'I – I don't know. Yes.' She dropped her bra on the table, and began to strip off her jeans.

Finn said, 'I'm terrified I won't be able to do it.'

'Oh.' Flora hesitated. Then she came across and touched him. 'You're fine. Really. You're out of practice, that's all.'

'You are – you are so beautiful!' He crushed her to him, kissing her face, her neck, her breasts. Somehow she was on the blanket with Finn lying on her, trying desperately to connect. She reached down and took hold of his erection, lifting herself on to him. Only then did she become part of the act, aware of herself and her feelings. Thoughts wandered in her head, like clouds. Suppose the others found out? Suppose she got pregnant? Suppose he stopped in a second, before – before – 'Oh! Oh. Oooohhhhh.' She closed her eyes against the light and wondered how she had lived without this feeling, how she could have forgotten what it was like. A slow pulse of pleasure spread out from her groin, right to the tips of her fingers and toes.

Gradually she came back to the world. The floor was hard and hot, and Finn's hipbone was digging into her side. Thank goodness the door was locked. If someone came in now they would see Finn's bare backside, his trousers round his knees, and Flora quite naked underneath him.

'We must get out,' said Flora, feeling almost drunk. 'They'll know.'

'I'm not sure that I care.' Nonetheless he struggled to his feet. Flora pulled on her clothes, doing her buttons up wrong three times. Finally she left them done up askew. Finn caught her arm as she prepared to leave. 'You're not upset, are you? You don't wish we hadn't done it?'

She knew she had to be honest. 'I do, rather. I was living without it, and I didn't mind. It's woken me up again.'

299

'If that's all —'

'I just hope to God I don't get pregnant.' She pulled out of his grasp and ran down the street. In the early morning light two or three people turned and watched her go.

Chapter Two

•

Try as they would to behave normally, there were no secrets in the village. Besides, it was hard to hide smiles and warm glances, cropping up without warning during the day. They made no arrangements to meet again; that would have been somehow sordid. But they both knew it would happen again, when the time was right.

Flora felt different, lighter, happier. When her period came she stared ruefully at the bloodstain and wondered why she didn't feel more relief. Perhaps she wanted a baby. The twins had been born when she was almost a child herself, and the woman she now was yearned for those years back again. But did she want Finn's child, did she want Finn's commitment? She didn't know.

An outbreak of cholera in the area put paid to everything but work. She was out every day in the jeep, and Finn took up residence in a village about twenty miles away, the centre of the epidemic. Government officials poured in, but they wanted to talk to Flora, not the victims. Barely a day went by without formal meetings and talks. One afternoon a visiting minister took her aside. He was a small brown man, bright-eyed, his tropical whites brilliantly clean. 'Tell me, Mrs Harrington, why are you wasting yourself here? There are so many large challenges in India, why devote yourself to this small one?'

She swallowed. The truth rose to her lips. 'For some reason I don't understand, nobody takes me seriously at Head Office. They know I'm competent, but the years go by and they leave me here. Perhaps I don't have the right friends.'

'Friends in high places, do you mean? You can count on me, Mrs Harrington. We don't only want ugly women in positions of power. It's time a pretty one was given a chance!' Flora laughed dutifully.

They went by car to the station. The train was already in, but for a minister of importance it would wait. Flora shook his hand, he took hold of his umbrella and ascended the steps. She stood waving as the engine puffed out of sight.

Dust settled on the station. All the clamour and bustle of moments before subsided into heat and lethargy. A woman, presumably from the train, was being importuned by two porters. She wore a large white hat, tight white trousers and a red tunic. It was Shalimar.

'What on earth are you doing here?' demanded Flora. She pushed her sweaty, dusty hair out of her eyes. As always Shalimar looked beautifully cool and composed.

'I've come to see you, darling! But you were busy with that charming gentleman and I hesitated to intrude. He seemed desperately important, I've never seen so many flunkeys. Do I take one or both of these porters, do you think?'

Flora rattled out some instructions, and the men at once stopped nagging and picked up Shalimar's bags. 'We'll get a taxi,' said Flora. 'Honestly, I feel a bit bewildered. You're the last person I expected to see!'

As they sat in the car Flora said, 'It must be odd for you not to be surrounded by hundreds of adoring fans.'

'It's a relief actually. No one knows me in India. Did you get my letter?'

'Yes. I've applied for leave at Christmas.'

'Oh. Oh, I see. And I've come all this way to persuade you to do just that.'

Their eyes met and they laughed. There was always some constraint these days, it came and went with the ebb and flow of conversation. Flora decided to get the thorny question out of the way first. 'How's Don?'

'I don't know.' Shalimar bit her finger. 'He – he rang me a couple of times in Singapore. He tries, Flora, he really does. But he's not interested.'

'I always told you he was only ever really interested in climbing.'

'And KORSEA. These days he's so thick with the government and everyone that he can't seem to go wrong. He did say that Malcolm hasn't improved. Are you sure you can't go home any sooner, Flo?'

Flora grimaced. 'I don't know. I'll try. He never replies to my letters or anything. And when I do go to see him he rants and raves, just as if it had all happened yesterday.'

'He's old. Perhaps to him it has.'

When they reached the bungalow Abdul was waiting with drinks.

302

Shalimar took her glass, and as Abdul shuffled away, said in a low voice, 'Am I right in thinking he's a leper? He's hardly got any fingers!'

'Not infectious, dear,' murmured Flora. 'You'll get used to him.'

But it was soon apparent that the aid people were going to have more trouble getting used to Shalimar. They, at least, knew who she was, and they sat on the verandah and stared at her in starstruck silence. She was one of the most talked about stars of the day, subject of dozens of articles and endlessly linked with this or that lover. The latest suspicion was that she was having an affair with Prince Charles, at a secret Scottish hideaway.

'Will you all stop gawping?' snapped Flora. 'Shalimar's my friend. If you can't talk sensibly go on about your business.'

All the same they peered round doors at her, and every now and then someone would ask for an autograph. 'For my sister – she's only ten.'

'Amazing how many only children have developed ten-year-old sisters,' said Flora with a giggle.

They went to sit on her bed and chat. It was amazing how soon the old camaraderie returned, with Shalimar turning her nose up at Flora's clothes and demanding to know what was going on. 'Cholera and cataracts,' said Flora expansively. 'The farm programme's coming on. And tigers are back in the swamp, people keep getting eaten. So everything's looking up.'

'Except for people on the tigers' shopping list,' murmured Shalimar. 'But tell the truth, Flo, any men? There must be someone.'

'Not really, no.'

'Flora! I know when you're lying. Who is he, not one of the toyboys?'

'Not on your life! It's hard enough making them concentrate on work as it is. It's a doctor, Finn McDonald. He's trying to decide if he's going to be a priest.'

'And he's doing that by screwing you?'

'Shhhhhh!!!' Flora flapped at her friend, the bungalow walls were like paper. Shalimar covered her mouth and giggled. It was just like talking after lights out with the gym mistress prowling the hallway.

'All right,' she hissed. 'What's he up to? A last fling before dark?'

'Quite possibly.' Flora leaned back against the pillows. 'He's nice. At the moment he's away, but if he was here you'd like him.'

'I'll be the judge of that,' said Shalimar darkly.

But to everyone's surprise Finn arrived that night, as they were all sitting down to dinner. 'Finn!' Flora got up as if to go to him, remembered herself, sat down, then got up and shook hands with him. Shalimar choked on a laugh.

'Hello, Flora. Wow, you look wonderful.' He kissed her cheek and Flora blushed scarlet, and everyone else made ostentatious efforts to pretend they hadn't noticed.

Flora put him on Shalimar's other side, but all the same he kept leaning across to talk to her. 'The epidemic's almost done, I think. Did you see the sunset last night? I'll swear the rains are coming early. Why don't we take the chance and go up to the lake and fish for an afternoon?'

'Yes,' said Flora. 'We could all go. Would you like that, Shalimar?'

'If you think I won't be in the way,' said Shalimar. 'You two obviously have so much to talk about.'

Flora gurgled with laughter. 'Don't be a pain! You're never in the way. Honestly, Finn, she's been dogging my footsteps ever since I was twelve. I've got no doubt I'll arrive at the Pearly Gates and Shalimar will turn up ten minutes later, wearing an utterly chic halo and making mine look like cheap brass. And she'll have me bunking off from choir practice and using my harp as a catapult.'

'Sounds just like Annie,' said Shalimar lugubriously.

'I didn't tell you, I had a letter from her. She sounds fine, just – well, you know. Adolescent. They've decided the headmistress is a lesbian.'

'She might be right there,' said Shalimar. 'I think the boyfriend is a cover. Don and I are taking bets, but I don't know how we resolve it.'

'Do you know Flora's husband?' asked Finn, breaking in on the girl talk.

Flora sipped her glass of water. 'Shalimar knows Don very well.' Her voice tinkled like ice cubes. Finn shot her a surprised glance.

When Flora took her late evening walk, Shalimar stayed at home, leaving Finn to decide that he too needed a breath of air. No sooner had they moved out of the circle of lamplight than he grabbed Flora, put out the torch and kissed her. She opened her mouth for his tongue and let her mind stop, blotting out everything except sensation.

'Is this the action of a future priest?' she murmured.

'At the moment I'm just a very randy man. Let's go to the clinic.'

304

'Are you sure? Everyone will know.'

'I don't think I mind.'

They were no longer new to each other, and Flora didn't expect passion. Nonetheless when they were skin to skin, arms and legs in a tangle of sweat and need, she was beside herself. It was as if they had breached a small hole in a dam, only to drown in the flood that broke down the wall and engulfed them. When they finished Flora was in tears.

'I don't know what we're doing,' she said helplessly. 'I don't know if it's you, or me. I can't think straight.'

'I never knew that sex could be this powerful,' whispered Finn. He flung himself back on the floor, arms outstretched. 'When you experience something like this you understand so much more of the world. It's just incredible.'

'I feel ashamed,' said Flora. 'As if I've taken off more than my clothes.'

Finn sat up and looked at her. 'What's your friend's relationship with your husband. Are they lovers?'

'They have sex. I don't know if there's any love there.' She got up and looked for her knickers.

'Unlike us,' said Finn. He caught her hand and held it. 'Unlike us.'

They heard on the radio that the rains were starting. Bridges were being washed away and railway tracks destroyed. 'I'm going in the morning,' said Shalimar. 'Hollywood needs me. And I think you ought to come too, Flo.'

'Not yet, surely!' Finn's stricken face was clear for all to see.

'I think I ought, Finn,' said Flora. 'I've got acres of leave due, and I really must go home.'

He looked thin suddenly, and very tired. He got up and left the room.

He came to see them off at the station. Everyone came, it was quite a party, and he was just one face amongst them all; the only one looking grim and unsmiling. Flora went up close to him. 'You haven't been doing much deciding,' she said softly. 'This is just the chance you need.'

'I thought I had decided. At the cholera camp, I decided to give it up. I never expected to have to give you up too.'

'I'm coming back, Finn! It's only a visit.' Not caring what anyone thought, she put her arms round his neck and hugged him.

305

When the train drew out she waved and waved and he watched her, his green eyes brilliant in a deadwhite face.

The castle seemed pale in the morning mist, an insubstantial mass of grey that might at any moment dissolve and disappear into cloud. The sunrise left long pink fingers in the sky, and the leafless trees lost their trunks in the mist, leaving a stark trellis of branches.

Flora had taken a taxi from the station. When she gave up her home she decided that she must also give up all the trappings that went with it: the private jets, the chauffeured cars, the designer dresses. No wonder Shalimar sneered at her clothes, they were utilitarian and tired. She had a sudden longing for wonderful things again; it would be nice if Don saw her at her best.

It was still very early, not yet half past seven. She paid off the taxi and rang the bell on the huge oak door. After long minutes Forbes came to open it.

'Miss Flora! Well, what a surprise! Marie, look who's come home!' She went in, pained to see Forbes struggling with her bags. But he would hate it if she helped him.

Marie said, 'It's good you've come, dear. Your father's not at all well. The children are away at school, of course. Will you be getting them home?'

'No, of course I won't. I'll go at the weekend, and then there'll be Christmas.'

'You're staying for Christmas?'

'If I can. If everyone will have me.'

There was a silence. Marie sniffed. 'He'll be having his breakfast,' she murmured. 'He's not at his best in the mornings.'

'Well, he's never at his best with me. I'll go and see.'

But her heart thumped as she turned the handle of the door. She went in quietly, and closed it behind her. He was reading the paper, he didn't look up. As always the sheer physical presence of the man took her breath away. He had the broadest shoulders of anyone she knew. One giant suited leg was slung casually over the arm of the gilt chair on which he sat.

'Hello, Don.'

His head snapped up. For a long moment his eyes bored into her, clear and grey and unforgiving. 'Flora. Thanks for letting us know.'

'I couldn't, I came away in a hurry. The monsoon was early, I didn't want to delay. I'm staying for Christmas, is that all right?'

'I'll make it alright. I'm going climbing.'

'Anywhere nice?'

306

'I'm sure I'll find it tolerably more pleasant than here.'

She winced. 'Do you mind if I pour myself some coffee?' She sat down without waiting for a reply, weighing the silver pot in her hand. The luxury of the castle had always amazed her. In the real world she forgot that such extravagance existed. Toast nestled under a quilted cover, at least ten different breads, although Don would only eat two at the most. She chose one for herself, borrowed his knife and buttered it.

'Feel free to make yourself at home.'

'Thank you. I will.' She munched for a moment but a gurgle of laughter forced its way into her throat. 'Oh, Don, you can be such a pig. Don't be so frosty.'

Their eyes met again, his cold, hers alight with laughter. The paper crumpled in his hand. He threw it down and stood up. 'I'll be back this evening. For God's sake find yourself something decent to wear. You look like a bloody refugee.'

He stormed out to the Bentley, a full half hour before he was expected. John began to struggle into his jacket. 'Don't bother,' snapped Don. 'I'll drive myself.'

'But, sir! You've appointments today – '

'Have I? Then take the Bentley in yourself. I'll drive the Porsche.'

The car had been a present to himself, a reward for at last putting KORSEA back in the front rank. Shalimar liked it, she always drove the thing when she was here, but it was small for him. Nonetheless he punched it into gear and sent it howling down the drive.

Damn her! Damn her to hell. If he had known she was coming he'd have made himself scarce. How could she walk in as if she owned the place, stroll in to breakfast looking tired and pale, but with that goddamned air of serenity? How dare she look so calm, so shabby so – beautiful? He lifted his foot and the speed fell away. She had violet shadows under her eyes, like thumb prints, and she did nothing with her hair any more, it was a mass of tangled red curls. Alex had her hair and Annie her shape of face. It was bad enough seeing them in her children without Flora herself turning up to confound him, to rock his hard won stability.

The mist was still heavy. He slowed right down, and found himself pulling the car in at the side of the road. Moorland stretched on every side, great tracts of heather and grouse. He got out and began to walk, feeling the dew soaking his legs halfway up his thighs. A thin autumn sun was struggling to fight its way through the haze, and the grouse were cackling hectically on all sides. On a day like this he should be glad to be alive, he thought, and he reached down to grab a handful of wiry heather. It came up by the roots, peaty and smelling of sour land. Suddenly he felt a surge of joy and he stopped to gulp down the cold wet air. From the road he heard John calling.

'Sir? Sir? Do ye need some help, sir?'

Slowly Don dusted his hands. Then he made his way carefully back to the car.

Flora slept for much of the morning. When she woke she lay for a long time, looking up at the cool blue ceiling above her head. The bed felt alien. She had been in the tropics for so long that any weight of covering seemed impossibly heavy. No mosquito net either, and no drone of flies. At last she got up and went to have a bath. It was delicious, hot, scented, and she crouched on all fours in the tub to immerse her breasts. It was a wonderful sensation. She was becoming a sensualist these days, she decided, and went back into the bedroom to root through her wardrobes. Did she look like a refugee? Looking at herself in the mirror she wondered how she had got so thin. Her ribs were quite visible.

She found a blue cashmere sweater, and a grey skirt. The skirt she remembered but the sweater she did not. Had one of the children put it in here? Sometimes they stored up her birthday presents and gave her a huge pile of things when she got home. But it was so long since she was home last, they might have unwrapped it and put it in the wardrobe for her to discover.

There was make-up too, on the dressing table, and she darkened her lashes. Since she was last in Scotland the fashions had changed, and eye make-up was darker and heavier. She liked the look, and added to it with a slash of plum-coloured lipstick. The Scottish Flora looked out at her, stylish and sophisticated, a far cry from the worn, tired aid worker that India knew.

When there was no way she could put it off any longer, she knew she would have to go and see her father. Even after so long her hands went cold and her stomach turned in fright. But there was no getting away from it, she had to go. Automatically shaking her shoes for spiders she slipped them on and left the room.

The nurse was indeed a dragon. She met Flora at the door. 'Mrs Harrington, I presume? He's sleeping and cannot be disturbed.'

'Oh. Oh, I see.' She resisted the urge to give in cravenly and forget it. 'I think he'll want to see me all the same.'

'I think the patient should be the judge of that. I'll tell him you called, and if he wishes to see you I shall let you know.'

'Why don't we ask him now?'

'He's asleep.'

'Are you sure? If he's asleep I could have a look at him, couldn't I? I am his only child.'

'I understand you haven't visited for many months, Mrs Harrington. I think at the very least you could wait until your father's awake.'

'I have been in India! Nurse, I really must insist.'

She met the nurse's fulminating gaze with her own cool stare. The habit of command was something which Flora had picked up quite inadvertently, but it was surprising how often it resulted in obedience. The nurse moved aside. 'Very well. I shall hold you responsible for any ill effects.'

'I fully understand that, Nurse. Thank you.'

The room was quiet, with warm, still air. Flora went to the bedside and saw that far from being asleep her father was lying with eyes half open, gazing dreamily out of the window.

'Hello, Dad,' she said softly. 'The park's lovely today. Full of autumn sunshine.'

He focussed on her, blearily. 'Flora. Help me sit up, girl.'

She put her arms around him and lifted him up. His head lolled against the pillow. 'I'm not getting any better,' he murmured. 'The old machine's running down. Time I was out of it.'

Flora said nothing. Experience had taught her that platitudes were useless in the face of death. No one wanted to hear trite phrases.

'Is the nurse bullying you?' she asked. 'Seems a tartar.'

'Sweet as sugar to me. Hell with everyone else, of course. Don't mind dying with her around. Prefer you. But not Lilian. She can come and admire me in the coffin.'

Flora chuckled. 'Keeping up appearances to the last.'

He closed his eyes for a second. When he opened them again he said, 'Have you seen Alex. Hell of a boy. I've left him everything in trust, and it's watertight, whatever Don keeps trying. He's been looking for a loophole for years, never did approve. Turned out a good man, Don did. You were the bad apple. The one that let me down.'

'No, I didn't, Dad. I've done what was right. Right for me.'

'Leaving your children? It was a crying shame. And it still is.'

'It wasn't doing them any good. Don and me fighting.'

'He never wanted them. He wanted you.'

She took in a sharp breath. 'Since he's been consoling himself with work, climbing and Shalimar, I don't think you need worry too much on that score. He's not a natural married man, Dad.'

'And who is, may I ask? What did you want for a man, a tame pussycat? Men are hunters, they're aggressive and wild. I've had

309

affairs in my life, I've slept around. But I never stopped loving your mother!'

'I only hope she appreciated it,' said Flora thinly. 'It wasn't Shalimar that finished us, Dad. She just marked the end, that's all. And I've been happy. Much happier than I thought I could be. And no one else has been nearly as sad as if I'd stayed.'

Kincaid's face contorted. He hadn't the strength to put up a hand to hide it. 'Except me,' he whispered. 'I miss you like hell, Flora!' She bent down and embraced him.

They spent the afternoon together, Flora sitting quietly by the bed. She got out some old photographs and they laughed at the fashions and faces.

'Do you remember when you gave me all those dolls?' she said. 'Ten of them. And I couldn't decide which I liked best, so I had them all in bed.'

'I took a snap of that, somewhere,' he said, and Flora hunted through until she found the picture. She looked small, overtired and almost tearful.

Towards evening the nurse came in and took Kincaid's blood pressure. Flora looked questioning, as if she should leave, but to her surprise the nurse motioned her to stay. It was very quiet in the room, with just the clock ticking and the soft hush of an old man's feeble breath. The last rays of the sun, breaking through the daylong cloud, fell on the windows and made a rainbow on the floor. Her father's hand tightened on hers, a brief pressure at once returned. His eyelids rose a fraction, as if for one last glance, before falling, closing, hiding a dying light.

'Dad?' whispered Flora, and waited for him to stir. But he was gone.

It was more of a shock than it should have been. In India Flora had become used to death: she had nursed two fatally ill aid workers as well as countless Indians. But the loss of her father seemed unreasonably hard. The suffering old man whose body lay at peace was one thing, she thought, but she had lost more than that; her father had been her life's central point from the day of her birth to this, the day of his death, and even if she took no notice of him and his demands, he had been there, fixed and immutable.

'He was waiting until you came,' said the nurse, more experienced even than Flora in these things. But to Flora it felt as if she had caused him to die. If she had stayed away he would still be alive, she told herself. And he was dead.

When Don came home, deliberately late, she met him in the front hall. He stared at her grimly. 'To what do I owe this honour?'

'Don, something's happened.' She clasped her hands in front of her, pressing the palms together. How little she wanted to say the words. 'My father's dead. He died this afternoon, quite peacefully. I was with him.'

For a long moment Don's face remained set. Then he swallowed, hard. 'Why didn't you call me?' he said huskily.

'I was with him, there wasn't any need.'

'And I've been with him for years! I should have been there! Don't you think I'd have wanted that?'

Flora took a shaky breath. 'No. Actually I didn't think you would. I'm sorry.'

He turned and made for the library, and when Flora tried to follow he shut the door in her face. She waited, listening, but there was no sound. After ten minutes or so she knocked and went in, and he was only sitting at the desk, looking at nothing, his fingers linking and unlinking paperclips.

'I thought perhaps you ought to tell the children,' she said diffidently.

'You do it. I always do the dirty work, you can have some for a change. I'm sick of you turning up like the fairy godmother. It's about time you did something real.'

'I do try and avoid being endlessly generous and nice,' said Flora. 'I'm sorry if I don't succeed.'

'And you can stop being so bloody reasonable! If there's one thing I hate it's your saintly reasonableness! Why can't you be a bitch occasionally? Then the rest of us could be allowed the odd foul emotion.'

'What sort of foul emotion did you want?'

He sighed and closed his eyes. 'Hate,' he murmured. 'Jealousy. Anger. I'm so angry that you were there and I wasn't. You gave up your right to be with him on the day you left. And I earned the right. He and I – we understood each other. We were friends. And I'm going to live on here in this damned big house alone. I shall miss him like hell.'

Flora said, 'It was easier to be friends with him than to have him for a father. You don't know how it was.'

'You only had to stand up to him! If you hadn't been so damned feeble you wouldn't have had a moment's bother. But you always blame everyone else for your own shortcomings, you never ever see how you could have been different.'

She found that her hands were shaking, and she clasped them together again. 'I'm a lot more assertive now, Don. And I won't stand here and have you take out all your rage on me. I'm going

311

to telephone the children.' She went out of the room, leaving the door wide open. A moment later she heard it slam resoundingly.

Phoning from her room, she spoke to Alex first. 'Darling? It's Mummy. Yes, I got home yesterday. Look, there's some rather sad news, about Grandad. He died this afternoon.'

Alex's voice, deeper than she remembered but erratically shrill at times, came hectically over the line. 'Grandad? Really? I bet the nurse poisoned him, she was foul. Is Dad all right?'

'Yes. Yes, I think so. Look, darling, I think the funeral's going to be on Friday. Do you want to come? I quite understand if you don't.'

'Friday? I can miss double maths. And I think I'd better. He was a great man, the greatest. The sixth form chaps are doing the growth of KORSEA in economics, they've got a picture of Grandad on the wall of the economics room. Mind you, it's only to cover the damp. Are you going to send the car or shall I come on the train? I'll fly if it's really urgent.'

'I'll see. Perhaps it'll be best to let the Head know. Talk to you on Friday, darling. 'Bye.'

He had taken it so calmly that Flora almost felt aggrieved. The old man had placed all his faith in Alex, only to have it received phlegmatically, as no more than due. Children have no yardstick by which to measure value, reflected Flora; the cardboard box is as attractive as the million pound computer which it contains. Would Alex ever realise quite how much devotion had come his way? Perhaps not. And perhaps that would be an altogether good thing.

She dialled Annie's school with growing trepidation. They didn't like calls from parents and were always unco-operative, but this time they made no more than a token fuss before putting Annie on.

'Darling? It's Mum. I'm home.'

'Well! Whaddayaknow! The wandering minstrel back from the wars, and about time too! You've got to get me out of this place. They are forcing me to eat meat, attend banal Church services and expose my legs.'

'I thought you liked exposing your legs. Your father told me you were wearing pelmet frills as skirts.'

'That was last hols. I've turned Buddhist.'

'Oh. Oh, I see.' Flora struggled with bewilderment. 'I know a lot of Buddhists, actually. Perhaps I can introduce you to some. They aren't all saffron-coloured monks.'

'It must be better than turning us all into perverts and idol worshippers. The headmistress here is a religious maniac.'

'I thought she was a lesbian.'

'That too. Oh, look, the history mistress is glowering. They're not supposed to listen to private calls but of course they do. Anything to liven up their dreadful frustrated lives.'

Flora felt she should take hold of this conversation before too late. 'Er — Annie dear, I've got some sad news. Grandad died this afternoon.'

She heard a sharp intake of breath. Then, shrilly, Annie said, 'Good. About time too. He was a useless old pillock who just got in the way of everybody.'

'That doesn't sound very Buddhist,' managed Flora, taken aback.

'Doesn't it? Well, it's the truth. Don't expect me to come to the funeral. He never liked me and I couldn't stand him. So there.'

The telephone banged down. Against her best intentions Flora was upset. She felt that her father was owed some real grief, they should all be united in loss. But Alex was unmoved, Annie enraged, and only she and Don were left to show what should be shown. Even Forbes and Marie were saying, 'It's for the best. He lingered too long.' And they had served here for forty years. Don had their allegiance now, he was the great white chief.

In need of a drink, Flora went downstairs. Don was still in the library, working, his whisky by his side. Flora went to the sideboard tray and poured herself one.

'Since when did you pour your own whisky?'

She took a large gulp. 'Since forever. It's medicinal in the tropics, God knows what bugs would get you if it wasn't for the drink. I've spoken to the children. Alex is unsurprised, and Annie won't come to the funeral.'

Don grunted. 'She will. I'll speak to her tomorrow.'

'And do what I couldn't, I take it.'

He met her eye. 'Yes. She doesn't buck me, she does as she's told. But then, I'm not out to be Mr Wonderful.'

'I wish you wouldn't fight with her so. I'm sure it makes her worse.'

'You know nothing at all about it.'

He returned to his work. People moved softly around the house, the doctor, the undertaker. Flora could hear them making preparations for her father to be taken away. 'Don't you want to see him?' she asked suddenly.

He looked up. 'Yes. Yes, actually, I think I do. Coming?'

Flora nodded. Don led the way upstairs.

'We'll make him look much better for the funeral,' apologised the undertaker, in the very act of measuring the body.

'I'd rather he looked like someone I know,' said Don scathingly.

313

'Don't turn him into an elderly choirboy.' He leaned over the bed and looked down at the dead face on the pillow. The undertaker cleared his throat and withdrew.

'He looks asleep to me,' said Don.

'I think he looks absent. I always think dead people look as if they've gone.'

'They don't on mountains. They look as if something has killed them, all the way through. There's nothing beyond this. Accept it.'

Flora said, 'Thanks, but I won't. And you shouldn't either.'

She went out and left him, it was clear he didn't want her there. For the first time she felt like crying, an unidentified sadness that had nothing to do with anything except her own grey mood. Downstairs again she poured herself another drink, and then when Don still stayed away she decided to take herself to bed.

Chapter Three

Don sent the car to collect first Alex and then Annie. They were disgorged at the house on Thursday evening, Alex calm and Annie indignant. Flora could hardly believe her eyes; Alex was only inches short of Don's height, a great lanky boy with a frame that would one day fill out to be every bit as muscled as his father's. As for Annie, she had a shock of black spiked hair, face powdered graveyard white, and from some dubious source she had obtained a school skirt that came down to her ankles. Add to that arms crammed from wrist to elbow with cheap brass bangles and she was a sight to behold.

'Mum! I don't want to be here. I'm going right now, I'm not staying an instant.'

'Oh. That's a pity. I did so want to talk to you. And of course, it's so near the end of term I was thinking you needn't go back.'

'Of course they go back,' snapped Don. 'One thing I won't stand is playing at education. They're at school to work.'

'You mucked around all the time until you were sixteen,' accused Alex. 'You're always telling us so.'

'There's no point at all in my going back,' said Annie, flouncing past them into the house. 'I'm probably going to be expelled anyway. I turned my breakfast plate upside down on the matron's head.'

'You did what?' Don's roar shook the windows.

'We know what she did, Don,' said Flora. 'But why, Annie? It wasn't bacon or something?'

'Sausages,' retorted Annie, from the depths of the hall.

'Darling, everyone knows there's almost no meat at all in school sausages! You've got expelled on behalf of a plastic skin and a handful of breadcrumbs.'

Alex chuckled. 'It is good to have you back, Mum. It's always fun when you're around.'

'And dull as hell when I am, I suppose?' accused Don.

Alex flushed. 'Of course it isn't! But you're responsible for us, you can't be fun. It's different for Mum.'

Later, when Don was settled in the library, Flora went in to him. 'I'm sorry,' she said. 'I didn't realise I was being quite such a pain.'

Don looked at her from under his brows. She was wearing a pale green cashmere sweater he remembered from years ago, and pink jeans. She might have been no more than a couple of years older than Annie. And suddenly he was so weary of carrying his burdens alone, burdens that should belong to both of them, equally. He put down his pen and sat back.

'I'm always going on at them,' he admitted. 'Especially Annie, she doesn't do a stroke. Buddhism's just the latest in a long line of crazes, she's always being something. I can't get her to understand that she's got to be sensible, make a life for herself. Alex is getting the firm, she's just got the wits she was born with.'

'I imagine that's half the trouble,' said Flora. 'You don't get over a slight like that very easily.'

'Don't give me your amateur philosophy!'

Suddenly she lost her temper. She banged her fist on the desk, meeting his pale eyes with her own hot blue ones. 'Look, Don. I wouldn't give you the time of day! But they are my children, and I do have the right to express an opinion without you jumping down my throat at minute intervals. Not one nice thing have you said since I got here, though I don't ask for anything except politeness. It doesn't do any of us any good to have you searching around for your meanest insult every time I open my mouth.'

'I didn't ask you to follow me in here,' he said thickly.

'But we have to communicate! These are our children, they need us both! Please, Don. Let's try not to be so bitter.'

As she leaned forward her breasts were clearly outlined against the sweater. He found himself thinking of sex, quite against his will. The children were playing music in their rooms, the servants were settled for their after dinner chat downstairs. Besides, there was a lock on the door – they'd made love here in the days before the twins. He felt desperately randy. 'I wish you'd take that sweater off,' he murmured.

Flora's eyes widened. 'What?'

'Take it off. You never used to be a prude. We are still married, you know.'

She straightened up, a dull blush staining her cheeks. 'I thought Shalimar took care of your libido. Isn't that what you use her for?'

316

'She's got nothing to do with this. Let's do it. No one need ever know. It won't hurt to be nice to each other for a change.'

He got up and came round the desk towards her. The muscles in Flora's lower belly tensed with unexpected desire. His size, his strength, reduced her thoughts to sluggish sensuality. 'Let's do it for the children,' he murmured, and slid his hands under her sweater, holding her ribs tight. Her breasts, heavy with arousal, seemed to swell over his hands. It was for the children – for Don – for both of them –.

'You'll have to lock the door,' she whispered.

Suddenly urgent, he let her go and did so.

He pulled her clothes down to her knees and began stroking her. She pushed him away and undressed completely, a woman who wasn't now prepared to let a man do only what he wanted. Her independence angered him. He grabbed her and let his fingers bite into her upper arms. He pushed her against the wall and started kissing her, feeling her hips writhe against him. He bent and sucked her right nipple, and she groaned painfully. 'Put it up me, will you?' she hissed.

He lifted his head. 'Since when were you this coarse?'

Meeting his eyes, almost drugged with need, she said, 'Since I found I needed a man. Please. I'm not a girl any more. I need it so much.'

He pulled his trousers open and put himself inside her. They stood, crotch to crotch, his legs bent at the knees, she on tiptoe and supported by him. Her breasts rubbed against his shirt. She pulled it open to let them touch his warm chest. He couldn't stop himself coming, but she was there too. She banged her head on the wall as the rigours ran through her.

When he let her go, she rubbed her head. 'Wow! You seem to know how to do it still.'

'So do you. Not in the least out of practice.'

She blushed. 'There is someone. We've only done it a couple of times, actually. And you've got Shalimar.'

He drew in his breath, feeling a distinct shock. 'Who is he?'

'Someone I work with. I met him again after years, and it was so strange.'

Don forced himself to ask mildly, 'Are you serious about this bloke?'

'I don't know. I'd been almost celibate for years. When we made love it was like starting again.'

A surge of rage, jealousy, uncontrollable emotion, almost silenced Don. Then he spat the words. 'I had you the first time. And you came. He couldn't do that to you.'

She went to Don and looked up into his eyes. 'You're not the only person who knows how to make love to me. I don't only need you to do it.'

'Yes you do! I had you first and there won't ever be anyone who knows you like I do. I know your body as well as I know my own!'

He flung off his shirt and trousers. Flora knew better than to try and resist. When he pushed her down on the leather sofa, the cold jabbing into her bare flesh, she closed her eyes so she couldn't see his face. It was as if he hated her, as if every stroke was stabbing her in the heart. But again she came, betraying herself. It seemed utterly dishonest, because she knew that she felt nothing for him. It was sex, for its own sake, because her father was dead and she needed a man, and whatever triumph he felt was his could only be made of stone.

The funeral was at twelve the next day. Flora dressed in a black suit with a stark white blouse, and went to see what the children were putting on. Alex was wearing his school suit and house tie, Flora noticed his sleeves were an inch too short. She made a mental note to get him smartened up before she went back. He was growing so fast he always looked gangling. He was going to be a very handsome man, she decided. But Annie was in red, bright red, long skirt and flowing jacket, with gold dangling earrings. She met her mother's eye defiantly.

'Oh dear,' said Flora, and sat on the bed.

'Don't expect me to change,' said Annie. 'I'm no hypocrite. He didn't think I was anything but second best.'

'I don't think that's the point.'

'Isn't it? There isn't another one.'

Flora sighed. 'Actually, there is. He's my father and I'm sorry that he's gone. Lots of his old cronies are going to be here today, and they'll be sorry too. It's going to upset them to see you dressed like that. And I know you wouldn't mind thumbing your nose at your grandfather, and it might be that he deserves it, but I know you. It's not in your nature to want to hurt sad old men who know it won't be long before they're in the coffin too. They'll hate to think their own grandchildren could feel the way you do.'

'They might,' said Annie sullenly.

'Yes. Perhaps they do. What a very sad day it's going to be.'

Annie pulled off her earrings. Then she flung open her wardrobe doors and said, 'OK then! What do you suggest?'

'How about that navy wool dress?'

318

'It's got a short skirt. I don't wear those any more.'

'You could wear navy tights with it. Very chic. And I'm sure I've got a blue pillbox hat somewhere. With a black belt to give that appropriate touch, you'll be a knockout.'

The outfit was assembled. 'I've got knobbly knees,' said Annie darkly.

'Have you, darling?' Flora stared at the offending objects. 'They were certainly knobbly last year. I think they've smoothed off now. Knees do, you know.'

'Oh. I didn't know.' Annie stared at herself in the mirror, tall, suspicious, and Flora felt her throat tighten with love.

Don said, 'Annie! You look fantastic.'

'Do I?' She looked anxiously down from the stairs.

'Yes. A real beauty. Come down and let me see you properly.'

He held her at arm's length and made noises of appreciation. 'Will you come to my funeral dressed like that? I'd be happy to go.' Annie laughed up at him.

Lilian arrived at eleven. She had taken the news with what seemed alarming calm, insisting on staying at home, wanting no one with her. But today Flora had sent the Bentley for her. Lilian got out stiffly, and for once she seemed truly old. John had to lend her his arm on the short walk to the house.

'Mother.' Flora went to kiss her cheek.

'Hello, dear.' Lilian stood and waited for the children's dutiful kisses, and then she and Don shook hands.

'Come and sit by the fire,' he said. 'You look tired.'

'Yes. I am. It's all been rather bewildering.'

Don led her to a chair, and Annie said in loud sotto voce, 'She didn't like him either. I don't know why all the performance.'

Lilian sat herself down. 'As it happens, Annie, I loved your grandfather very much. But I know, it's difficult to understand. You look most elegant, dear, and I do admire your legs. I thought we were never going to see them again.'

Annie's face flamed and Flora said smoothly, 'Goodness me, Mother, fashions change every five minutes. I liked her long skirts. But the short ones look more sophisticated, a bit less drooping hems in the pigstye.'

'I didn't think you could follow fashion in India,' said Lilian, accepting a glass of sherry from Forbes. 'I recognise that suit, it's at least ten years old.'

'At least,' said Flora. 'But it still fits.'

Alex took her hand, still young enough to make spontaneous

319

physical contact. 'I wish you would buy some new stuff, Mum. You'd look great.'

'I don't need to look great in India! Jeans and T-shirts are all I wear. They're easy to put on.'

'And take off,' said Don.

Lilian cut across the silence. 'Would somebody go and see if there's a walking stick in the hall cupboard? I might need one today.'

Both children made a face, but Don said, 'Go on, you two. You're getting so lazy you'll take root to the floor.'

When they were gone Lilian said mildly, 'Please don't bring up your differences in front of the children. It's so dreadful.'

'There are many things a great deal more dreadful than that, I can assure you,' said Don. 'Like having your wife getting into bed with every Tom, Dick and Harry that comes along.'

'His name's Finn,' said Flora grimly. 'And he's none of your business.'

Their eyes met. Don let out his breath. 'OK, it's none of my business. But the stupidity of this situation, with your children here, needing you, and you out there wasting your time with some randy guy who sees his chance of a good lay –'

'Please, Don, I wish you wouldn't,' said Lilian. 'She won't change, whatever you say. And if you think of what she was before and what she is now, you'd see she was right. Flora's a whole person now.'

'Thank you, Mother.'

'And what about the rest of us?' Don's voice cracked. 'Her children? How whole are they, growing up without their mother?'

He turned and went out. Flora put her hand to her mouth, forcing back tears. 'He's upset,' said Lilian. 'The children are fine, both of them.'

'I don't know.' Flora blinked her eyes hard, trying to dispel the drops that threatened to fall and make her mascara run. 'I find them easy, Don finds them hard. He wants everything from them, I want nothing but their happiness. If we were together we'd have raised the most balanced pair you could wish for. As it is – I wish I knew what would happen to them.'

'I think they manage very well as they are,' said Lilian calmly. 'Of course you feel guilty. You should. But the situation was impossible. At least you've spared them the horror of a truly broken home. At least you and Don still speak to each other.'

Flora thought how much more they had done. It had been such a mistake. All the pain and anger was back at the surface, breaking throught the layers of time and other experience they had laid on it.

320

More people began to arrive, forgotten cousins and ancient aunts. And Shalimar. Dressed in black trousers and jacket, buttoned low across a bare chest, she got out of her taxi and strode into the castle. A diamond brooch shaped like an apple was pinned to her lapel. It was enormous and fabulously expensive. Annie, at the sight of her, scuffed her shoes. 'Oh. It's you.'

'Shalimar!' Flora came across to embrace her. 'I didn't think you'd come.'

'Well, I wasn't sure I should. But there was a seat on Concorde, so I took it.'

Don came in with Alex, they had been organising seating in the cars. 'Oh, hi,' said Don, and came across to peck Shalimar's cheek.

'Don't be too effusive,' she said thinly.

'What? It's good to see you. Glad you could come.' It was so clearly a lame effort at welcome that Shalimar grimaced and turned away.

'Mum's here now,' said Annie nastily. 'You can't expect him to slobber over you.'

Flora linked her arms through her daughter's and her friend's. 'I'm so glad we can all be here,' she said determinedly. 'I expect you all to sing very loudly. Dad deserves a good send-off. Look, it's time to go to the chapel.'

Halfway through the service Lilian turned to Flora and whispered, 'I keep remembering your wedding. Your father was so proud of you.'

'Was he?'

'And when you were young. There was nothing he wouldn't do to make you happy.'

'I know.'

Lilian took a shuddering breath. 'I find it hard to accept − that it's the end. We won't ever be able to talk again. We barely saw one another and yet he was the most important person in my life. The world feels quite empty.'

Flora held her mother while she wept. Don caught her eye and lifted his brow questioningly. Flora shook her head, there was nothing to be done. They would stay right through, however harrowing it seemed, because afterwards there would be calm. She glanced round the church and saw the black-coated men, all Kincaid's business acquaintances and many of Don's paying tribute to a grand old man. He had been grand, she thought. However bitterly they had fought these last years, however unforgiving he had shown

321

himself, he would never lose her admiration. Even in adversity he'd not gone down.

A sense of party came over them afterwards. It was relief from the dreadful business of mourning, and the fires crackled, the wine flowed, and people gossipped with friends and relatives they hadn't seen in years. Lilian went to lie down upstairs, and the twins snaffled half a bottle of white wine and knocked it back behind the curtains of the window seat on the upstairs landing.

'Ooh, I do feel strange,' said Annie.

'I don't suppose you get drink at that school of yours,' said Alex, for once the more worldly wise. 'We have beer all the time. Some of the blokes bring it in.'

'I wish I knew some boys,' said Annie disconsolately. 'You ought to bring someone decent home, someone older.'

'Oh yeah! I can't ask fifth formers! They'd think I was wet.'

Annie giggled. Then she cocked her head and said urgently, 'Shhh! Someone's coming.'

Giggling silently, they pulled the curtains closed around them, leaving a crack at either edge for them to peer through. Don came into view, and holding his hand was Shalimar.

'Come on,' he was saying. 'We've only got ten minutes.'

'And I don't want a ten minute screw! It's tactless. It's Malcolm's funeral, the house is full of people, and Flora's here.'

'And for those good reasons, let's do it.'

Shalimar still held back. 'I don't know why you're so angry at Flora.'

'I bet you do know why. His name's Finn, I'm sure she's told you about him.'

'She didn't tell you, did she?' Shalimar sounded shocked. 'My God, sometimes Flora amazes me.'

Don suddenly seemed weary. 'Look, love,' he said, 'can't we give each other a little affection? Malcolm's dead, the house is full of misery, and my wife's in bed with another man. If ever I needed some help it's now. Please.'

'I'm not the health service,' said Shalimar.

'You are for me. And I am terribly, terribly grateful.'

Before the twins' amazed eyes he unlooped the button of Shalimar's jacket and exposed her breasts. Then he put one hand over each and squeezed hard. Shalimar groaned. 'All right,' she murmured. 'But make it quick. I don't want to be missed.'

When they had gone neither of the twins spoke. Annie wouldn't look at her brother, her face was buried in the fabric of the curtain. At length Alex said, 'We always knew they did, anyway.'

322

Annie's voice was muffled. 'But today! With Mum in the house. And he's so disgusting!'

'He wasn't really. That's what people do, touching and so on.'

'At least they could be in bed!' She struggled with herself. At last she burst out, 'And he said that about Mum! As if she would! She's working for charity, she doesn't do things like that. Everyone out there only thinks of helping people. She's like a saint.'

'I don't think it can be true about Mum,' agreed Alex. 'I mean, Shalimar's like that, she does films and things. Mum isn't.'

'I don't think I ever want to speak to my father again.'

By four o'clock the only people left were the family and Shalimar. Lilian was still feeling shaken, and Flora arranged for her to be taken home in a car. 'Oughtn't we to ask her to stay?' suggested Don, but Flora shook her head.

'She'll be better in her own home. I'll visit her in a day or so.'

Shalimar said, 'Why don't we play a board game? You too, Alex. I know you've got lots.' She put an affectionate arm round Annie.

'Don't touch me!' Annie threw off the embrace. 'I don't want to play anything with you. Get away from me. Go and cuddle someone with your sort of tastes! You must know lots of prostitutes!'

'Annie!' Flora was taken aback. She looked from her friend to her daughter and felt a ghastly suspicion. Surely not today – not today? Shalimar raised her eyebrows a fraction. Her wry grimace spoke volumes. 'Come upstairs, Annie,' said Flora, controlling her voice with a massive effort of will. 'I want to talk to you.'

'No.' Annie ran for the door. 'No! I don't want to talk to any of you ever again!'

At nine that night Flora went up to knock on Annie's door. After much persuasion she was at last admitted, bearing a tea tray and a new box of tissues. Annie was still sobbing, her wet pillow bearing witness to the hours of tears that had gone before.

'Did you see Dad and Shalimar?' asked Flora bluntly, pouring them both a cup of tea. 'It's all right, you know. It doesn't upset me. I don't let it. They both need someone to love, and they're not going to get married or anything. But I wish you hadn't seen. It's hard to understand about that sort of sex when you're thirteen.'

'He undid her clothes and touched her!' burst out Annie, flinging herself on Flora in a paroxysm of grief. 'Alex and I were behind the curtain, we saw him do it. It was so disgusting!'

Flora cradled her daughter and tried to explain. 'Dad needs someone,' she ventured. 'He hasn't got me and you can't expect him to do without anyone. Men and women, grown-up men and women, need that sort of love.'

323

'I wouldn't mind if he loved her!' flared Annie.

Flora sighed. 'Yes. It's all a bit one-sided, I'm afraid. She's terribly fond of him, you know.'

Annie pushed her wet hair out of her eyes. 'How can you not mind? She's your friend and she's doing that with him, here, in this house! You ought to send her away and not let her back. She's a terrible, terrible person.'

'She isn't, and you know she isn't,' said Flora grimly. 'And she loves Dad.'

Suddenly Annie was crying again, a river of tears. 'Why don't you?' she sobbed. 'If you loved him it would all be perfect. You wouldn't go away and help the starving, you'd stay home and help us. And I don't believe what they said about you, I know you haven't got anyone else. You wouldn't. You just wouldn't.'

Flora felt as if the ground had opened before her. If she admitted about Finn Annie would hate her, and if she didn't, not only would she be lying but she would be living a lie. The children would set her up against Don. She had to tell the truth.

'There is somebody,' she said stiffly. 'He's a doctor, and he's called Finn McDonald. We may be thinking about getting married.'

Annie swallowed. Her eyes were wide and unblinking. 'But you don't − he doesn't touch you?'

If only she could have said no! She tried a feeble defence. 'Annie, Finn and I care about each other. It's all part of that.'

The girl seemed to fold in on herself. Flora busied herself with the room, throwing away tissues, finding a dry pillow, settling her daughter down for the night. At last she said. 'Do you want to talk some more?'

Annie shook her head.

Downstairs Flora found Shalimar and Don sitting silently in front of the television. 'The twins saw you,' said Flora bluntly. 'Annie's hysterical. I suggest you talk to Alex, Don.'

He sighed. 'You're not the only one with perception. I already have. Fortunately if these schools do nothing else they make them men of the world. I think he wants help with technique, the morals don't seem to bother him.'

'Good Lord, you don't believe that?'

Don withered her with a glance. 'He wants me to believe that. And I won't invade his privacy.'

Shalimar got up suddenly. 'Look, I'd better go,' she said. 'This is all my fault and I'm only making things worse.'

Don said, 'It wasn't you at all. I took you upstairs, you were all for staying with the party.'

324

'But the children won't want me here now,' said Shalimar thickly. 'Oh Don, this is such a mess!' Tears began to pour down her face.

It was the signal for him to get up and comfort her. He rose to his feet and embraced her, patting her heaving shoulders. But there was a distance between them; he was doing as he ought, not as he wanted. He was conscious of Flora's face, rigidly expressionless, and suddenly the whole stupidity of the situation became clear to him. He let Shalimar go.

'This is the end,' he said thickly. 'I'm sorry, but it is. I don't want it to be like this, I'd give anything for it to be possible for us – but it doesn't work. And I'm using you, and it's time I stopped.'

Flora said, 'I'll just go out – ' but neither of them heard her.

Shalimar was shaking with sobs. Flora put her hands over her ears and fled.

'I'm going to die without you! I can't live on my own.'

'That's a line from a film,' growled Don.

She looked at him in anguish. 'But I mean it! I know you don't believe me, but I do!'

He didn't want to believe her. And yet she had the most beautiful face he had ever seen, eyes and bones and shadows, she was a dream of a woman. But she was not his dream, and never had been. He had never led her on, never offered her more than friendship, but still she had hoped, expected – he tried to soften the blow. 'It's my fault. I'm just not made right. You're a girl who can have anyone, I'm not such a big deal. I work and I climb and sometimes I get you into bed and make love. That's no life for you.'

'That's all I want. We could have a baby and be happy. I'm not like Flora, I wouldn't want anything else. We could be married.'

Don felt as if his head was splitting. The vague sense of guilt he had always felt with Shalimar had at last grown to giant proportions. 'I've got a wife already.'

She shuddered as he said it. Then she looked up at him, her face streaked and anguished. 'It's over and you won't see it. She doesn't want you, she's got a new man. Everyone knows how they feel, you only have to look at them. So why are you waiting for Flora?'

He closed his eyes suddenly. 'Flora and I are finished,' he said thickly. 'I don't know why I said that. There isn't going to be a happy ending and I'm not sure that I want one any more. But this – this isn't right. If you really want to go on as before, then we will, but I can't give you any more than that. Perhaps I'm some sort of pervert, perhaps being married to someone who isn't here is my sort of thing. Whatever happens, I'm not going to marry again.'

'Why don't you say it?' Suddenly she was screaming at him. 'Why don't you say you don't love me, tell me I'm just a good fuck? That's all I've ever been to you, with the added advantage that I always know what Flora's doing, so you get pillow talk about your wife while screwing your mistress. No wonder you find me such a turn-on. Bastard! Bastard.' The tears poured down her face. She fell on her knees and sobbed.

Don went to her, hating himself. Why couldn't he love her? She was beautiful, kind, generous, the sort of woman that turned heads whenever she entered a room. She deserved to be loved, honestly, truly, and he gave her second-hand emotion. He sat in a chair and drew her on to his lap, a long slender baby. Gradually she cried herself out.

'Do you want to go home?' he asked. 'I'll get the plane for you.'

'But you won't let me come back.'

'You can come here any time. And you know me, I can never set eyes on you without wanting to take you to bed.'

'And nothing else. Never, ever anything else.'

He rocked her, saying nothing. At last, staggering a little, she got up and left.

Chapter Four

In the morning, Annie was gone. There was her bed, the pillow still damp, and next to it yesterday's teatray, just as Flora had left it. But the pictures of Alex, Don, Flora, even those of her ponies, had all gone. So had her night things and her money.

'She's taken her bank book,' said Flora tightly. 'She can't draw money on her own, can she?'

'Yes,' said Don. 'They both can. It gave them some independence.'

'And now she's run away! What sort of independence is that?'

'There's no need to get hysterical.'

'Oh, you would say that. After all, it's your fault she's gone, so best to blame someone else, anyone else. You were seen screwing someone in the middle of a funeral, someone you don't even like, but that's just natural lust, we're not supposed to disapprove!'

Don shot out a hand and grabbed her. Flora gave a squeak and was silent. 'If you had stayed home I would never have slept with anyone but you,' he said softly. 'The blame's at least half yours. So accept it and start thinking where she might be.'

When he let her go she slumped into a chair. Once she left here she would never ever come back again, she decided. Famine and hardship were as nothing to this. Here, people took out your soul and lacerated it.

Alex came in. 'She'll be going to London,' he said.

Don's head came up. 'Why do you say that?'

'She's always talking about it. And that's where everyone goes, isn't it? She'll be expecting to take drugs and live in a squat.'

'That's what happens to you, you don't aspire to it!' shrieked Flora.

'She thinks it's glamorous,' said Alex stoically.

When they talked to the staff they discovered that one of the maids

327

had seen Annie trudging down the drive with her suitcase, and when they called the bus company someone remembered a young girl saying she was going to Edinburgh.

'She'll be getting the train from there to London,' said Alex matter of factly. 'She knows you'd find her in Aberdeen.'

'We'll find her in Edinburgh too,' said Don. 'Or London, or Timbuktu. Come on, Flora, we'll take the Bentley.'

'I'm coming,' said Alex. 'She's my twin.'

So the three of them drove out of the castle. Frost still lay on the fields, thick as snow under the hedges. The hips and haws were bright on the bushes, hanging in great clusters, tangled in the beech hedge. Flora thought she had never felt so desolate in all her life. From time to time Alex played rock music on the radio, until Don said finally, 'Cut it out, Alex. I can't think straight.' So they sat in uneasy silence all the way.

They didn't find her in Edinburgh. They went first to the station and then drove round and round, looking. 'She'll have got the first train,' said Alex. 'We could fly down and be there before her.'

Don looked at him in surprise. 'So rugby hasn't quite addled your brain then.'

Alex grinned. 'There's the odd cell left, Dad. Have to be if I'm going to run the firm.' Don ran a hand throught the shock of his son's red hair.

Their own jet had taken Shalimar, so they were reduced to chartering from a private firm. It took time. Flora was haunted by the thought that Annie would escape from the station and be lost. But at last they were airborne, the plane shaking a little in the turbulence, the pilot strange and the passengers silent. Alex ate Toblerone to pass the time, his teeth crunching like a cement mixer.

The journey from Heathrow into town by taxi seemed to take an age. Don was scanning the train timetables. 'We could miss her,' he said tightly. 'If she got the first possible train.'

'We should contact the police,' said Flora, feeling on the verge of hysterics. 'If she gets lost in London we could never see her again. She could be killed, anything.'

'Not the police,' said Don. 'She'd never forgive us for getting her arrested.'

'I don't care if she never forgives us. I just want her home.'

As they neared King's Cross the traffic snarled up into a stationary tangle. They leaped out, Don throwing money at the driver, and raced into the concourse. Thousands of people stood around; people sat on chairs, on the floor, they lay in the waiting areas or stood with their bags round their feet looking expectant.

'When's the Edinburgh train due?' demanded Don of a porter.

'Came in ten minutes ago,' he said laconically, and Flora burst into tears.

Don looked wildly around. All that he knew he could identify was her black hair, Annie could be wearing anything. What would he do if he arrived here? Waste time for a bit perhaps. He made for the take-away cafe, where the red seats and fast food beckoned the kids. Sitting at a corner table, white-faced and scared, was Annie.

He sat down without a word. Then he got out his handkerchief and blew his nose. 'Don't mind if I cry, do you? I've never been so relieved in all my life.'

Annie said, 'I don't want to talk to you. Any of you.'

He nodded. 'I know. Your parents are behaving like fools and the world's gone mad. I'm sorry about what you saw, love. Shalimar and I are just about finished, it never was right.'

'What about you and mum? Why isn't she home with us?'

He shrugged. He couldn't speak. All at once he got up, made a clumsy rush and embraced Annie's head, pressing it into his chest. 'Don't you ever do anything like this again,' he threatened, shaking her with rough affection. 'You nearly killed me with fright!'

They didn't talk much on the way home. Night fell as they landed in Scotland, and the drive to the castle was a long, dark trail. Both children fell asleep in the back, their mouths covered in Toblerone smears, like three year olds.

'Had I better go?' said Flora. 'I seem to be causing such upsets.'

Don slowed for a corner. 'I've got a better idea. I'll take Alex climbing, you stay at home and do girl things with Annie.'

'Suppose she wants to climb?'

Don grinned. 'She can if she wants. But I don't think she'll want. She feels dizzy looking out of the top deck of a bus.'

'She's never been on one!'

'Yes she has. I took them once for a treat.'

Flora turned to look at their children. 'It isn't getting any easier, is it?' she said.

Don gave a strangled laugh. 'No, it is not! The last year's been hell, actually. When they're little it's all so straightforward. There's the odd major upset, but nothing you can't resolve. If they don't like the school you change it; the friends, you find them something else to do so they make new ones; the work, you get a tutor in. But now, we make the messes and watch them trying to come to terms. KORSEA launched a recycling project at Annie's school last year and she was furious with me for embarrassing her. And Alex was mad

329

because he wanted it at his school to impress his mates. And I try, and I try — sometimes I feel like leaving the whole lot and going climbing forever.'

Flora laughed. 'You take your big brawny son off climbing and enjoy yourself then. Annie and I will stay at home and admire you.'

Don said, 'You know, that almost sounded affectionate.'

'Did it? I'm sorry, I didn't mean anything.'

'No. I don't suppose you did.'

It took Don days to accept that his son wasn't a natural climber. He was big, strong and brave, but the effortless relation of muscle to sinew that Don possessed, the ability to exert strong pressure at the limit of his reach, was missing in Alex. In place of it he had enthusiasm, and might ultimately have technique.

'I'm not very good, am I, Dad?' Alex said breathlessly at the end of one troubled and clumsy pitch.

'Climbing's learned,' Don assured him, and tried to forget that he had been born knowing how. Perhaps he should have started the boy earlier, he thought. At least he hadn't acquired Flora's fear of heights.

On the way down, hiking across bog and grassy moor, he said, 'You do want to do this, don't you, Alex? If it isn't your thing then say so, boy. I don't want you putting up with it for my sake.'

Alex looked at his father's strong face. He kept a picture of him at school, cut from a magazine, showing Don in the Himalayas, wearing a sweat band round his forehead, a duvet jacket dripping with gear and an expression of hawklike intelligence. Alex adored his father, he worshipped everything about him. His only regret was the sure and certain knowledge that he would never, ever, be as much a man. But he was certainly going to try. 'It's all right, Dad,' he said happily. 'I mean, it's super. I really love it.'

'Good. Good. I sometimes think this is the best bit, hiking home after a long day, with a warm fire and some good conversation to come. It's great having you out here too, Alex. Really great.'

Alex almost wished that he wasn't too big to hold hands. He felt a great sense of pride, that his father thought him man enough to be brought here and taught the things that made his father what he was. As they descended into the valley a barn owl swooped low above the buildings, and they could look into the cottages to see people watching television or having their tea,

'Looks good after a day on the hills, doesn't it? said Don. 'Don't worry about being scared. Everyone is. You learn to cope with it.'

'I'm not scared,' said Alex indignantly.

Don laughed. 'Then don't be too cocky! When all's said and done the gear won't always save your life. The rock will. If you learn how to live with it.'

They went to their lodgings, leaving boots and gear stacked in the porch. The landlady knew Don only as one of the many climbers she had over her threshold, and she babied Alex, bringing him hot chocolate and buns. Later his father took him out to the pub, and he sat in a corner drinking lemonade topped up with a splash of his father's beer, and listened to the men, the hard men of the hills, talking and laughing together. He knew then, with joyful certainty, that he would give anything to enter this world as one of them. Nothing would stop him.

Flora took Annie to buy clothes, but it wasn't a success. All the warm intimacy was gone. Anything Flora liked her daughter hated on principle.

'You are being a pig,' said Flora in the end. 'If there isn't anything you want then let's give up. We can go and have lunch and visit a gallery or something.'

'All right. If you want.' Annie was deliberately bored.

She warmed up over an elegant lasagne taken in one of those gilt-chaired cafes that cater solely for expensive ladies on shopping expeditions. 'It makes me feel rich and idle, eating in here,' said Annie. 'Especially since I should be at school.'

'I think having time together is more important just now,' said Flora. 'Will you look at that old lady! Don't turn round — you can see her in the mirror. She's dripping with dirty diamonds.'

Annie turned her attention from the wrinkled lady in the mirror to her smooth-skinned and bright-haired mother. Flora had dressed up today, in a green coat and black hat. 'You've got lots of diamonds,' said Annie. 'You never wear them.'

'No.' Flora realised she was going to have to be more open, and it was uncomfortable. 'I — I don't like putting on the trappings of Kincaid's daughter, or Harrington's wife, when I'm only pretending. I'm not what either of them wanted, you see,'

The pudding trolley arrived and Annie selected an enormous chocolate eclair. 'I think you're just like Grandma Lilian,' she said decisively. 'You turned out like her despite everything Grandad did to stop you. I'll probably be the same.'

Flora was taken aback. 'Do you want to be?'

'No, not really. I'd like to be one of the women here, the happy ones. Coming out to lunch to buy things for their families, and going home with lots of bags. And everyone together at Christmas, and no rows. And my husband buying me diamond brooches that I'd love to wear.'

Flora felt suddenly ashamed. Why couldn't she too have been happy with such a life? 'You can have that if you want it,' she said shakily. 'There's no family tradition of escape that you have to follow.'

'You'd be ashamed of me, living like that,' said Annie, with a shrewd glance at her mother's face. 'You'd think I was wasting myself.'

'I wouldn't be so presumptuous! It's up to you to decide who you want to be darling, don't spend your life living up to some mythical concept of what I want for you. The trouble with me and your father, if you must know, is that he wouldn't let me be anything! He kept me at home, stifled me, while he did whatever he liked. Which, as always, was climbing.'

'That didn't stop you doing anything you wanted. He was away, he couldn't object.'

Flora stared blankly at her daughter. At the time her life had seemed stifling, but was it like that, really? Now, her adult self looked back at those times and wondered why she had felt that sense of unendurable waste, as if her life had been pouring away down a drain.

'It was awful,' she said feebly.

'No, it wasn't. You were spoiled. You were used to having everything your own way.'

'I had nothing my own way! Ever! You should have tried living with those men, with their expectations. For God's sake, Annie, I don't have to explain myself to you!'

Annie recoiled, and people at the next table stared in disapproval. There was no excuse for yelling at your daughter in public, they seemed to say. What an uncontrolled woman, venting sour spleen on the unresisting head of her child.

Flora pulled herself together and asked the waitress for the bill. They went out without speaking, and at the gallery trailed round staring listlessly at the pictures. In one small room there was a modernist canvas of mother and child, a picture of love and unity. Flora felt all the world's reproach. She turned to Annie. 'I should never have left you. I wouldn't have done it if there had been anything else I could do. I'm so sorry.'

Annie took a long breath and let it out slowly, visibly relaxing. She gave a beatific smile. 'It can all be put right,' she said. 'Shalimar's gone and we'll have Christmas together and you and Dad can start all over again. Alex and I will make sure Dad doesn't do anything you don't want. Mum, we're going to be so, so happy!'

Flora's smile froze on her face. 'But Annie — what about my life? What about Finn?'

'Well, you can't care about him more than us, can you?'

Flora began to walk at furious speed out of the gallery, Annie jogging at her side. 'It isn't possible,' she hissed. 'I've my work, my friends. I don't want to come back to your father.'

'Well, you ought to want to! You're such a cheat, pretending to be good and kind. If you don't come back it's because you don't love us, and you can't keep popping in for a week or two and pretending any more. Dad's got rid of Shalimar, so obviously he wants to try again. He didn't even want you to go in the first place. And it wouldn't be so bad if you really were looking after starving people, but you're just having it off with this horrible, horrible man.'

Flora stopped on the pavement, frantically trying to flag down a taxi. 'Don't use that vulgar expression.'

'Why not? What other one would you like? Screwing? Fucking? Putting his leg over?'

'Annie, stop it!'

A taxi drew up and Flora fell inside. Annie still stood on the pavement. 'Now what?' said Flora hysterically. 'What do you think you're doing?'

'John's here with the Bentley,' said Annie. 'Honestly, I think you're cracking up.'

Flora scrambled out of the car again. 'If I am, it's your fault. Just let's stop talking and get home.'

Over the next few days they developed an uneasy truce. Together they dressed two trees, one for the hall and one for the sitting room, and they tied up bunches of holly and spruce. Annie was surprisingly artistic, making wreaths out of wire and decorating them with fruit and leaves sprayed silver, and all the presents she bought were wrapped in confections of paper lace. One wintry afternoon they went down to the kitchen and helped Marie make mince pies and shortbread, and that evening, before the curtains were drawn, they watched flakes of snow dusting the grass. 'I ought to get my mother here before the weather really starts,' said Flora.

'She wouldn't want to come. Grandma hates me and Alex being noisy and objectionable. And her hating makes us worse.'

'I can't leave her alone for Christmas,' said Flora. 'Not this year.'

333

'You've left us alone often enough,' said Annie.

It was hopelessly difficult. Flora went up to her room and sat on the bed, crying to herself. She hadn't realised how much she valued her daughter's good opinion, how she had unconsciously conformed to Annie's idea of her as an unworldly woman with a mission to help. She hadn't got a mission any more. After all these years she was left with none of the fluffy ideals of the aid worker, she was down to bare metal, polished through constant rubbing against life. She was so far from being a saint, she thought. Stupidity, greed, wilful hatred of all things western be they videos or vaccinations, all these things enraged her. Sometimes she almost hated the people she tried to help, because they seemed so hopeless and dull-witted. And yet even the most stupid of them could amaze her by suddenly taking up an idea. In the old Biblical analogy, she was a sower of seeds, and she could not tell where they fell, or indeed which would grow. But in nursing her tender plants abroad, she had neglected those at home. One at least was in danger.

When Don and Alex arrived back three days before Christmas, Flora welcomed them effusively. 'It's been so odd without you,' she declared. 'We'll have a special dinner, and the children can have a glass of wine.'

'I've been driving her frantic, Dad,' said Annie.

'At least you don't keep it all for me. You look thin, love, eat some chocolate or something.'

'I want to be thin. I'm going to get anorexia and waste away to nothing. If I ate chocolate I'd only go and throw it up again in the bathroom.'

'Try that and you get your bottom pounded,' said Don phlegmatically. 'Go and talk to Alex. He can tell you all about the gull that spat in his face.'

'Yeah!' agreed Alex. 'They regurgitate food if you frighten them. And it did! All over me, a gallon of puke! Yuk!'

Don and Flora went into the sitting room. She sat down on the sofa, closed her eyes and shuddered. 'It's been terrible. She talked me into a corner and tried to make me say that you and I should try again. She's absolutely determined, nothing I say convinces her that there's any reason for me to go. She keeps saying I can't love her, or Alex or anyone.'

Don said, 'I imagine that might be true.'

'What? That I don't love them? Come on, Don, don't you start.'

He leaned against the fireplace. 'You don't love them enough to

334

give anything up for them. This friend of yours, for instance. Not that he appears to be keeping closely in touch. Heard from him?'

'I didn't give him my address.'

'You sleep with a bloke, but you don't know him well enough to get letters from him. I see. Let's hope he's more into French letters, or you'll be in the club. And that would be hard for Annie to understand.'

'Oh, do shut up, Don! I'm sick of your stupid jealousy.'

She stormed out into the hall, her lunch churning in her stomach. Her forehead felt clammy with sweat. This visit was turning into a nightmare! She went into the downstairs cloakroom and rested her forehead against the tiles. After a while she felt better. She would go for a walk in the garden, she decided, by herself. At least there no one could get at her.

Don stood at the window and watched her. He wondered if she locked her door at night. Her bottom moved under her skirt, round and erotic. When they said hello this afternoon she had put her hand on his shoulder so she could kiss his cheek. She smelled of old-fashioned roses, the richest scent.

Annie came into the room behind him. 'I think it's time you told Mum she's got to stay home.'

Don turned and grinned. 'You know she never listens to me.'

'Yes she does! She said such nice things about you. Said you were a wonderful man and she was sorry she'd hurt you so. If she'd been more mature she wouldn't have done it. That's what she said.'

Only half-believing, yet wanting to believe, Don said, 'Annie, are you sure?'

'Yes, of course I am. This other man isn't anything. She hasn't sent him one letter, and he hasn't written her any. I think she's making him up.'

'Well, I suppose it might be possible.'

He looked out of the window again. She was walking the riverbank, with two or three ducks quacking in her wake, hoping for food. She had grown so poised and graceful that she daunted him at times, he found it easy to imagine her running some aid station in the middle of nowhere. She had the appearance of someone who could handle anything, who was almost beyond surprise. He said her name to himself, Flora, Flora, and to him she was all gentleness and warmth. Yet there was no one in the world who could make him more angry.

They had a family meal that night, and for once it was just right. Alex had his tales to tell: 'I made a shambles of it at first, but Dad showed me what's what. And the blokes in the pub all offered to

335

take me along any time I'm up there. They all want to get on one of Dad's expeditions, of course.'

'Are they all hairy?' demanded Annie. 'In the photographs they always seem to have beards.'

'Of course they do!' said Flora. 'It's so cold they daren't shave, for fear of frostbite. Your father had a beard when I met him. Or at least, the second time I met him. He'd grown it in between. And he smelled dreadful!'

'You said you didn't mind,' objected Don. 'You smelled very strange for that matter. You'd been washing your hair in some local herb. It was like cuddling up to a sage bush or something.'

'When I go back to India I always think the place smells strange,' said Flora. 'And then in an hour I don't notice it. But I'd love to go back to Nepal.'

'It must have been so romantic,' said Annie softly.

Don and Flora found themselves exchanging glances. 'Yes,' murmured Flora. And Don said, 'It certainly was.'

At nine o'clock Annie began yawning ostentatiously. 'I'm exhausted,' she declared. 'And so must you be, Alex. All that climbing.'

'We stayed up till midnight most nights,' said Alex. 'The blokes wanted to talk and so on.'

'So you must be tired now,' said Annie, and fixed him with a gimlet stare.

Alex made a face at her. But he climbed to his feet.

'It is jolly early,' said Flora. 'You haven't got school, remember.'

Annie yawned again. 'Holidays are more tiring than anything. We'll only be bad tempered tomorrow if we don't get enough sleep. Come on, Alex.'

When they had gone Don got up and poured them both another glass of port. 'One of Annie's more subtle moves,' he remarked.

Flora giggled. 'The girl's an absolute steamroller when she sets her mind to something. Alex is so good, he just lets her get on with it. Anything for a quiet life, don't let the women ruin the beer. Was he really good at climbing?'

Don nodded. 'He was OK, yes. Loved it. Rattling off the jargon with wild abandon − laybacks and handjams, cams and screws. You can't help but laugh, the kids are all the same. Five minutes after they find out what something is they're chatting about the damned thing as if it's as familiar as their teddy. And Alex had to be forcibly restrained from dressing up in everything, every last rope and sling, every time we went out. He looked fit to conquer

336

the Eiger just to go to the pub.' He chuckled and shook his head.

Flora sighed fondly. 'He is such a darling. They both are.'

'Even scheming minx Annie.'

Flora said nothing, merely turning the stem of her glass in clean, slim fingers. They were so much whiter than when she arrived, thought Don. She was leading the life of a soft and pampered lady. It had never suited her before. He tried to frame the words he wanted to say, and they literally stuck in his throat. He coughed, and Flora lifted her eyes from her glass, those dark unfathomable eyes.

'Why don't we start again?' he said jerkily. 'For the children and for us. Your father's gone, the slate's wiped clean, there's only you and me left. We owe it to Alex and Annie, if no one else.'

Flora took a shallow breath. 'You don't have to do everything Annie wants,' she said stiffly.

'I thought of it as something for us, for the family. You're needed here. And, quite honestly, you don't seem all that desperate to get back to India.'

'Don't I?' She sighed. 'This isn't real life.' Then, before he could say anything, she rushed on: 'I know it's real to you! But it has so much, so many things and ways of living. Out there it's like worn leather over rock, basic, uncomfortable and going into holes. And I'm not only helping them, I'm helping me. I need that life. It's important to me. At the moment I'm banging my head against a brick wall out there, because I want a bigger job and no one's giving it to me. If you must know I'd love to drop out and give up, it would be so luxuriously easy. And it would be wrong.'

'You wouldn't have to give up altogether.' He made his voice indifferent, hard, the antithesis of pleading. 'You could still be away a lot. But you'd come back. We'd be together again, a caring, loving family. This family's real, we need real things, real people. Luxury, money, they're no damn use at all.'

Suddenly Flora bent her head. Sobs shook her. She pressed her fingers to her eyes to hold back the tears. 'Don't, don't! It can't happen, it won't happen. There are things you don't know about.'

Don half stood, looming across the table at her. 'What things? Is it this man? I'm beginning to doubt that he exists. He's just a convenient excuse for you to hide behind, when the truth is you don't want to live here. We can have good sex, we can have good living, we've got two fabulous children, and you won't. Flora, why not?'

She looked up at him, drowned in tears. 'I'm pregnant,' she said flatly. 'And I'm afraid Finn isn't imaginary, he's a real man and we had real sex and we didn't make any use of those French letters you so wisely advised. But then neither did you, that short time ago. I

337

don't know if this baby is yours or his, Don, and I've no idea what I'm going to do about it.'

The colour drained from his face as she watched. 'It can't be his. I – I won't let you have another man's child.'

'I told you, I don't know if it's his. I'm not often all that regular. It could be yours, we did it twice! And it's so stupid to be in this mess, I could kick myself black and blue, as if I shouldn't know better! I've been celibate for years and years, and then two men in one month. I so wish I hadn't let you touch me!'

Don turned on her. 'What? So you could be sure it's loverboy's? Then you could go back to your lovenest and tell him what a big boy he is to have put you up the spout, and you could rear your little nestling on carrot water and lentils, alongside your pathetic and treacherous principles!'

'I betrayed him more than you,' said Flora thickly. 'I didn't mind doing it with you, I thought he'd never know. It's like having an affair, cheating on your lover with your husband. But now I don't know what to do. Don, don't shout at me, tell me what I should do!'

He got up and went to the fireplace, staring down into the glowing pile of logs. Little flames came and went, sparking the bark into luminous shards of light. He felt physically sick, as if someone had hit him in the stomach with a baseball bat.

'Do you want me to say I don't care if it's his? Because I do care. I care so much that if you have this child I never want to see it, never want to know that it's alive. No child deserves to be hated as much as I hate this.'

Flora said shrilly, 'I don't know why you should. You don't love me, and you haven't for years. To you I'm just a thing, something you own, an old car you keep in the garage to take out for a spin occasionally. You don't need me, but you like to know I'm there.'

'Some garage! Half across the world!'

'But you still keep tabs on me. You still see me as a wife. You still think I should keep my sexual favours for no one but you.'

Don said nothing. He went to the side table and poured himself a whisky, adding only a splash of water. 'What does this Finn character look like?'

Flora looked up. 'You can't expect to hold an identification parade in the labour ward! Or were you planning on blood tests. On one side we have the family welcome, on the other the orphanage. Don't get too fond of it Flora, the results might come out wrong.'

'Oh, for Christ's sake, Flora, I am not the Gestapo! I'm not even your father! I just asked what the bloody bloke looked like!'

'I'm sorry.' She swallowed, trying to compose herself. 'He's smaller than you. Quite a bit. Slimmer. Green eyes, black hair and beard. Looks a bit elfin, somehow. A bit other world. Actually he's an obsessive character if anything, he does everything to extremes. When I met him in Nepal he stayed in the villages for years, immersed himself in local language and culture. Since then he's done research, campaigned for reform of health care in prisons, and in the hospital he ran he transformed it from a monstrous cess pool to a caring, relevant institution. And now he's thinking of becoming a priest.'

Don's mouth fell open. At last he said, 'I take it that sex with you helped make up his mind.'

The ghost of a smile crossed Flora's face. 'I don't know. Possibly. It just sort of happened, Don, because we wanted it to. The afterwards didn't seem very important.'

'No thought of the afterwards. A bloody doctor! I expect more sense of Alex, damn it!'

Flora sank her forehead into her hands. 'We are two people used to things being organised. I didn't expect nature to sneak up on me like this, not at my age.'

'You're not exactly an old age pensioner, Flora. You're not even thirty-five, you must have realised you could get pregnant!'

'Perhaps I did. And perhaps it was just a romantic idea, I didn't think what it truly meant. Oh Don, Don, What am I going to do?'

She began to cry in earnest, putting her head on her arms. Don thought his head would explode. The thoughts thundered round like a herd of angry buffalo. 'What would you do if it was mine?' he heard himself say.

'I don't know! How can I? Anyway, it would probably be the signal for Annie to go completely off the rails. Perhaps I'd have an abortion, I don't know.'

'Christ! You'll keep the brat if it's this priest that's the father, but if it's me you'll bash it on the head!'

'I didn't say that,' said Flora wearily. 'I tell you, I don't know! Perhaps I'd go off by myself and have it in secret and not ever speak to any of you ever again.'

'That's always your solution.' Don felt his throat tighten. 'You always run away.'

Chapter Five

All at once Christmas was upon them. Lilian came and any rows or discussions were shelved for three days. Don gave Annie a white kitten, and she was ecstatic. Suddenly their almost punk daughter was reverting to baby talk.'I love you forever, don't I, dinkums? Itty bitty kitty.' She put her face so close to the little cat that his blue eyes crossed as he stared at her.

Alex was bored. He nagged his father to take him for a scramble on a nearby rock outcrop, and when he said no Alex mooched around the house desultorily kicking the furniture and scowling. Don didn't want to go. He would give anything to be with Van now, he thought, somewhere cold and very dangerous. He wanted no time for thought, and certainly none of Alex's inane chitchat. But in front of Lilian he and Flora were forced to maintain some semblance of a conversation, and that was worse. So he gave in, and went out with Alex, heading for the nearest stiff climb.

Flora sat sewing by the fire with her mother. It was a pastime she had taken up seriously in India, copying the exquisite silk embroidery with which the country abounded. She found it soothing, whereas in her youth it had seemed a waste of time. So many things changed with the years, she thought.

'What is the matter, Flora?' asked Lilian gently. 'You and Don can barely look at one another.'

Flora glanced up. 'It's only the usual,' she said smoothly. 'I'll be off soon. We can't spend much time together, we get on one another's nerves.'

'I rather thought he was going to ask you to stay,' remarked Lilian. 'And on reflection, I think you should.'

Flora tied tiny knots to secure seed pearls no bigger than caviar. 'I'm afraid, Mother, there's someone else,' she said.

Lilian didn't seem surprised. 'Don't you think that's all the more reason for you to stay? Darling, when all's said and done, you owe the children something. They need you. I might not have lived with you, Flora, but I wasn't halfway across the world. Annie needs help growing up. She needs your help.'

The needle stuck into the fleshy part of Flora's thumb. She left it there for a long moment, then twisted and pulled it out. The pain felt justified. 'Mother, I'm pregnant and I don't know who the father is,' she said flatly. 'It could be my friend and it could be Don. I let him make love to me when I first came home.'

Lilian's face remained fixed. The only sign that she had heard was a slight thinning of the skin over her nose. 'I take it Don knows,' she said finally. Flora nodded.

They sat in silence. At last Lilian said, 'The answer has to be an abortion. For you, for the children, even for Don. He doesn't deserve to have you treat him like this.'

'He was the one that wanted sex, Mother!' flared Flora.

'And you are quite old enough to know what happens!' retorted Lilian. 'This is only a potential child, it's nothing yet. If you want a baby afterwards then have one, with Don or this man or whoever. The very least you owe your children is to let them know who fathered them.'

'It was an accident,' moaned Flora.

'And you want me to believe that at your age you were swept away by passion. First with this man, and then with your husband!'

'Yes! Yes!' screamed Flora. 'I've tried to deny that part of me and I can't! I went with Finn because I care for him and it was good. And I went with Don because even if I hate him it's always good. I can't stop wanting him just because we're separated.'

'But you could control yourself, Flora. You could think sensibly!'

'But I didn't think it would hurt anyone. And I regret it so much.'

Later, as it was getting dark, Annie came in from riding. The three of them settled down in the firelight, toasting crumpets and listening to the wind at the window. 'I hope the men get back soon,' said Flora, sleepily.

'Dad's bound to come back early,' said Annie. 'He loves coming back when you're here.'

'Don't make things up, you schemer.' Flora smoothed the hair over her daughter's ear and Annie hunched her shoulder.

'I'm not. It's lovely when everyone's here and we're all together.'

She looked so frail, sitting there, knees hunched up to a pointed

341

chin, her hair again spiked as a thistle. 'Eat another crumpet,' said Flora, but Annie shook her head. Perhaps she would get anorexia, thought Flora, perhaps this lovely young thing would wither and die. Fear clutched at her heart. She didn't know if she wanted the risk of another child. She didn't know if she wanted more, so that Annie and Alex might matter less. Except that she loved them both with all her heart, and would love another one also without taking one morsel away from them. In that moment, looking down at her daughter, she had a deep yearning to have this baby, and love it and treasure it, giving it everything Annie had lacked. Whoever else could claim it, the child was first and forever her own.

'Sometimes,' said Lilian, 'I see your father in you, Flora.'

'Only in looks,' said Flora.

'Oh no,' said Annie. 'More than that. He had ideas and he liked to follow them. He never did things by halves.'

'I wish I was more cautious,' said Flora, sighing. 'I get myself in terrible muddles.'

'Like what?' demanded Annie, leaning on her mother's knee.

Flora sighed. 'I don't know. Things. I do wish the boys were back.'

But it was eight o'clock before they finally returned, brought in a police car. Flora stood in the doorway, framed in light, as Don was helped into the house. Alex followed him, white faced.

'What happened?' Flora stared in disbelief at Don's arm. It was in plaster past the elbow. There were grey lines of pain drawn under his eyes.

'I fell,' said Alex. 'Dad saved me.'

'It was my fault,' said Don tightly. 'I let him lead, I forgot he was a novice.'

'And I forgot what he told me,' said Alex, desperation clear in his voice.

'Only a busted wrist,' said Don. 'Could have been worse.'

The policemen were invited in for a wee dram to warm themselves, and the family listened to their chatter in silence. 'Lucky to get down they were, by all accounts. The rescue people should have been called out, you know. But Mr. Harrington doesn't need to bother with those, I dare say.'

'We all have our moments,' said Don thinly. He sat down, and Flora knew he was exhausted. Whatever had happened had taken everything from Don. But he didn't want Alex to know.

She ushered the policemen out and sent Alex upstairs to bathe. 'It's common enough in climbing,' she said airily. 'Chipped this

342

and broken that. I'm glad it's happened, Alex, perhaps you'll be properly careful.'

The boy smiled, beginning to be reassured. His natural ebullience was returning, soon he would indeed believe it was nothing. Flora went back to where Don and Lilian still sat.

'All right,' she said tensely, 'how did you nearly let that boy kill himself?'

'Flora, that's unnecessary,' said her mother.

'But it's true,' said Flora. 'He took him on something too hard, and Alex fell. What happened next I don't know, but I can guess.'

'He nagged to try a hard move,' said Don wearily. 'I didn't want him to. He's like a young bull, no fear and no finesse. He shouldn't have led, of course. He'd put in a cam but he must have done something wrong because when he fell it came out. I stopped him, the rope went round my arm. And that's when the fun started.'

'I hope it's put him off for life,' said Flora vehemently. 'It's a bloody, bloody sport.'

'It was hell getting him down that face,' murmured Don. He closed his eyes against the memory. 'I was in a mess and he didn't know what to do. Pride apart, I'd have sat and yelled to be rescued if there'd been anyone to hear. There never is when you need them.'

Flora put her hand on his shoulder. 'Thanks,' she said briefly.

He opened his eyes. 'I didn't do it for you.'

Forbes brought a tray and poured Don an enormous whisky. He downed it and held out the glass for another. It was a quick, if dangerous way to relax.

Lilian got to her feet. 'I'll leave you and go home. John can drive me. Might I suggest you discuss what you intend to do about Flora's condition? These things don't go away.'

'However much we might wish they did,' said Flora shakily. 'Are you sure you won't stay, Mother?'

Lilian sighed irritably. 'Don't recite platitudes. I want to go and you want to see the back of me. So we shall agree to part. Let me know what you decide, darling. Goodbye, Don. You have my admiration.'

When they were alone, Don said, 'What do you think she meant by that?'

Flora put her chin in her hands. 'At present, she thinks you are behaving very much better than me. I've decided to go back to India.'

'And?'

'And – I don't know. Mother thinks that since I don't know

343

who fathered my child, I should have an abortion. But I'm not sure it matters. After all, it's my child. If either of you wants to be involved with it afterwards, then that's up to you.'

Don said, 'Are you going to tell him about me? I suppose you'll pretend it was a drunken fumble in the dark. You'll never sell two consenting adults enjoying an orgiastic hour of bodily contact.'

'You were furious the second time,' said Flora. 'Behaved as if you wanted to stab me.'

Suddenly he grabbed her hand and pulled it down to his lap. She felt his erection, and she turned her head away, while he still gripped her hand. After a moment he said, 'It's mine, you know. I'm sure of it. Tell him that and he won't want you. He can go and be a priest and forget about things he doesn't understand.'

'It could easily be his,' said Flora, and Don's fingers closed like a vice on her wrist. 'You ought to be in bed,' she said steadily, and after a long second he let her go.

She helped him undress, and there was an odd, strained eroticism in the air. As she guided his legs into pyjama trousers he said, 'You like having me helpless.'

'Do I?' Kneeling, she looked up at him. He put his good hand gently on her hair.

Then he said, 'If this child's mine then it's as much mine as Alex or Annie. I want you to remember that. You won't bring it up on your own.'

'Then I hope it's Finn's,' she snapped. 'At least then I can do what I like.'

'He can't be much of a man,' said Don.

'I sometimes wish you weren't so much of one.'

He was swaying with weariness. She helped him to his bed, and as he lay down he almost groaned. The hair on his chest was like young wheat, she thought, and suddenly she was wishing that she could stay. She had been so young before, she hadn't known that the only walls that contain you are the ones you build yourself. If the child was Don's then she would stay, she thought. If she knew that the child was his. But she couldn't know until it was far, far too late to change anything.

When she went to see to the children they were both asleep. Alex's curtains were open and she drew them on the cold, starlit night. A great wave of thankfulness swept over her, that Alex had come safely home. Don took good care. She only brought conflict into this house, nothing more.

Annie's hair looked like ink against her pillow. Flora touched it briefly, her heart going out to her wild, romantic girl. Her pictures were once again on the table at the bedside, and from somewhere Annie had found one of the wedding photographs. Don and Flora stood together, smiling at each other. 'Oh, Annie,' whispered Flora, 'I'm sorry. There isn't a right thing to do any more, everything's wrong. And I can't bear to make you sad.'

There was no way she could say goodbye. She went to her room and began to pack, taking only the things she had brought with her. All the cashmere and silk, the satin and lace, would be left here once again and she would make do with jeans and bush gear, and perhaps one cheap dress for official functions. All at once she felt dizzy and sat on the bed for a moment, wishing that she felt well enough to deal with this dreadful situation. If only she knew whose child it was! The fates had inveigled her into this and now they were laughing at her, watching her try to extricate herself from an impossible tangle. A sudden image of a baby occurred to her, Don's hair, Finn's eyes, her own mouth. It was a nightmare thought, and not the only nightmare she had to endure. She could lose her job over this. She could lose everything.

Flora rang down to Forbes, and asked for the car. The only thing she could do for her family, the most loving thing, was to go.

A sweet, almost damp breeze brushed Flora's cheek. The people in the carriage were laughing and singing, oblivious to their children asleep on the floor. Indians accepted children in a wholly un-Western way, as something inevitable and abundant. Flora moved a toddler carefully aside, got up and made her way into the corridor. She felt slightly queasy, and her head ached from the incessant noise. What's more her waistband felt tight and she speculated on whether she should wear a sari and conceal her state for at least a month or two. But after that there would be no escape, and she doubted very much whether anyone would be willing to speak out for her. The girls who got pregnant always lost their jobs.

Her thoughts centred on Finn. He must help her, he must advise. She felt that she must go to him and confess everything, and that he would judge. In her mind's eye he seemed almost saintly, so different from Don, from any man that she knew.

A white man was squeezing past in the corridor, and he seized the opportunity to rub himself against her buttocks. She pretended she hadn't noticed, but when he came back she moved into the carriage again. Two women were having an argument, and Flora was asked to referee. She politely declined.

It was five in the morning when they arrived. Flora climbed stiffly down from the train, exhausted and dry-mouthed. Fortunately the rickshaw man knew her and took charge of her baggage, and she sat in the cart watching him pedal, thinking that exhaustion made everything seem like a dream. When they arrived at the bungalow she sat for some moments before stirring, and paid the man off in a daze. The doors were locked and she had to knock to get in, but eventually one of the boys opened up.

'Good Lord! We weren't expecting you for weeks. There's someone in your bed.'

'There can't be. I've got to have somewhere to sleep.'

'They'll be getting up in an hour or so. I'll whistle up some tea for you or something.'

She felt unequal to suggesting anything else.

Abdul appeared, smiling and delighted, and made her cups of delicious tea. She drank it black and lay in one of the long verandah chairs, listening to the sound of India waking up. Street life began in the cool of the morning, the sweepers shuffling about on stick thin legs. Closing her eyes, she was drifting into sleep when someone said, 'Flora!' It was Finn.

'Hello. I'm back.' She looked wearily up at him. In the lamplight he looked pale, his eyes a fierce green. He was wearing a brown dressing gown that had seen better days.

'I wish you'd given me your address. I wanted to write.'

'Has something happened?'

'Yes. Yes, I think it has.'

He took her hand and squatted down beside her. 'You're my greatest friend,' he said softly. 'And you are so tired.'

'So tired I can barely think. Everything seems so much the same, it's as if I haven't been away.'

'You'll be surprised, we've had lots of changes. Come and sleep in my bed. I'll get up and start the day.'

Within minutes Flora found herself curled up in the blessed peace of Finn's bed. The sheets smelled of him, faintly. She took deep breaths, wondering if the foetus growing inside her would in some way respond. In a little time, a very little time, she would tell Finn and he would know what to do. It was like being a child again, and bringing your problems to Daddy.

She woke in the afternoon, hot and sweating. She borrowed Finn's dressing gown and went in search of her own bathroom, only to find it full of other people's gear. That was the worst of communal living, it was so often far too communal. She showered, dressed, and asked Abdul to lay claim to her room for her again. The place was getting sloppy, she decided, looking about her. A pile of photographs of the orphanage lay in a dusty corner, and

346

files were left about on chairs. She ordered some more tea and a clean-up, before settling down to read her correspondence.

Halfway through, Finn came back. She got up and held out her hands and he took them, bending to kiss her. 'You look wonderful,' he said. 'Have you found out, yet?'

'What?'

'Your promotion. You're Director of Operations for the State.'

'Don't pretend, Finn. Women who run obscure stations don't get jobs like that.'

'They do when they impress ministers. Look, here's the letter.'

He pulled out a deceptively flimsy piece of paper from the waiting pile on Flora's desk. She scanned the lines quickly, and then again, with great concentration. It was true. At last, after years of patient toil, she was to have her reward.

'That's wonderful,' she said dully. 'A wonderful challenge.'

Finn looked down at her. 'You won't be needing an obscure doctor around in a job like that.'

'Oh, Finn!' She laughed up at him. But something in his face held her back. 'Finn, what do you mean?'

He took her hand again and led her to sit down. 'I've decided what to do,' he said. 'I had a call − it was so strong and clear, that this time I couldn't deny it. And you were the instrument, that I do so truly believe. The physical sensuality of that contact alerted some part of my brain to what was there all the time if I'd had the wit to see. When you left I felt alone, cold almost. I felt that I had no one to turn to. I couldn't even write, you hadn't left me your address, I could do nothing to make contact with your warmth, your love. It was a form of desolation. And in that time I turned fully for the first time, to God.'

Stiffly, Flora said, 'But I'm back now. Suppose we made love again?'

He smiled warmly into her face. 'It wouldn't matter. I'm not making a choice between God and woman, not yet anyway. I've no doubt that I will make that choice, in two, perhaps three months, but now, if I chose to love you there'd be no thunderbolt. God isn't that petty. But − it would be pale. Before it was the most vivid and transforming experience of my life, it awakened me to a new level of thought, feeling, everything. Now I see it was just the opening bars of a great overture, that what we experienced was no more than the reflection of this panoply of wonder that is God's. I am called, Flora. I've been given a blessing more truly great than any I have ever known. Certainty.'

She got up and paced the room. 'But what will you do, where

will you go? Is it the end of your medical career? Surely you're not going to journey through India trying to print your own brand name on other people's religions?'

Finn laughed. 'You know me better than that, Flora. I'm no evangelist. But I've got strength now, and direction. I know that whatever I should do will become plain. No more struggling, no more questions, I will be shown a clear path. I feel that for the first time I am using His strength!'

Flora took a deep breath. 'It's wonderful, Finn. I've never seen you so sure of anything. Will you be ordained here or in Scotland?'

'Scotland, probably. I need balance in my life, too much India's no good for anyone. But I may well be back, trying to do my bit, pleading with the great lady in charge to let me have some space on her patch.'

Forcing herself to laugh, Flora said, 'I shan't be too kind, Finn. After all, you're deserting me.'

His thin face became soft. 'My dear girl, until I loved you I couldn't love at all. You set me free.'

She went to her room and sat on the bed, feeling numb with shock. What use was it now to tell him about the child? It would embroil him in something he couldn't put right. She almost laughed to herself. What had she been expecting him to do? There was no magic wand to wave, no amount of instant expertise that would give him the power to tell who had fathered this child. She couldn't ask him to be responsible for it, any more than she could ask Don. She alone must bear the responsibility.

Chapter Six

'Now I've got this appointment,' Flora wrote, 'I hope to be coming home quite often on business, so of course I'll mix it with pleasure and come and see you. Darlings, I do hope you're working for your exams. It really is an important year.'

The train lurched and stopped. Sooner or later she was going to have to stop beating about the bush and tell Alex and Annie about the baby. She waited until the swaying lessened, and then tried. 'By the way, I've got some exciting news. I'm having a baby. Your father knows, of course, and I'm sure you'll all be pleased to see it when I bring it home. Who knows, it could be twins, like you two.'

She stared blankly at the page. What a cop-out. She implied that Don was the father, and then left him to sort out the mess. What's more, this baby apparently qualified for her care. Was she going to trail it with her round India? She could. Her new position meant she could do very much as she liked. Only the vaguest lie would be needed to imply that she and her husband had decided to have a late addition to the family. It didn't really matter whether she was believed or not.

Putting down her pen, she let her imagination rip. Her baby, pink, smooth, loving her. Who cared who the father was? She was the mother, and out here that was all that mattered. Millions of babies grew up fatherless. She would love it as much as any baby has ever been loved, she would make it absolutely her own.

The train was picking up speed. She put away her writing things and pulled the window to, ignoring the hands that stretched down from the roof asking for food, drink, anything the rich people in the carriage might offer to the poor ones riding on top. The constant swaying was making her queasy, this was turning out to be a very sick pregnancy.

Flora forced herself to open a file and concentrate on the problems of corruption in the electricity supply to one of the largest squatter camps in her region, something that required an urgent appeal to the officials. Since they were probably keeping their families on the proceeds she would have to use considerable muscle to get an investigation, she decided. Was it worth it? Threats, contacts, the whole paraphernalia of persuasion and coercion, were best saved for the truly important issues. In this instance it was probably best for the aid workers to galvanise the weary people into demonstrating, which was obviously political involvement, and therefore not done, but would nonetheless prove effective. Flora made an obscure note, in code.

The train was still swaying, almost violently now. A lady with a gold nose ring fell against Flora, but before she could apologise a suitcase was flung down from the rack. It burst open, revealing clothes, brushes, a pot of jam that smashed messily on the floor. People were starting to scream and shout. Flora hung on to the window with one hand and with the other clutched at her file. A figure flashed past the edge of her vision, she thought for a moment someone had fallen from the roof. But another man went, and another. They were jumping, all of them, leaping to safety from the train. They were going to crash!

The screaming became ear-splitting. She had the sensation that they were plunging wildly down, and then up, up, the world was turning and twisting to the sound now of screeching metal. There was an intolerable weight on Flora's chest. She pushed and it shifted, as everything was shifting, slower, slower, gradually coming to rest. Flora took in a breath of hot, dust laden air, the first it seemed for minutes. Next to her the woman with the nose ring was sobbing, her ring gone, ripped out to leave a bloody gash. Far away someone was still screaming, this time in pain, not fear. The carriage seemed to be full of things, things everywhere, with people scattered above and below them. Suddenly Flora realised what had happened. The carriage was on top of the one in front. It had mounted it on the slide, ripping open the roof and sinking down on to the people below. The scene was ghastly, the foul imaginings of an eastern Hogarth.

The windows had been put out, she didn't know when. Gradually sliding up her seat she managed to crouch by it, and looked down some twenty feet to the ground. People were running around aimlessly, and in the distance was part of the train, presumably still on the track. Only the engine and some carriages had plunged off, then. Carefully she wriggled through the window, clinging on to a piece of metal that cut into her hands. As she climbed down, moving past the crushed windows of the carriage below, a hand clutched at her, begging for help.

'I will bring help soon.' said Flora. 'I promise. Very soon.'

Once on the ground she tried to run, but her ankle gave way. A bad bruise, no more, she decided, and hobbled up towards the line. The guard was wandering distractedly to and fro, she caught his arm and deluged him with questions. Where were they? Where could they get help? Could someone go now with a message?

Some of her people worked near here, they would be best placed to mobilise rescue. She scribbled a note on a piece of paper someone offered her, and when it was safely on its way she went down the slope again. 'Bring water,' she told the guard. 'Get everyone to help.'

Some villagers had appeared, to stand staring at the wreck. Flora commandeered two buffalo and made the owner pull a girder away from some windows. Three children crawled out, but no adults. Some shocked-looking chickens were pecking around, released from baskets in the train. Flora made someone chase them away, they were pecking dazedly at the corpses they laid on the grass. She made snap decisions – put this one here; that one there, he won't survive. Labouring in the drum-beat heat of the day she felt dehydration stalking her and gulped down warm water from a bottle. 'I'll suffer for that,' she thought, feeling grit on her tongue. But for once the present was all that mattered. Tomorrow was a lifetime away.

Hours later, almost a day later, she lay in a cool bath and tried to relax. Shock was making her teeth chatter. She reached out and turned on the hot tap. She felt weak as a kitten, probably because of the diarrhoea that had followed on from the water. She didn't want to take too much for it, because of the baby, but it was desperately debilitating.

Eventually she got out of the bath and dressed herself. A servant in a white uniform knocked and brought in a pile of files, her files, from the train. 'I am sorry to see them so stained, madam,' he said politely.

Flora murmured her thanks. When he had gone she looked at the brown stains and started to cry, but a moment later there was another knock and she was forced to pull herself together. It was a Western television crew, after a statement about the crash. She vaguely remembered their presence at the scene yesterday. She had sent them away and told them to talk to her later. This was later.

Sitting on a desk, pretty, strained, she gave a short moving interview that was beamed around the world.

Don pressed the record button on the video, forcing himself to use his bad arm. This he would keep. He stared at Flora's calm, gentle face, wondering how she could have survived the world's worst train crash and be serene. Even so, she looked tired and pale, perhaps not very well. Suppose she had died, he found himself wondering. What then? He tried to imagine a world in which Flora no longer existed. Her face faded from the screen in front of him, but it remained more than vivid in his head.

The 'phone rang, and Don switched off the television and answered. He would watch Flora again later, he decided, saving it up as some sort of treat. He caught himself in mid-thought, and almost decided to erase the tape. He was barely interested, of course. But the children ought to watch.

'Yes?' He snarled down the 'phone.

'It's only me. I am not the debt collector.' It was Van.

'Thought you were the office. You OK?'

'More OK than you. I don't have an office. Arm fixed?'

'Yup. Good as new. Got anything?'

'Annapurna.'

Instinctively Don found himself stretching out in his chair, a long, steady relaxation. To hell with Flora, the kids, an arm still only just set, the baby that might or might not be his. Annapurna. 'When?'

'Autumn. But I thought maybe you could go out early and see Flora. I saw her on the news.'

'Did you? I didn't look. She's got some bloke out there. A doctor.'

'Oh. Well, you wouldn't look then. But maybe you'd want to have a chat perhaps. Didn't look happy on the news, white as a corpse.'

'She had just been in a train crash.'

'I thought you didn't look?'

'Clever bastard.'

Van chuckled happily and hung up.

But it wasn't until the last moment that Don positively decided to see Flora. The twins were being bad-tempered about being left in the middle of the summer holidays, and Alex saw no reason why he could not go to Annapurna too.

'You're too damned young,' said Don at last. 'I didn't get to the Himalayas until I was in my twenties, and even if it was

352

safe, which it isn't, I'm damned if you're getting everything on a plate.'

'Kids today don't know they're born,' chimed in Annie, and Alex linked arms with her and they chanted, 'Bread and dripping, bread and dripping, that's all *we* used to get for tea!'

Don laughed, and considered the subject closed, but Annie said, 'You shouldn't go when we're on holiday. It's the one time you promised you wouldn't ever go.'

It was true. He made it a rule normally never to leave the children in the holidays. But they were older, out more than half the time, it was August and he'd already endured two weeks in France with them, boring himself rigid on a beach. 'I'm going early so I can see your mother,' he said tightly.

There was silence. 'Oh,' said Annie. 'I see.'

'You might have said,' added Alex. 'I mean, it does have something to do with us. Remember to tell her I'm in the First XV.'

'You can write letters.'

'Well, it sounds a bit boastful coming from me.'

Don turned on them suddenly. 'Listen, you two! Your mother and I are not getting back together. Not ever. I'm going to see her because when all's said and done she's my wife, and your mother, and we've got things to discuss.'

'You should get divorced and marry again,' said Annie slyly. 'Children our age need a mother.'

'You need a scold's bridle,' grumbled Don. 'I'll marry Shalimar and see how that suits you.'

But Annie was already on another tack. 'I think we should come too. We could stay with Mum and then come home when you'd finished climbing. Terribly educational.'

'I'm sure it would be,' said Don, thinking that the sight of Flora at eight months' pregnant might prove more instructive than they might wish. 'But you've got GCSE's, you can't miss the start of term. Sorry and all that.'

'Pig, pig, pig!' Annie stuck her tongue out and then slammed out of the room.

'She can be very immature,' said Alex, doing a somersault along the back of the Chesterfield. He sent a lamp flying, and Don swore at him.

India was like a cauldron full of mice, thought Don, a boiling, struggling mass of living things. He found himself reading a lot, retreating into another world away from the endless movement, the endless begging, the endless need. He had intended to fly,

353

but somehow, once he arrived, he thought he would travel as he used to, when he first came to the country, and rode the trains in a permanent state of wonder. But he had got out of the habit of wasting time, the years had turned him into the sort of man who expected life to unroll before him in a seamless carpet of efficiency and well-spent hours. He needed to go back a little, he decided. Besides, he needed to prepare himself to meet Flora.

She was waiting on the platform, her body swollen like a plum. He shouldered his rucksack and climbed loosely down from the train, unable to think what he would say to her, his face already stiff with strain. Flora watched him approach, her heart pounding. He was such an incredibly good-looking man, towering above everyone, his face like icy rock. Somehow the KORSEA aura came with him still. He exuded power and expectations.

'Don.' She stepped forward, put her hands on his shoulders and leaned up to kiss his cheek. Her belly brushed against him, round and hard.

'You look terrible,' he said flatly. 'Exhausted.'

'I'm not that bad. It's the heat, that's all.'

She led the way from the station, automatically taking it upon herself to hail a taxi. Don put her aside and did the job, repulsing porters, rickshaw men and other taxi drivers with ease.

'I forgot you'd been in India before,' said Flora. 'I was going to impress you.'

He grunted. 'What does the agency think about your state?'

'They think it's you and me having a late aberration. Are you going to tell them different?'

'I see no need to tell anyone anything. Except I should like to know what's happened to your friend. The priestly doctor.'

Flora went pink. Then she giggled. 'Oh, won't you be pleased! He's gone back to Scotland to study for the priesthood. Which put me firmly in my place. So there didn't seem a lot of point in telling him about the mess I was in. It would only have made everything terribly complicated.'

Don said nothing for a moment. But he settled more comfortably into the worn seat, and looked interestedly out at the scenery passing by.

'You don't have to be quite so delighted,' said Flora peevishly. 'I thought I might make a new life for myself. I was tired of being lonely.'

'That's the price you pay for doing your own thing,' said Don. 'We both know that.'

He met her eyes. Sunlight was striking through the window behind her head, she seemed to be wreathed in golden light. He felt sudden buoyant happiness, and was amazed at himself. It was to do with nothing and everything, it was because of and despite the peculiar mess they were in. He reached for Flora's hand and squeezed it. 'It's good to see you,' he said.

She gave a tremulous smile.

Flora's bungalow was impressive in an old-fashioned way. Built of teak some fifty years before, it had stately, badly-plumbed charm. Roses rioted over the verandah, legacy of some long gone gardening lady, and the effect was a sort of oriental English production, like perfumed tea. She had brought her servant Abdul with her, and he brought drinks as soon as they arrived, insisting that Flora sit down and rest. She scanned her feet thoughtfully, one of the ankles ballooned by swelling.

'I twisted it in a train crash I was in,' she remarked. 'And it doesn't like the heat. How I wish this pregnancy would end.'

'Had any tests done?' said Don, taking a sip of his gin fizz.

She shook her head. 'I won't. This is my baby. And if you want to like it too, then you can, whatever colour it's eyes are.'

'If it's my child it should be at the castle,' said Don. 'You can't bring a kid up here.'

'Oh, Don, you're not going to be difficult, are you?' She looked at him helplessly. It was the old Flora, unsure of herself, trying to oblige. Pregnant as she was, he wished she'd oblige him in other ways.

He was sleeping with a woman solicitor who worked for KORSEA. She was divorced with no children, and once a week he took a room in an hotel, had dinner from room service and had sex. It suited them both, neither of them wanted any ties. But he said to Flora, 'Do you know how Shalimar is? I don't hear.'

'Oh. Well, she's OK. Doing a play somewhere. Actually, she seems pretty miserable. She wrote this letter about having a baby. She wants to apply for the sperm of some genius and do it artificially. I think she's mad.'

Don said, 'She always wanted children. She ought to get herself a decent bloke and have some. Or be like you, and sample the available beds.'

'Beast.' She took a slice of lemon from her drink and threw it at him. He caught it, put it in his mouth and munched. 'You're worse than Annie.'

'You drive us both to it.'

They dined that evening with a number of the agency top brass. Don was impressed. They were intelligent, pragmatic and calm.

355

'Do you still keep your young girls in purdah?' he asked lazily. 'When I first met Flora she was being chaperoned by a dragon of a woman.'

'Winifred,' giggled Flora. 'She thought you had designs on me. She was right. And we are still careful, some of the people out here are incredibly young. First sniff of freedom and they go mad.'

'Don't you find it a strain being so much apart?' asked Henry, Flora's immediate boss.

'Not particularly,' said Don, scooping curry on to a *chapatti* with native ease. 'When she comes home it's so much fun. Isn't it, darling?'

'Er – yes. ' Flora tried to avoid looking at anyone. A subdued snigger ran round the table.

Afterwards everyone left except Henry. 'I really am glad to meet you after all this time,' he said to Don, cradling his whisky affectionately. 'We worry about Flora, you know. Not hard-bitten, you see.'

'She can bite hard enough,' said Don lazily. He wished Henry would leave. He wanted to go to bed.

'I take it you're staying for the birth?'

'I shouldn't think so,' said Flora, smoothly. 'Don's going climbing. I shall be fine, Henry. Don't worry about me.'

'But you're hardly going to be fit to come back to work straight away, are you, my dear?'

'Yes.' Flora leaned back and put her swollen feet on a stool. 'I'll get an ayah. And Abdul does everything for me, I lead a life of total ease. Besides, we've got the start of the farming reform programme, I have to see to that. It should be very simple.'

'And I may come back this way,' remarked Don. 'It might be best if I take the baby back to Scotland with me.'

'No!' snapped Flora.

'But, darling, you can't bring a baby up here.'

'My own thoughts exactly,' said Henry.

Flora said nothing. These men were conspiring against her. She looked from one to the other, and hardened her resolve. They would not now herd her into their sort of life. She would live her own way, with her own child, without them. 'Perhaps after a year.' she said, smiling. 'Babies need their mothers at least until then.'

Don's face became unreadable. 'You don't say.'

When Henry had gone, Flora blazed: 'You are not stealing this child! And don't think you men can band together, I won't have it! In all probability it isn't even yours, but you're laying claim to it, you're determined to stamp it with the Harrington mark.'

356

'If it's mine, I want it,' said Don.

'What for? To do me down, I suppose.'

'Because, believe it or not, I love my children! I won't allow them to be brought up on the other side of the world!'

Flora got up, blinded by sudden tears. 'Stop it,' she said shakily. 'I've had enough, it isn't fair. You've only been here five minutes.' She blundered across the room, caught her swollen ankle in the trailing edge of the rug and fell.

Don picked her up and called Abdul. They put her to bed and at first she seemed fine, but soon her back was aching. Contractions started at four a.m., and she hobbled through to tell Don.

'I'm going to lose it,' she said. 'It's four weeks early.'

'Nonsense. That's nothing these days.'

'It is in India.'

He got out of bed and put his arms round her. If he hadn't shouted — if she hadn't made him so cross — what was he doing here, comforting a woman who might be bearing another man's child? They sat on the bed together, briefly at peace.

The hospital was small and clean, a maternity home run by nuns. Within its walls there was little sound except for the crying of babies, but beyond could be heard the unmistakable sounds of India, the shouts, the wails, the singsong murmur of voices. Flora sat on a bed in a short white nightgown, and a nun tried to shoo Don away.

'I prefer to stay,' he said.

'I am sorry, that is not permitted.'

'I'm sorry too. I'm staying.'

Eventually they gave him a gown and mask, and made him stay by Flora's head in case he should see anything shocking. She wasn't in great pain, the contractions were frequent and shortlived. Her body was expelling its burden with brisk efficiency, like an unwanted growth. 'I thought I'd lose it after the train crash,' she murmured 'I had diarrhoea for weeks. It isn't fair to go this far and have it go wrong.'

'It may not be so small a baby,' said the nun, smiling. She put a delicate hand on Flora's inner thigh. 'We can see the head, Mrs Harrington. Dark hair.'

'Shit!' said Don.

'My daughter has dark hair,' said Flora desperately. Suddenly everything was beyond her, she felt herself parting in two. Don gripped her hands, and she hung from him, suffering one last great convulsion. The child was born.

357

'A boy,' said the nun. She wrapped him in a towel and lifted him on to Flora's stomach. 'There. A little boy.'

They looked down at the tiny wet face. He was a scrap of life, no more than that. Eyes of misty blue, but all babies have blue eyes, a squashed red face.

'What do you think?' said Don.

'He's so small. He should be in an incubator.'

'We shall bring one shortly,' assured the nun. The cord was cut and the baby put fully into Flora's embrace. He was breathing in short, quick gasps.

'He needs help now,' said Don. 'Go and get someone. The baby's ill.'

The nun looked up at Don, and then again at the baby. She hurried from the room. 'He's going to die,' said Flora. 'There's something terribly wrong.'

She held the baby tight to her breast, willing him to take breaths, to struggle, to enter fully into life. But, like someone looking into a room and deciding not to come in, he opened his eyes a little, closed them, and retreated. The baby quietly died.

The doctor arrived some ten minutes later. He took the little corpse and examined it. Then he wrapped it again and gave it back to Flora. 'He would not have lived, even at full term. His lungs are damaged. Some illness you had, perhaps. You can have more children.'

'She wanted this one,' said Don. He sat on the bed and moved the towel away from the still face. He recognised nothing of himself. The doctor, helpless, moved away to talk to the nun, and Don said. 'Was it his, then? I can't tell.'

Flora shook her head, wordlessly. 'No more his than yours. A baby, that's all. A dead baby.'

She wouldn't stay in the hospital so he took her home. The next day he went alone and saw the child buried, accepting the birth certificate that marked so brief a life. He gave the child a name, for official purposes. He called him Malcolm. Malcolm Harrington.

Chapter Seven

The air tasted good at last, thought Don, stopping to draw gulps of it into him. He wasn't acclimatised as yet, he had been away from here too long. But after India, the oven-hard plains of that clamouring nation, he drank in peace and cold oxygen.

He caught up with Van in the next dozen strides. Van said, 'Hey, man, you look better. When you came I thought you were going to die, you know? You looked like death.'

'Well, you know how it is.'

'You're a bloody fool, man. That woman needs you.'

Don almost laughed. 'What a load of balls!'

'You think so? Without you she'd crumble. Believe me, I know these things.'

Don stopped and looked across a valley thick with mustard flowers. A bird hovered below him, still thousands of feet above the valley floor. 'Flora's two people,' he said suddenly. 'I married one of them. The wrong one, the good dutiful daughter. The other Flora is sexy, reckless and terrified of being trapped. I trapped her, and all she's done since is escape.'

'Aah,' said Van owlishly. 'She likes escaping. She doesn't like to be free!'

Don aimed a casual punch at his friend's chin. Van swayed back an inch and it brushed through his beard. 'I take it you're sleeping with a psychologist.' Don had started off again.

'No, a fat housewife. Not so fat, though. Katya. She's very, very warm. Katya, Katya, I adore her great thighs. She enfolds me like a sausage in bread, she feeds me soup and buns, I may find I have to marry this woman.'

'She'll stop you climbing.'

'I shall have it written in the contract: he must have good sex, good food and good climbing. But soon I shall be too old for

359

anything but food. Those boys are too young, they annoy me.'

On the trail in front the young bloods in the party were forging ahead. Don sometimes thought them a joyless, egotistical bunch, interested in nothing but their own performance. Alex wasn't like that, thank God. Unbidden the thought came − Alex wasn't that good. He needed practice, Don decided. He'd send him off next summer to a school where they taught good, basic stuff. He was trying to copy his father, missing out on the simple, muscle and confidence building grind. He needed to climb to his own standard, not a watered down version of his father's.

Catching the thought, Van said, 'How long before Alex comes with us, hey? He's a lucky kid, born in the right place. You going to mind when he beats you, Don?'

He laughed. 'Yes. No. If he got up something good the pride would kill me. He's a great kid, all guts. Annie's the dangerous one, made out of nitro-glycerine. Handle carefully or she explodes.'

'Katya will only have boys. I forbid girls, they worry me.'

'Oh Christ, it's that close, is it? Romance, at last.'

The young boys ahead stopped to drink *chang*. Don chivvied them on and had a word with the Sirdar. Some of the porters were wasting time, and two had already sold their boots. One was plugged into a Sony Walkman. Countries changed, Don thought, you left them and they had the impertinence to progress. Then he turned at a movement and saw a Sherpani giving an unmistakable invitation. He grinned and shook his head. They didn't change that much.

It was a relaxed expedition from the first. People got on with their work, professional and committed. The route could quite literally be a killer. They were loaded with gear, every technical aid known to man, and they would need it all. Hard, sustained climbing at high standard in thin air would take all that they had and more. Beneath the calm atmosphere was an electric tension, as everyone feared they might let themselves and others down.

Don led quite often in the early days, in good weather and on good rock. It was total pleasure. Sometimes he remembered Flora, India, the whole sad mess, and it seemed a lifetime away. He restored himself on rock, he drew strength from its indifference. Below, waiting to come up, Van was singing to himself, and on a sudden whim Don started a traverse, deciding at that moment to take a quick, hard passage up a pillar.

Down in camp one of the boys said, 'They've still got it, whatever you say. Tough as hell.'

The weather closed in after the first week. A blizzard raged for

360

three days, without once slackening. When at last it cleared the mountain was heavy with snow, and avalanches roared down almost hourly. They sat in camp and watched them, tracking their routes down gullies and across faces. An acceptable level of risk, Don felt. He decided they would get going.

'Hey, man! You mad? Give it a day, we'll be killed.'

Don was taken aback. Van had never chickened out in his life. 'We can hack it,' he said mildly. 'You not feeling so good?'

'I'll feel better tomorrow.'

Don didn't challenge him. Instead he took one of the others up with him, leading alternate pitches. The snow roared down from time to time, and they clung to their stances, heads down, while it cascaded across their backs. Don's broken arm began to ache. He was reminded of Alex, falling. Then a rock bounced down the face. It struck his second and he yelped.

'You OK?' yelled Don, when the world stopped falling.

'I've broken my bloody finger!'

'Shit.'

Nothing for it but to go down. It was the beginning of frustration, as if the mountain itself was determined to resist whatever they could do. Injuries were minor − fingers, frost nipped toes, an altitude headache − but they were always inconvenient. The weather beckoned them on to the mountain each day and drove them off each night. One of the boys was seen one day hanging from a rope and kicking the face he was trying to climb. 'Sod you, sod you, sod you!' he was yelling. 'Will you just bloody give in?'

But the mountain held out, shrugging them off with a sly, dishonest grin.

Don sat in camp and wrote to Flora:

I think we'll be home in time for Christmas. If you could come again the children would love to see you, I know. And it might do you good. This is good for me, in a teeth-gritting sort of way. Each yard we make is won from the mountain, we seduce her into yielding − like a moral woman giving in to passion.

I think about you a lot. Hope you are well.

Yours,

Don.

Flora read the letter in the evening on the screened verandah. Moths battered themselves against the gauze screens and the lamp flickered, struggling with a temperamental electricity supply. He might hope she was well, out there on that barren rock, but she

361

was as unwell as she had ever been. Body and mind hurt, and she dragged herself through every day like an automaton. Abdul worried about her, tempting her with delicacies that she could not bring herself to eat. Only the work helped, blotting out thought and feeling, leaving only weariness.

She travelled all the time, tirelessly visiting children's homes, hospitals, farms and villages. One day she caught sight of herself reflected in the dirty window of a shop and she stopped in amazement. Hair dulled by dust, her face thin, her arms thinner. Bush clothes bleached colourless by washing and the sun. She looked like Winifred, she realised. Old and stringy.

Prakash Raj, one of her Indian project managers, climbed smiling out of a dry ditch beside the road. 'Mrs Harrington! I didn't expect you so early.' Oxford-educated, he spoke with a slight drawl, like the languid son of a millionaire peer. It seemed incongruous coming from a flashing-eyed oriental farmer. 'We're having a dreadful snake problem,' he explained, waving at his boots and thick breeches.

'Oh no. Have many people been bitten?'

'Dozens, dozens. But no one's died yet. The trouble is one's conservation principles vie with the instinct for survival in this case. In England we'd be declaring this a Site of Special Scientific Interest, no doubt, and sending out scientists to count krait and cobra. In India we are so stupid as to attempt to grow rice paddy, of course. Our foolish desire to eat!'

'Do you mind if we talk somewhere else?' asked Flora, eyeing the dry ditch with anxiety. 'I can't bear snakes.'

'Really? I confess, they fascinate me.'

They drove in his jeep around the farms and villages. It was a good year, Flora realised. The snakes were one manifestation of abundance. India was changing, and old problems gave way to new. Famine was almost a thing of the past, and in its place they had over-population and grinding urban poverty. Every city had its shanty town, its open sewers, begging children, infant prostitutes. Much as she would like to stay here and look at success, they had to move on.

'You're finished her, Prakash,' she said thoughtfully. 'You've worked yourself out of a job.'

He glanced at her. 'But there's much more to do. Many projects.'

'I'm sure there are. Someone else can see to them. I want you to come back with me today. I want you to work with me, and then I shall recommend that you be sent to Bombay.'

362

'But I come from Bombay.'

'I know. I hope that may help.'

For a moment his composure seemed shaken. 'You are asking so much,' he muttered.

'It's a compliment to you, Prakash.'

He tried to laugh. 'I hope I don't let you down.'

She took him with her back to base. Aware that he was being promoted, many people gave him farewell gifts, some of considerable value. He rejected all but the most trivial offerings, and even these he left behind. He was giving visible proof to Flora that he would not fall victim to that most insidious of Indian faults, corruption. It was what she was asking him to tackle in Bombay.

They arrived at the bungalow, tired and hot. Someone was waiting for them. In a demure white dress, fanning herself with a peacock fan, sat Shalimar.

'My dear Flora, you look terrible,' she declared.

'Shalimar. Oh, Shalimar!' Forgetting her dignity, Flora stumbled up the steps and embraced her friend. Prakash Raj stood uncomfortably, watching his formidable boss giggle and squeak like any fifteen year old.

'I'll go to my room,' he said diffidently.

Flora turned. 'Prakash, I forgot you. This is Shalimar, my oldest, dearest friend. Shalimar, Prakash Raj.'

'How do you do?' they both said, and shook hands.

He was an inch or two the shorter, and stood very straight to compensate. 'Won't you have some of this delicious lemonade?' asked Shalimar. 'Abdul's been keeping me constantly supplied.'

'A glass would be welcome,' said Prakash. 'And then I must shower. Do you come from India, may I ask? I hail from Bombay.'

'My mother came from Hyderabad,' said Shalimar.

'We went to school together in Britain,' supplied Flora. 'And now Shalimar's terribly famous and lives in Hollywood.'

'I'm not in the least famous,' said Shalimar indignantly. 'Out here I'm just nobody. Not important at all.'

'Oh. Sorry,' said Flora. Apparently she had said quite the wrong thing. She left them exchanging histories and went to change.

Shalimar came in when Flora was lying on the bed in her robe, still damp from her shower. 'You look like something the cat's dragged in,' said Shalimar, sitting on the bed. 'You look ill. And what's wrong with your foot?'

'I hurt it months ago,' said Flora sleepily. 'It doesn't get better. I'll have it X-rayed when I go home next.'

363

'Go to Delhi and have it done now. Really, you can't live with an ankle the size of a football, it's disgusting.'

'It's not so bad in the mornings.' Flora eyed her foot distastefully. In an attempt to distract her friend, she said, 'Don was out here, recently. He's on Annapurna just now, but he popped in.'

'How very cosy,' remarked Shalimar.

'I just meant — I know things have fizzled out. He asked after you. I told him about your silly idea.'

'It wasn't silly.' Shalimar put her chin in her hands. 'It was a good idea but it didn't work. I'm probably barren.'

'I think it probably works better if you do it the proper way,' said Flora. 'You know, wine and flowers and romance. What baby, however much a genius, wants to start life in a plastic tube?'

'Every other one, these days.'

Shalimar stretched out, taking up more than her share of the space. 'What a delicious man you've got in tow.'

'Prakash? He's one of my staff. Please don't touch, he's going to Bombay to take charge of one of our shanty town clean-ups. He'll need his wits about him — half his relatives are involved in graft at all levels. I'm asking him to unravel it. He's going to have to impose quite unrealistic standards of honesty on himself. He can't be distracted.'

'He seems very nice,' wheedled Shalimar. 'You won't talk about films and things, will you? It might put him off.'

Flora sat up. 'Look,' she said. 'I'm glad you've got over Don, but Prakash is quite above your touch. Double first at Oxford. Likes snakes. One false move and he'll engage you in a discussion of Proust in the original French. He'll leave you standing, dear. I only cope because I'm his boss and he's not allowed to put me down.'

'Anyway, I'm taller than him,' said Shalimar disconsolately. Then she brightened. 'Perhaps he won't mind. I'll wear flat shoes.'

'Oh God!' Flora turned her face to the pillow and groaned.

At dinner she was almost silent. She sat, thinking her own thoughts, picking at the food before her. Prakash and Shalimar were discussing ayahs, laughing together at songs dimly remembered from babyhood.

'If you'll excuse me, I think I'll go to bed,' said Flora. The others watched in silence as she left.

In the morning Shalimar said, 'Well, how about getting a flight on Friday? You could square it with your boss by then, I suppose?'

'A flight where?'

'To Delhi. You need some time off, and you must have that ankle

364

looked at. Prakash says he's got some leave coming, so we could all go.'

'I don't want to play gooseberry to you and Prakash Raj,' said Flora crossly.

Shalimar laughed. 'Don't worry. We won't let you.'

Flora objected, and complained, and in the end refused outright.

Shalimar went over her head to Henry, and Flora was ordered to Delhi, to rest and have fun. 'I really don't want to go,' she kept insisting, even as Shalimar propelled her to the plane. 'I much prefer working.'

'Yes, well, you always were strange,' said Shalimar absently. 'Prakash dear, do you think you could buy some sweets? My ears pop so on planes.'

He went off and Flora said, 'Prakash dear, Prakash dear,' in an exaggerated tone. 'Do you want all Prakash, or just his reproductive ability? I knew it was a mistake to tell you about the double first.'

'I want my children to be clever,' said Shalimar aggrievedly. 'You realise he's a rake? No skirt unlifted in Oxford when he was up. You miss all these things when you're in charge.'

'I think you're making it up,' said Flora in shocked tones. 'He's probably got an arranged marriage coming up.'

'Oh, probably,' said Shalimar. 'But these things can be unarranged, you know.'

They sat three abreast on the plane. Prakash and Shalimar talked all the way, smothering laughter in their hands when they thought Flora was asleep. She wasn't. She lay wondering how long it would be before each day seemed more than a desperate trial of strength, an obstacle to be overcome. A baby in the rear of the plane began to cry and she felt her eyes prick with tears. It was all such a waste.

On their first morning in Delhi Flora went to the hospital while Shalimar and Prakash explored. The day was still only pleasantly warm. They strolled amongst the elegant shops and Shalimar bought silks and embroideries for her Hollywood home. They walked in a park, with tiny birds flitting amongst brilliant red flowers.'

'Why on earth do you work for the agency, Prakash?' asked Shalimar at last. 'It can't pay well.'

'I get an allowance from my family. So the money doesn't matter too much.'

'I know why Flora does it,' went on Shalimar. 'She started off full of ideals, but they fell apart a bit under the strain of real life.

But by then she realised she was good at this sort of work, much better than everyone else. She's naturally practical, you see. This is her element. But I don't know if it's yours.'

Prakash said nothing for a moment. 'India's my element,' he said finally. 'Although I'm too English for India, really. Working for the agency puts those two things together, I think. I'm learning to be Indian again. Eventually I shall go into politics. Unlike Mrs Harrington, I still have ideals.'

'But she's a realist,' said Shalimar softly. 'She knows what she can do, she's given up trying to make things perfect.'

'I won't ever give up. For me, there has to be the possibility of perfection. That, surely, is the aim of mankind? The pursuit of the absolute, through this life and many lives. But you won't believe that, Hollywood actress.'

'I'm not entirely shallow.'

She began to walk away from him, quick in her flat shoes. He caught her hand. 'I didn't mean to be unkind.'

'I'm sure you didn't. You mean to flirt and take me to bed, that's all.'

'But that's all you've asked of me! We both have more to us. If you want we can explore it, but if not we can laugh and have fun. Do you want to tell me about your sadnesses?'

'Yes,' said Shalimar. 'I'm tired of pretending I only laugh.'

'When you've told me, we'll laugh again,' said Prakash. 'And then we'll go to the hotel and make love. I warn you, after months on the farms, I am very much in need of good sex.'

He shocked her a little. She smiled at him anxiously, and he drew her arm through his. 'We'll go and find a good cup of tea,' he said, as cosily as any English colonel. Bewildered and off balance, Shalimar knew she was in danger of falling in love.

'The ankle's been broken and reset,' said Flora, looking ruefully down the bed at her suspended foot. 'I broke it before and took no notice. No wonder it hurt.'

'You really are an idiot,' said Shalimar. 'How are you feeling?'

'All right. I'm going to have to stay here for three weeks. You'll have nothing to do.'

'Prakash is entertaining me,' said Shalimar, straightfaced. But suddenly she couldn't pretend. 'He's wonderful!' she burst out. 'Such a lover, such a friend! I adore him, and you're right he's a million times cleverer than me. Hindu, of course. But, Flora, he's ten years younger than me.'

'Good Lord, is he?'

366

'Not only that, but he's supposed to be getting married in two months. An absolutely huge wedding. I know he likes me, and he likes sleeping with me, but he's going to go off to some teenage virgin and never think of me again.'

'Yes, I imagine he is.'

Shalimar eyed her friend with distaste. 'You can be so mean,' she declared.

'But honest. Of course that's what he's going to do. If he stayed with you everyone would be scandalised. Besides, there's your career. You don't want to live in India.'

'I wouldn't care where I lived if it was with Prakash,' said Shalimar in a small voice. 'I'd give anything to have his children. Shall I try and get pregnant?'

'No! He might never forgive you.'

'I probably couldn't anyway. Oh, Flora, he won't want to be bothered with an ageing, barren actress with a list of lovers as long as your arm.'

'I thought he was bothering,' said Flora. 'You look as if you've had a wonderful day.'

'And tomorrow, and tomorrow, and tomorrow,' sighed Shalimar. She put her arms round herself and hugged. 'At least we've got a little time. He's so wonderfully clever, and charming, and kind – oh, Flora, I'm so, so in love.'

When she had gone Flora turned her face into the pillow and cried. She cried for two hours, a gentle and persistent flow of tears. Afterwards she sat up, dried her eyes and asked for some tea. She felt better, calmer and less desperate. It occurred to her that she hadn't written to the children for some time, and she got out her paper and began:

Dearest Alex and Annie,

Sorry to have been so long writing. I'm in hospital having my foot mended. Apparently it's been broken for months and I didn't know. Anyway, Dad and I had a nice time when he was here, and now he's on Annapurna. I had a letter, he's doing his usual thing. I suppose he's written to you about pitches and traverses and leads and so on, but he knows I don't understand and doesn't bother.

All my work is going to pile up while I'm in hospital, so it doesn't look as if I'll be home for Christmas. Let me know if there's anything special you want, otherwise I shall ask Santa Claus to see if he can find something out here you might like. This is such a fascinating country. A wedding procession is going

367

by in the street, with jugglers and snake charmers and jangling dancing girls. There's a plague of snakes at the moment, I'm quite glad to be in hospital. Write soon.

All my love

Mum

Thank God she hadn't told them about the baby, she thought. Actually, she regretted telling them about Finn. She should never have told Don about Finn, or the baby, or anything. But she wasn't naturally secretive or devious, nor was she naturally sad. She opened a file on one of the agency's orphanages, and deliberately stared at the pictures of smiling children and dark-eyed babies. The world was full of children, too many by far. Her little boy's death, or more honestly, his lack of life, left her with love that she could not give. She must give it away, she decided, lavish it on babies that no one loved, fight back against despair. There were many tragedies in India, but hers was not one of them. She lay back in her hospital bed, stared balefully at her foot, and recovered.

Prakash Raj sat in the lobby of the hotel, waiting for Shalimar. He watched the people passing by, some good-looking, most plain ordinary. When Shalimar came she would turn every head, an incredible woman. She was the perfect blend of east and west, her skin a creamy gold, her hair a mass of abundant fine strands, her eyes huge and expressive. But underneath, what was she? American aggression, English reserve, Indian fire? He never knew which she might display. And lately, tearing at his heart, she had been all feminine pleading.

It was all dreadfully out of hand. His mother would never countenance a liaison with an actress, however beautiful. Shenaz was seventeen and had been expecting all her life to marry him. He was fond of her, and she came of a very good family, as he did himself of course. But Shalimar, Shalimar — she bewitched him, and he was in love.

Today she was wearing a sari, in red and gold, but even in that demure dress she demanded attention. She had a presence that he couldn't define, the filmstar aura he supposed. And when she was there she turned his world diamond bright with expectation.

'Prakash.' She bent her head that necessary fraction to brush his cheek with her lips. 'Darling Prakash.'

'You look so respectable I can't believe it.' He held her hand and admired her. 'Even my mother could not disapprove.'

'You should let me meet her, then.'

'My mother is in Bombay.' He paused on the hotel steps. 'I am going to Bombay soon. To discuss my marriage.'

Shalimar's eyes flooded with tears. Quickly Prakash hustled her into the hotel gardens, fumbling in his pocket for a handkerchief. She was choking on sobs, trying to smother them down with her hand. 'I'm sorry, I'm sorry,' she burst out. 'I know you must go. But it breaks my heart.'

'And mine. If you only knew, it is destroying me!'

'Then why must you go? Prakash, I love you so.'

She was torturing him. He had four days before he had to leave, but he knew that this must be the last time he saw Shalimar. They had no future together. He sat on a bench with her and tried to explain, and she understood, that was the worst of it. She knew he had to go.

'At this moment I feel as if I will never have a moment's happiness without you,' he said at last.

'I suppose we'll be happy again,' said Shalimar. 'You'll have children, they'll make you happy. I long to have children. Your children, Prakash.'

'Don't. Don't, you make me hate my future. If we only could!'

'Perhaps we can. I don't ask for marriage, I don't want it. I'm rich, I don't need money, any sort of help. Give me your child!'

She was on her knees, pleading with him. One of the gardeners stopped in his work and watched in amazement, but neither of them saw. Prakash held her face and kissed her, she put her arms around his neck and clung like a child herself. In a while they got up and went back to the hotel. That evening, Prakash left for Bombay.

Flora stumped crossly about the room on crutches. 'If you really are pregnant you could ruin his life,' she declared. 'Imagine how his wife's going to feel, when you appear with photographs and so on of the first born.'

'I won't. I wouldn't.'

'I bet you would! Shalimar, it's one thing having the child of a man you don't know. Quite another if it's a man you love.'

'I don't think you know about either situation,' retorted her friend.

Flora sorted through the mail that had collected while she had been away. There was the telltale grubby envelope from Don, covered in the fingerprints of dozens of porters, mailmen and delivery boys. She opened it and saw a Polaroid photo of Don covered in snow, furiously angry and in the act of throwing an ice axe at the cameraman. On the back he had written, 'One of the more pleasant moments of the trip. Complete failure, going home. Wonderful therapy, you should try it some time. Don.'

She passed the picture to Shalimar. 'Why do you need therapy?' she asked.

'He probably thought I looked dreadful. I do. I need a remake, I'm a mess.'

'Couldn't agree more, love. Want me to take you in hand?'

Flora grinned. 'Not now, thanks, I'm too busy. Next time I go home. Now, I've got reports to write on our regional managers. Just think, someone used to write them on me. I shall drip with friendly understanding.'

Shalimar sighed and went out on to the verandah. The tropical night was descending with all its unexpected speed. She had wasted so much time with Don. Why? It had been clear from the start that he could give her very little. Don wasn't an island, entire of itself, but he wished to be. He made only the contacts he couldn't avoid, took what he needed and moved away. Perhaps she was that sort of woman, she decided, settling only for unattainable men. If Prakash could be hers perhaps she wouldn't want him. But she wrapped her arms around herself and knew that she would, she would.

Her breasts prickled. Imagination, she thought. What chance did one afternoon encounter have? She had tried to become pregnant and failed, she had been reckless and never once got caught. It wouldn't work. She couldn't expect that it would. But, three weeks later, arriving back in New York, Shalimar was rewarded. Her pregnancy test was positive.

Chapter Eight

Annie lay on the upstairs window seat watching the postman's van approach. Alex, in the next window, said, 'This is it, then. The end is nigh.'

'If he hasn't got them I shall die,' muttered Annie tensely.

She uncoiled her long legs, today in red and white striped leggings. She was wearing a tunic so short that it was almost a jumper, and people might be forgiven for thinking she had forgotten her skirt. But at sixteen, Annie refused to be overlooked. Eyes as pale and grey as her father's were outlined in thick black, her hair was a long black tousle and she wore silver hoop earrings that brushed her shoulders.

'I'll go down,' said Alex. 'If the postman sees you he'll faint.'

'I know I'm going to faint,' said Annie. 'It's all right for you, the young master can be thick as a plank and no one cares. But I'm going to Cambridge.'

'You should go to a decent Scottish university,' shouted Alex over his shoulder. 'None of this defection.'

'No one's going to look at me if I don't pass,' squeaked Annie. 'Hurry up, Alex. I'm going to be sick!'

The postman rang the bell, as always. Coming all this way to deliver the mail, he usually received at the very least a cup of coffee, and sometimes, on cold days, a wee dram. But even with today's east wind blowing the young master only seized the letters, said 'Thanks' and shut the door. Which meant no morsel of refreshment until the end of the village. He slouched off in a temper.

'They're here,' said Alex, and his voice cracked.

'Bring them up,' whispered Annie. 'I can't bear to look.'

Alex went slowly up the stairs, and held an envelope up to Annie's reaching fingers. She scrabbled frantically with the seal. 'B's! Only B's! One lousy A! Oh God!'

371

'You've opened mine, you ninny. Look. You've swept the board. Distinctions in everything.'

'Really? No. Not in maths too?'

They exchanged papers and sat on the top stair. 'Thank God I can drop history,' said Alex. 'I never wanted to take the bloody subject in the first place.'

'You're not sad about the grades, are you?' asked Annie anxiously. 'I mean, it's not that I'm cleverer or anything. But they make you work at my school. And all you do is climb and play rugby.'

'I'll try harder now,' said Alex. 'I got distinction in maths, and that's good. I can take economics, I'll need that for KORSEA. We'd better phone Dad.'

But the phone was already ringing. 'Don't say they haven't come,' said Don, when Alex picked up the receiver.

'They've come,' said Alex. 'Annie's got straight A's, just like we said. I got an A in maths and B for everything else.'

'Lazy sod,' said Don. 'You even passed history?'

'Yes. Great isn't it?'

'Wonderful. Well done, Alex. Put Annie on, will you? The family genius.'

'He says you're a genius,' said Alex, passing over the receiver.

'I deserve a medal,' retorted Annie, and Don said, 'I reserve those for your teachers. Those poor women have suffered so much. Do you want to send your mother a telegram?'

'You send it,' said Annie. 'She likes to hear from you. Are we going out tonight?'

'Yes, get John to bring you into town around seven. We'll have champagne and eat rich food. Unless you'd rather go to a disco or something foul.'

'We'll do everything,' said Annie. 'Oh, Alex thinks he deserves to go climbing this weekend, in Cairngorm. He's going to be more of an absentee chairman than you, Dad, and it's all your fault.'

'If I get the blame then I get the credit too. Well done me, for getting you through your exams.'

'We triumphed despite our broken home,' said Annie, and put the phone down.

The rest of the morning was filled with telephoning, as they spoke to friends and compared stories. But Annie became increasingly less jubilant. 'They've all done worse,' she told Alex. 'I can't crow when people are going to have to do retakes and things.'

'I bet they're still pleased for you,' said Alex. 'Especially Juliette.'

'She tried. But she's failed maths and French, she might get

372

chucked out. I hate being Little Miss Silver Spoon, living like this and brains too. Even I think it isn't fair.'

'You just like being miserable,' said Alex. 'You're a manic depressive, that's what you are. Go and moon in the stables or something.'

'I'm a bit old to be cheered up by a pony.'

Nonetheless Annie got up and wandered off. She got out her results sheet again. She had been meaning to photocopy it and send it off to Flora, but now, after all the waiting, the actual paper seemed trivial. She wished her mother was there. Men were never quite the answer at times like this, and Juliette, her usual confidante, was out of bounds. The paper was annoying her, she was sick of staring at it. She crossed the hall to Don's office, and opened the drawer in the walnut filing cabinet where he kept the family files. All the birth certificates, health forms, passports and so on were kept in one huge box file. Annie pulled it out, meaning to slip the results form in the front, but an envelope caught her eye. It was sealed and the letters MH were written in her father's handwriting. Without giving herself time to think, Annie ripped it open.

The certificate smelled of India, although the scent probably came from a flower disintegrating into dust in a corner of the envelope. She read the details at first without comprehension – then she looked at the date. Somehow she had expected a long-ago family secret, but this was not even two years ago. She read it all again, wondering if she had misunderstood. But it was all so clear. A baby, Malcolm Harrington, had died in India, soon after birth.

She pushed the paper back into its envelope, slammed the file shut and put it away. Forbes was ringing the bell which meant afternoon tea. It was a meal she normally loved, but today she didn't want it. Instead she went out to the stables, not bothering to change. No one was there. She put her arms close around the neck of her pony and hid her face.

That evening, the celebration evening, she was unnaturally quiet.

'What's the matter, Annie?' Don kept asking. 'Look, we can go to a disco after dinner if you want. I'll sit in the corner and pretend I don't know you. I don't know what you're going to do with Alex, though. No one's going to come near you if they think you're with him.'

'I'll wander round looking like a bouncer,' said Alex, who had the barrel chest that normally goes with the part, and Annie smiled dutifully.

She was so quiet, despite the champagne, that Don took them

home early. He went into the library and poured himself a whisky, the after a moment he took it upstairs and knocked on Annie's door. She was sitting on the bed, still dressed, leafing through a magazine.

'All right if I talk for a bit?'

She shrugged, and did not look up. Don felt a sudden longing for Flora. What was he doing trying to talk to this tall, lanky, beautiful girl? How could he understand what went on in the mind of his daughter? She hadn't been clear to him from the word go.

'I don't know what's bugging you, Annie, but please tell me what it is.' He sat in her bedside chair, fully expecting her to give him the usual 'Nothing' response. He never got anything out of Annie by asking. But to his surprise she stopped turning the pages of her magazine, looked up and said, 'Who was Malcolm Harrington? How did he die?'

Don's face froze in shock. He picked up his whisky from the table and drank it down in one. He said, 'How dare you open sealed envelopes in my private files.'

'It wasn't private, it was the family file. I was putting my results away.'

'The envelope was sealed! I don't expect to have to lock things away from my own family.'

'You locked a secret away. Was it Mum's baby? Mum's and yours?'

He rubbed a hand over his face. 'It died soon after birth.'

'I bet it was killed. I bet someone murdered it.'

'Annie, don't be ridiculous! The baby died. I was there. Your mother had been ill during the pregnancy, the baby was damaged. Obviously she was upset, but − well, I had to go climbing. I saw it buried, took the certificate and came away.'

'So it wasn't yours,' said Annie.

Words failed him for long seconds. He stared at his daughter and she stared back with his own pale eyes. There was no deceiving her. She knew when he lied. 'It − might not have been,' he conceded. 'Annie, your mother had an affair with someone in India. When she came home − she and I slept together. I don't know why, I really don't.'

'You're married,' said Annie. 'It's the other man she shouldn't have gone with.'

'Really? I don't know. It's the love that counts, not the legal situation. And − and she was pregnant. You were younger then. We couldn't explain. God help me, I wish I wasn't explaining now!'

374

There was a silence. Then Annie said, 'You never think of anyone but yourself. That was our brother. We had a right to know about him. We've got a right to know what's going on in our lives. My mother hasn't been home in ages because of this, and you didn't say. You didn't think we should know. It never occurs to you to wonder what we think about this terrible — terrible situation!'

She started to cry. Don looked down at her bent head and felt his heart twist for her. 'What goes on between your mother and me has nothing at all to do with you,' he said thickly. 'We've always tried to stop you getting hurt. She left to stop that.'

'You wish we'd never been born,' sobbed Annie. 'You'd have got divorced and never seen each other again if we hadn't been around.'

'I should hate never to see your mother again,' said Don.

Annie looked at him, her eyes drowned by tears. 'What?'

'You heard. If I never saw Flora again I should be deeply, deeply unhappy. Oh, Annie, you're big enough to understand, aren't you? We made a mess of being married, she was too young and I wasn't ready. I hadn't done all the things I wanted to do, and I wasn't going to stop doing them for anyone. But I loved her. I love her still.'

'Is that why you called it Harrington?'

'Yes. I suppose so. And also because it was the smallest, most defenceless little thing you ever saw. I wanted to do something for it, and there wasn't anything else.'

Annie swallowed hard. 'So why doesn't Mum love you?'

Don shook his head. 'I don't know. I don't think she ever did. We married to please her father and to go to bed together. Lust is a very powerful motivator, and we had it in plenty. But on her side there wasn't anything else. I'd stopped her living her life, and the life I had and the life she wanted just couldn't match. So it ended. And then we had that brief fling, and she got pregnant, and now you know.'

He stared down into his empty whisky glass. Annie said, 'You expect us to have principles, and you haven't any yourself. Shalimar, this, I bet you've got someone else now.'

'I don't have to discuss my sex life with you, Annie. I'm a man first, a father second. Even I'm allowed some privacy.'

'Then don't expect me to tell you anything. I can have privacy too, and I can sleep around. If my parents are anything to go by I can do exactly what I bloody well like!'

'Annie, stop it.'

'Stop what? What shouldn't I do? You and Mum have done

375

everything. Next thing you'll be telling me not to get knocked up, and she did, she did, and she didn't even know who the bloody father was!'

'Annie, will you shut up! You'll wake Alex.'

'She already has.'

Don turned to see his son standing in the doorway. 'Are you going to tell him or shall I?' shrieked Annie.

'I will. But I need another whisky. Come downstairs, Alex, we've got to talk.'

Alex lifted his eyebrows at his distraught sister. She heard them talking softly together as they went downstairs, two men leaving her to scream and cry herself out. Sometimes they made her feel like an alien. If only she had her mother, the mother she used to have, pure and good, loving and faithful. Someone so different from this other woman her father knew. She couldn't imagine her mother pregnant, couldn't think of her lying with her father, or worse, with another man.

Shivering, she crawled under the bedclothes, still fully dressed, and pushed her head into the darkness under her pillow. Her parents took her world and broke it, and never told her. They hoped she wouldn't see. There was nothing certain to hold on to, nothing sure. She shivered, and hid, and a long, long time later, she slept.

The headmistress's office had the chintzy, book-lined feel of a country house, let down by a miserable little fire and a passing smell of school dinners. Photographs of past girls stood on shelves, their eager scrubbed faces a parent's joy. Don recalled Annie as he had seen her ten minutes before: pink eye make-up, hair in a purple bow, floor-length skirt. The sixth form were permitted out of uniform, but as always Annie was going too far. He tried not to feel nervous.

'Ah, Mr Harrington. Sorry to keep you waiting.'

He had never liked the headmistress. Tall, unmarried and horse-faced, she had the femininity of Attila the Hun. He wasn't in the least surprised the girls gossiped about her.

'How do you do?' The handshake was almost a trial of strength.

'Do sit down. Now, you have seen Anabel? Dear me. Who has not seen Anabel? She can hardly go unnoticed, I fear.'

'She's always a snappy dresser,' said Don feebly.

'Snappy. Yes. One wonders whether snappy is quite what one looks for in an Oxbridge candidate.'

'They dress far worse than that at university,'

376

'Exhibitionism has never featured very high on the list of essential qualities to get in, though.'

Don met the headmistress's eye. Not for the first time he wondered if the woman saw any further than the figures on the school report, boasting of this or that many girls offered up to the best universities. The anorexics, the attempted suicides, the sad failures, all these were disregarded. Success counted here, and nothing else.

'Annie's had a difficult time,' he said. 'Her mother hasn't been to see her in over a year, nearly two years. It's hard for a girl her age – '

'If she will not work, Mr Harrington, then she must leave. Anabel has shown herself capable of intense study. What she appears to lack is the motivation. We can't work miracles. If Anabel will not choose to work then she must leave.'

'Look.' Don put his hands on the desk, trying to sound reasonable. 'She's working hard enough to pass the exams, I'm sure. She can get into other universities, any other university I should think. If Cambridge is beyond her then so what? I don't give a damn if she goes, it was her idea in the first place.'

'We're not interested in second best, Mr Harrington. Anabel is Cambridge material, and as such that is our aim. There is no safety net in this instance, I want you to understand that. If she thinks she can get away with this laziness, rudeness, sheer disruptive behaviour and still get into university, then we might as well give up now. We will give up. As I said, either she buckles down and shows us what she can do, or I must ask that she be taken away.'

Don resisted the urge to hit the woman. It was a common sensation. When someone criticised either of the children he found himself longing to pick up a table lamp and brain them. The woman was right, that was the sickening thing. Annie had the ability, if only she would apply it!

'May I talk to her, please?' he said.

'Of course.' The headmistress got up, baring her teeth in a travesty of a smile. 'I'll send her in.'

The room was quiet, and outside girls could be heard talking and laughing. 'Shut up! The old trout'll hear you,' said one in a loud whisper.

Another said. 'Oh, fuck! It's French and I haven't learnt it.'

Did Annie say fuck, he wondered? She probably taught it to the first formers. He turned as the door opened. It was Annie herself.

'Hello, love.'

'Hi.' She stood watching him defiantly.

377

'Is the room bugged?' he asked. 'Do we have to run taps or something?'

'I don't care if the old bat hears everything I say. Is she chucking me out? I hope so. I've had enough of it.'

'She's threatening. Look, if you like you can leave and go somewhere else. I don't mind if you don't make Cambridge.'

Annie made a face. 'You wouldn't. You probably think I ought to get married and have babies instead. You tried to pin Mum down, but you won't succeed with me.'

Don took in his breath. 'I'm not trying to do anything to you, love. If you want to stay and work, then you can. If you don't want to work, you can leave. You'll have to, she's giving you the push if you don't buckle down.'

Annie suddenly blazed. 'Did she say that? Did the old battleaxe actually say she'd sling me out if I didn't read fourteen French novels a week, and Shakespeare crits till I'm blue, and translate Chaucer until I can rattle it off in my sleep? Because that's what she wants, you know. Enough is never enough, she wants me sick of working, working so hard I can't sleep. She doesn't care if we all drop dead from the strain, just so long as we make her damned statistics look good.

'Like I said,' managed Don, 'if you don't like it you can leave.'

'Oh! That's always your solution! Put the girls out to grass.'

Don lost his temper. 'All right, Annie,' he roared. 'Do what you fucking well like! Stay and work if you want, leave and give up if you want, or leave and find somewhere whose ambience suits your finely tuned temperament. Because I don't know what suits you. I've been hauled in here when I should be overseeing an oil rig tow, when the Minister of State for Scotland is on my list of people to call back, when one of our ships is staggering back into port with a man with head injuries, but don't worry about it! I've got plenty of time. I'll just stand here while you knock seven bells out of anything I fucking well say!'

Annie eyed him thoughtfully. 'You realise everyone can hear if you yell like that? The first formers are right over this room, and they swear quite enough as it is.'

Don turned away. Laughter was threatening to choke him. This girl, this maddening, adorable girl!

'I'm glad you find me so amusing,' said Annie stiffly.

'I'm not laughing.'

'I don't expect you to take me seriously. After all, my future isn't important to you, I've always known that. Grandad didn't think I mattered and you don't either. I imagine you'll be off

378

to see how Alex is doing this afternoon. He's got a match you know.'

'Since I was nearby, I was going to look in,' said Don patiently. 'Why don't you come? We can have some lunch, chat, talk things over. If you really do want to go to Cambridge you're going to have to work, love, these things don't come to anyone on a plate.'

'You got the business on a plate,' said Annie. 'Or was it on a bed? All that lust you were telling me about.'

He crossed the room in a stride and hit her. It was a sharp slap across the cheek, leaving his handprint clear on her white skin. Annie put her fingers to it, looking at him in wide-eyed horror. He had never touched her in anger in all her life, not even when she was tiny. 'You hit me,' she said, and her eyes started to fill.

Don was shaking. 'I'm sorry. Annie, I'm sorry. You touched a nerve. Love, you can't just say things and not expect them to hurt. I shouldn't have hit you. I'm sorry.'

The tears welled up until they must surely fall, but Annie watched him unblinking. Then she turned and ran from the room.

He wanted to go after her, but when he went to the door there was just the oak-panelled hallway and a dozen exits. A couple of small girls watched him curiously. He couldn't face the headmistress now, and admit he had lost his temper with his sixteen-year-old daughter to the point where he had struck her. They put kids into care for less these days. How could he have done it? How?

He made for the front door and left. John was polishing the Bentley and as soon as he saw Don he leaped into the driving seat. 'All settled, sir?' he asked brightly.

'Shut up, John,' snarled his employer. 'We'll go and see Alex.'

'Yes, sir.' John stole a glance in the mirror at his fulminating employer.

Don calmed watching rugby on a damp afternoon. Alex was brilliant, a powerful front row man with a good turn of speed when it came to a run for the line. Partisan members of the school stood on the touchline chanting 'Harring-TON, Harring-TON' as Alex thundered down the field, dodging and weaving amongst lesser men. Why wasn't Annie this simple? Don asked himself. Why would she never let him experience this uncomplicated level of pride?

Afterwards Alex came out of the shower, steaming and tousled. He had a graze down his cheek and there were stud marks on his thigh.

'You're not indestructible, you know,' said Don mildly. 'The body needs some consideration.'

379

'Ah well, nothing's smashed,' said Alex philosophically. 'Any chance of a beer?'

'No. I'm in enough trouble today without getting you thrown out.'

Alex grinned. 'Let's go for tea then. I take it you've seen Annie.'

Don sat in a tea shop and watched his son hoover up vast mounds of food. In between mouthfuls Alex made pertinent comments as Don told the tale. 'She'll be very upset,' he said at last, spreading cream on a scone. 'What do you bet she runs away?'

'Not again,' said Don. 'I can't stand it again. Look, you'd better phone her and talk. She always talks to you.'

'I'll ring when I get back. You handled it all wrong, you know.'

'Tell me something new! She wouldn't agree to anything. I was prepared to let her leave if she wanted, but that wasn't right, nothing was right.'

Alex eyed him with undisguised contempt. 'Can you not see what she wanted, Dad? It's not hard. She wanted you to listen to her telling you how terrible it was, say she could leave if it really was too much but that you'd be terribly proud if she'd tough it out. She wanted you to say you really wanted her to make it to Cambridge, that it mattered to you. And all you said was that she could do what she bloody well liked.'

'I just wanted her to do what made her happy!'

'But she wants to do what makes *you* happy! Oh, Dad, you don't understand her at all.'

Don closed his eyes for a second. 'I don't know what I'd do without you, Alex,' he murmured.

'You'd be in a bloody mess, that's what.'

'Will you stop swearing! You kids have got mouths like sewers these days.'

'Bit bloody much, isn't it?'

Don reached up and thumped Alex's ear. They both laughed.

Don drove back to see Annie after that. With Alex's words of wisdom ringing in his ears he felt sure he could sort her out. But the moment he set his hand on the knocker he knew something was wrong. The headmistress herself answered the door. 'Following your assault on your daughter, Mr Harrington,' she declared, 'Anabel has seen fit to run away. And I for one have no idea where to look for her.'

Chapter Nine

At sixteen, Annie made none of the errors of her thirteen-year-old escape. This time she left no trail. She might be in London, Edinburgh, even Timbuktu for all the trace there was. In a cold, frosty January it frightened Don witless to think what might happen to her; the warmth, the bed, offered by a man who saw his chance to touch something young and vulnerable; the drugs that might take the edge from a frowsy bedsit or stinking squat. She hadn't anything like enough money.

After a week they still knew nothing and Don realised he had to tell Flora. He hated the thought, hated admitting that it was his fault, he had failed. But there was nothing else for it. He put through a call to Delhi, which would be relayed to her in as much as twelve hours or as little as three. Then he waited, jumping each time the telephone rang. 'Let it be Annie,' he whispered, again and again. 'Just let it be her.' But it was the police, ringing to say they had no news, or the private detective with the selfsame message, or Alex suggesting this or that place she might have gone.

Eventually, at three in the morning, it was Flora. 'Don? I've been trying to get through for hours. What's the matter?

The sound of her voice unmanned him and his throat closed. 'Don? Don, are you there?'

'Yes. It's just − Flora, Annie's gone. She's run away.'

'Not again! Please, not again! When did she go, have you looked for her?'

'We've been looking for over a week.'

He heard Flora's sharp intake of breath. At last she managed, 'Why? What happened?'

'A lot of things. First, she found the baby's death certificate, and being Annie, jumped to the right conclusion. Then she got in trouble at school for not working, and when I was hauled in to give her the hard word I made a balls of it. I slapped her. It was the worst thing I could have done. By the time I'd calmed down she was gone.'

'She must have said something awful to make you do that.'

'It wasn't that awful, I'm an adult, I'm supposed to be able to control my temper. But she just caught me wrong, and nothing I said was right, nothing I offered suited her. And now —'

'Poor Don,' murmured Flora. 'Look, I'll come back right away. I'm sorry it's been so long. You should have told me Annie knew about the baby. Why didn't you?'

His head felt as if an iron band was tightening round it. 'God knows! I can't talk any more, Flora. It's the middle of the night here, KORSEA is taking over a salvage company that's fighting like hell, Alex can't work for worrying and all I can think about is Annie, so don't ask me questions I can't answer.'

'I'm sure she'll be all right Don,' said Flora.

'I wish I was so bloody sure.' He slammed down the receiver.

Flora replaced hers more slowly. It was morning, and she was phoning from the local Post Office. She felt slightly sick, as if she was getting some sort of tummy bug. She picked up her hat and bag and went out, wondering how soon she could get a train to an airport, find a seat, begin the long slog home. It was a bad moment to leave, when a row was brewing about agency involvement in strikes. Add to that the vitriol that was flowing her way because of Prakash Raj and his corruption purge, and it would look as if she was making a hasty escape. There had been two assassination threats aimed at her, and Prakash posted a guard outside his home, to protect his wife and baby.

On the way back she called at Henry's bungalow. He was home, recovering from a bad bout of one of those nameless fevers India has in plenty. White and drawn, he looked far more in need of a trip home than she did, thought Flora. They talked, and of course he gave her permission to go, although since she was due months of leave, it wasn't strictly required. As she prepared to leave, he said. 'Actually, it might be a good time for you to get out. Perhaps you should go for good. Far too many people are gunning for you, Flora.'

'Isn't that all the more reason for me to stay?' She tried to smile, but her face felt stiff and unresponsive. All her life was falling apart on the same day.

'I don't want to see you hurt, my dear. A bit of time out of the field wouldn't do you any harm at all. We can find someone else to take over here. We won't let up, but at least with you gone, they might think we will. The pressure will be off. And you can see your children and catch up with your life again. Perhaps even catch up with that jetsetting husband of yours.'

Flora swallowed. She was being moved on, gently but firmly pushed out of the limelight. 'Haven't I done a good job, Henry?' she asked suddenly. 'Tell me honestly.'

He took in his breath, and his thin hand waved incredulously. 'I don't know how you can ask that,' he managed. 'You, of all people!'

Flora was bewildered. 'Why shouldn't I?'

'My dear girl, you've become a legend! Nobody thought a woman could be tough enough to do this job. Everyone expected you to get embroiled in love affairs and emotional traps, to cry over the beggars and the maimed children, to alienate politicians and their wives alike. And you've done none of that. You've danced over the top of all the swamps and messes that beset aid workers. You don't have rows, you don't have conflicts, you don't seem to have an ounce of self-importance. No one but you could have got so far without getting murdered. When at first you were charming, I worried that you couldn't be tough. But you're tough enough. And sweet enough so no one notices.'

Shakily, Flora said, 'That is such a load of hogwash, Henry. But the compliments were lovely. Thanks.'

He tried to get up from his chair, and after a moment's struggle sank back, exhausted. 'I'll be going home soon.' he said wearily. 'Try to shake off these damnable fevers. Incidentally, who do you think should take over from you?'

'Prakash Raj,' said Flora at once. 'He needs to get away from Bombay, he's done all he can. You're right, it's time we all moved. His wife's expecting their second baby, and in Bombay it's hard for him.'

'Right then. Prakash Raj it is.'

Leaving, her trunks packed and strapped, Abdul in tears, friend after friend coming to give her presents, she felt that India was lost to her. The clear mornings, hot afternoons, the thundering rain of the monsoon, all these she would never see again. Everything was happening so quickly she hardly had time to absorb it, until she stood at her bedroom window and looked out at a clear tropic moon, suspended by magic against a velvet sky. Tomorrow she would be gone, and Prakash Raj and his young wife would live in this house, sleep in this bed. Shenaz was sweet, and inclined to hero-worship her husband, so Prakash led a pampered and

383

somewhat narrow life. If it had been Shalimar, thought Flora, and looked around at her modest home. No, it wouldn't have done. She lived at Malibu now, on the Pacific Ocean, her days centred around her beautiful little boy. She worked, she came home, if she had lovers they were nowadays utterly discreet. Did Prakash ever look at his wife and wonder? Flora thought. She would never know.

A small procession escorted her to the station in the morning. The train belched and snorted. She stood on the iron steps and bade farewell to her friends, deliberately not looking beyond to the blank and sullen faces of her enemies. If everyone loved her she would know she had failed, she told herself. People didn't suffer because the world was too poor to care for them, they suffered because of greed and poor management and war. You couldn't put all, or even much of that right, but as the years passed she knew that she had learned to be better than nothing. Even by her own long yardstick, she had done well.

The train began to move out, and she stood waving, waving, until the platform was hidden by steam and dust. It was over. She had ended one part of her life, and now stood in limbo, looking towards the next. Children working in the fields waved to her, and she waved back. They, at less than ten, survived in a harsh world, so how could Annie, years older, not survive? The double standards of Europe and Asia assailed her. It was hard to feel anxiety for an educated girl of sixteen when she was only mildly concerned about an illiterate four year old who lived by grubbing with her brothers on a tip. But, as the miles passed, as she was absorbed into the Western world of speed, efficiency and cold, hard values, her perceptions changed. She began seriously to worry.

'My God,' said Don. 'You look appalling.'

Flora waved a grubby hand. 'I'm tired, that's all. Have you heard anything?'

'Yes, actually.' Don brandished a letter. '"Dear Dad, Just to ask you not to worry about me. Not that I imagine you will. Now you and Alex can have cosy chats and not have to bother about me being difficult and getting in the way. Think of all the money you'll save not having to pay for me at Cambridge. Don't try and find me, I don't want to be found. Yours, Annie."'

He tossed it on to the table.

'Oh.' Flora's lips twitched. 'What was the postmark?'

'Edinburgh. But I doubt she's there. She got her friend Juliette to forward it, and I've nearly wrung Juliette's neck and she won't say where she is. Gutsy kid, actually. Flunked her exams and got a job in retailing. And she's about a hundred years less competent than Annie.'

Flora sank into a sofa. She felt weak and unprepared for all this. 'So you've decided she's all right.'

'I've decided nothing of the kind! She ought to go to bloody Cambridge. It's what she wants. And all the time she's doing whatever it is she's up to, she isn't doing the work! Christ, Flora, if I had thought that letting you go would result in this I would have bloody well chained you to the bed!'

'I bet it wouldn't have made any difference.' Flora yawned. 'Annie's the sort that's bound to make heavy weather of growing up.'

'I like the way you can be so objective,' said Don with heavy sarcasm. 'You haven't seen her in years.'

Flora went upstairs to bath and sleep. What would Don say if he knew she wasn't going back to India? She had at least six months off, more if she wanted. And when they met he had given her the briefest peck on the cheek.

She stripped off and stared at herself in the bedroom mirror. Did she really look so terrible? Thin, certainly, and her hair was a mess, tangled and dirty, with no recognisable cut. She was going grey at the temples, too, which was annoying. Her fingernails were broken, and her face was drawn with weariness, but her eyes were the same, surely? He'd always liked her eyes and she'd made them up especially on the plane. But these days she didn't know any of the fashions, and it didn't look right. Not yet forty, and she felt old and worn and unlovely. It was stupid to mind, and even more stupid to cry.

Once in the bath, deep in hot water and truly warm for the first time since leaving India, she thought about Annie. Where might she be? A town, certainly. Perhaps she'd got a job in a shop, in her letters Annie seemed to find inexhaustible interest in shops and shopping. She might even be a cinema usherette, but let her not be a nightclub hostess, Flora prayed. A photograph of Annie in the school play, dressed in a rakish French maid's outfit, showed her to be admirably suited to such a role. She had the legs for one thing.

In the morning she would go and confront Juliette, Flora decided. Or perhaps Alex should talk to her. He appeared to be something of a heart-throb with Annie's friends. But for all she knew about her children from their letters, if they walked in now she might not recognise them. Suddenly she felt tearful again, because she had missed out on so much of their lives, through her own decision, her own fault. But if she had had her way the twins might never have been born, she remembered. It was Don's idea.

She lay back in the bath and let her hair trail in the water. Bliss. Things might have been much worse if she had been home with Annie. It might have been Alex who chose to be difficult. Dear, dependable Alex. Her head rolled, and sunk into her steaming bath, she fell asleep.

Annie was making a pet of a herring gull, feeding it every day at the same time and in the same place. She lay at night and worried in case it didn't come, because it was very lonely here. There were only sheep and gulls, and the sheep looked at her with flat yellow eyes and ran away.

It was hard to imagine that the peat she burned in the fireplace was the peat her mother had cut when they were babies, dried to superb condition in the barn. When they were small, and Marie had told the tale, it was a fairy story of life in a cottage by the sea, living in simple happiness. The reason for their mother's retreat to such a place had never been investigated, but they demanded again and again to hear how their mother made them porridge on an open fire, and took them to the edge of the sea to see the seals playing, until their daddy came to take them home once more. The magic of Eryn Cottage had lasted years and years.

Sometimes she saw a man walking the beach in the distance. She always turned and walked the other way. People out here frightened her, when the loneliness only made her sad. If a disaster happened, if her leg was broken, that would be troublesome, but if a stranger came into her house, closed the door behind him and said 'Nobody will hear if you scream,' that was a waking nightmare. When she saw the man, walking far down the beach, she thought about him for the rest of the day.

Juliette had come with her on that first day, They had hired a taxi and loaded it with food, telling the driver they were both staying to do work on a geography project on the seashore. Later Annie had walked her friend to the village and the bus, and she went back home in the gathering dusk. It was very lonely here. Each day when she went out walking she looked for the man on the beach.

Some two weeks after she ran away, she finished all her books. She would reread Chaucer, of course, and the Shakespeare, but to have nothing fresh was terrible. The village shop boasted one guide book and a copy of Robert Burns, but she knew all the poems and felt distinctly uninspired at the thought of long dissertations on local earthworks dating from the fourth century BC. Did the man on the beach read? She wondered. What was he doing here? For herself, she was staying until home and school fully realised what they had done to her, but from the way the man walked he wasn't that young. He wore a long black overcoat, and he walked up and down, sometimes stopping to throw stones into the sea. Perhaps he was a ghost, she thought. Perhaps he wasn't there at all. Perhaps under that long coat he carried a letter which he must give to an innocent virgin, and she would then be haunted for the rest of her natural life!

Her walks began to move down the beach somewhat. She wished she had a dog, because then there was a point to a walk and even the smallest terrier might feel some compunction to save its mistress from eternal haunting, or whatever. As it was, the gull wasn't suited to a stroll, and so her only companion was the leatherbound copy of Chaucer her father had insisted on buying for her. Everyone else had tatty editions, and only she had tooled leather, much to her embarrassment.

'You'll have it all your life, it might as well give you pleasure,' he had said to her, dropping it into her lap. That was Dad for you, he never made a proper occasion out of anything. Except when he made too much of one.

When she was within a hundred yards of the man she couldn't decide if she should go on or go back. At this distance he looked worse than ever, black hair, black beard, black coat. But younger than she had thought, her father's age or less perhaps. He was walking away from her, and so presumably didn't know she was there. Instinctively Annie walked more quickly, so that if she did decide to go on there was less distance between them. When she was within twenty yards and had quite decided to stop and go back, he turned suddenly. 'Hello,' he said.

Annie was taken aback. She hadn't expected him to sound friendly. It could be a trap, and this friendliness was only to make her drop her guard, so that he could lure her to his den and eat her bones. Except these days it would be rape and murder, she would never go home again!

'Windy day, isn't it?' he said.

Annie nodded slowly. 'I was following you,' she said.

'I know,' said the man. 'But I wasn't surprised. When there are only two people on a vast and empty beach it's hard not to be intensely curious about each other. I've been worried about you.'

'Oh,' said Annie.

She turned her book in her hands. 'I've run out of things to read,' she said. 'This is Chaucer. My father bought it for me.'

387

'Oh. May I see? It's years since I read Chaucer.' He held out his hand and Annie meekly gave him her book. Suppose he kept it? she thought. Never mind. If he took her book she would murder him, and he would be the one who would never go home.

The man chuckled. 'I do so love the rhythm. And the vulgarity. When I was at school I was shocked by it. The years have made me a little more broad-minded, I hope. Are you doing it for exams?'

Annie nodded. 'But I'm not taking them any more. I was going to Cambridge. But not any more.'

'Oh. That's a pity. You'd like Cambridge.'

'But my family don't want me to go.'

'Does it matter if they want it?'

The girl shrugged. 'I don't know. I thought it did. But now I'm not sure.'

'I always think you should do what you want, regardless of anyone or anything else. Within reason, of course. But I tried for years to do what other people thought I should. In the end I did what I wanted, I listened to an inner voice telling me what to do, and it all came right.'

'I haven't got an inner voice,' said Annie aggrievedly. 'I'm no Joan of Arc. It's easy, with an inner voice.'

'Your inner voice is telling you to go to Cambridge.'

He held out her book and she took it back. He said, 'If you come here tomorrow I'll bring something for you to read. I brought lots of books with me.'

'What are you doing here?' asked Annie.

'The same as you, no doubt,' he said. 'Listening to my inner voice.'

She grimaced at him and laughed. He laughed too. 'Wrap up well,' he said. 'It's a nasty east wind blowing. See you tomorrow.'

'Yes. 'Bye. See you tomorrow.'

They walked away from each other, back to back, brisk and determined down the beach. When she got home Annie made a pot of tea and baked some scones in the oven, and tidied round her house to make it as smart as she could. Tomorrow she would invite him home with her, to eat scones before the fire.

He took to coming every day. First she would meet him on the beach and then, after a walk, she would extend her invitation. He never assumed he would come, and she was never quite certain that he would. But when he sat in the cottage and they talked about books and the complexities of life, Annie felt safe and secure. Gradually, without knowing that she did so, she told him about her life. She told him about her dreadful mother, who had abandoned

388

her when she was small to go off and do good works and have affairs. 'She's been – ill,' she said. 'And still she wouldn't come home. Dad went out to her and everything, but she didn't care, just kept on doing what she wanted.'

'I suppose it's always a shock when we discover our parents are real people,' he said.

'Oh, I know I'm supposed to be seeing her as a woman and not a mother,' retorted Annie, 'But most women don't behave like her. I don't know anyone else who has a mother like her.'

'What, one that follows her own convictions? Not many women would leave home and family to do something they felt they should. Perhaps you feel she neglected you.'

'Well, she did. But Dad didn't. I suppose she knew he'd be a brick.'

'You must love him very much.'

Annie shot him a withering glance from under her mop of hair. 'Of course I do! He's super, Dad. And he tries terribly hard, but he doesn't understand me. He thinks he can put things right for me, and I don't want him to put them right! I just want him to know that it isn't always plain sailing, it isn't always easy for clever old Annie. They think I can do the work standing on my ear, they think I can go to Cambridge just if I want, and if I don't want I needn't.'

'You do make things difficult for yourself. You want everybody behaving just right.'

'Do I?' Annie grinned. 'Perhaps. My parents are too active, that's the trouble. They won't stay still so I can get used to them. Always doing something else. Mum's got this terribly important job, did I tell you? In charge of half India. And of course Dad's thick as thieves with the government and everything, but he doesn't give a damn about that, always off climbing things. You'd think he'd grow out of it, wouldn't you? I mean, most fathers do.'

'Annie, you want your parents old! You should be ashamed of yourself.'

She put her chin up at him. 'Why? It's jolly hard to live up to parents like that. What were your parents like?'

He considered. 'Quiet, settled – yes, they were old. I may take after them, doing less and thinking more as the years go by. We were a very thinking family. You obviously come from a long line of doers.'

'We do think as well,' retorted Annie. 'Why are you spending so much time wandering up and down this beach? I've got an excuse, but you haven't.'

'But mine is the same excuse! Time out, between rounds. Next week I'm off to begin something very big and very difficult, so I'm gathering myself. Listening to the inner voice. Making quite sure that I'm prepared.'

'Chatting to me and eating scones doesn't do that.'

He laughed. 'Yes, it does. It helps you and it's a treat for me. I've learned to be kind to myself, enjoying what the good Lord sends my way. You should learn that. You're too eager to wear your crown of thorns.'

The fire was glowing red, enclosing a rosy cavern that led towards infinity. The gull tapped at the window, and beyond was the sea, endlessly sucking and pulling at the shore. Annie felt timeless, as if she was locked in a moment that could belong in any century, any world. The fire, the sea, two people letting their minds touch and pull away. A great calm seemed to spread in her, soothing her very soul. 'Will you go home, Annie?' he said softly. 'It would be a kindness to yourself.'

She looked up and smiled at him, and for that second he saw Annie as she would become, settled, poised, brilliant. 'So it would,' she said.

They did not light the lamp. They sat, saying nothing, and the fire began to fall away into ashes. They would move soon, but they clung to the moment. In the midst of it they heard feet approaching the door, and a hand knocked, nervously. Annie got up, pushing her hair out of her face.

'Who is it?' she called out, her voice young and shrill with fear.

'Annie? Annie, it's me. Mum. Annie, please let me in.'

When she turned the lock and lifted the latch they stood staring at one another. 'Oh, Annie,' said Flora at last. 'Annie, I'm so sorry. I'll go away if you want, but I had to see that you were all right.'

'Don't go away,' said Annie. 'Did you come home because of me?'

'Yes. Right away. And your father was in such a state I couldn't leave him to worry all by himself. Oh, Annie, he'll be so relieved.'

They stood looking at each other, still not touching. Annie was taller than her mother now, an inch, perhaps more. 'You look terrible,' said Annie.

'I wish people wouldn't keep saying that,' said Flora in exasperation. 'I shall have to dye my hair.'

'You ought to buy some clothes,' said Annie. 'They look like flour sacks.'

'Do they?' Flora gazed down at her washed out skirt and top. 'Well, they might. You could help me, I suppose. But your father

390

won't like that. He's desperate for you to get into Cambridge.'

Annie stood up straight. 'No he isn't! He doesn't care.'

'I think he cares terribly, but he thinks it's wrong to put pressure on children to succeed. Even brilliant ones. You oughtn't to waste time going shopping.'

'I might be able to spare the odd half day,' said Annie.

She remembered her visitor, and stood awkwardly aside at last to let her mother into the room. 'I'd like you to meet – a friend,' she said lamely. 'This is my mother.'

'How do you do?' He rose and stood. Dark, bearded, unsmiling. 'How – do you do?'

Her mother and her friend stood staring at each other. 'I'm delighted to meet you,' he said. 'Annie's told me so much.'

'Thank you for listening to her,' she said.

'It seemed the least I could do.'

'Are you – staying round here?'

'Only until Sunday. Then I go abroad. The Lebanon.'

'Oh. Oh, I see. May I wish you luck? Or would that be considered unnecessary?'

'Not in the least. Any blessing is always welcome.'

Annie, a little confused, said, 'He's been really kind. We've talked for hours and he lent me loads of books.'

'That was very kind,' said Flora. 'Thank you again.'

'Simply a favour returned.' He moved to go, and then at the door, stopped. 'I gather things haven't been easy in the last year or two,' he remarked. 'I'm so sorry.'

Flora swallowed audibly. 'These things happen. We survive. Sometimes it's all for the best.'

'Ah, yes – the great panacea. God and his knitting pattern, the odd dropped stitch makes for the beauty of the whole. For myself, I prefer a less brutal theory. Random suffering, relieved by the struggle for good. My blessing on both of you. Goodbye.'

He walked quickly through the door. Annie picked up a book and ran after him, calling, 'Please! I still have your book.' But he didn't stop and come back for it. She returned to the room, saying, 'You know, Mum, I know he seemed odd, but he wasn't like that before. Perhaps he's a hermit of some sort. Not used to company.'

'Yes,' said Flora stiffly. 'He did seem strange. How much did you tell him?'

Annie flushed. 'Lots. Not everything. Not – you know.'

'Oh.' Flora took a long breath, and said brightly, 'He seemed a remarkable man. You expect saints to be like that somehow. The beard and so on.'

391

'He ate far too many scones to be a saint! Anyway, I used to think you were one.'

'And then you learned better!' Flora caught her daughter's hand and lifted it to her cheek. 'Dear Annie. I'm glad you came here. This cottage is made for people in trouble. It looks after them, and then it lets them go.'

'Back to the dreadful, dreadful school,' said Annie lugubriously, pulling away.

'With Cambridge to follow. Remember that, darling. The icing on an otherwise tasteless cake.'

Together they packed Annie's few things. The gull was flying around irritably, and they gave it a pile of food, most of the things remaining in the cupboard. But Annie left a few tins, some wood to light the fire and a packet of tea. 'Someone's going to want this house again,' she said. 'We want it to be ready for them.'

In the car, Flora looked at her daughter's calm face and was amazed. It had all been so easy, as if Annie had made her own reckoning at last. Was this the end then, of the tantrums and screams, the end of childhood? She thought how often children are exhorted to grow up, and how painful it is when they do. 'I hope you're not terribly angry with me,' she said breathily.

Annie turned her head. 'I don't know. Sometimes. You shouldn't have had a baby and not told us. We had a right to know.'

'I didn't want you to see the mess I'd made of things. It's very tempting to let your children think you're perfect. Dishonest, but tempting.'

'And it's very silly,' said Annie. 'It gives them unreal expectations.'

They drove in silence for a few minutes. Then Flora burst out, 'Good Lord, you're going to be a much better parent than me. You're going to be wonderful! And I shall be a ramshackle old bat that you hate to have to stay.'

Annie sighed happily. 'I always love the first day you come home. It's exciting, the best time, as if everything in the world is going to come right.'

Instinctively Flora reached for her daughter's hand. Their fingers locked.

Chapter Ten

Prakash Raj found it hard to love Flora's bungalow. It was built a foot off the ground, for the better circulation of air, but still for a family it was small, hot and cramped. Born to wealthy parents, he had been brought up in a whitewashed mansion, with marble floors and high ceilings cooled by the constant motion of the punkah. Nowadays of course his parents had moved to an apartment with air conditioning.

Air conditioning was a mixed blessing, decided Prakash. Before its advent the heat was to be endured, if you could not get away to the hills or the lakes. Today you were tormented by the knowledge that in this shop, that office, someone's private home, you could be cool, and the transition from misery to release was too easy. You learned to hate being hot, you lost the ability to accept it.

But, as in all his daily life, he sought humility. Aid workers did not merit air conditioned homes, it could not be justified in a land where so many had no home at all. That his parents could buy him comfort a thousand times over was of no importance. This was the way he had chosen, and he would resign himself.

But Shenaz, heavily pregnant and missing her family, found it harder to cope. She had taken to lying on her bed in the hot afternoons and crying, becoming so distraught that Prakash was beginning to feel he dared not be away from home for even so much as two hours together. He had sent for her sister to keep her company, but the girl was at college and couldn't yet come. Not for the first time he wished Shenaz had gone to college. She might seem less – provincial. It was an unkind word, and he at once rejected it. She wasn't all that bright, he had realised that early on, but she was loving and sweet, and a wonderful mother.

When he went home that afternoon, there were many people in the bungalow. 'What is it?' he demanded. 'Shenaz?'

The agency doctor was there, another Indian, a woman. 'Baby on the way,' she said cheerfully. 'Coming in rather a rush, Prakash. Be a good chap and sit on the verandah while we get on with our job.'

In the bedroom Shenaz was calling for her mother.

'Do you think I should go to her?' asked Prakash worriedly. 'She gets very upset. She doesn't like it here, she's from Bombay.'

'She's a sweet little thing,' said the doctor patronisingly. 'You leave her to me. I'll see if I can stop her making such a fuss.'

He felt annoyed. They felt sorry for him, married to his silly little girl, who wanted her mother and the pet dog she had left behind, who hated this place because it was so hot. His son was crying and the nurse was trying to soothe him. Prakash went and picked him up and took him out to the verandah. Abdul, the leper, poured lemonade and made soothing noises to the baby. Somewhere nearby people were quarrelling violently, almost drowning out the sound of Shenaz's squealing. The quarrellers moved away, leaving only the squeals, and suddenly they too were silenced. There came the thin, reedy wail of a crying baby.

'A new brother or sister for you,' Prakash told his son, and old Abdul said, 'A girl, for sure. I can tell by the cry.'

It was indeed a girl, a princess, as everyone said when they congratulated him. Thank goodness he already had a son, they added. Shenaz was delighted, and invited half her family to come and stay. Prakash thought of them crammed into the small bungalow and shuddered, but it made her happy and that was that. When they arrived he seized his chance to travel for a few days, because he had been far too desk-bound during these last months. Flora had always been on the move, it was part of her success, and he must not let all she had achieved fall apart. He attacked his work zestfully, determined to shake off the shackles of home and family. He was very lucky, he told himself. Very lucky indeed.

In the bungalow, Shenaz's mother was holding the baby while Shenaz was in the bathroom, washing her hair. They talked through the open door, gossiping about this and that.

'You must get Prakash to come back to Bombay,' said the older woman. 'If he hadn't made such a nuisance of himself before, you would not have had to leave. He should stop working for this agency and join his father, you could live as you should. This horrible, horrible house.'

'I know. It's too hot. But I can't tell Prakash what to do.' Shenaz, her long black hair over her face, reached blindly for the shampoo.

'He has no right to coop you up here. No proper facilities at all. Everything primitive, and you're not used to such things. This baby is getting hungry again, Shenaz. Shenaz? Shenaz?'

There was no answer. The small brown snake retreated back behind its cracked tile, and slithered away into the space beneath the house. They often came into bathrooms in these old houses, attracted by the coolness and damp. The girl stared at her wrist, at the two small punctures in her smooth, firm flesh. Already it was swelling.

'Shenaz?' Her mother appeared in the doorway.

The girl started to scream.

In India there is no waiting around for days, it is all done quickly. So the funeral was over before Prakash even came home, and he stood in the house, staring at his distraught mother-in-law, wondering if any of this was real. 'There were nests of snakes under there, and it is your fault, yours for bringing her here. She should never have left Bombay. We should never have let her marry you. All this India, India, why can't you be civilised and live as you should?'

'Wasn't there a doctor? Someone?

'Living out here, how are we to find anyone? How are we to know what to do? My daughter is gone, gone, and not one tear have you shed, no sign of sadness at all!'

He went out, he couldn't bear any more. There were boxes of snakebite serum at the clinic. Why hadn't Shenaz gone straight there? But he could guess at the scene, the screaming, the chaos, and no one to act rationally. They would have wasted time, and little Shenaz, weighing so little and weak from childbirth, presented no great resistance to poison. She had died at home, while messengers ran to fetch help that couldn't possibly come in time. Her life was gone. Her children were motherless. He sat down on the verandah and wept.

On the other side of the world, in a garden full of flowers and sweet grass, Shalimar sliced an apple into perfect segments. She gazed at the woman opposite with a serene and challenging frankness. 'I like my life,' she said. 'I live here with my son Liam and I'm happy. It may be difficult for your readers to understand, but I don't have any need of a man. I have that wonderful thing, complete independence.'

The interviewer scrabbled with her notepad. She wanted to make her name with this interview, find some crack in the perfect shell of the filmstar facade. So far there was nothing, not even a picture of Prince Charles, and it would be yet another 'alone but happy' piece, with an inevitably stunning picture. Shalimar always photographed well. Perhaps they could do a shot with her lying on her back holding the baby above her head – but of course that too was a cliché. Wasn't there anything new?

'About your next film – won't you mind being cast as an older woman?'

'I am an older woman,' retorted Shalimar. 'By film standards at any rate. But, since I seem to be staving off the ravages of old age, they're going to stick on some fake wrinkles. I shall enjoy it. There is nothing so seductive as one's own good looks. We should all get used to doing without them.'

'Right.' The interviewer scribbled again, and Shalimar yawned. This was oh, so boring. She wondered why they never sent men to talk to her any more. It was so much more fun to play at seduction, even if it got no further than perspiration. The pieces were always better too, full of excitement and might-have-beens.

The earnest girl before her said, 'Don't you feel a boy should have a man around the house? As a role model?'

'He's got lots of role models. A butler, a gardener, film directors, producers, actors.'

'But nobody really important. No father figure.'

Shalimar decided to dislike this girl thoroughly. 'Did you have a father figure?' she demanded.

'Well, actually yes.'

'Was your father important?'

'He's a senator. Actually.'

'Oh.'

Shalimar allowed herself a grin, 'That is a worry for me,' she conceded. 'Liam doesn't have enough to do with men. I don't like introducing him to every boyfriend I have, it's too confusing. They come and go, come and go. I think I may send him to boarding school in England, but it would break my heart.'

'... break my heart ...' scribbled the girl assiduously and Shalimar said. 'Do stop taking all these notes. The best interviews are never word for word, they catch the spirit of a person, not every last syllable.'

The girl looked up. 'What would you write about you, then?'

Shalimar sighed. 'My greatest tragedy – perhaps everyone's – is that you may have the ability to do many things but life insists that you only investigate your talents in one direction. I might have been

396

a brilliant wife and mother, under different circumstance. I might have enjoyed it very much. I might have been a writer, director, businesswoman, whatever. But I'm an actress. That's all I am. I find it limiting.'

'Oh.' The girl started writing again and Shalimar decided she had had enough.

'Time to go,' she declared. 'Liam needs his nap.'

The girl looked doubtfully at the wide-awake toddler climbing around on the grass, playing with his wooden building blocks. 'I could wait,' she ventured.

'No, you couldn't. I'm a very conscientious mother, I sit with Liam for at least half an hour when he naps.'

When the girl had gone, still scribbling, Shalimar went back into the garden and lay on the grass with Liam. He tangled his fat hands in her hair and said, 'Mum. Tory. Now.'

'I'll read you a story in a minute. What did you think of that lady? Wasn't she a pain?'

'Tory. Now.'

'Self-centred, like all men, I see.' She poked his warm tummy and he gurgled.

Later that evening, walking barefoot around her cool house, she sipped a Martini and considered. Only twice in her life had she ever wanted to marry, and on each occasion she had chosen someone who could not marry her. Didn't that say something fairly significant? She had always imagined herself as someone who wanted marriage but just couldn't achieve it. Perhaps the truth was that she always put that state carefully out of reach.

She sat herself down in her rocking chair and swung backwards and forwards. What did she need marriage for, anyway? She was happy on her own, she had security, a child, a good sex life when she wanted it. In the mornings, when she woke up alone, she had no one's difficult little habits to contend with. Liam gave her love, her job gave her wealth, her strength of mind ought to give her contentment. She was content. Very content. There was nothing more that she needed.

Flora looked worriedly at herself in the mirror. 'I don't think it's quite me.'

'You ought to be more adventurous, Mum. You'll be wearing a kilt and a twinset if you're not careful.'

'Oughtn't I to wear that? At my age?'

'No. You're not even forty. And if you were fifty, it would still be boring. You've got a super figure, you should show it off.'

'Not in this.'

Moving with difficulty, Flora extracted herself from a skintight leather dress. It moulded so closely to her body shape that underwear could not be worn, and she was forced to confront a silhouette in which nipples, ribs and stomach featured prominently. 'Your father would be appalled,' she panted. 'It's the sort of thing Shalimar wears.'

'He'd have liked it on Shalimar,' said Annie darkly.

They set off once more to trudge the streets. Flora was unimaginably bored by shopping, and it was all Annie could do to keep her keeping on. Without constant shepherding she would dart off into a bookshop, coffee shop or art gallery, and every time she spied the Bentley making its stately way in pursuit, hoping to receive non-existent parcels, she had to be restrained from hailing it and going home.

'I've changed shape,' moaned Flora. 'I used to have curves, and now I've got angles. I can't look good.'

'You'll probably have curves again soon,' said Annie. 'Let's pretend you've got them already.'

'You're going to stuff old nylons into my bra,' muttered Flora darkly. 'All I want is a cord skirt and things. A blouse or two.'

'And a balldress,' said Annie, and swept into another shop.

Flora argued even as she was poked and prodded into a dress. 'I do not need green taffeta. Annie, be reasonable. No one needs a skirt four feet wide!'

'It looks great. You ought to have it.' The assistant was blank-faced and down to earth.

'I shan't go to any balls,' protested Flora.

'There's the KORSEA dance coming up,' said Annie. 'Dad usually takes me and Alex. Now you can go.'

'It wouldn't be right,' said Flora, constrained by the presence of the assistant. 'Everyone would think – they'd assume – .'

'We'll have it,' said Annie, turning her back on her parent. 'And we'll try the cream suit, please. And the black velvet. And that delicious thing in the window, the dark blue with a peplum.'

'But I need things for everyday!' complained Flora.

'We'll get those at Marks and Sparks,' declared Annie. 'You're a pain, Mum. Totally indecisive. Think of others for a change. Alex and I don't want a mother who embarrasses us.'

'Oh, thanks.'

Flora allowed herself to be bullied into the blue dress, and the cream suit, not to mention the brown leather brogues that had suddenly become hugely fashionable. 'You'll be telling me next I should wear them with the taffeta,' she said aggrievedly, but Annie simply held out a pair of shot silk pumps. Everything was going on the pile, item after item.

'No!' Flora turned her back and started to scrabble for her old clothes. 'I will not have so much money spent. It's obscene.'

'You're married to a millionaire, Mum,' said Annie. 'And Dad's always supporting charities. He must be saving whales by the hundred.'

'And there are people starving for want of a few pounds. I won't have it, Annie. No! I'm going home.'

Almost hysterical with panic, Flora rushed out of the shop, her buttons done up wrong and her hair flying.

'Bit wrong in the head, is she?' asked the assistant.

'Oh, bats in the belfry,' said Annie. 'Look, I'll pay for all this. And put in that scarf and the two jewelled haircombs. My conscience can stand it.'

Flora sat in the car in stony silence while Annie filled the boot with parcels. 'You needn't worry,' said Annie, when all was at last stowed away. 'I'll do your hair myself and save a fortune. At least ten pounds.'

'You have spent hundreds!' muttered Flora. 'How do you have so much money?'

'I talked to Dad this morning. I knew you'd be difficult. It isn't going to help the starving if you walk around in rags, you know. If Dad spent all his money on India it wouldn't be enough. You've got to keep a sense of proportion.'

'Oh, do shut up!' Flora sank into her corner, feeling beleaguered. Annie tapped on the glass. 'Stop at M & S, John,' she called out. 'My mother can stay in the car.'

It was like childhood, thought Flora. Premature senility. Annie would undoubtedly come back with something so dreadful that she would look a complete fool.

'Nothing like Balenciaga, to my mind,' mused John. 'But a St Laurent suit takes some beating.'

'We're spending quite enough already,' said Flora frostily. 'Enough to keep a hundered Indian families for years.'

'Aye, but there's good Scots families need people to buy clothes here,' said John irrefutably. 'And good French families making the clothes in Paris. These things are no so simple as they seem.'

'Thank you for that kind advice,' said Flora, and was ashamed of her sarcasm. She wasn't nearly so guilt stricken as she made out. Underneath everything she felt panic, that she had lost whatever looks she had ever possessed, and would never look pretty again. She was almost too scared to try.

At home, ignoring her mother's protests, Annie turned her attention to Flora's hair. She sliced off eight inches of split ends and kept the mirror away, so Flora could not see the worst. Then she plastered the remains with glutinous dark red dye, and Flora shrieked: 'You'll make me look a complete fright! Annie, have some consideration!'

'Oh, be quiet, do,' said Annie. 'I haven't done this before and I have to follow the instructions. You don't want green hair, do you?'

'I may have to learn to live with it.' She sat, glumly dripping, for the required space of time.

But the reward was worth it. Even Annie was pleased. Flora's hair was alive again, bright with streaks of reddish gold. Newly washed and rebellious, it surrounded her face like a soft bush. Taken by surprise she sat back and let Annie make up her face, with gentle brown lines round her eyes and the softest touch of eyeshadow and lip gloss. Finally, she dressed in a new crisp white shirt, a silk scarf at the neck, tweed trousers and a wide leather belt. 'And the brogues,' advised Annie. 'And some jewels. You can wear your diamond and pearl clusters, they always go. And the diamond pendant. I've never seen you wear that at all.'

Flora stared at herself in the glass. Light touched her diamonds, her eyes, her shining lips and hair. The clothes held crisp shape, giving her waist and shoulders definition. 'I shall be cold,' she murmured, and Annie held out a cashmere cardigan, acquired from somewhere. Her mother was past protesting.

They did not appear until the family was gathered for dinner. Annie had dressed in a short black jumper and knee-length black trousers, like a Japanese puppeteer. Alex was in jeans and said, 'I didn't know we were going to dress up. Shall I go and change?'

'You'd only find another pair of jeans,' said Don. 'Stay as you are. Flora, you look – amazing.'

'All Annie's work,' she said shyly, and took a sherry from Forbes.

'She's bought a dress for the ball,' declared Annie. 'So Alex and I can stay at home instead of struggling round the floor pretending we know how to dance the foxtrot.'

'You can dance the foxtrot,' said Don. 'I sent you to the lessons, remember?'

'But the people we dance with can't,' retorted Annie. 'They only think they can. And we fight our way round, like wrestlers.

400

Everyone's going to be thrilled when you and Mum turn up.'

Flora felt herself blushing. 'She's being silly, of course,' she said. 'It isn't my place. Everyone would imagine things – '

'They've imagined enough of those in the past,' said Don mildly. 'Yes, you'd better come. Stop all those rumours about you being mad or dead or disgraced. Alex, will you stop kicking the furniture!'

The twins dominated the meal, chattering and going into peals of laughter over shared jokes. Don and Flora said little to each other. When Flora passed the salt and their hands touched, they both apologised.

'What shall we do now?' demanded Annie, as they finished and stood up. 'We can play a game. Trivial Pursuit, something like that.'

'I'm going for a walk,' said Don. 'Want to come, Flora?'

She glanced at the twins. Their faces were bright with expectation.

'I'm not dressed for it,' she said feebly, but Annie said, 'You only have to put on a coat and change your shoes. Really, I find it hard to believe you did such an important job. I think you made it up.'

'I know what you mean,' said Don. 'I well remember the time she nearly sold off two tugs at knockdown prices. I saved her at the last minute.'

'You caused it, you mean,' snapped Flora, stung. 'I was naive in those days and allowed you to bully me. The myth of the incompetent little woman was dreamed up by my father and fostered by you.'

'You were incompetent,' said Don coolly. 'Soft as butter, anyone could walk over you. Who could tell that you'd turn into a harridan?'

'I am not a harridan!'

The others all laughed. Sometimes she felt excluded, they had an everyday understanding that she couldn't match. Shared experience was the stuff of family life, and she had shared so little. She went huffily to get a coat and boots, and too late realised that the children weren't coming. She and Don were walking in the moonlight alone.

The air was cold and frosty. A culvert was running strongly, and their boots splashed through water. A deer, creeping from the wood under cover of the dark, was betrayed by the moonlight and fled. A rabbit sat up all surprised and stared at them.

'You're making Annie happy,' remarked Don. 'All this dressing up.'

'She won't take no for an answer,' said Flora. 'I'm sorry, I know it's desperately extravagant.'

401

'The money's yours by right. You don't have to ask me if you can spend it.'

'No. I suppose not.'

In the shadows, he caught her hand and held it. 'You look so pretty.'

'Thanks. I feel — odd. Not me. Don, there's something I should tell you. Several things in fact. You know the man Annie met at the cottage, the man who talked to her? It was Finn. Finn McDonald.'

He took in his breath. After a moment he said, 'That must have been cosy. Meeting him again after all this time.'

'It was nothing of the sort! We only spoke for a moment. I was on tenterhooks in case Annie had told him about the baby. I don't want him to know, ever.'

Don dropped her hand. 'Yes, of course, we can't upset poor Finn now, can we? Me, the kids, everyone, they don't matter. But the sainted Finn remains inviolate.'

'You do talk rubbish,' she said dispassionately. 'I only meant — look, Don, I don't want him, and if he knew what had happened he might think he should revive things. They died a natural death. We both manage very well on our own. He'll be a marvellous priest, you know. He's off to the Lebanon.'

'Oh, well,' said Don cheerily, 'that's the last we'll see of him, then. He's going to die a fairly unnatural death, I should imagine.'

'Do you have to be so foul?' snapped Flora. 'He looked after Annie quite marvellously. If it hadn't been for him I don't think she'd have come home, you know. Haven't you any gratitude?'

Don moved away. She couldn't see his face, misty in the pale light. He said. 'I don't know the man. But you loved him, and so did Annie. I feel jealous as hell.'

Flora took a sharp breath. 'If I did love him, it was only like Annie,' she whispered. 'He's a very good man. The sex was just loneliness and need. You can't go on giving everything and getting nothing back. The well runs dry. In the end, you have to look after yourself.'

'I'd have looked after you.'

She went to him and touched his hand. 'And that's the trouble, isn't it? I don't want to be looked after. I want to take care of myself.'

When they returned to the house Don was quietly furious. The children had expected romance and were upset. Alex muttered, 'What did you say to him, Mum? I never knew anyone rattle him like you do.'

'I didn't say much.' She took off her boots, kicking them viciously into a corner. 'He wants things his way all the time, that's all.'

'So do you,' said Annie, overhearing. 'One thing this marriage has taught me is the importance of compromise. You two don't know the meaning of the word.'

Flora stuck her tongue out at her, and flounced into the sitting room. Don was pouring himself a whisky. 'The other thing I meant to say,' announced Flora, 'which you didn't wait to hear, of course, is that I'm home for at least six months. Sorry and all that, but I've finished in India and I'm taking accumulated leave.'

Whisky spilled from the decanter on to the floor. 'Shit!' Don mopped at it. 'How dare you announce a thing like that? There's no way you can stay here for six months.'

'Of course she can,' said Annie, casting herself on to the sofa. 'You're bound to get used to each other again.'

'We were never used to each other at all,' wailed Flora. 'But you can go climbing or something, can't you, Don?'

'I will not absent myself from my house at your convenience.'

'It was my house before ever it was yours. And you absented yourself often enough at my inconvenience!'

Alex crossed the room and switched on the television, deliberately turning it up very loud. Flora felt shaky and near to tears. She was looking her best tonight and no one noticed, no one cared. Everything she said infuriated Don.

'I won't come to the ball,' she said shrilly, and Don turned on her.

'Damn it, you'll come! You'll come if I have to drag you! For once you can be some damned use.'

She descended the stairs carefully, afraid that she would fall over her skirt. It swished around her in exhilarating folds of green shot with black and silver. Although in the shop it had seemed pretty, now that her hair was done and she was made up and sparkling, it had become a stunning dress. The silk pumps Annie had insisted she buy were so flat that she felt almost diminutive. Don was waiting for her in the hall, superb in dinner jacket and scarlet bow tie. When she stood next to him she felt weak suddenly. She wanted to put her arms round his neck and have him hold her. Hot colour surged into her cheeks.

'Ready then?' He was grim and unsmiling.

'Perfectly ready. You look wonderfully distinguished.'

'You don't. Soft and sweet, that's you. What a deceiver.'

She reached up and touched his cheek. 'Don't be mean. I won't be. This is your night, I made Alex dance the foxtrot for hours this morning, and Annie's been coaching me in getting on down. But if I do I shall never get up.'

'Why do you always talk as if you're old?'

She shrugged. 'I'm quite old, in Indian terms. You have to readjust back here. And anyone with two huge children has to feel old.'

Without warning he put his forefinger into her cleavage. 'But you were a child bride. It's very warm in there.'

'Stop it.'

She pulled away and went out to the car. They must not do this, must not again fall into the trap of following where their bodies led. Even if she avoided pregnancy the emotional traps were every bit as dangerous. But he pulled the velvet curtain across the glass partition and opened the cocktail cabinet to pour them both some champagne.

'Let's just enjoy ourselves,' he murmured.

'Let's not,' retorted Flora. 'Don, we are not doing it. Not again. We just can't.'

'I haven't suggested anything of the sort,' he said lazily. 'And if I did, what would it matter? A bit of fun. Some pleasure. For old times' sake.' His hand touched her ankle and moved slowly up under her dress. When he reached her knee she clamped her legs together.

'No. It doesn't work.'

'Once didn't work. What about twice, or three times – or every night?' He put his hands on her hips, gently moving his thumbs against the taffeta, and beneath it, the bone. Her lips parted and she drew in her breath. Trust him to be so good at this – so wonderfully, lazily enticing.

'Stop it,' she murmured. 'If you don't I shall pour this champagne all over you.'

To her surprise he let her go. 'No time, anyway. There's always later. And I'm sick of trying to live like a monk. I'm owed something, for God's sake.'

She turned away from him, but he leaned his shoulder against the door to watch her face. He had aroused her, and he knew it. There was something about the way her eyelids drooped over those huge navy eyes.

He felt a rising contentment, his pride soothed by the knowledge that she still needed him. He hadn't known her very well when they married, he wouldn't say that he wholly knew her now, but he had certainly learned enough to know that tonight was full of promise. He could wait. Half the fun was in waiting.

The ball was to be held at an hotel, and Flora went first to the cloakroom to tidy her hair. Other KORSEA women were there but no one recognised her. When she went into a toilet cubicle someone said in a low voice, 'I hear he's brought his wife. Is that her?'

'Could be. What a glamourpuss! Patricia's going to be upset. He's not been near her in weeks, she says.'

'Well, you can understand it. She always was pushy.'

Flora waited until they had gone before she came out. Another mistress then, another Shalimar. Her colour was very high, she went to the basin and splashed her face with cold water, dabbing it with a monogrammed linen towel.

Don was waiting for her in the hall, talking to several men, most of them in kilts. He reached an arm for her and introduced her easily, 'You remember my wife, Flora?'

Against her will she was forced to stand with his arm on her shoulders. His fingers gently caressed her bare skin and a small, dark woman across the room, watching with fierce attention, turned suddenly away.

Champagne flowed. Flora's glass was replenished again and again as she and Don made the rounds, speaking to everyone that mattered. Dorothy, his secretary, was there, and said brightly, 'He's been looking very strained since you came home, Mrs Harrington. You've been upsetting the applecart, no doubt.'

Flora was taken aback. 'I try not to upset him,' she said. 'It can be difficult.'

'He has a lot of responsibility,' said Dorothy in reproach. 'It doesn't do to have him worried by things at home. Your father wouldn't have wanted that.'

'No. No, indeed.'

Moving away, she hissed to Don, 'That woman has been giving me a lecture! Says you're all upset.'

'I am,' he murmured. 'Sexual frustration is very upsetting. You just wait until I get you alone. I'm going to screw you to the bed.'

Her face flamed, but he moved smoothly towards the next group, making the introductions as if he wasn't aware of Flora's colour. She began to feel really cross with him, as his hand touched her bare shoulder, her wrist, even straying to her cleavage to remove an imaginary hair. 'Will you stop it?' she hissed. But he smiled blandly and continued on.

The dancing began, and it was left to Don and Flora to take the floor. No one else joined them and she muttered, 'We don't have to do an exhibition performance, do we?'

'Seems like it.'

405

It was the dreaded foxtrot. Flora gritted her teeth, trying to remember the wealth of information the children had imparted. Big steps, they said, and those heel turn things. 'Don't worry,' said Don. 'If the worst comes to the worst you can stand on my feet.'

'Like a little girl at a wedding!' She laughed up at him and they began.

She had forgotten how good a dancer Don was. Perhaps she had never known, it might be one of those things acquired with years. But for a big man he always moved with poise and precision. She began to relax, leaning back in his arms on the turns so that her dress billowed out and her hair swung. Although traditionally after the first few turns of the room everyone else joined in, this evening they did not. Instead they watched an apparently perfect couple, and when the music ended they all clapped.

'That's enough of that,' called out Don. 'Next year we'll get a cabaret. And we need some decent whisky.'

Glasses appeared from nowhere and he toasted Flora. 'Well done, Mrs Harrington.'

'I return the compliment, Mr Harrington, sir. I must stop drinking, I'll fall over.'

'I'll catch you.'

Their eyes met. Flora felt her heart stutter. Why, oh why, was Don such an attractive man? They were to be together for at least six months. Would it be better or worse if she slept with him? She knew the answer to that. It hadn't worked then and it wouldn't work now.

One of the directors asked her to dance a reel and she accepted. Don had gathered a young team around him, a band of driving men who needed no prodding, only restraint. As each took his turn dancing with the boss's wife they tried with varying degrees of subtlety to impress her, ask for things, make the case for this or that pet project. When at last Flora found herself next to Don for a moment's peace, she murmured, 'I didn't know you were into property development.'

'We were. We're getting out, the market's falling. My property bloke's losing his job, he's just been told.'

'Oh, the poor man! I didn't realise.'

'He's getting a fistful of money and a glowing reference. Get a job anywhere. Once you've worked for KORSEA everyone wants you, they all know I give everyone tons of responsibility.'

'In marked contrast to my father.'

'Indeed.' He grinned down at her. 'Thanks for coming. I haven't enjoyed one of these do's for years, I'm always trying to stop the twins doing something they shouldn't. One year they poured jelly into the tombola drum, and it sprayed across the room like slimy bullets. The dry cleaning bill ran into hundreds.'

Flora giggled. 'But you let them come the next year? You must be mad.'

'Well, it was bloody funny. These things can be so boring, you've no idea.'

It was suppertime, signalled by a piper playing a skirl and the arrival of the haggis. Don settled Flora in a corner by a palm and went to fetch her some food. Two ladies on the other side of the tree, unable to see her, were talking.

'Well, something's certainly working in that marriage. Do you see the way they look at each other? Up to his tricks again, no doubt.'

'The woman ought to have more discrimination! He's a complete bastard. You know he's been sleeping with Patricia Makepeace? And he's sacked James Talbot, without so much as a by your leave, I hear. At least he's left those ghastly children at home this time. God knows why we have to put up with their antics.'

Flora felt her fingers tensing into claws. She got up and went to meet Don, who was carrying two plates of food. She took one. 'We're being talked about. Or at least, you are. You're randy, dictatorial, and you've got two dreadful children.'

'About sums it up, I should think.' He grinned down at her and Flora giggled. 'Ought we to talk to people?' she asked, waving her champagne glass at the throng.

'They much prefer watching us flirt, don't you think?'

'We're not flirting! Or at least I'm not. Don, don't.' She held a wineglass in one hand and a plate in the other. He put down his plate, placed his free hand behind her head and kissed her. It wasn't passionate, it wasn't rushed, just a thoughtful exploration of her mouth by his tongue. She felt blood start to rush noisily through her head.

'That wasn't fair!' Everyone was watching them. She wanted to die.

'But it was so enjoyable.' He picked up his plate again and munched a turkey vol-au-vent. 'What do you say we book a room upstairs? We always seem to be conducting our sex life in clandestine meetings, somehow.'

'We don't have a sex life,' said Flora desperately. 'Not a shared one, at any rate. You have a series of mistresses and I just have the occasional disastrous liaison.'

'I'm between mistresses, and you're between disasters, so why not?'

407

Flora looked across the ballroom, her face considering. 'You'll have to use something,' she murmured.

'What? I don't want to fiddle with a rubber johnny at my age!'

'I'll help you fiddle,' said Flora. 'But we'll have to stay at least until midnight.'

Their eyes met. 'OK,' he whispered.

They left the food half eaten and began to circulate once more. The disco was starting and the lights going down. The younger members of staff were intent on ignoring the rest and having fun. Raucous laughter came from the bar, and some of the men were beginning to acquire the glazed look of the seriously drunk. Flora went to the ladies and passed a couple in a clinch behind yet another palm. It was the dark girl and the property man, James Talbot. Consoling themselves, no doubt.

The shrieking began as she was washing her hands. The ladies headed in a rush for the door, and Flora followed, still carrying her towel. The palm was on the floor, James Talbot was looking bemused and an unknown woman had Patricia Makepeace by the hair. 'You bloody harpy!' she was yelling. 'I'll teach you to tamper with my husband!'

The two women wrestled noisily, and everyone stood, transfixed. It was such an unusual occurrence that there seemed no proper method of dealing with it.

'Stop them, someone,' called out a woman, but no one did.

James Talbot caught his wife's arm. 'Come on, Jennifer,' he said angrily. 'Stop that now.'

She let go the other woman and swung round on her husband. Her fingers caught his cheek, scoring deep fissures in the skin, and while her back was turned Patricia picked up a free-standing ashtray and threw it at her. The bottom was weighted and the hall was showered with sand, old cigarettes and the clattering pieces of ashtray.

Don erupted from the ballroom, closely followed by two or three of his henchmen. 'What in God's name's going on?'

James Talbot, drunk, his face bleeding, his wife hysterical, turned and saw him. He lunged forward, arms flailing wildly, and hit Don hard on the chin. He fell back, dazed, while Talbot wrestled with the men trying to restrain him. He kneed one in the groin and he fell like a shot stag: there was a crunch as the other's nose went.

Don let out a roar and went for the man. He hit him once in the gut and as he doubled caught him under the chin. As the man crumpled Jennifer Talbot leaped shrieking into the fray, though whether to kill her husband or to save him wasn't clear. The Makepeace woman began to laugh hysterically, and suddenly there was fighting

408

everywhere, whether between KORSEA people or complete strangers no one knew. It was Saturday night and the drink was flowing. The men threw off their sophistication and remembered that nothing had pleased their Scots ancestors more than a fight and were they not, tonight, wearing the tartan? As the giant mirrors shattered and fell, somebody called the police.

Chapter Eleven

'I thought you told me the KORSEA parties were boring?' Flora sat in the Bentley, pressing the damp towel from the Ladies on to Don's swelling cheek.

'Did I say that?'

'Yes. What with jelly in the tombola and police raids, it's all rather more than I'm used to. Oh, I'm so tired.'

Dawn was breaking. Her feet ached in her new shoes, there was a sour taste in her mouth and her hands were still dirty from the compulsory fingerprinting they had undergone at the police station.

'Some little old lady is sure to ask questions at the AGM,' muttered Don. 'Why is there open warfare at the KORSEA dance? Does this indicate lack of management control? Yes, it bloody well does! I want to crucify someone.'

'You can start with Patricia Makepeace,' said Flora sourly. 'She's rapacious. Steals people's husbands at a moment's notice.'

'At least a decade, in your case.'

He took the towel and threw it in the corner. 'So much for our night of passion.'

'Yes,' Flora sighed. 'It wasn't a good idea, you know. We fight if we sleep together or not, and if we are sleeping together then it just ups the stakes. It hurts more. There's more involved.'

'Balls!' Don pulled open the cocktail cabinet and extracted the remains of last night's champagne. He poured them both a glass but Flora grimaced. 'We agreed,' said Don grimly.

Flora took the glass. 'When the night was young. Not in the grey dawn with flat champagne and fistmarks. No, Don. I'm sober now. I've got my head together. I don't want to sleep with you.'

He sat looking at her as they drove. Her hair was in a mess, her dress was stained and there was a mark on one bare shoulder where

410

some flying missile had hit her. She had violet shadows beneath her eyes. He felt his breath catch with the force of his emotion. 'You don't know what you do to me,' he whispered.

She pushed her hair back from her face. 'I don't do anything. Just sometimes I'm not as strong-minded as I ought to be.'

'God, but you make me sick! What terrible crime are you going to commit by going to bed with me? What awful retribution is going to fall on your head? We can discount pregnancy, you've already got me promising to behave like any schoolboy, so what else is there? What are you afraid of?'

The car was nearing the castle entrance. Flora said nothing, looking away, pretending he wasn't there. He caught her arm and shook her, but still she wouldn't look at him. When the car drew up he flung open the doors and dragged her out on to the gravel.

'Don, stop it! You're behaving like a madman.'

'You're enough to drive me mad! I love you, Flora, and I've never stopped loving you, and you give me nothing in return. What do you want of me? You're tearing apart my soul!'

His fingers were gripping her arm to the bone. His swollen cheek gave him the look of a gargoyle, a wild creature. 'You mustn't do this,' she said feebly. 'It isn't fair to the children.'

'They're not children any more. I won't live this half-life with you, I won't spend my time trying to seduce you into bed. It isn't worth it. For Christ's sake, *you're* not worth it. There must be another woman in this goddamned world to make me happy!'

He dragged her up the steps to the open door and threw her across the polished floor. She fell hard against the stairs and lay there, silent and watchful. 'Damn you,' muttered Don. 'Don't look at me full of all that shaky courage, it makes me want to kill you.'

'Are you going to?' she asked.

'You know I won't. You know I can't hurt you. You know you can do anything and still I won't hit back. Flora, I want to get away from you, I want my life to myself, I don't want you haunting me like this! Go to bed, will you? For once I don't care if I never see you again.'

She crept quietly up the stairs. If the household had heard there was no sign. She heard Don go into the library and get a drink, when he was drunk enough already, surely. It was the drink that made him wild, she told herself. That and the fight. The KORSEA men had thrown off restraint and entered into battle like any warrior band, standing by their king, and afterwards had lied valiantly to the police. None of them had thrown a punch, officer, certainly

411

not Mr Harrington. It was all a ghastly mistake. And this was a ghastly mistake.

Never before had he said he still loved her. She had long ago decided he did not, when she needed him and he left her, time and again. She had bought herself freedom, offering up her children to him so that he would let her go.

Did he really think she could make him happy? It was a mad delusion. They each fought to persuade the other to give up what they most wanted to do. But the years had gone, rolling away like pebbles down a hillside, and those pebbles had built something. If only she could tell what it was.

She bathed and then slept for an hour or so, coming down around nine. Don was in the hall, wearing jeans, his rucksack at the bottom of the stairs.

'You can't go climbing now,' said Flora dully.

'I have to go climbing now. I meant what I said last night, we can't go on like this.,'

'I know you meant it.'

She sat down on the stairs and watched him. Alex, coming down, said 'Are you off, Dad? Hey great, I'm coming.'

'No you're not. I'm going to the Alps, I don't want a green kid.'

'Oh, thanks! What happened to the fun we used to have together?'

Don sighed, not meeting Alex's eyes. 'We'll have it again. I need some time to myself, that's all. I've got to sort out a few things.'

'I wish you'd talk,' said Flora.

'I can't talk to you. I can't talk about – what I feel. I know we're all supposed to do it nowadays, get out our guts and hang them on a washing line for the world to gawp at, but I can't. I only know that I will not live like this a moment longer.'

Alex sat on the step above Flora. Annie appeared on the landing, wearing a canary yellow dress. 'What's going on?' she asked uneasily.

'Dad's leaving,' said Alex.

'I'm going climbing,' said Don. 'But you're right, I might not come back. You'll manage, all of you I'll be somewhere around.'

Flora said, 'I'll go. This family won't exist without you.'

He met her eyes for the first time. 'There isn't a family any more. Just four people, doing their own thing. And I have to get out, before all I have left is an empty shell that used to be me. I did the job I was taken on for, sorted the business, raised the kids. And now I'm off. You can do what you like.'

'All because I wouldn't sleep with you!' burst out Flora. 'I don't understand why you think it's so important!'

'It isn't,' said Annie. 'Dad just wants you to love him, that's all.'

Flora burst into tears. Alex said, 'I can be ready in five minutes, Dad. I really think I ought to come.'

But Don shook his head. He fastened the last strap on his rucksack, picked it up and walked out of the door.

In the evening Flora sat by the fire, staring at nothing. The house felt strange, almost unfamiliar. Don had been absent many times, but never like this. Even the house seemed to sense that he wouldn't come back.

Alex came in. 'We've got to talk,' he said.

She looked up, dully. 'All right. If you want. But there isn't anything to say.'

'You must have upset Dad terribly last night.'

'No I didn't! Or at least, if I'd known it would upset him – I didn't think he minded so much, Alex.'

'No. Nor me. But Annie says we're stupid.'

'Well, Annie would.'

She tried to think clearly about all the conversations she and Don had had over the past couple of years. After the pregnancy she hadn't once thought that he would wish to try again. Before that he'd toyed with the idea from time to time, more to make her accept her responsibilities than anything else – perhaps even to put her in the wrong. So it had seemed anyway. But lately – if only the fight hadn't happened. If only, in the car, she'd had the sense to look behind his words at what he meant, rather than what he said. He wasn't an easy man to understand. And the house felt so empty.

'Oh dear.' She found she was crying, and she sniffed and fumbled valiantly for a tissue.

'I've packed my rucksack.' said Alex.

Flora blew her nose. 'Don't be silly, darling. He wants to be on his own. He'll probably ask Van to come out, anyway.'

'His wife's having a baby, he's not climbing before the spring. Dad's obviously going to his usual guesthouse first, so I could go out and hang around for a bit. I think I should, Mum.'

'Why? You don't think he's going to kill himself, do you?' Her voice rose in panic.

'No! Not Dad. Honestly, Mum, he's got more guts than anyone, and you don't know him at all. He'll calm down in a day or so, and if I'm there to talk to him, chances are he'll come back.'

She smiled blearily. 'Alex, the wonder worker. He meant what he said, you know. I just don't see why he couldn't tell me he was tired of the way things are. We could have talked – if we knew how to talk. There's never any time, somehow. Someone else, something else, something getting in the way. Oh, Alex, if I write him a letter, will you give it to him, please?'

Alex was surprised. 'If you think it'll help, Mum. Annie's writing. She's dead scared she had something to do with him going. Thinks he might not know she loves him, and all that stuff.'

'It wasn't her fault, it was me,' wept Flora. 'Oh, Alex, I'm sorry to be so stupid. You go first thing in the morning. I'll write now.'

She sat for a long time before the words came. Even then each was cranked out at a snail's pace, wrenched from some inaccessible corner of her mind.

Dear Don,

I let Alex come because he says he knows where you are and he can always talk to you. I wish you hadn't gone. If I'd known not sleeping with you would upset you so much I'd have stripped off then and there and got on with it, but honestly I didn't think it mattered that much. I've learned to do without it, you see. And last time was such a disaster. I didn't want to go back to fighting when we'd been getting on so well!

I don't know what I think about sex, actually. I know it's supposed to be free and unencumbered by guilt and all that, but for me it isn't and never has been. I always give in to it, and then feel that I shouldn't sleep with people. You don't get all tangled up.

I wish you hadn't said you loved me. Love is what we had when we started, and it was young and excitable and delicious. I don't know what we've got now. If that was love, what is this? Or wasn't that love? I only know that you've gone and it hurts me because this time you mean not to come back. When Dad died my mother said she couldn't imagine a world in which he wasn't there, and I know what she meant. If you really, really want to be free of us all then I shall stay here and do everything I should in your place, but if you'll only come back home I'm sure we can get rid of the children and the staff and the business for long enough to talk. I don't know what I want to say. But it hurts me so much to see you hurt and I'd give anything to stop that, for both of us.

Yours,

Flora.

414

Alex was ready to leave at six the next day. Annie pressed an envelope in his hands, black with pink spots. Flora's neat business white seemed uncaring in comparison, like giving money instead of a present. She took it back and searched out an old gift pack, and put the letter in a pale blue envelope lined with blue tissue, with a little angel printed on the flap.

'Dad's going to think you've flipped,' said Alex dubiously.

'The other thing looked like a maintenance demand, or something. You will be sure to tell him how upset everyone is, won't you? I mean, Annie. And me. Especially me.'

'It's not going to make any difference to your life,' said Annie scathingly. 'We're the ones left without good old Dad to look after us. And none of the books say how you cope when your father's love affairs go wrong. *He's* supposed to be coping with *our* heartbreak.'

'We weren't having a love affair,' said Flora tearfully. 'We had an argument, that's all. We always have arguments. I don't know why this one had to be so terribly different.'

Alex picked up his rucksack. 'I can trust you to look after KORSEA and everything, I suppose, Mum?' he asked. 'Normally I'd step into the breach, of course.'

Annie snorted. 'They don't need help sweeping the floors. You know perfectly well they can go for months without Dad being around, it's a model of efficiency. I think a chimpanzee could inherit KORSEA and it wouldn't matter.'

'If it comes down to you they'll be home and dry then, won't they?' said Alex, and Annie put her tongue out at him. 'Hope you break your neck,' she yelled as he got into the car. He waved a long arm, and she waved back.

There wasn't much snow that year. Skiers were bussed from town to town, and snow blowers worked long into the night trying to make up for nature's paucity. Don's guesthouse, high up, was for once almost full of people eager to find some snow in the narrow clefts normally left to climbers. But he knew some of the blokes who were there to climb and bunked in with them. Their chatter got on his nerves.

Any one of them would have been happy to go with him, but for once Don wanted to be entirely alone. It was dangerous, of course. But he was reclaiming his life, grabbing it back from the demands of other people, and if he wanted to risk death then no one else need care. But he didn't want to die. It was the possibility that excited, turning the sunshine into brightest gold, the snowy rock into a cherished possession. He loved the world most when there was the chance, almost the likelihood, that he was looking at it for the last time. Then he left misery aside.

The weather was changeable, light snow on the tops turning to rain further down and causing great wails of anguish from the skiers. In the evening they sat around getting drunk and discussing the greenhouse effect, whether in ten years' time there would be Alpine skiing left. Don went and sat in the empty dining room, spreading a map on a table and studying a route. One of the guides came and talked to him for a while, remembering old times, old friends. 'You were in the party with Neil Kindler, when he fell? Yes, I thought it was so.'

'Never climbed again, of course.'

'Really? I never heard anything. He was one of the best.'

They ran through a list of mutually admired climbers. It was disconcerting to realise how many were dead. The accidents seemed rare enough but the men were picked off, one by one, ensuring the constant rise of a new and young succession. Don yawned and accepted the offer of a glass of schnapps before bed. As he sipped it Alex arrived.

He came in looking diffident, with none of his homebred confidence of manner. For a moment Don watched him without Alex knowing he was there. He felt exasperated. Try as he would to get free they insisted on tracking him down. Then Alex turned and saw him, and his whole face lit up. He threw back his shock of red hair with a careless hand.

'Dad! I knew you'd be here somewhere. Full, isn't it? They say there isn't room for me.'

'I'll fix you up in the next village. It's only ten miles or so.'

'Why don't you ask them to sort out something here? You know they always do things for you.'

Don leaned back in his chair. The black mood that only lifted when he was on the face seemed to settle more steadily over his mind. 'I didn't want you to come, Alex. Don't you ever do as you're told?'

'Most of the time, yes. Annie's sent you a letter. And Mum.'

Don sighed and closed his eyes for a second. 'I don't want their damned letters,' he said finally. 'Look, you can have my bed for tonight. I'll get them to put me in the attic. It's freezing cold but at least it's empty. You can go back in the morning.'

'No thanks. Even if you don't want to see me, I'm duty bound to keep an eye on you. I promised the girls.' Alex leaned back in his chair and put his feet on the table. Don swiped them off.

'You'll get served up as stew if you indulge your mucky habits here. Look, Alex, I don't want you around. I know that's a shock to your ego, but just for once I want a few days unencumbered by family. I want to live by myself, climb by myself, and decide what I want to do. I don't need you sheepdogging me back home.'

Alex was silent for a moment. 'You oughtn't to go out by yourself,' he said at last.

'I've taken the greatest care not to get killed while you were growing up, so now I can do what I like. And I won't get killed. I've an aversion to it.'

'You didn't take any care! You were just lucky.'

Don grinned. 'Yeah. Perhaps I was. As it happens the worst injury I ever had was with you, so how come you're here to take care of me?'

'I've improved masses since then. But it's OK, Dad, I'll hang around and ski if you won't take me climbing.'

'You'll go back home,' said Don, with quiet menace.

'No can do. You said yourself I'm grown up. If I want to stay and enjoy some winter sport, that is up to me. Isn't it?'

Don felt very tired suddenly. He had escaped teenage wrangling only to have it follow hard on his heels all the way here. He got up, saying shortly, 'I'm going to bed.'

'Here.' Alex pulled out the letters and dropped them on the table. Don scooped them into his pocket without another word.

The attic was icy, but in his altitude bag Don wasn't uncomfortable. In fact the lady of the house was all for putting some of the others up there and letting Don share with his son, but the thought appalled him. In the cold, lifeless air under the roof, listening to the snow freezing outside, he could at least think.

KORSEA rarely needed him any more. The challenge was long past, these days the firm was a byword for efficiency and solid progress. The children were in the process of launching off into free flight, and soon they would be gone. Perhaps it was that which had precipitated things. For years the children had used up energy and emotions, had stopped him wanting more from any woman than simple sex. Now, as they prepared to go their own way, they left him aware for the first time that he was heading for a desert of human contact.

In all his life he had walked in and out of relationships at his own will. When he wanted people he found them, when he wanted solitude he found that. Strong, attractive, resourceful, he had never known what it was to be without friends and companionship on his own terms. Flora had been his one resounding defeat. Perhaps he

417

loved her because of it, although he didn't think so. More likely he was that not so rare creature, the monogamous male who married once and married for life.

It was strange that society fostered the view that men were not naturally given to lifetime pairings. Even the most promiscuous member of the sex could be relied upon to consider his life blighted when his wife finally walked out, and violent drunkards haunted women's refuges begging their wives to come back. Men might not look after their marriages, thought Don, but they expected them to last. In all these years he had lived expecting that, come what may, eventually Flora would find it was time to remember she was married to him.

It was humiliating to acknowledge it, even to himself. All these years, waiting for a woman who in the end had closed the lid of the chocolate box with the merry grin of someone who doesn't at that moment fancy an orange creme. Suddenly he fumbled for his torch and switched it on, then ripped open Flora's letter. The jokey envelope enraged him, trust her to be flippant. Could she never for one moment take anything seriously?

But as he read the letter, he calmed. He could almost see her struggling to write it, one slim hand tangled in her hair, stopping now and then to blow her nose on a linen handkerchief. Sometimes she seemed as young and gentle as the day they met, and sometimes too it was as if the years between had been spent baking her into toughness. Suddenly, now, she was sorry that he was hurt. What about all the times before? But, battling, they had each made sure the other never saw the wounds.

He opened Annie's letter and scanned the page. Typical Annie. One moment declaring that he was the best father in Christendom, the next threatening not to go to Cambridge if he didn't come back and stop disrupting her life in this insensitive way. He was grinning as he switched off the torch. Trust the kids, each true to form. For Annie the impassioned letter, while pragmatic Alex simply packed up and did what he thought was best.

Lying in the dark, with the wind blowing frozen grains of snow around the chimneys, he wondered what he was going to do. A voice tempted him: Go home, try once more, this time she'll be different — and all the time common sense shouted, 'No! You should have learned by now! That woman won't ever be yours, she only belongs to herself!' But he wanted her, he had always wanted her, and that need had shaped his life. There was such humiliation in it. You could fail to climb any mountain and no one mocked the failure, but this — this. He hated this one-way love affair. If she could love him there would be nothing more to want, but some half-hearted emotion — what did she want him to do?

He thought how pleasant it was to have the whip hand for once. He had waited a long time to get it, and would not run back home the moment she asked. Let her worry a little, let her decide how much she wanted him back. In a day or two, perhaps a week or two, he'd go home. Until then his life was his own. He snuggled down in his bag and sank into comfortable sleep.

Chapter Twelve

The day was very bright and clear, with the air so cold that it stung as it was drawn into the lungs. Everyone was up early, drinking hot chocolate and coffee, stamping into ski boots or festooning themselves with ropes and slings. Alex had found himself a climbing partner, someone with a spare pair of skis, and they were even then poring over a map plotting to get to some remote col. They would ski to the climb and enjoy themselves.

Don took his son by the shoulder and shook him roughly. 'Be careful. I know you're good, but off piste is dangerous.'

'We're not stupid, Dad. It's freezing hard.'

'Now it is, but what about later? I won't say don't go, but do watch out. And on the climb, don't – well, don't do anything stupid.'

'Thought you'd given up being a parent?'

'I have. A momentary relapse, that's all.'

They grinned at each other. Don remembered taking Alex for his first ski lessons, remembered how he roared when he fell and fell again. His first climbing lessons, when he'd been so big and clumsy. And now he stood watching his big, brawny son pace out across the snow and then with an expert flick of his poles swoop away through the throng. A twist, a turn, and he arrived in a flurry at the lift. They would leave at the top, make their way over a ridge and across a glacier edge to the snow-filled col.

In the early morning the trees were iced with six inches of frost and the ground was dense with untrodden white. As he walked up the hill Don thought about joining them for the climb. But he wasn't so good a skier: unlike Alex he hadn't started in his cradle. He would hold the others up. And it was soothing to let the sounds of the guesthouse fall away behind him, to be alone in the white, cold day. He tramped for an hour, almost two, and

420

gradually the sun began to melt the icicles that had formed around his mouth and nose.

He was following a ridge that was blown clear of snow in parts. The rock was cold and grey, he preferred moving on the ice, front-pointing. When at last he reached the start of the climb, at the foot of a steep chimney thick with snow and green glacier ice, he was breathing hard. Getting old, he thought, and then remembered he had climbed this with Van nearly twenty years ago and they'd almost given up before they arrived.

But the climb found him out. It was tough and exhausting. He became dizzy from gazing at reflections in ice that reflected more ice. He couldn't move with any rhythm, he felt encumbered by clothes and gear. He stopped on a precarious stance and dumped his jacket, tying it to a spare axe, and when he went on he felt better. But thoughts kept intruding. Suppose he went home tonight? Supposing he never went home? Supposing he went off to the States and saw Shalimar?

A crampon slipped and he hung in space trying to fix it. There wasn't far to fall, a hundred feet or so. It was killing distance, but didn't look alarming, unlike the clear views you sometimes had of a valley thousands of feet down. The crampon slipped again and he cursed and stopped once more. He felt very cheerful. Yesterday he'd been lost in gloom and misery, on a far better climb. This was boring hard work, and his gloves were getting wet. The day was warming up, that was the trouble. Everything was trouble. Suppose he wrote back to Flora, to see if she would write again? He toyed with a dozen enjoyable possibilities.

When he got to the top, around midday, he barely glanced at the view. It was getting warm and though this valley was partially shaded his route home was in full sun and might be sliding. Every now and then he heard the dull boom of controlled avalanches started by explosives. He hoped Alex and his pal were keeping out of trouble. The authorities were noted for being unsympathetic to those who went without a guide.

Suddenly he was tired of the climb and wanted to get home. It was a bore coiling rope and making sure he had all his protection, and still more of a bore going down in a steady, measured stride. He felt the urge to go quickly, he found he was almost having to restrain himself from running. Something was happening, he found himself thinking. Something was about to happen. If he could only get down this hill he would know.

His feet slipped on ice and he fell, rolling ten, fifteen yards. He picked up and went on running, remembering Alex as he had seen

421

him that morning, long-legged and ebullient. Let it not be Alex, he found himself thinking. Not Alex. But his sense of doom mounted with each stride.

As he came out near the top of the ski lift he turned quickly up towards the col where Alex had gone. Someone yodelled to him from below. He turned and waved to indicate his intention. The lift was half buried, he realised. There were dogs, people, they were digging for people in the snow.

He had no room to think of anyone but Alex. He made for the col, ignoring the calls from below, following smeared ski tracks that seemed not to have been crossed by people coming the other way. There was an odd atmosphere, a sense of expectancy, as if the air was quivering with silence. Sunlight sparked off every surface, slowly, secretly loosening the bond of rock and snow.

He came through the narrow cleft that led to the col, and saw them, Alex and his pal, racing down the far side. He dared not call out. He watched them descend in a flurry into the basin, gradually ploughing their way into deep snow and a stop. He saw them push up their goggles and stand laughing together, and in horror he saw the slope they had descended begin to fall. It came in a piece, like the detaching of some giant wallpaper, and it hung in the air for long, long seconds.

'Alex!' he roared, and anguish made his lungs crack. 'Alex!!!!'

They heard, turned, and knew it was coming. But nothing could get them out of the way, nothing could help them escape. They began stumbling through the snow, and Don began scrambling towards them, and the avalanche came down on them with hurricane ease. The roar, vast, triumphant, like a thousand mountain souls, filled the col with echoing power. Snow boiled up and over, there was a stick, a leg, a wildly gasping head. In an instant they were gone, and in less time still the snow was at rest once more, jumbled, blank, uncaring.

Don made it down in seconds, sobbing, praying. He used his hands to dig, and it was futile. Six feet of snow and rock lay on top of what was there before. After five minutes he found a ski pole, and frantically began prodding and calling. Scrabble, prod, scrabble, prod. He dared not stop to go for help in case they were down there suffocating. They could be dead already, he was taking so long! He extended the stick at the limit of his arm, and at the same time put out all his soul in prayer. He felt something.

He dug like a madman, like something possessed. When he saw the arm and then the head he dragged at them, and saw that Alex had somehow managed to cup his hands to give himself air. 'Alex?

422

Alex?' he yelled, and his voice came back from the hills around. 'Alex? Alex?' There was a yodel again. He looked up and people were standing in the cleft. They had heard the fall. They had dogs. He waved them down, yelling and screaming for help, and went back to Alex, pushing his wet red hair away from his face. Was he breathing? He put his hand in front of his son's mouth and felt a faint warmth. Tears began coursing down his cheeks, an uncontrollable flood of pain and relief and joy.

They took Alex down on a stretcher, still unconscious, his legs like pieces of bleeding string. Don had to stay with the search, directing the dog that had been sent to help. He floundered in the snow, deliberately holding back thought. The dog quartered the ground energetically, and finally began to dig in a vast drift of snow. They all joined in, and after half an hour they uncovered a body. He was dead, his neck broken and his mouth crammed full of snow.

'I don't know who he is,' said Don quietly. 'French, I think. A climber. My son borrowed some skis from him. They both wanted to try climbing here. Someone's boy.'

'Your son was lucky to get out alive. Go and see how he is. There's no one else here.'

Don nodded and began the long slog back out of the col. He was exhausted suddenly, the adrenaline draining away to leave nothing but weariness. He had been going to have a drink or two with Alex tonight, eat some food, a fondue perhaps, talk. They might have gone home tomorrow. The stretcher party met him halfway down the snowed-up lift track, and one of them said. 'Your son's in the hospital. They said to be quick about getting there.'

Anxiety began again, flooding back like a tidal sea. He'd been conscious, or nearly. Legs like spaghetti. My God, they'd need consent to operate and the poor kid would be going through hell! He began almost to run down the hillside.

But the doctor was in no hurry. He sat at his desk and shuffled a fistful of X-rays. Don said, 'I was here once before. It isn't his back, is it?'

The doctor glanced up. 'No. His legs, I'm afraid.'

'If that's all! Broken legs! You can fix that, can't you? Any number of pins and screws. The boy's so fit, a real outdoor type, a crack rugby player. Wanted to climb. Wanted to be − like me.'

The doctor's mouth made a small 'o' of polite interest. He shuffled the X-ray plates like cards and selected one. 'This is the main bone,' he explained, pointing. 'This is the nerve. You see?'

'You can pin all this together,' said Don, hanging on to his control. 'I've seen pictures of legs worse than that.'

'But not when the nerve has been severed. Three places, you see?'

'Nerves repair,' said Don. 'If there's the slightest chance, we have to take it.'

'At the very least he will lose his foot,' said the doctor.

Don was silent. At last he said, 'I want a second opinion. Ten, twenty opinions. I'll fly someone out from England tonight.'

The surgeon nodded. 'Of course. But this was the good leg, Mr Harrington.'

Numb, Don stared in silence at the other plate. The knee-joint, smashed beyond recognition, the femur like gravel, a mass of pebbles.

'What – what – ?' he muttered.

'We hardly know where to begin,' said the doctor. 'Mr Harrington, in this instance we should welcome any expertise you can bring to bear. But with the best will in the world, I must tell you that in my view, whatever happens, your son is crippled.'

Don said nothing. The doctor found himself taking a dispassionate interest in the reaction of the man opposite. It was minimal, and that was strange, almost as if he was absorbing data before he would respond. A man used to emergencies, perhaps, accustomed to accident and crisis. 'You will wish to see your son,' he said, and Don looked up sharply.

'No. Not until I've got myself together. Tell him – tell him I'm out with the rescue.'

He went out into the corridor and leaned his head on the wall. He was alive, that was the main thing. What were legs? He felt a sob rising up in his throat. If he could have put himself under the snow and spared Alex, he would have done it. He went into a side room and found a telephone, rang Flora almost without thought. What time would it be there? Five, six?

'Flora? It's me.'

'Don? Oh, hello. I've been so hoping you'd call.'

'There's been an accident. Alex. His legs are smashed.'

'What?' He heard her swallow, knew that she had suddenly sat down.

'Alex? Has he broken his leg, what?'

'Both legs, very badly. It's serious. We've got to find the best specialist on offer, I don't care how much it costs. I'll get KORSEA on to it. You'd better come out, you and Annie.'

'Yes – yes, of course. But if it's just his legs – it's not that bad, is it, Don? Don't say it's that bad?'

He drew in his breath, it felt like knives. 'They may have to amputate. But I'm getting the best man there is. Someone's going to save him.'

'You mustn't let them touch him!' Flora was screaming down the 'phone. 'I'm coming at once, don't let anyone near him! I won't let them do that to Alex!'

He put down the 'phone and stood for a moment with his eyes closed. This morning, a few hours since, Alex had been fit and well. Let the tape rewind, let the day be undone, let it all be some ghastly imagining. How often had he stood in hospitals and talked, unintentionally, about things like this? He thought of Neil Kindler. He thought of Mike.

A great anguish rose up in him. How had he let this happen to his boy, his dear, cherished boy? It must not happen. Something must be done to stave off this disaster, to put right what he had permitted to go wrong. He took up the phone again, punching out the number for KORSEA, and when that was done set about commandeering a secretary, a fax, another telephone line. The thoughts were pushed aside, to be considered later. If someone was to be found who could save Alex, he had no time to lose.

'Hello, darling.' Flora clasped her son's big hand. He moved his head slightly on the pillow and tried to smile. His parents tried to look cheerful.

'Hurts,' said Alex huskily.

Don said, 'They'll give you something for it in a while. But they want you out of the anaesthetic. You were under for twelve hours.'

'What have they done?'

There was a long pause. 'Quite a bit,' managed Flora at last.

'They've pinned your legs,' went on Don. 'You'll need a new knee joint eventually.'

'Shit! I'll be laid up for weeks, then. My foot hurts. Terrible pins and needles. Can I have something for my foot?'

'I'll go and tell the nurse,' said Flora hurriedly, and tried to get up.

Don put his hand on her shoulder, restraining her. 'Feels a bit odd, I suppose,' he said tensely to Alex. 'It's bound to.'

Alex rolled his head on the pillow and met his father's eyes. They had always had such complete understanding. 'Why?' he whispered.

It had to be said. He had let it happen, he couldn't shirk this duty. 'They've taken it off, son. The nerves had gone. You were getting gangrene. They amputated just above the ankle.'

The boy's hand, in Flora's, suddenly gripped. She closed her eyes on a flood of tears, but they fell on his hand despite herself. She wept in silent horror. 'It was only a bloody avalanche,' said Alex wonderingly.

Don tried to master his voice. 'Bit of a bastard, avalanches. The experts seem to think you won't have too much of a problem with the foot, they can fit you with something artificial quite easily. Your other knee's the bugger, apparently. Going to be a long haul.' He watched his son's face, not knowing what he looked for. The faint down of boyhood still marked his cheeks.

'Bang goes the rugger,' said Alex thickly. 'And you won't have to put up with me on the end of a rope any more. I wasn't any fucking good, was I?'

'I thought you were great.'

Flora said in an utterly false voice. 'There'll be lots you can still do, darling! You see people doing things all the time, people who can't – people with – '

'Cripples,' supplied Alex. 'I'm a one-legged cripple. Dad, tell the nurse I'd like something for the pain, will you?'

Don nodded and went away. Acting on sudden instinct, Flora rose and cradled Alex's head, burying his face against her. He was crying, huge, babyish sobs. She held him, soothing, petting, loving him, shedding her own tears on to his bright hair. This was a tragedy, no less, and Alex must grieve for his lost self. The mirror of his future had been snatched from him, and in its place there was a dark fog of pain.

Don came back and stood watching them. If only he had let Alex go with him. If only he hadn't come out at all. The guilt was his, of that he had no doubt. He had declared himself tired of parenthood and responsibility. He had taught his son about the mountains, he should have taken care to be with him in them, not in the company of some half-baked friend who knew even less about avalanche and danger.

Alex was calming. Flora found some tissues and mopped his face and her own, saying, 'I was told not to cry. I'm disgracing myself.'

'Bet you never thought you'd have Long John Silver for a son,' muttered Alex.

'Perhaps we can get a parrot,' said Flora. 'I've always wanted a parrot. Do you know if they bite?'

'Yes. They're savage as hell, a bloke at school's got one. My God, I shall never face them at school.'

'There's no shame attached to it,' said Don harshly. 'You've lost a foot, not your manhood.'

426

Alex looked up at him and grimaced. 'I'm not going to be the Don Juan of the highlands with a wooden leg, Dad. No one's going to want to sleep with a cripple.'

And Flora said, 'The important bit is quite intact, I understand. You make love lying down, dear, the condition of your legs is immaterial.'

'All those dancing lessons,' muttered Alex. 'What a waste.'

It was all a waste. All those years of love and care, to come to this. He was so young, so terribly young. Flora said, 'Perhaps you'll still dance. They can do wonders nowadays.' But she knew that none of them believed her.

The nurse came in with an injection. Alex said, 'Would you mind going now, please? I'm a bit tired.'

Don nodded, and brushed his son's forehead with his hand. 'See you, tiger.'

Flora bent and kissed him. 'We'll come tomorrow. Love you.'

Outside the hospital, she sat heavily on a snow-covered bench. Don said 'Annie's waiting. We've got to get back.'

Flora looked up at him. 'Not yet. I feel as if my legs have been cut off. They hurt so.'

'I wish mine had been cut off. Anything rather than have him suffer like this. Alex! That boy has never done anything unkind in his whole life! I deserve to be shot.'

Flora was bewildered. 'It wasn't your fault. It was a terrible day. Lots of people were hurt, there were six people killed! He isn't dead, Don. We could be here mourning his death.'

His pale eyes met hers. 'He might be better off. There's nothing more for him. Say what we like, this world is made for people with strong bodies, and if you don't have that then you've nothing. I don't want him living a second-class life. If I couldn't get him out whole I should have left him there and not got him out at all.'

Flora leaped to her feet and struck at him, catching him on the shoulder. 'How dare you! My boy is more than just his legs! You might think life's all doing and running and climbing, but I don't. He's got a brain, he's got a heart, he's got a soul, and I love him and Annie loves him and we won't be the only ones! How dare you say he isn't worth a light!'

But Don stood looking at her, his face drawn and hopeless. 'It's not what I think, it's what he thinks. What he's going to think. Believe me, Flora, I've seen it before. They'd rather be dead than maimed and crippled. You remember Mike, on Everest, broke his leg? Not much that, few broken bones, that's what everyone

427

thought. Got a thrombosis and ended up in a chair, minus both feet. Couldn't work, let alone climb. Killed himself last year, getting on for twenty years after it happened, got a shotgun and blew his head off. What does that say about his life?'

'It says a lot about him,' muttered Flora. 'He didn't have Alex's guts.'

'For Christ's sake, Flora! Do you want your son to have to steel himself to face every sodding day? And it's my fault. All my fault. If I had taken better care it would never have happened. And once it had I should have had the courage to let him die. But I was too selfish. I couldn't face the world without him.'

He started to walk away and Flora ran to keep pace. 'Too damn right, you're selfish. You see everything your very own way. Just because you never learned to be happy without doing something aggressively physical, it doesn't mean he can't. Like − like a swami, or a monk, learning to rise above the things of the flesh. You wallow in them. You think that's all there is.'

'He's seventeen, Flora!'

'Yes. Just the age to change.'

A taxi came and Flora flagged it down, pushing her husband into it. He seemed almost unaware, his hands were like ice. They were staying at a skiing chalet twenty minutes away, with cheerful girls coming in to cook and clean. The holiday atmosphere jarred on Flora's nerves, but at least they were spared an impersonal hotel. She felt a rising sense of panic. Alex was enough to cope with: she couldn't face it if Don cracked up. She hadn't enough strength for all of them.

Annie was on the telephone when they got in, sprawled in front of the fire. 'Right, so you'll come on Friday. I'll meet you, and you can have some skiing afterwards. But you have to visit him every day − and remember, get the leaflets. I'll send you back if you forget. 'Bye.'

'We don't want visitors,' snarled Don. 'Your brother's crippled and you're holding a bloody party.'

'Two of Alex's mates and two of my girlfriends,' agreed Annie. 'They've sworn not to pal up. They're here for Alex, nothing else. And Juliette's bringing a whole load of stuff about artificial limbs, muscles flexing through electrical impulses, that sort of thing. Alex, the transistorised man, that's who he'll be.'

'He's not feeling very well yet,' interposed Flora. 'He's only just been told.'

'We're not going to make a nuisance of ourselves! But he's bound to be feeling like an outcast. Juliette's hoping he'll finally take some notice of her. She can get in the back door, with sympathy and available sex.'

Flora started to laugh. But Don yelled, 'For Christ's sake, haven't either of you any idea what this means? For the rest of his life he's condemned to staggering about as a cripple, in pain, an outcast, with all the fun of life gone. There is absolutely nothing you can do that will make it better. It's time you grew up, Annie, there's no happy ending. Alex is finished.'

White-faced, Annie said, 'It doesn't have to be like that. If we don't think of it like that it won't be. He's got enough courage.'

Don's face contorted. 'He'll waste his life being brave. The most godawful waste.'

He went to the cupboard and picked up a bottle of whisky. Before Flora could say a word he went into the bedroom and locked the door.

Later, Annie and her mother sat by the fire writing letters to people, telling them what had happened. Annie said, 'I hope they put a guard on Alex's room. I wouldn't put it past Dad to bump him off.'

'That's a horrible thing to say.'

Her daughter looked at her honestly. 'But he might. He wouldn't want to go on living like that, and he thinks Alex won't either. You know how physical he is.'

'Yes.' Flora looked down at her hands. The easy obedience of his body was vital to Don, so much so that he disregarded it. He wasn't a health fanatic, or a dietary weirdo, simply a man who regarded a fit, whole body as the only acceptable tool. He and his set mourned death far less than disability.

He would take it far less hard if it had been himself. He might even have come to terms with it. But for this to happen to Alex seemed to Don to be a clear sign that he had betrayed his trust, fundamentally failing his son. Don had seen so many men hurt and broken, he had so much more experience of this sort of thing than she. Flora felt her heart suddenly contract with fear. Was Don right? Was it terrible to ask Alex to go on living?

The words she had written leaped up at her. They were to her mother. 'Obviously we're terribly upset, but it isn't the end of the world. He'll adjust, no doubt, and find things he can do which he enjoys. I hope he'll come to see what has happened not as a tragedy but as a damned nuisance. That's what we all hope, anyway.'

She put her hands over her eyes. 'I'd give anything to be back before it happened. I'd give anything not to know.'

429

'I get a headache thinking about it,' agreed Annie. 'But if I don't think of it I feel guilty. Poor Alex. I bet he can't forget.'

'They're giving him stuff,' said Flora. 'He doesn't want us around. I hate you children growing up and telling me what to do.'

Annie, sitting on the carpet by her mother's knee, reached out her arms. Flora enfolded her.

At bedtime, in her dressing gown and slippers, Flora hammered on Don's door. 'Don! Don, let me in. Don? Don?'

There was no reply. Eventually she went into the kitchen and found a hammer and chisel, set the chisel against the lock and thwacked it. The wood splintered expensively, but the door swung open. Don was lying on the bed, the whisky bottle empty beside him.

'Is he OK?' asked Annie cautiously from the doorway.

'Pallatic. You go to bed, love, I'll see to him.'

'He's not dead, is he?'

'No, he certainly isn't. Go to bed, Annie.'

When at last Annie went, Flora hauled Don off the bed and dragged him bodily into the bathroom. She pulled off his shoes and his jacket, pushed his head into the shower and turned on the spray. He started to moan and mutter, and she struggled to strip off more of his clothes, getting herself soaked in the process. When she pulled his underpants over his brown, ridged thighs she was afflicted, suddenly, by the strength of his legs. They were so like Alex's, such long and healthy limbs ending so appropriately with enormous feet. The toes were exquisite, she realised, long and beautifully formed. She had never considered feet before. As he lay unconscious she slumped down in the water beside him, cradled his feet in her lap and cried.

Alex was quiet the next day, and every day. He hardly spoke about his legs, enduring the agonies of treatment uncomplainingly. If he did respond it was to Annie and her cronies, not his parents. To them he seemed shut off, erecting an iron wall of private thoughts. Flora was hurt, but nowhere near as hurt as Don. Night after night he drank himself into a coma. In the mornings he was bleary-eyed and lethargic, still smelling of whisky. Juliette, Annie's friend, was heard to say, 'Honestly, Annie, you never said your father was a lush!'

Annie, a committed pacifist, hit her. Juliette burst into tears and rushed to her room, Annie burst into tears and rushed to Flora, and Flora disentangled herself and went to talk to Don.

'You are causing the most awful trouble,' she said flatly.

He was sitting at a desk, looking through old photographs of the children. He must have asked Dorothy to send them out. He didn't say anything.

'Juliette thinks you're a lush. Annie says one's parents should have the decency to have their nervous breakdowns in private. She hit Juliette, by the way.'

Still he sat without speaking. He looked terrible, she realised, the skin of his face seemed puffy and unhealthy. She had never once seen him look so ill. 'It doesn't help to have you behaving as if his life is at an end,' she said desperately. 'It isn't, you know. Honestly, truly, it is not.'

He said, 'If it was me I'd want to die.'

'I don't believe you. You'd come to terms, you'd fight, because people love you and need you and want you around. It doesn't do any good to make things worse than they are. It happened, you couldn't have stopped it. Truly, it isn't your fault.'

He said, 'I keep thinking of Mike.'

'I don't know why. You didn't like him much when he was alive. Why don't you blame yourself for that. Didn't you fetch him down?'

'Yes, but that was different.'

'Why?'

'I didn't want to fetch him down.'

Flora snorted. 'Honestly, I don't understand you. And I don't understand climbers, I never have. We could have been happier you know, if you'd had to give it up.'

Don shook his head. 'I doubt it. I'd have put you through hell. I don't know what it is, I don't know why − it's just something I need. All the times I left you when I should have stayed, I used to sit in some stinking tent and wonder what I was doing. Sometimes I meant to pack up in the morning and go back. I never did. It's like a drug that you can't give up.' He turned to Flora, his eyes suddenly blazing. 'Suppose he kills himself? Suppose in twenty years he decides he's had enough? It might not take twenty years. I couldn't bear it, Flora, I know that.'

'You do talk rubbish.'

She put her hand on his arm and left it there, a warm, reassuring contact. He hadn't talked to her so honestly in years, perhaps ever. 'I wonder what would have happened if I'd insisted on going on those trips with you?' she murmured.

'What? At the beginning?' He almost laughed. 'I can't imagine it. Or at least, I couldn't then. We were so damned stupid. Everything

431

this or that, no compromise. I look at the children and think – ' he paused.

'Yes,' said Flora gently. 'You think how narrow their view is. How many more opportunities there are than they understand. Alex isn't so bad, you know. Better, with Annie and the others. He's in pain, you can't expect him to rise above that. When the pain stops, then he'll be Alex again.'

He said, 'I never thought he'd need something I couldn't give. I thought you were the one thing in life I couldn't fix, and now Alex as well. Alex! My boy.'

He dropped his head on to his hands and shook with sobs. Flora went to him, cradled his head against her, murmured into his hair. First Alex, now Don, she thought. Where did she find the strength to give this comfort? All the years and years of giving had strengthened her. She was trained to stand fast when everyone else had crumbled. She had seen so much suffering, real and unrelieved disaster, and she knew that this was not the same. All she could do was help her family to hold on, struggle through, until they too realised it.

'We'll go and see him with Annie tonight,' she said. 'Show Juliette you're human, for one thing.'

'I'd rather not.'

'And I'd rather do anything than sit there in silence. He hates it, we hate it. Let's go with the kids.'

'I don't think I want to see him again. I was planning on going home.'

She was silent. Then she moved away across the room, and played with the window cord. Outside a machine was moving last night's snowfall into tidy piles at the sides of the road. 'I never thought you'd be this weak,' she said. 'You've hauled bodies off mountains, you've faced death, you've even faced my father when the business was on the rocks, and you can't even go and talk to your poor hurt son.'

'He doesn't want me to talk to him!'

'Perhaps he doesn't. But you know you should go. Bringing up Alex has been so easy up to now, he's been the loveliest boy. Annie might have driven you mad, but Alex never did. You were friends, the greatest friends. And now, when he's meeting the first real challenge of his life, perhaps the biggest challenge of his entire life, you want to turn your back on him. Of course he's difficult, of course he's upset! You mustn't be.'

He got up, furious at her stupidity. 'Oh, for Christ's sake! It's all right for you. But it's my fault! If I hadn't had a tantrum, if I

432

hadn't thought my own piddling little problems were important, if I'd had the sense to take him out with me instead of wanting to be by myself, commune with nature, leaving him to the tender mercies of some inadequate Frenchman – '

'Why don't you blame me?' asked Flora quietly. 'Why wasn't it my fault for refusing to go to bed with you when I promised? That was the thing that upset you. And as for not letting him go off on his own, he was allowed to do just that on his damned school skiing trip, and no one said a word! He knew what he was doing, Don! The weather changed, that's all, and by the time anyone realised it was too late.'

'You don't understand,' said Don thickly.

'Yes, I bloody well do! You want to wallow in self pity, blame yourself because it's easier than helping him. I don't know how you can, Don, I don't know how you dare, and I won't let you. I won't, I absolutely won't!'

She came up close to him and started pushing at him, punctuating each word with a shove, pinning him against the wall. He caught her hands and they wrestled, with real venom. He pushed her in turn and she resisted, until forced back inch by inch to the desk. He bent her backwards over it, still gripping her hands, until she was lying on the photograph album, his face inches from hers. 'Bitch,' he whispered.

She licked her lips. 'I know. What are you going to do about it?'

She lifted her feet from the floor and wrapped her legs around him. He let out a low groan, and she spread her arms, and his too. He let himself come down on her breast, his lips brushing her own.

'What are you going to do about it?' she asked again.

'Is this your idea of therapy?' he murmured.

She moved her pelvis from side to side. 'It might work. Anything's better than watching you drink. I want to do it with you. Please.'

He got off and put a chair under the door handle. Flora stepped out of her underclothes, and stood by the desk, barefoot, waiting. He came across to her and lifted her skirt. She stood looking into his face while he touched her. When he came close and she felt him, naked, she heard herself start to moan. It had been so long. Locked together in the act, clinging to him, she felt caught up in a whirl of emotion. Sadness and joy ran side by side, tension and release conspired together. Loving this man, hating this man, all she needed from him now was this. He began kissing the cleft between

433

her breasts, hunched over her and in her, like a giant parasite taking nourishment. She began to shudder and he wrapped his arms round her to lift her up, moving her against him for his pleasure. They fell against the sofa, locked together in mutual anguish, until suddenly he was finished. Flora lay with him spreadeagled between her knees. She felt replete.

Chapter Thirteen

Juliette, small, brown-eyed, scuttled along beside Alex's wheelchair.

'They're going to be furious, Alex! You know you're not supposed to leave the hospital.'

'Stop wittering, Jules. I'm not staying cooped up here for the rest of my life. We're only having a coffee and a look round the shops.'

'I hope your mother doesn't see us.'

'You don't have to be frightened of her. She likes you.'

'She might not, after this. And I couldn't bear it if they sent me home.'

She hung on to the back of the chair as Alex sent it hurtling down a ramp and into the street. His legs were like just-set jelly, and he was forbidden to put any pressure on them at all. If he fell from the chair everyone would blame her, she knew, but he wouldn't let her push or do more than act as a brake on steep slopes. She tried to walk nonchalantly along at his side.

'I feel as if I'm escorting an escaped convict,' she muttered.

'Why don't we rob a bank? Not many cripples turn out criminal, you know. I could start a precedent.'

'You could get arrested, you mean. My mother always said you were a bad influence. She said you were like your father, only half tame.'

Alex chuckled. Juliette was very flattering to his ego. He pushed himself along the pavement, trying to see in windows, exhilarated by the fresh air. Everything was always so immaculately clean here, he felt untidy just cluttering up the street. His single foot on the rest seemed horribly obvious, and he forced himself not to care. He saw a cafe with huge glass windows and he headed for it. 'Time for some calories,' he announced. 'Got some money, Jules? I'll get some off Dad and pay you back.'

'I don't mind paying. I don't pay for meals or anything while I'm here, everyone's terribly kind.'

'They're saving your virgin flesh for me,' said Alex, and grinned wolfishly. Juliette blushed.

They ate strudel and drank coffee. A couple of girls were watching them, and Juliette said tensely, 'I wish they wouldn't. They're awfully pretty.'

'I hadn't noticed,' lied Alex. 'Anyway, you're prettier. These foreign girls are always a bit hard.'

'Do you think so?' Juliette brightened. Then she said breathlessly, 'Are you going to dump me once you're out of the chair, Alex? I bet you are.'

'I should think you'd rather dump me. After all, you can't go on being kind to me just because I've lost my foot.'

Juliette looked down at her plate. 'I don't see that your foot matters at all. I know you think it does, but if you can walk that's enough, isn't it? I know I'm a pain, always hanging round hoping you're going to notice me, but I'm not doing it because I feel sorry for you or anything like that. I love you, Alex.'

He felt himself blushing. The two girls across the room were looking at him again, and Juliette was watching him with her pretty brown eyes. 'I'm not a romantic figure, you know,' he heard himself say.

She sighed. 'You've always been romantic. You're a romantic family. And I just know you're going to go on being romantic and famous and daring, all your life. And I'll be married to some boring man who's not romantic at all.'

'You don't have to marry someone boring!'

'If I can't have you I might as well.'

The two girls left, and one of them waved behind Juliette's back. Alex tossed his shock of red hair back from his face. Juliette was gazing at him in melancholy adoration.

'We'd better get back,' he said. 'My parents will be coming in soon.'

'I thought you didn't want to see them?'

'Oh, I think I'd better. They worry about me. Think my life is ruined, and all that.'

She walked beside him back to the hospital. Standing on the doorstep looking disconsolate were Flora and Don.

'Hello, you two,' said Flora. 'I thought you were making a run for it.'

'Not without my plastic knee,' said Alex. 'Jules, why don't you go and do some shopping or something? Dad can take you back when he goes.'

436

'Yes. All right. I'm sorry, Mrs Harrington. Alex did insist that we go out.'

'That's all right, Juliette. See you in half an hour. 'Bye.'

When the girl had gone, Flora said, 'Have you been upsetting her, Alex?'

He grinned. 'No. Well, not intentionally. It might be time she went home, Mum, she's getting a bit intense.'

'What's wrong with that?' asked Don.

'Not a lot. But I want to play the field and with Jules breathing down my neck it's a bit difficult.'

'Play the field!' shrieked Flora. 'Your bones have hardly set!'

'Yes, and very glamorous it is too. The young hero, maimed at so early an age. His brave smile above the bandages, his gallant facing up to his broken life – it's real bird pulling stuff, Mum, I promise you. Don't look so surprised, Dad. There's more to life than climbing mountains, you know.'

Flora looked at him over Alex's head. 'Your father wouldn't know about that, Alex,' she said.

Don grunted. He said, 'Actually, I've been thinking. Do you want to come straight into KORSEA? I know you were going to college but under the circumstances – I mean, you can learn on the job.'

Alex swivelled in his chair, the better to look at his father. 'You don't need two feet to do a degree, Dad. I'll get back to school and take the exams, if it's all the same to you. You don't have to provide me with a cosy little niche, away from the cold winds of life. I'll come into KORSEA when I'm good and ready.'

'I didn't mean –'

'Yes, you did. And I'm sick of being treated like a has-been. I know at first I thought – well, it was a shock. You don't expect something like this to happen. But I can talk, I can think, I can even pull the birds, and soon I shall be able to walk. And I never was going to be anywhere near as good a climber as you, and we both know that's true. So it doesn't matter. Or at least, it doesn't matter that much. A damned nuisance, that's all.'

Flora bent down and put her arms round him. 'I am so proud of you,' she whispered. 'And I know I'm an embarrassment but I don't care. You're terrific.'

But Alex was staring up at his father. 'What about you, Dad? Was it worth hauling me out alive?'

Don swallowed a giant lump and said hoarsely, 'If you think so. It was always worth it for me. I don't care if you can't move an eyelid, but I care about you. If you can make a go of it then good luck to you, son. And don't get anybody pregnant.'

Alex laughed and Flora said, 'That is just awful. Alex, if you lay one finger on Juliette I shall cast you off with a shilling. Or at least – perhaps we'd better send her home. You can take up with some loose-living continentals, I'm sure everyone here's too clean to have AIDS. But the poor girl's going to be heartbroken.'

'I'll see her when I get back,' said Alex. 'Look, you two should go as well. I've got to study and you must have things you should be getting on with. I'll ring you if anything crops up.'

Walking away down the street, Flora said, 'You realise we've been dismissed?'

Don grinned. 'In favour of women. He's got guts, hasn't he?'

'Certainly has. Just like my father and just like you. None of you knows what to do with a bad hand except play it.'

He turned to her. 'I haven't had any bad hands.'

'Except me.'

He took her hands and held them, gazing down into her face. Lines fanned gently from the corners of her eyes, but the bones of her face, hidden in girlhood, made heart-stopping angles and curves. 'You're the best thing that ever happened to me,' he said.

'Liar!'

'I don't tell lies. We might not have the most conventional marriage, but we haven't split up. We might not know how to live together, but we've made a good thing of living apart. Our children like us, and we like each other.'

'We didn't used to. I thought we were all washed up. I thought you were leaving.'

'A lot seems to have happened since then.'

They walked on. A chill spring breeze was blowing and she wrapped her coat closely round her. Don took her hand and put it in the pocket of his sheepskin. 'I hated you being in love with someone else,' he said. 'That was the worst time.'

'Oh yes, Finn. We'd both had an overdose of celibacy. I can't have been that much in love, I was only too keen on getting into bed with you. And then I got into such a dreadful mess.'

He gripped her hand tightly. 'Children make all the problems,' he burst out. 'Nothing but problems and worry from the moment you know they're on the way. And I'd have another dozen tomorrow.'

'Would you?' Flora looked up into his face.

'Yes. Wouldn't you?'

She felt a blush starting to spread from her toes to her hair. Don said, 'It's not so obscene a suggestion. Between two married people who love each other.'

'Do we?'

438

He shrugged. 'Don't we? There's no one else knows me as well as you. And OK, we're not starrry-eyed, we don't live in each other's pockets – but I think it's love.'

She let out her breath. 'It's a very workaday thing, then. Like good beer instead of champagne.'

'We had the champagne. You can't live on it.'

Flora laughed up into his face. 'You're the most amazing man. There should have been thunderclaps when I married you, warning me of what was to come. Oh Lord, look, there's Juliette, we forgot her.'

'Remember, we're supposed to send her home, before Alex gets trapped between those perfumed thighs, plaster casts and all.'

'She is not trying to trap him! At least – yes, we'd better send her home.'

It was an odd evening. Juliette was doleful because of her imminent departure. Annie and the others had long since left to go back to school, but Juliette would count any job well lost for Alex. So Flora and Don made polite conversation and looked at each other over the salad.

'I remember when I first met Alex,' murmured Juliette. 'It was when Annie took me to watch him play rugby.'

'I first met Don in Nepal,' said Flora. 'I had a stomach upset.'

Don laughed. 'That wasn't Delhi belly, it was love. There's little difference.'

'You can't cure love with milk of magnesia.'

'Have you tried?'

She made eyes at him. 'Many times.'

'You ought to go back,' said Juliette. 'Have a sort of second honeymoon.'

Don looked at her with new respect. 'What a sensible idea, Juliette. You must come and see us when Alex is home. Come and stay. We can find you a room near his.'

'No we can't,' said Flora. 'I mean – we should love to see you, Juliette. You can share with Annie.'

'Thank you. That's really kind.'

When at last she had gone to bed Don poured them both a brandy and threw another log on the fire. Sparks raced up the chimney and into the night. 'You can fly direct to Kathmandu nowadays.'

'Couldn't we call in on Prakash Raj instead? He's got my patch, you know.'

'Aren't you finished with all that?'

She shrugged. 'I don't know. Perhaps – for the time being. But

439

in the end there'll be somewhere in the world where I can be useful. Ethiopia, for instance. I could do a lot in Ethiopia.'

He came behind her and put his hands on her breasts. 'Don't you want to have more children?'

She took in her breath. 'You know I do. But the two we've got are going to be shocked. And Mother's bound to be appalled.'

He nuzzled her neck. 'To hell with them. If we can have a second honeymoon, we can have a second family. And you can go to Ethiopia later.'

She turned in his arms and began to press kisses on his throat. 'I keep thinking that we're being terribly irresponsible,' she murmured.

'Rubbish! We may not always be together at dinner but we're together when it counts. Flora, Flora, you're heaven.'

The log was crackling in the hearth, she could taste brandy and skin. Through all the years, through all the partings, they remained exciting to one another, the magic had never gone. Like two chemicals that meet and react, they gave off light and fire and energy. Once she had thought they destroyed each other, but instead they were fused in the flames, drawn together, twisted around, inseparable.

When had she stopped trying to be rid of him? When had she ever really tried? He was the enemy that was almost a friend, the lover to whom you never dared surrender. She had never known what it was to put down her weapons, lay aside her armour, and give herself totally to this.

The Land Rover was hotter than Hades, and full of flies. When they stopped dust settled over them, like a fine net, coating their lips and eyelashes. They were loaded down with water, and every few miles Don stopped and emptied petrol cans of the stuff into the radiator. Children crept out from the huts, arms stretched to beg, and Don perfected the art of throwing money at the last minute.

'You shouldn't,' said Flora sternly. 'It encourages them.'

'You're getting hardbitten. That little girl's got scabies or something.'

'Yes, but — oh well, do it if you like. It's a drop in the ocean, you know. Much better to spend on health care and workshops and education —'

'All right, all right. Since I'm not spending on those you can allow me my little bit of charity.'

She subsided, easing her back off the seat, feeling the sweat run in trickles down her spine. She was like an old warhorse scenting battle, itching to get involved. They had stopped the previous day at one of the clinics she had established, and there it was, running beautifully, just as she had planned. It was a strange feeling, seeing an idea come to fruition. Her time away had given her a new perspective.

It was too hot even for them to keep driving in the heat of the day. They stopped at a village and drank fruit juice while resting on thin grass under a tree. Flora went to the pump and rinsed her arms, face and hair, and Don watched her easy confidence with the villagers, chatting and making jokes. A new sensation assailed him. Pride. He was suddenly aware that he was immensely proud of his wife. He had married a pretty girl, never thinking she would one day be this beautiful, this intelligent, this accomplished.

When she came back he said, 'Do you think I've changed over the years?'

She considered. 'Yes. Not hugely, though. You've mellowed. You don't want to spend every waking minute hanging off a cliff. You still need it though, your occasional fix. I once thought I could stop you going. Now I think if I did, you'd be unliveable with. It's your escape route, your antidote to family life.'

He rolled on his back and looked at her, the sun like a halo behind her head. 'What would you know about family life?'

They ate a mango, getting sticky with juice. When they had washed it was time to go on, with the heat of the day waning to a steady throb. The village was coming to life again, and as they left a woman on her way out to the fields stopped and waved.

They arrived in the early evening. Flora was taken aback, everything was different and yet the same. Her bungalow was so much smaller than she remembered, and the climbing rose was in a muddle over the door. When Abdul saw her he burst into tears and put a towel over his face, keening loudly. Two small, bare-bottomed children came out and stood, watching in silence, and a moment later Prakash himself appeared, wiping his mouth with a napkin.

'Mrs Harrington! Flora! What a surprise.'

'Hello, Prakash. I'm so sorry, we were going to telephone but when we tried we couldn't get through.'

'That doesn't surprise me. The telephones have been dreadful lately.'

'May I introduce my husband?'

Prakash extended his hand. 'How do you do, sir. Do come in. Abdul, may we have some drinks, please?'

As the greetings were made Flora cast surreptitious glances around. Things were not as she had expected. The children looked messy and in need of a bath, and Prakash himself had old stains on his sleeve, when once he had been immaculate. He gave orders and more food

441

was brought, but the rice was gritty and the chapattis slightly sour. An air of seedy disorder hung over the place, from the dead flies on the verandah to the stains in the bath.

'Is your wife away visiting, Prakash?' enquired Flora at last.

He looked uncomfortable. 'I thought you knew — my wife died shortly after the baby was born. Snakebite.'

'Oh. Oh, I see. How terrible, I am so very sorry.'

'It must be difficult with the children so small,' said Don, and Prakash nodded. 'My wife's mother came for a time but we didn't get on. It was suggested Shenaz's sister come, but she's studying and it wouldn't have been right. We should have had to marry, and — but a charming girl, of course. Most charming.'

'So you just muddle along,' said Flora. 'Don't you find it difficult, travelling?'

'I — I find it difficult to do much travelling nowadays. Of course I should do more, but under the circumstances —'

Flora said, 'Yes. I do see.'

That night, in the unfamiliar guest bedroom with Don hot beside her, Flora said, 'I feel it's my fault. I recommended him for the job and he's letting things go.'

'Blame the snake,' said Don sleepily. 'Or the ayah, or the cook. The food was foul and the kids need a bath.'

'Don't they just.' She put her cheek against Don's back, and then moved because he was radiating warmth. 'Do you think Shalimar would like it out here?'

'Good God, no. She'd hate it. Dust and snakes and no ice.'

'You know Prakash is Liam's father?'

Don rolled over and stared at her. 'She got him from some sort of sperm bank, didn't she?'

Her hair brushed his arm as she shook her head. 'She got him from a whirlwind affair. She wanted to marry him but he wouldn't upset his family. He went off and got married to the family choice and she went off and had Liam. And as far as I know, they haven't sent each other so much as a Christmas card since. I don't think he even knows she had a baby at all.'

'And you have been sitting on this information all this time? That's appalling.'

'Wasn't my secret. Are you jealous or something? Prakash Raj making out on one of your old stamping grounds.'

'Don't be stupid. I care about Shalimar.'

'Oh, do you? Or is your nose out of joint because she actually found someone other than you to be in love with?'

'Now you're being really stupid,' he said scathingly.

442

Flora sat up, pulling the sheet over her naked breasts. 'I always did think it was disgusting, getting into bed with my best friend,' she said in a shrill voice. 'I suppose you'd have obliged her by fathering a child if you'd known she was that keen. Awfully decent of you, old chap. Nothing like keeping it in the family.'

'She never suggested anything of the sort! Obviously, if we'd married –'

'Oh, so you were thinking about it! Why didn't you take the plunge, get yourself someone really spectacular.'

He caught her shoulders and held her. She glared up at him in the dim light. 'What are you so mad about? I didn't marry her. I couldn't, I was married to you. And I'm still married to you.'

Flora flung herself down. 'I hated you sleeping with her.'

'I'm not a monk!'

'But Shalimar! My best friend! It was terribly bad manners, if nothing else.'

Don yanked the sheet back and lay down. 'Oh, sorry! Afraid I must have trangressed! If you weren't going to sleep with me I should have taken to self-abuse and not found what comfort I could in the bed of someone discreet and loving and intelligent.'

'And beautiful. Why not say beautiful? Admit it, Don, you're more than half in love with Shalimar and you always have been. What's more, you're jealous of Prakash Raj!'

'She's your best friend, Flora. Aren't you the one that's jealous?'

Flora choked on a sob. 'If I am I've a right to be. I never tried to pinch anyone that belonged to her. It's just – oh, go to sleep, Don.'

'Look, if you want to fight then let's fight. I'm not going to spoil your fun. This is ancient history, but don't let that get in your way.'

'I don't want to fight. I just think you think a lot more of Shalimar than you're letting on.'

'What do you want to do, attack my soul with a buttonhook?'

'What's that supposed to mean?'

'You want jam on it, Flora, you really do!'

They lay side by side, hot and angry. One of the children was crying somewhere in the house and the nurse was comforting it. The plumbing gurgled and in the hot night beyond a million insects chirruped and whirred. Eventually, as the night at last grew cool, they slept.

Over breakfast Prakash asked if they had slept well. 'Yes – yes,' said Flora, although her eyes were puffy and shadowed.

443

'The bungalow is very hot,' said Prakash. 'Sometimes it can be uncomfortable.'

'You should get air conditioning,' said Don. 'No point in wearing unnecessary hair shirts.'

'I doubt it would look well in the community,' said Prakash. 'The other aid people don't have it, you see.'

'You're the boss. If you get it then they'll have something to aim for. By the way I didn't know you knew Shalimar.'

Prakash looked self-conscious suddenly. Then he smiled. 'Yes, we knew each other well. Before I married. Her mother came from Hyderabad.'

'You don't say. Well, you must have been a ladies' man.'

Flora sliced the top off her boiled egg. 'And he's not the only one.' Prakash looked bewildered, but he was diverted by his son toddling into the room clutching a potty and followed by his nurse.

'We have visitors! This isn't right! Please, I shall come directly the meal is over!'

Flora and Don left straight after breakfast. 'I never thought I'd see that slick performer reduced to this,' said Flora, tying a scarf round her hair. 'I don't know how you can be jealous of him.'

'I'm not in the least jealous.'

'Well, piqued, then.'

'Flora, will you please shut up!' He drove for five minutes in silence. Then he said, 'OK, so it offends me. I'd got used to being adored.'

'I knew it!' Flora folded her arms and stared blankly out of the window.

'Wasn't that what you wanted me to say?'

'Yes! No! At least I had the decency to fall out of love. You're just spending your life hovering tantalisingly on the brink.'

'I am in love. With you.'

'And Shalimar. With me and Shalimar both.'

He looked at her tense profile. 'With you a lot – and Shalimar a little. A very little.'

Flora started to cry. 'Oh, for Christ's sake,' said Don. 'Send her a telegram and tell her to go and see Prakash Raj. She might like to set up house on some baking Indian plain.'

'You'll hate it if she does.'

He considered. 'No, I won't. What I hate is you staring at me as if I was turning into Bluebeard. If you hadn't left I'd never have looked at Shalimar.'

Flora looked at him balefully. 'You sound like Alex, humouring Juliette.'

444

He laughed. 'Put it this way: I'd never have looked at her seriously. Will that do?'

She retied her scarf. 'I suppose it's going to have to. Oh, Don, I'm sorry to be such a fool.'

The Land Rover was hired and they left it at an airport late the following day. Before they got on the plane to Kathmandu they sent a telegram to Shalimar. It read: 'Imperative you go see Prakash Raj. Wife dead, two children motherless, life in chaos. Flora.'

The trails were busier than Flora remembered them. The world's holidaymakers had discovered Nepal, and the Everest route was thick with young and not so young explorers. Don decided he and Flora would go to Namche Bazar and then branch off into the endless mountains. The evening before they left Namche they ate with some Sherpa friends and drank and sang. Smiling Sherpa faces shone in the firelight, young girls giggled and old men reminisced. They were such cheerful people, thought Flora. On an evening like this they gave no hint of dangerous or difficult lives.

The next morning was bright and dry. They took a tent and some food, rejecting the many offers of portering. Flora had a headache but Don seemed fine, he strode ahead with effortless strides. She couldn't keep up and he had to wait at every bend, although he was carrying the heavy pack and she just a light one.

'You're getting flabby in your old age,' he teased.

'I am not! You've got longer legs. You and Alex have legs like giraffes, both of you.'

Don grunted. 'We're whittling Alex down inch by inch.'

'Don't! Just — don't.'

They walked in silence for a mile or so. The air was heavy with the scent of flowering shrubs and lentil bushes. Their trail was carved on a narrow ledge, and to the right stretched the valley, every inch farmed even on its steep mountain edge. Women were carting fodder for penned buffalo, and hens were pecking aimlessly round their feet. So little had changed in all these years, she could be nineteen again, on the brink of life.

That night they camped in the lee of some rhododendron bushes, with a stream trickling past inches from the door. It was cold. Their breath formed clouds as soon as the sun went down. They ate rice and eggs and some dried rations Don swore by, which Flora thought disgusting. She ate a Mars bar and then made her teeth ache by cleaning them in the freezing mountain stream.

'Come to bed,' said Don. 'It's the only warm place.'

'It isn't eight o'clock yet.'

445

'I'm getting you up at dawn.'

She slid fully dressed into her sleeping bag. 'It isn't very friendly for a honeymoon,' she objected.

'I was rather thinking the same. Are you prepared to risk frostbite?'

She giggled. 'I'm sure it only attacks the extremities. And I've got fewer than you.'

'Bodily contact is always advised in these cases. The only thing.'

'Really?'

'Without a doubt.'

They undressed with giggling haste, and Don got back into his bag. Flora slid in on top of him. 'Is this going to ward off frostbite?' she murmured.

'I doubt it. We have to do exercises.'

'Oh, I see. I'm glad you're an expert. Do you do this at altitude?'

He laughed. 'No. Up there we put on an extra pair of socks. Boring, don't you think?'

'Yes. Terribly.' She held on to his shoulders, pillowed by her breasts. It was warm and strange and exhilarating. Suddenly she giggled. 'Oh, Don, Winifred was absolutely right about you. You're a terrible influence!'

They wandered the mountains for days, sometimes camping, sometimes staying in villages, strolling hand in hand along the trails. They grew brown and healthy, and in one village there was a wedding and Flora had her hair hennaed and her hands painted. They wrote letters to the children and sent them back with one of the runners who still worked the trails of Nepal, carrying goods and messages, news and gossip. 'We're having a wonderful time,' wrote Flora. 'We should have done this years ago, Dad and I are getting on simply splendidly. I do hope you're behaving Alex, and Annie, if you're going to fail your Cambridge exam do let me know in advance – Dad will need careful handling!'

Don read the letter and complained. 'You make me sound like an unexploded bomb.'

'Nothing like an incentive to do some work,' said Flora, tweaking the page from his fingers. 'Are we going to have to go home soon?'

He sniffed. 'I suppose so. Next week. Or the week after. OK?'

She nodded and passed him a mug of tea. She felt unreasonably happy.

As they meandered the trails Don said suddenly, 'Why don't we pop in on Prakash Raj on the way home. See if Shalimar's turned up.'

'Oh yes?' Flora glowered.

'Not still feeling insecure, are you?'

She considered. Without doubt the last weeks had set the seal on something. They were like boxers who had finally, after many bloody bouts, come to respect each other. The contest was over and no one had won and no one had lost. 'Do you think you're going to get bored with me?' she asked suddenly.

Don blinked. 'Er — no. Not bored. I've said a few things about you, but never that you were boring.'

'Good. Because I should hate to admit to loving you only to have you stop loving me.'

'Oh, please don't admit anything that's going to incriminate you,' he said with heavy sarcasm. 'When you leave me I'll be able to throw it at your head. "She said she loved me, officer! And we've got a family of five!"'

'How many?'

'I was just rounding it up. So, we go and see if Shalimar turned up.'

Flora sighed. 'Oh, all right. But I bet she stayed home.'

When they arrived at the bungalow there were rugs hanging on a line, being beaten by a small boy in a dhoti, a gang of workmen digging a hole in the lawn and another couple fixing new screens to the verandah.

'Shalimar,' said Don.

'Probably Prakash's mother,' retorted Flora. But she squeezed past the workmen and ran into the house.

Shalimar was supervising the scouring of the kitchen. She was wearing tight trousers and a tunic in purple brocade, an outfit quite unsuited to house-cleaning chaos. 'So you did come,' said Flora.

'Oh, darling, hello!' Shalimar held out her arms and enfolded her friend. Then they stood back and giggled.

'You look singularly inappropriate,' said Flora.

'I'm dressing for the life I intend to lead here. Not this dreadful mess.'

'Why are they digging holes in the garden?'

'My dear girl, it's something disgusting to do with sewers. Quite foul. Now, Prakash is working and the children have gone for a walk with the ayah. Liam is so American, I hadn't realised, Demands hamburgers and french fries, not to mention peanut butter. He's suffering terrible culture shock.'

'But you are staying?'

Shalimar's lovely face was creased by a frown. 'I really don't know, darling. It's all so desperately uncomfortable. I was perfectly happy, you know, I didn't need to be summoned to help.'

447

They wandered out to the comparative quiet of the sitting room. Don was sipping a drink and leafing through a newspaper. Shalimar coloured. 'I didn't know you were here.'

'Yes. Flora and I have been having a second honeymoon.'

'Oh. Oh, I see.'

'No you don't,' said Flora. 'We've buried the hatchet. Finally and forever.'

'I bet it isn't,' said Shalimar.

Flora glanced at her. 'Thanks for your vote of confidence. I think we've done all the fighting we possibly could. Peace has broken out.'

Don threw down his newspaper. 'I like your friend Prakash. Charming guy.'

'He isn't "my friend" as you call him,' said Shalimar abruptly. 'He was once. But as you know, friendship doesn't last.'

He winced. 'Ouch! Actually in my experience friendship lasts a hell of a long time, it's passion that causes problems. All that fire and agony.'

'You made very sure we never had any of that,' snapped Shalimar.

Flora said, 'Do stop squabbling. Look, Don, let's go into town and find a hotel. Prakash and Shalimar can come and join us for dinner tonight. We can treat them.'

Shalimar turned her stunning profile haughtily away. Don laughed. 'Come on, old girl! It could be fun.'

The evening was more than fun, it was perfect. Ensconced in one of India's many elaborate hotels, they dined beneath lazy fans, in an immense and beautiful hall, waited on by a dozen men in dazzling white. Prakash was in his element, full of wit and charm, the harassed single parent a lifetime distant. Shalimar, her hair piled into a towering chignon, looked from Prakash to Don and was delightful. Flora felt a little dowdy in comparison. But she wore a silk blouse that matched her eyes, and a pair of brass earrings, and Don said, 'You had a pair like that when we met. I adore you, Flora.'

'Ah, Flora is always adored,' said Shalimar.

Prakash took her hand. 'And you are always worshipped. A goddess amongst women.'

Shalimar suddenly remembered how lovely Prakash was. Next to Don he had seemed small and harassed, a poor second best, but tonight, in the candlelight, in starched shirt and gold cufflinks, he was again the man she had loved. His eyes reminded her of Liam, and there was the same lift to his mouth.

'I so much want Shalimar to stay,' said Prakash. 'But she has so good a life in America.'

'She's not all a good time girl,' said Don. 'Shalimar has always hankered after home and family.'

'I've got them,' she said sharply. 'At least − Liam and I are very happy.'

'So you see, I can't press her,' said Prakash. He looked forlorn for a moment, and Flora said, 'I think you ought to press her. This is the sort of chance you shouldn't let go.'

They drank champagne, cold as a glacier and as exhilarating. A band came and played stately tunes just for the four of them, and they danced in strict tempo. Shalimar felt more conscious of her height than she remembered from before. When they changed partners and she danced with Don, she said, 'What do you think I should do?'

Don whirled her round a corner. 'Marry him. Do you both good.'

'I don't need to be done good. Are you and Flora really making a go of things? It's not just some temporary backlash from Alex's accident?'

He shrugged. 'If it is then so be it. But I don't think so. We've grown up. We've considered the alternatives. When all's said and done we're happier together than apart. And right now we're very happy.'

She said nothing for a moment. Then she burst out, 'Sometimes I am so jealous of Flora I could spit.'

'Don't waste your energy. You've got a good man there, make the most of him. Liam won't want you hanging around when he's twenty.'

'Beast.' She looked dispassionately to Flora and Prakash, chattering and dancing in careful rhythm. She sighed. 'We had some good times, didn't we?'

'You know we did.'

'What a pity you were always thinking of Flora.'

They parted and went back to the table. Flora and Prakash came back, and Don put out his arm and drew his wife close. They stood side by side as Prakash and Shalimar prepared to take their leave. Prakash took Flora's hand. 'Thank you so much, Don, Flora, for sending Shalimar to me. It's the best thing that could have happened.'

'That's what we thought,' said Don.

'And Shalimar will think so too,' said Flora. 'Once the plumbing's working again.'

449

Shalimar smiled. 'I'm sure you're right. Let's hope it doesn't take us twenty years to get happy.'

When they had gone Don led Flora out on to the verandah. Scented air came in from the gardens, jasmine and bougainvillea. 'Did it really take us twenty years?' asked Flora.

He nodded. 'About that. What were we fighting about? Really?'

'Being us,' said Flora. 'Being our own people. But you don't keep people by hanging on to them, only by letting them go.'

'I'd rather you stayed,' whispered Don.

'I will if you will.'

He drew her into his arms and held her.

It was blowing a fine Scottish gale when they came back to the castle. The park was full of leaves and whirling branches, and the ducks insisted on struggling into the air, to be tossed and ruffled and to crashland back on the river. Flora fell into the hall and Don pushed the door closed behind them, silencing the wind.

'Good God,' he said.

Flora shook her tangled hair out of her eyes. Alex was standing by the stairs, one hand resting on the balustrade. Annie hovered close by, squeaking, 'Don't rush it, Alex. Keep quiet, you two, and wait.'

They all waited, breathless with tension. Slowly, carefully, Alex put his artificial foot forward, and followed it seconds later with the real one. One step, another, he let go of his support and walked free. As he wavered, ten steps on, Don rushed forward and engulfed him in a hug. Alex clung on to him, laughing and triumphant. 'Watch it, Dad, I'm a work of art!'

'You're a bloody miracle, boy. You could have told us. We might have died of shock.'

'Ah, why intrude on your elderly idyll?' enquired Annie, and Flora said, 'Ooh, Annie, you beast. Go and do your homework or something.'

'Not till we've had some champagne,' said Don. 'Have you seduced the adoring Juliette, Alex? Or are you saving yourself?'

'Forbes won't let her come and stay till Mum's home,' declared Annie. 'And now you're home we don't want any strangers cluttering the place up. Alex will have to control himself.'

'I need a Swedish masseuse,' said Alex.

'You'll get a Scottish physiotherapist and like it,' snapped Flora.

They gathered in the library for the toast. Alex insisted on standing, hanging an arm round Don's neck in a casual gesture of support. They waited for Don to speak but Flora realised that

450

he was beyond words. He was choked with emotion. She raised her glass.

'Here's to all of us,' she declared, her voice high and clear. 'Here's to courage, and love, and kindness. May we all have enough to go round.'

They raised their glasses, each to the other, and drank.